THE SUBTLE KNIFE

THE GRAPHIC NOVEL

PHILIP PULLMAN

THE SUBTLE KNIFE

THE GRAPHIC NOVEL

Adapted by Stéphane Melchior,
art by Thomas Gilbert

ALFRED A. KNOPF  NEW YORK

THIS IS A BORZOI BOOK PUBLISHED BY ALFRED A. KNOPF

Visit us on the Web! rhcbooks.com

Educators and librarians, for a variety of teaching tools, visit us at RHTeachersLibrarians.com

Library of Congress Cataloging-in-Publication Data is available upon request.
ISBN 978-0-593-17693-1 (trade) — ISBN 978-0-593-17694-8 (lib. bdg.)
ISBN 978-0-593-17695-5 (ebook) — ISBN 978-0-593-17692-4 (trade pbk.)

MANUFACTURED IN CHINA

January 2022
10 9 8 7 6 5 4 3 2 1
First American Edition

Betrayed by Mrs. Coulter, rejected by Lord Asriel, and devastated by the death of their friend Roger, Lyra and her dæmon cross into the new world. She and Pantalaimon are determined to discover more about Dust. This mysterious substance has been the source of so much consternation, the subject of hideous experiments. But if it is feared and reviled by their enemies, Lyra and Pan feel it must be good, and worthy of protection.

Behind them lie pain and death and fear; ahead of them lie doubt and danger and fathomless mysteries. They'll be on their own in this new world, without their friends the gyptians, the adventurer Lee Scoresby, the witch Serafina Pekkala, and, most of all, the magnificent armored bear Iorek Byrnison. But they have the alethiometer to guide them. And they have each other.

And they are about to discover that they are not the only ones with a destiny. . . .

The word "dæmon," which appears throughout the book, is pronounced like the word "demon."

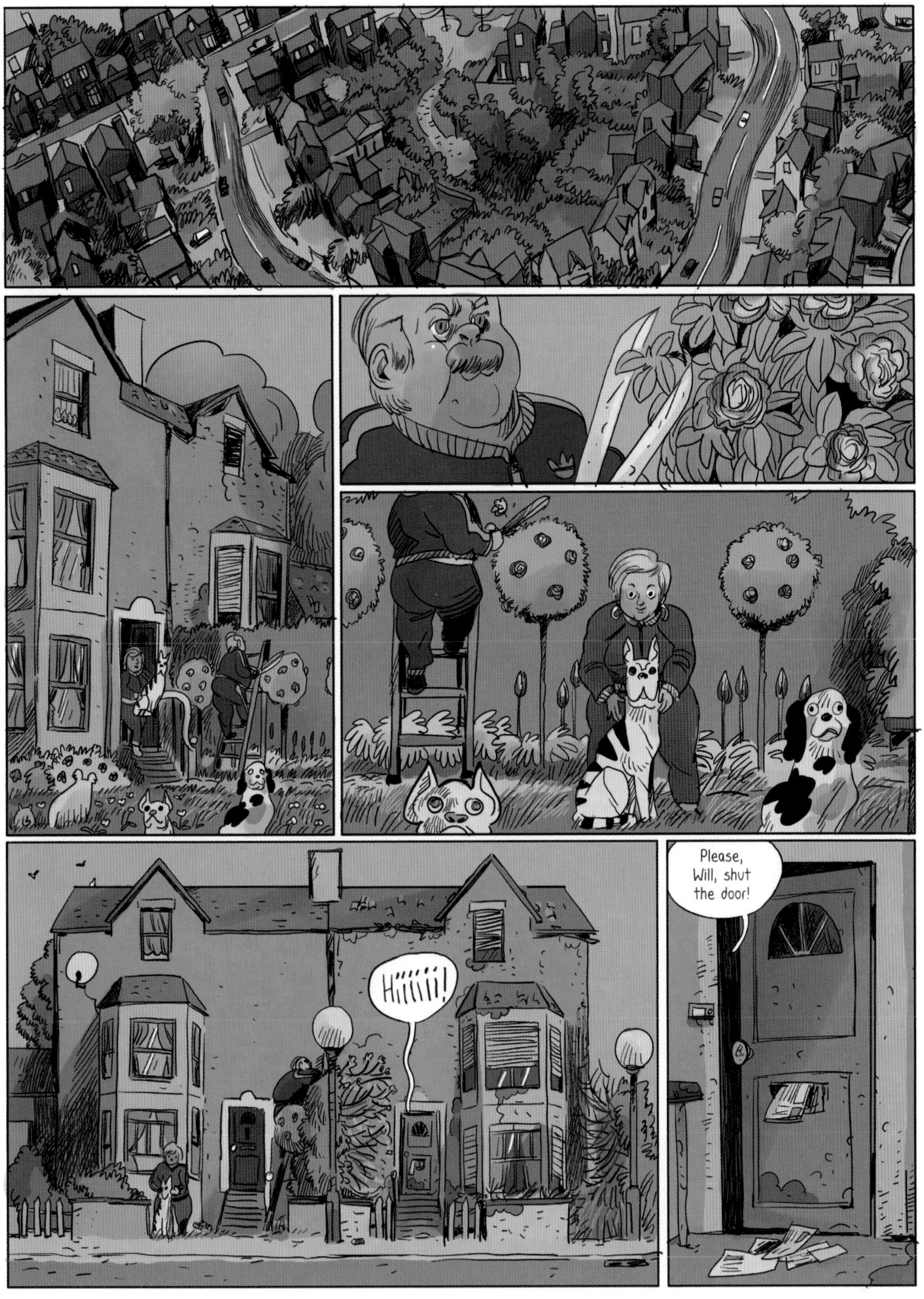
Hiiiiii!
Please, Will, shut the door!

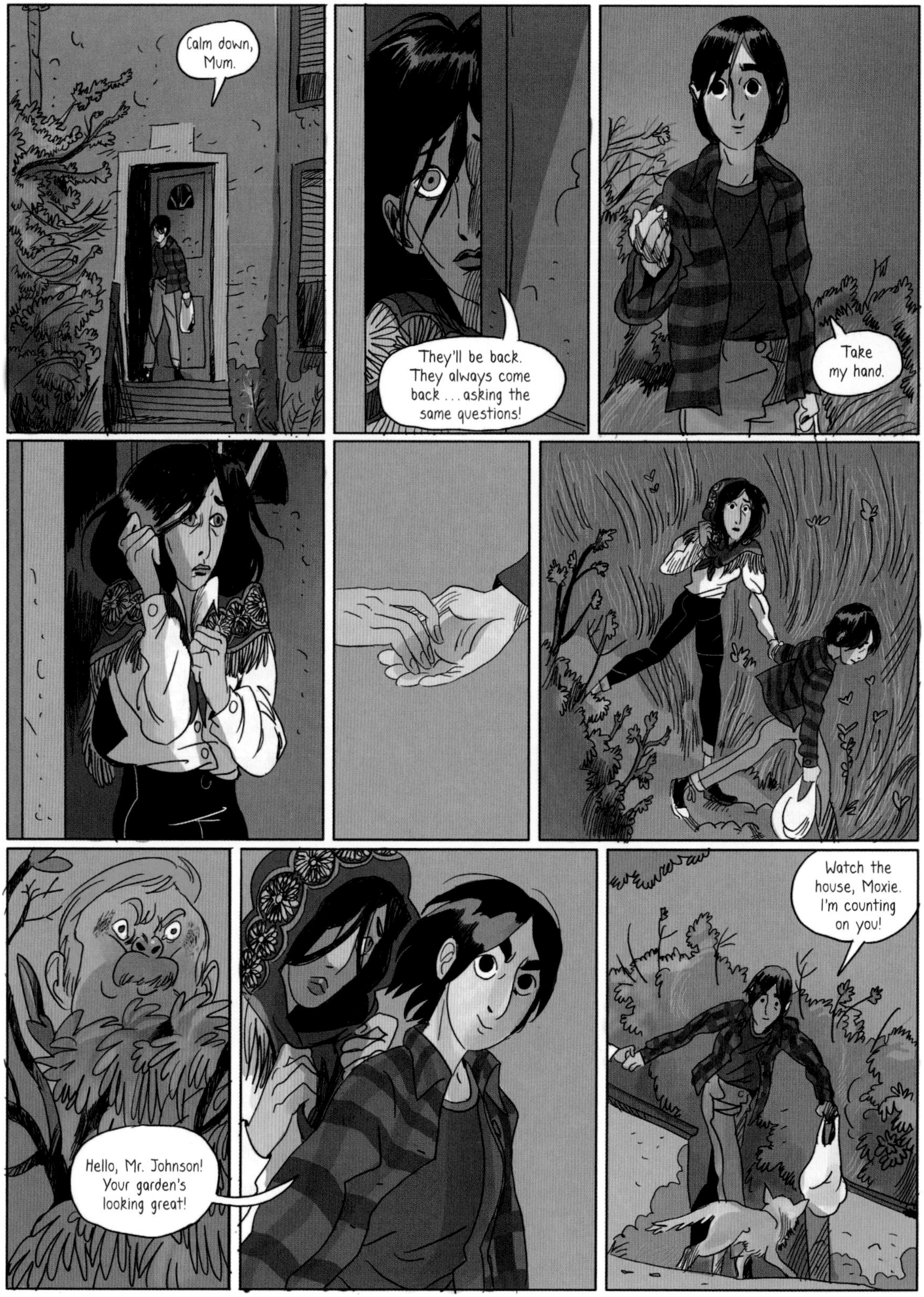
Calm down, Mum.
They'll be back. They always come back . . . asking the same questions!
Take my hand.
Hello, Mr. Johnson! Your garden's looking great!
Watch the house, Moxie. I'm counting on you!

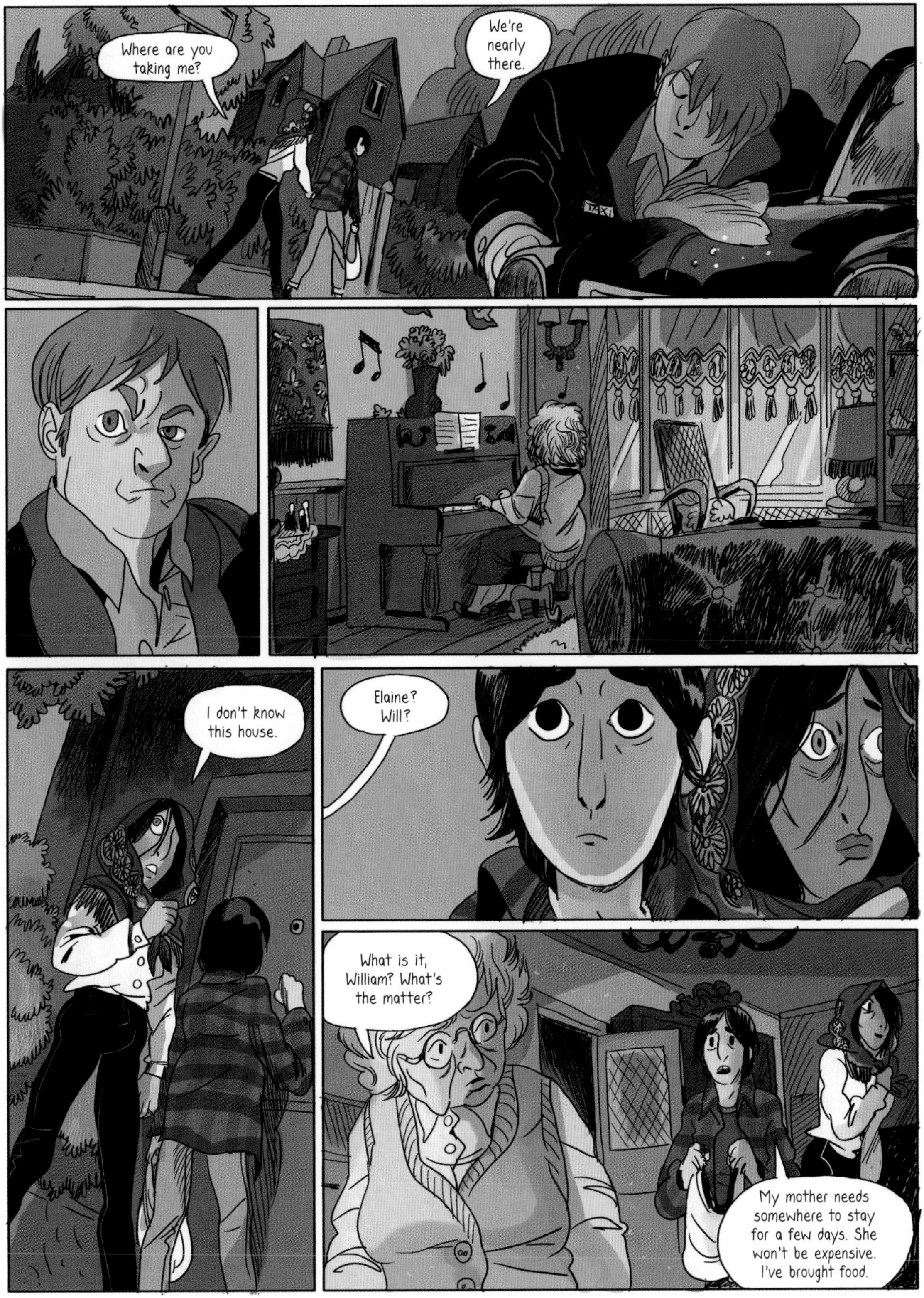
Where are you taking me?
We're nearly there.
TAXI
I don't know this house.
Elaine? Will?
What is it, William? What's the matter?
My mother needs somewhere to stay for a few days. She won't be expensive. I've brought food.

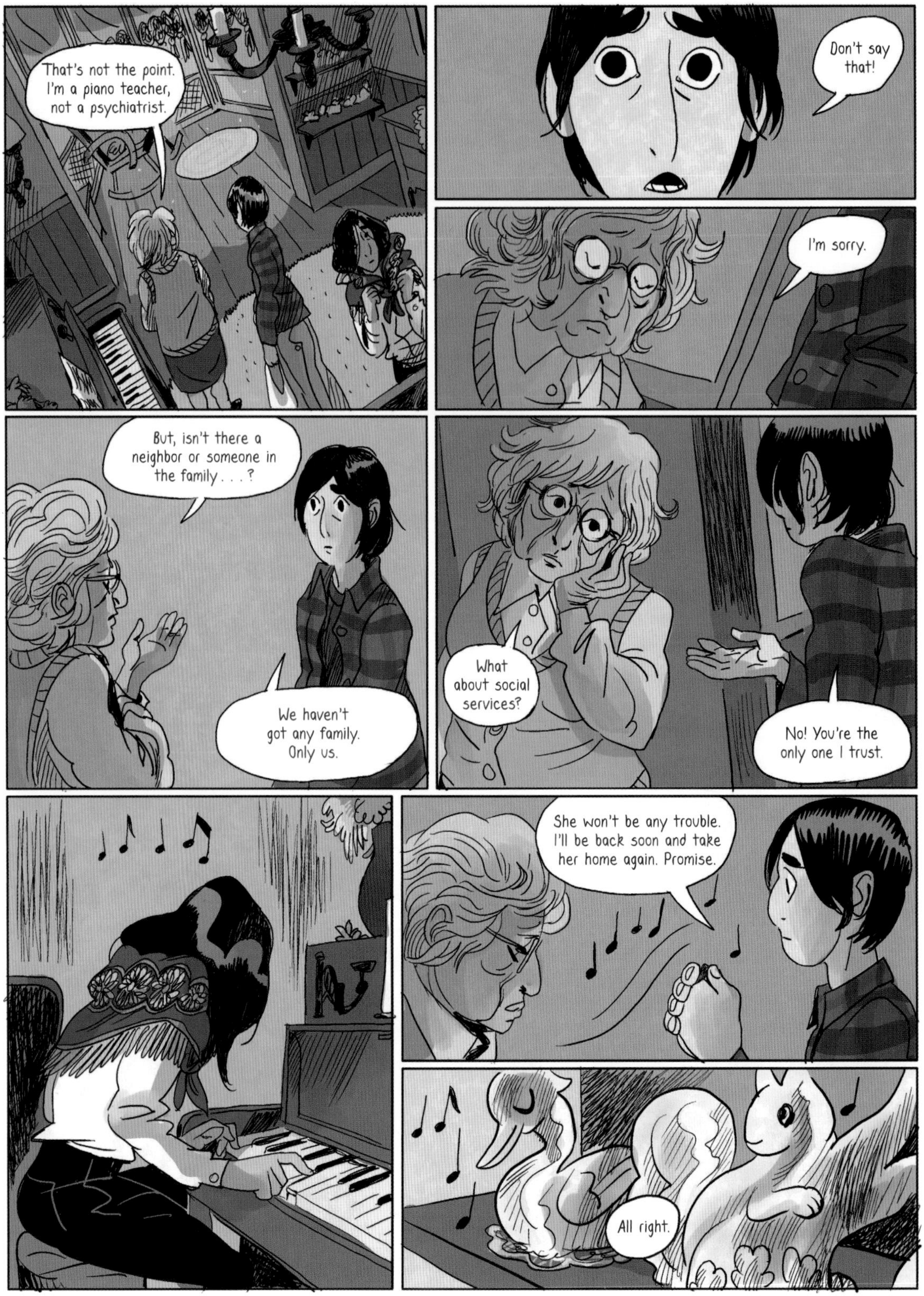
That's not the point. I'm a piano teacher, not a psychiatrist.
Don't say that!
I'm sorry.
But, isn't there a neighbor or someone in the family . . . ?
We haven't got any family. Only us.
What about social services?
No! You're the only one I trust.
She won't be any trouble. I'll be back soon and take her home again. Promise.
All right.

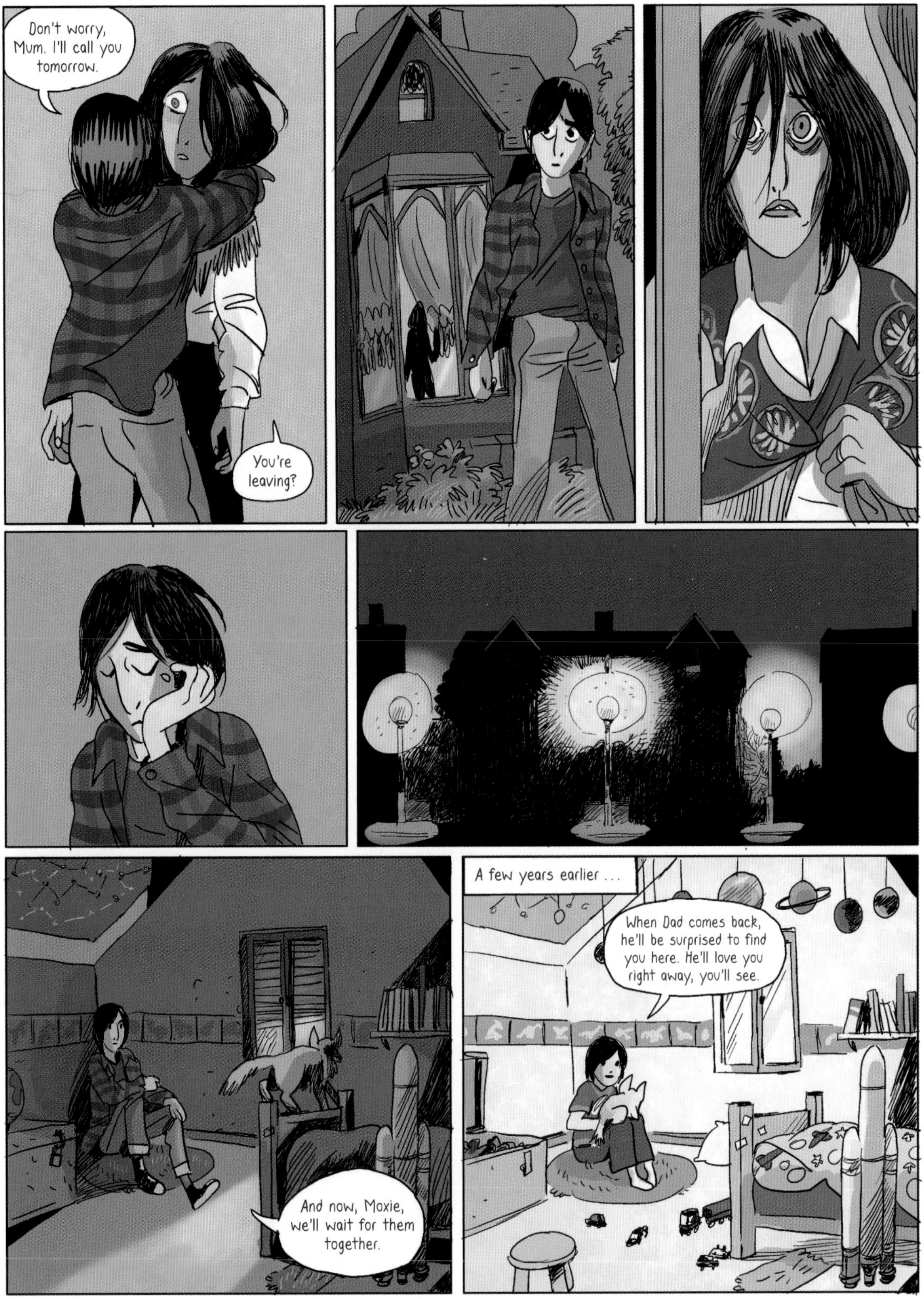
Don't worry, Mum. I'll call you tomorrow.
You're leaving?
A few years earlier . . .
When Dad comes back, he'll be surprised to find you here. He'll love you right away, you'll see.
And now, Moxie, we'll wait for them together.

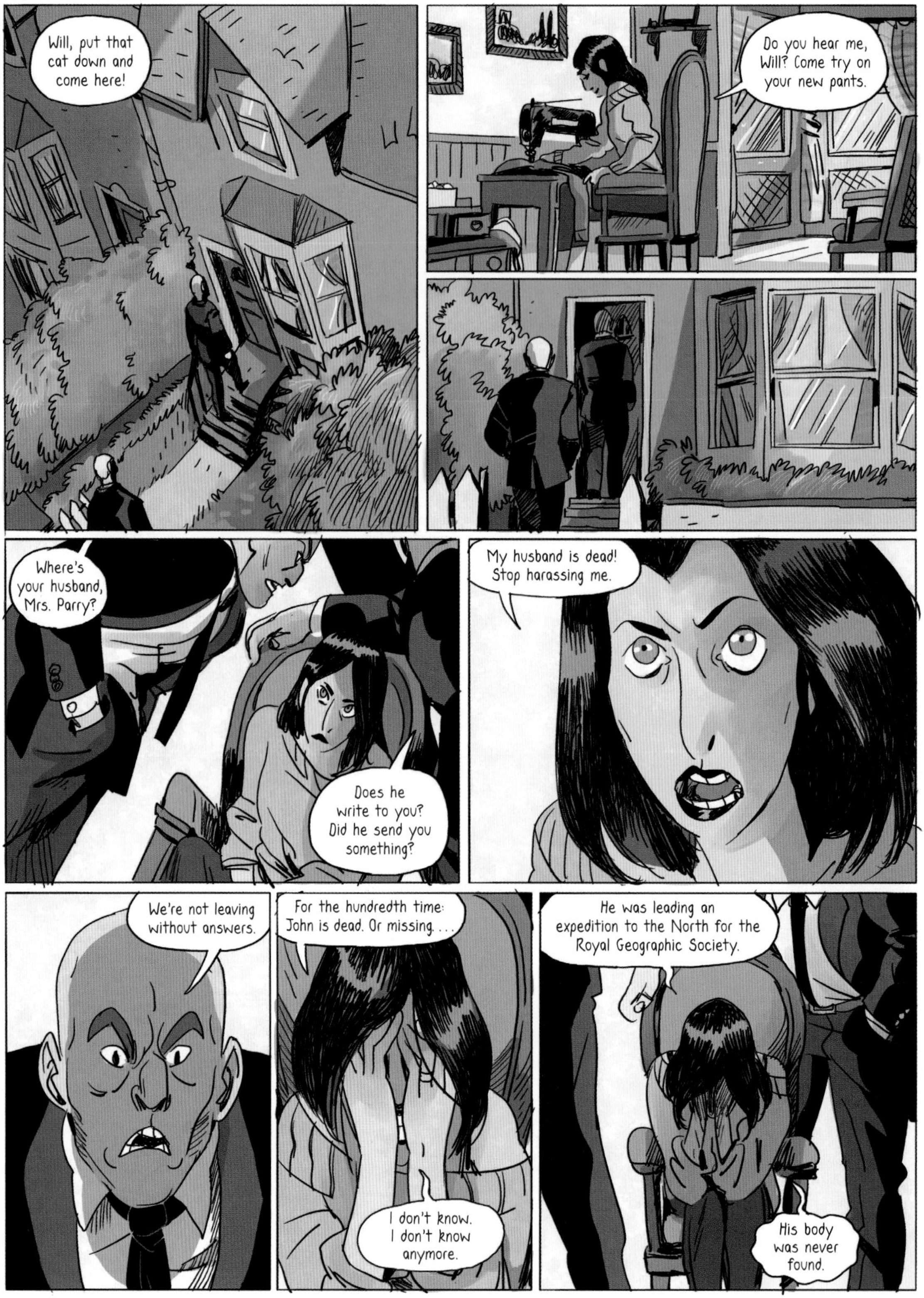
Will, put that cat down and come here!
Do you hear me, Will? Come try on your new pants.
Where's your husband, Mrs. Parry?
Does he write to you? Did he send you something?
My husband is dead! Stop harassing me.
We're not leaving without answers.
For the hundredth time: John is dead. Or missing. . . .
I don't know. I don't know anymore.
He was leading an expedition to the North for the Royal Geographic Society.
His body was never found.

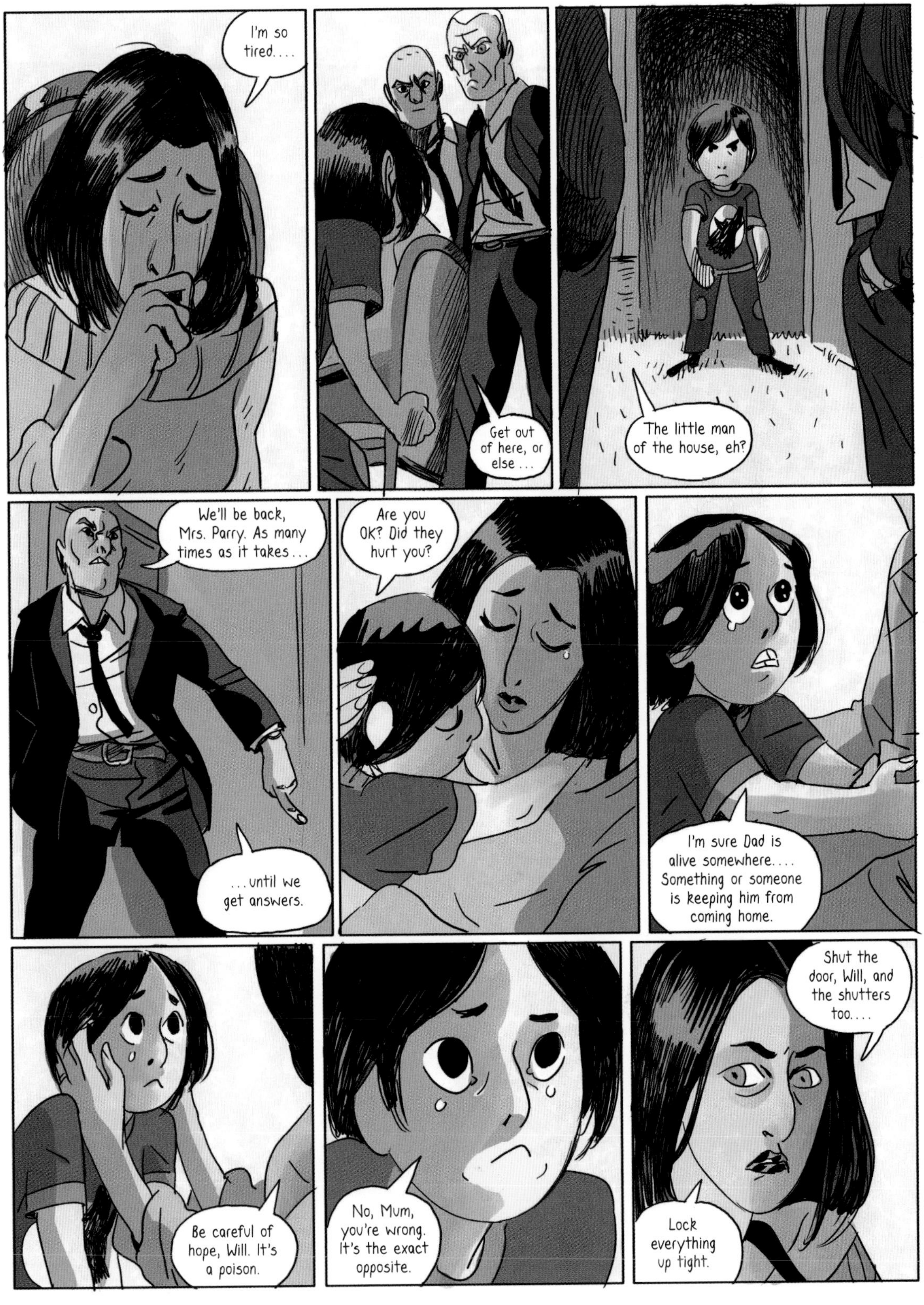
I'm so tired....
Get out of here, or else...
The little man of the house, eh?
We'll be back, Mrs. Parry. As many times as it takes...
...until we get answers.
Are you OK? Did they hurt you?
I'm sure Dad is alive somewhere.... Something or someone is keeping him from coming home.
Be careful of hope, Will. It's a poison.
No, Mum, you're wrong. It's the exact opposite.
Shut the door, Will, and the shutters too....
Lock everything up tight.

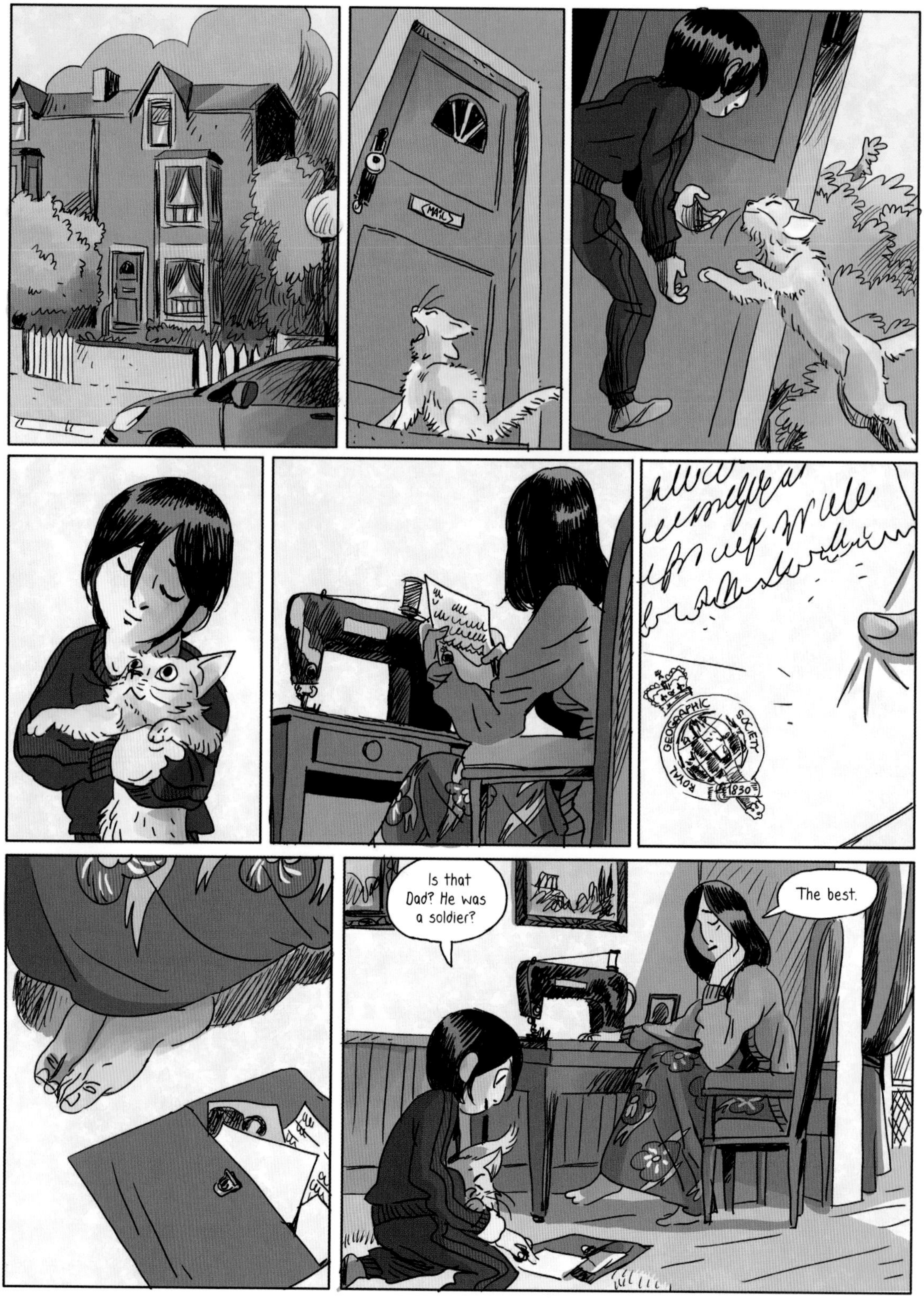
MAIL
ROYAL GEOGRAPHIC SOCIETY
1830
Is that Dad? He was a soldier?
The best.

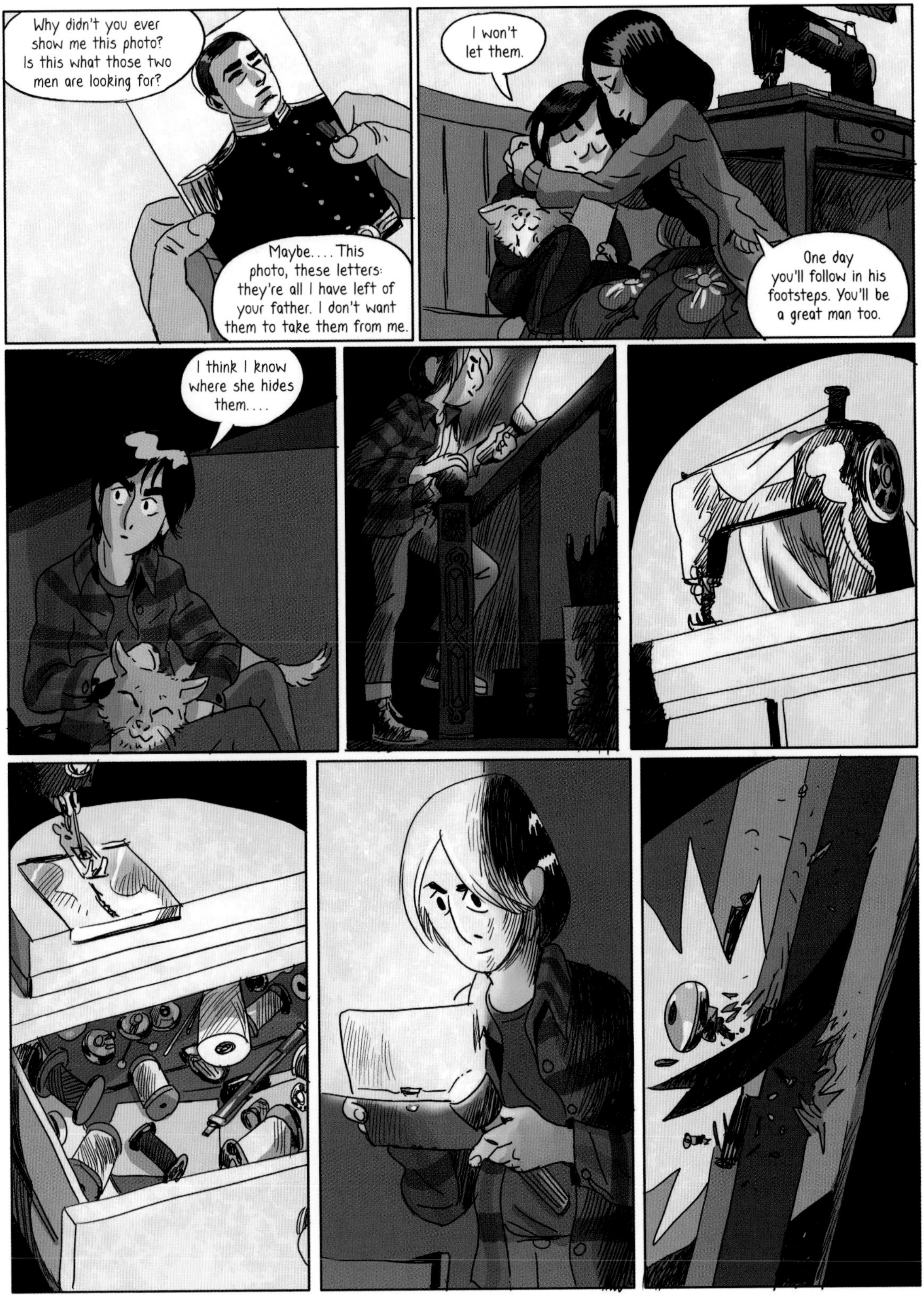
Why didn't you ever show me this photo? Is this what those two men are looking for?
Maybe.... This photo, these letters: they're all I have left of your father. I don't want them to take them from me.
I won't let them.
One day you'll follow in his footsteps. You'll be a great man too.
I think I know where she hides them....

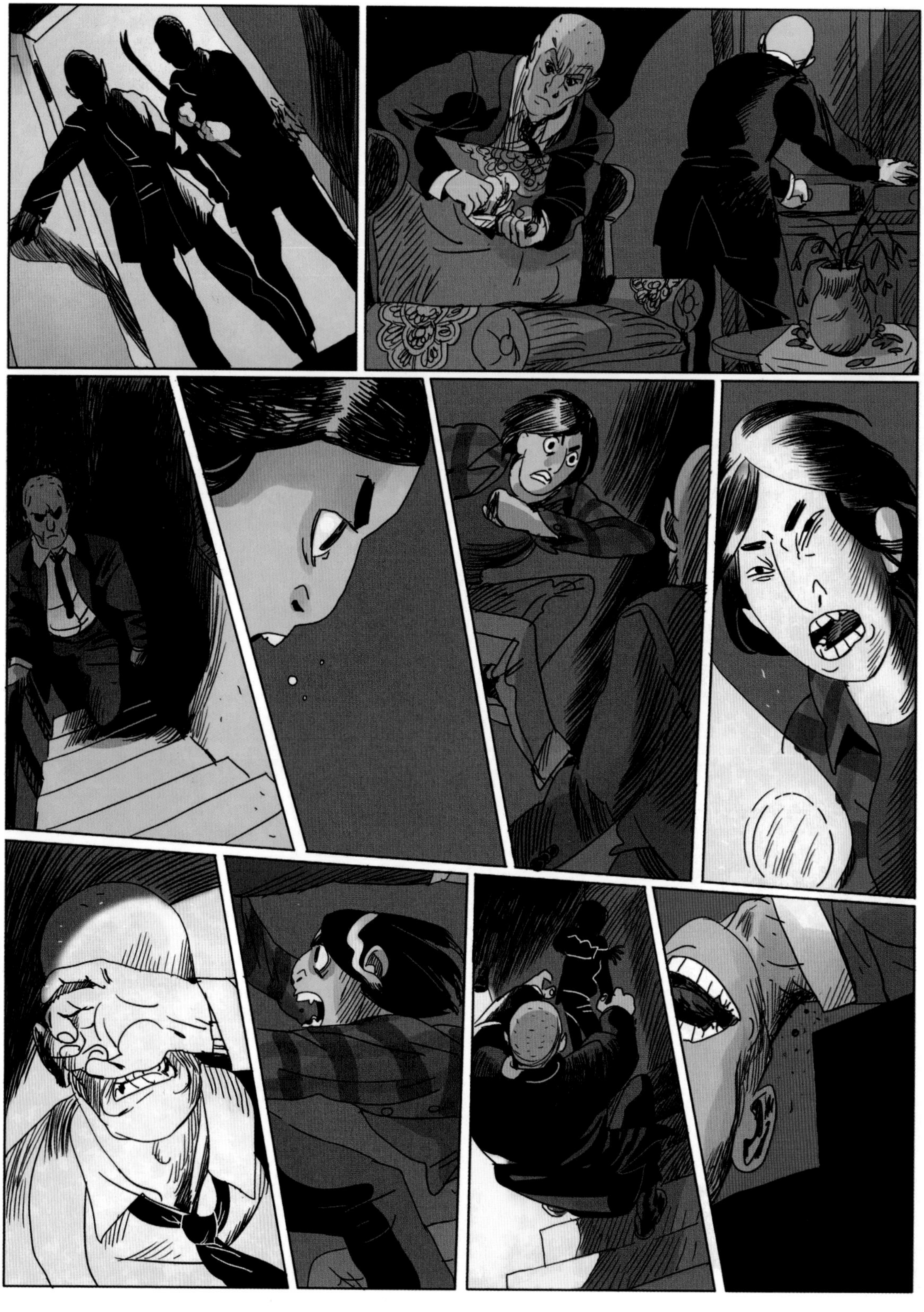

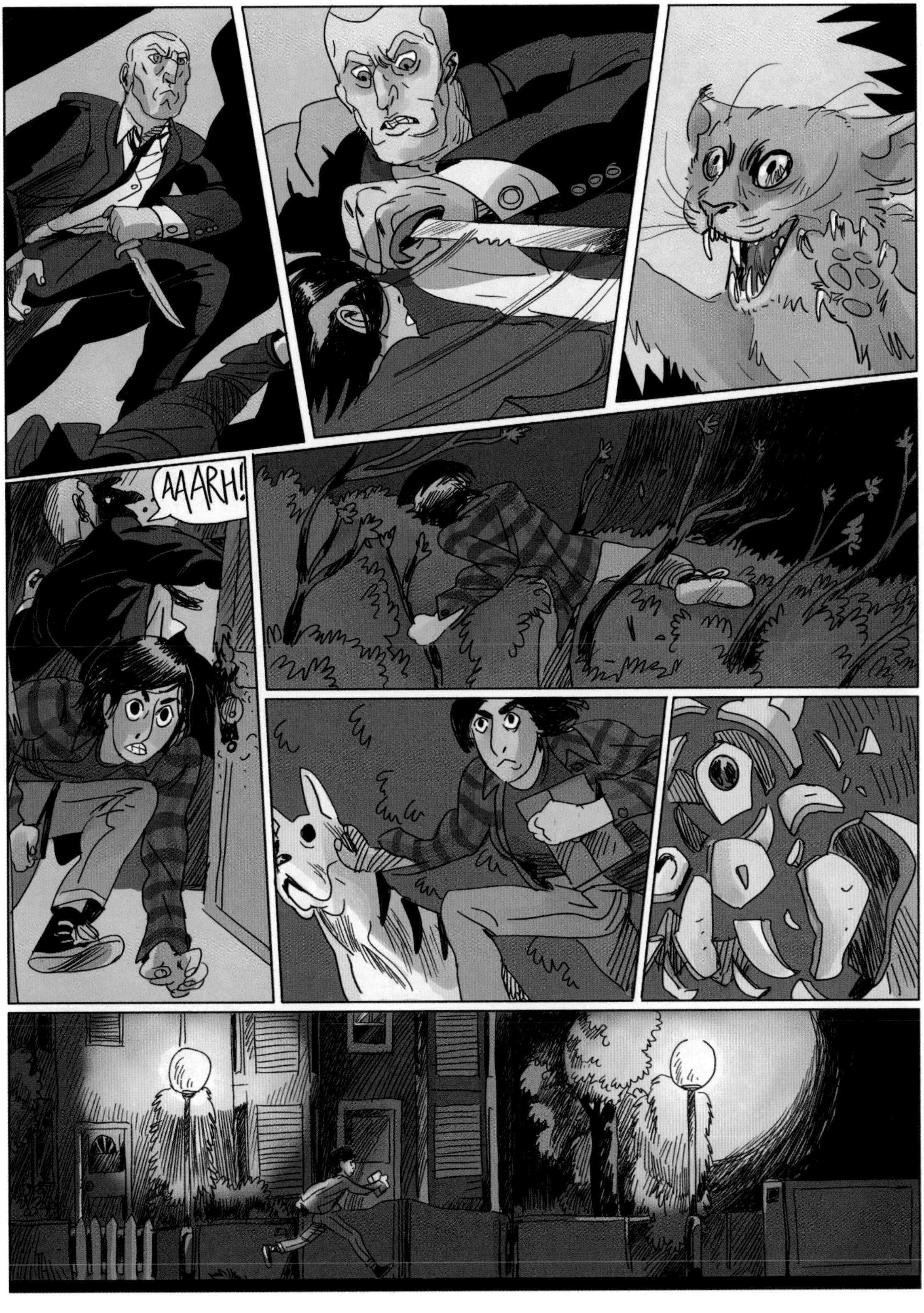
AAARH!

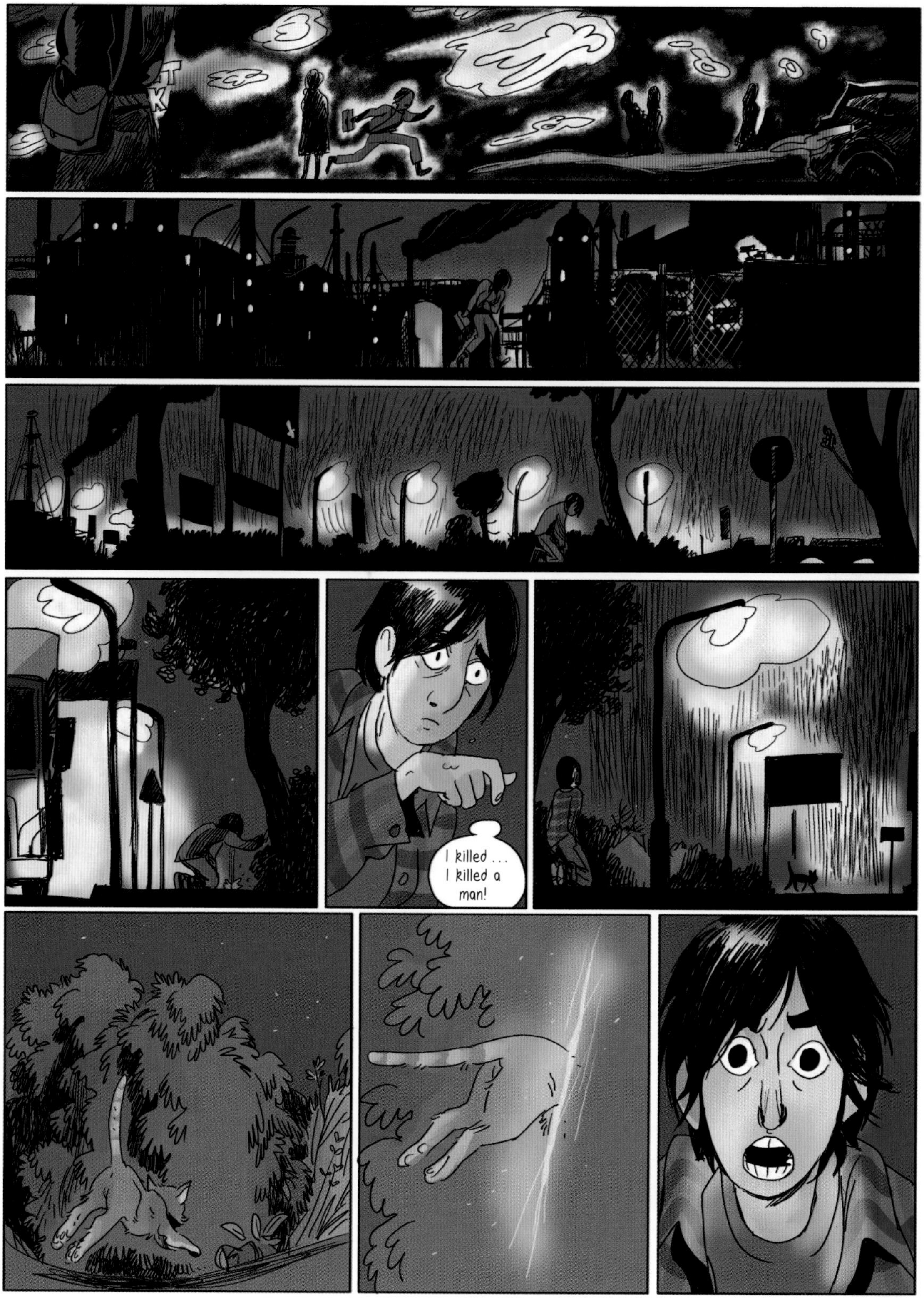
TK
I killed . . .
I killed a
man!

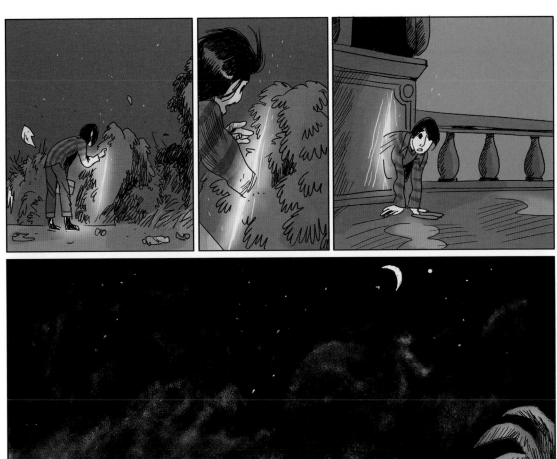

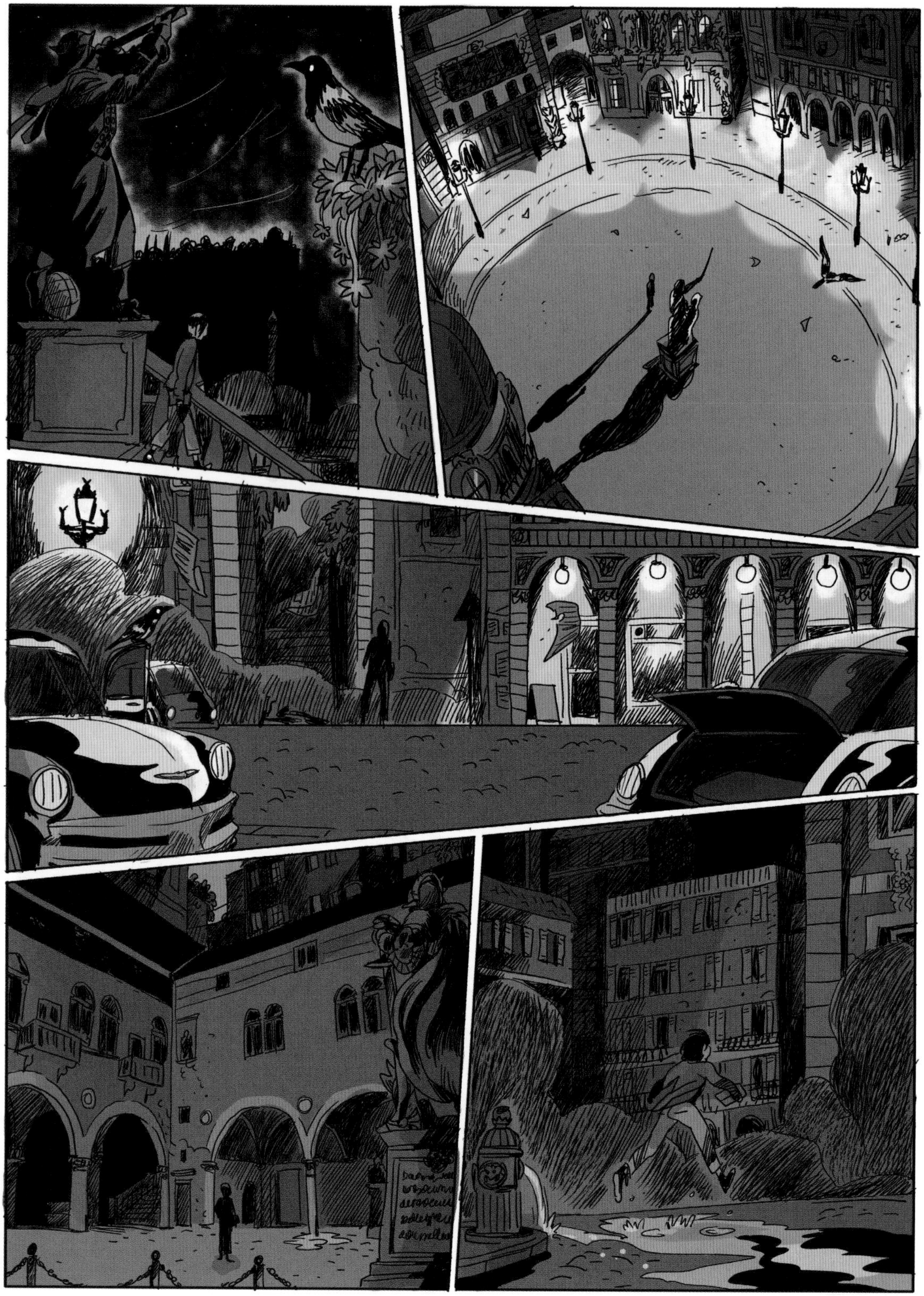

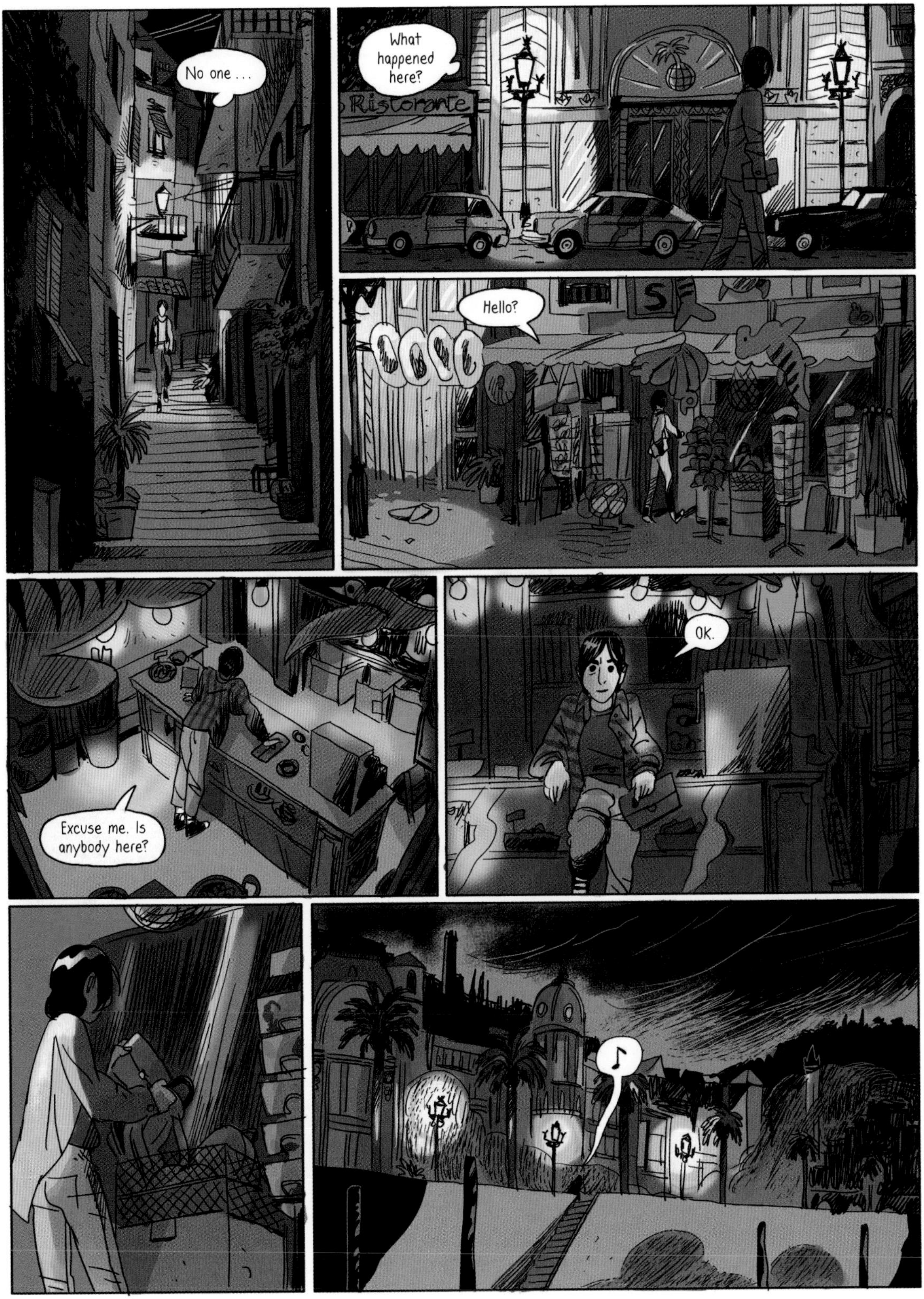
No one . . .
What happened here?
Ristorante
Hello?
Excuse me. Is anybody here?
OK.
♪

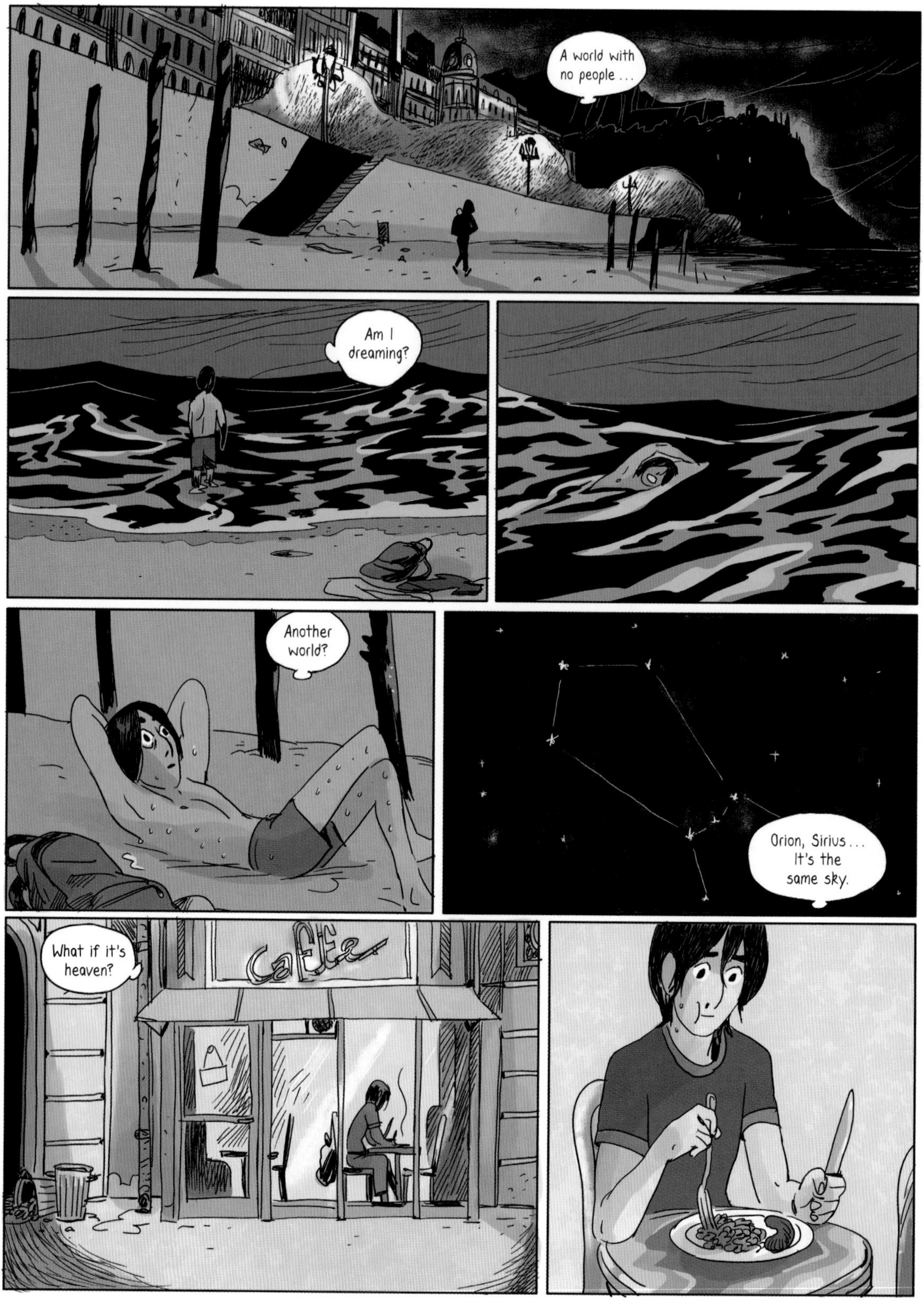
A world with no people . . .
Am I dreaming?
Another world?
Orion, Sirius . . . It's the same sky.
What if it's heaven?
Café

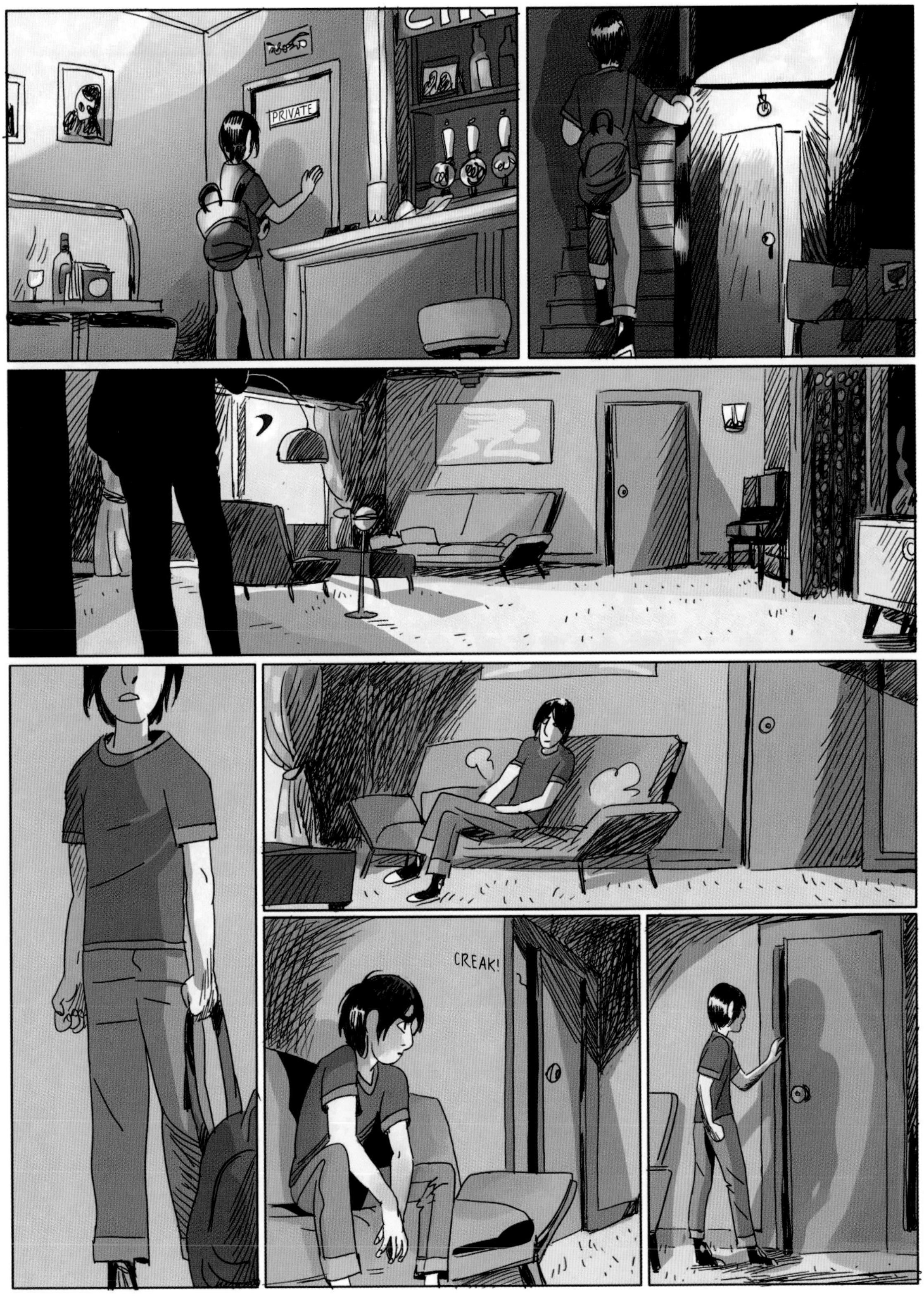
PRIVATE
CREAK!

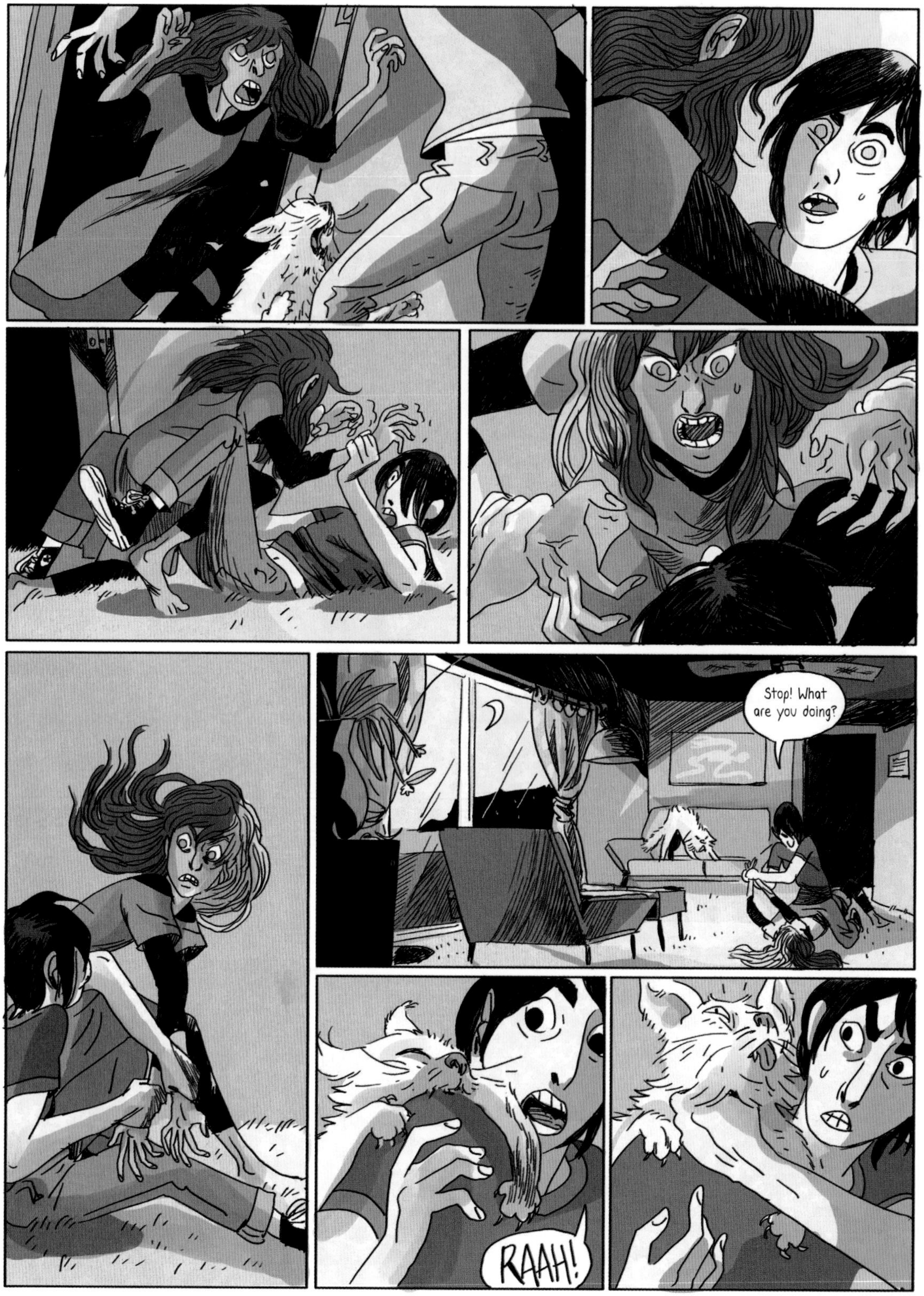
Stop! What are you doing?
RAAH!

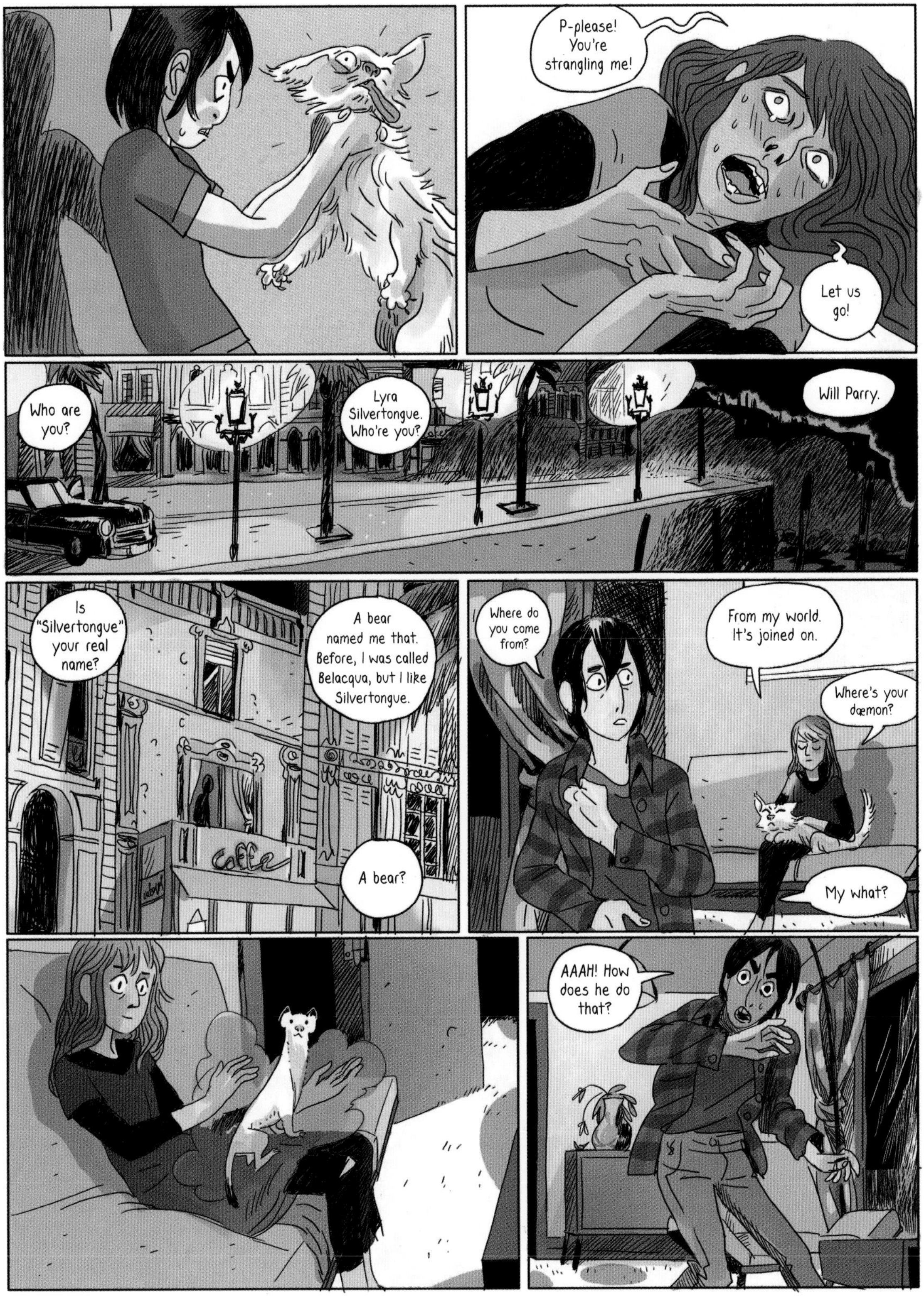
P-please! You're strangling me!
Let us go!
Who are you?
Lyra Silvertongue. Who're you?
Will Parry.
Is "Silvertongue" your real name?
A bear named me that. Before, I was called Belacqua, but I like Silvertongue.
A bear?
Where do you come from?
From my world. It's joined on.
Where's your dæmon?
My what?
AAAH! How does he do that?

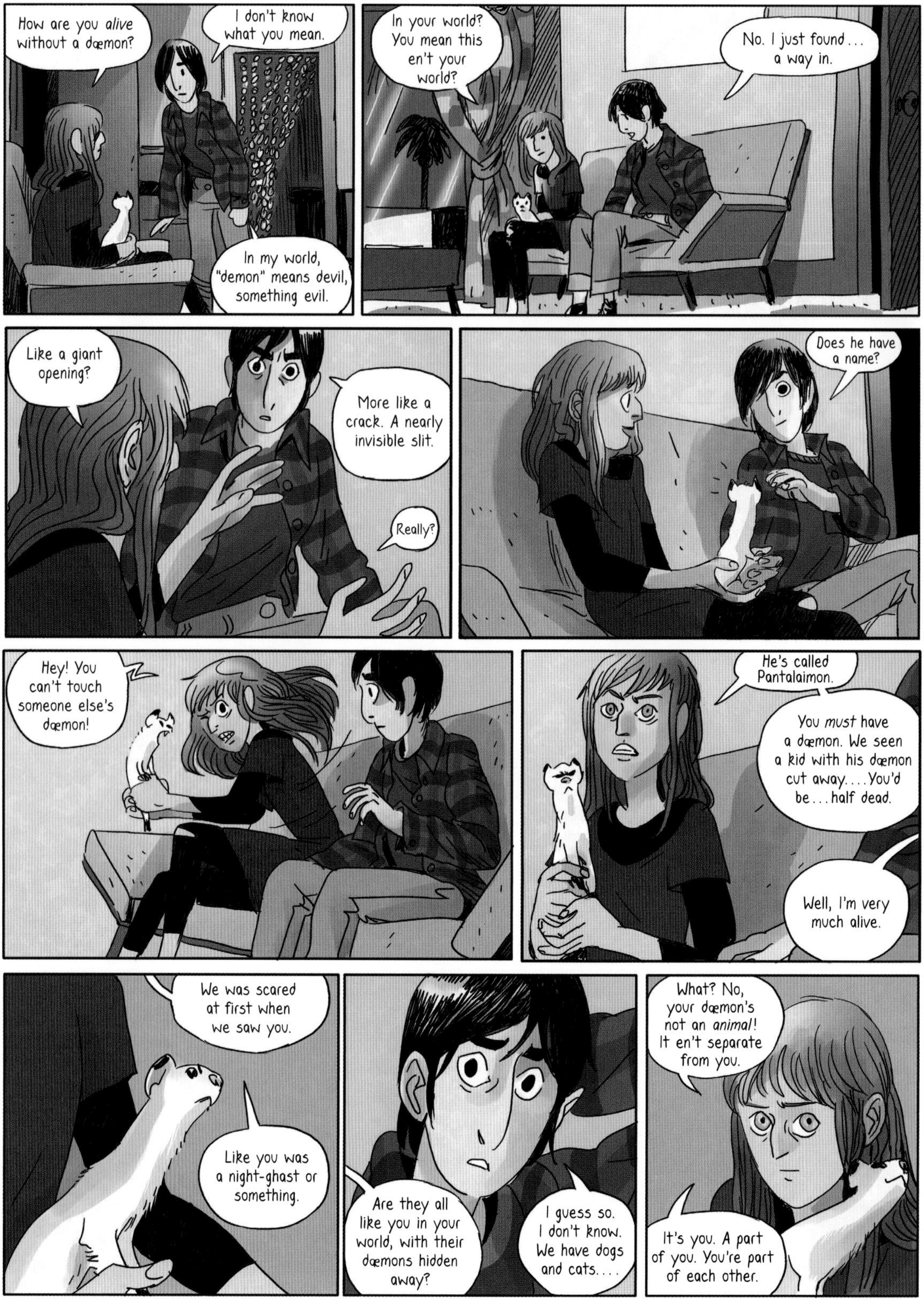
How are you *alive* without a dæmon?
I don't know what you mean.
In my world, "demon" means devil, something evil.
In your world? You mean this en't your world?
No. I just found . . . a way in.
Like a giant opening?
More like a crack. A nearly invisible slit.
Really?
Does he have a name?
Hey! You can't touch someone else's dæmon!
He's called Pantalaimon.
You *must* have a dæmon. We seen a kid with his dæmon cut away. . . . You'd be . . . half dead.
Well, I'm very much alive.
We was scared at first when we saw you.
Like you was a night-ghast or something.
Are they all like you in your world, with their dæmons hidden away?
I guess so. I don't know. We have dogs and cats. . . .
What? No, your dæmon's not an *animal*! It en't separate from you.
It's you. A part of you. You're part of each other.

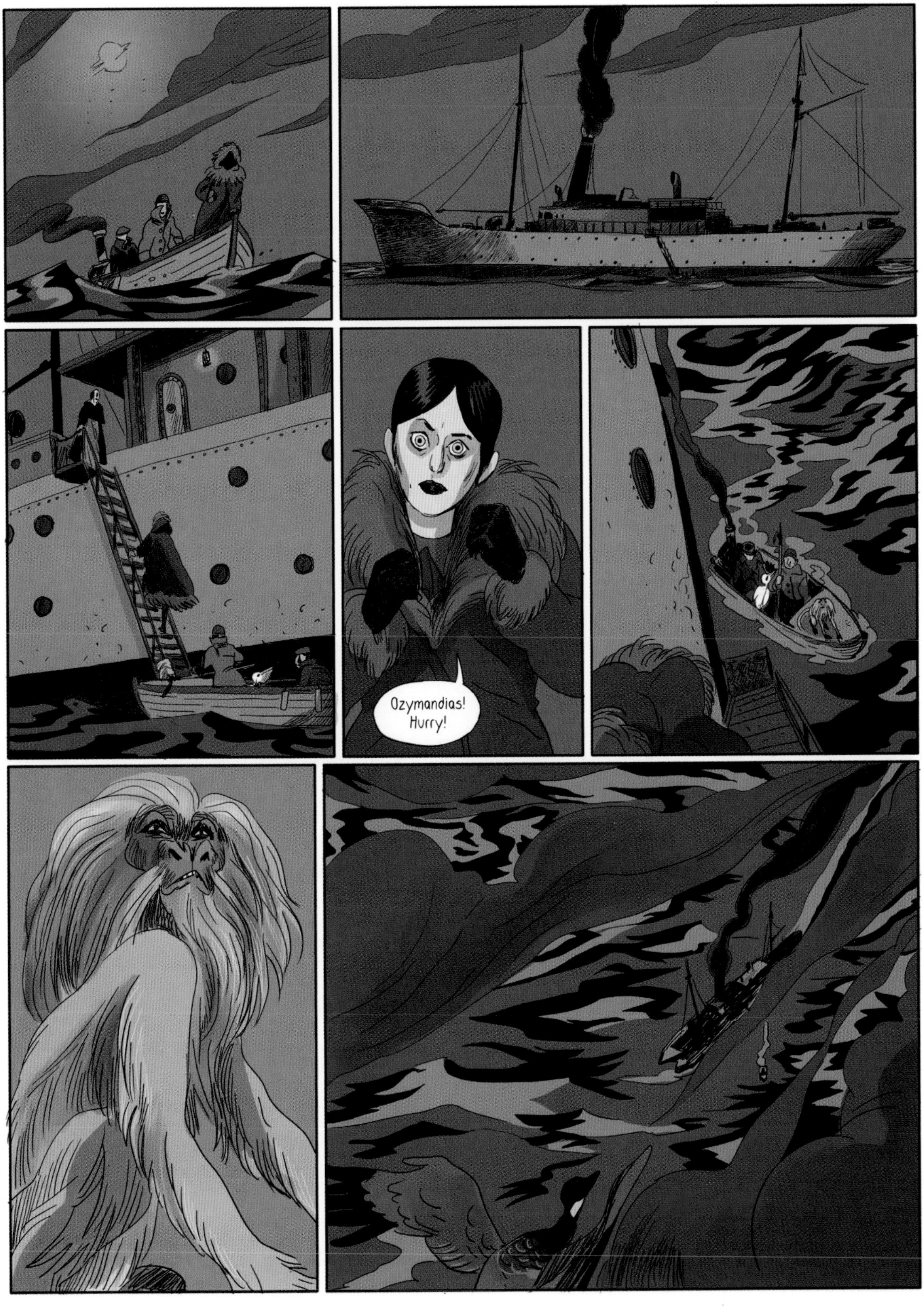
Ozymandias! Hurry!

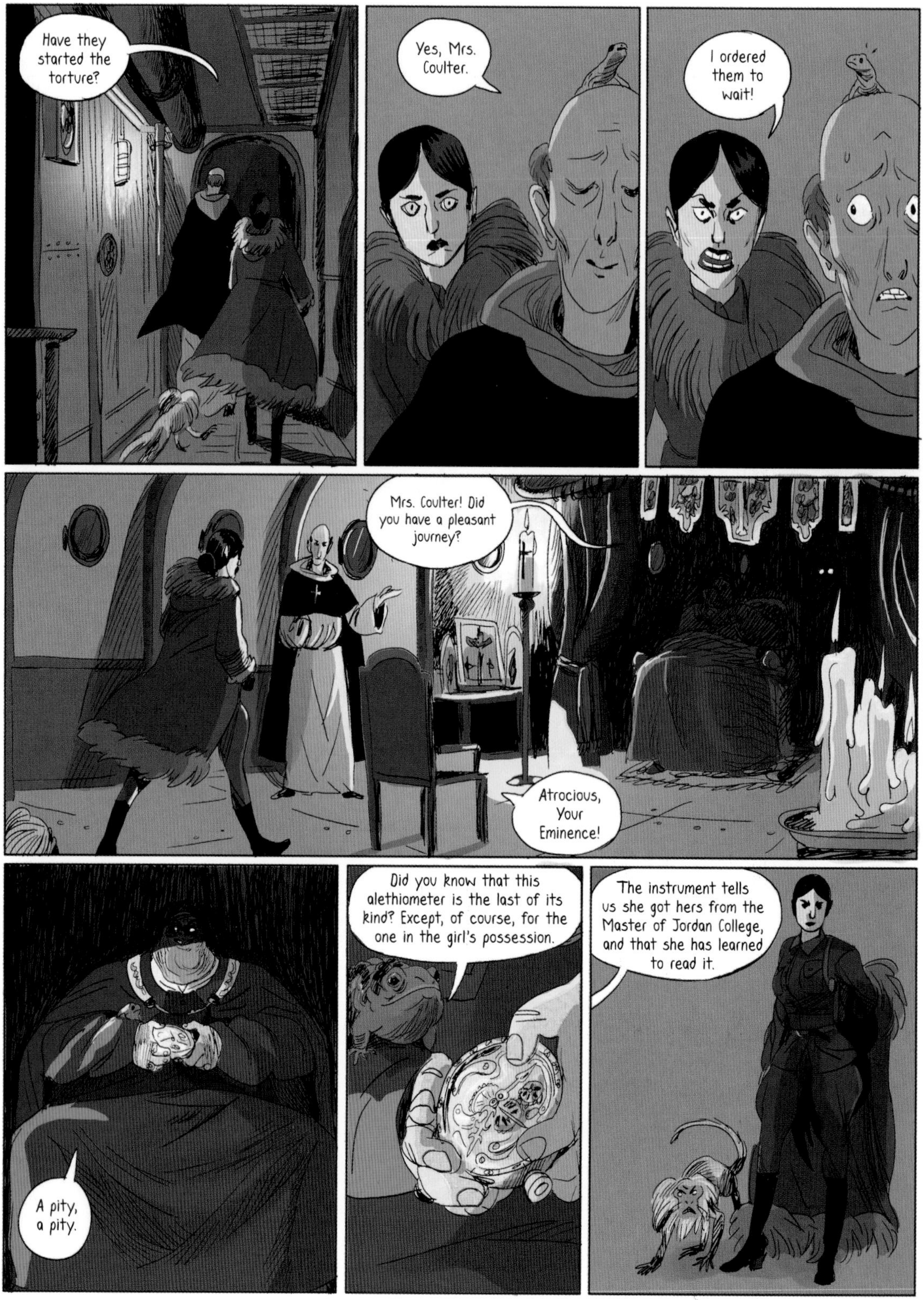

Have they started the torture?
Yes, Mrs. Coulter.
I ordered them to wait!
Mrs. Coulter! Did you have a pleasant journey?
Atrocious, Your Eminence!
A pity, a pity.
Did you know that this alethiometer is the last of its kind? Except, of course, for the one in the girl's possession.
The instrument tells us she got hers from the Master of Jordan College, and that she has learned to read it.

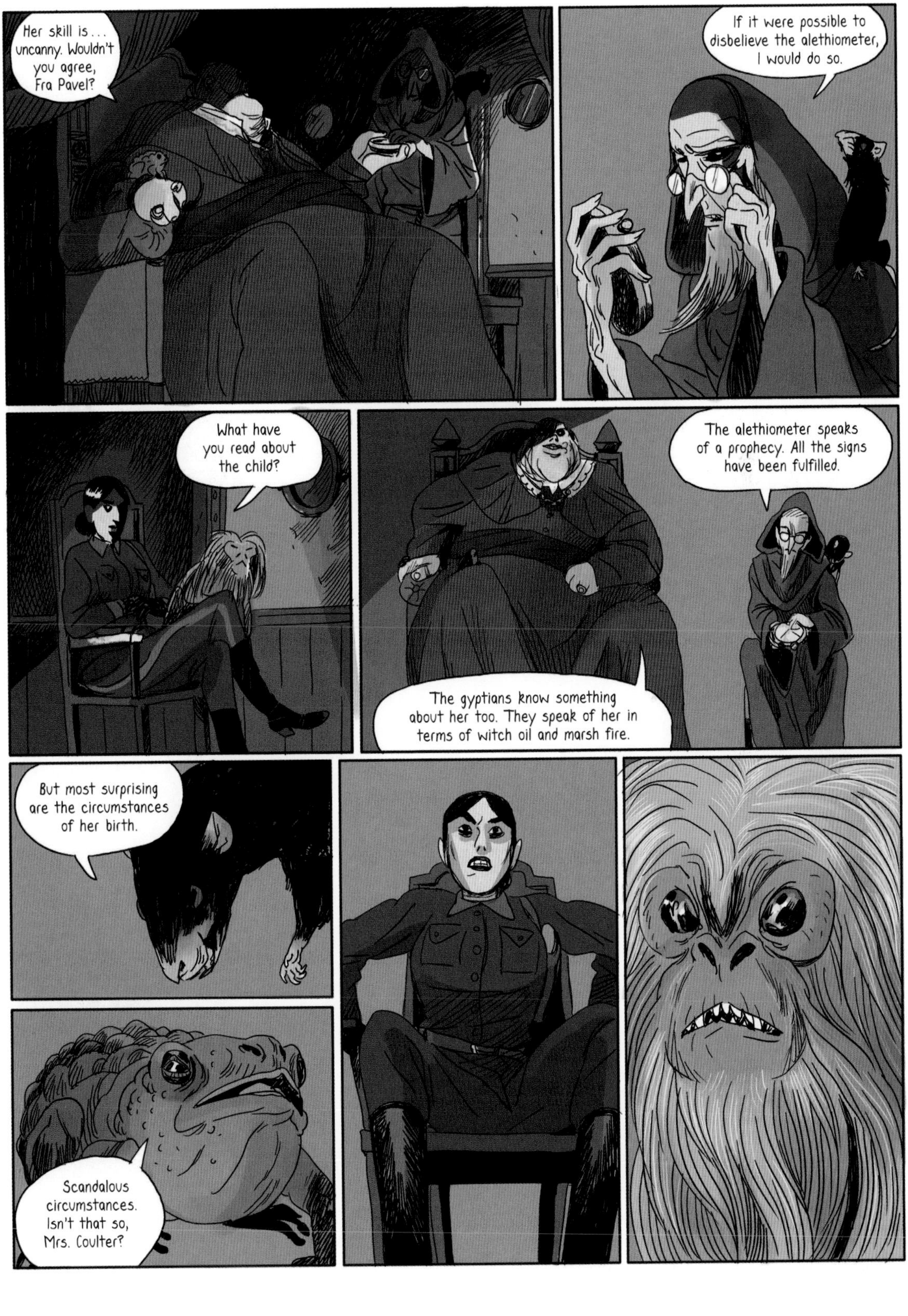
Her skill is . . . uncanny. Wouldn't you agree, Fra Pavel?
If it were possible to disbelieve the alethiometer, I would do so.
What have you read about the child?
The alethiometer speaks of a prophecy. All the signs have been fulfilled.
The gyptians know something about her too. They speak of her in terms of witch oil and marsh fire.
But most surprising are the circumstances of her birth.
Scandalous circumstances. Isn't that so, Mrs. Coulter?

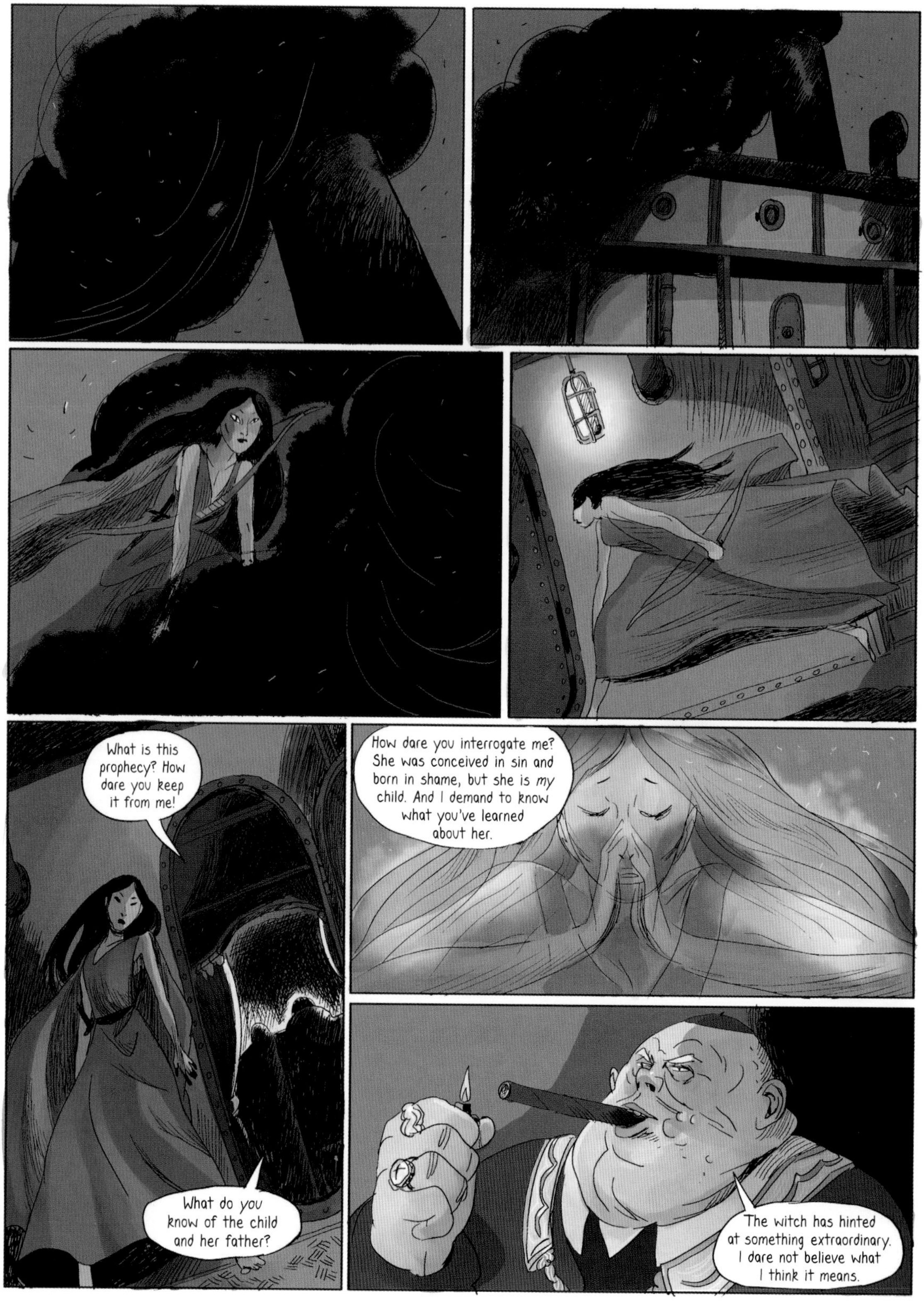
What is this prophecy? How dare you keep it from me!
What do *you* know of the child and her father?
How dare you interrogate me? She was conceived in sin and born in shame, but she is *my* child. And I demand to know what you've learned about her.
The witch has hinted at something extraordinary. I dare not believe what I think it means.

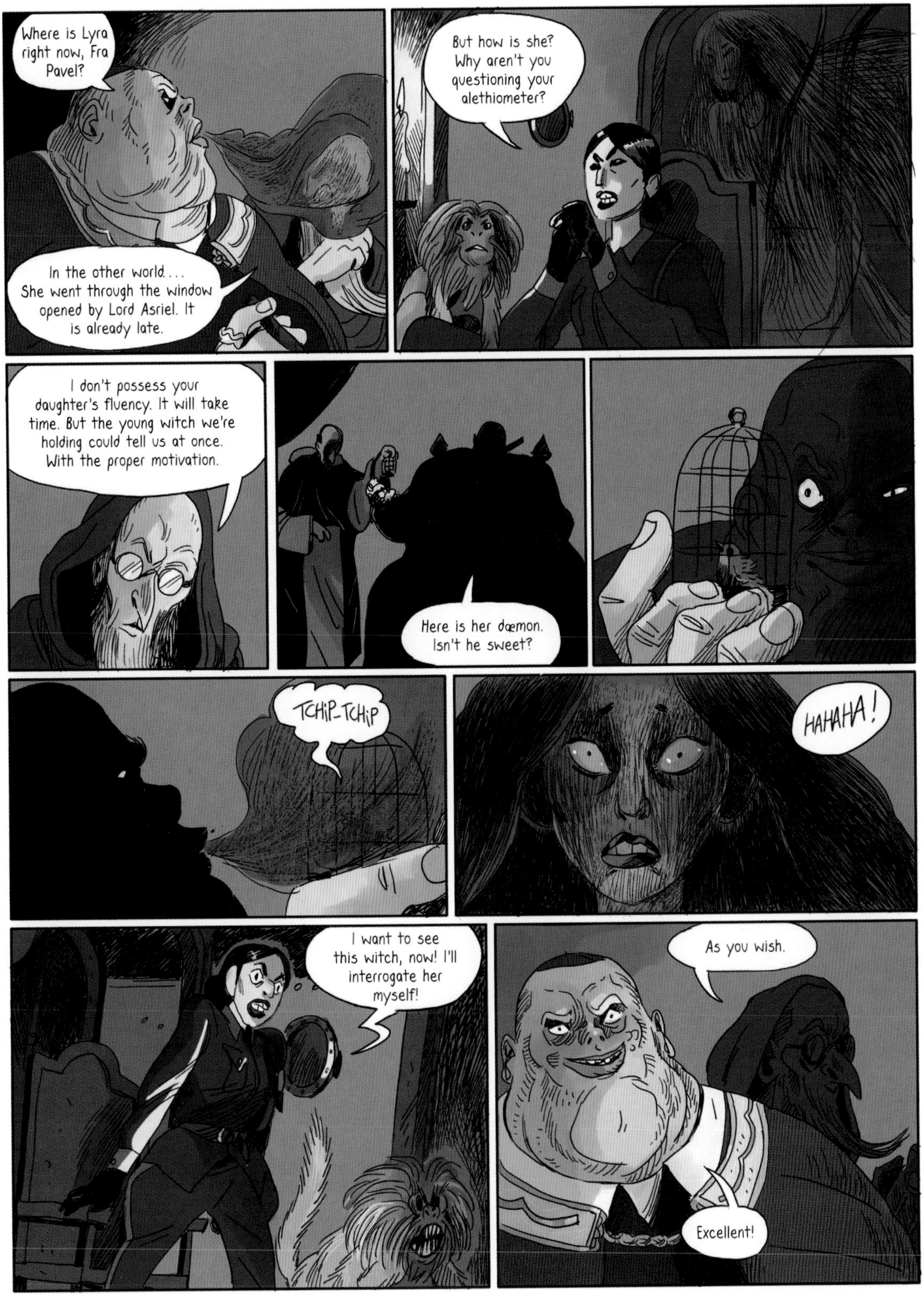

Where is Lyra right now, Fra Pavel?
In the other world.... She went through the window opened by Lord Asriel. It is already late.
But how is she? Why aren't you questioning your alethiometer?
I don't possess your daughter's fluency. It will take time. But the young witch we're holding could tell us at once. With the proper motivation.
Here is her dæmon. Isn't he sweet?
TCHIP-TCHIP
HAHAHA!
I want to see this witch, now! I'll interrogate her myself!
As you wish.
Excellent!

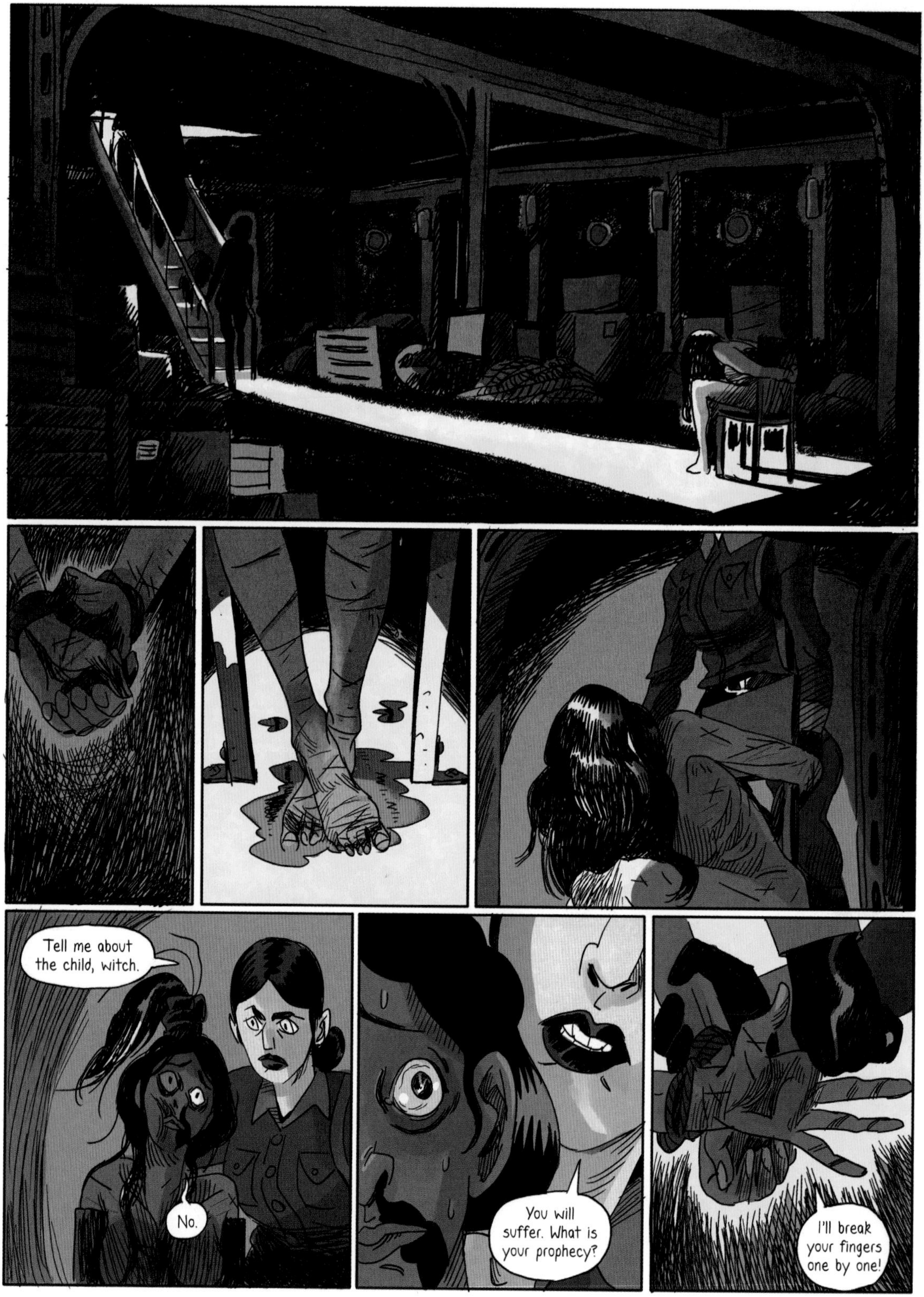
Tell me about the child, witch.
No.
You will suffer. What is your prophecy?
I'll break your fingers one by one!

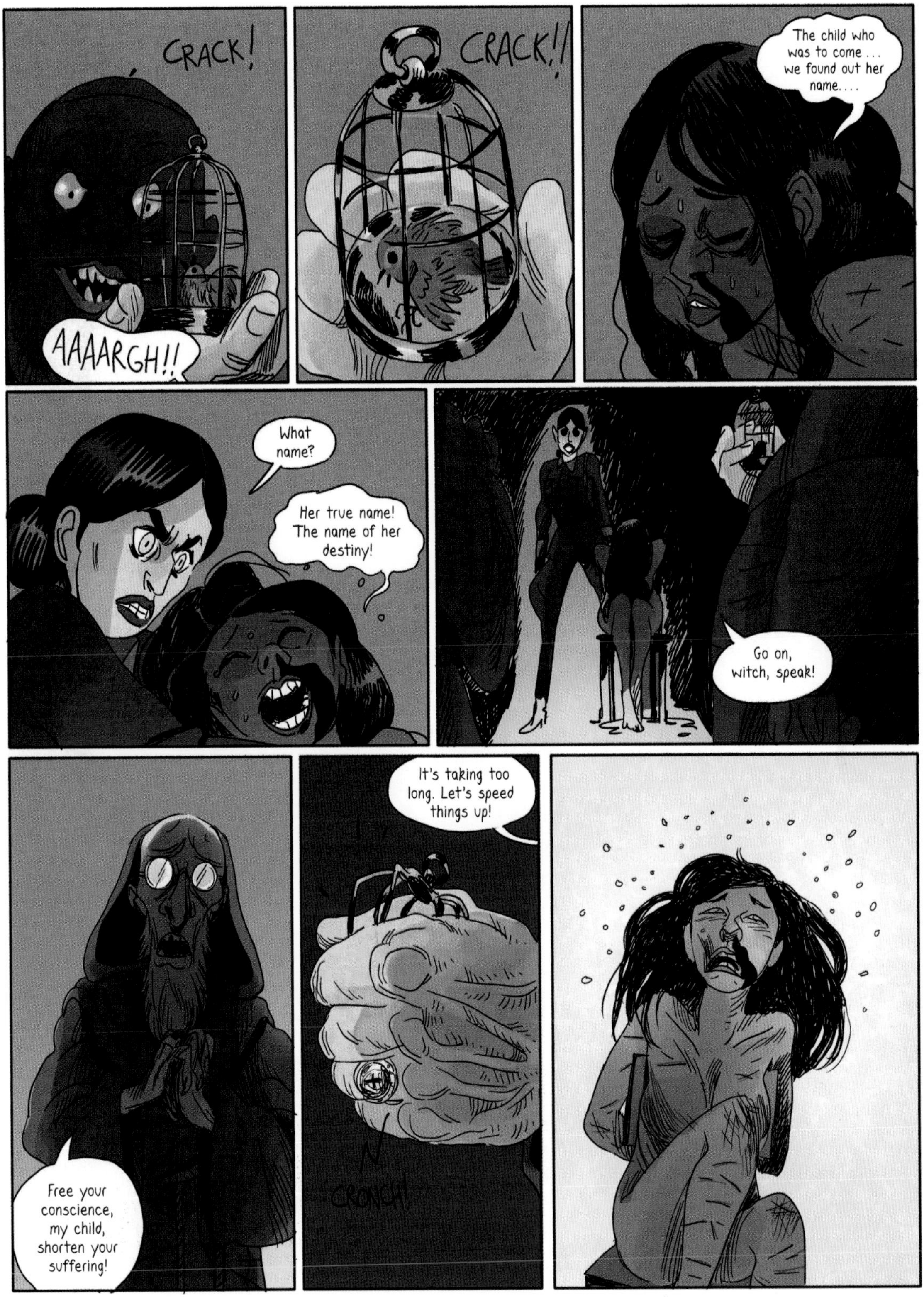
CRACK!
AAAARGH!!
CRACK!!
The child who was to come . . . we found out her name. . . .
What name?
Her true name! The name of her destiny!
Go on, witch, speak!
Free your conscience, my child, shorten your suffering!
It's taking too long. Let's speed things up!
CRUNCH!

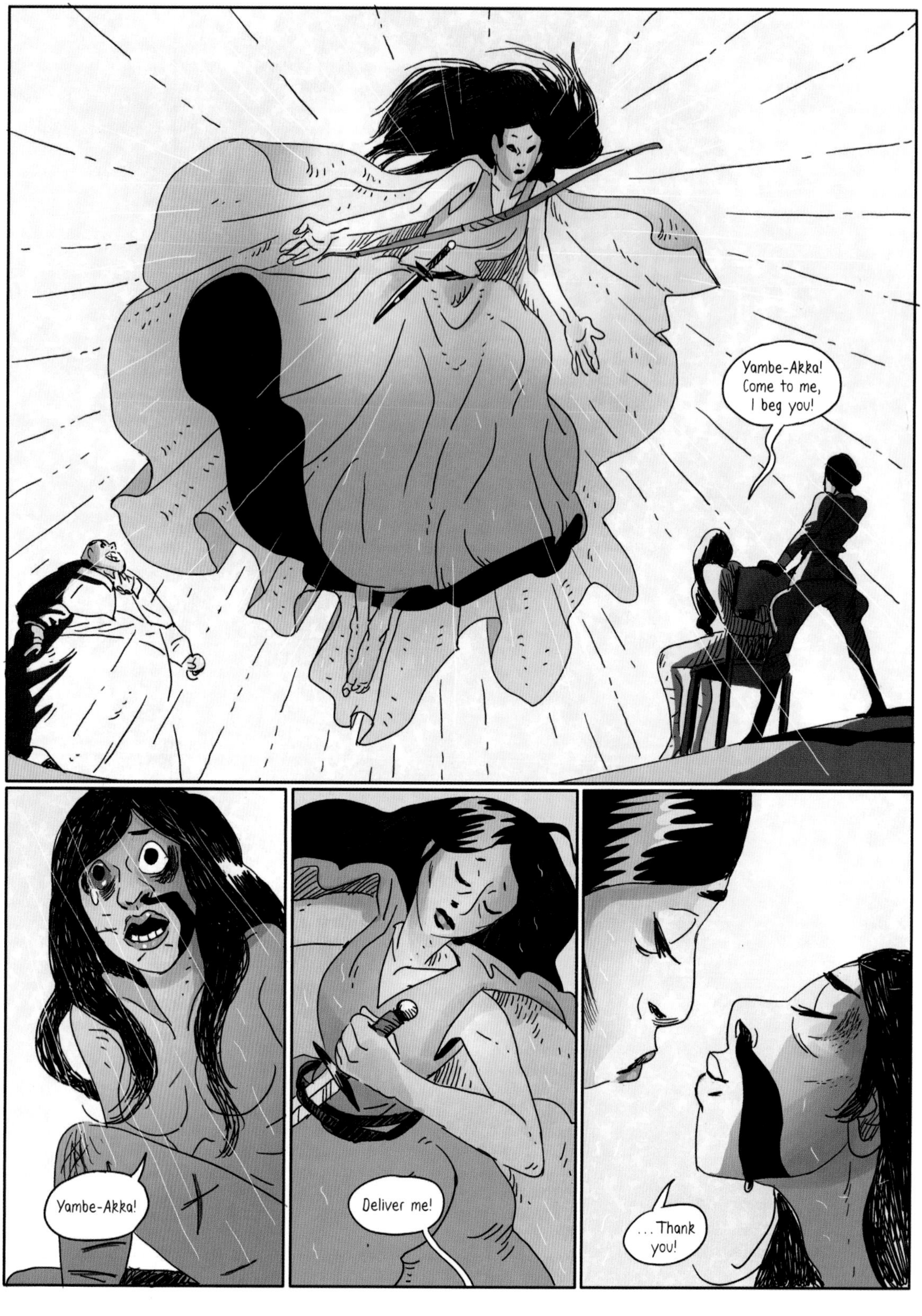

Yambe-Akka! Come to me, I beg you!
Yambe-Akka!
Deliver me!
...Thank you!

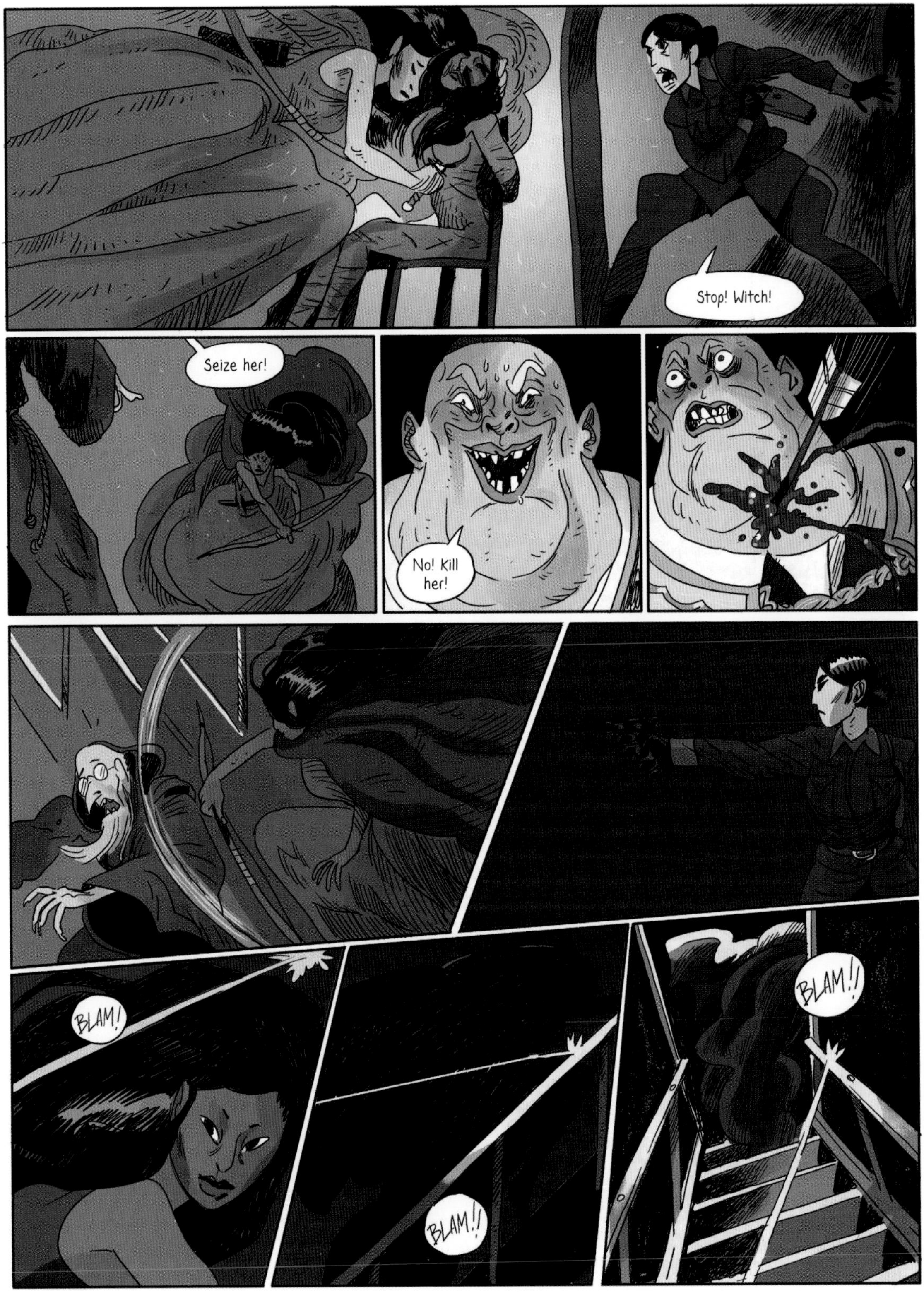
Stop! Witch!
Seize her!
No! Kill her!
BLAM!
BLAM!!
BLAM!!

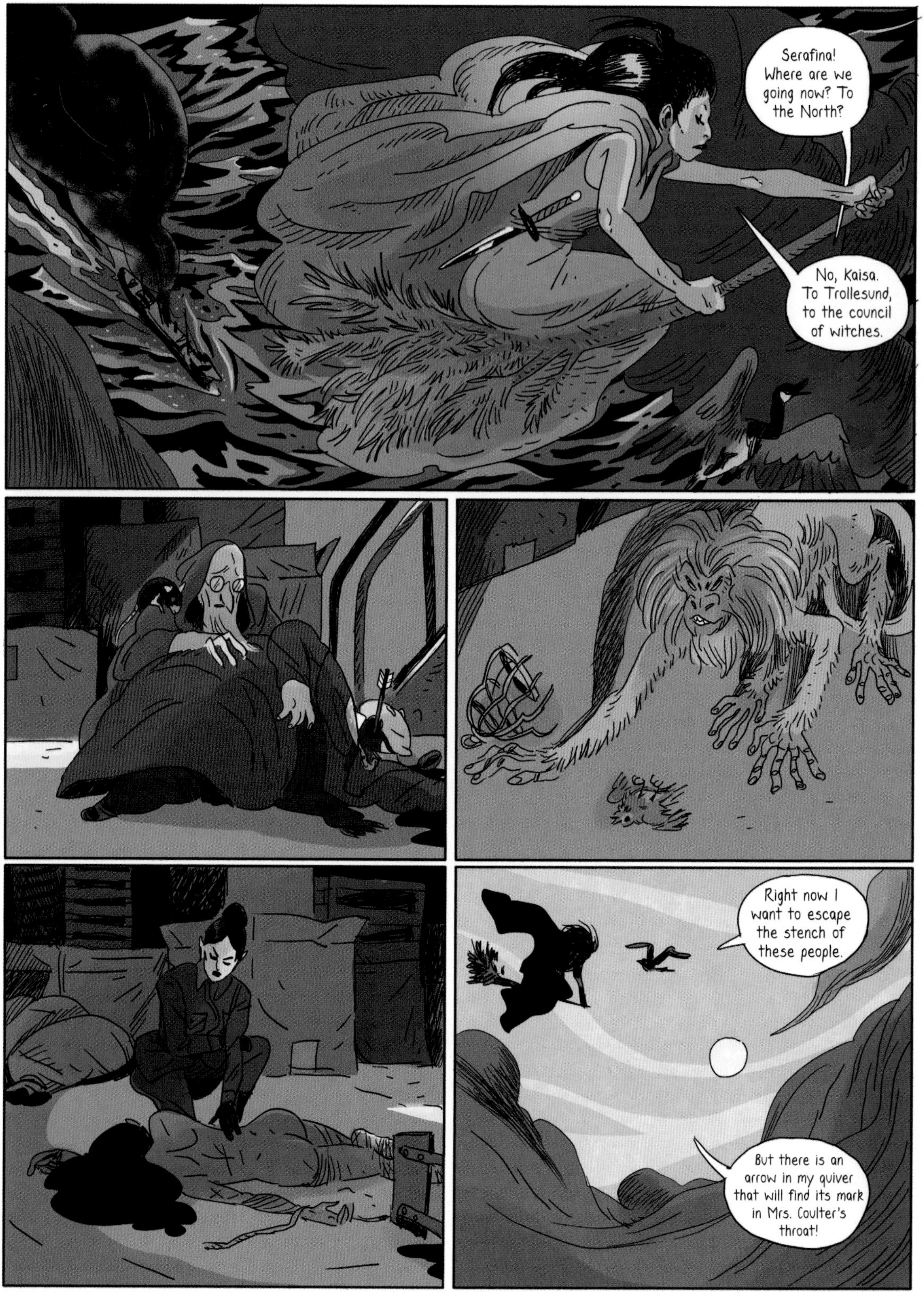
Serafina! Where are we going now? To the North?
No, Kaisa. To Trollesund, to the council of witches.
Right now I want to escape the stench of these people.
But there is an arrow in my quiver that will find its mark in Mrs. Coulter's throat!

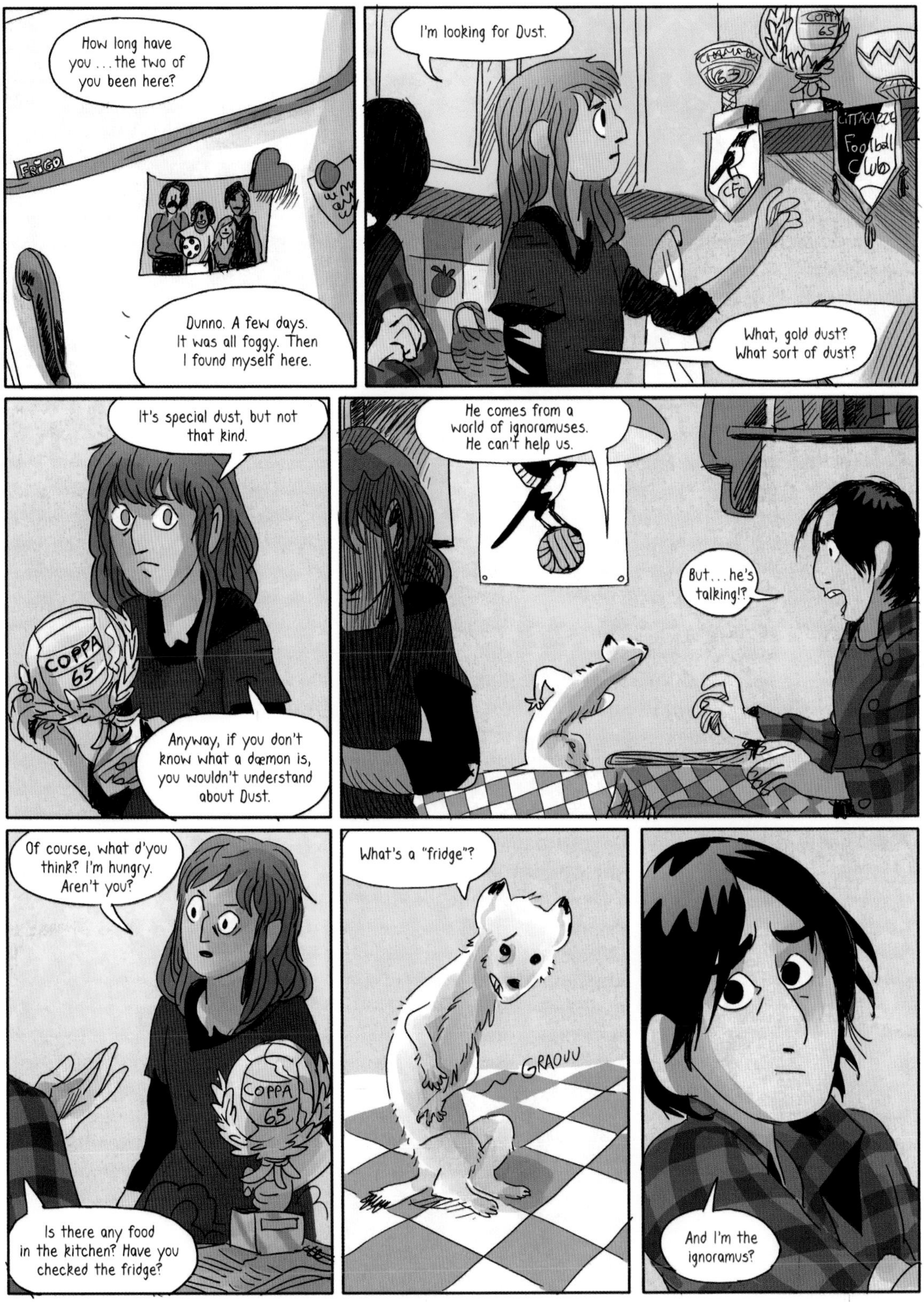
How long have you . . . the two of you been here?
FRIGO
Dunno. A few days. It was all foggy. Then I found myself here.
I'm looking for Dust.
COPPA 65
CITTAGAZZE Football Club
CFC
What, gold dust? What sort of dust?
It's special dust, but not that kind.
COPPA 65
Anyway, if you don't know what a dæmon is, you wouldn't understand about Dust.
He comes from a world of ignoramuses. He can't help us.
But . . . he's talking!?
Of course, what d'you think? I'm hungry. Aren't you?
COPPA 65
Is there any food in the kitchen? Have you checked the fridge?
What's a "fridge"?
GRAOUU
And I'm the ignoramus?

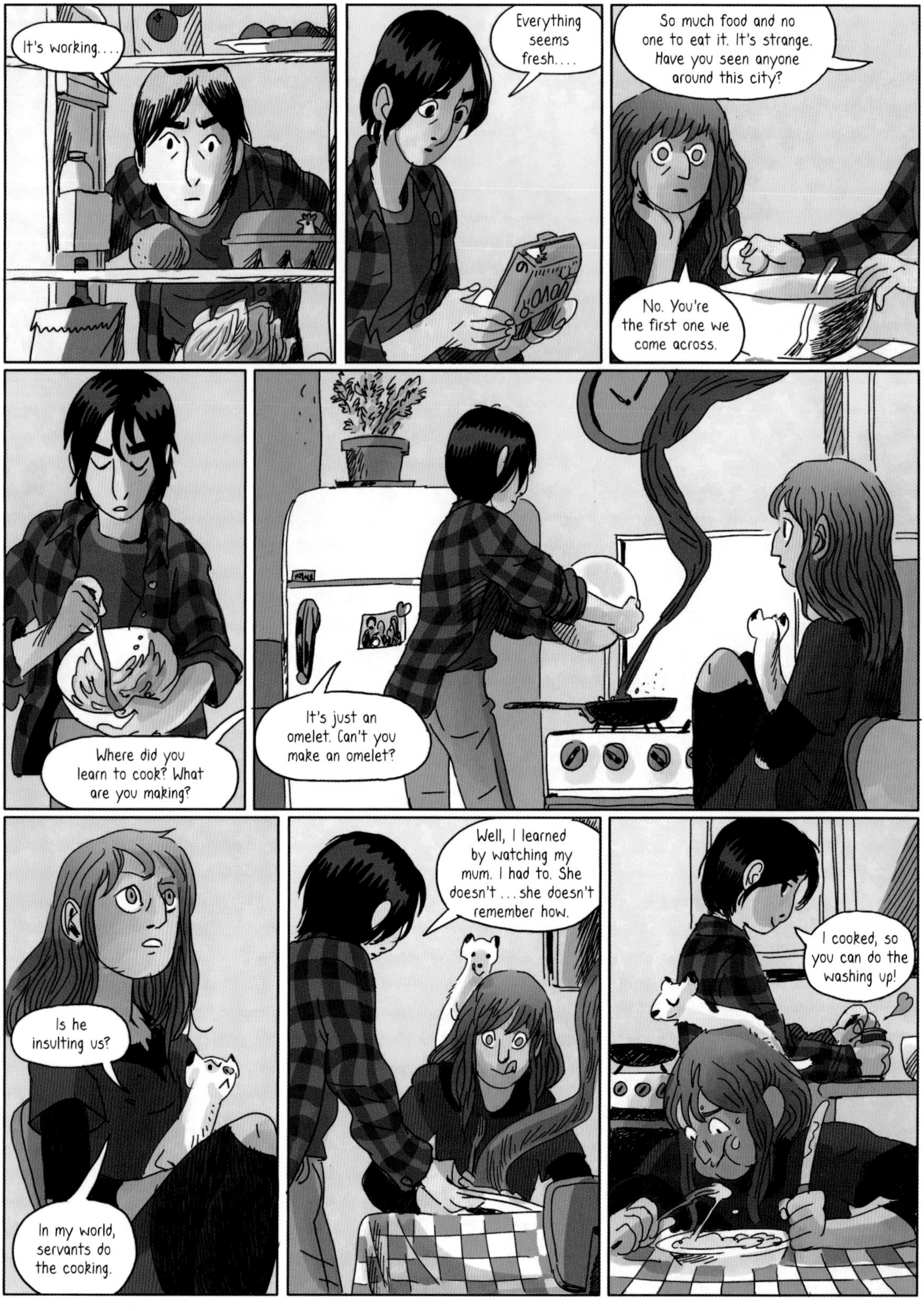
It's working. . . .
Everything seems fresh. . . .
So much food and no one to eat it. It's strange. Have you seen anyone around this city?
No. You're the first one we come across.
Where did you learn to cook? What are you making?
It's just an omelet. Can't you make an omelet?
Is he insulting us?
In my world, servants do the cooking.
Well, I learned by watching my mum. I had to. She doesn't . . . she doesn't remember how.
I cooked, so you can do the washing up!

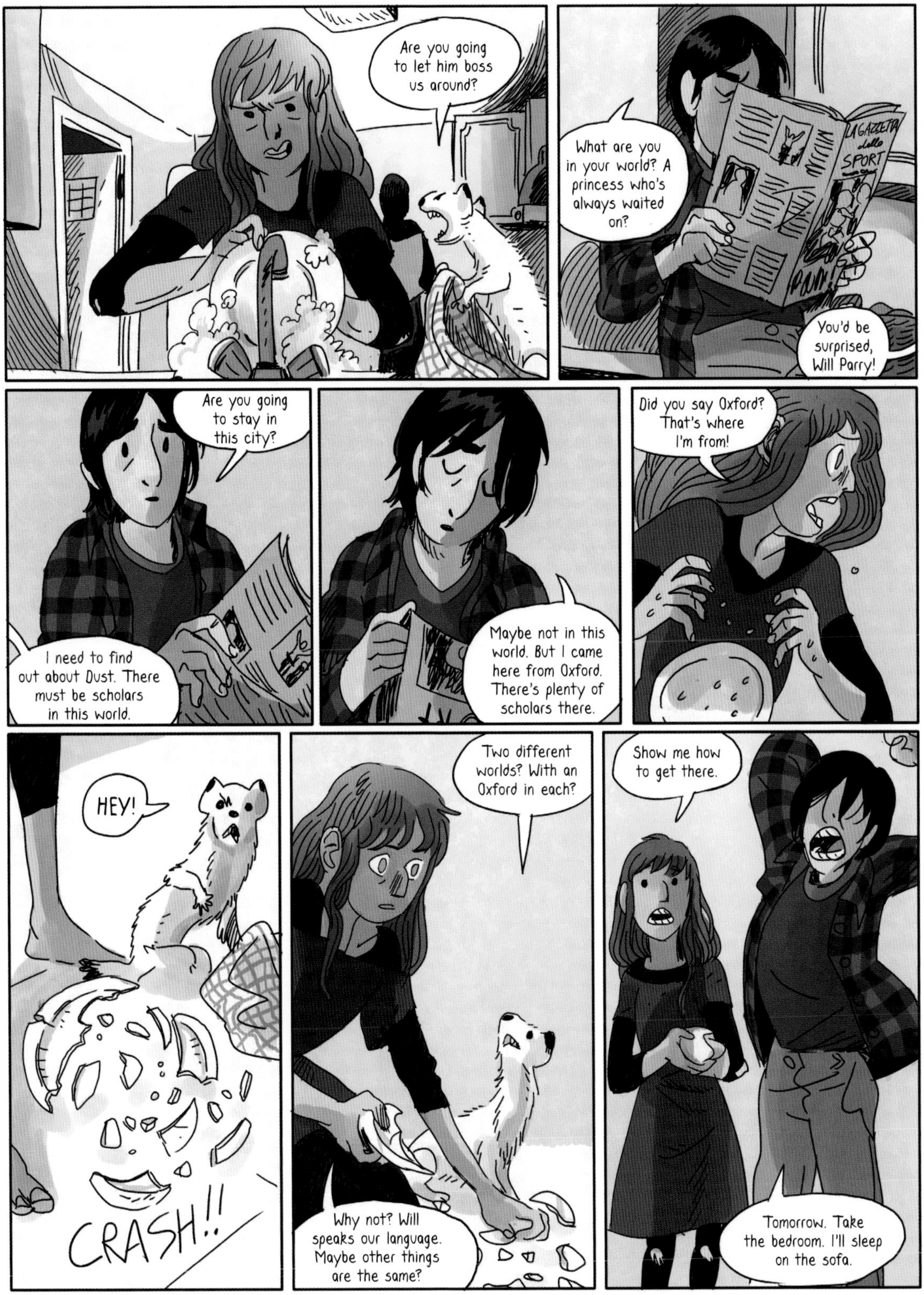
Are you going to let him boss us around?
What are you in your world? A princess who's always waited on?
You'd be surprised, Will Parry!
Are you going to stay in this city?
I need to find out about Dust. There must be scholars in this world.
Maybe not in this world. But I came here from Oxford. There's plenty of scholars there.
Did you say Oxford? That's where I'm from!
HEY!
CRASH!!
Two different worlds? With an Oxford in each?
Why not? Will speaks our language. Maybe other things are the same?
Show me how to get there.
Tomorrow. Take the bedroom. I'll sleep on the sofa.

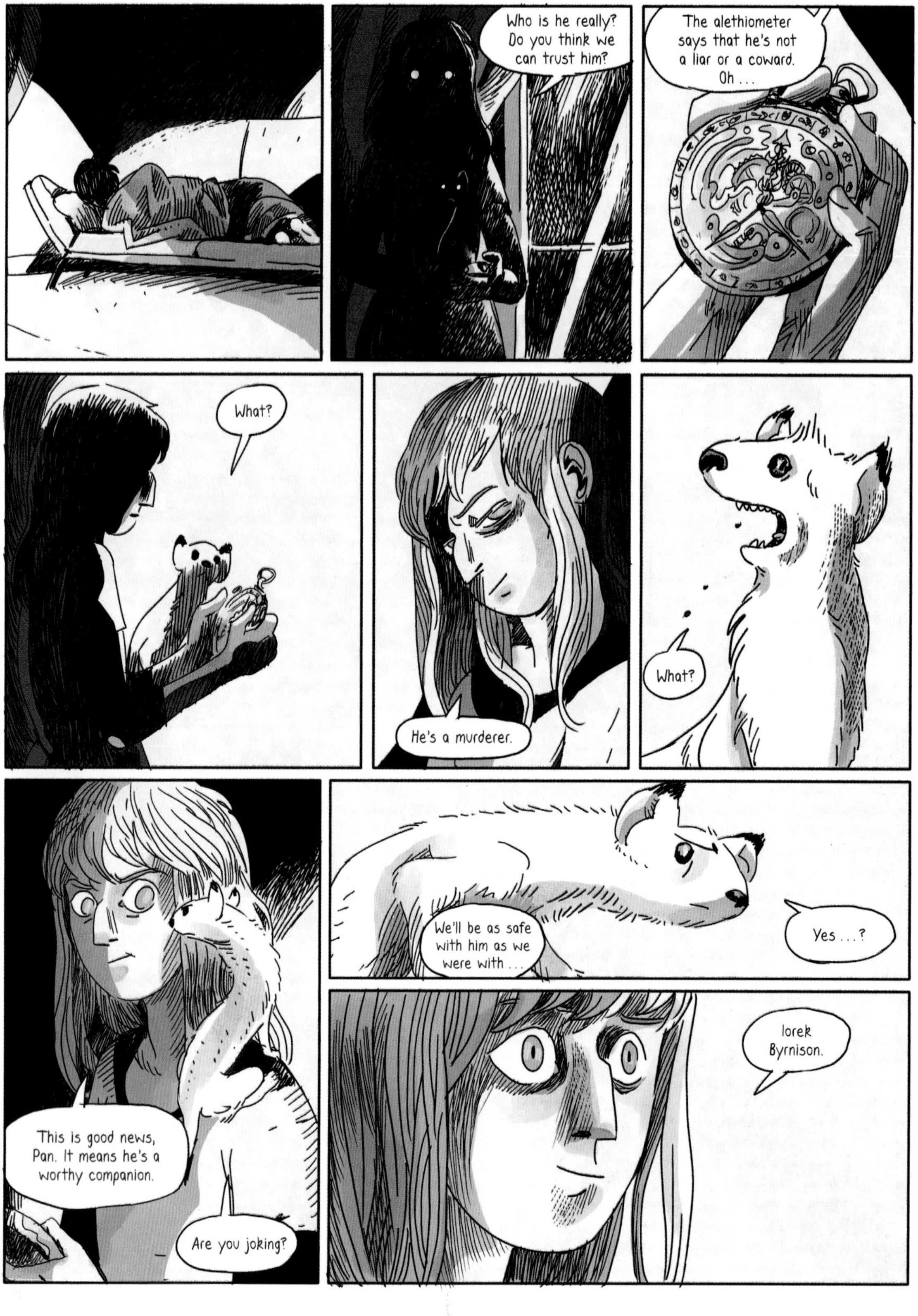
Who is he really? Do you think we can trust him?
The alethiometer says that he's not a liar or a coward. Oh . . .
What?
He's a murderer.
What?
This is good news, Pan. It means he's a worthy companion.
Are you joking?
We'll be as safe with him as we were with . . .
Yes . . . ?
Iorek Byrnison.

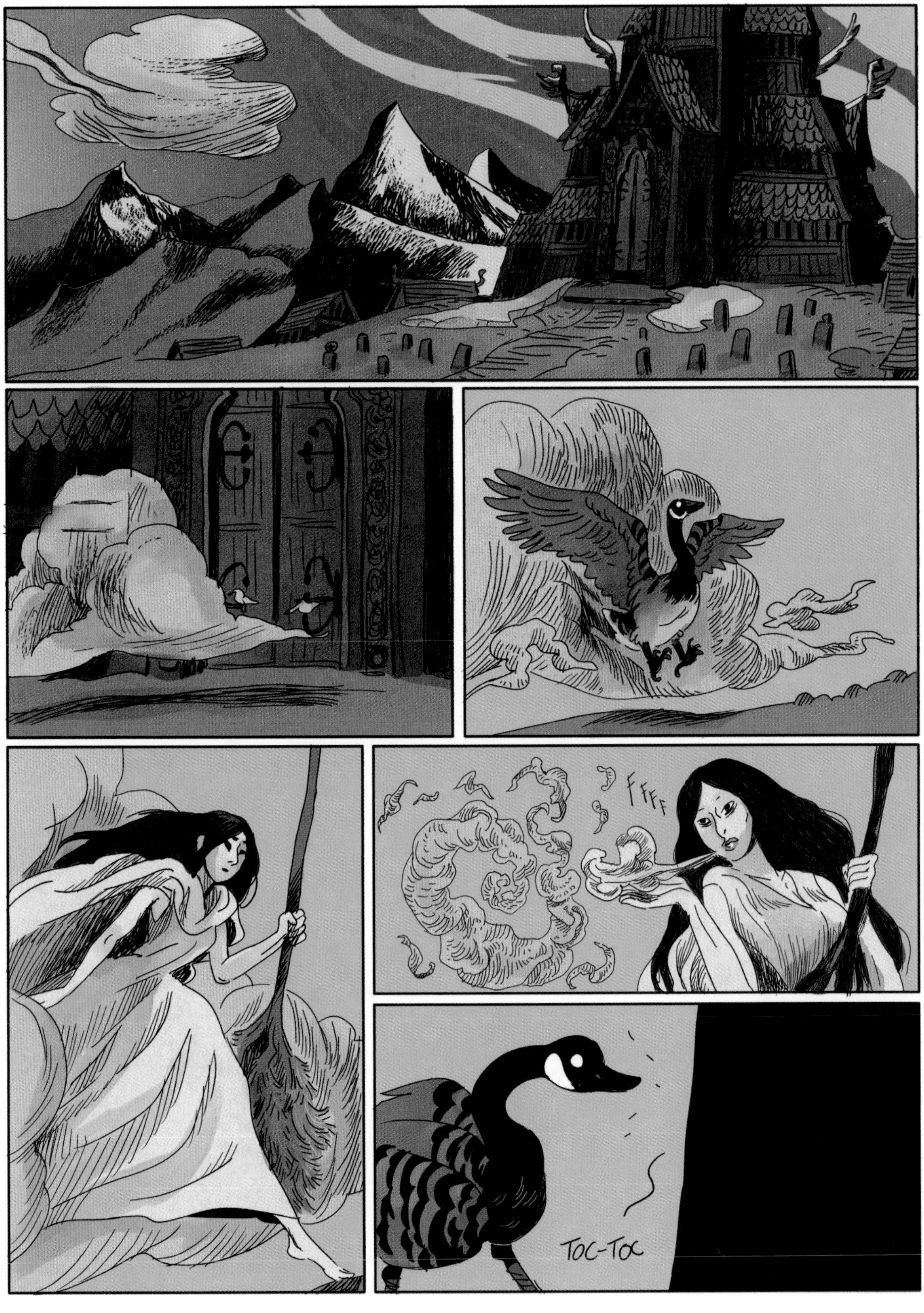
FFFF
TOC-TOC

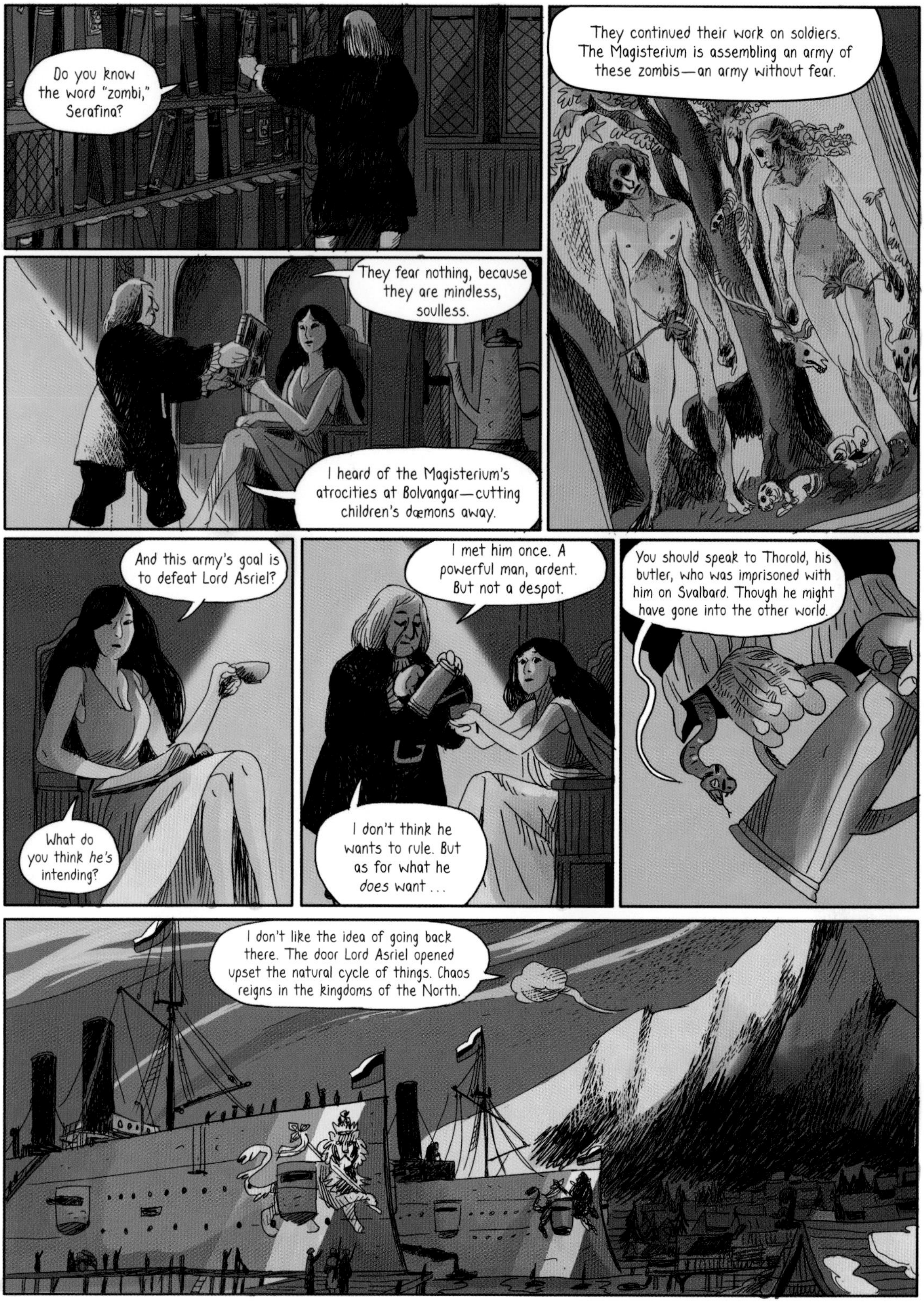
Do you know the word "zombi," Serafina?
They continued their work on soldiers. The Magisterium is assembling an army of these zombis—an army without fear.
They fear nothing, because they are mindless, soulless.
I heard of the Magisterium's atrocities at Bolvangar—cutting children's dæmons away.
And this army's goal is to defeat Lord Asriel?
What do you think *he's* intending?
I met him once. A powerful man, ardent. But not a despot.
I don't think he wants to rule. But as for what he *does* want . . .
You should speak to Thorold, his butler, who was imprisoned with him on Svalbard. Though he might have gone into the other world.
I don't like the idea of going back there. The door Lord Asriel opened upset the natural cycle of things. Chaos reigns in the kingdoms of the North.

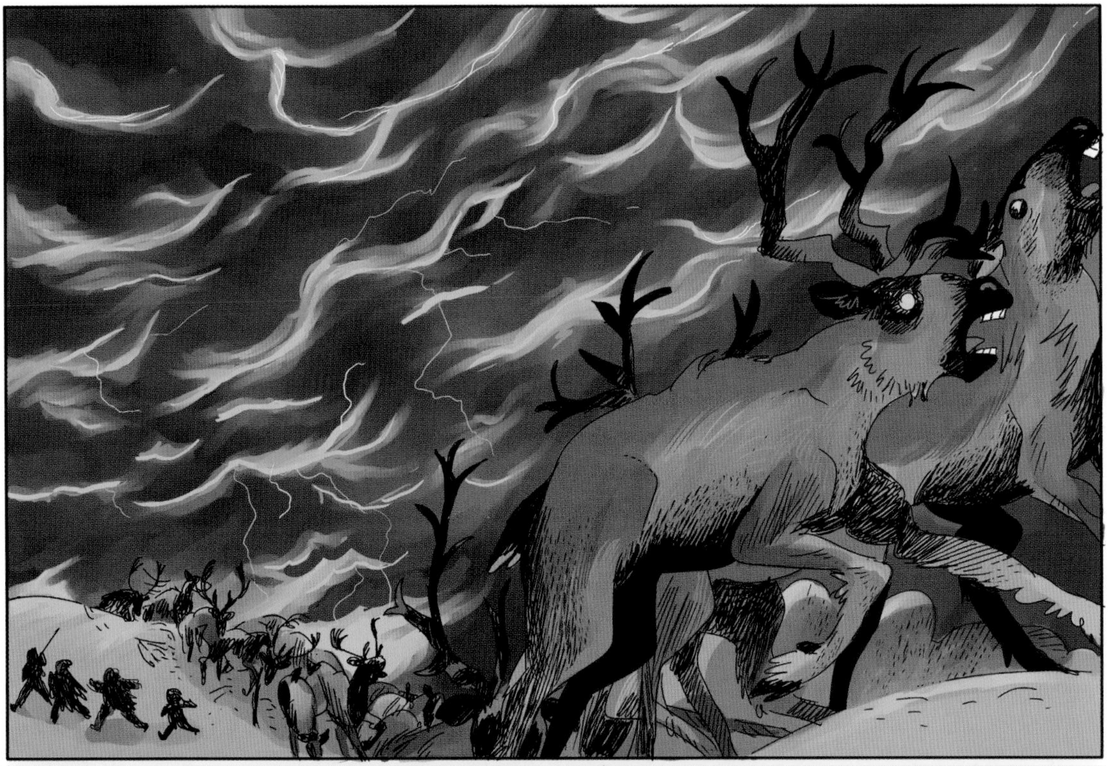
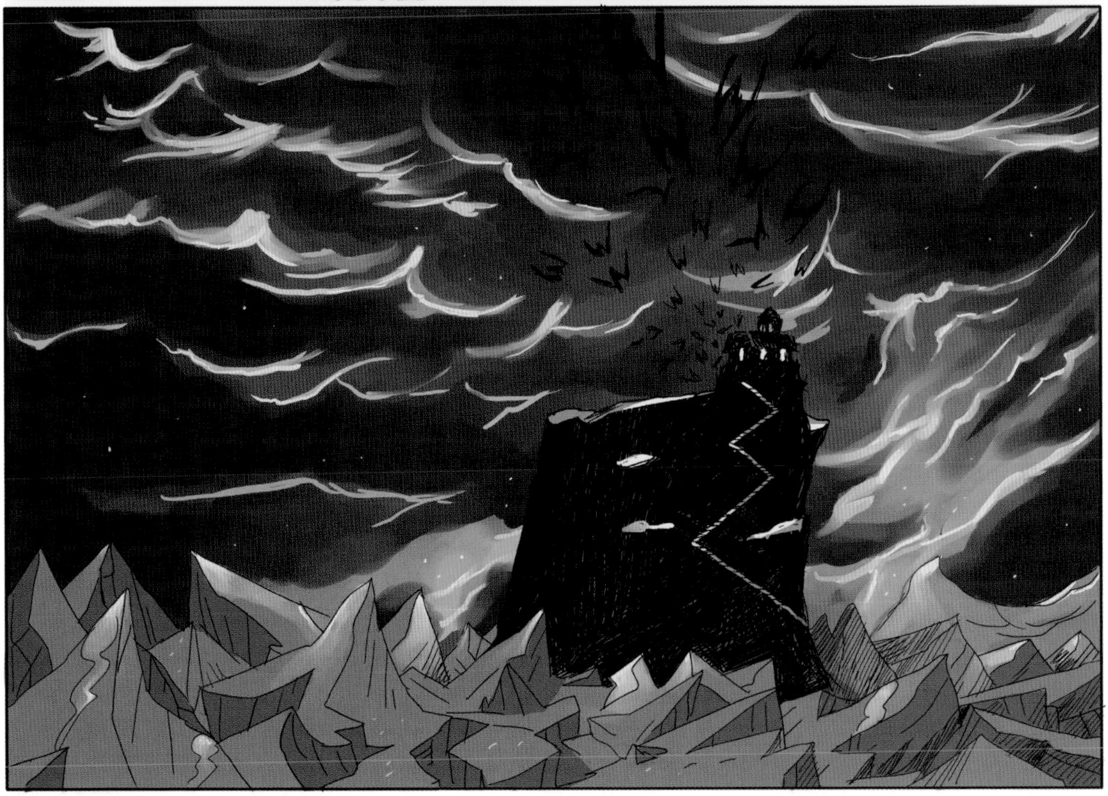

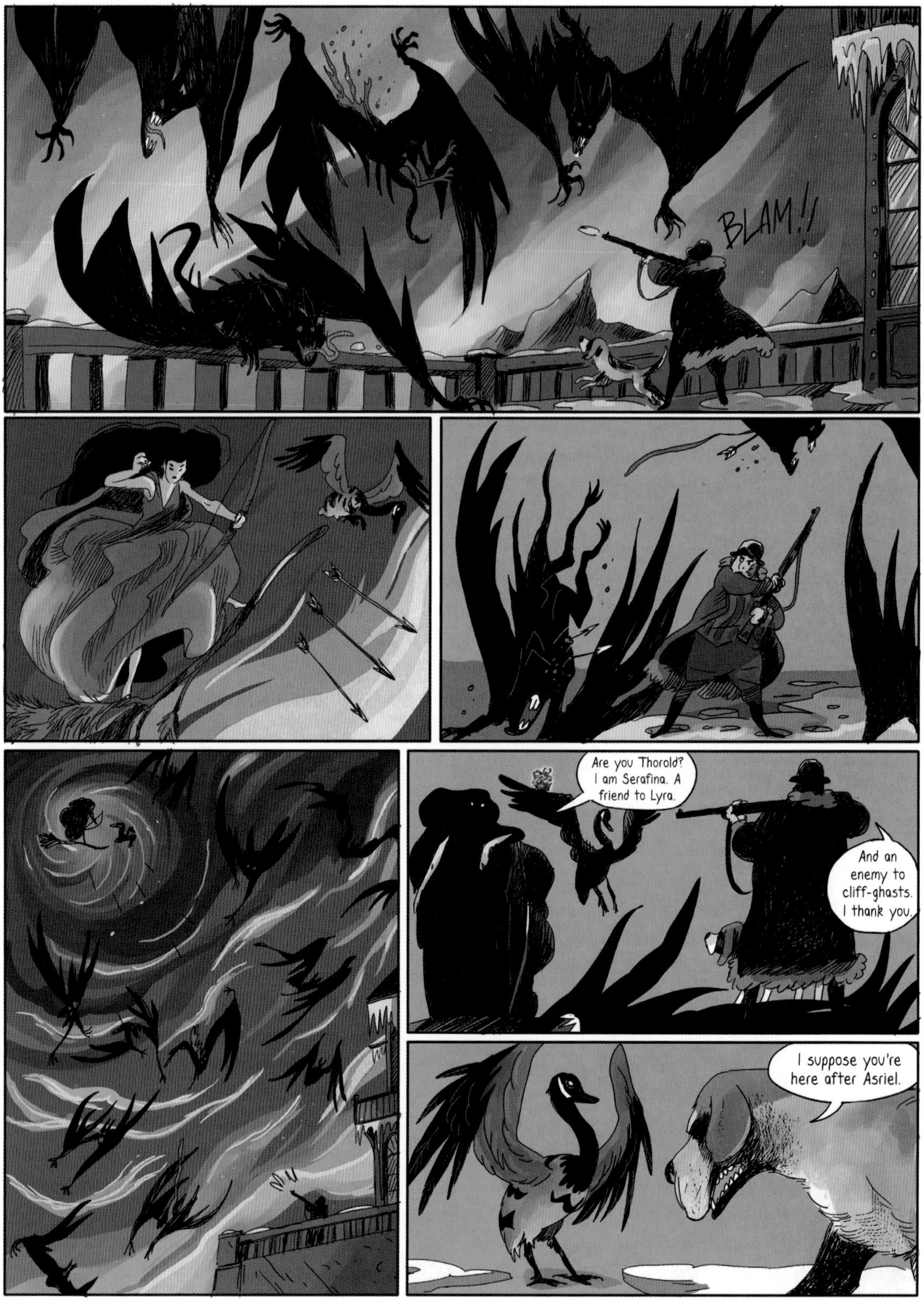
BLAM!!
Are you Thorold? I am Serafina. A friend to Lyra.
And an enemy to cliff-ghasts. I thank you.
I suppose you're here after Asriel.

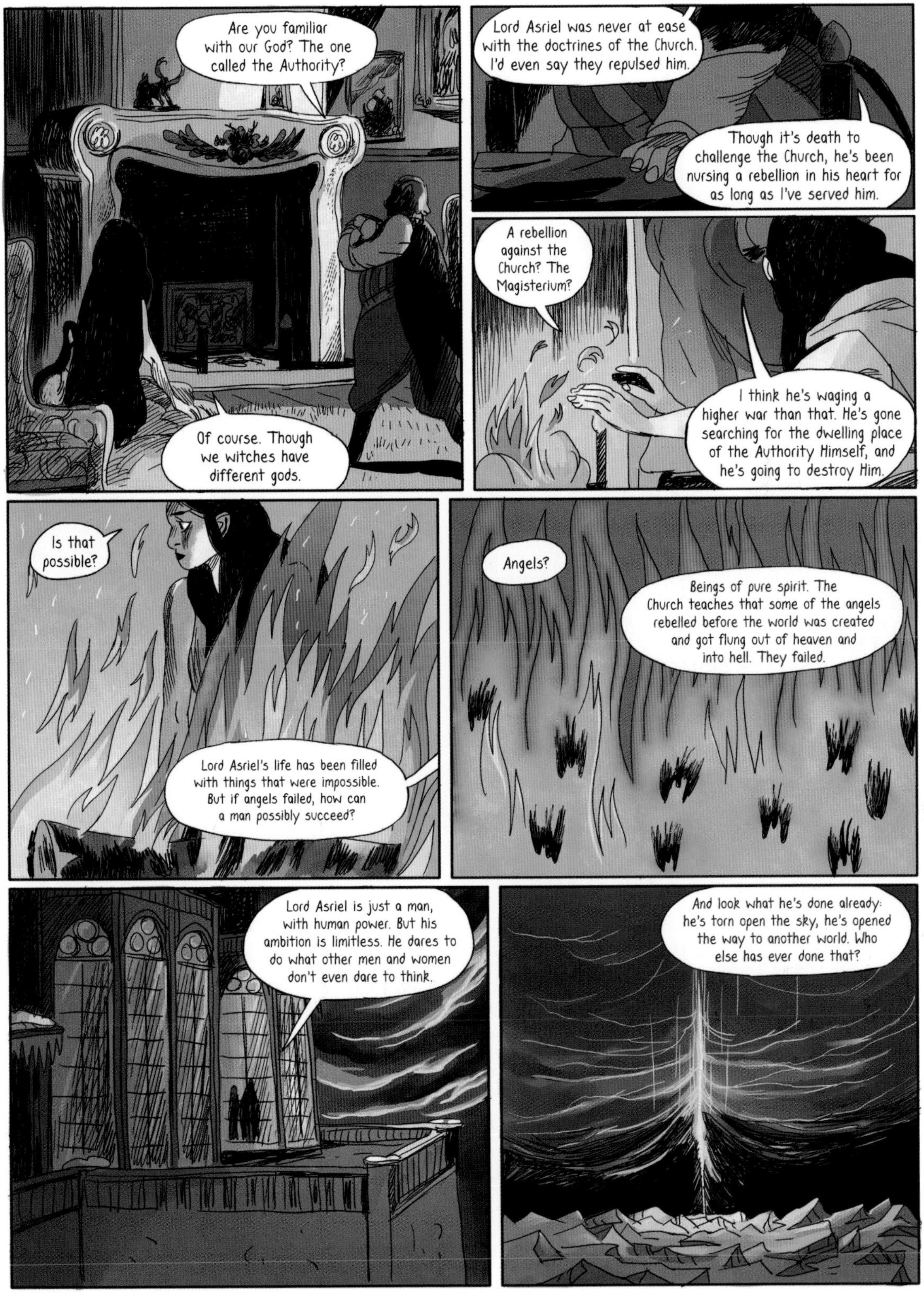
Are you familiar with our God? The one called the Authority?
Of course. Though we witches have different gods.
Lord Asriel was never at ease with the doctrines of the Church. I'd even say they repulsed him.
Though it's death to challenge the Church, he's been nursing a rebellion in his heart for as long as I've served him.
A rebellion against the Church? The Magisterium?
I think he's waging a higher war than that. He's gone searching for the dwelling place of the Authority Himself, and he's going to destroy Him.
Is that possible?
Lord Asriel's life has been filled with things that were impossible. But if angels failed, how can a man possibly succeed?
Angels?
Beings of pure spirit. The Church teaches that some of the angels rebelled before the world was created and got flung out of heaven and into hell. They failed.
Lord Asriel is just a man, with human power. But his ambition is limitless. He dares to do what other men and women don't even dare to think.
And look what he's done already: he's torn open the sky, he's opened the way to another world. Who else has ever done that?

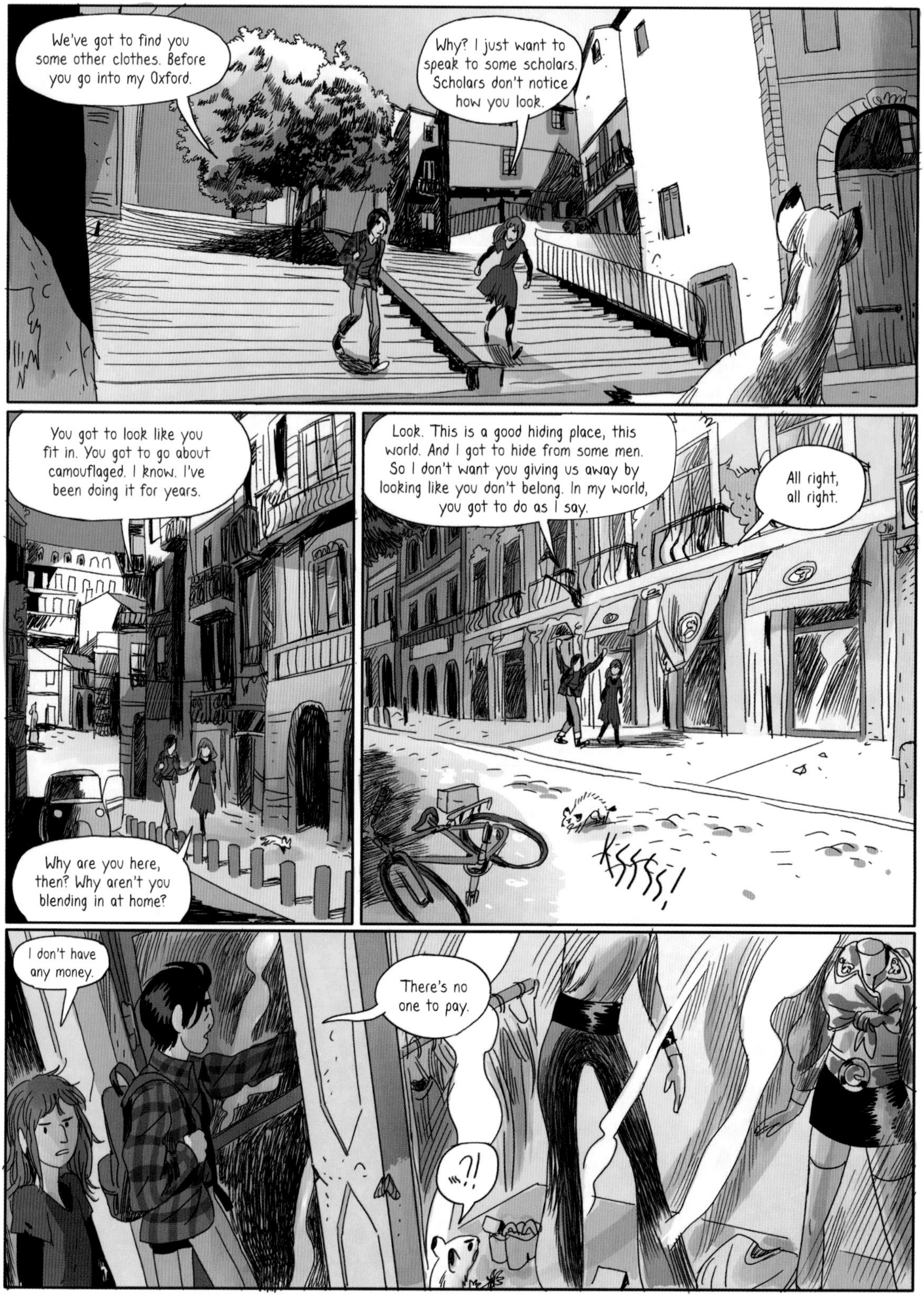
We've got to find you some other clothes. Before you go into my Oxford.
Why? I just want to speak to some scholars. Scholars don't notice how you look.
You got to look like you fit in. You got to go about camouflaged. I know. I've been doing it for years.
Why are you here, then? Why aren't you blending in at home?
Look. This is a good hiding place, this world. And I got to hide from some men. So I don't want you giving us away by looking like you don't belong. In my world, you got to do as I say.
All right, all right.
KSSSS!
I don't have any money.
There's no one to pay.
?!

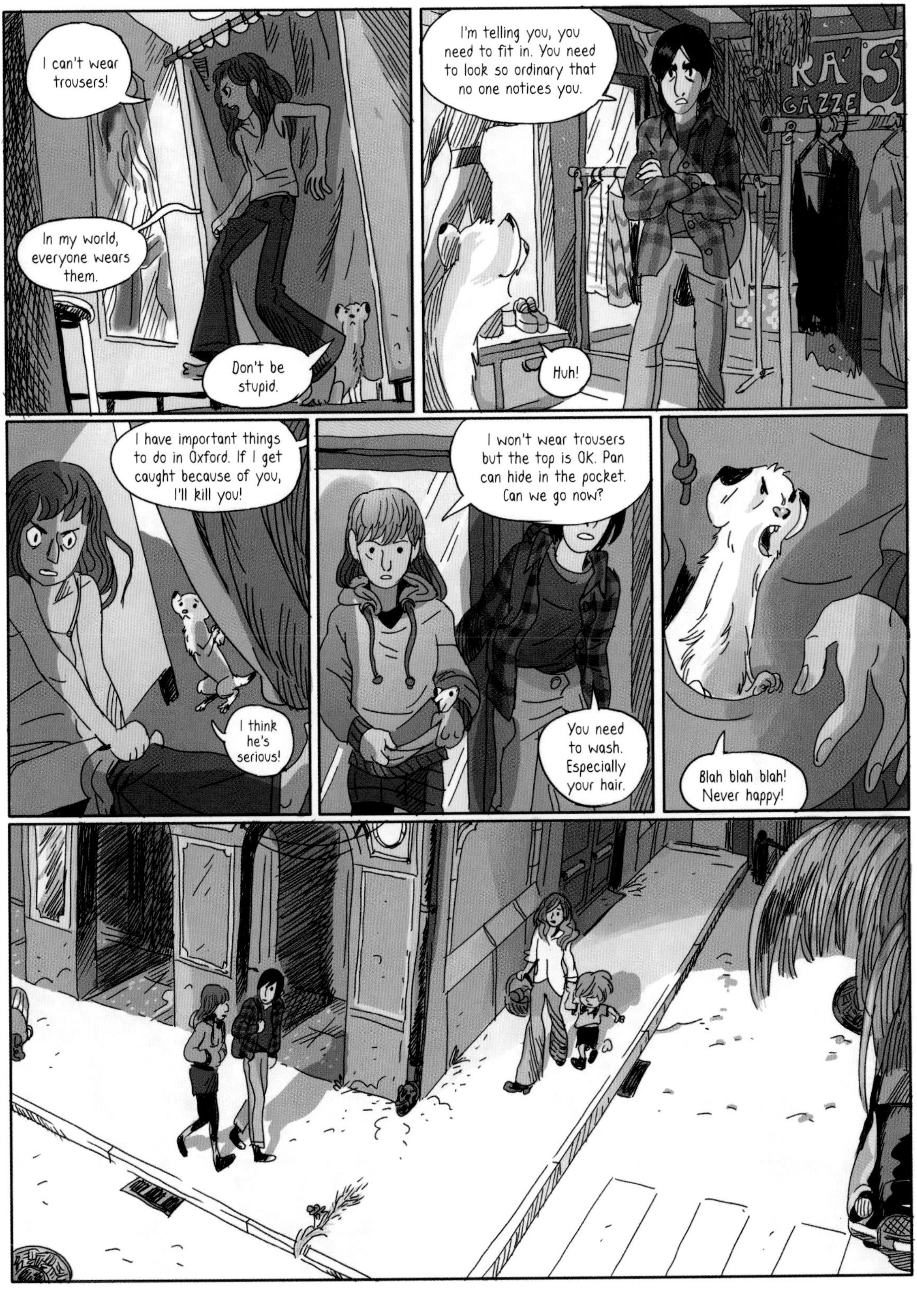
I can't wear trousers!
In my world, everyone wears them.
Don't be stupid.
I'm telling you, you need to fit in. You need to look so ordinary that no one notices you.
Huh!
I have important things to do in Oxford. If I get caught because of you, I'll kill you!
I think he's serious!
I won't wear trousers but the top is OK. Pan can hide in the pocket. Can we go now?
You need to wash. Especially your hair.
Blah blah blah! Never happy!

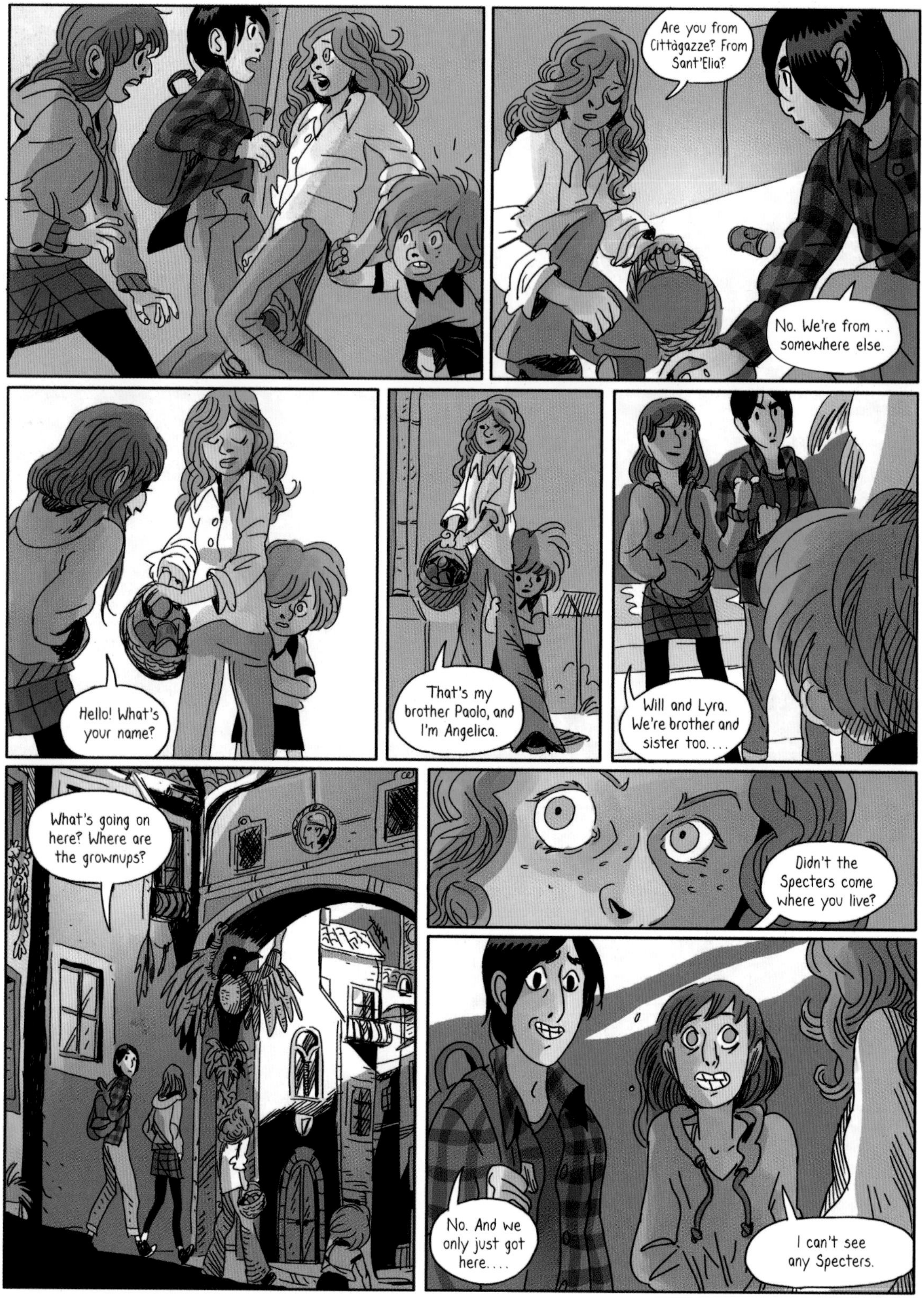
Are you from Cittàgazze? From Sant'Elia?
No. We're from . . . somewhere else.
Hello! What's your name?
That's my brother Paolo, and I'm Angelica.
Will and Lyra. We're brother and sister too. . . .
What's going on here? Where are the grownups?
Didn't the Specters come where you live?
No. And we only just got here. . . .
I can't see any Specters.

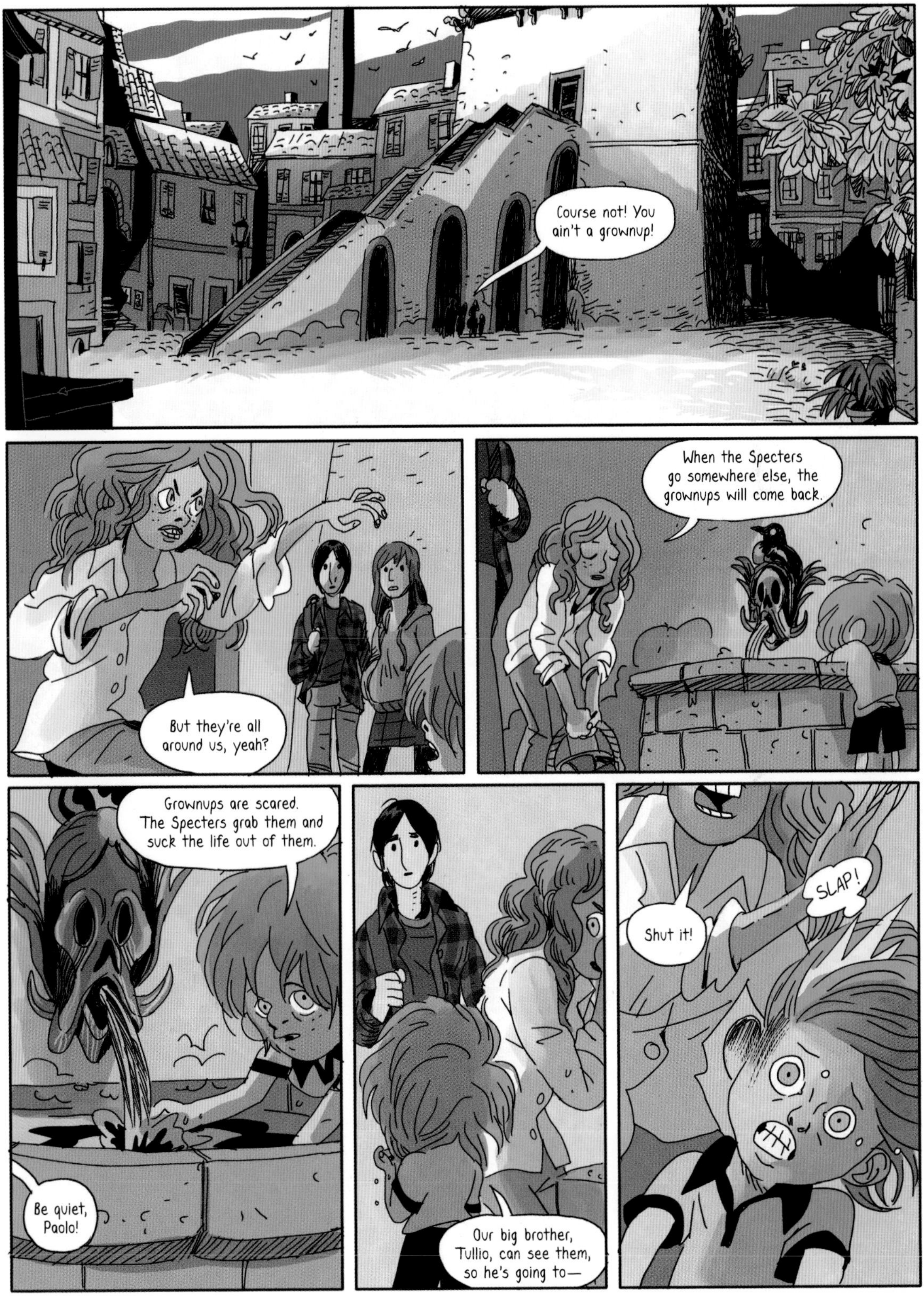
Course not! You ain't a grownup!
But they're all around us, yeah?
When the Specters go somewhere else, the grownups will come back.
Grownups are scared. The Specters grab them and suck the life out of them.
Be quiet, Paolo!
Our big brother, Tullio, can see them, so he's going to—
Shut it!
SLAP!

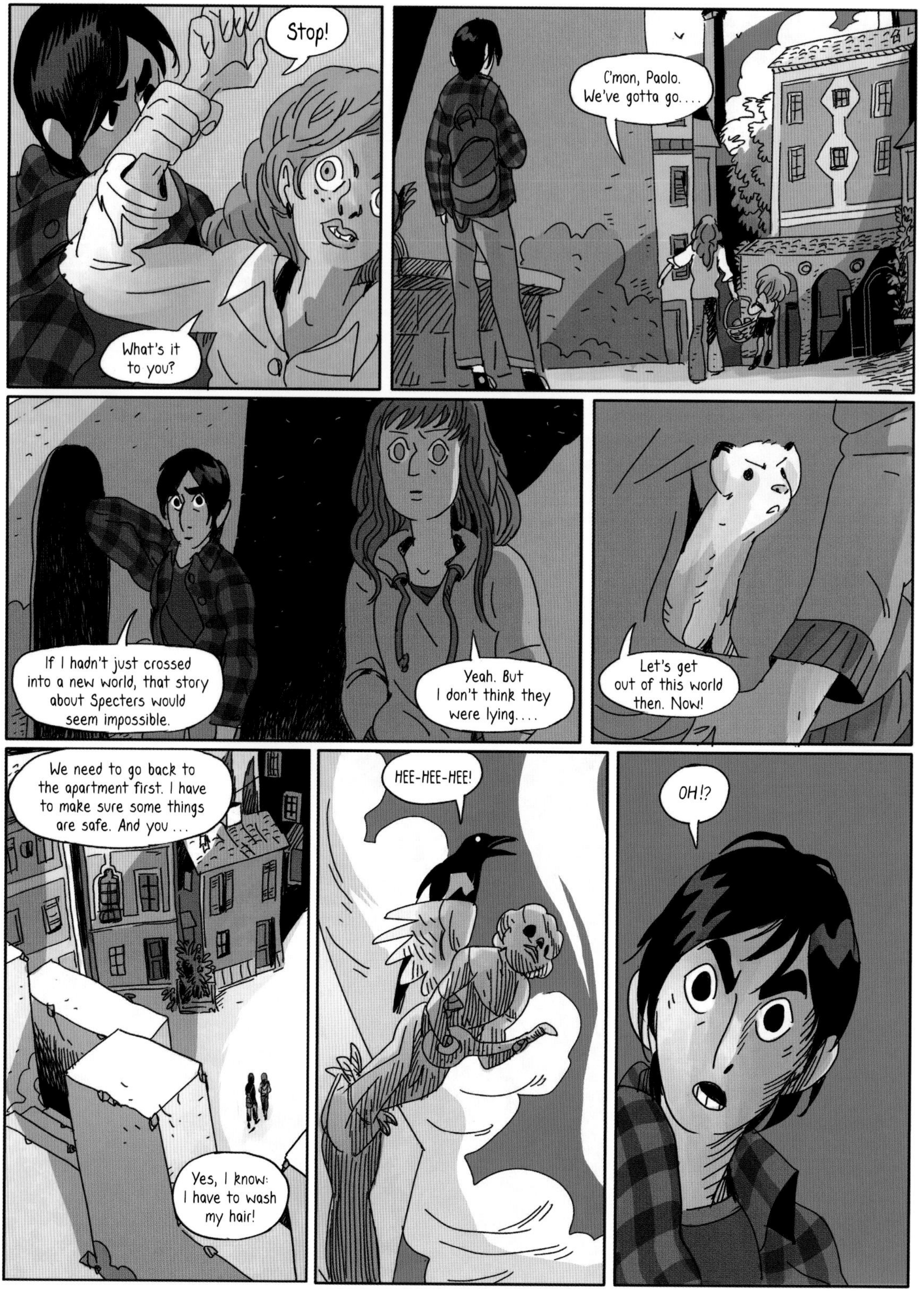
Stop!
What's it to you?
C'mon, Paolo. We've gotta go. . . .
If I hadn't just crossed into a new world, that story about Specters would seem impossible.
Yeah. But I don't think they were lying. . . .
Let's get out of this world then. Now!
We need to go back to the apartment first. I have to make sure some things are safe. And you . . .
Yes, I know: I have to wash my hair!
HEE-HEE-HEE!
OH!?

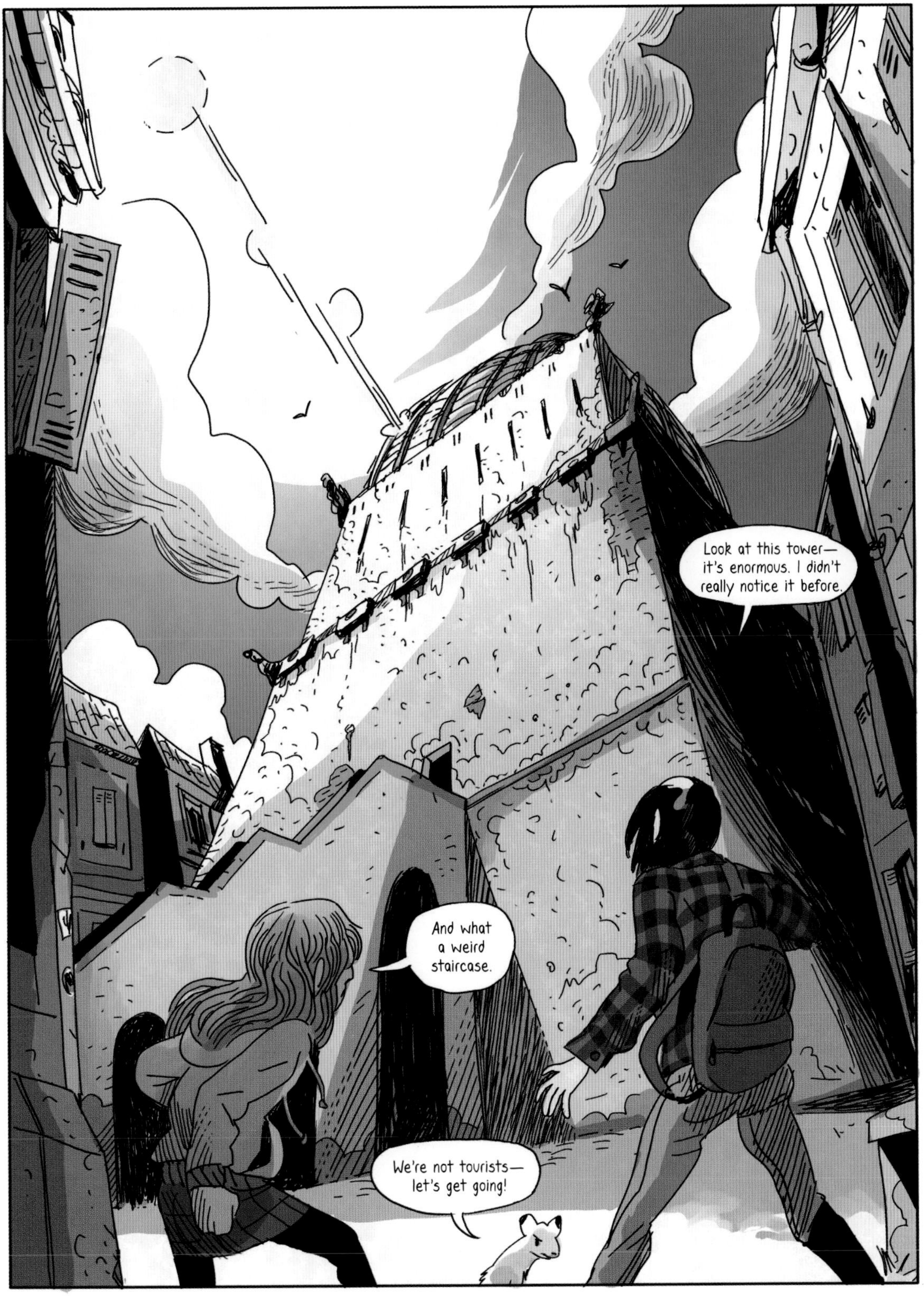
Look at this tower—it's enormous. I didn't really notice it before.
And what a weird staircase.
We're not tourists—let's get going!

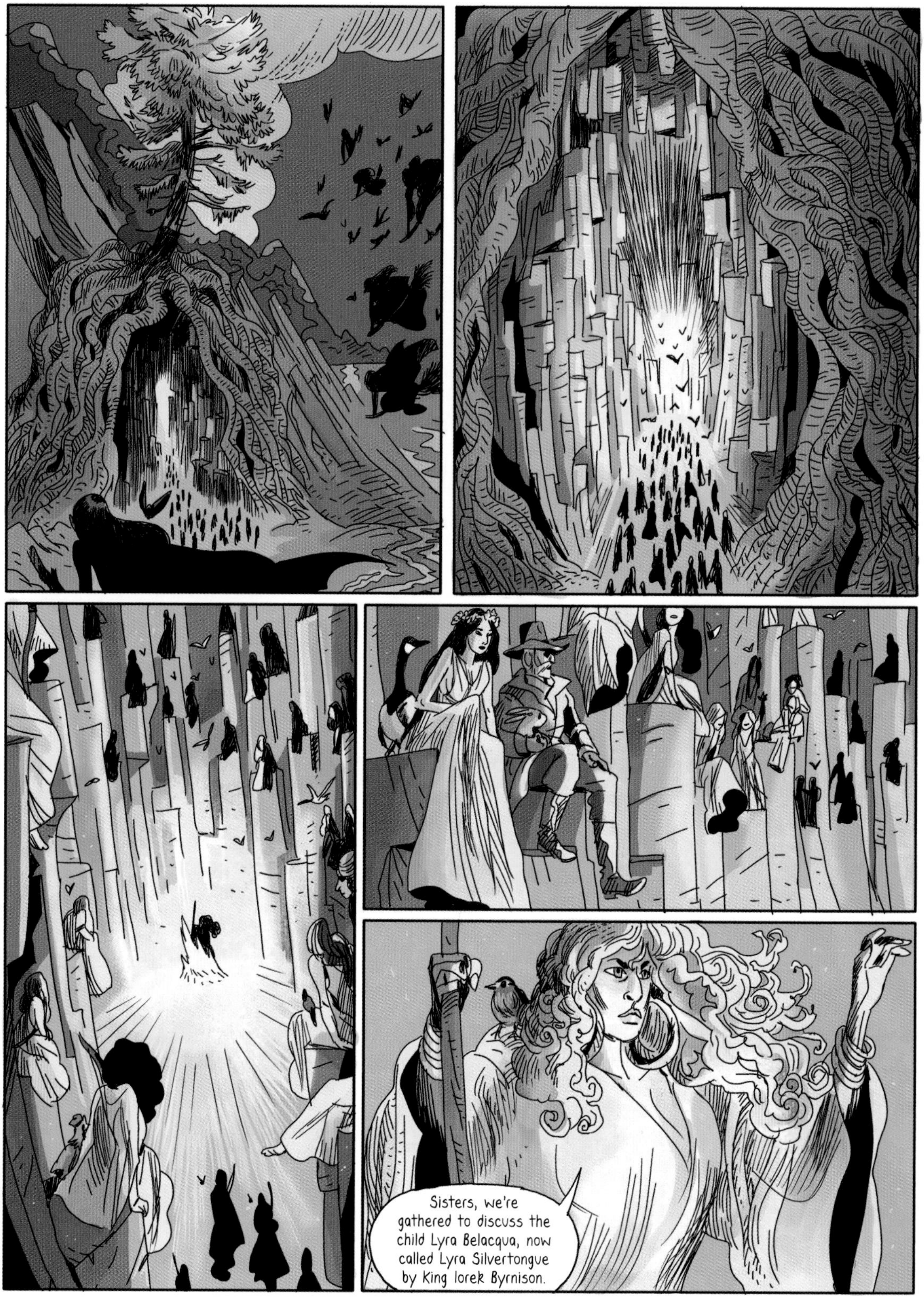
Sisters, we're gathered to discuss the child Lyra Belacqua, now called Lyra Silvertongue by King Iorek Byrnison.

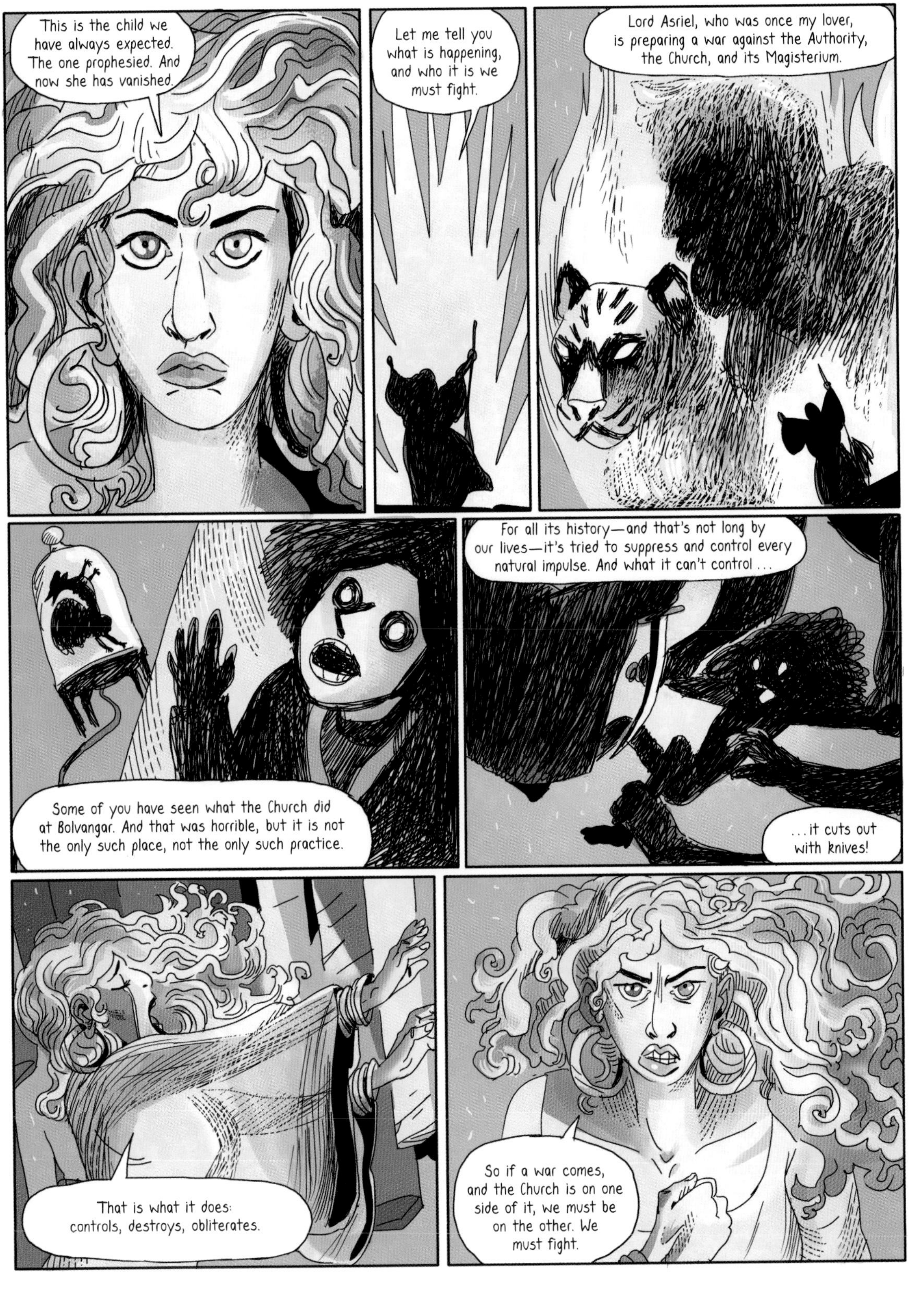
This is the child we have always expected. The one prophesied. And now she has vanished.
Let me tell you what is happening, and who it is we must fight.
Lord Asriel, who was once my lover, is preparing a war against the Authority, the Church, and its Magisterium.
Some of you have seen what the Church did at Bolvangar. And that was horrible, but it is not the only such place, not the only such practice.
For all its history—and that's not long by our lives—it's tried to suppress and control every natural impulse. And what it can't control . . .
. . . it cuts out with knives!
That is what it does: controls, destroys, obliterates.
So if a war comes, and the Church is on one side of it, we must be on the other. We must fight.

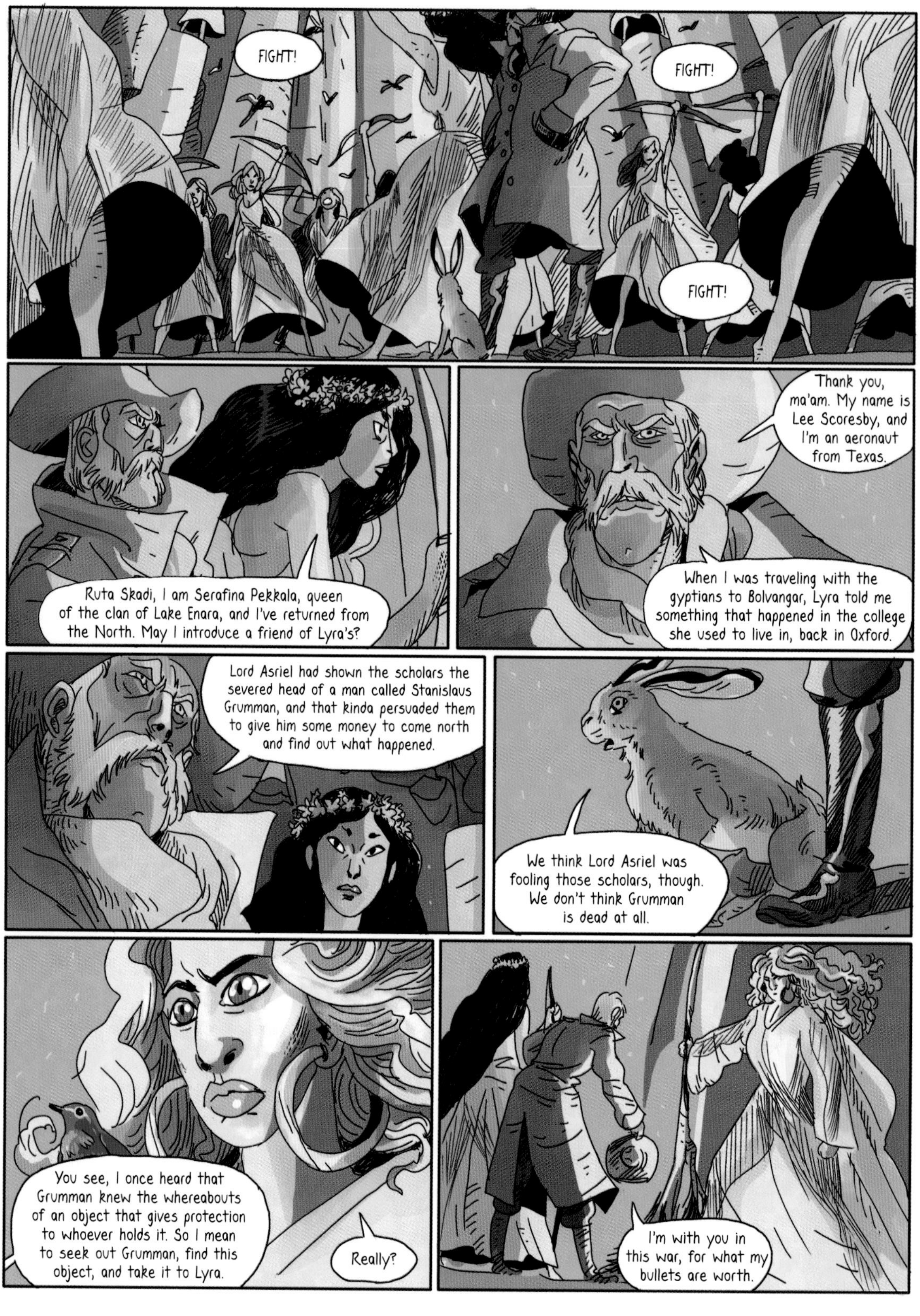
FIGHT!
FIGHT!
FIGHT!
Ruta Skadi, I am Serafina Pekkala, queen of the clan of Lake Enara, and I've returned from the North. May I introduce a friend of Lyra's?
Thank you, ma'am. My name is Lee Scoresby, and I'm an aeronaut from Texas.
When I was traveling with the gyptians to Bolvangar, Lyra told me something that happened in the college she used to live in, back in Oxford.
Lord Asriel had shown the scholars the severed head of a man called Stanislaus Grumman, and that kinda persuaded them to give him some money to come north and find out what happened.
We think Lord Asriel was fooling those scholars, though. We don't think Grumman is dead at all.
You see, I once heard that Grumman knew the whereabouts of an object that gives protection to whoever holds it. So I mean to seek out Grumman, find this object, and take it to Lyra.
Really?
I'm with you in this war, for what my bullets are worth.

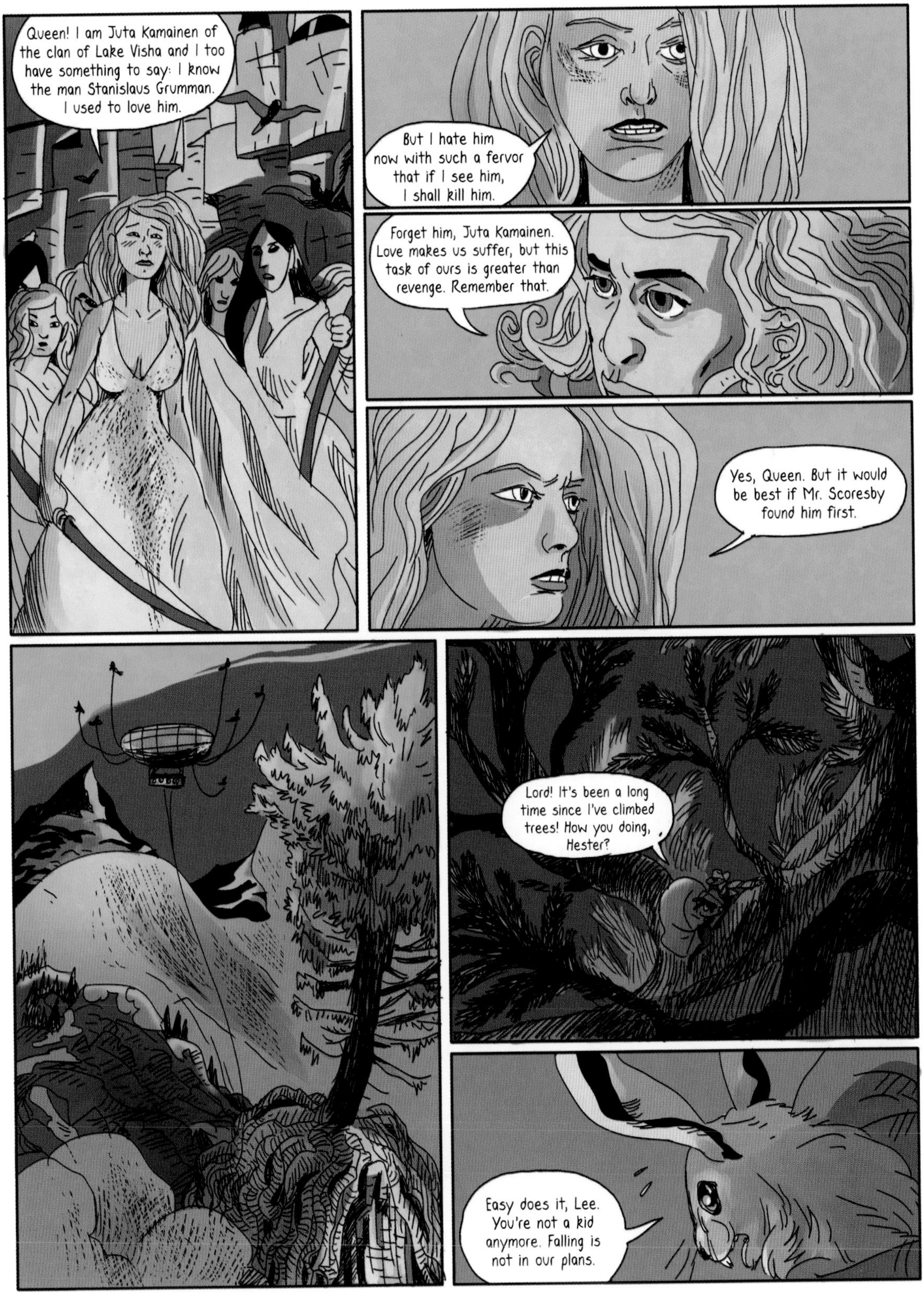
Queen! I am Juta Kamainen of the clan of Lake Visha and I too have something to say: I know the man Stanislaus Grumman. I used to love him.
But I hate him now with such a fervor that if I see him, I shall kill him.
Forget him, Juta Kamainen. Love makes us suffer, but this task of ours is greater than revenge. Remember that.
Yes, Queen. But it would be best if Mr. Scoresby found him first.
Lord! It's been a long time since I've climbed trees! How you doing, Hester?
Easy does it, Lee. You're not a kid anymore. Falling is not in our plans.

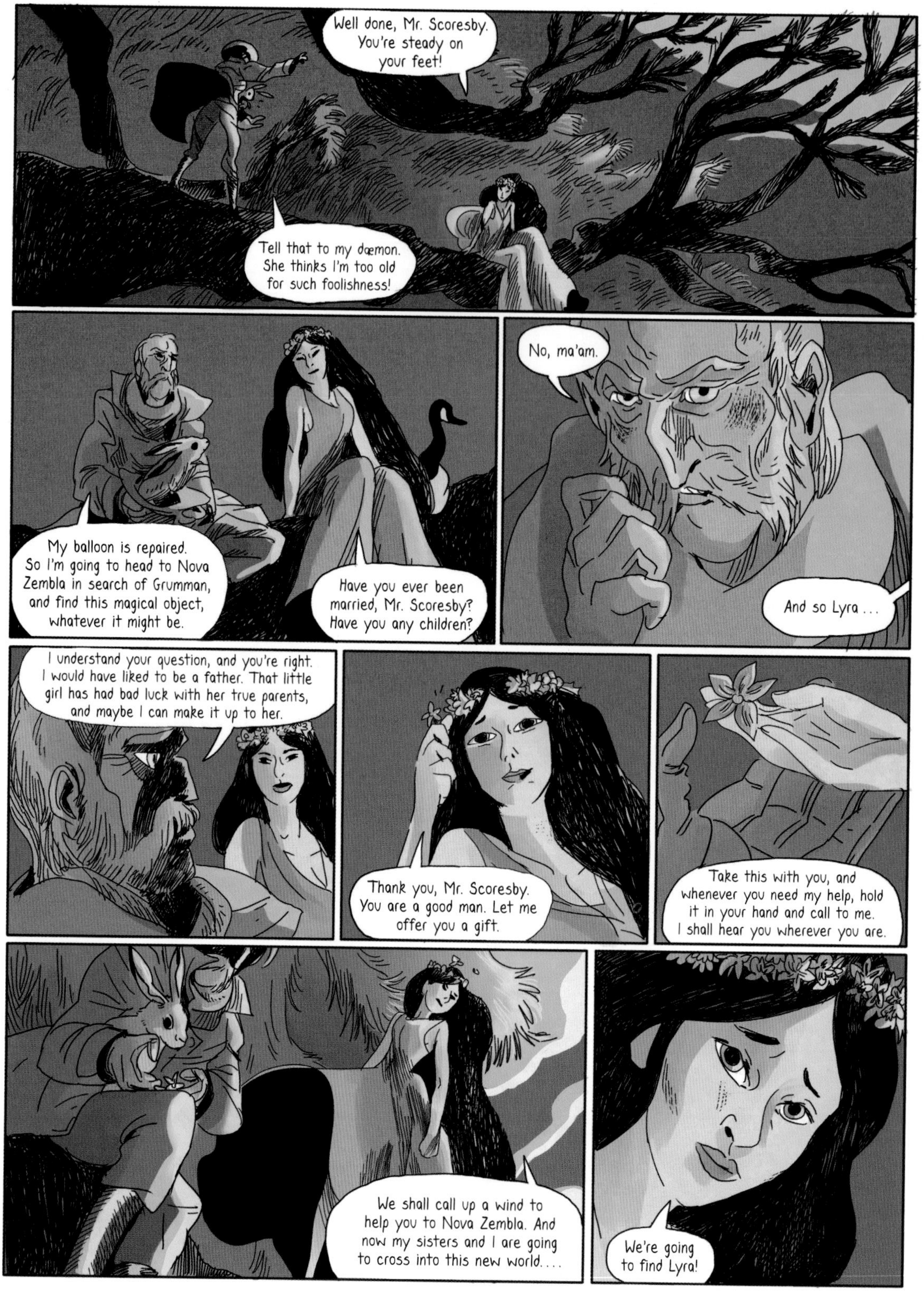
Well done, Mr. Scoresby. You're steady on your feet!
Tell that to my dæmon. She thinks I'm too old for such foolishness!
My balloon is repaired. So I'm going to head to Nova Zembla in search of Grumman, and find this magical object, whatever it might be.
Have you ever been married, Mr. Scoresby? Have you any children?
No, ma'am.
And so Lyra . . .
I understand your question, and you're right. I would have liked to be a father. That little girl has had bad luck with her true parents, and maybe I can make it up to her.
Thank you, Mr. Scoresby. You are a good man. Let me offer you a gift.
Take this with you, and whenever you need my help, hold it in your hand and call to me. I shall hear you wherever you are.
We shall call up a wind to help you to Nova Zembla. And now my sisters and I are going to cross into this new world. . . .
We're going to find Lyra!

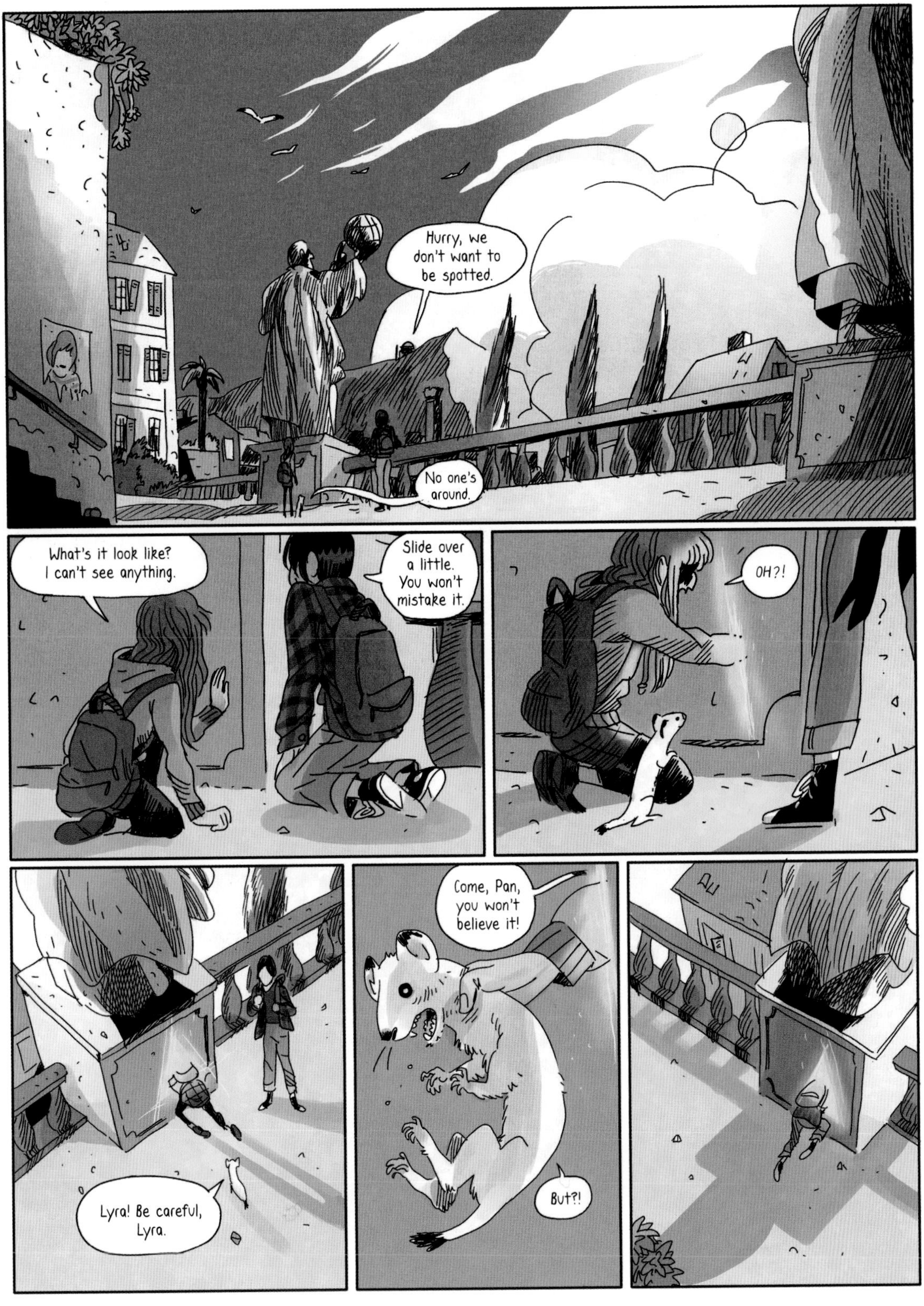
Hurry, we don't want to be spotted.
No one's around.
What's it look like? I can't see anything.
Slide over a little. You won't mistake it.
OH?!
Lyra! Be careful, Lyra.
Come, Pan, you won't believe it!
But?!

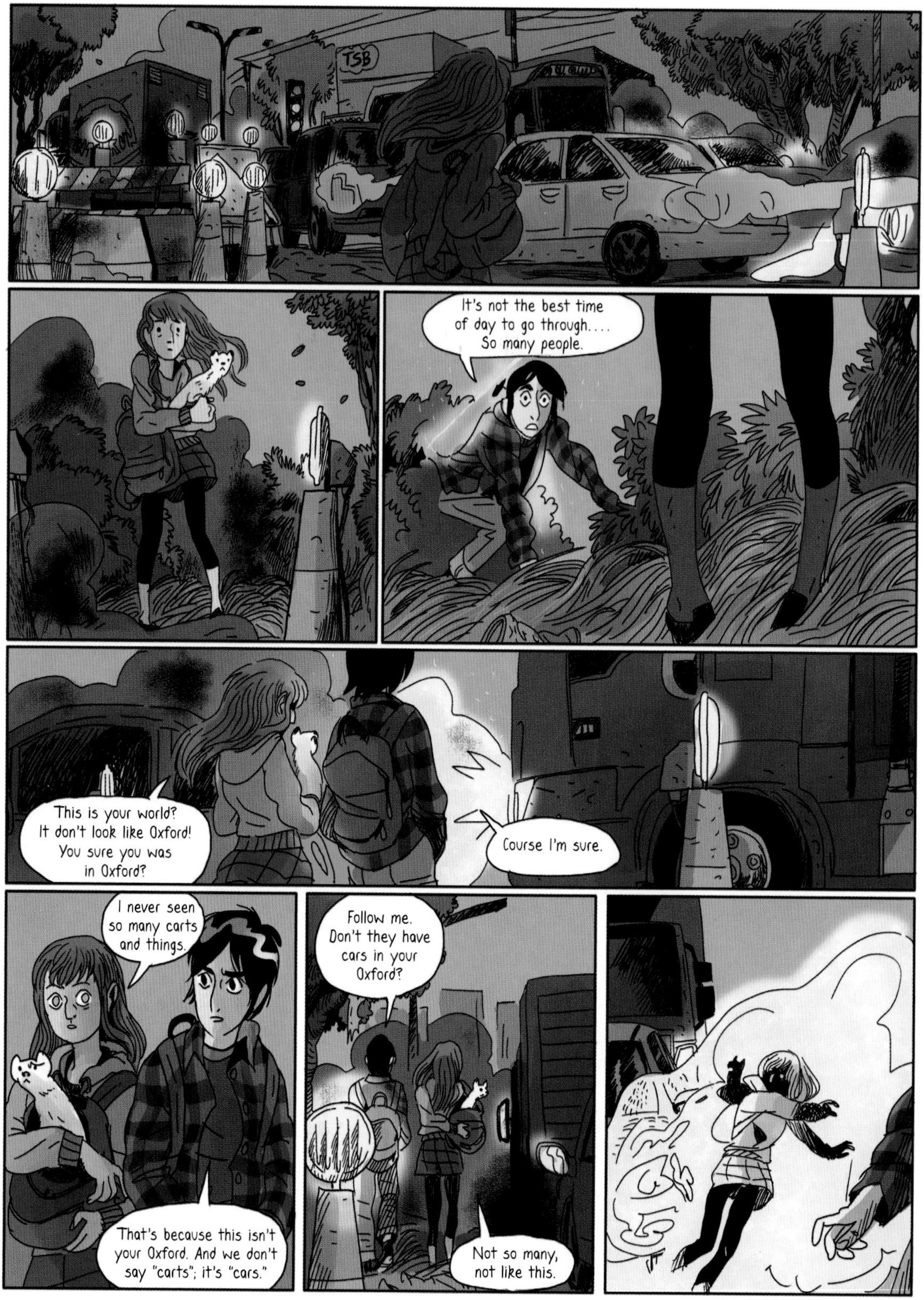
TSB
It's not the best time of day to go through.... So many people.
This is your world? It don't look like Oxford! You sure you was in Oxford?
Course I'm sure.
I never seen so many carts and things.
That's because this isn't your Oxford. And we don't say "carts"; it's "cars."
Follow me. Don't they have cars in your Oxford?
Not so many, not like this.

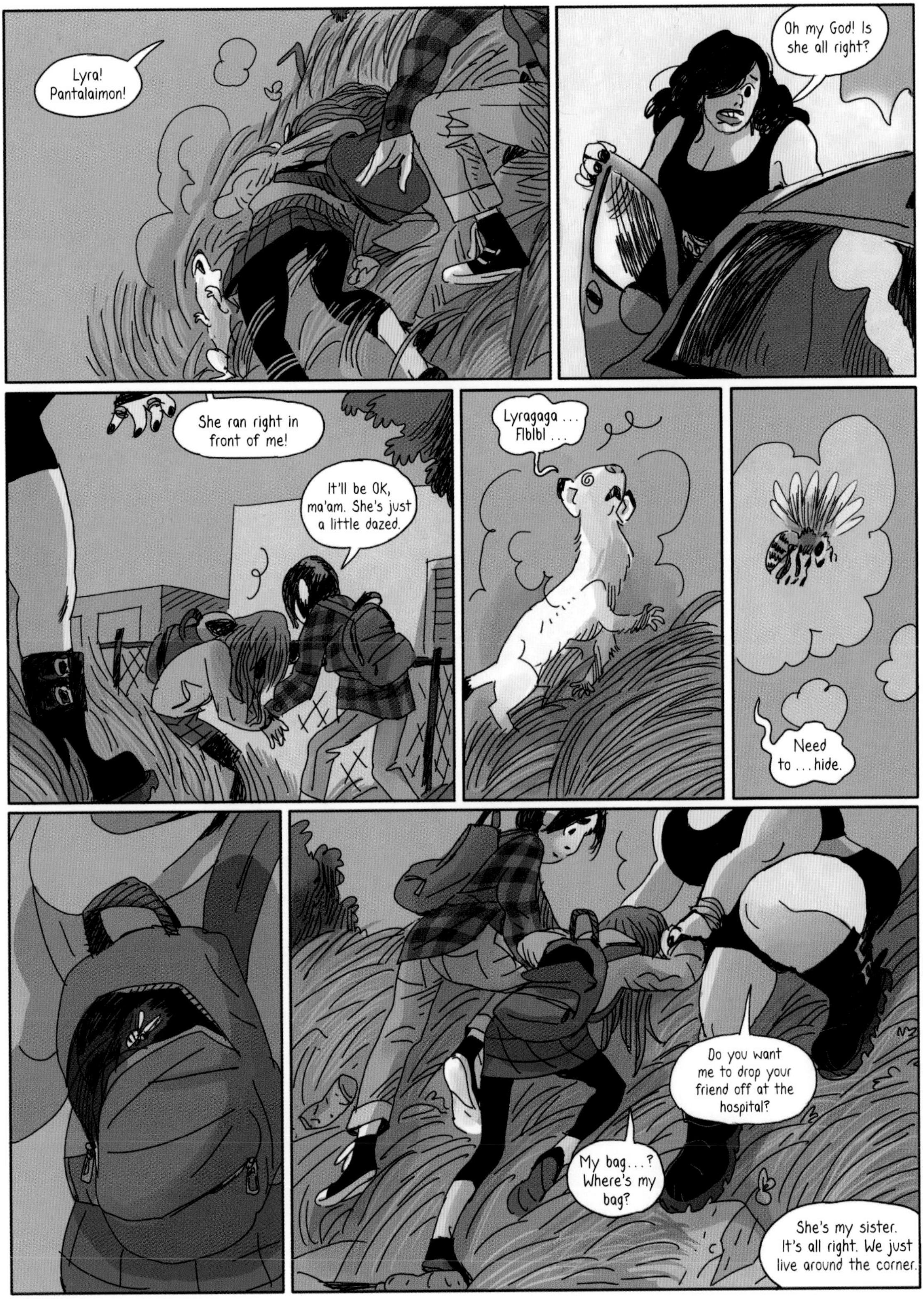
Lyra! Pantalaimon!
Oh my God! Is she all right?
She ran right in front of me!
It'll be OK, ma'am. She's just a little dazed.
Lyragaga . . . Flblbl . . .
Need to . . . hide.
Do you want me to drop your friend off at the hospital?
My bag . . . ? Where's my bag?
She's my sister. It's all right. We just live around the corner.

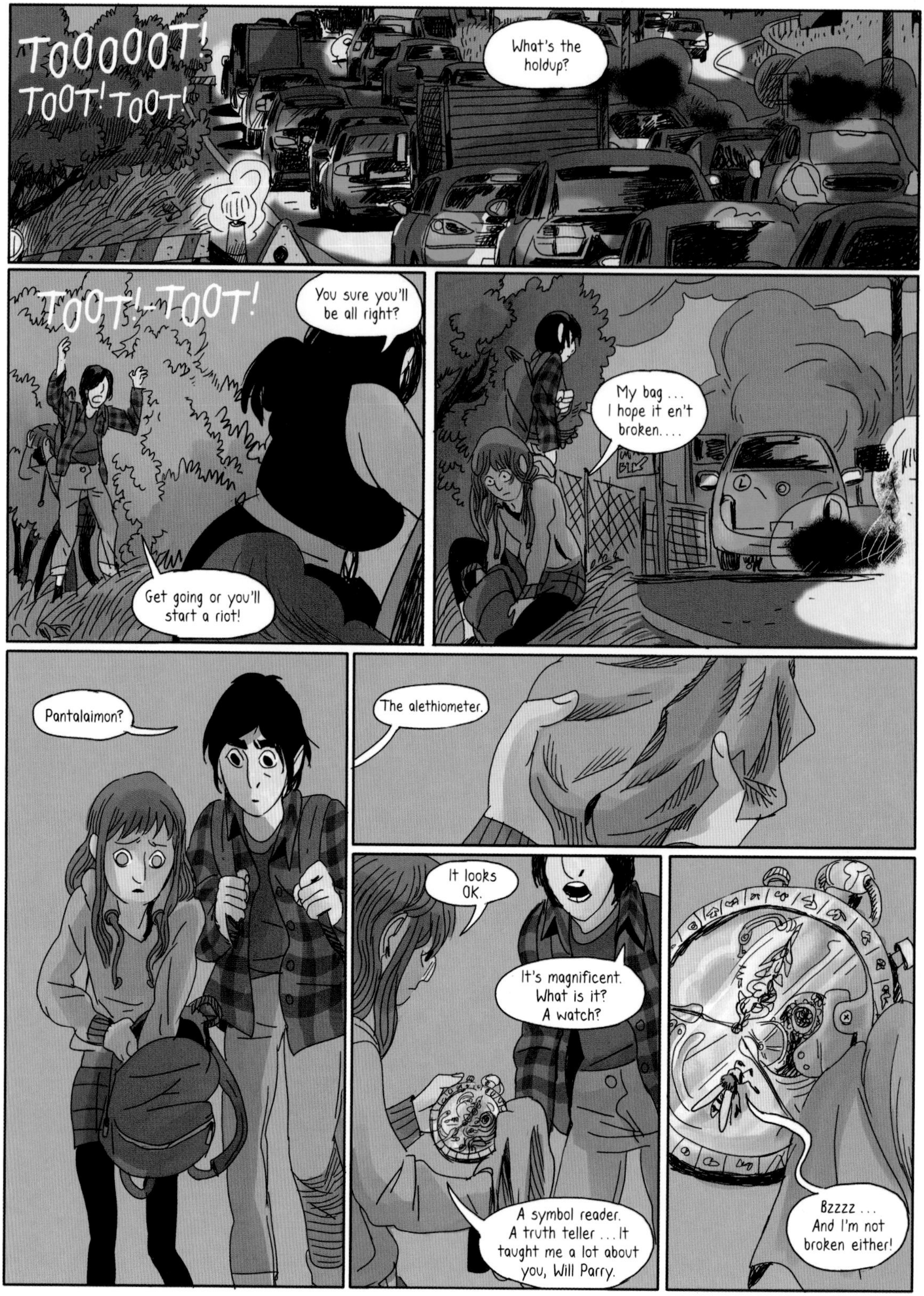
TOOOOOT! TOOT! TOOT!
What's the holdup?
TOOT!-TOOT!
You sure you'll be all right?
Get going or you'll start a riot!
My bag . . . I hope it en't broken. . . .
Pantalaimon?
The alethiometer.
It looks OK.
It's magnificent. What is it? A watch?
A symbol reader. A truth teller . . . It taught me a lot about you, Will Parry.
Bzzzz . . . And I'm not broken either!

I recognize some street names but ... where is Jordan College?

I told you, Lyra.

That en't right. It's all changed.

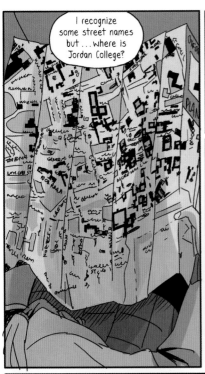

It isn't your Oxford.

Here ... you'll need some money.

You have a queen? We have a king.

If anyone asks, I'm Mark ... Mark Ransom. And you are?

That, and I'm wanted.

A fake name? That's logical for a fake Oxford. . . .

I'll be Lizzie. I used that before, I can remember that.

Lizzie Ransom, of course, since we're brother and sister.

We'll meet up later in front of the university library. Will you be OK?

I've already crossed two worlds. I'm sure I can manage without you.

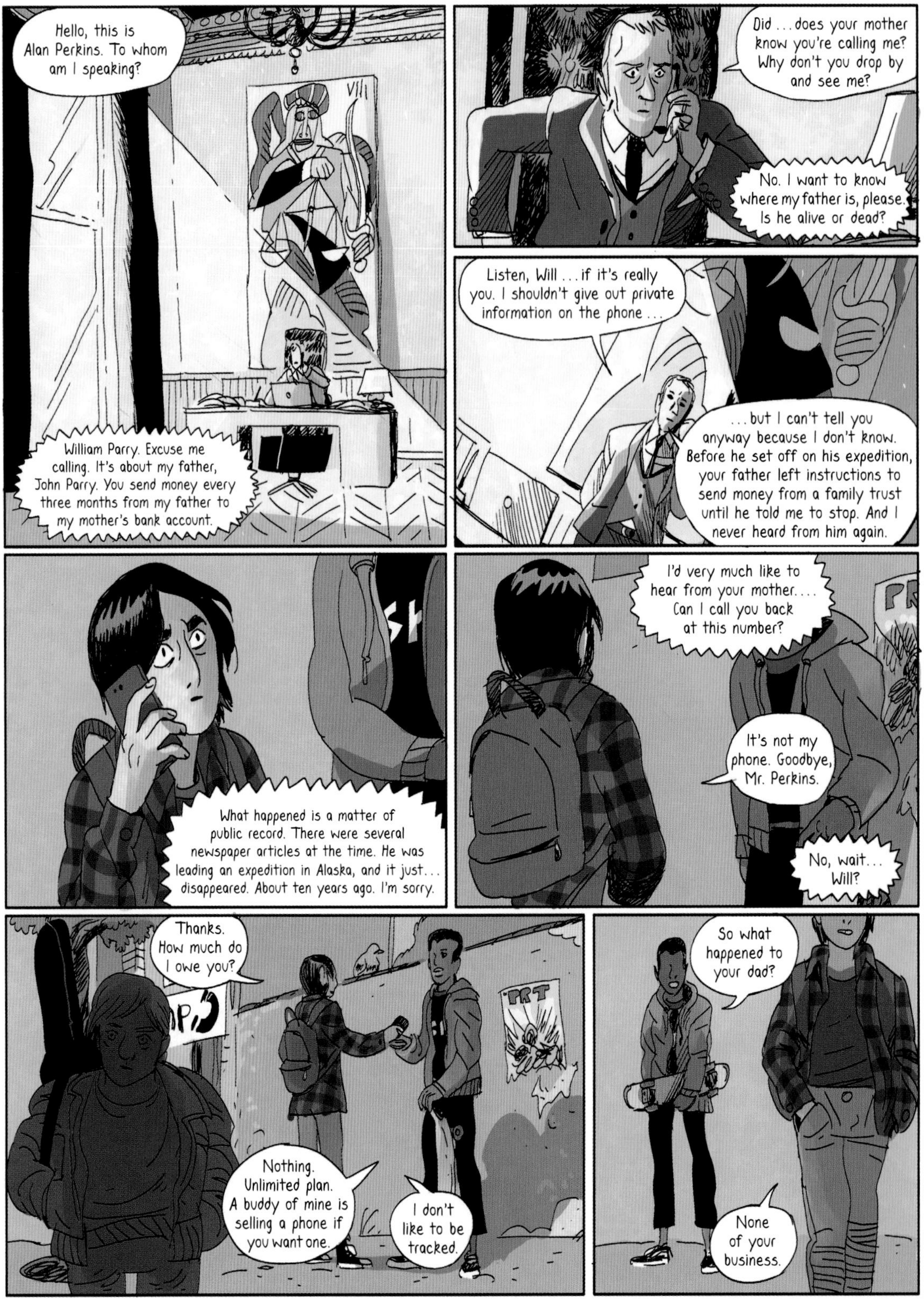
Hello, this is Alan Perkins. To whom am I speaking?
William Parry. Excuse me calling. It's about my father, John Parry. You send money every three months from my father to my mother's bank account.
Did . . . does your mother know you're calling me? Why don't you drop by and see me?
No. I want to know where my father is, please. Is he alive or dead?
Listen, Will . . . if it's really you. I shouldn't give out private information on the phone . . .
. . . but I can't tell you anyway because I don't know. Before he set off on his expedition, your father left instructions to send money from a family trust until he told me to stop. And I never heard from him again.
What happened is a matter of public record. There were several newspaper articles at the time. He was leading an expedition in Alaska, and it just . . . disappeared. About ten years ago. I'm sorry.
I'd very much like to hear from your mother. . . . Can I call you back at this number?
It's not my phone. Goodbye, Mr. Perkins.
No, wait . . . Will?
Thanks. How much do I owe you?
Nothing. Unlimited plan. A buddy of mine is selling a phone if you want one.
I don't like to be tracked.
So what happened to your dad?
None of your business.

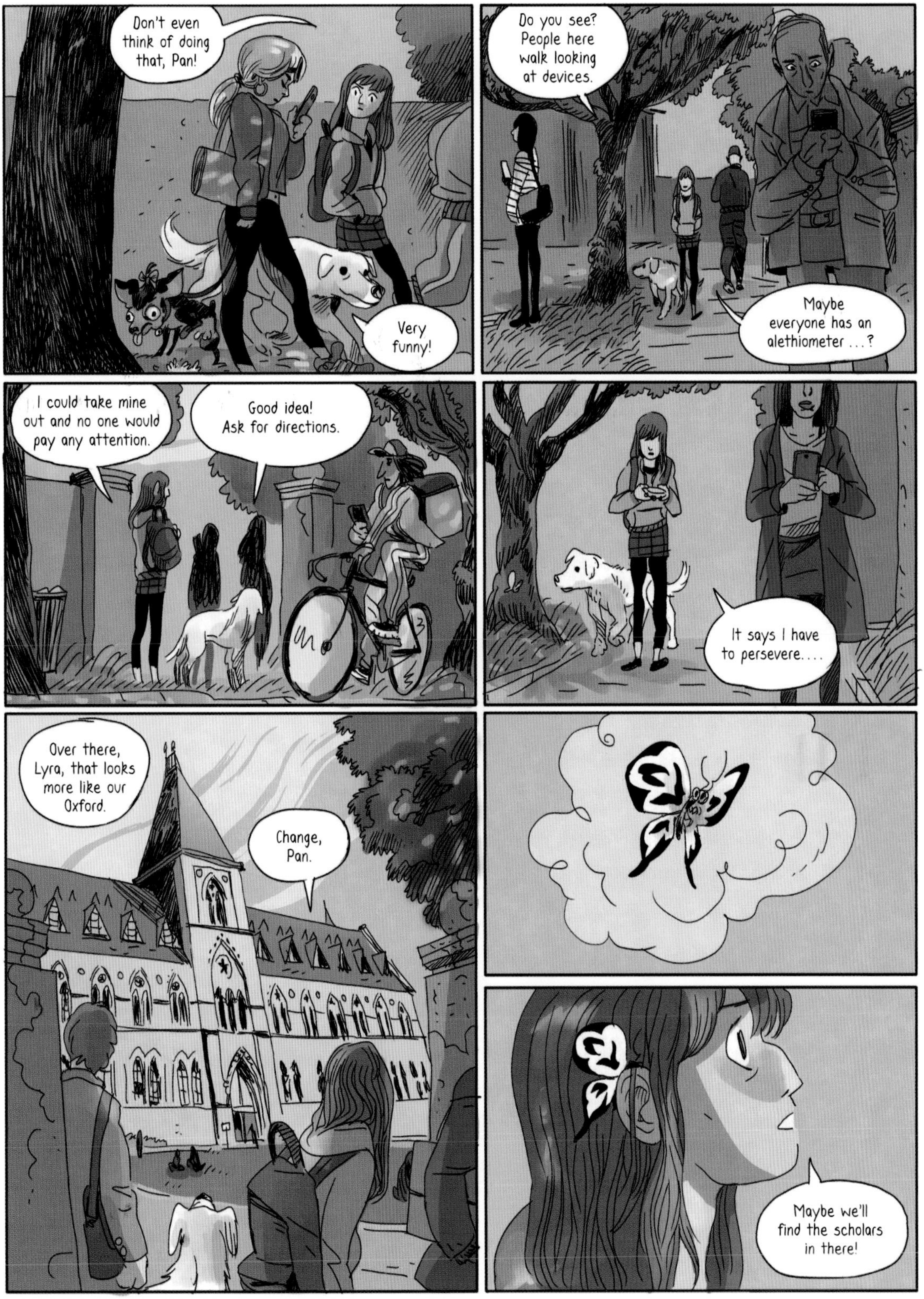
Don't even think of doing that, Pan!
Very funny!
Do you see? People here walk looking at devices.
Maybe everyone has an alethiometer . . . ?
I could take mine out and no one would pay any attention.
Good idea! Ask for directions.
It says I have to persevere. . . .
Over there, Lyra, that looks more like our Oxford.
Change, Pan.
Maybe we'll find the scholars in there!

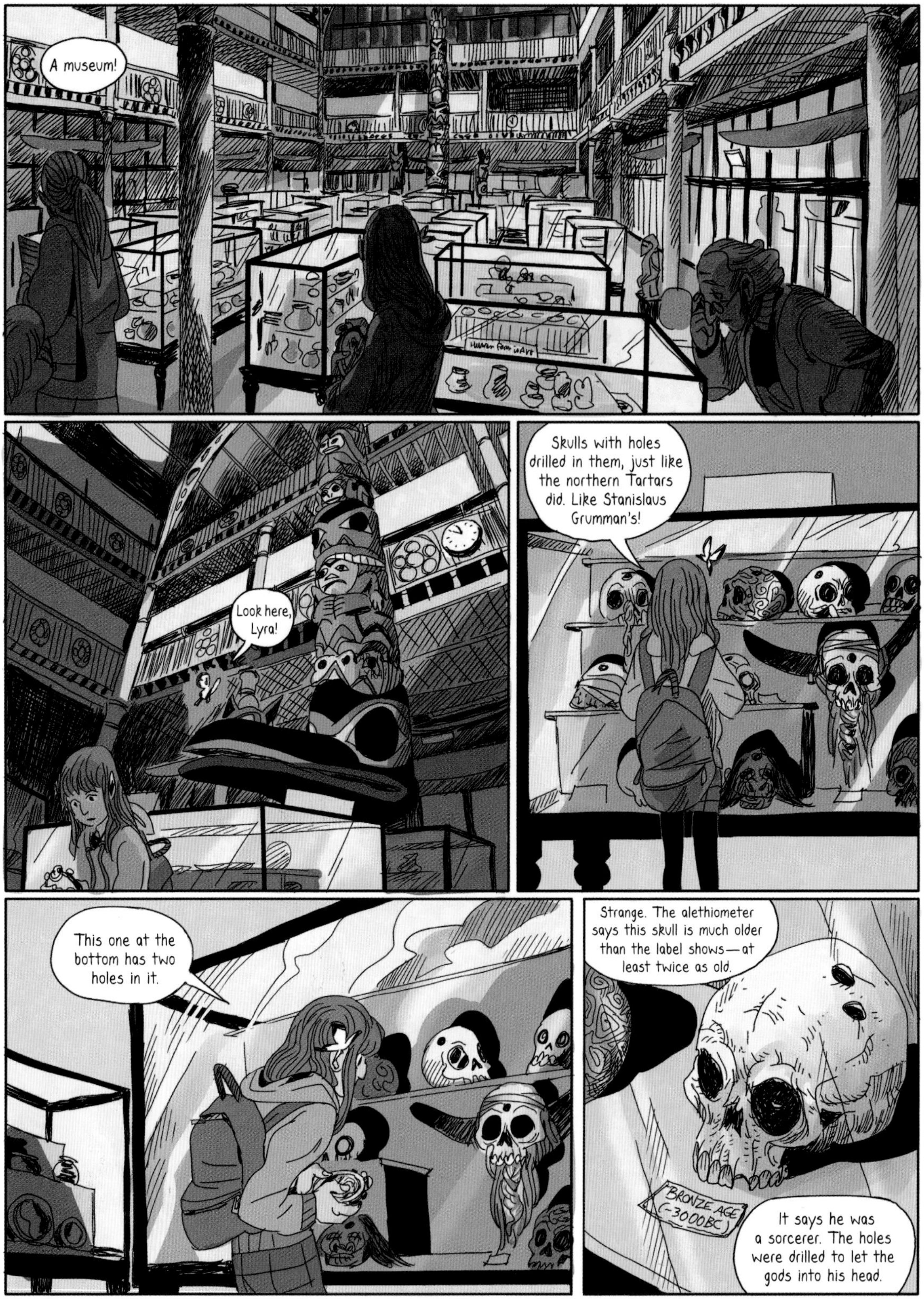
A museum!
Look here, Lyra!
Skulls with holes drilled in them, just like the northern Tartars did. Like Stanislaus Grumman's!
This one at the bottom has two holes in it.
Strange. The alethiometer says this skull is much older than the label shows—at least twice as old.
BRONZE AGE (~3000BC)
It says he was a sorcerer. The holes were drilled to let the gods into his head.

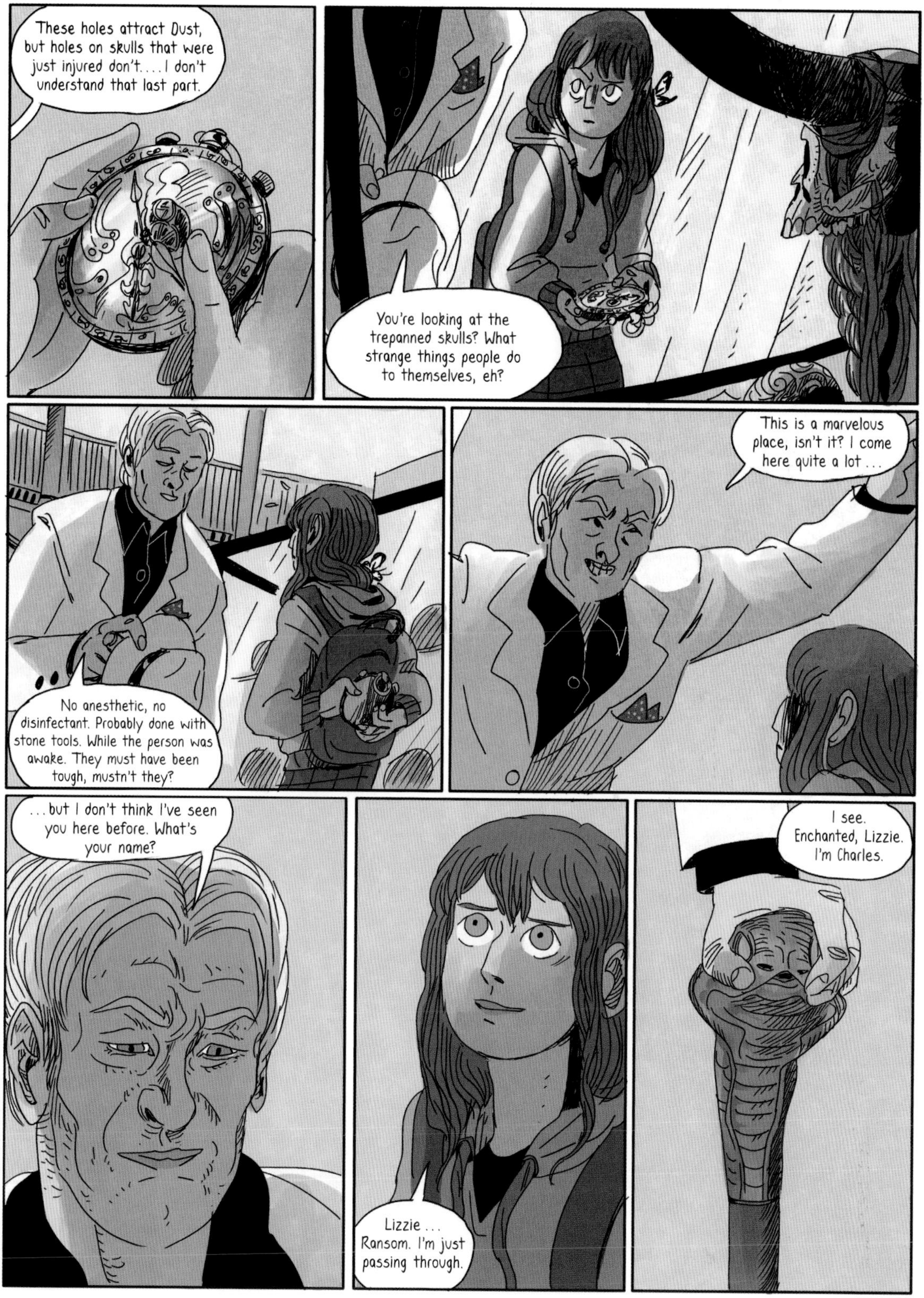
These holes attract Dust, but holes on skulls that were just injured don't. . . . I don't understand that last part.
You're looking at the trepanned skulls? What strange things people do to themselves, eh?
No anesthetic, no disinfectant. Probably done with stone tools. While the person was awake. They must have been tough, mustn't they?
This is a marvelous place, isn't it? I come here quite a lot . . .
. . . but I don't think I've seen you here before. What's your name?
Lizzie . . . Ransom. I'm just passing through.
I see. Enchanted, Lizzie. I'm Charles.

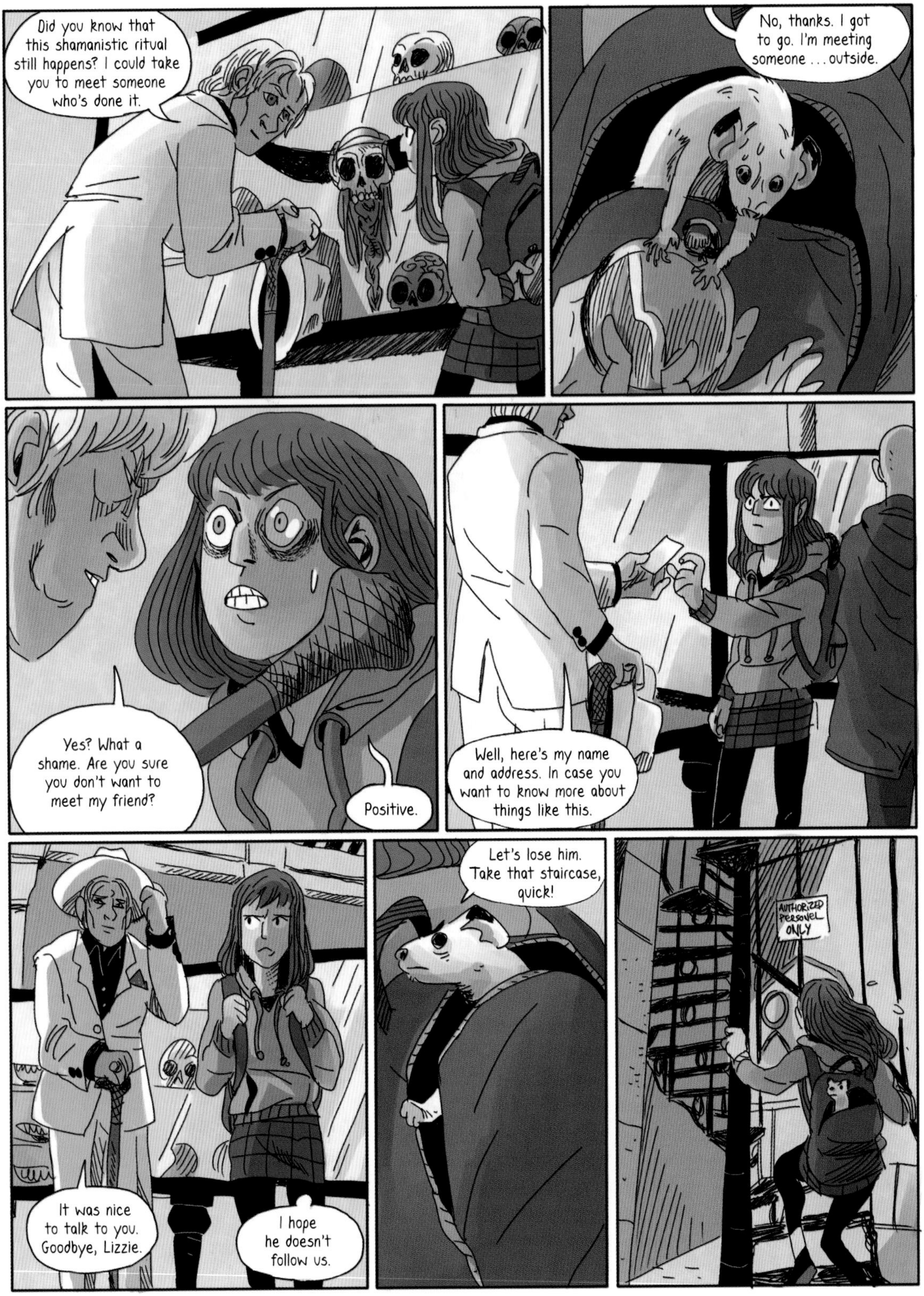

Did you know that this shamanistic ritual still happens? I could take you to meet someone who's done it.
No, thanks. I got to go. I'm meeting someone . . . outside.
Yes? What a shame. Are you sure you don't want to meet my friend?
Positive.
Well, here's my name and address. In case you want to know more about things like this.
It was nice to talk to you. Goodbye, Lizzie.
I hope he doesn't follow us.
Let's lose him. Take that staircase, quick!
AUTHORIZED PERSONEL ONLY

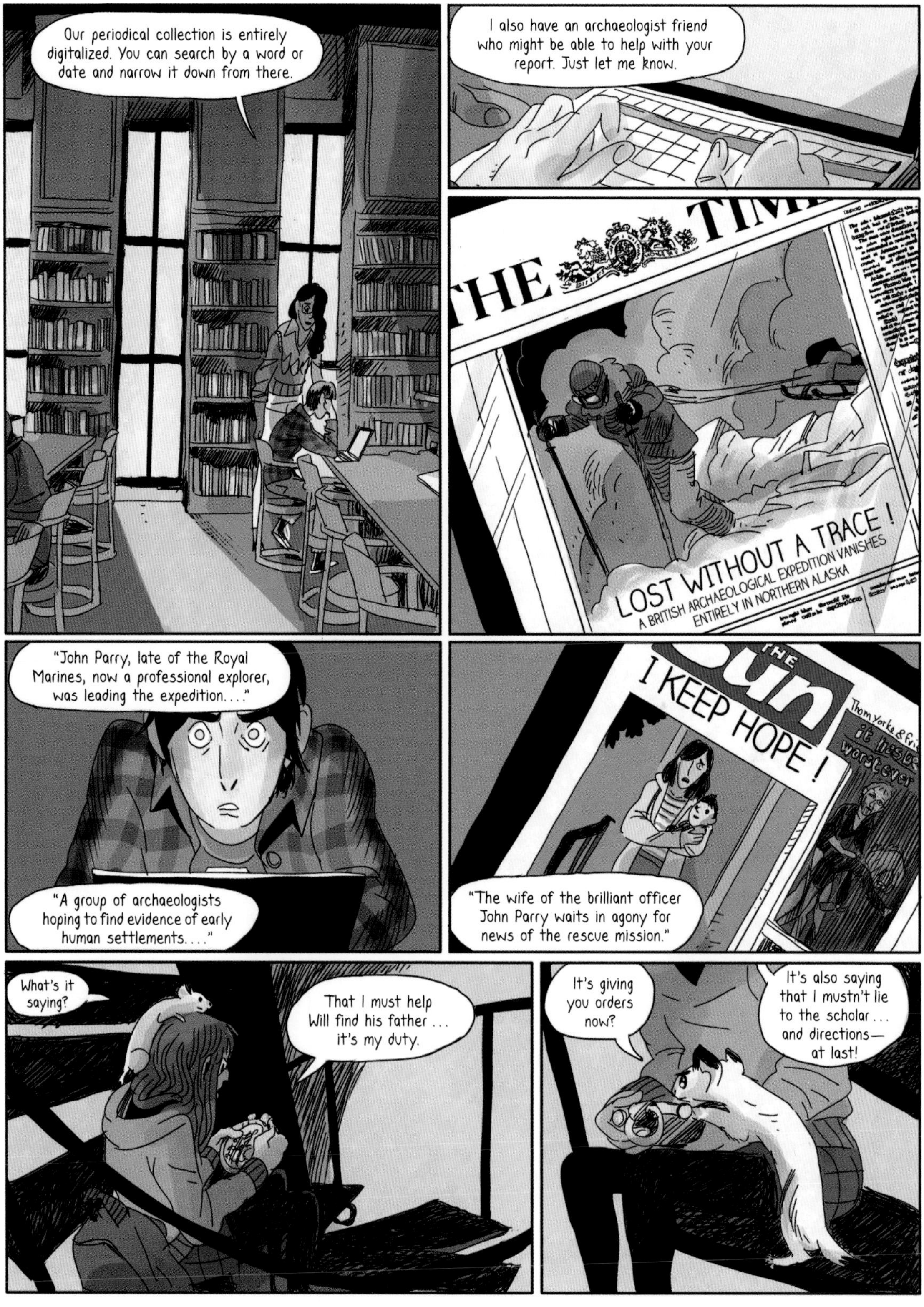
Our periodical collection is entirely digitalized. You can search by a word or date and narrow it down from there.
I also have an archaeologist friend who might be able to help with your report. Just let me know.
THE TIM
LOST WITHOUT A TRACE !
A BRITISH ARCHAEOLOGICAL EXPEDITION VANISHES ENTIRELY IN NORTHERN ALASKA
"John Parry, late of the Royal Marines, now a professional explorer, was leading the expedition. . . ."
"A group of archaeologists hoping to find evidence of early human settlements. . . ."
THE Sun
I KEEP HOPE !
"The wife of the brilliant officer John Parry waits in agony for news of the rescue mission."
What's it saying?
That I must help Will find his father . . . it's my duty.
It's giving you orders now?
It's also saying that I mustn't lie to the scholar . . . and directions— at last!

You're the second person this month to ask me about this Arctic expedition. I looked it all up for that journalist, so I suppose I can tell you too.

There was a big to-do about it at the time. It was a preliminary survey, not a proper dig. Half a dozen blokes, I think, each looking for different things in the area.

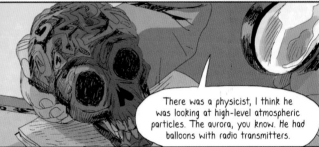

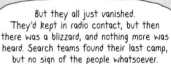

There was a physicist, I think he was looking at high-level atmospheric particles. The aurora, you know. He had balloons with radio transmitters.

And there was a professional explorer, ex-Marine, leading the scientists. They were going into some wild territory, and polar bears are always a danger in the Arctic.

But they all just vanished. They'd kept in radio contact, but then there was a blizzard, and nothing more was heard. Search teams found their last camp, but no sign of the people whatsoever.

The journalist who came to ask you about the expedition, what did he look like?

Look like? Well, he was a big man, square jaw, albino, I think ... very pale anyway.

A military man too, if you want my opinion, despite his press credentials.

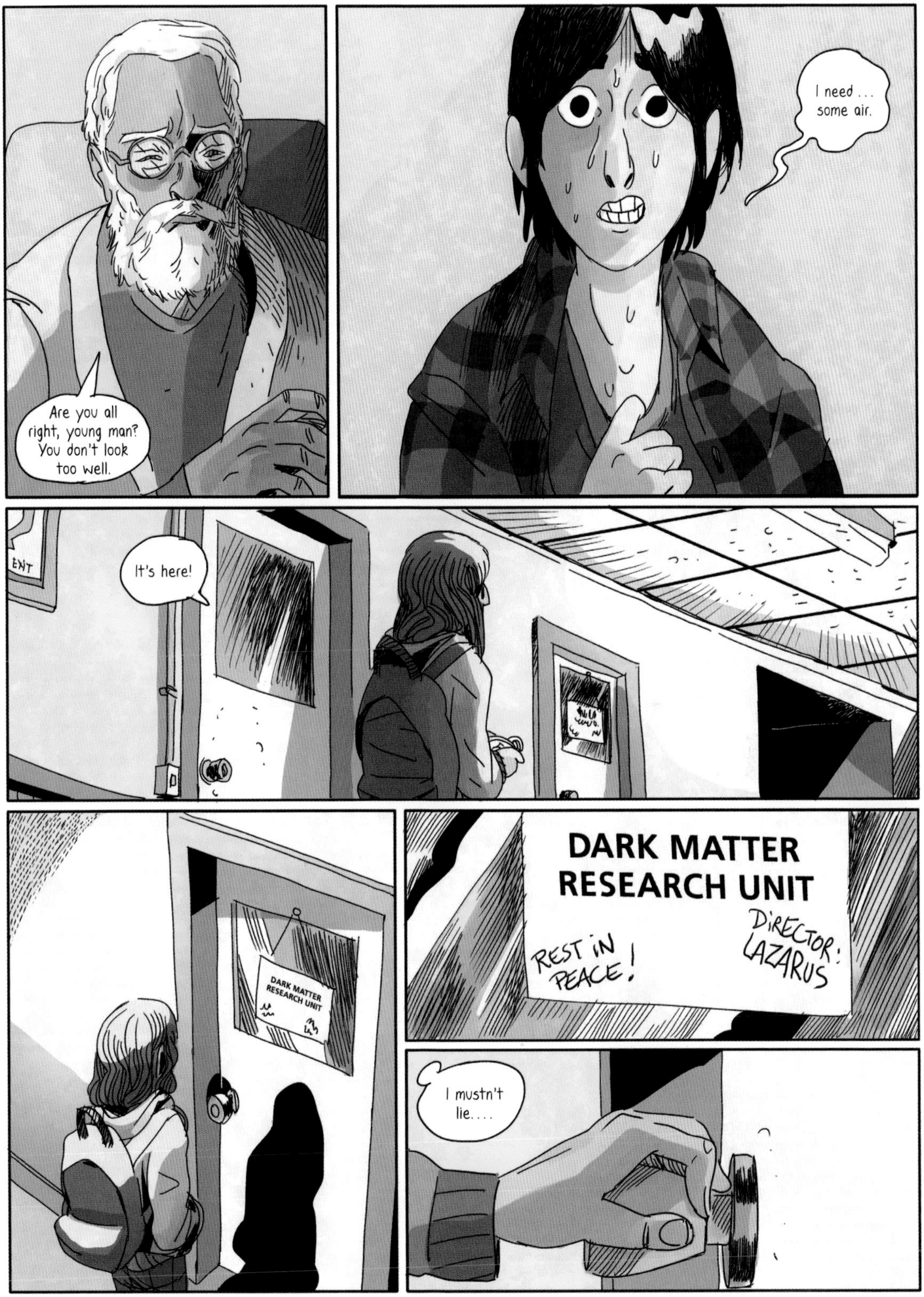
Are you all right, young man? You don't look too well.
I need . . . some air.
EXIT
It's here!
DARK MATTER RESEARCH UNIT
DARK MATTER RESEARCH UNIT
REST IN PEACE!
DIRECTOR: LAZARUS
I mustn't lie. . . .

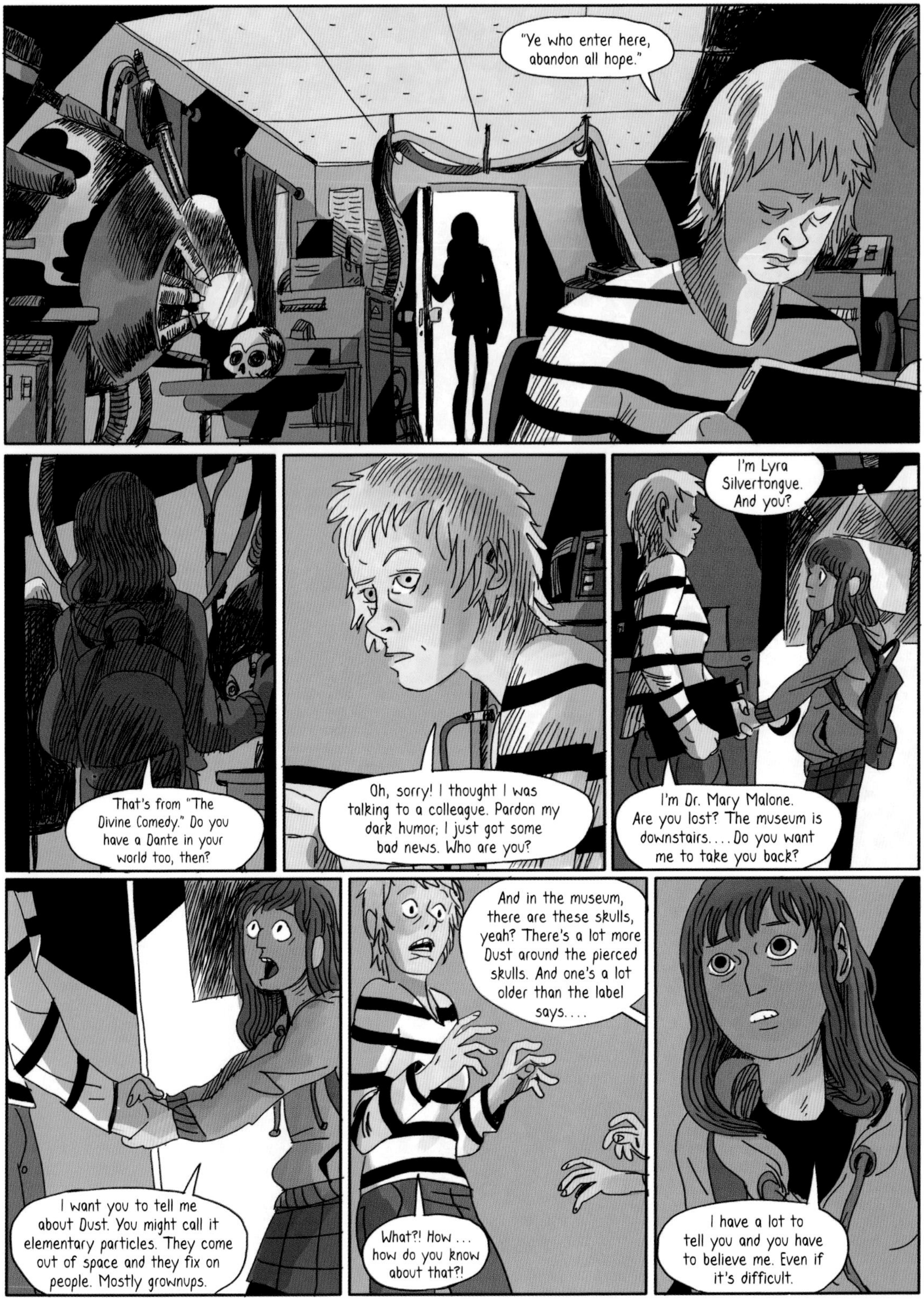
"Ye who enter here, abandon all hope."
That's from "The Divine Comedy." Do you have a Dante in your world too, then?
Oh, sorry! I thought I was talking to a colleague. Pardon my dark humor; I just got some bad news. Who are you?
I'm Lyra Silvertongue. And you?
I'm Dr. Mary Malone. Are you lost? The museum is downstairs. . . . Do you want me to take you back?
I want you to tell me about Dust. You might call it elementary particles. They come out of space and they fix on people. Mostly grownups.
And in the museum, there are these skulls, yeah? There's a lot more Dust around the pierced skulls. And one's a lot older than the label says. . . .
What?! How . . . how do you know about that?!
I have a lot to tell you and you have to believe me. Even if it's difficult.

Orphan . . .

Murderer and fugitive . . . I can deal with all that.

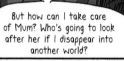

But how can I take care of Mum? Who's going to look after her if I disappear into another world?

OXFORD

Dear Mum,
I am safe and well and I will see you again soon.

. . . I hope everything is all right. I love you. Will.

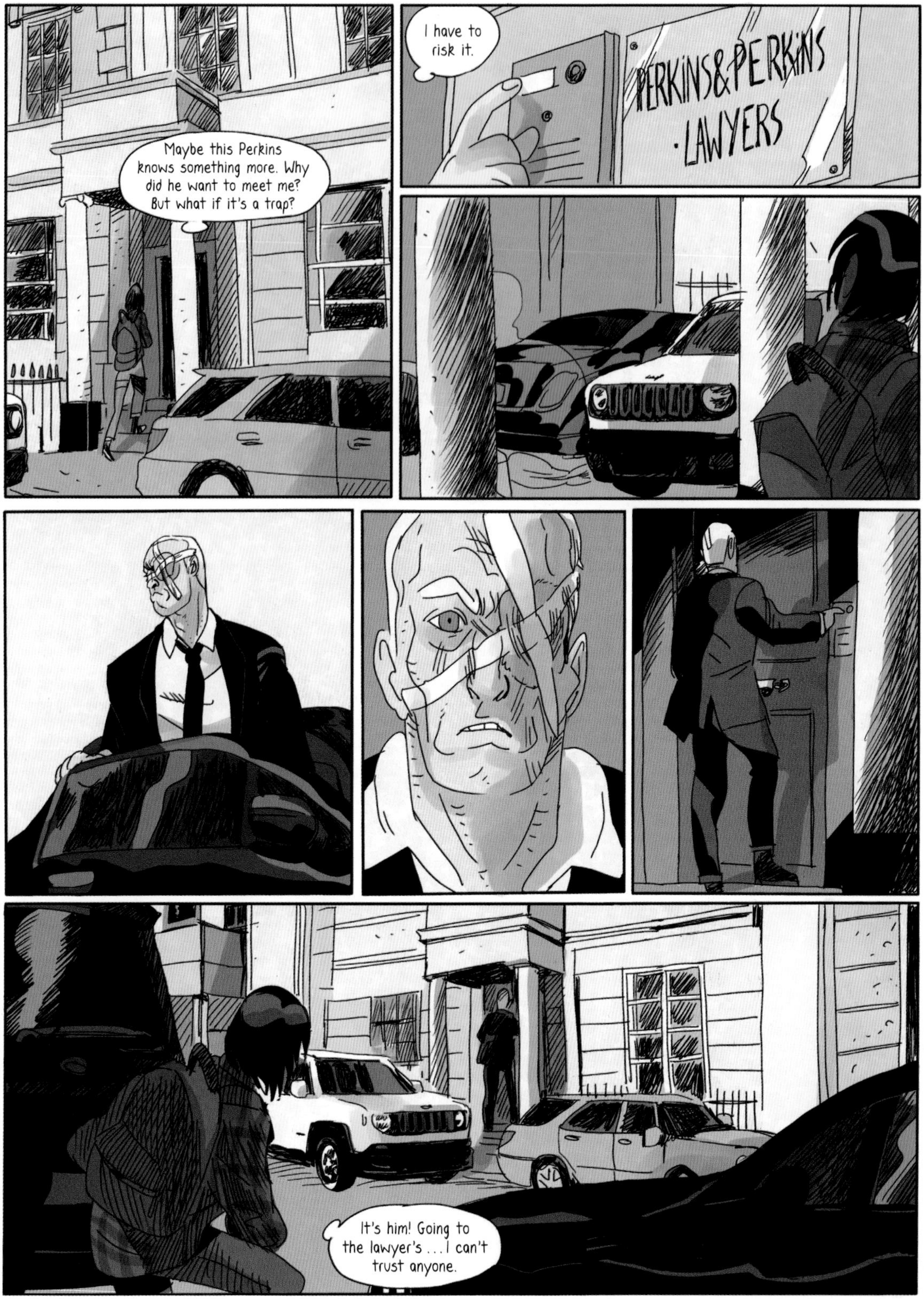
Maybe this Perkins knows something more. Why did he want to meet me? But what if it's a trap?
I have to risk it.
PERKINS&PERKINS
·LAWYERS
It's him! Going to the lawyer's . . . I can't trust anyone.

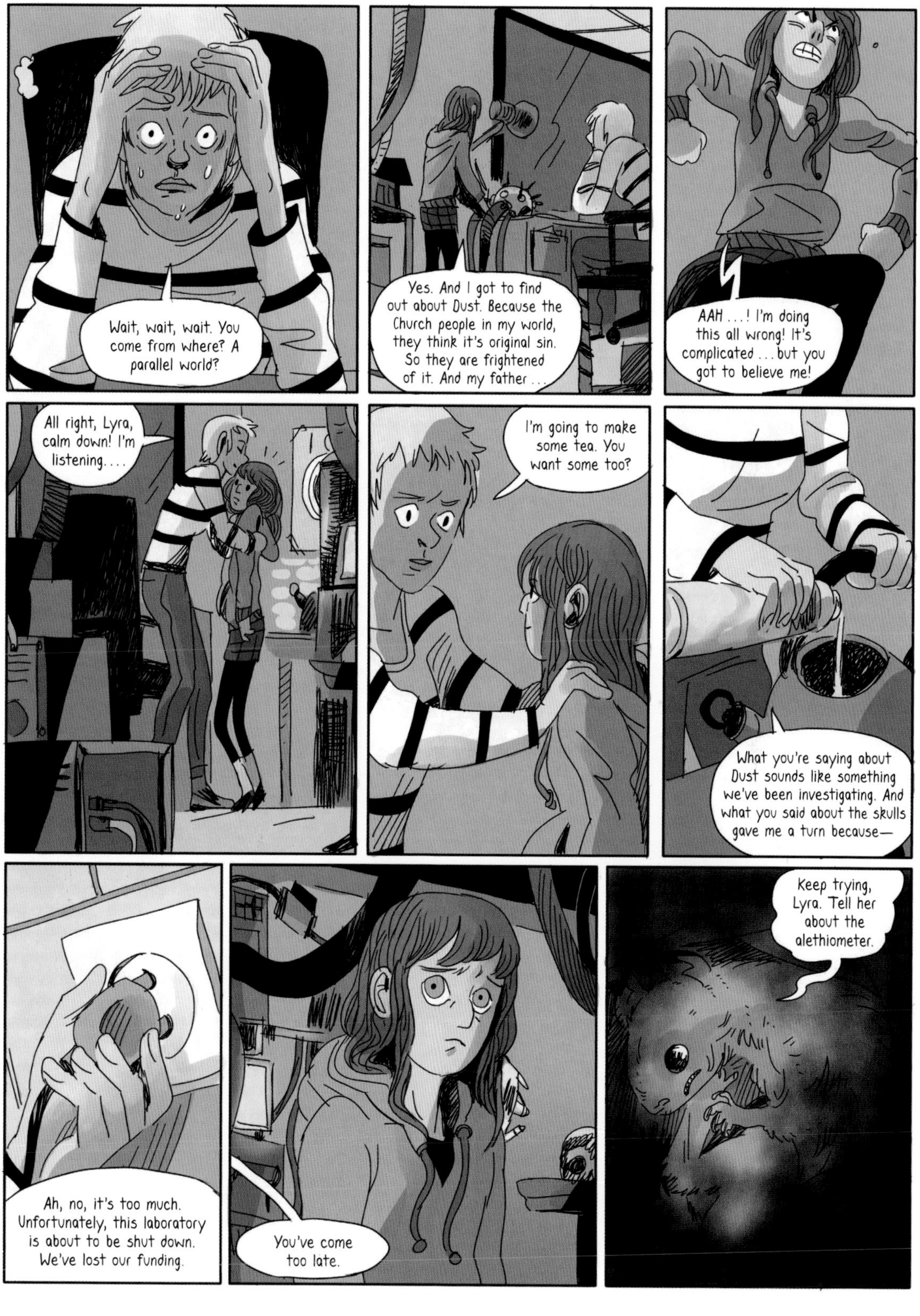

Wait, wait, wait. You come from where? A parallel world?
Yes. And I got to find out about Dust. Because the Church people in my world, they think it's original sin. So they are frightened of it. And my father . . .
AAH . . . ! I'm doing this all wrong! It's complicated . . . but you got to believe me!
All right, Lyra, calm down! I'm listening. . . .
I'm going to make some tea. You want some too?
What you're saying about Dust sounds like something we've been investigating. And what you said about the skulls gave me a turn because—
Ah, no, it's too much. Unfortunately, this laboratory is about to be shut down. We've lost our funding.
You've come too late.
Keep trying, Lyra. Tell her about the alethiometer.

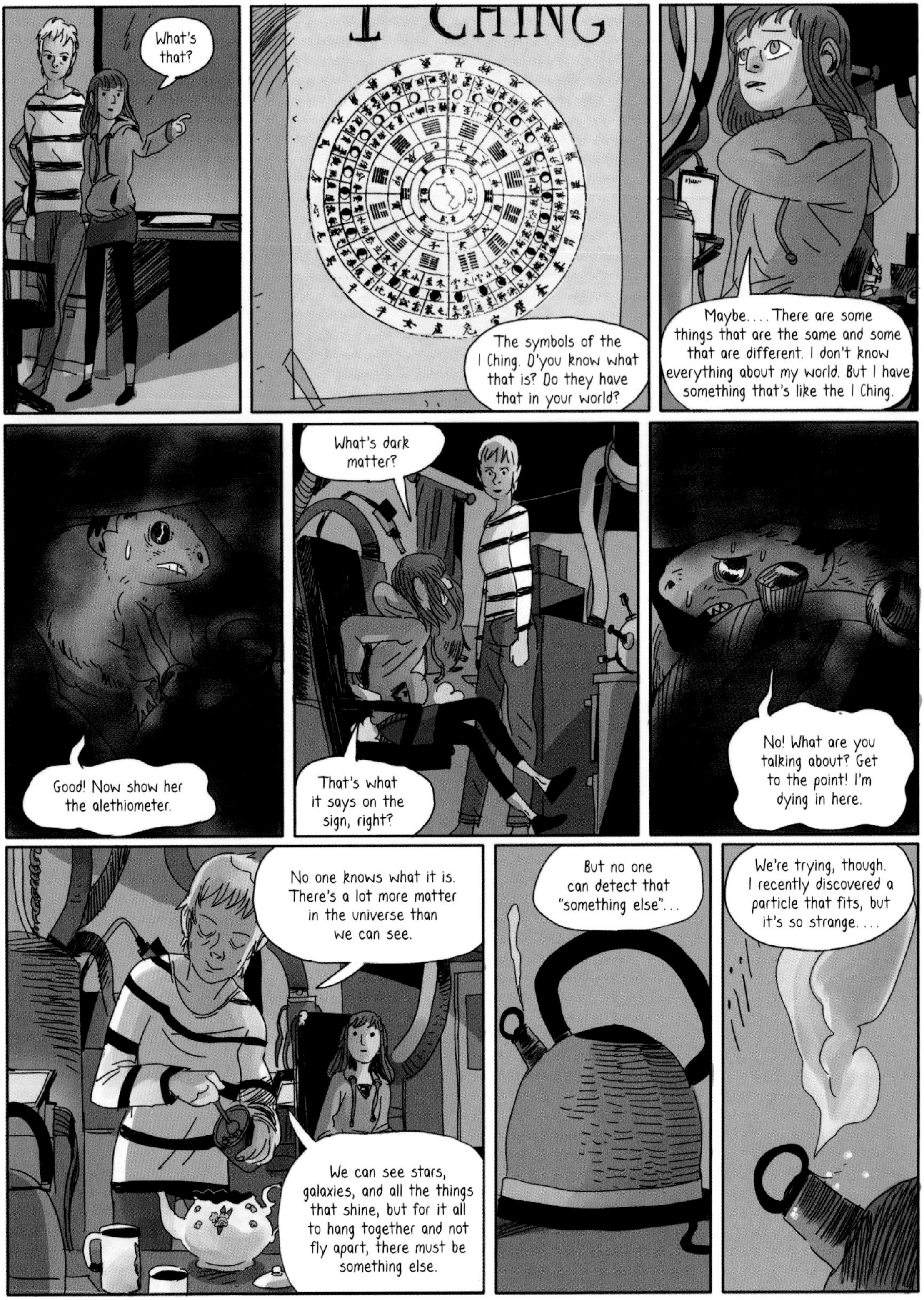
What's that?
I CHING
The symbols of the I Ching. D'you know what that is? Do they have that in your world?
Maybe. . . . There are some things that are the same and some that are different. I don't know everything about my world. But I have something that's like the I Ching.
Good! Now show her the alethiometer.
What's dark matter?
That's what it says on the sign, right?
No! What are you talking about? Get to the point! I'm dying in here.
No one knows what it is. There's a lot more matter in the universe than we can see.
We can see stars, galaxies, and all the things that shine, but for it all to hang together and not fly apart, there must be something else.
But no one can detect that "something else". . .
We're trying, though. I recently discovered a particle that fits, but it's so strange. . . .

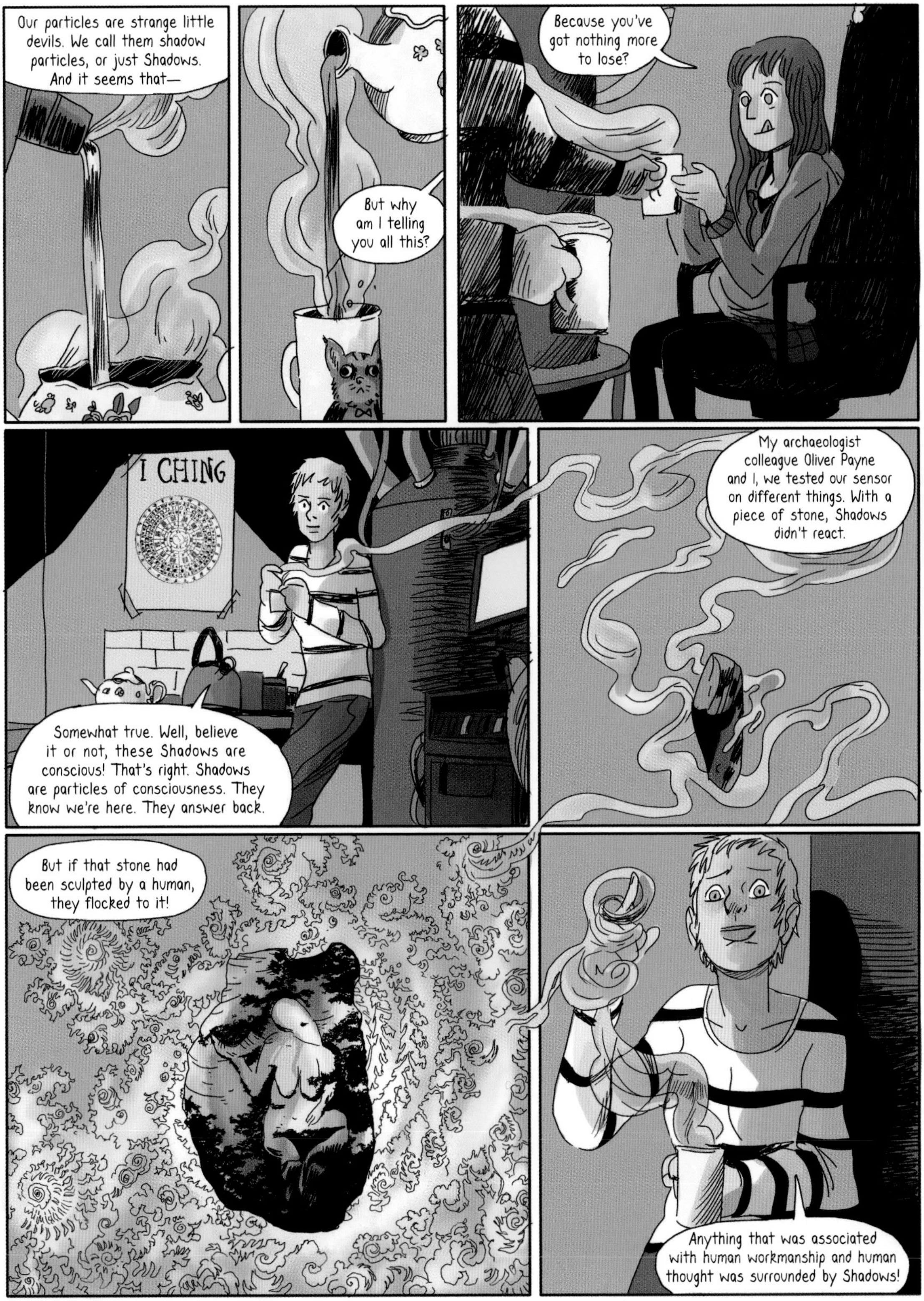
Our particles are strange little devils. We call them shadow particles, or just Shadows. And it seems that—
But why am I telling you all this?
Because you've got nothing more to lose?
I CHING
Somewhat true. Well, believe it or not, these Shadows are conscious! That's right. Shadows are particles of consciousness. They know we're here. They answer back.
My archaeologist colleague Oliver Payne and I, we tested our sensor on different things. With a piece of stone, Shadows didn't react.
But if that stone had been sculpted by a human, they flocked to it!
Anything that was associated with human workmanship and human thought was surrounded by Shadows!

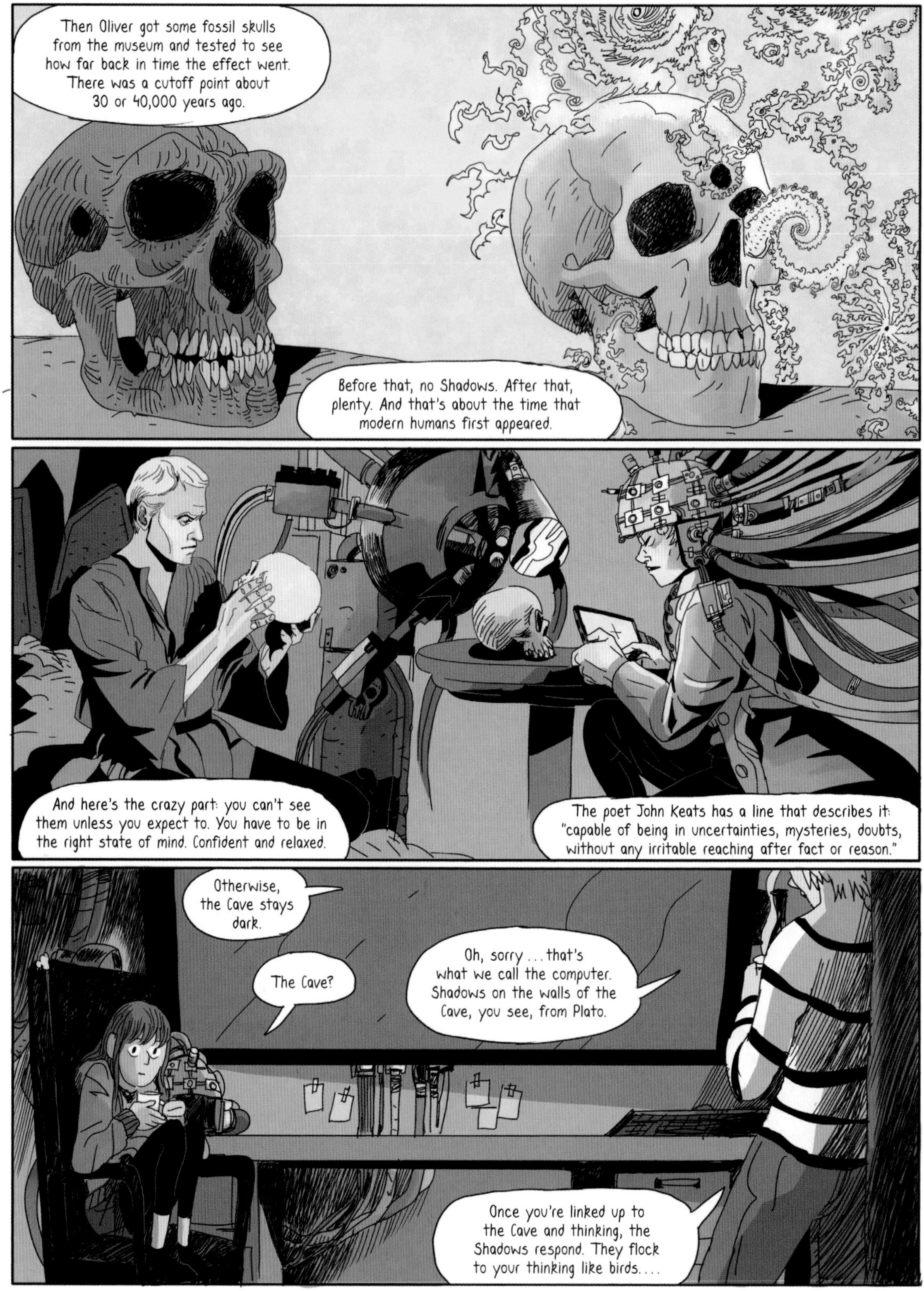
Then Oliver got some fossil skulls from the museum and tested to see how far back in time the effect went. There was a cutoff point about 30 or 40,000 years ago.
Before that, no Shadows. After that, plenty. And that's about the time that modern humans first appeared.
And here's the crazy part: you can't see them unless you expect to. You have to be in the right state of mind. Confident and relaxed.
The poet John Keats has a line that describes it: "capable of being in uncertainties, mysteries, doubts, without any irritable reaching after fact or reason."
Otherwise, the Cave stays dark.
The Cave?
Oh, sorry . . . that's what we call the computer. Shadows on the walls of the Cave, you see, from Plato.
Once you're linked up to the Cave and thinking, the Shadows respond. They flock to your thinking like birds. . . .

I want to see the Cave.

But why?

Please, I want to try it. I know what I'm doing. It's Dust, I know it. I have another way to read it.

Impossible. You'd need very sophisticated tools for that.

Like this.

About time!

It's made of solid gold! Where on earth did you ...?

I didn't steal it if that's what you're thinking. It was given to me.

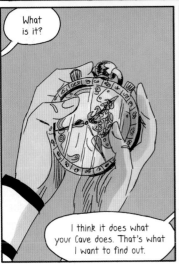

What is it?

I think it does what your Cave does. That's what I want to find out.

If I can answer a question truly, something you know the answer to and I don't, can I try your Cave then?

What, are you a fortune-teller now?

Are you afraid I'll find the answer ...?

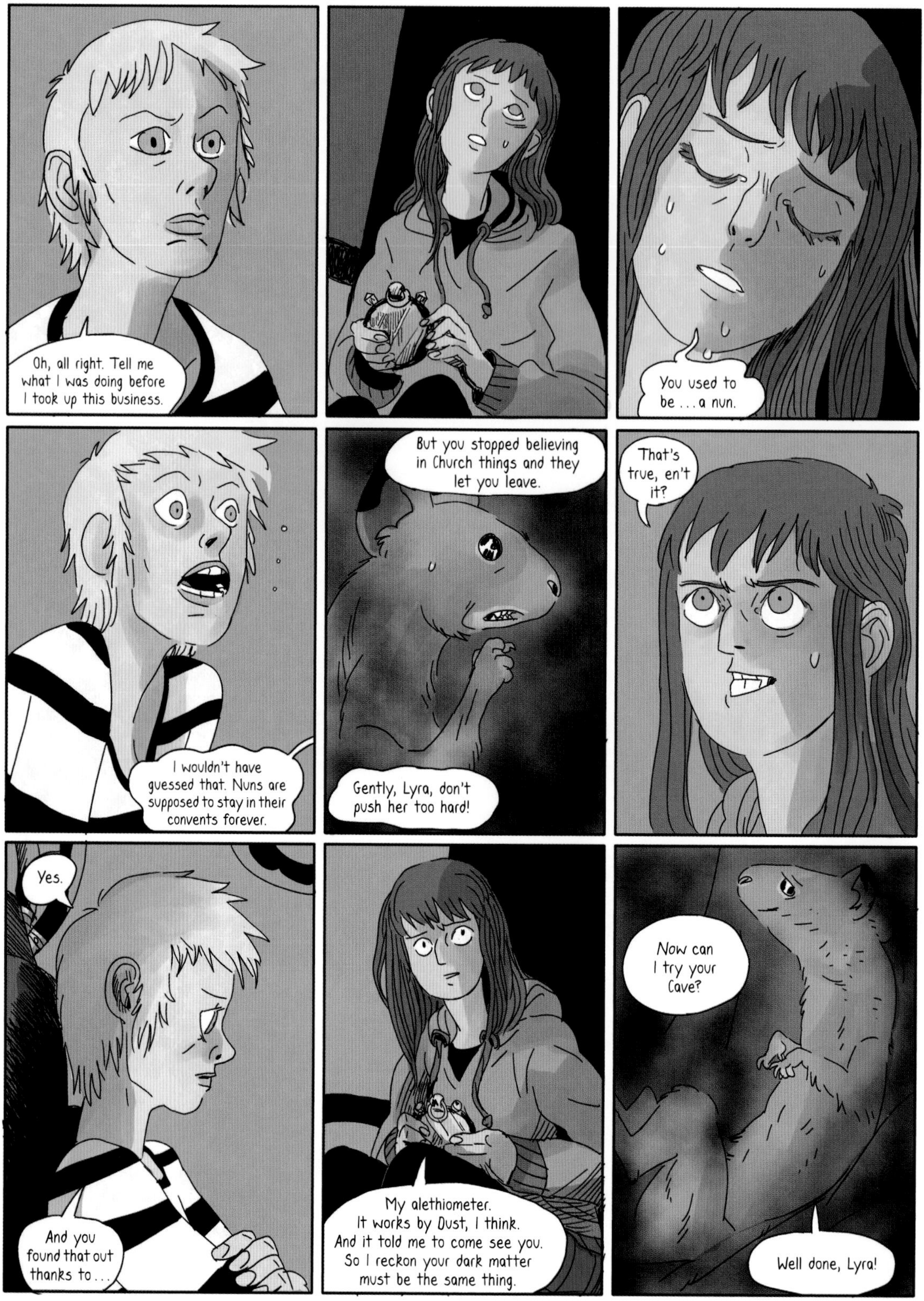

Oh, all right. Tell me what I was doing before I took up this business.
You used to be . . . a nun.
I wouldn't have guessed that. Nuns are supposed to stay in their convents forever.
But you stopped believing in Church things and they let you leave.
Gently, Lyra, don't push her too hard!
That's true, en't it?
Yes.
And you found that out thanks to . . .
My alethiometer. It works by Dust, I think. And it told me to come see you. So I reckon your dark matter must be the same thing.
Now can I try your Cave?
Well done, Lyra!

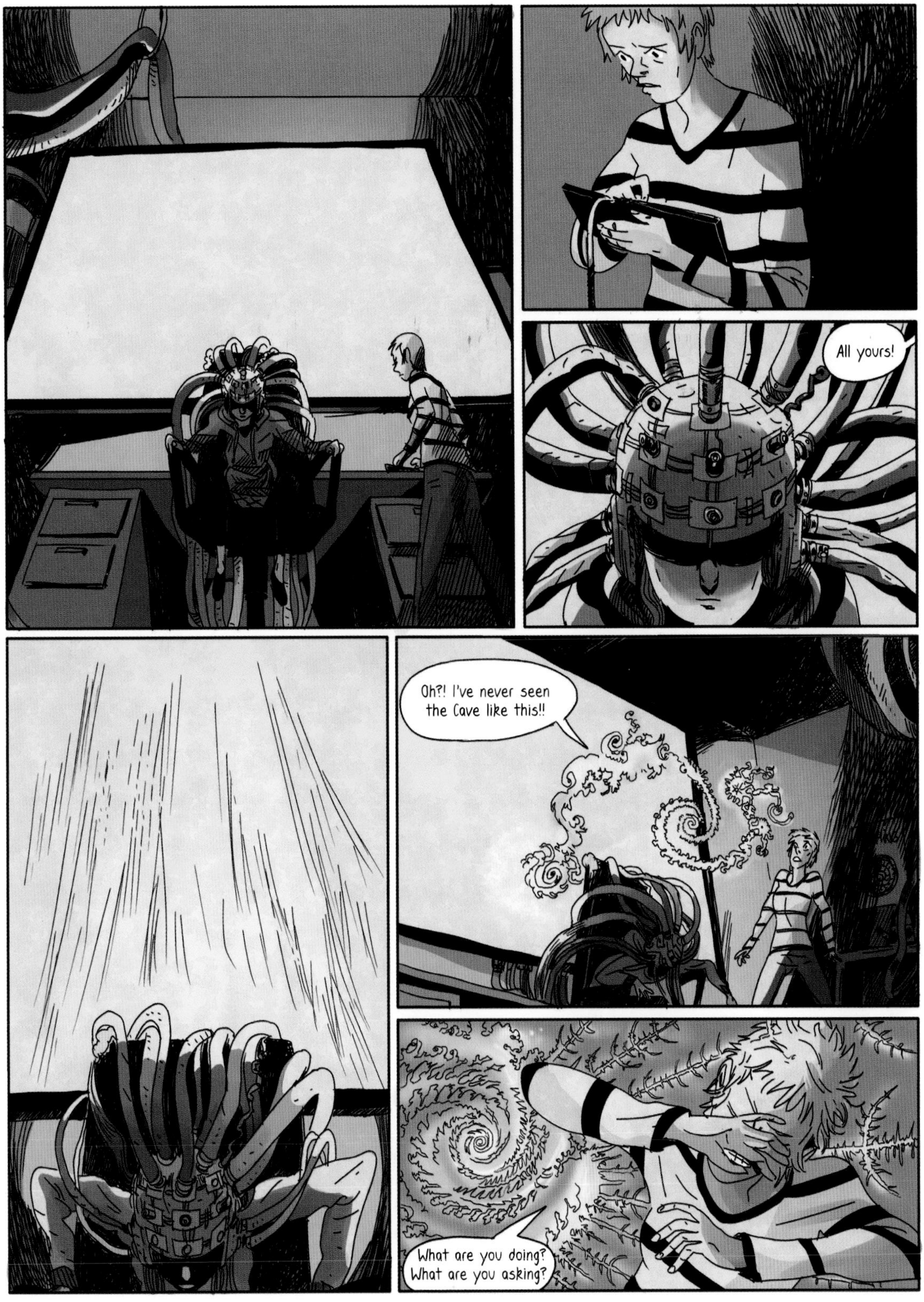
All yours!
Oh?! I've never seen the Cave like this!!
What are you doing? What are you asking?

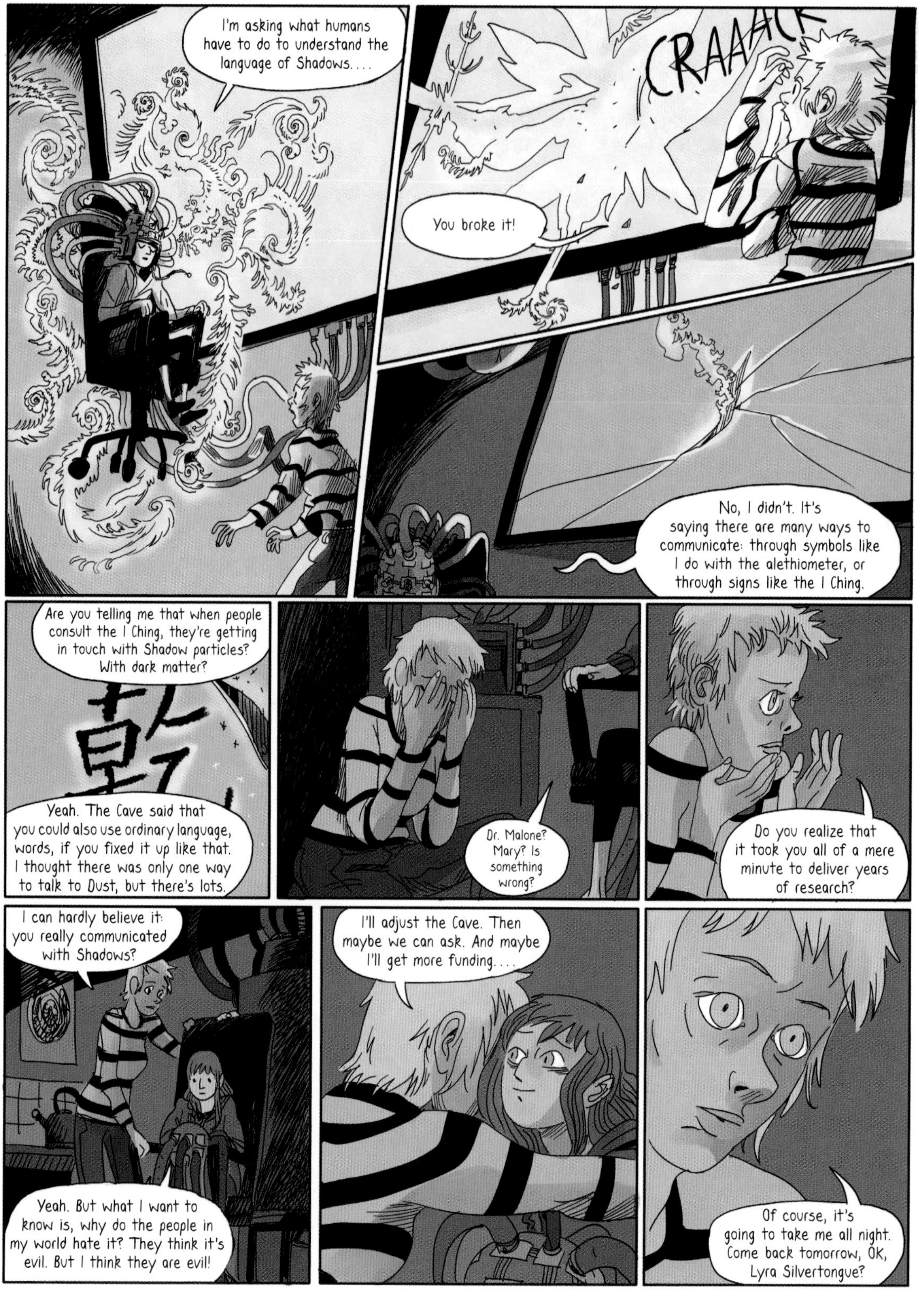
I'm asking what humans have to do to understand the language of Shadows....
CRAAACK
You broke it!
No, I didn't. It's saying there are many ways to communicate: through symbols like I do with the alethiometer, or through signs like the I Ching.
Are you telling me that when people consult the I Ching, they're getting in touch with Shadow particles? With dark matter?
Yeah. The Cave said that you could also use ordinary language, words, if you fixed it up like that. I thought there was only one way to talk to Dust, but there's lots.
Dr. Malone? Mary? Is something wrong?
Do you realize that it took you all of a mere minute to deliver years of research?
I can hardly believe it: you really communicated with Shadows?
Yeah. But what I want to know is, why do the people in my world hate it? They think it's evil. But I think they are evil!
I'll adjust the Cave. Then maybe we can ask. And maybe I'll get more funding....
Of course, it's going to take me all night. Come back tomorrow, OK, Lyra Silvertongue?

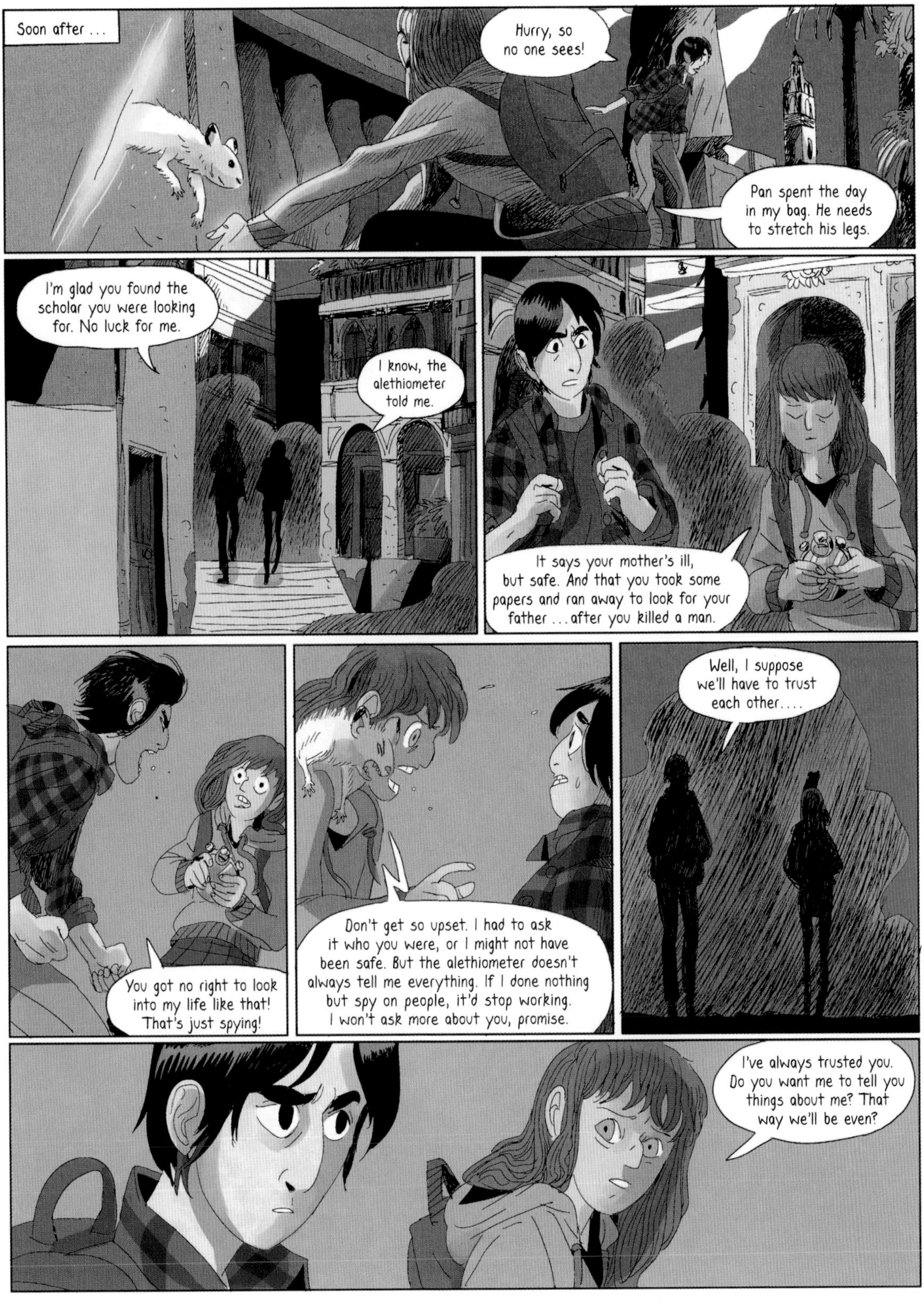
Soon after . . .
Hurry, so no one sees!
Pan spent the day in my bag. He needs to stretch his legs.
I'm glad you found the scholar you were looking for. No luck for me.
I know, the alethiometer told me.
It says your mother's ill, but safe. And that you took some papers and ran away to look for your father . . . after you killed a man.
You got no right to look into my life like that! That's just spying!
Don't get so upset. I had to ask it who you were, or I might not have been safe. But the alethiometer doesn't always tell me everything. If I done nothing but spy on people, it'd stop working. I won't ask more about you, promise.
Well, I suppose we'll have to trust each other. . . .
I've always trusted you. Do you want me to tell you things about me? That way we'll be even?

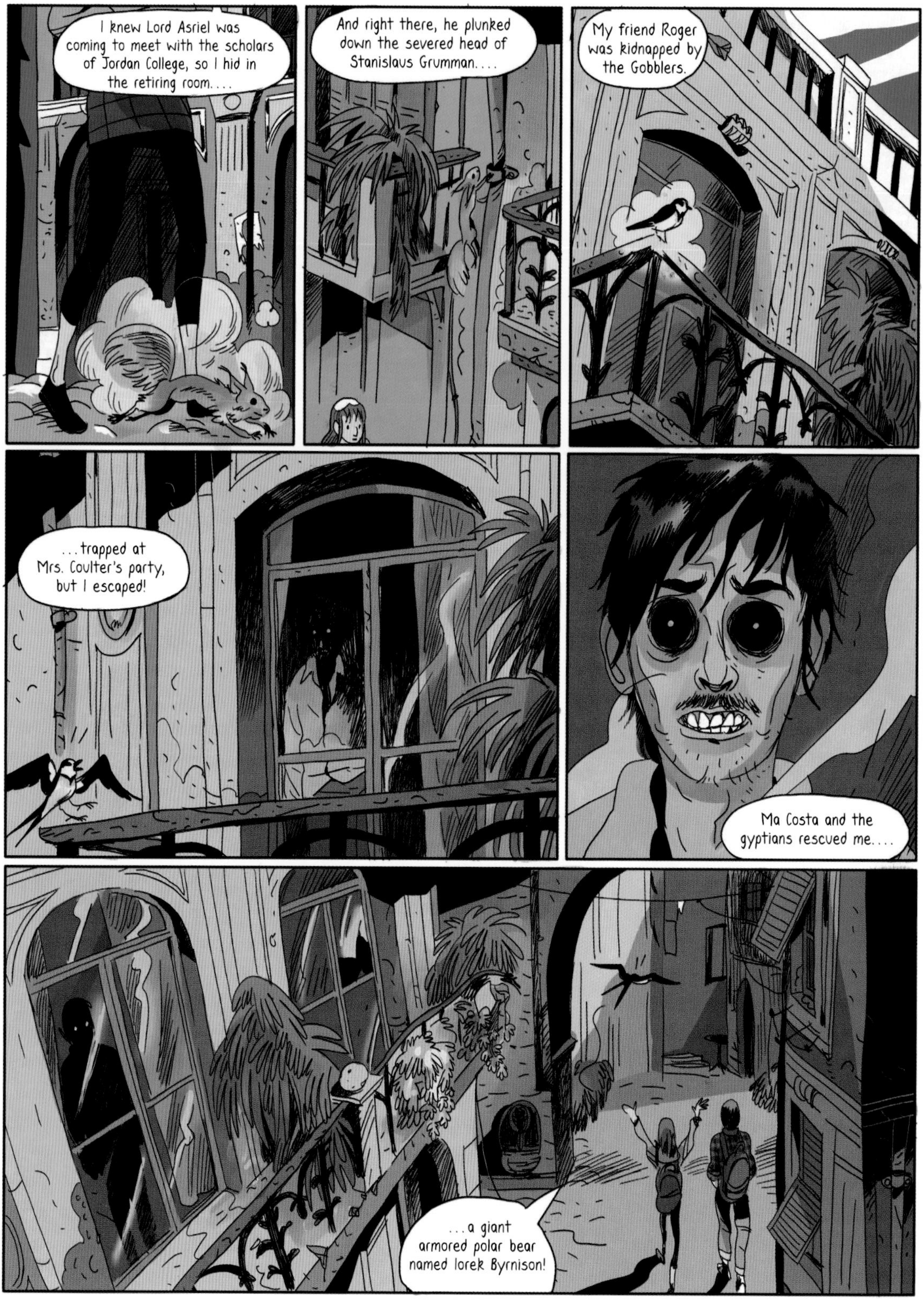

I knew Lord Asriel was coming to meet with the scholars of Jordan College, so I hid in the retiring room. . . .
And right there, he plunked down the severed head of Stanislaus Grumman. . . .
My friend Roger was kidnapped by the Gobblers.
. . . trapped at Mrs. Coulter's party, but I escaped!
Ma Costa and the gyptians rescued me. . . .
. . . a giant armored polar bear named Iorek Byrnison!

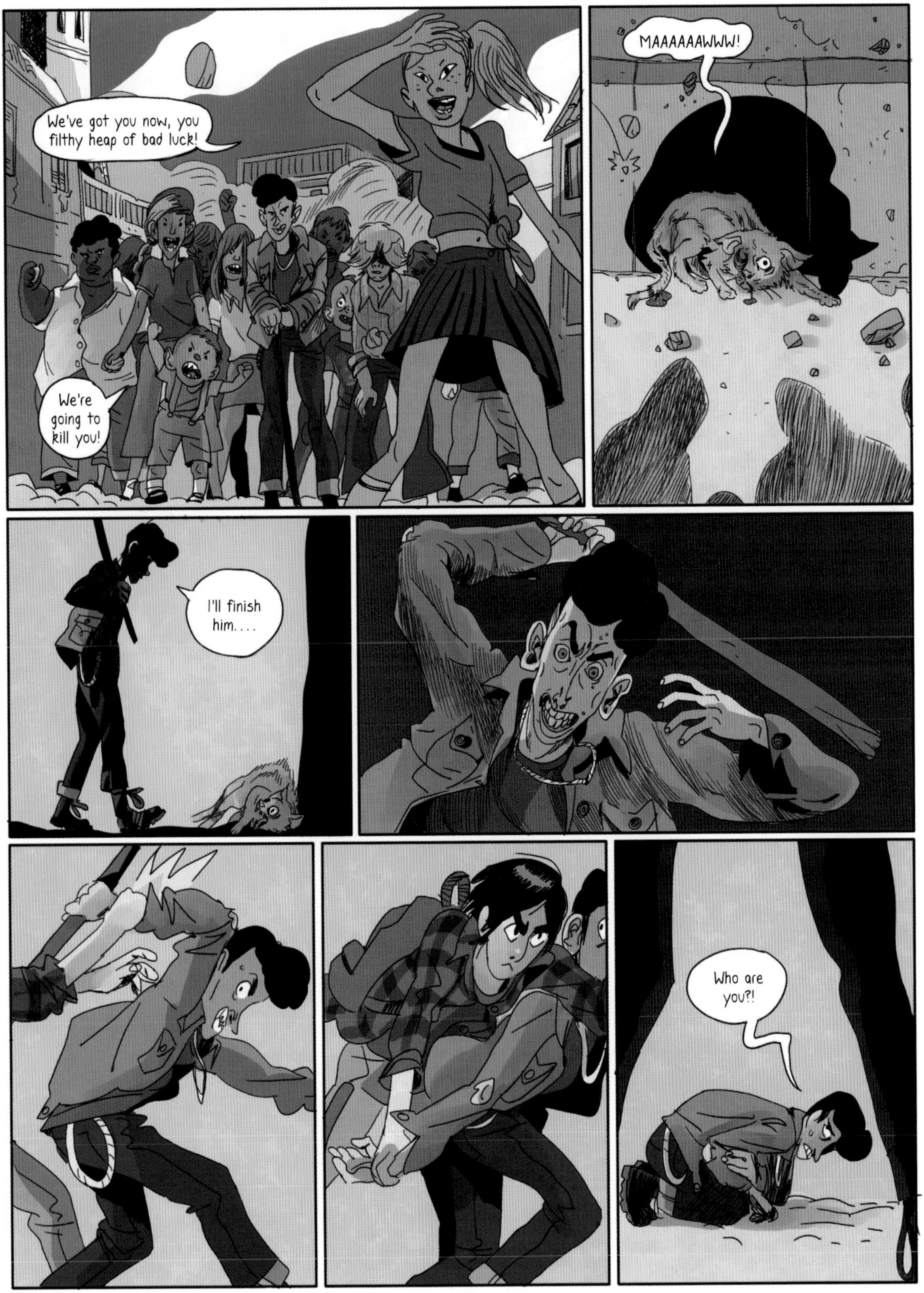
We've got you now, you filthy heap of bad luck!
We're going to kill you!
MAAAAAAWWW!
I'll finish him. . . .
Who are you?!

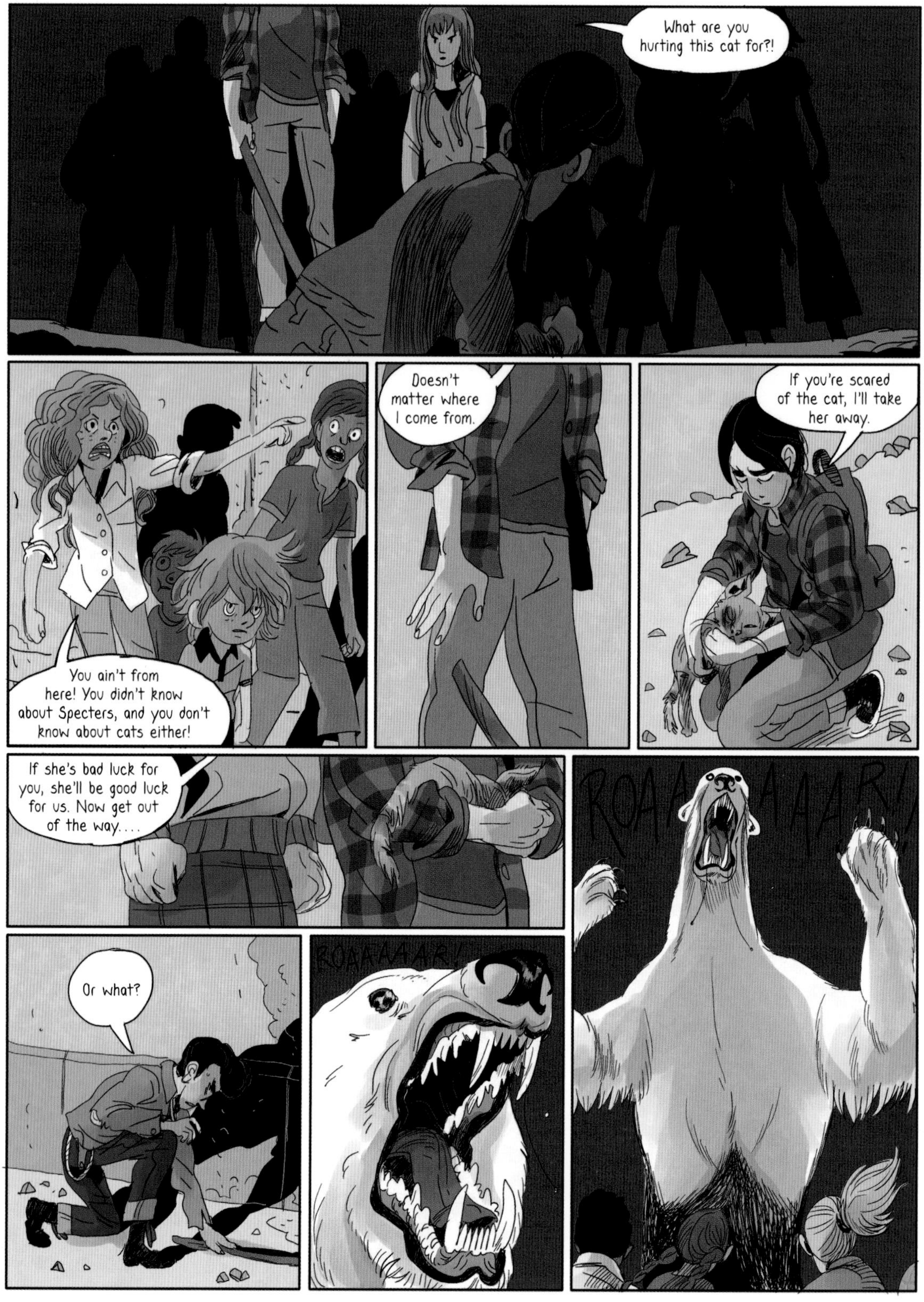
What are you hurting this cat for?!
You ain't from here! You didn't know about Specters, and you don't know about cats either!
Doesn't matter where I come from.
If you're scared of the cat, I'll take her away.
If she's bad luck for you, she'll be good luck for us. Now get out of the way. . . .
ROAAAAAAR!!
Or what?
ROAAAAAR!

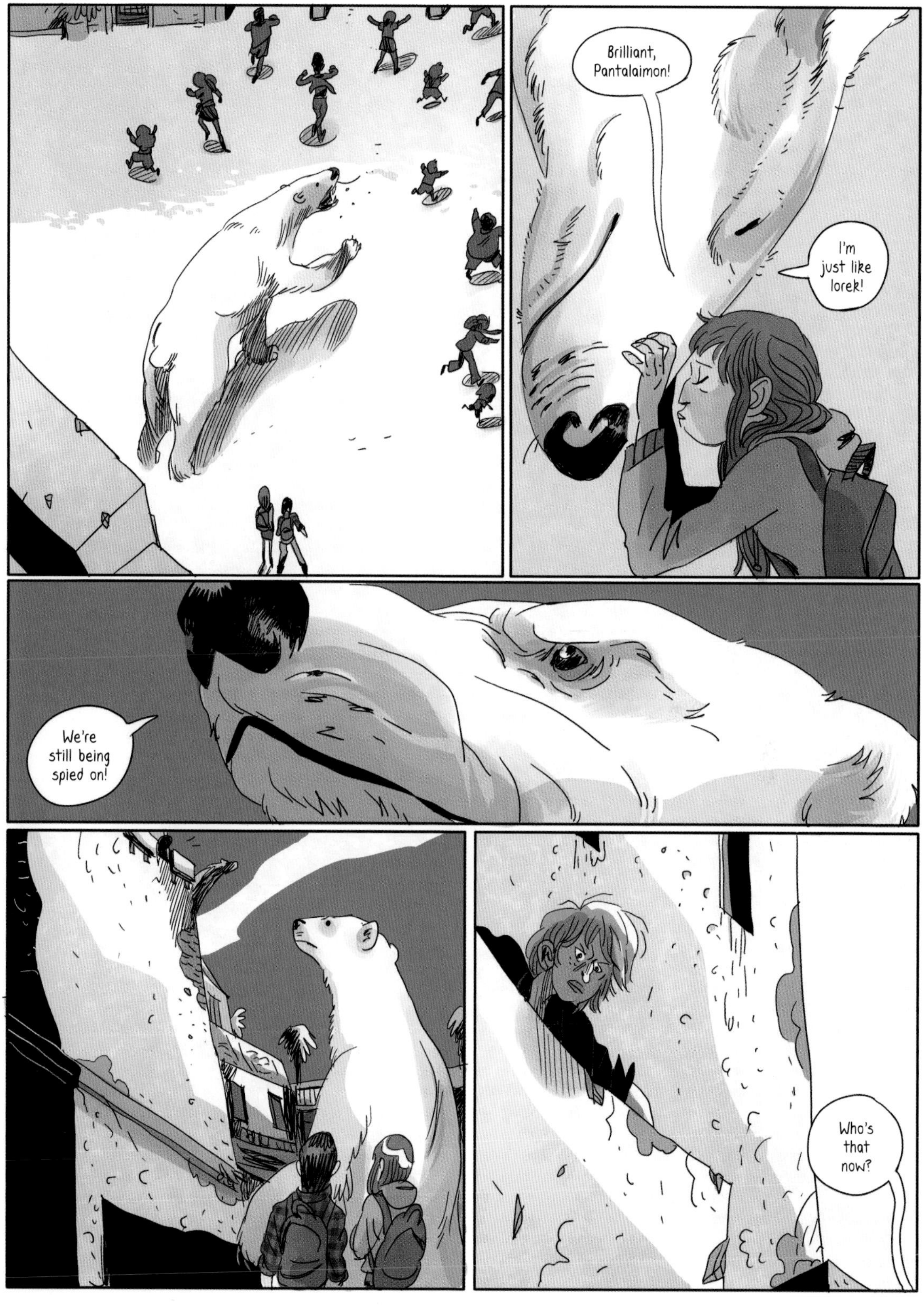
Brilliant, Pantalaimon!
I'm just like Iorek!
We're still being spied on!
Who's that now?

It's the cat I saw the night I left Oxford. The one who led me to the window.

They were wild. They would have killed her. I never seen kids being like that.

I have.

Slag!

Loon!

Loony slag!

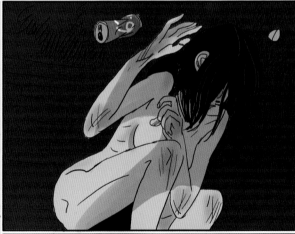

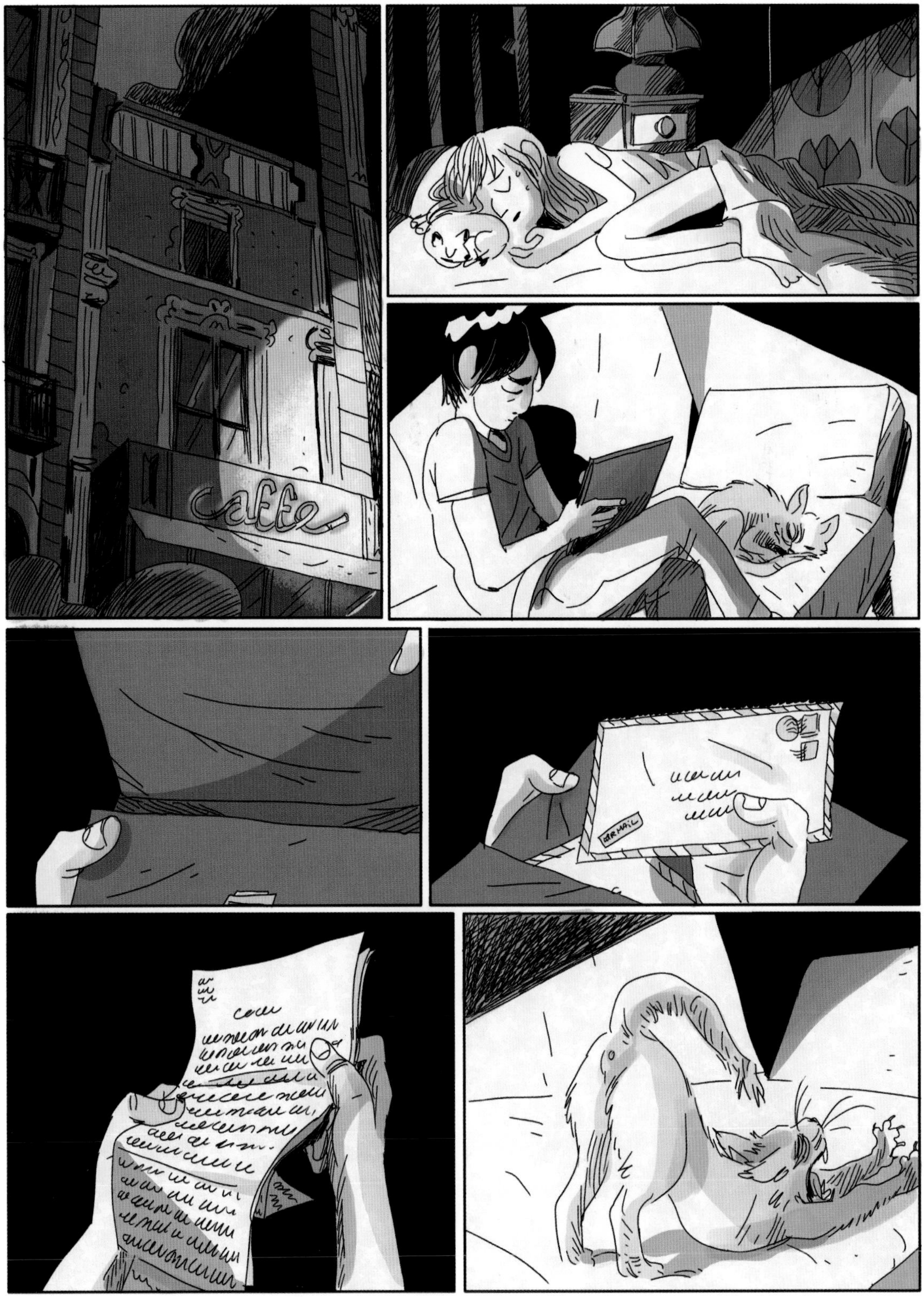
caffe
AIRMAIL

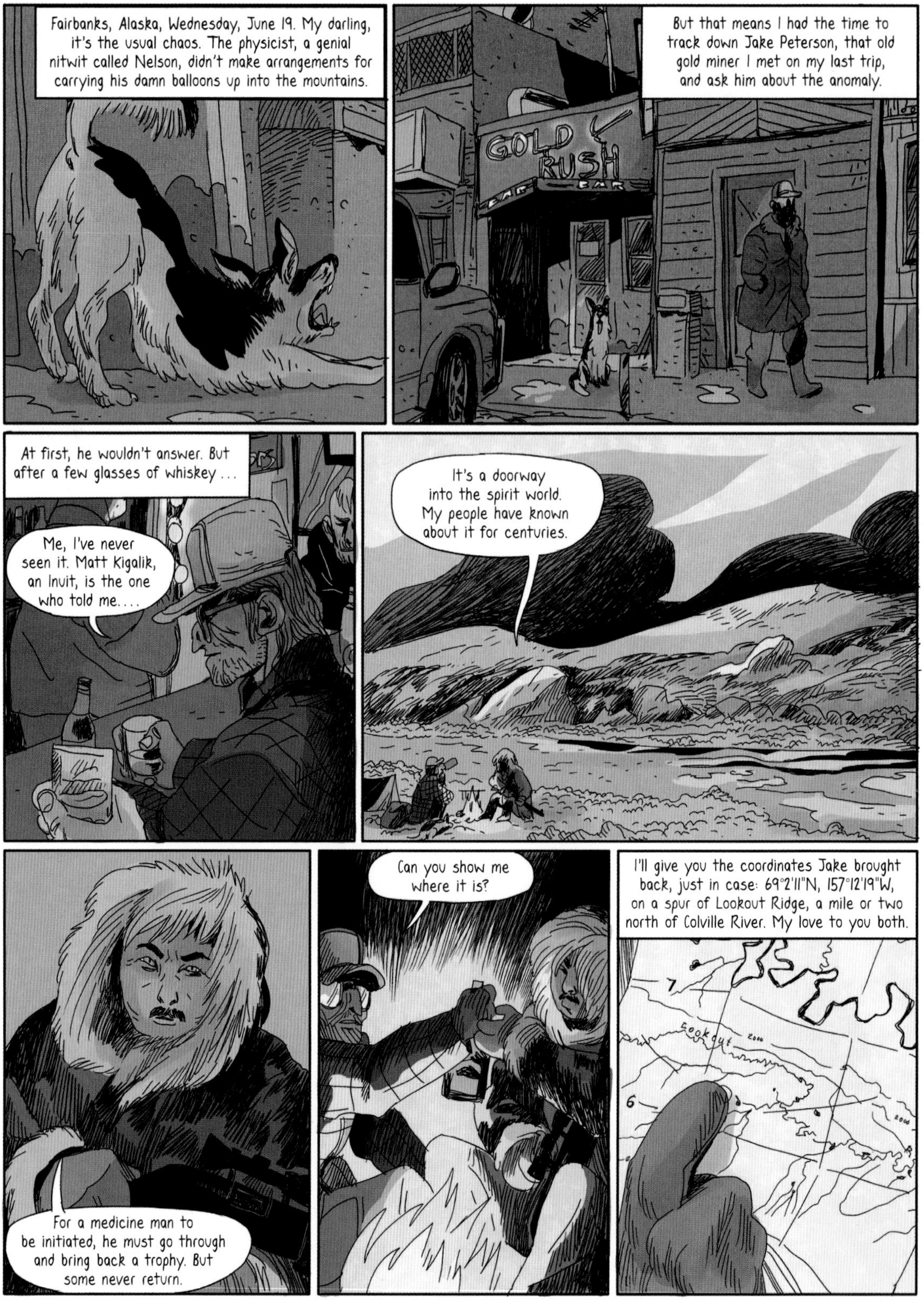

Fairbanks, Alaska, Wednesday, June 19. My darling, it's the usual chaos. The physicist, a genial nitwit called Nelson, didn't make arrangements for carrying his damn balloons up into the mountains.
But that means I had the time to track down Jake Peterson, that old gold miner I met on my last trip, and ask him about the anomaly.
GOLD RUSH
BAR
At first, he wouldn't answer. But after a few glasses of whiskey . . .
Me, I've never seen it. Matt Kigalik, an Inuit, is the one who told me. . . .
It's a doorway into the spirit world. My people have known about it for centuries.
For a medicine man to be initiated, he must go through and bring back a trophy. But some never return.
Can you show me where it is?
I'll give you the coordinates Jake brought back, just in case: 69°2'11"N, 157°12'19"W, on a spur of Lookout Ridge, a mile or two north of Colville River. My love to you both.

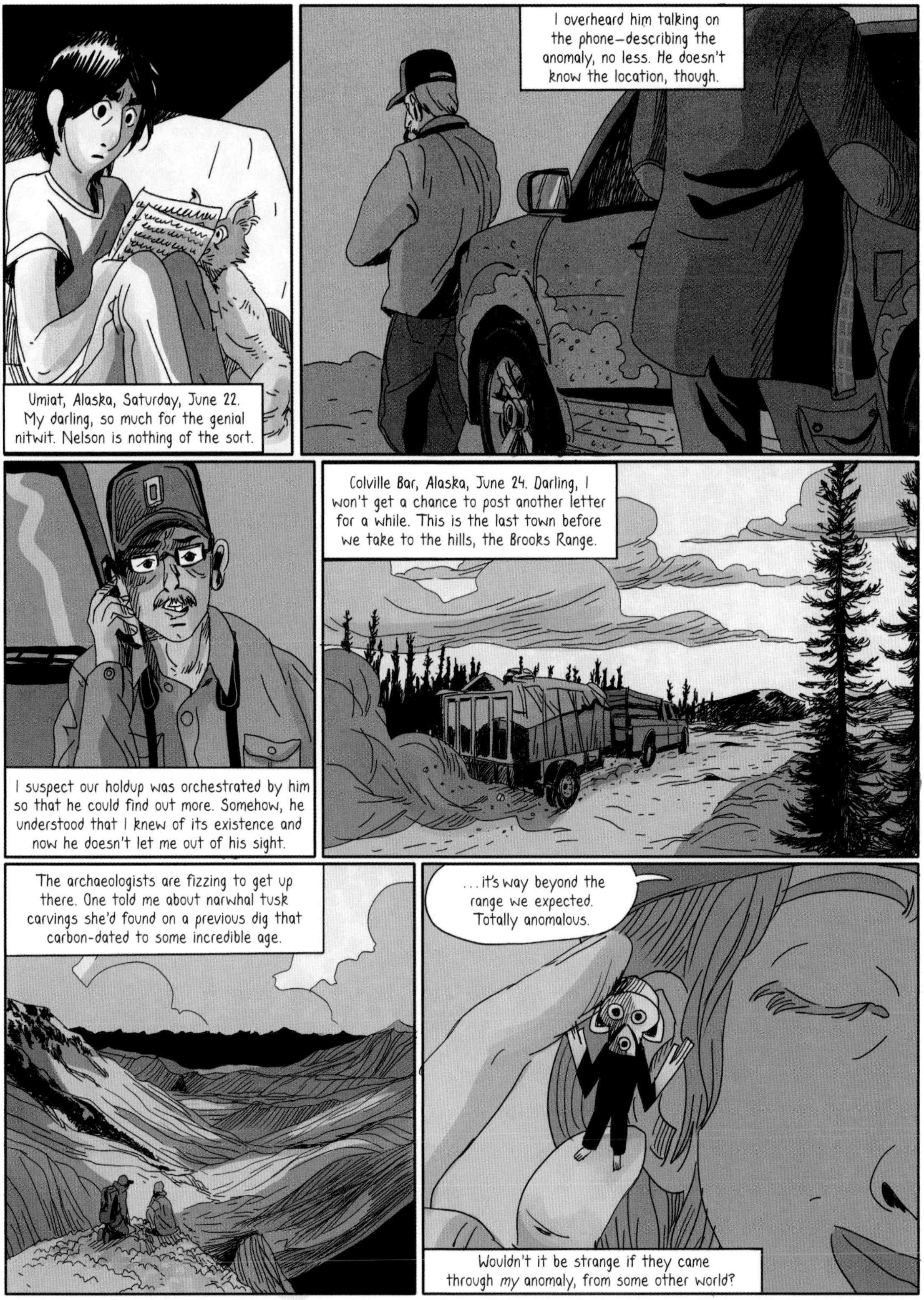
Umiat, Alaska, Saturday, June 22. My darling, so much for the genial nitwit. Nelson is nothing of the sort.
I overheard him talking on the phone—describing the anomaly, no less. He doesn't know the location, though.
I suspect our holdup was orchestrated by him so that he could find out more. Somehow, he understood that I knew of its existence and now he doesn't let me out of his sight.
Colville Bar, Alaska, June 24. Darling, I won't get a chance to post another letter for a while. This is the last town before we take to the hills, the Brooks Range.
The archaeologists are fizzing to get up there. One told me about narwhal tusk carvings she'd found on a previous dig that carbon-dated to some incredible age.
...it's way beyond the range we expected. Totally anomalous.
Wouldn't it be strange if they came through *my* anomaly, from some other world?

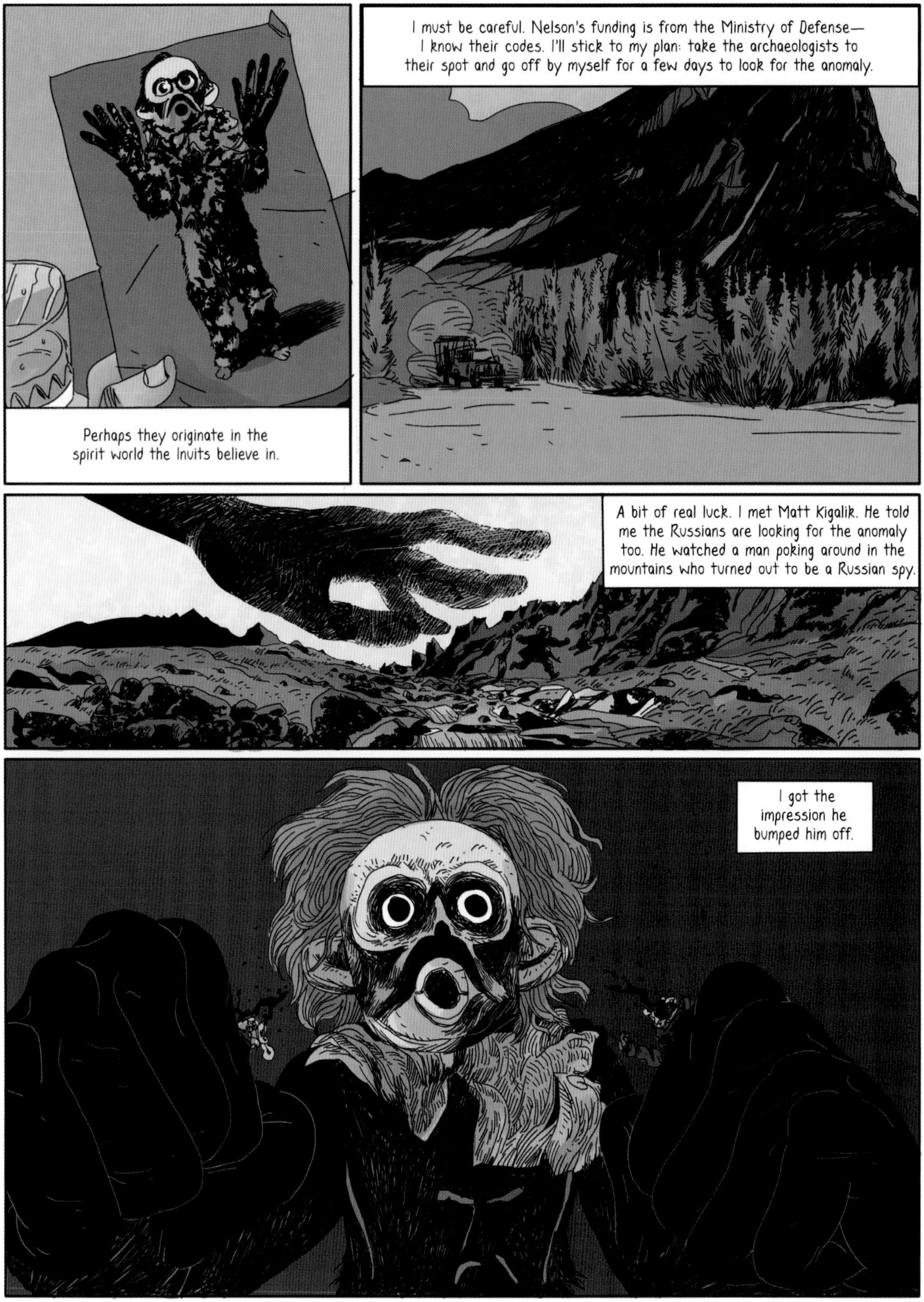
Perhaps they originate in the spirit world the Inuits believe in.
I must be careful. Nelson's funding is from the Ministry of Defense— I know their codes. I'll stick to my plan: take the archaeologists to their spot and go off by myself for a few days to look for the anomaly.
A bit of real luck. I met Matt Kigalik. He told me the Russians are looking for the anomaly too. He watched a man poking around in the mountains who turned out to be a Russian spy.
I got the impression he bumped him off.

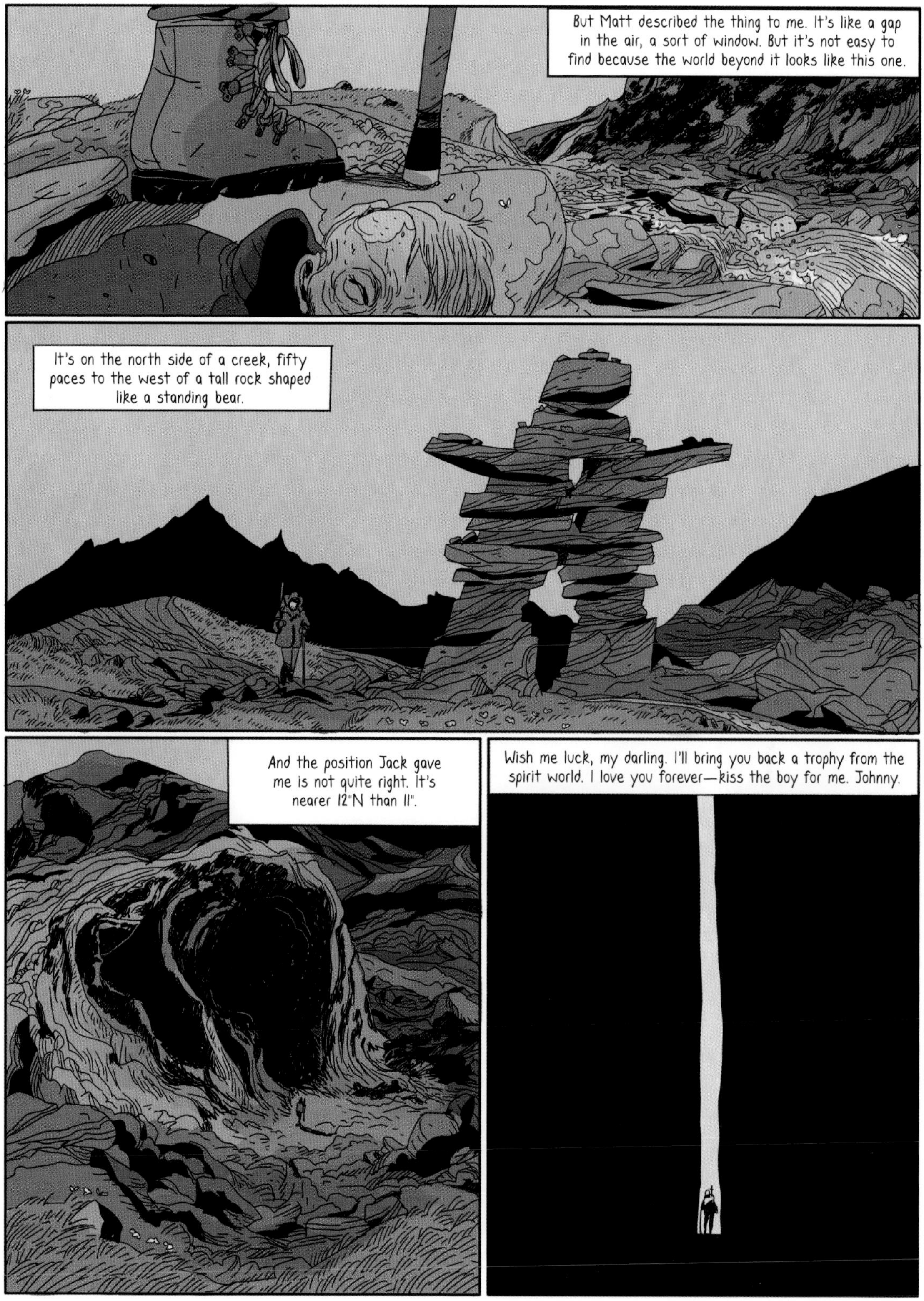
But Matt described the thing to me. It's like a gap in the air, a sort of window. But it's not easy to find because the world beyond it looks like this one.
It's on the north side of a creek, fifty paces to the west of a tall rock shaped like a standing bear.
And the position Jack gave me is not quite right. It's nearer 12"N than 11".
Wish me luck, my darling. I'll bring you back a trophy from the spirit world. I love you forever—kiss the boy for me. Johnny.

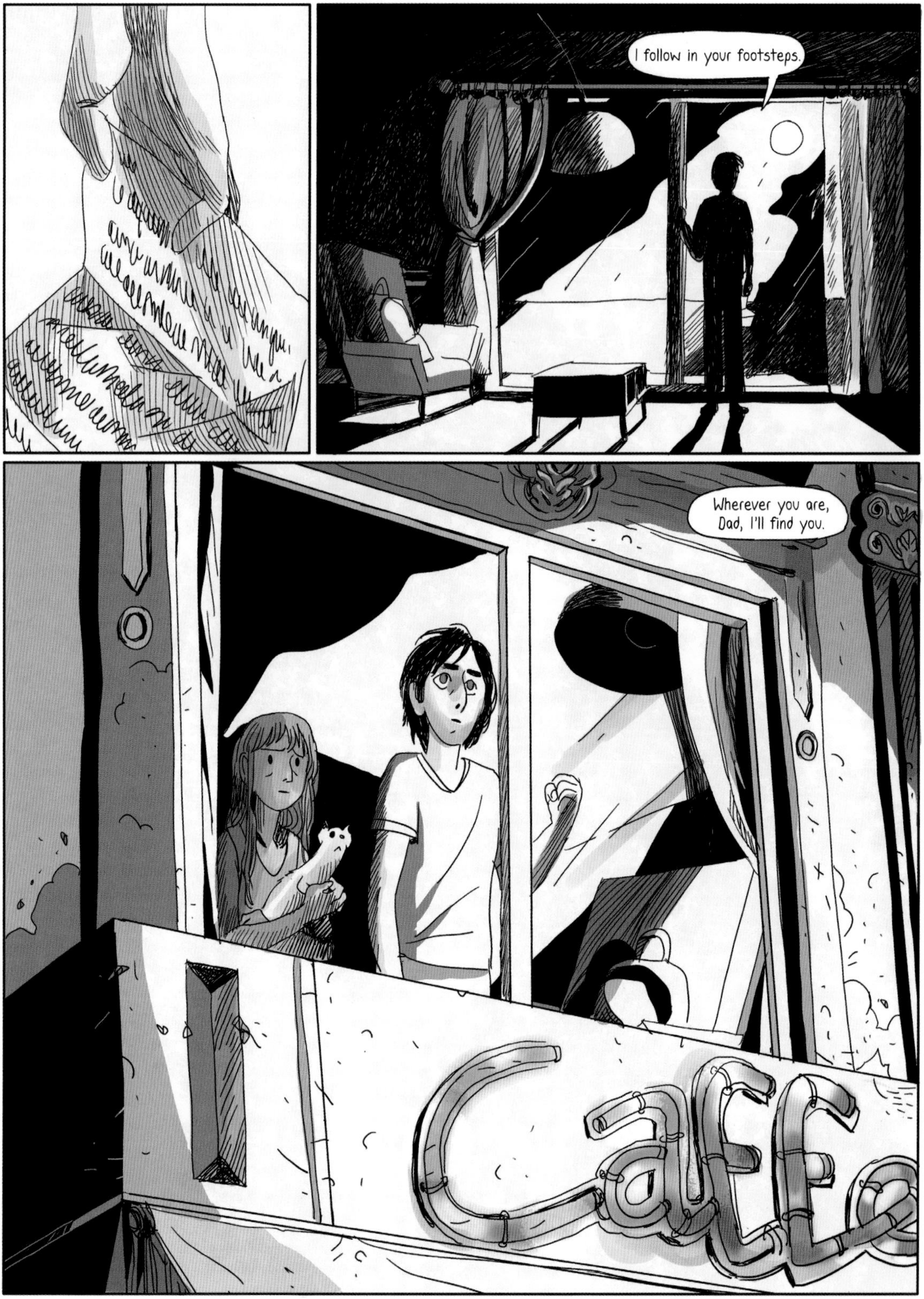
I follow in your footsteps.
Wherever you are, Dad, I'll find you.
Caffe

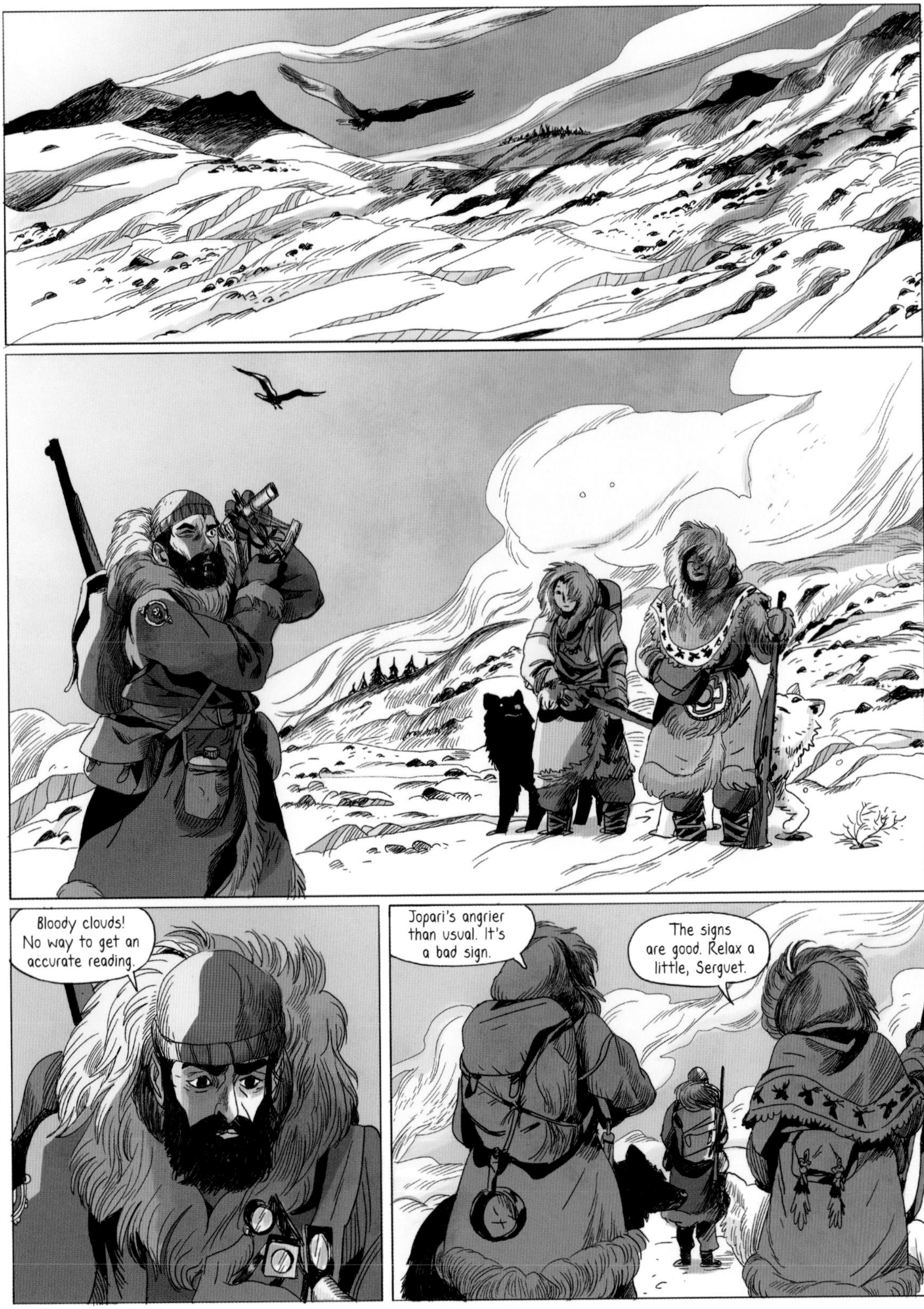
Bloody clouds! No way to get an accurate reading.
Jopari's angrier than usual. It's a bad sign.
The signs are good. Relax a little, Serguet.

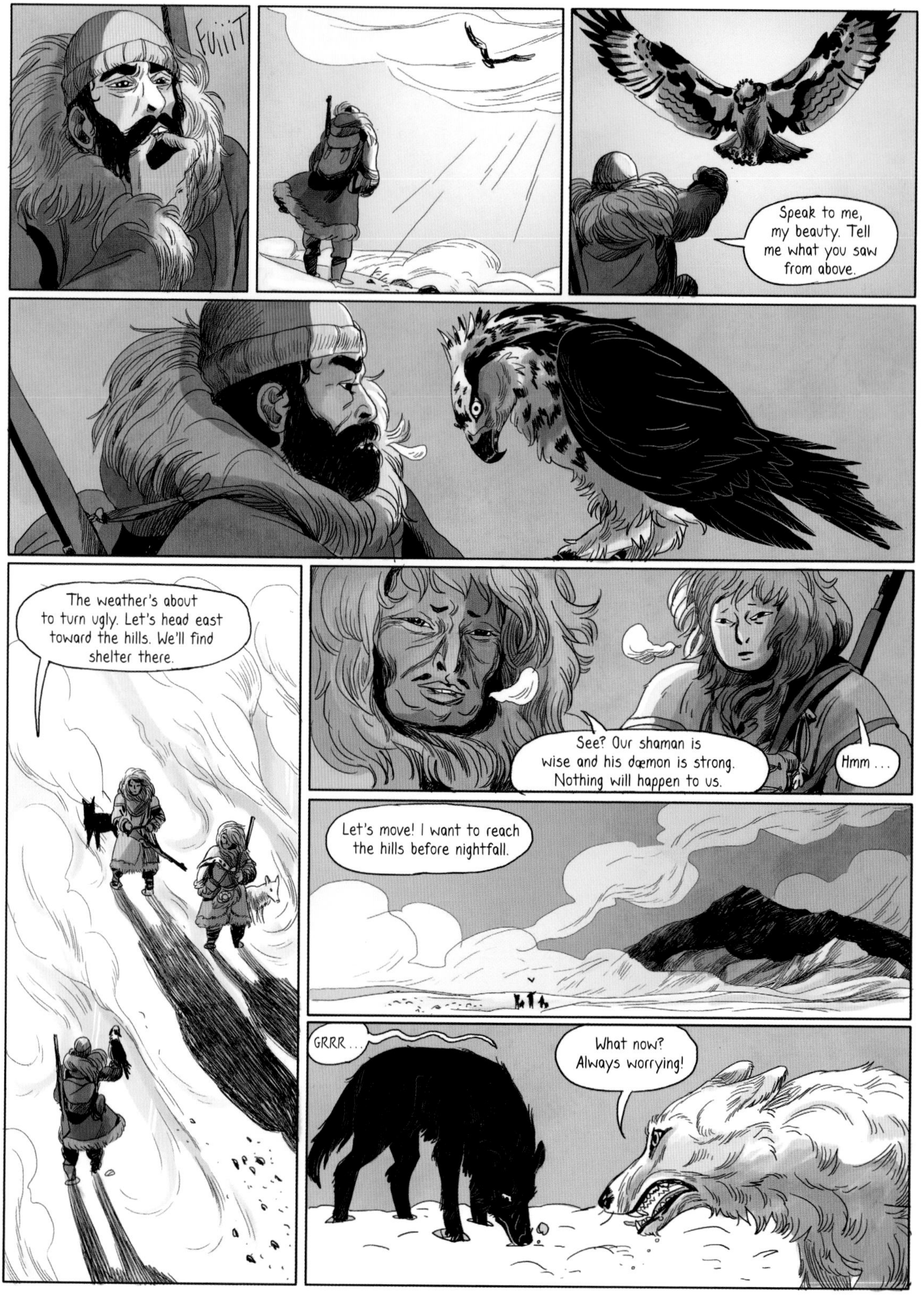
FUIIIT
Speak to me, my beauty. Tell me what you saw from above.
The weather's about to turn ugly. Let's head east toward the hills. We'll find shelter there.
See? Our shaman is wise and his dæmon is strong. Nothing will happen to us.
Hmm . . .
Let's move! I want to reach the hills before nightfall.
GRRR . . .
What now? Always worrying!

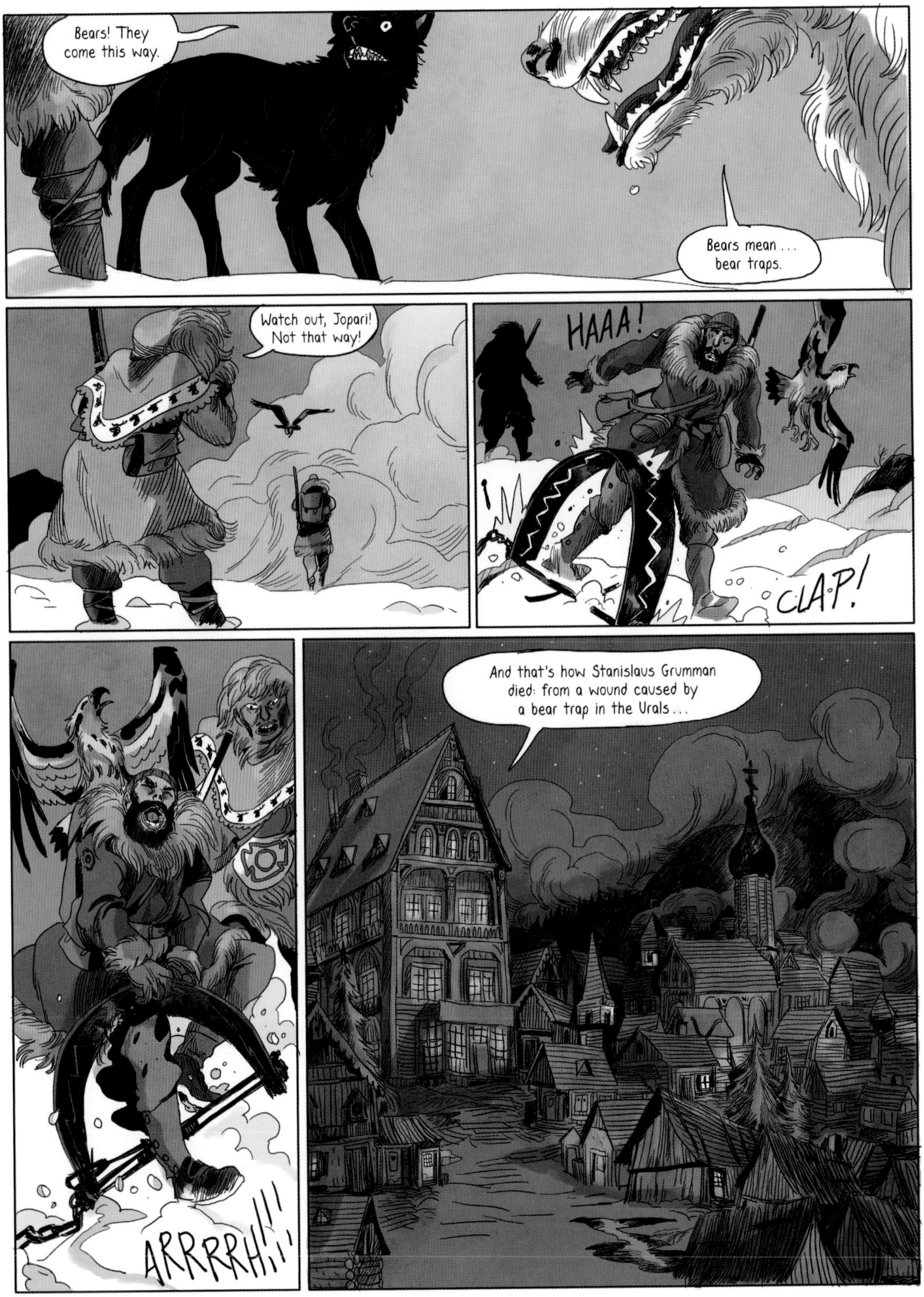
Bears! They come this way.
Bears mean . . . bear traps.
Watch out, Jopari! Not that way!
HAAA!
CLAP!
ARRRRH!!!
And that's how Stanislaus Grumman died: from a wound caused by a bear trap in the Urals . . .

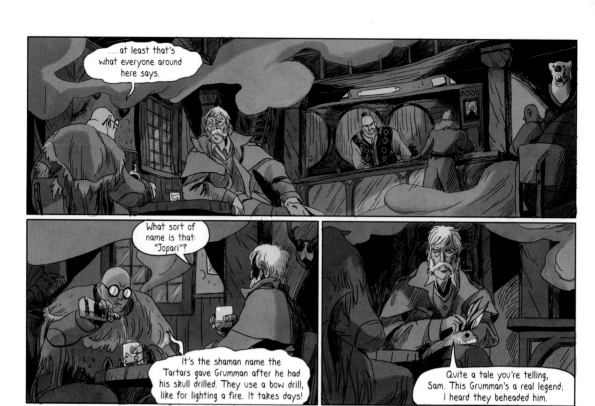

...at least that's what everyone around here says.

What sort of name is that: "Jopari"?

It's the shaman name the Tartars gave Grumman after he had his skull drilled. They use a bow drill, like for lighting a fire. It takes days!

Quite a tale you're telling, Sam. This Grumman's a real legend; I heard they beheaded him.

Strange man. There was a witch who wanted him for a lover, but he turned her down!

Another legend?

Not this time. I was there!

A witch offers you her love, you should take it.

If you don't, it's your own fault if bad things happen to you.

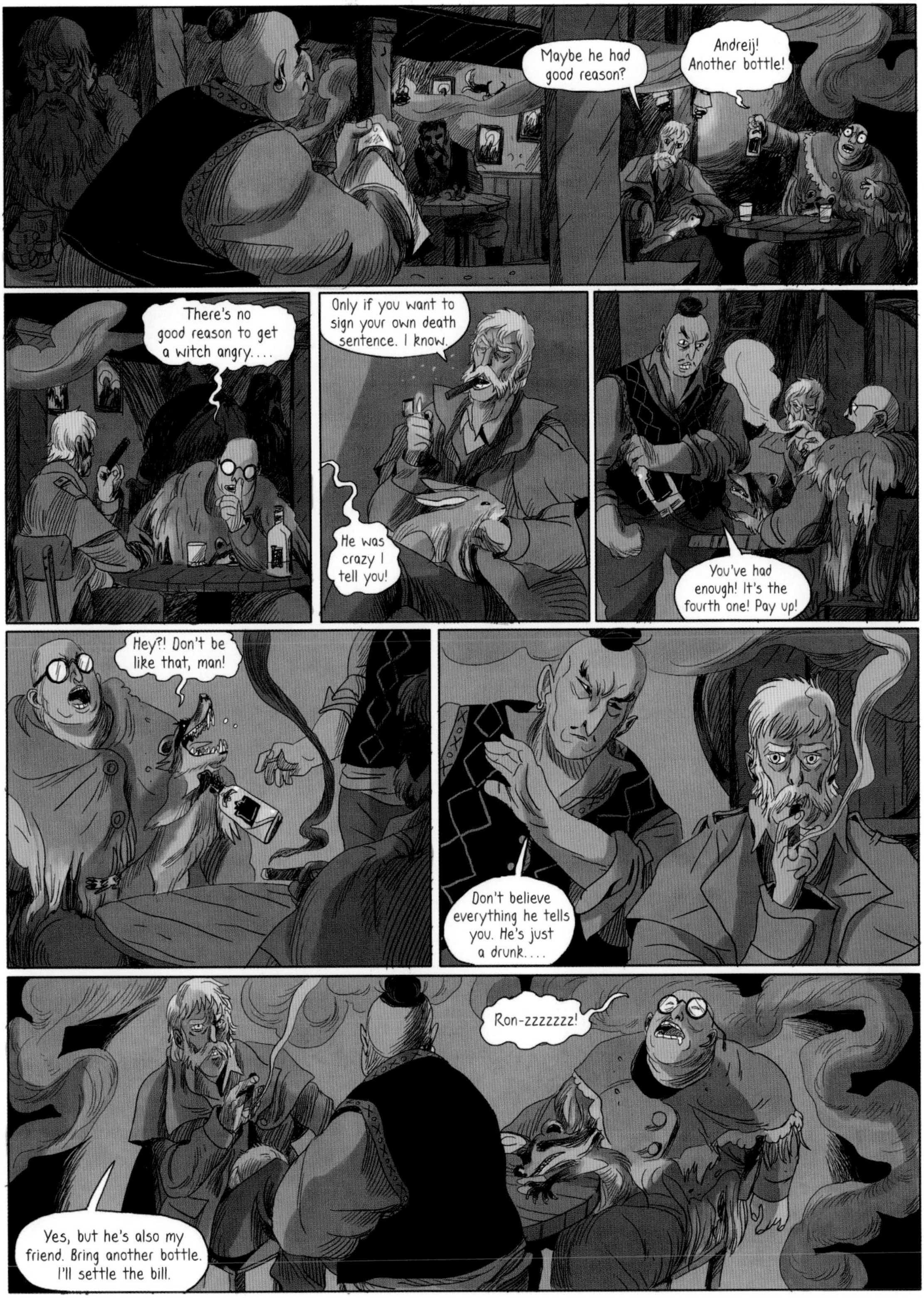
Maybe he had good reason?
Andreij! Another bottle!
There's no good reason to get a witch angry....
Only if you want to sign your own death sentence. I know.
He was crazy I tell you!
You've had enough! It's the fourth one! Pay up!
Hey?! Don't be like that, man!
Don't believe everything he tells you. He's just a drunk....
Ron-zzzzzzz!
Yes, but he's also my friend. Bring another bottle. I'll settle the bill.

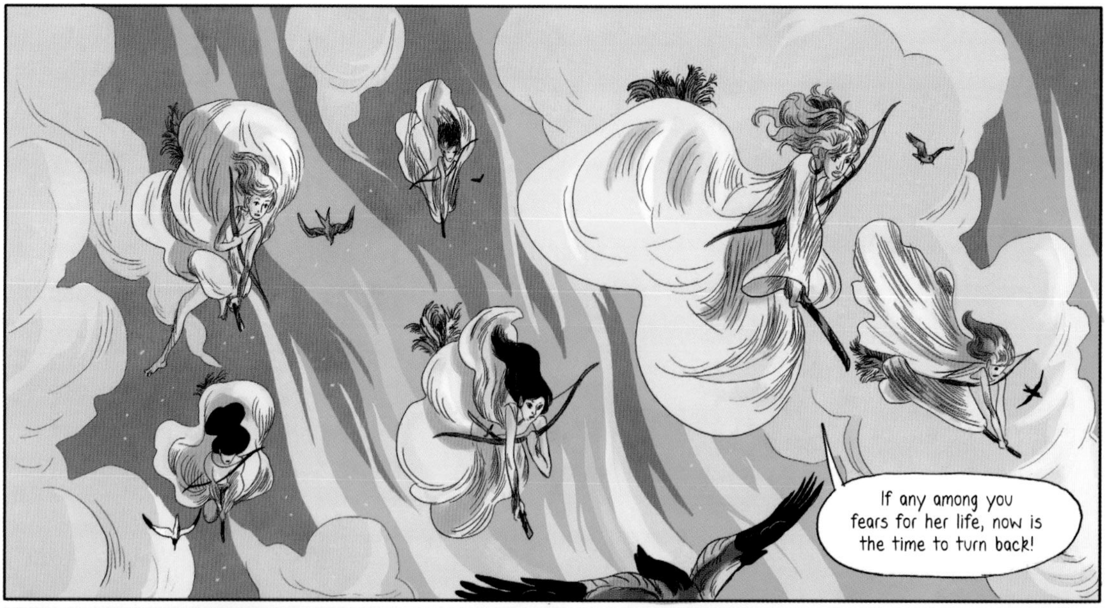
If any among you fears for her life, now is the time to turn back!
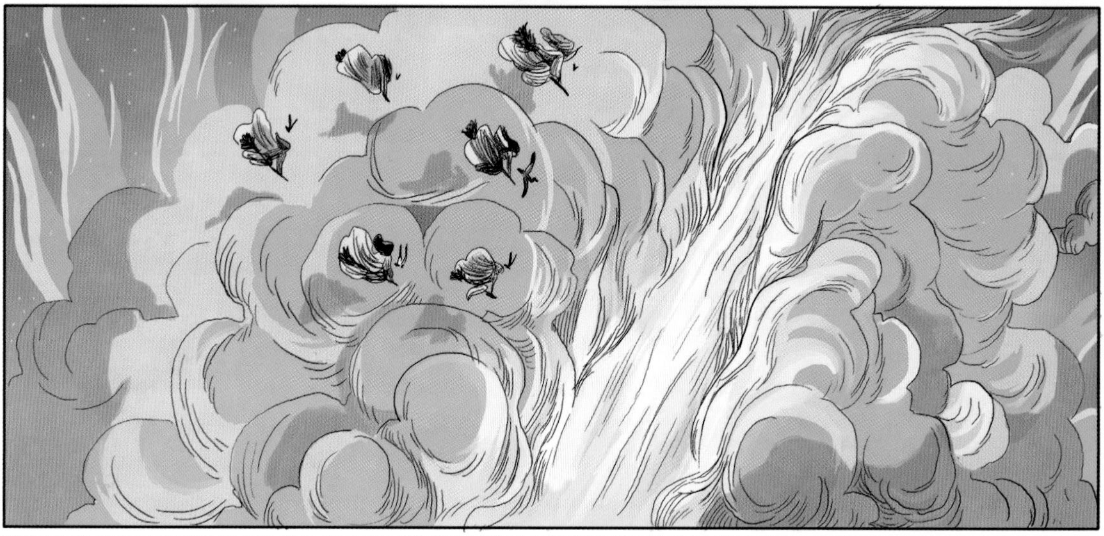
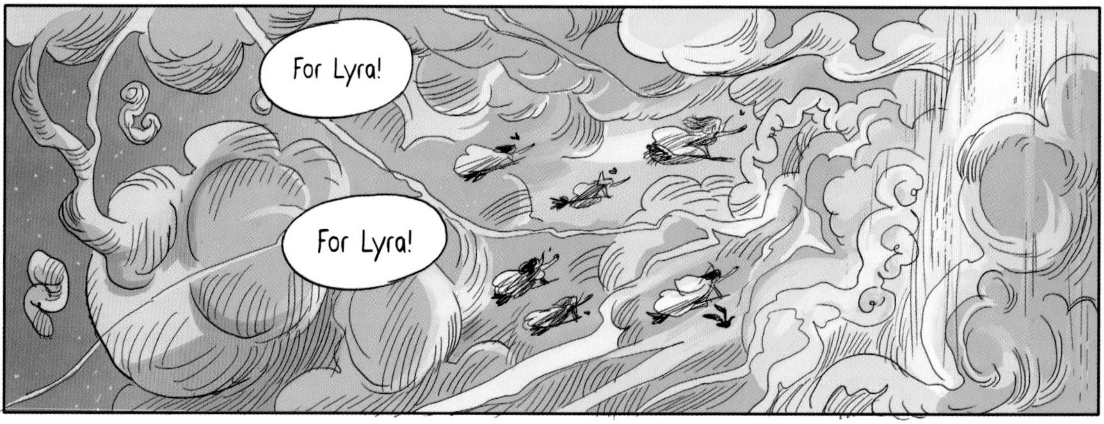
For Lyra!
For Lyra!

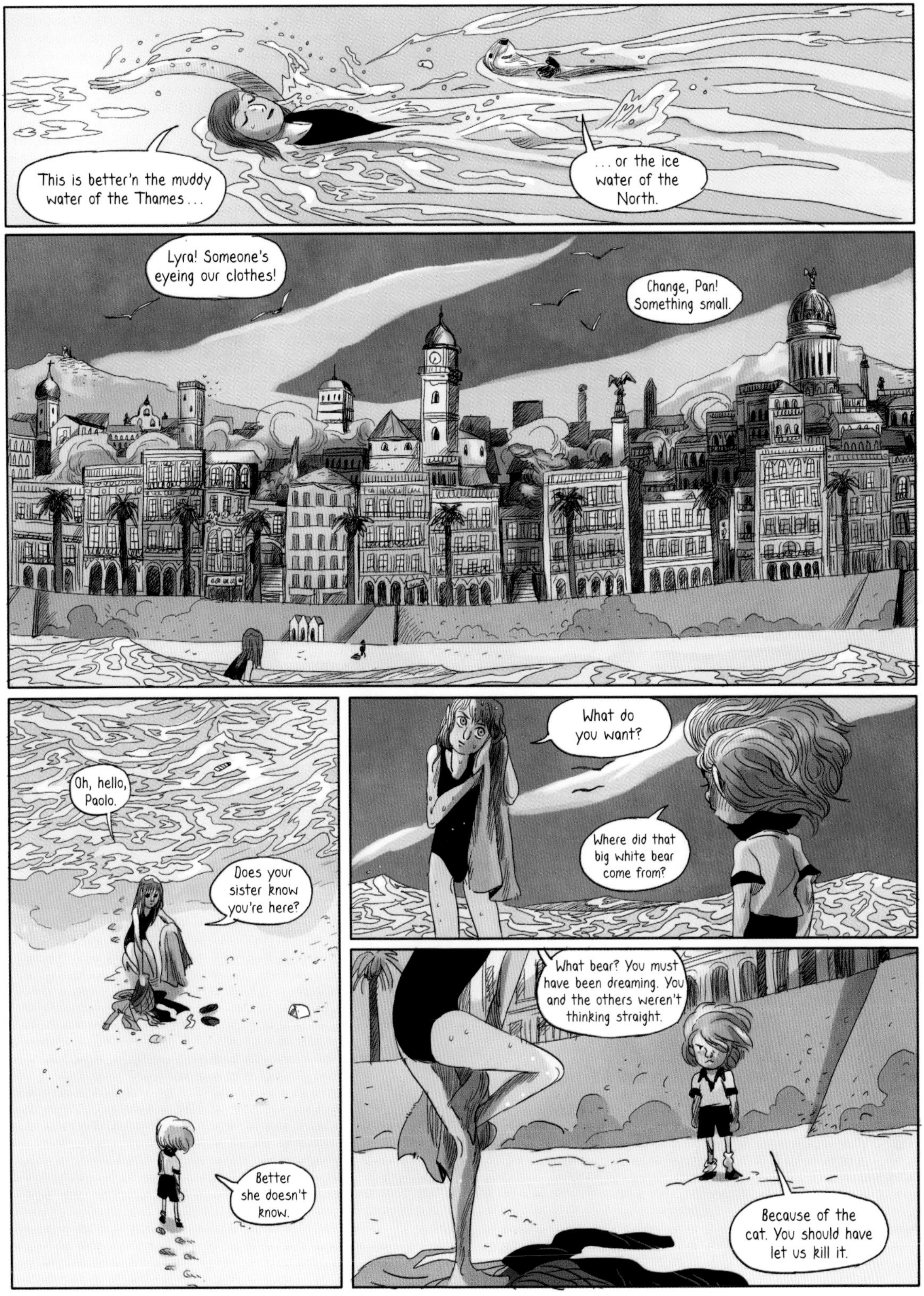
This is better'n the muddy water of the Thames . . .
. . . or the ice water of the North.
Lyra! Someone's eyeing our clothes!
Change, Pan! Something small.
Oh, hello, Paolo.
Does your sister know you're here?
Better she doesn't know.
What do you want?
Where did that big white bear come from?
What bear? You must have been dreaming. You and the others weren't thinking straight.
Because of the cat. You should have let us kill it.

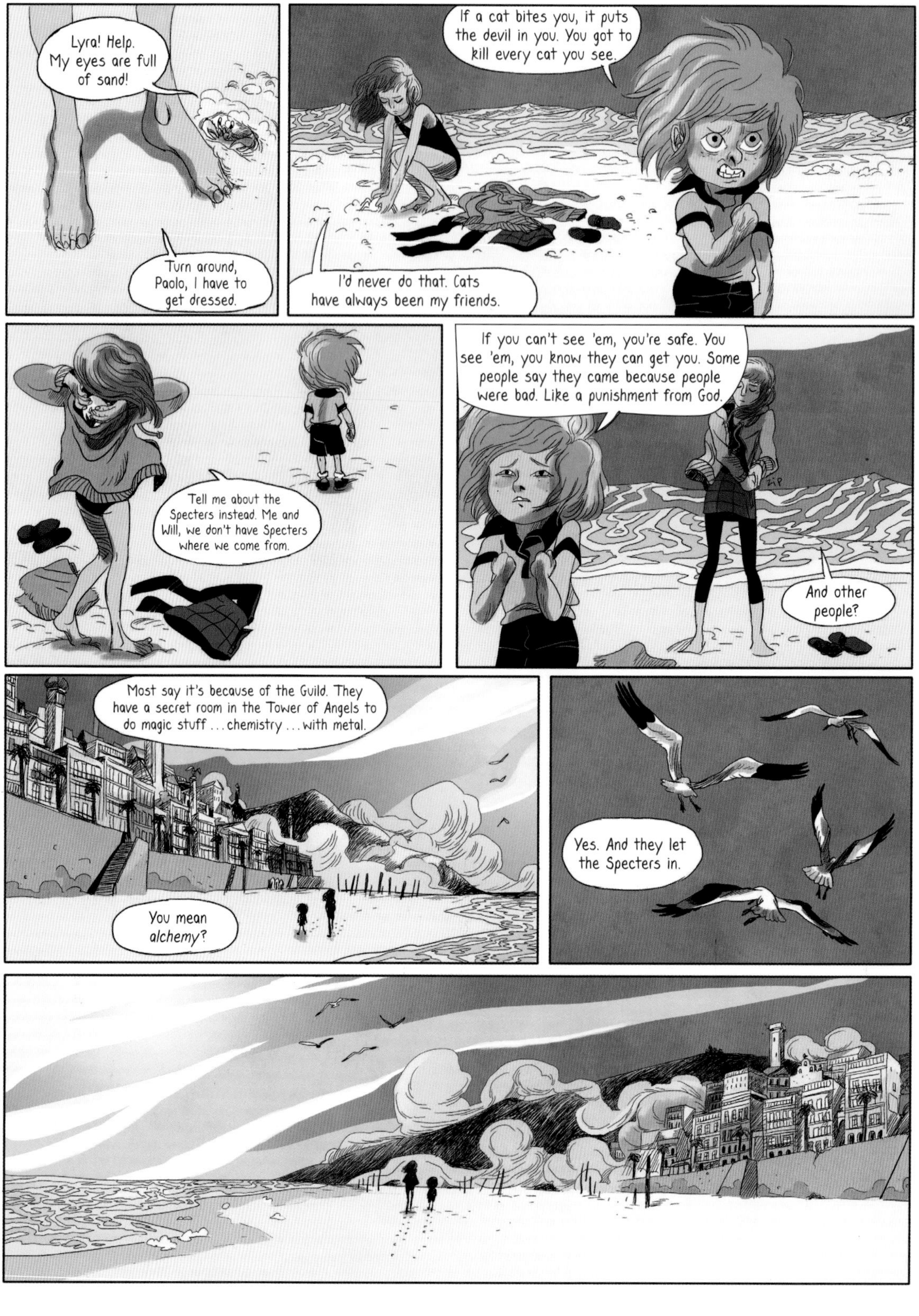
Lyra! Help. My eyes are full of sand!
Turn around, Paolo, I have to get dressed.
If a cat bites you, it puts the devil in you. You got to kill every cat you see.
I'd never do that. Cats have always been my friends.
Tell me about the Specters instead. Me and Will, we don't have Specters where we come from.
If you can't see 'em, you're safe. You see 'em, you know they can get you. Some people say they came because people were bad. Like a punishment from God.
ZIP
And other people?
Most say it's because of the Guild. They have a secret room in the Tower of Angels to do magic stuff . . . chemistry . . . with metal.
You mean alchemy?
Yes. And they let the Specters in.

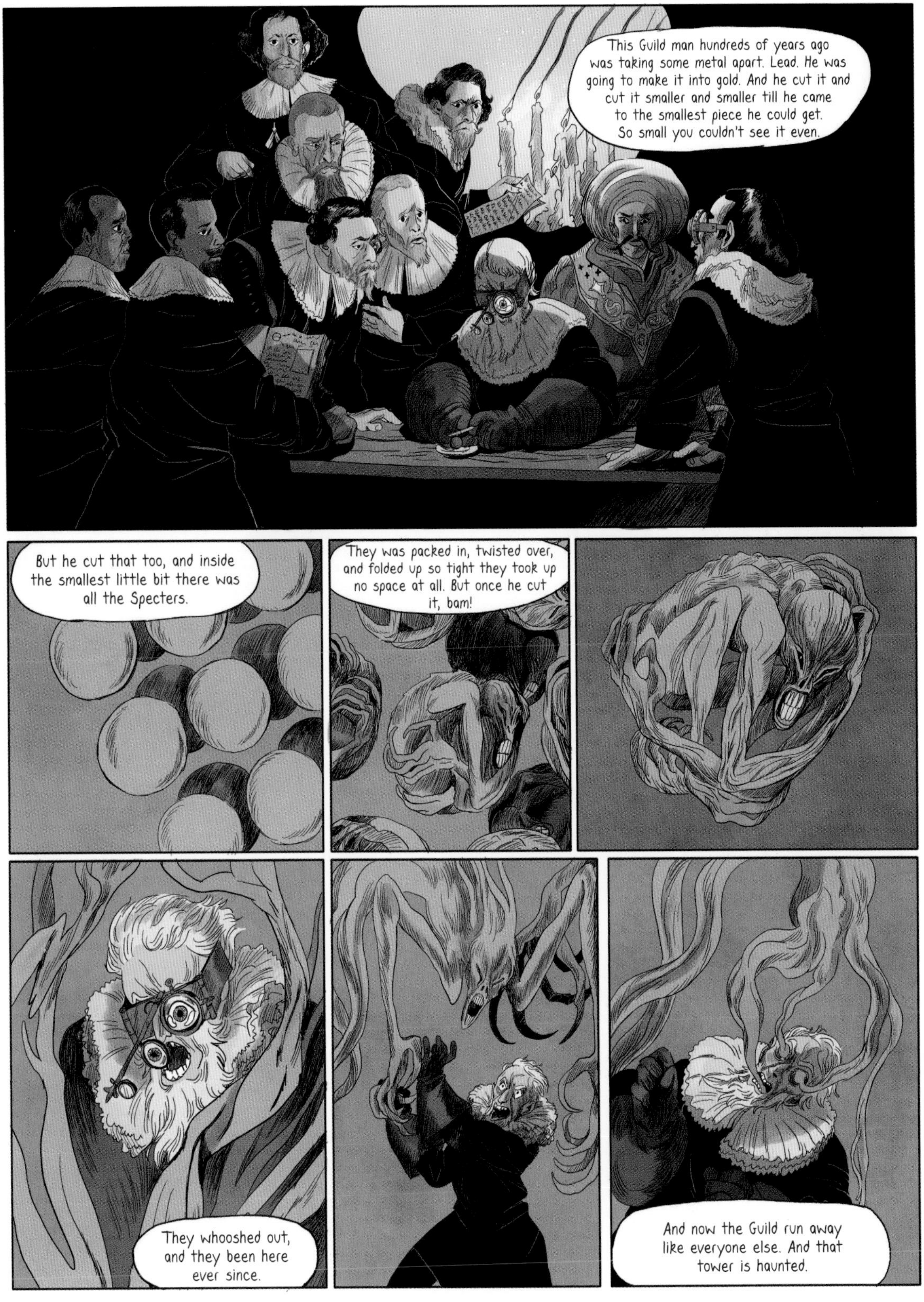
This Guild man hundreds of years ago was taking some metal apart. Lead. He was going to make it into gold. And he cut it and cut it smaller and smaller till he came to the smallest piece he could get. So small you couldn't see it even.
But he cut that too, and inside the smallest little bit there was all the Specters.
They was packed in, twisted over, and folded up so tight they took up no space at all. But once he cut it, bam!
They whooshed out, and they been here ever since.
And now the Guild run away like everyone else. And that tower is haunted.

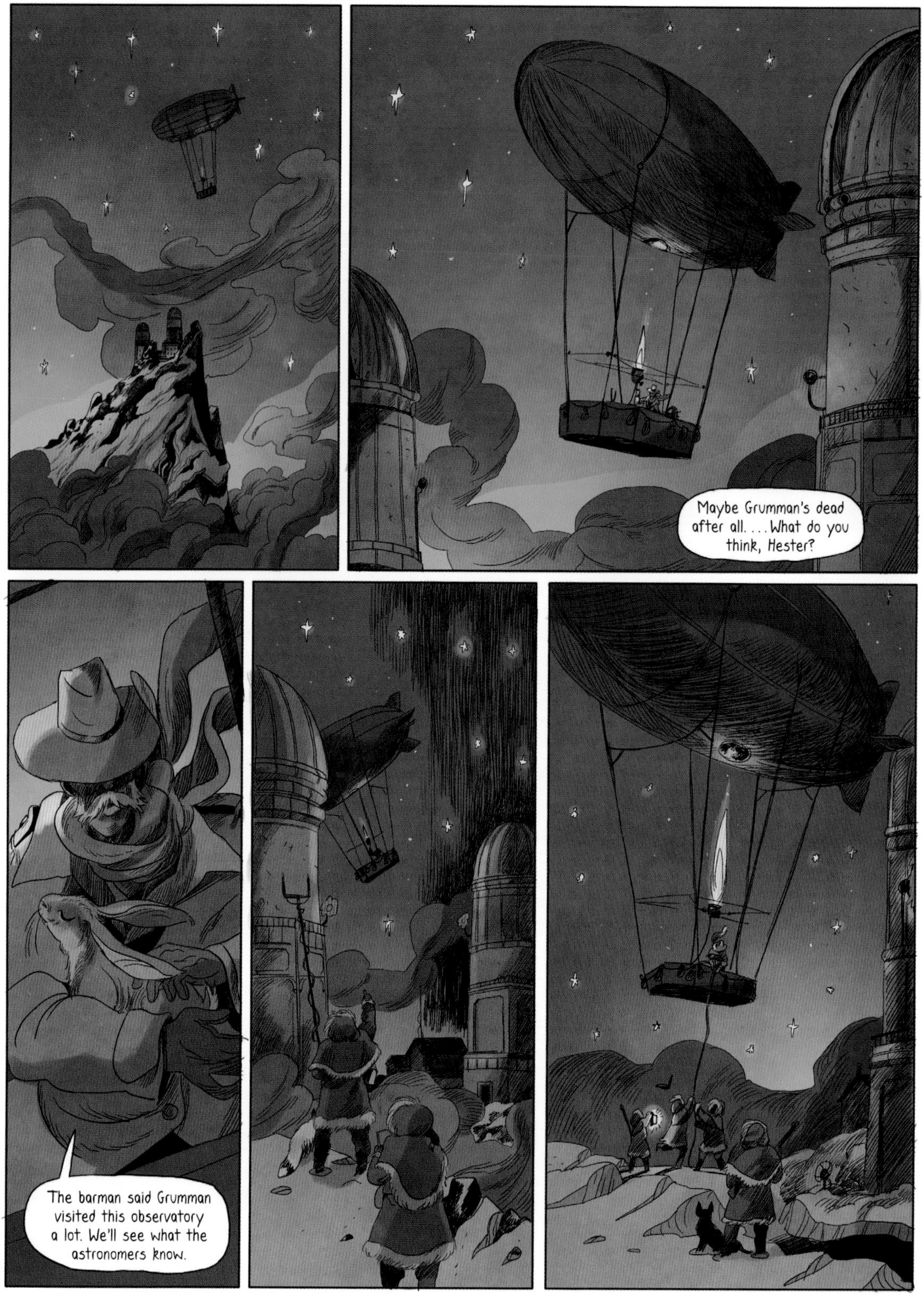

Maybe Grumman's dead after all. . . . What do you think, Hester?
The barman said Grumman visited this observatory a lot. We'll see what the astronomers know.

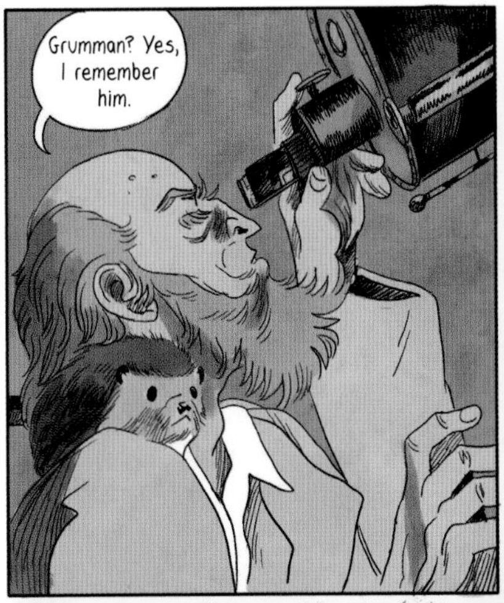
Grumman? Yes, I remember him.

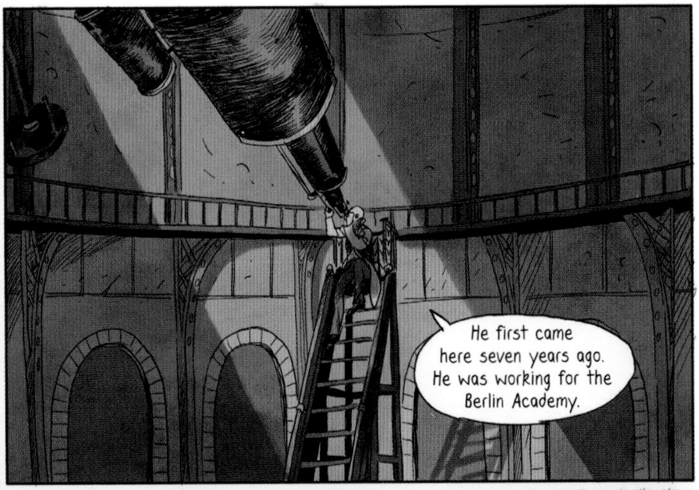
He first came here seven years ago. He was working for the Berlin Academy.

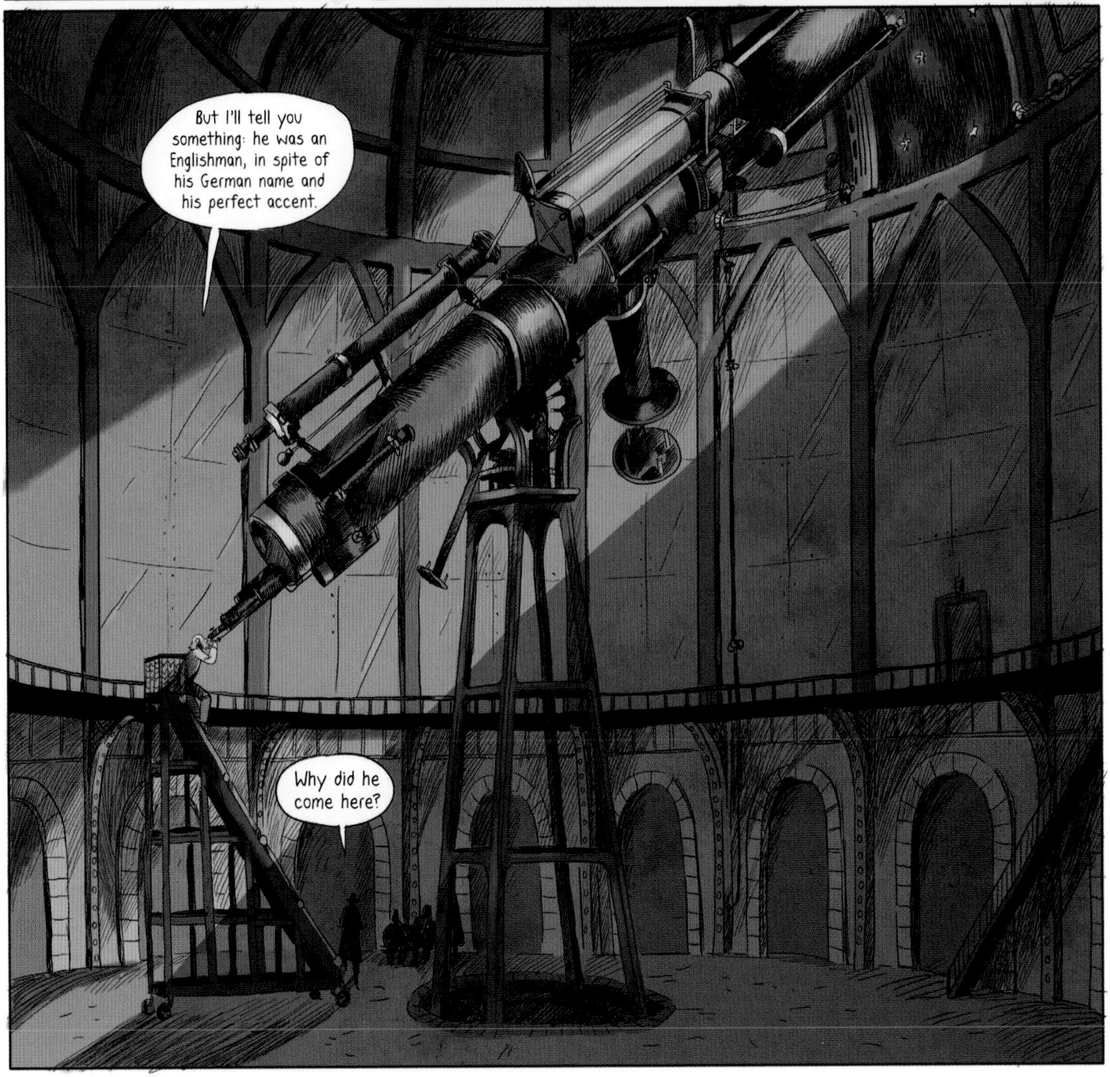
But I'll tell you something: he was an Englishman, in spite of his German name and his perfect accent.
Why did he come here?

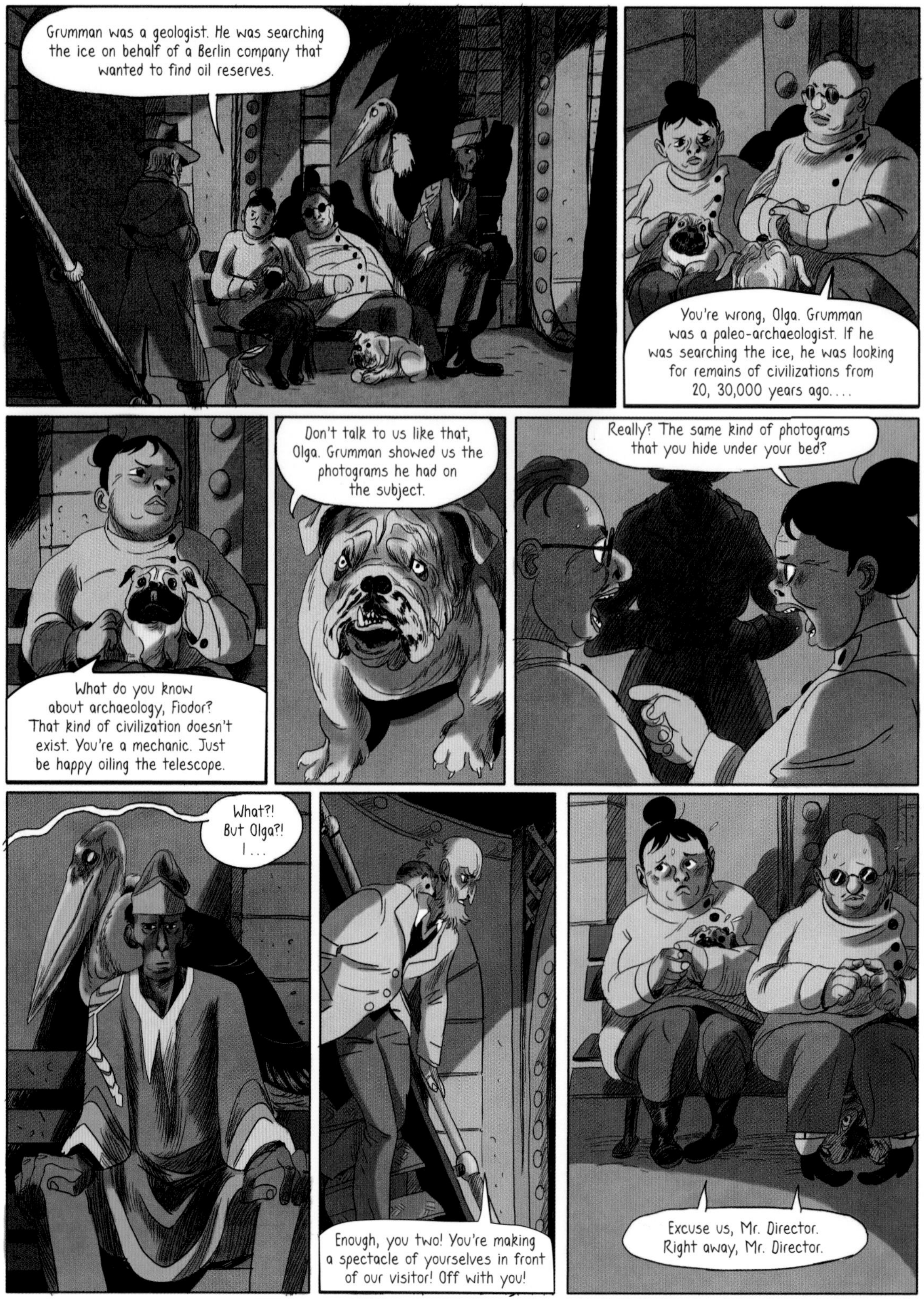
Grumman was a geologist. He was searching the ice on behalf of a Berlin company that wanted to find oil reserves.
You're wrong, Olga. Grumman was a paleo-archaeologist. If he was searching the ice, he was looking for remains of civilizations from 20, 30,000 years ago. . . .
What do you know about archaeology, Fiodor? That kind of civilization doesn't exist. You're a mechanic. Just be happy oiling the telescope.
Don't talk to us like that, Olga. Grumman showed us the photograms he had on the subject.
Really? The same kind of photograms that you hide under your bed?
What?! But Olga?! I . . .
Enough, you two! You're making a spectacle of yourselves in front of our visitor! Off with you!
Excuse us, Mr. Director.
Right away, Mr. Director.

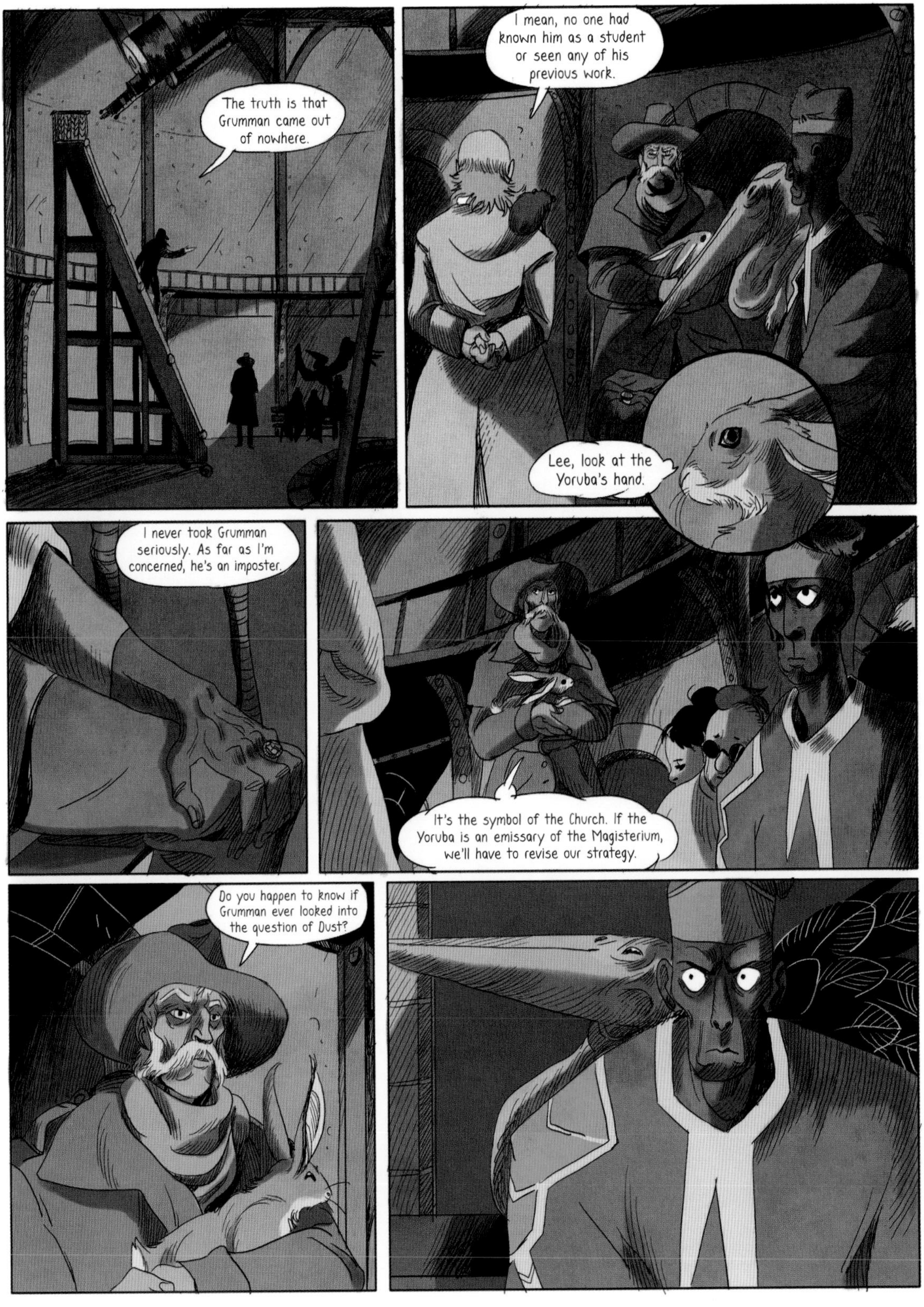
The truth is that Grumman came out of nowhere.
I mean, no one had known him as a student or seen any of his previous work.
Lee, look at the Yoruba's hand.
I never took Grumman seriously. As far as I'm concerned, he's an imposter.
It's the symbol of the Church. If the Yoruba is an emissary of the Magisterium, we'll have to revise our strategy.
Do you happen to know if Grumman ever looked into the question of Dust?

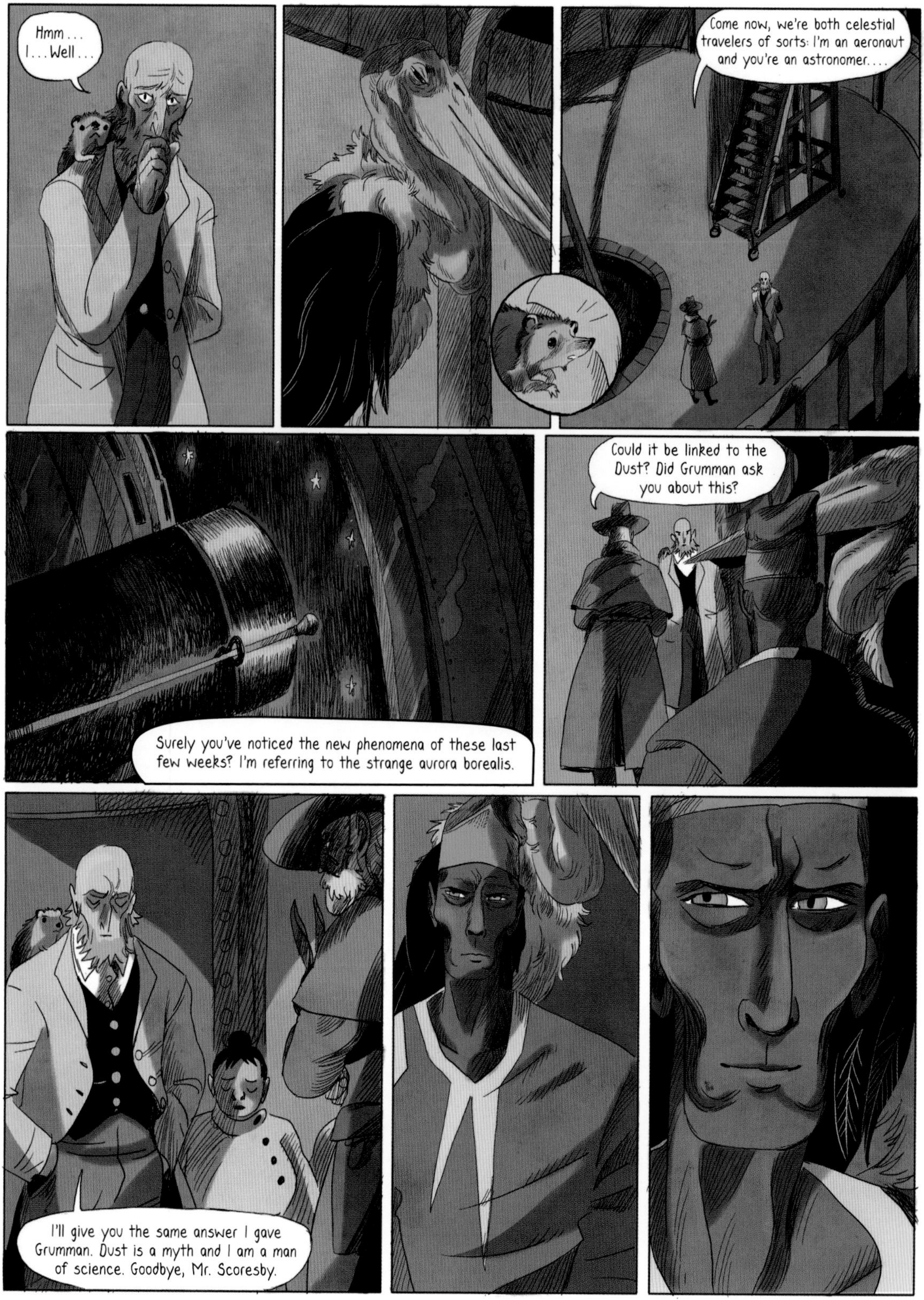
Hmm . . .
I . . . Well . . .
Come now, we're both celestial travelers of sorts: I'm an aeronaut and you're an astronomer. . . .
Surely you've noticed the new phenomena of these last few weeks? I'm referring to the strange aurora borealis.
Could it be linked to the Dust? Did Grumman ask you about this?
I'll give you the same answer I gave Grumman. Dust is a myth and I am a man of science. Goodbye, Mr. Scoresby.

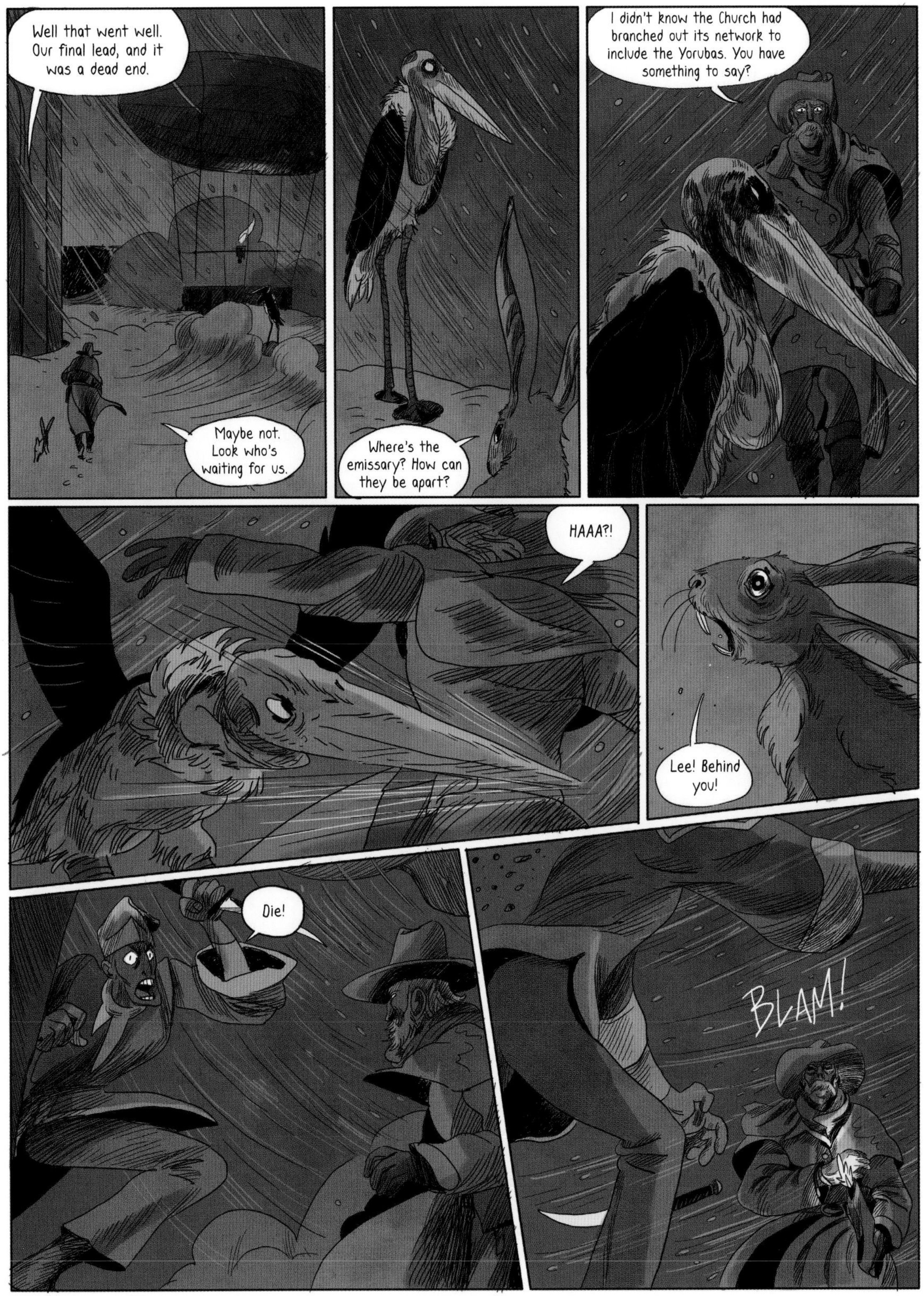
Well that went well. Our final lead, and it was a dead end.
Maybe not. Look who's waiting for us.
Where's the emissary? How can they be apart?
I didn't know the Church had branched out its network to include the Yorubas. You have something to say?
HAAA?!
Lee! Behind you!
Die!
BLAM!

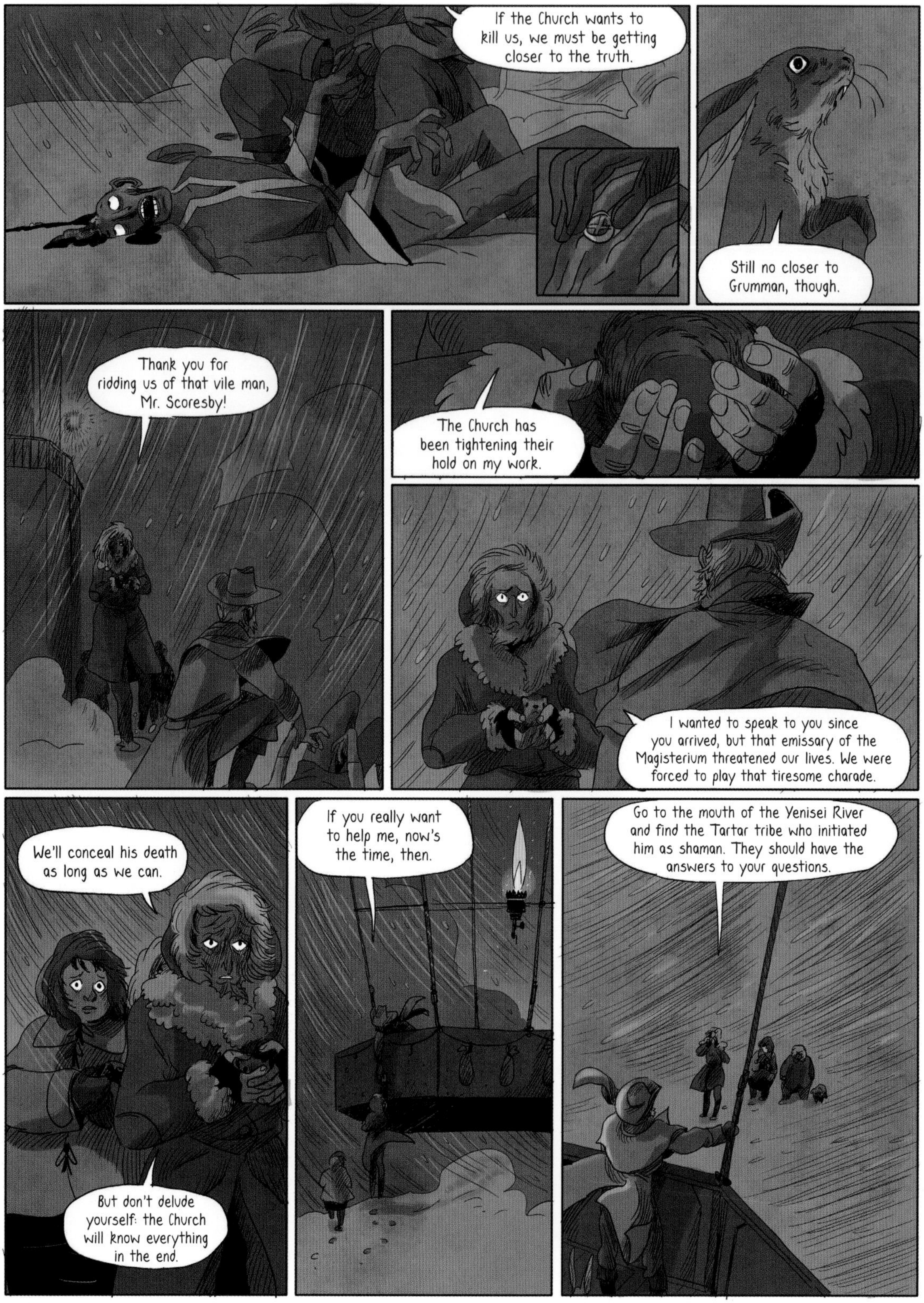
If the Church wants to kill us, we must be getting closer to the truth.
Still no closer to Grumman, though.
Thank you for ridding us of that vile man, Mr. Scoresby!
The Church has been tightening their hold on my work.
I wanted to speak to you since you arrived, but that emissary of the Magisterium threatened our lives. We were forced to play that tiresome charade.
We'll conceal his death as long as we can.
But don't delude yourself: the Church will know everything in the end.
If you really want to help me, now's the time, then.
Go to the mouth of the Yenisei River and find the Tartar tribe who initiated him as shaman. They should have the answers to your questions.

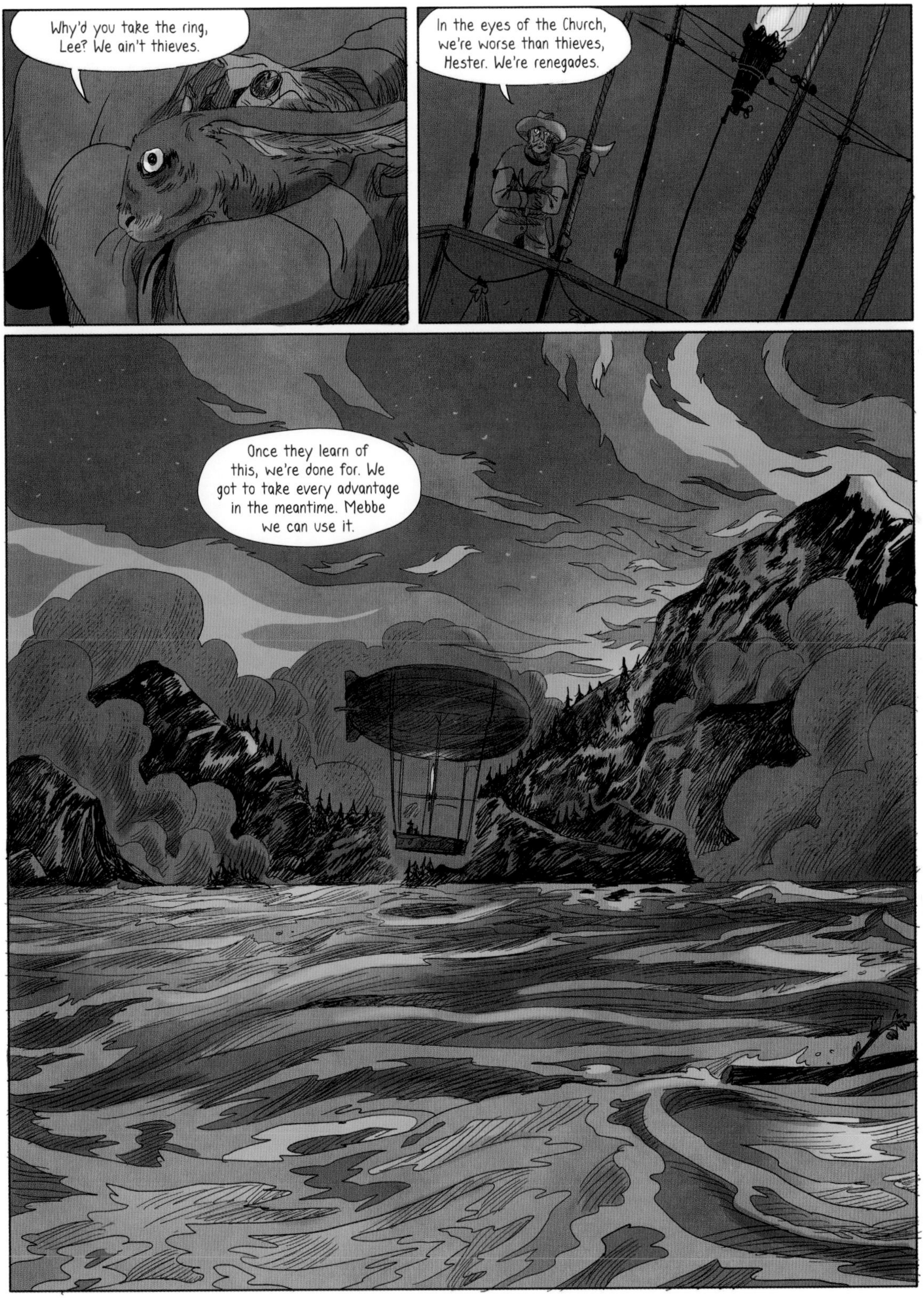
Why'd you take the ring, Lee? We ain't thieves.
In the eyes of the Church, we're worse than thieves, Hester. We're renegades.
Once they learn of this, we're done for. We got to take every advantage in the meantime. Mebbe we can use it.

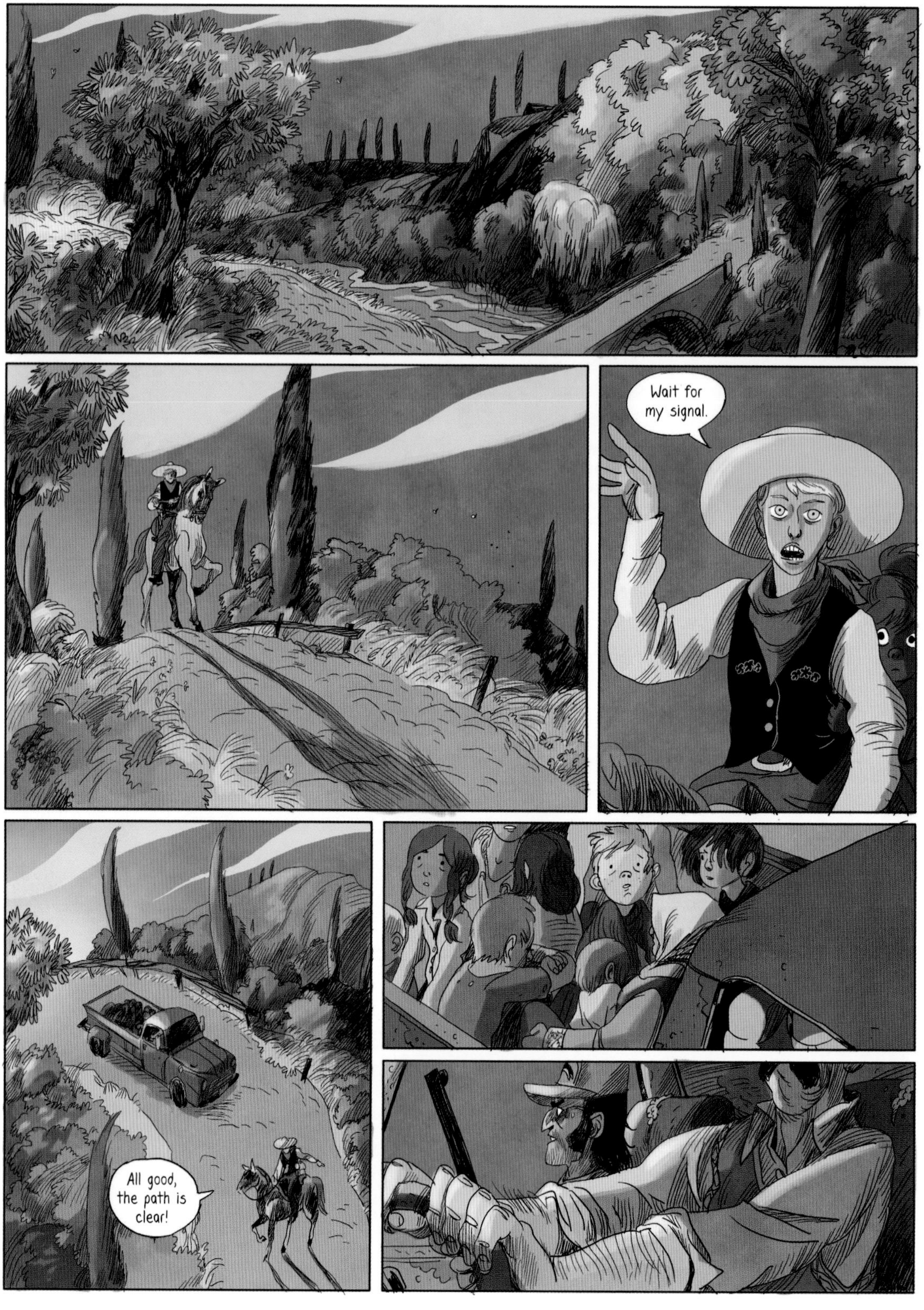
Wait for my signal.
All good, the path is clear!

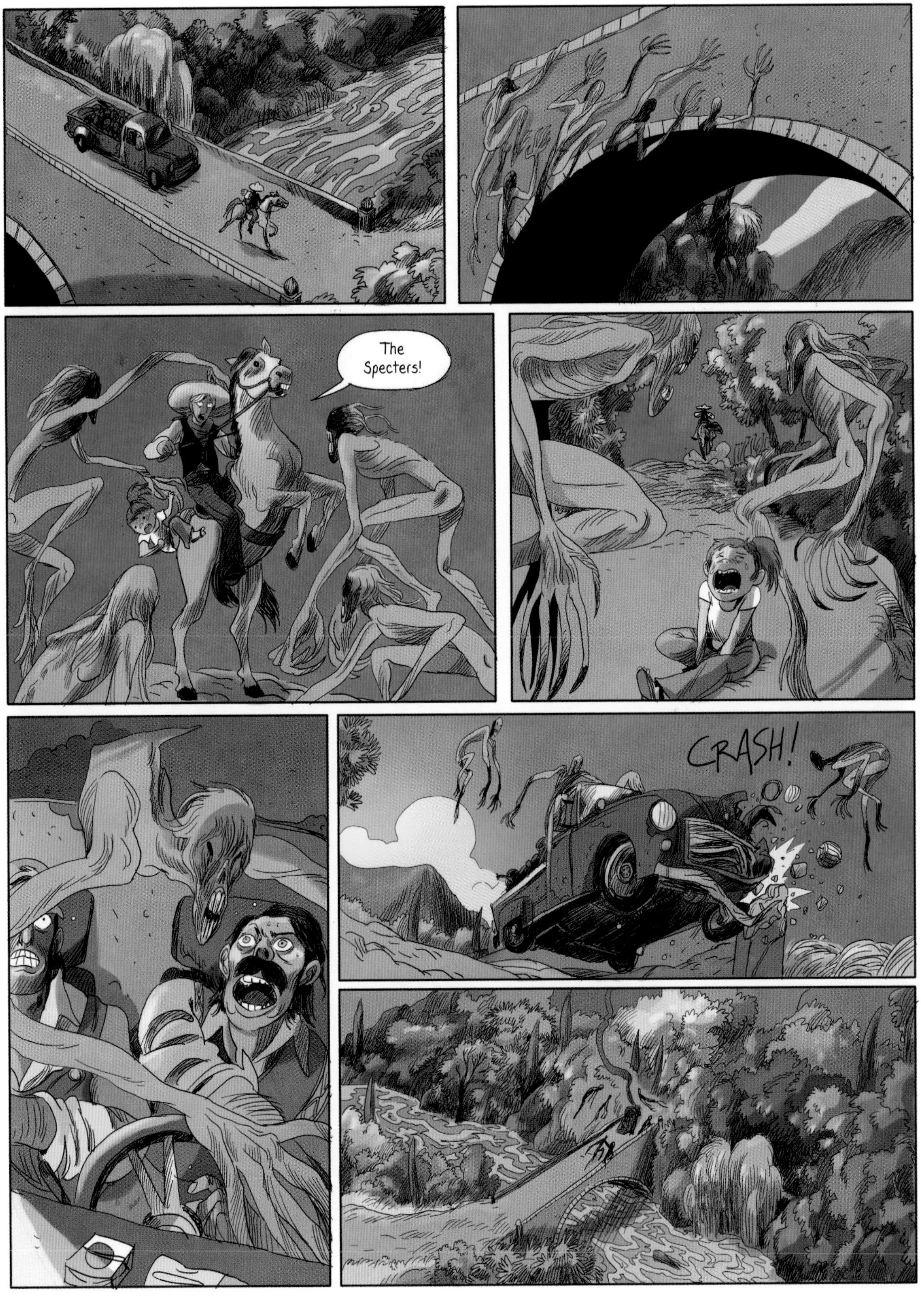
The Specters!
CRASH!

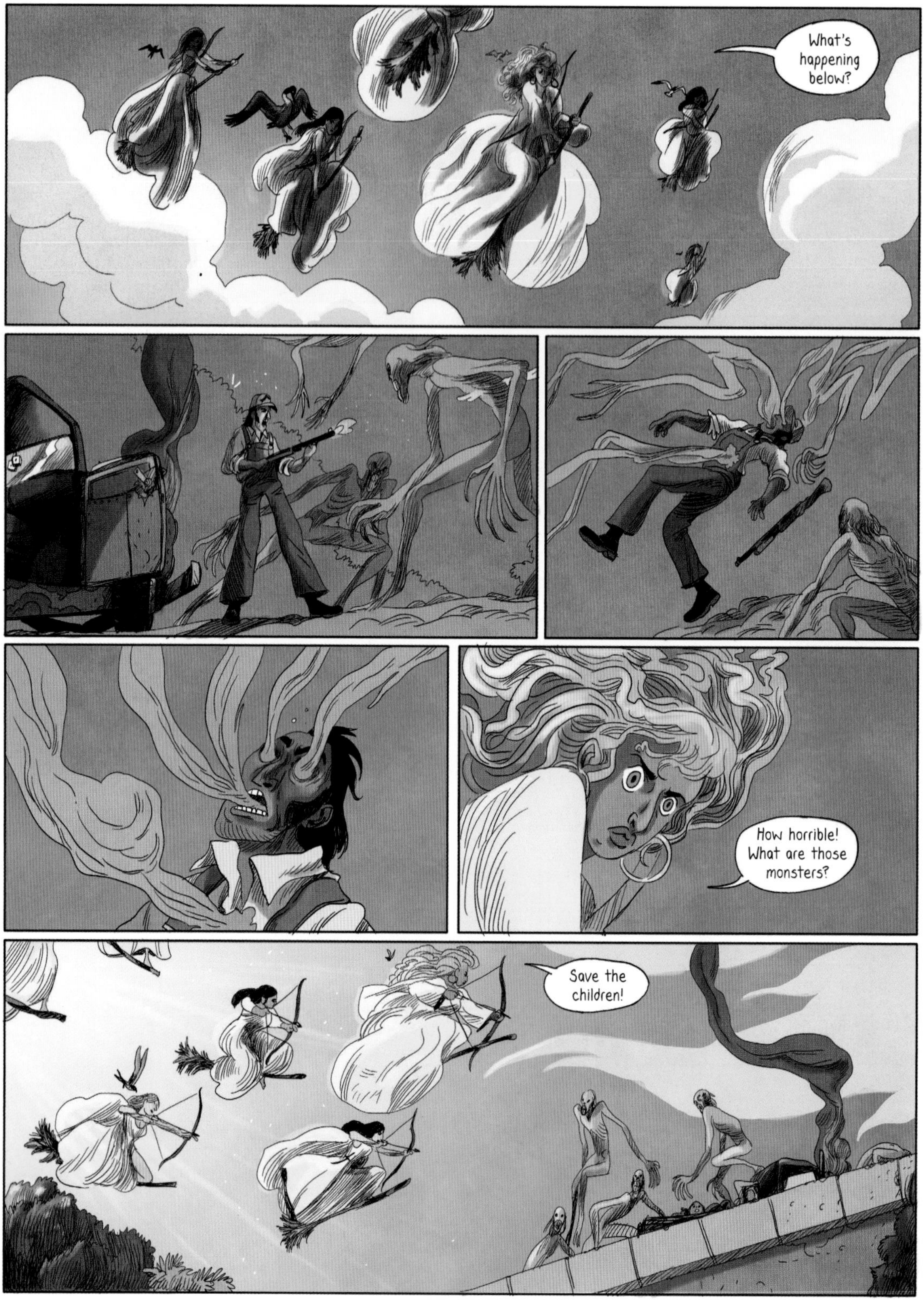
What's happening below?
How horrible! What are those monsters?
Save the children!

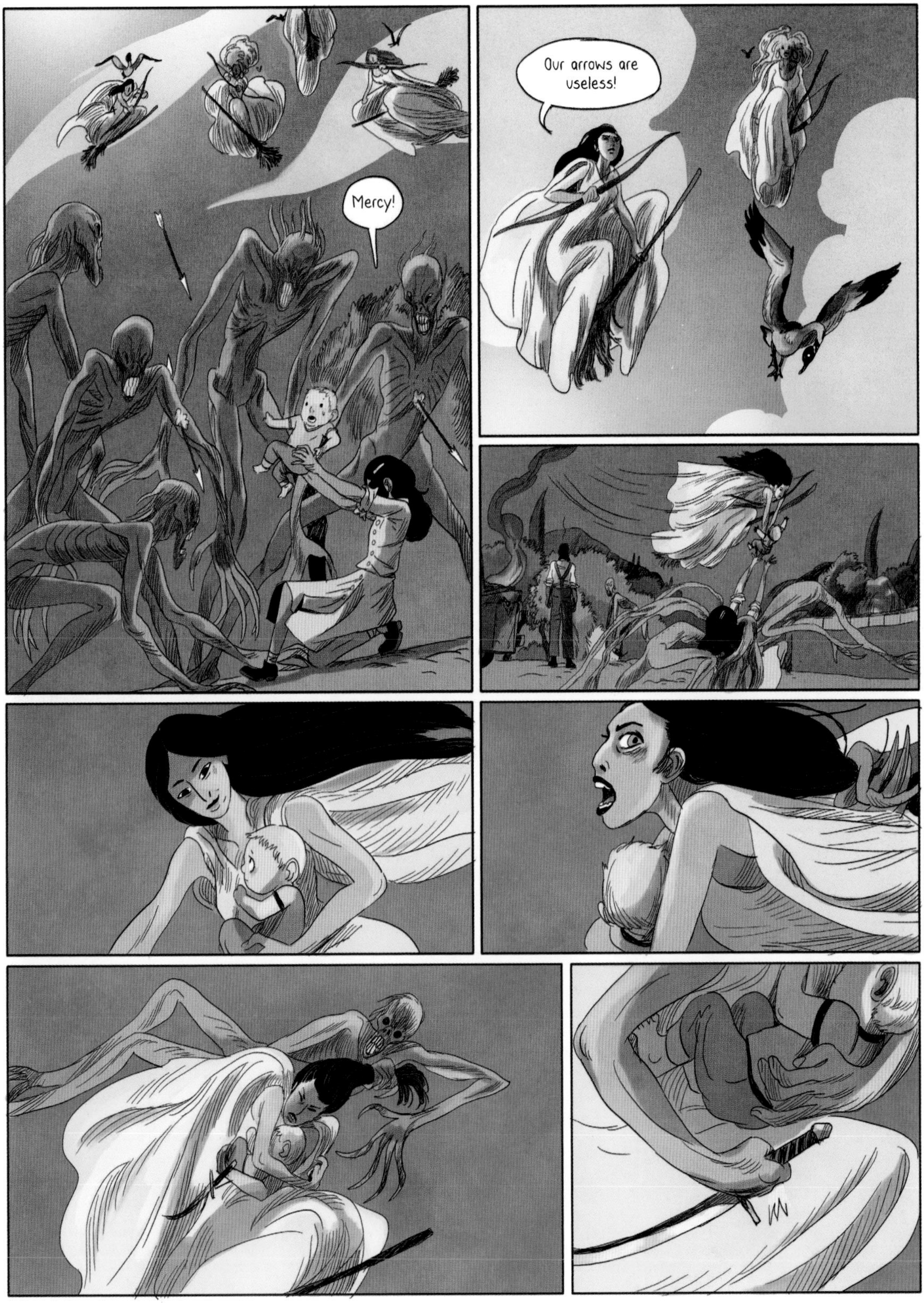
Mercy!
Our arrows are useless!

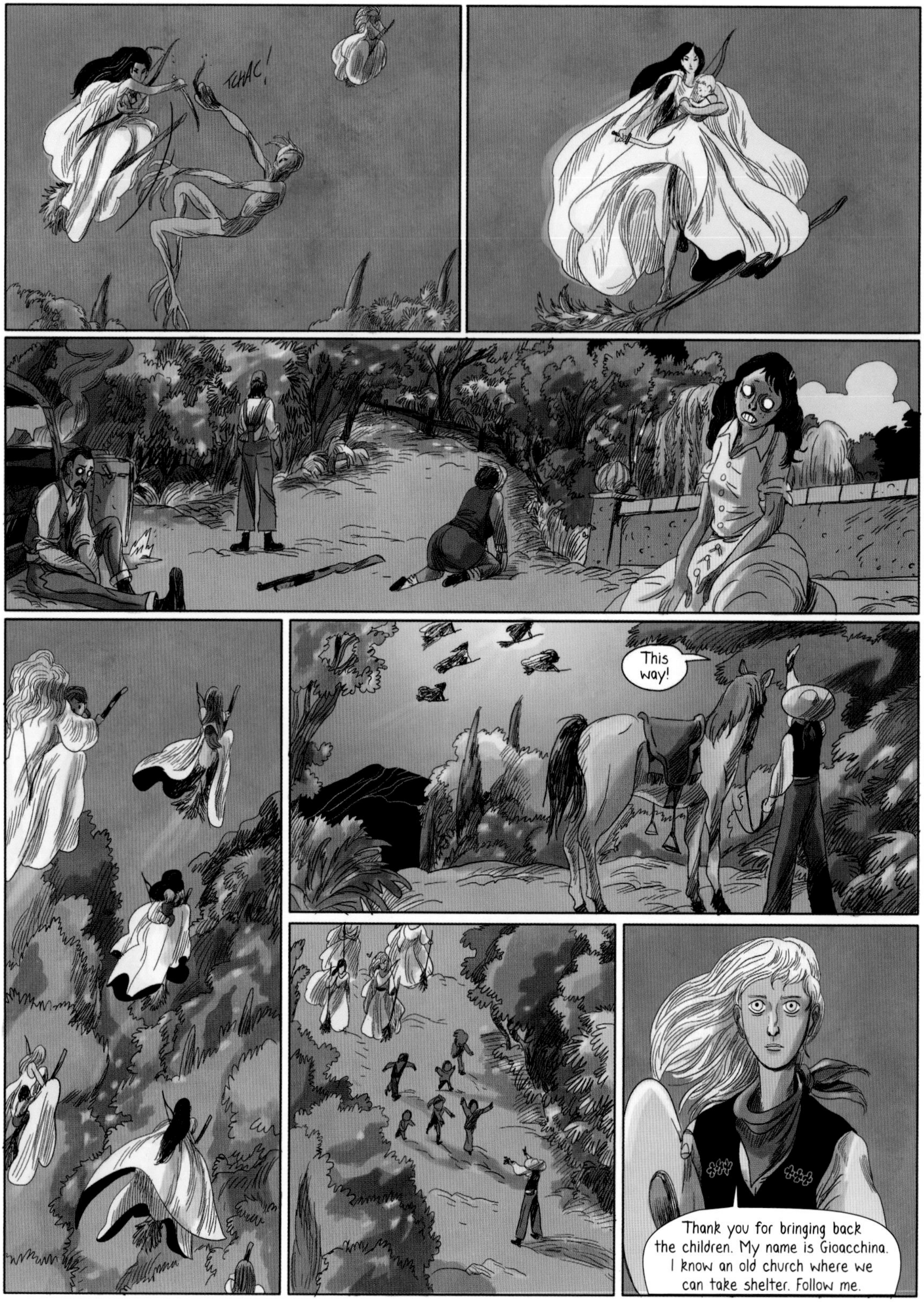
TCHAC!
This way!
Thank you for bringing back the children. My name is Gioacchina. I know an old church where we can take shelter. Follow me.

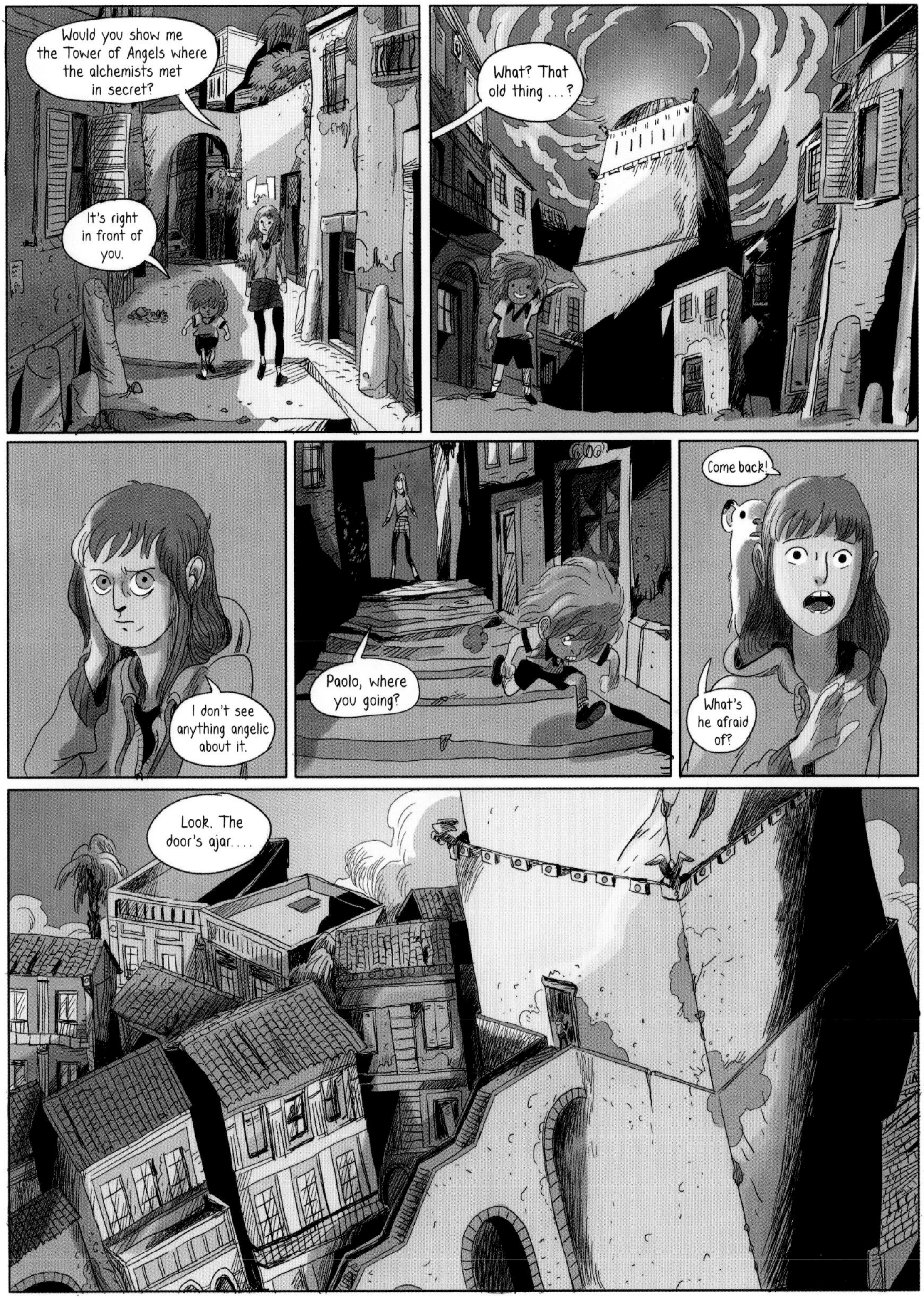
Would you show me the Tower of Angels where the alchemists met in secret?
It's right in front of you.
What? That old thing . . . ?
I don't see anything angelic about it.
Paolo, where you going?
Come back!
What's he afraid of?
Look. The door's ajar. . . .

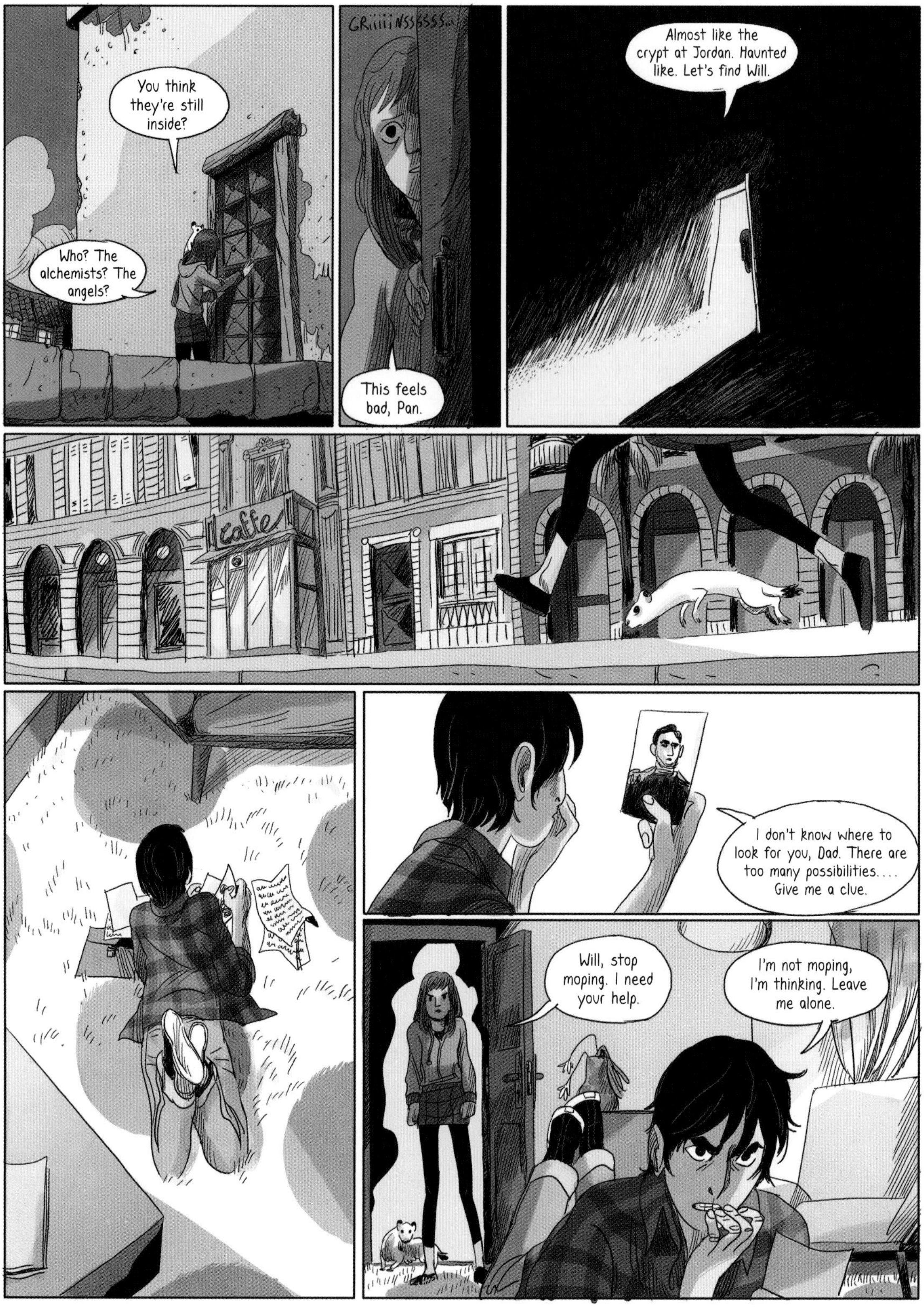
You think they're still inside?
Who? The alchemists? The angels?
GRiiiiiNSSSSSS...
This feels bad, Pan.
Almost like the crypt at Jordan. Haunted like. Let's find Will.
Caffe
I don't know where to look for you, Dad. There are too many possibilities.... Give me a clue.
Will, stop moping. I need your help.
I'm not moping, I'm thinking. Leave me alone.

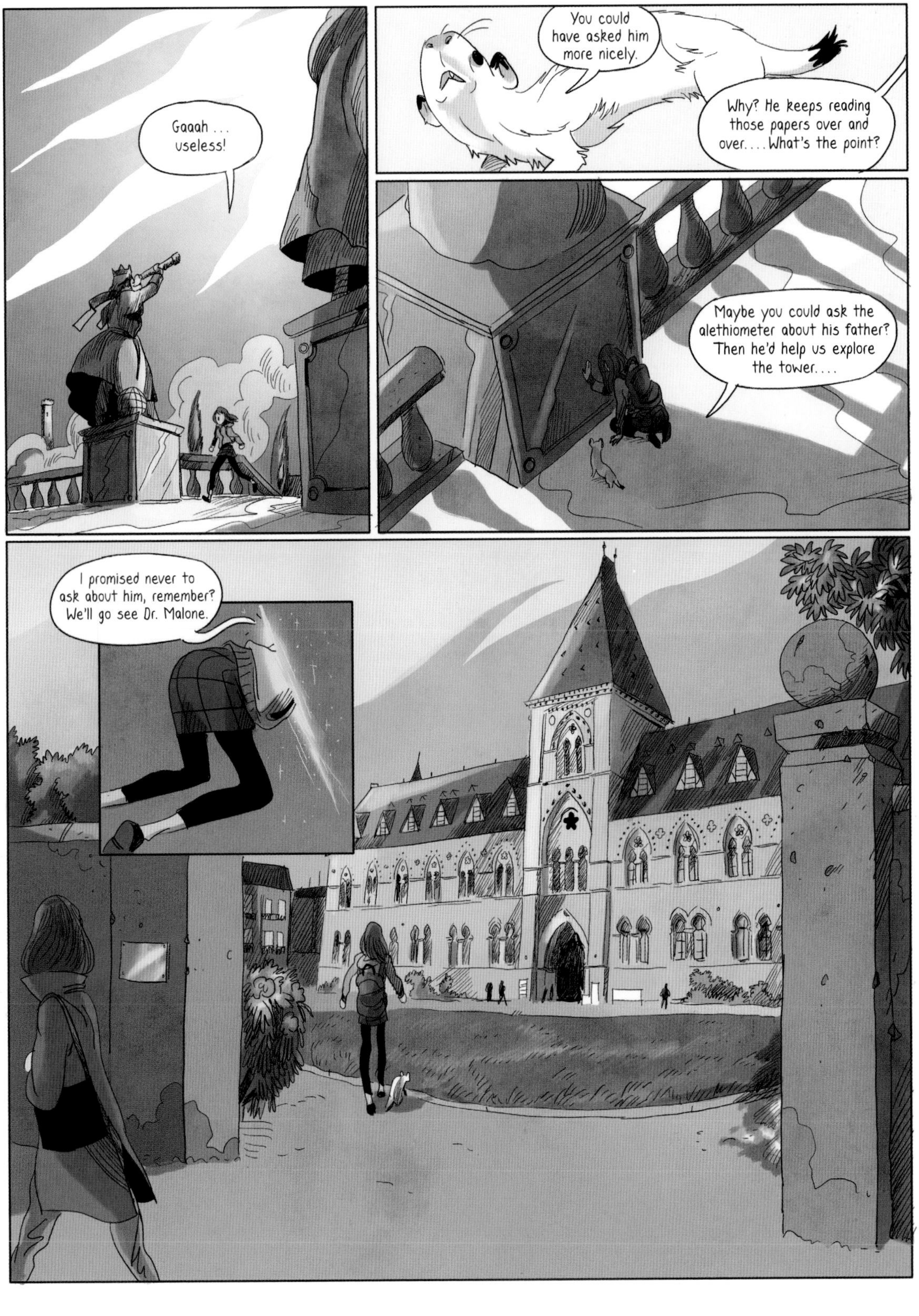
Gaaah . . . useless!
You could have asked him more nicely.
Why? He keeps reading those papers over and over. . . . What's the point?
Maybe you could ask the alethiometer about his father? Then he'd help us explore the tower. . . .
I promised never to ask about him, remember? We'll go see Dr. Malone.

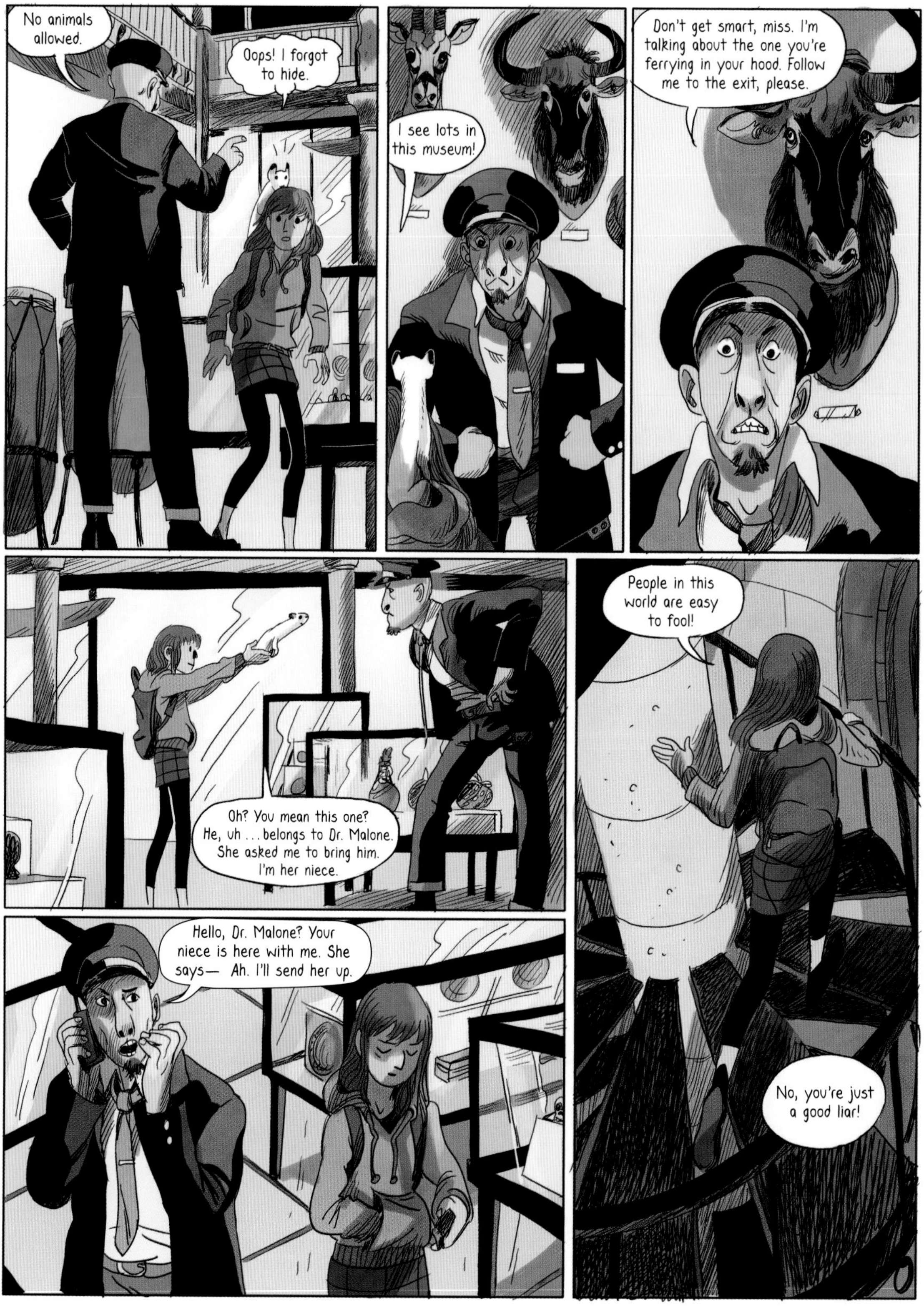
No animals allowed.
Oops! I forgot to hide.
I see lots in this museum!
Don't get smart, miss. I'm talking about the one you're ferrying in your hood. Follow me to the exit, please.
Oh? You mean this one? He, uh . . . belongs to Dr. Malone. She asked me to bring him. I'm her niece.
Hello, Dr. Malone? Your niece is here with me. She says— Ah. I'll send her up.
People in this world are easy to fool!
No, you're just a good liar!

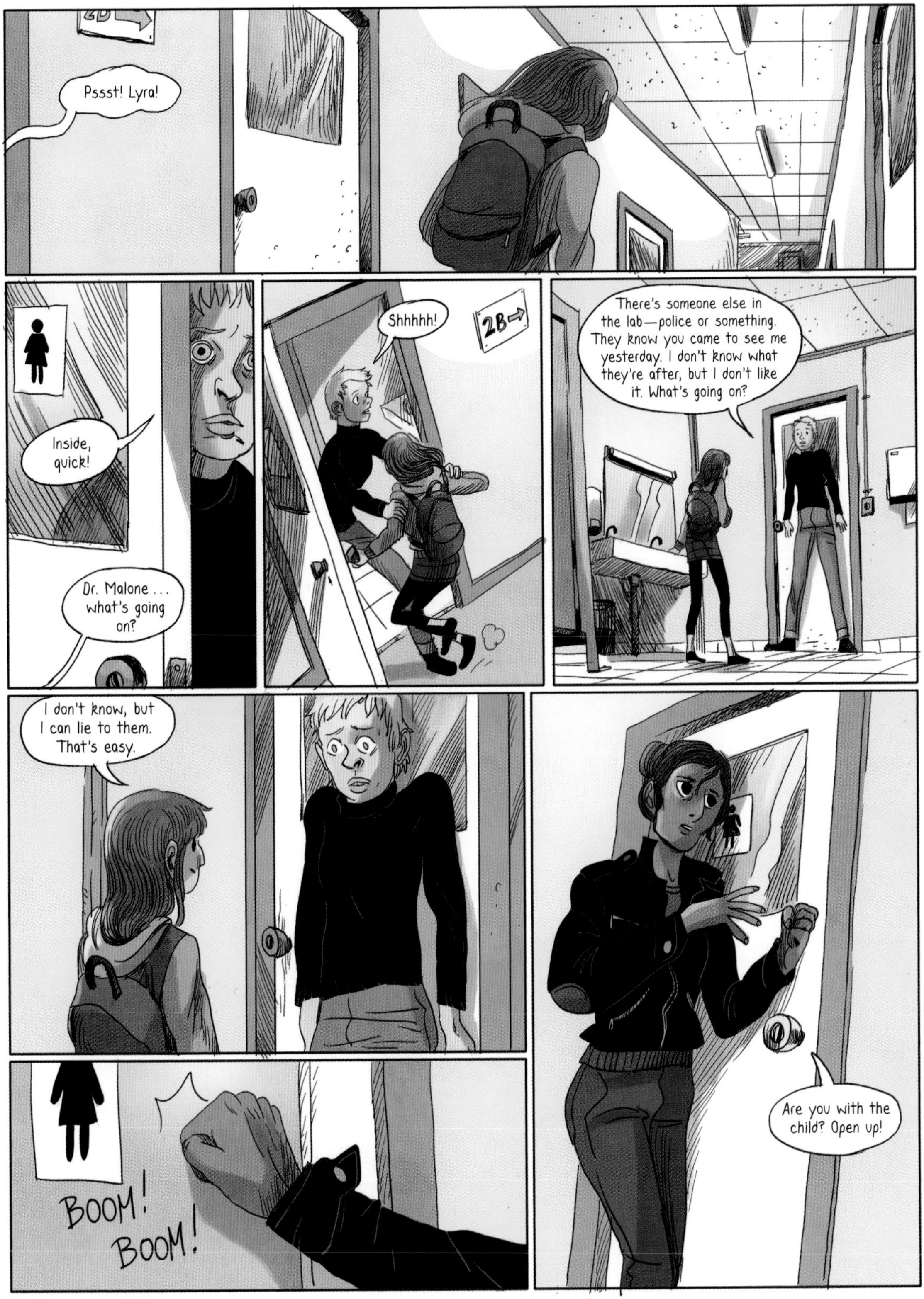
Pssst! Lyra!
2B
Inside, quick!
Dr. Malone . . . what's going on?
Shhhhh!
2B
There's someone else in the lab—police or something. They know you came to see me yesterday. I don't know what they're after, but I don't like it. What's going on?
I don't know, but I can lie to them. That's easy.
BOOM! BOOM!
Are you with the child? Open up!

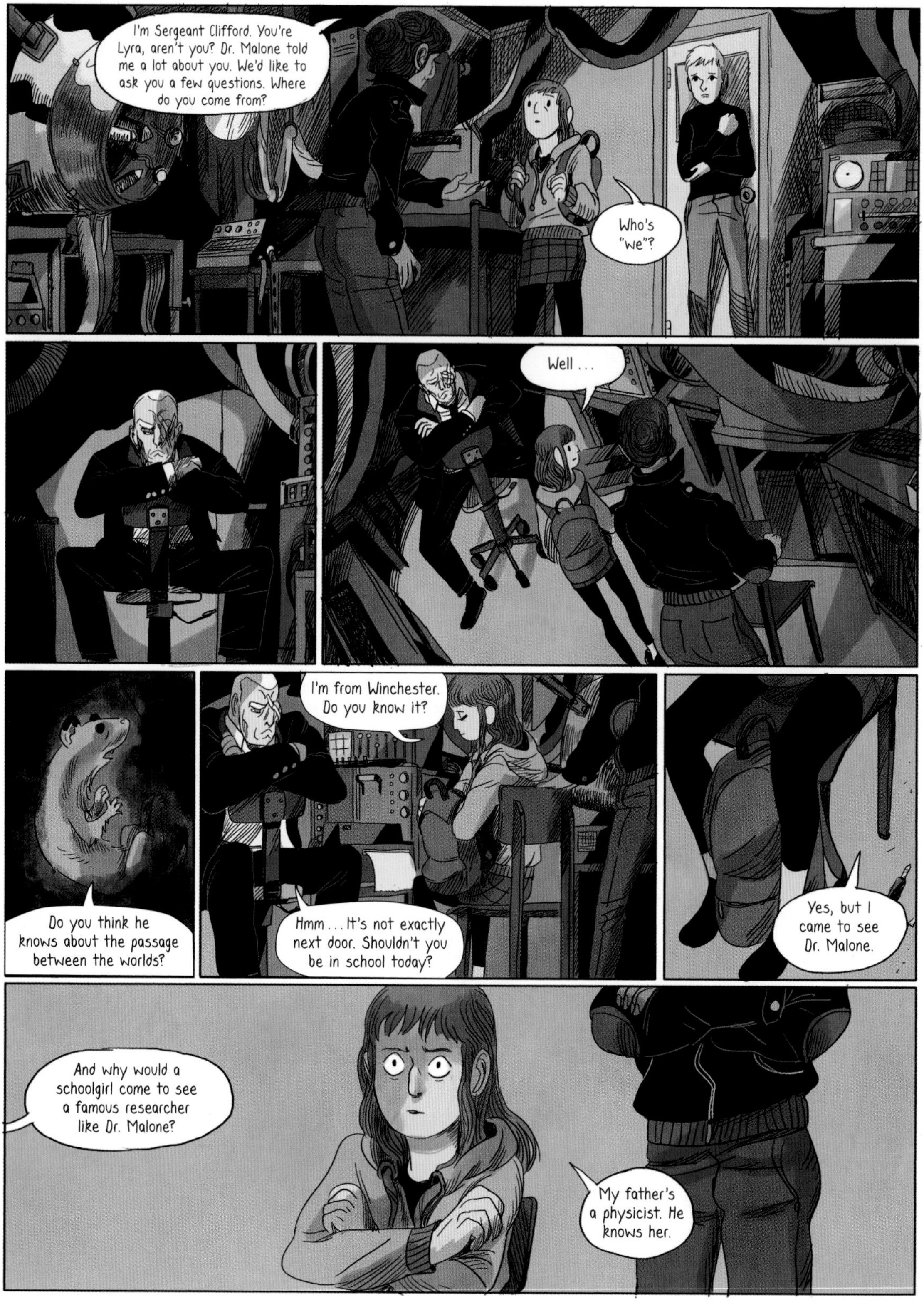
I'm Sergeant Clifford. You're Lyra, aren't you? Dr. Malone told me a lot about you. We'd like to ask you a few questions. Where do you come from?
Who's "we"?
Well . . .
Do you think he knows about the passage between the worlds?
I'm from Winchester. Do you know it?
Hmm . . . It's not exactly next door. Shouldn't you be in school today?
Yes, but I came to see Dr. Malone.
And why would a schoolgirl come to see a famous researcher like Dr. Malone?
My father's a physicist. He knows her.

Did Dr. Malone show you what she's working on?

Yeah. The engine with the screen...all that. My father does the same kind of work, but he doesn't use the same methods.

He's looking into dark matter, then?

Yes. He can do some things better, but that engine with the words on the screen—he hasn't got one of those.

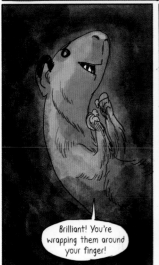

Brilliant! You're wrapping them around your finger!

And Will? Does he know Dr. Malone too?

Well, no... because...

Because?

He...he...

He got you! Run, Lyra, run!

ARRHH!

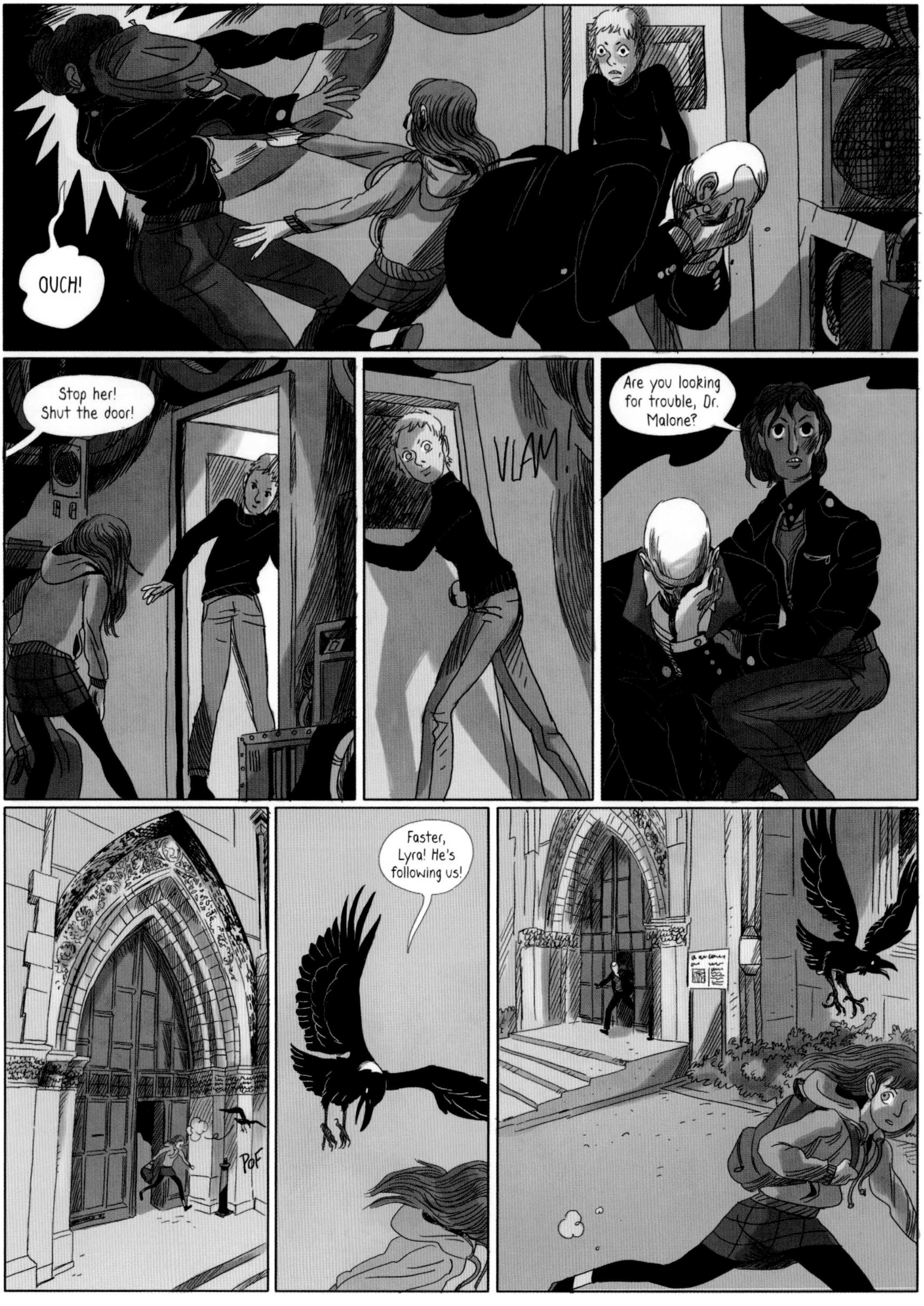
OUCH!
Stop her! Shut the door!
VLAM!
Are you looking for trouble, Dr. Malone?
POF
Faster, Lyra! He's following us!

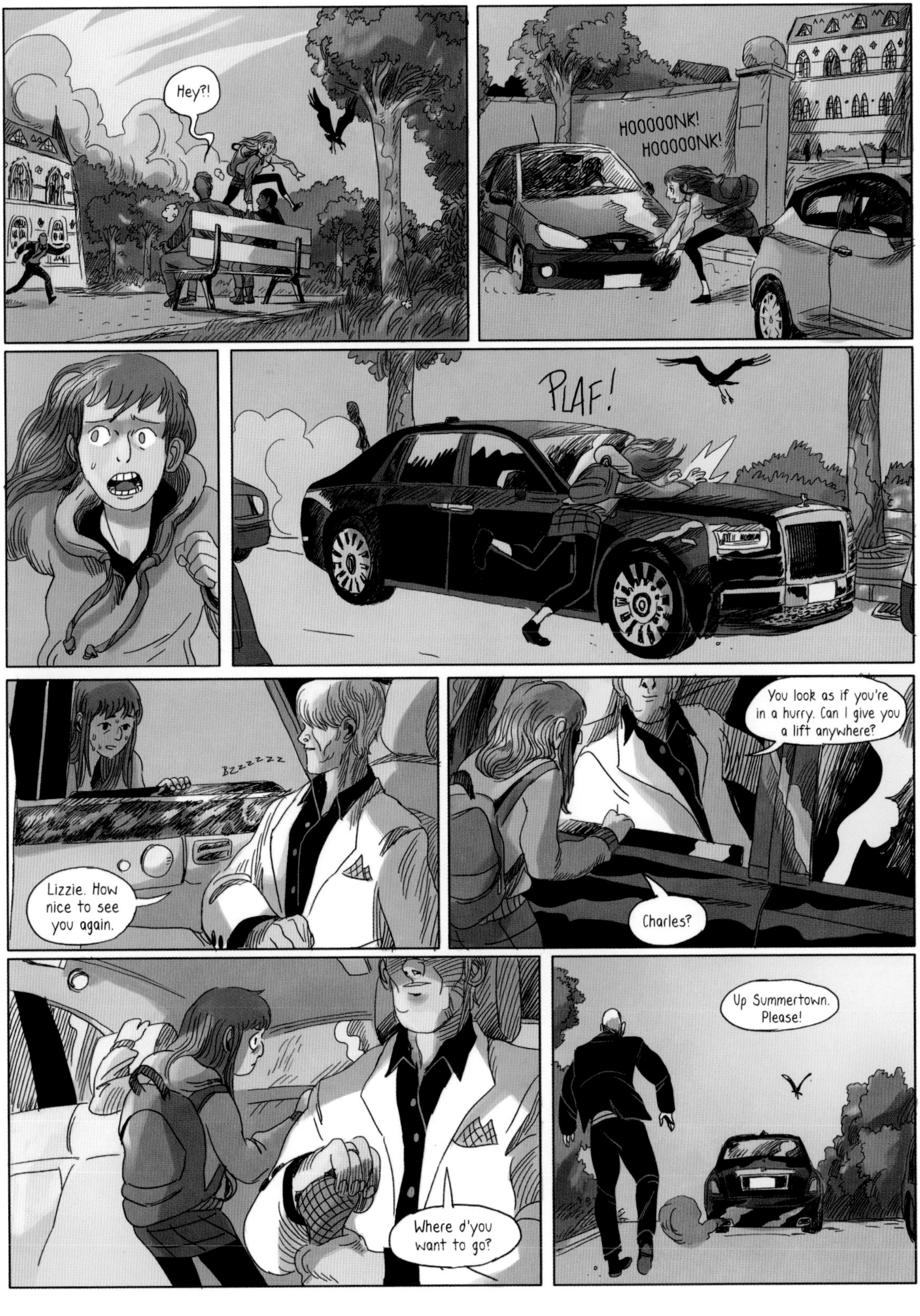
Hey?!
HOOOOONK!
HOOOOONK!
PLAF!
Bzzzzzz
Lizzie. How nice to see you again.
Charles?
You look as if you're in a hurry. Can I give you a lift anywhere?
Where d'you want to go?
Up Summertown. Please!

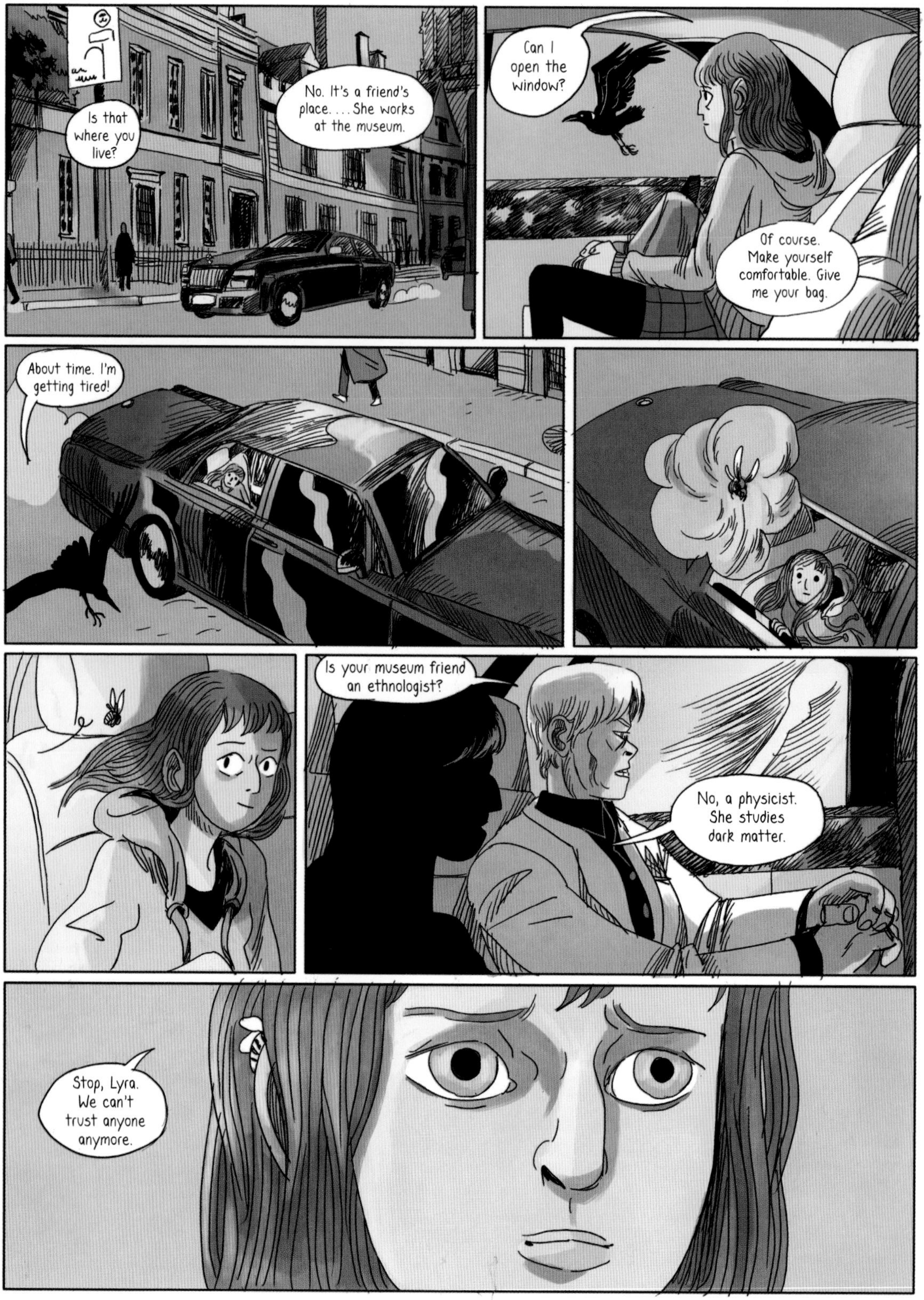
Is that where you live?
No. It's a friend's place. . . . She works at the museum.
Can I open the window?
Of course. Make yourself comfortable. Give me your bag.
About time. I'm getting tired!
Is your museum friend an ethnologist?
No, a physicist. She studies dark matter.
Stop, Lyra. We can't trust anyone anymore.

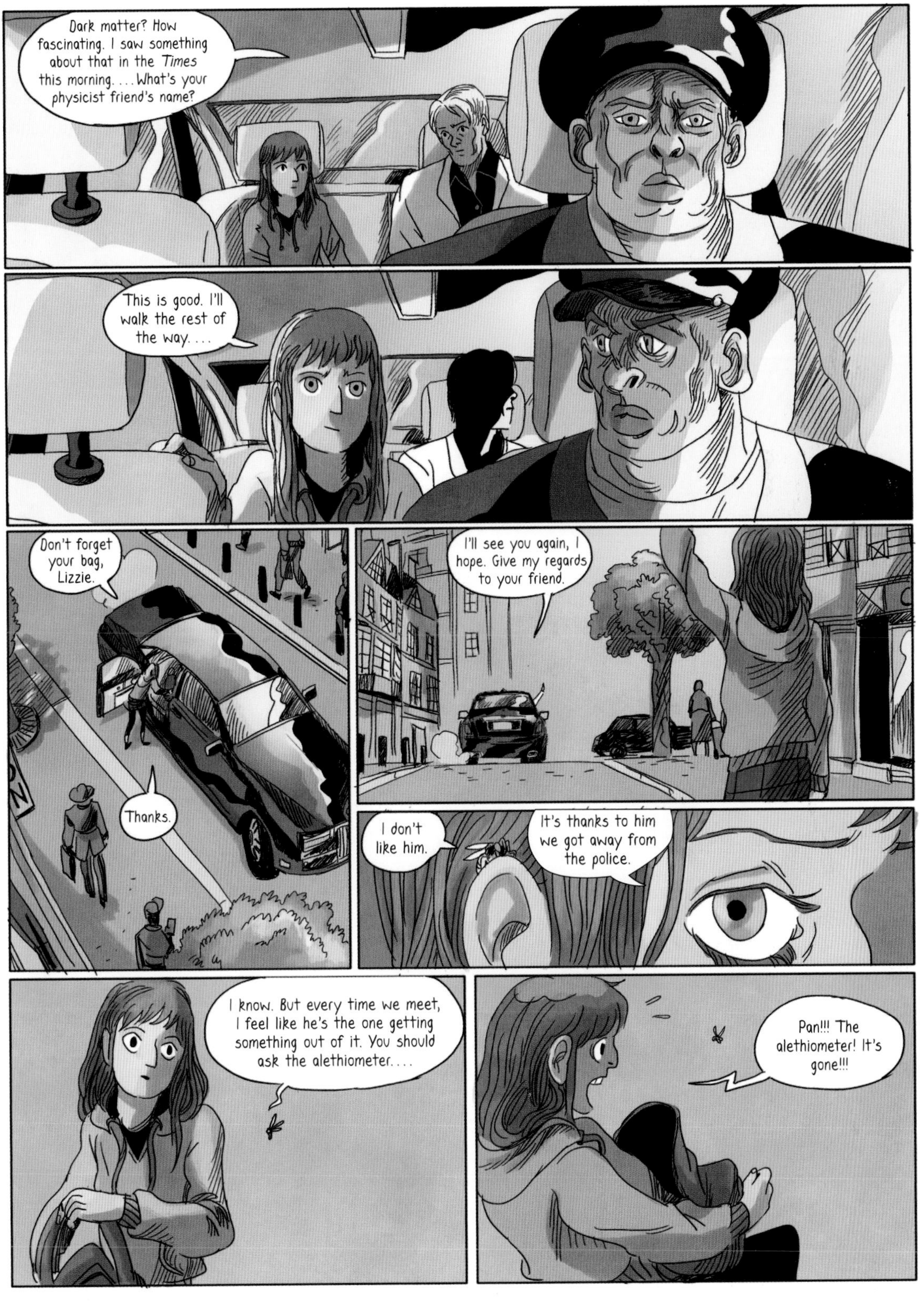
Dark matter? How fascinating. I saw something about that in the *Times* this morning. . . . What's your physicist friend's name?
This is good. I'll walk the rest of the way. . . .
Don't forget your bag, Lizzie.
Thanks.
I'll see you again, I hope. Give my regards to your friend.
I don't like him.
It's thanks to him we got away from the police.
I know. But every time we meet, I feel like he's the one getting something out of it. You should ask the alethiometer. . . .
Pan!!! The alethiometer! It's gone!!!

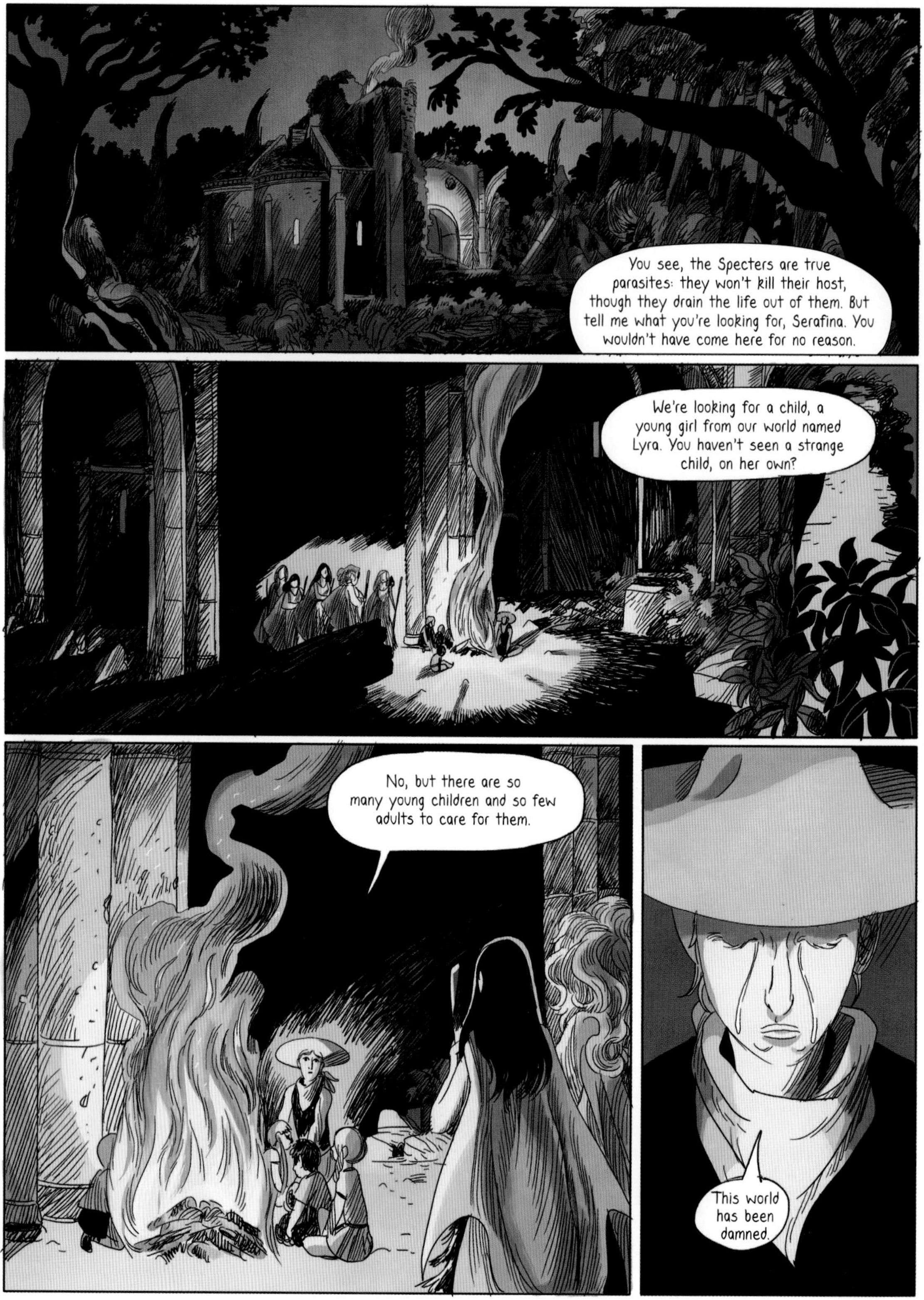
You see, the Specters are true parasites: they won't kill their host, though they drain the life out of them. But tell me what you're looking for, Serafina. You wouldn't have come here for no reason.
We're looking for a child, a young girl from our world named Lyra. You haven't seen a strange child, on her own?
No, but there are so many young children and so few adults to care for them.
This world has been damned.

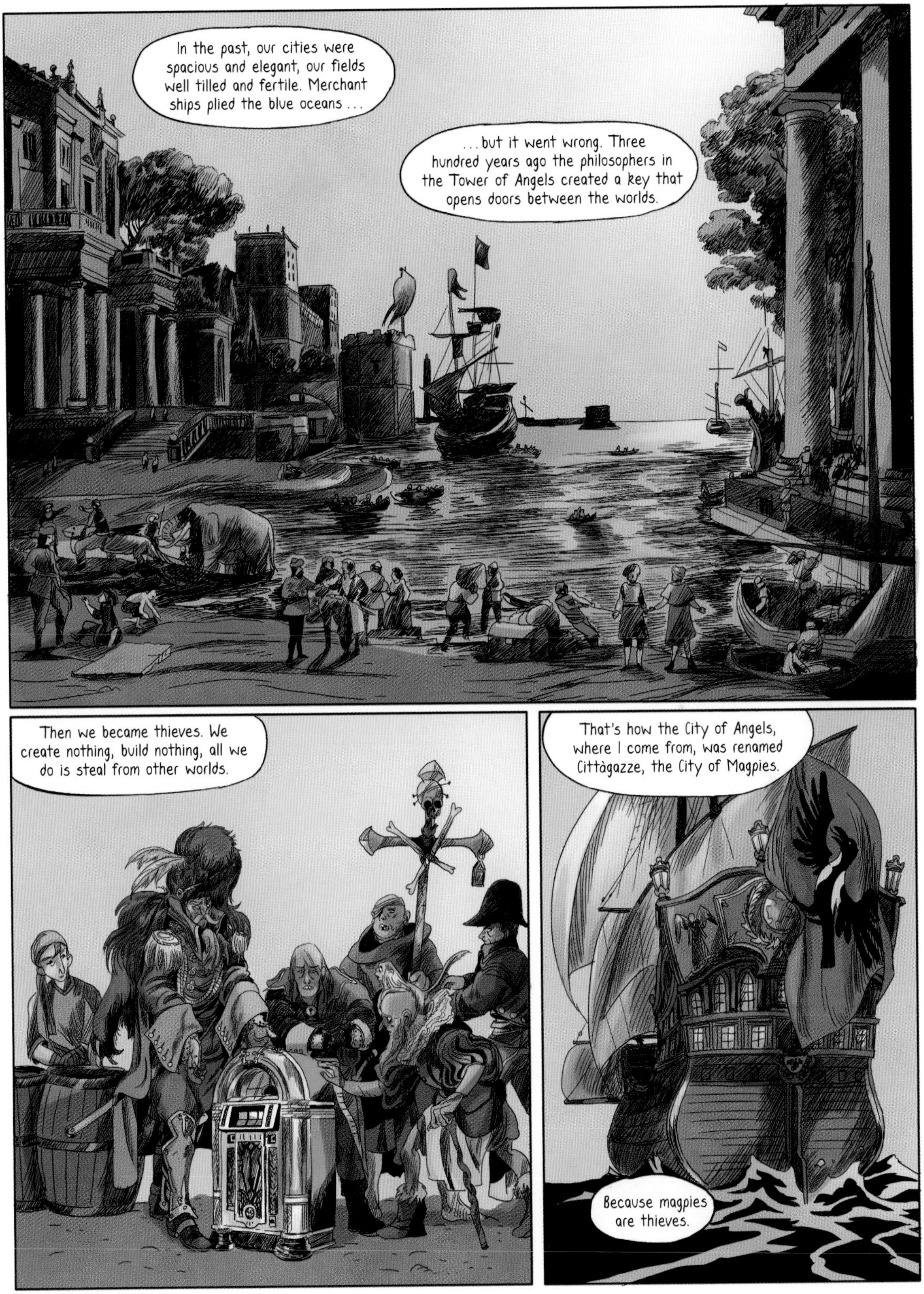
In the past, our cities were spacious and elegant, our fields well tilled and fertile. Merchant ships plied the blue oceans . . .
. . . but it went wrong. Three hundred years ago the philosophers in the Tower of Angels created a key that opens doors between the worlds.
Then we became thieves. We create nothing, build nothing, all we do is steal from other worlds.
That's how the City of Angels, where I come from, was renamed Cittàgazze, the City of Magpies.
Because magpies are thieves.

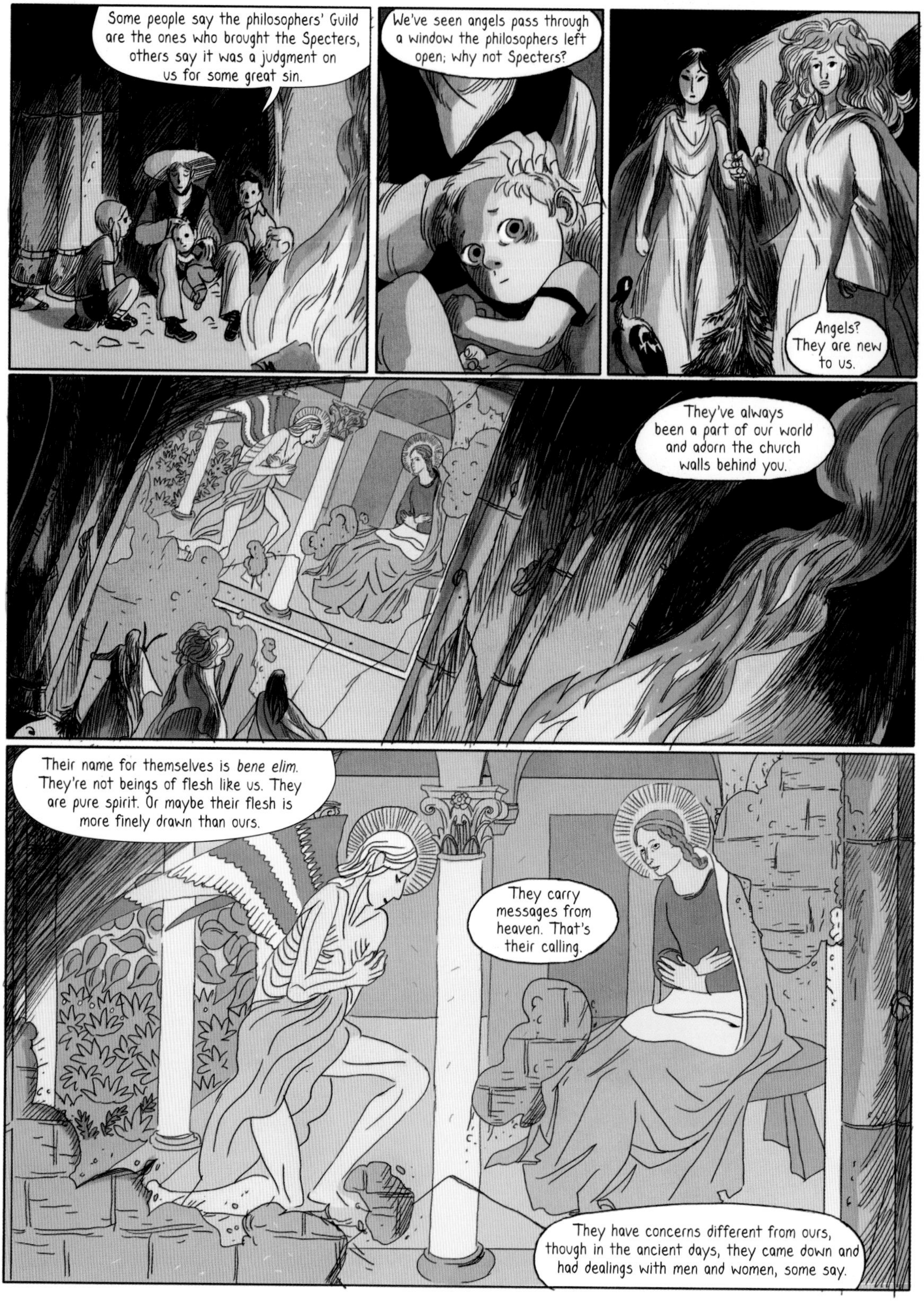
Some people say the philosophers' Guild are the ones who brought the Specters, others say it was a judgment on us for some great sin.
We've seen angels pass through a window the philosophers left open; why not Specters?
Angels? They are new to us.
They've always been a part of our world and adorn the church walls behind you.
Their name for themselves is *bene elim*. They're not beings of flesh like us. They are pure spirit. Or maybe their flesh is more finely drawn than ours.
They carry messages from heaven. That's their calling.
They have concerns different from ours, though in the ancient days, they came down and had dealings with men and women, some say.

Now we see them sometimes in the sky, passing through this world on the way to another, shining like fireflies way up high.

And when the fog came, after the great storm, I heard voices above me, cries of anger and alarm, and wingbeats too.

WAAAH!

WAAAH!

Then, the other night, we saw them, among the stars, making for the Pole, like a fleet of mighty ships under sail. Something is happening.

There could be a war breaking out. There was a war in heaven once, immense ages back. It wouldn't be impossible if there was another.

The devastation would be enormous, and the consequences for us . . . I can't imagine it.

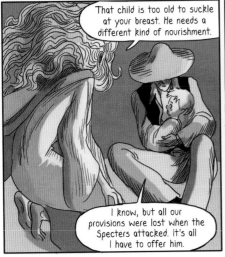

That child is too old to suckle at your breast. He needs a different kind of nourishment.

I know, but all our provisions were lost when the Specters attacked. It's all I have to offer him.

Sisters, what were we thinking?

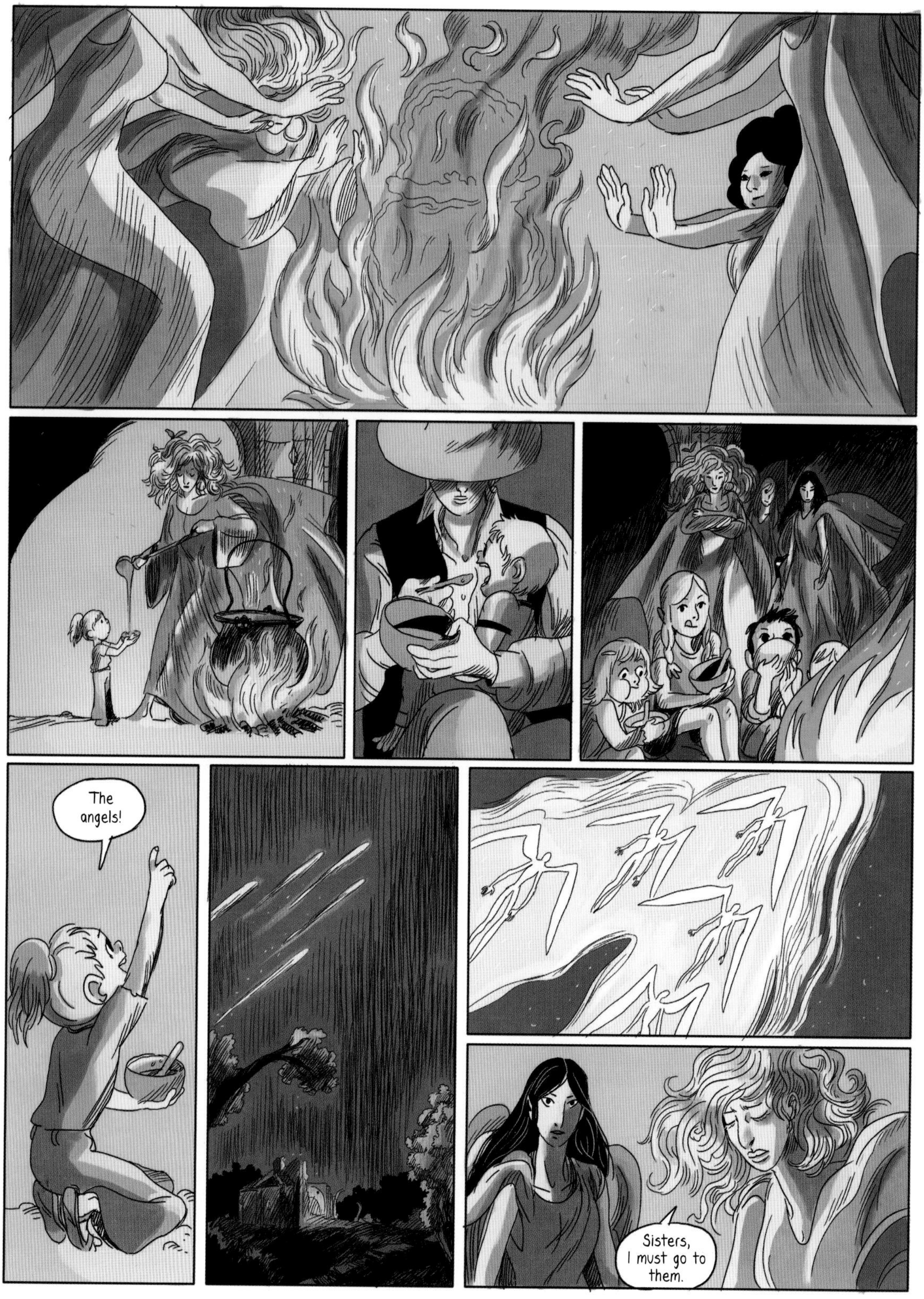
The angels!
Sisters, I must go to them.

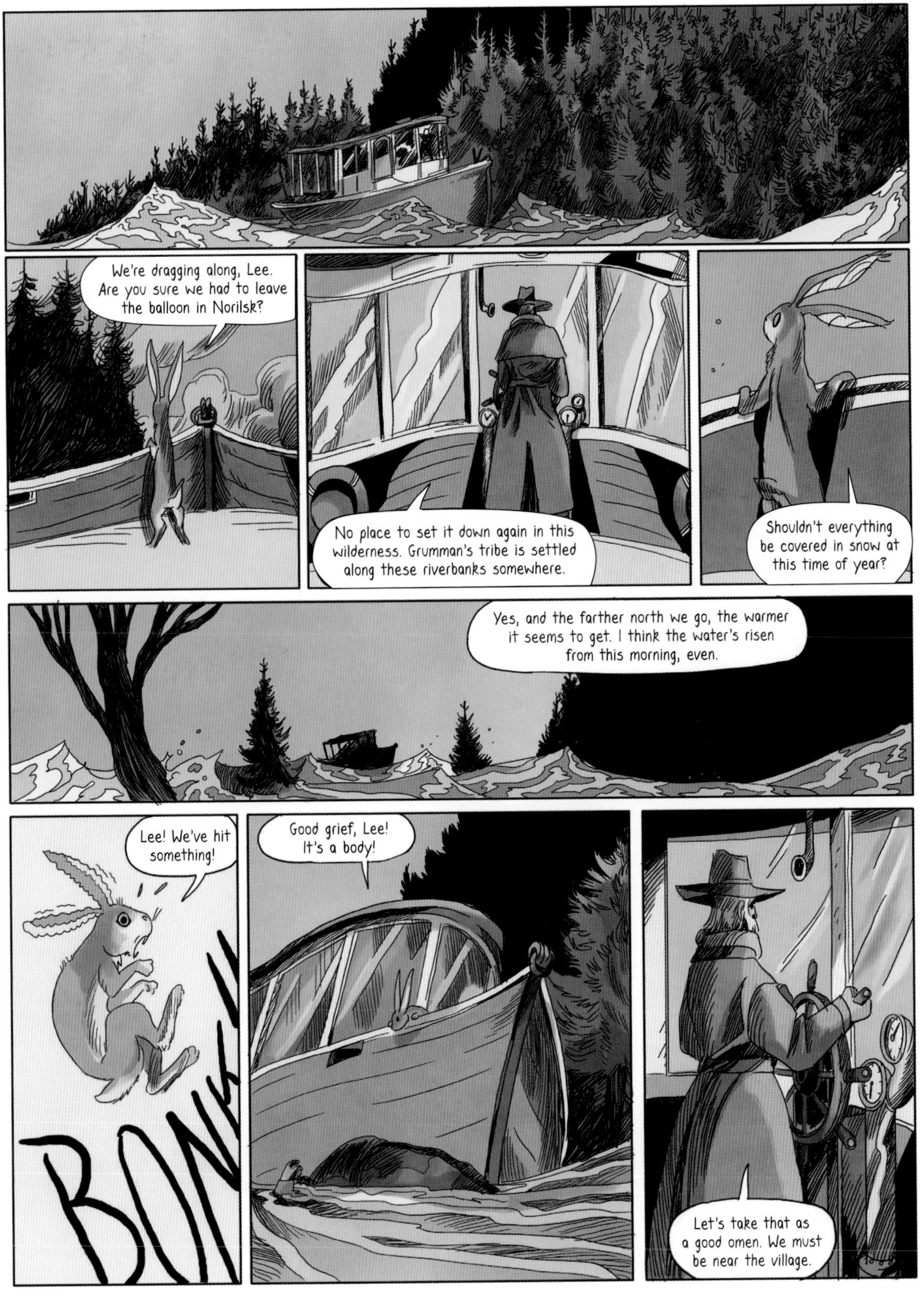
We're dragging along, Lee. Are you sure we had to leave the balloon in Norilsk?
No place to set it down again in this wilderness. Grumman's tribe is settled along these riverbanks somewhere.
Shouldn't everything be covered in snow at this time of year?
Yes, and the farther north we go, the warmer it seems to get. I think the water's risen from this morning, even.
Lee! We've hit something!
BONK!!
Good grief, Lee! It's a body!
Let's take that as a good omen. We must be near the village.

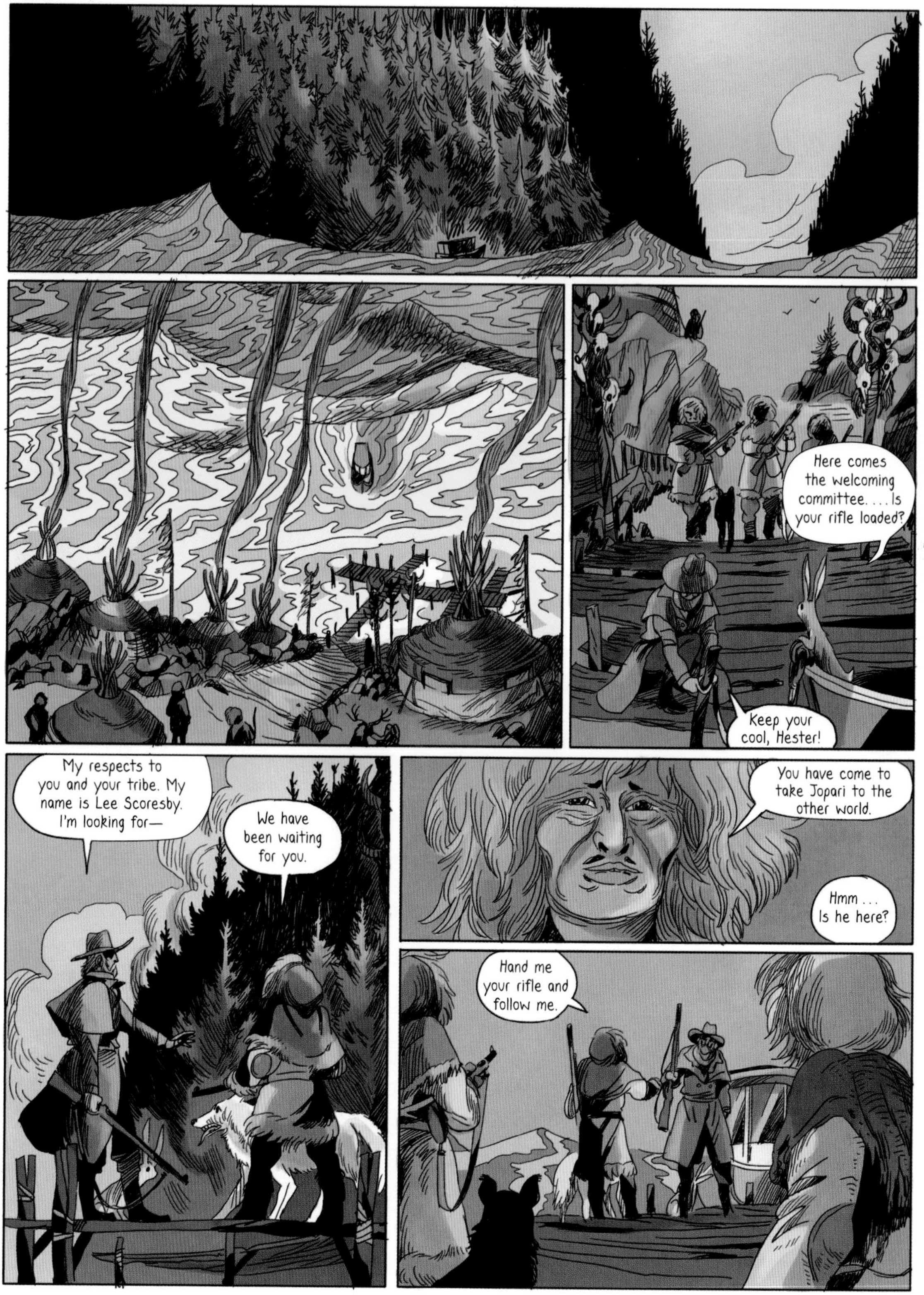
Here comes the welcoming committee. . . . Is your rifle loaded?
Keep your cool, Hester!
My respects to you and your tribe. My name is Lee Scoresby. I'm looking for—
We have been waiting for you.
You have come to take Jopari to the other world.
Hmm . . . Is he here?
Hand me your rifle and follow me.

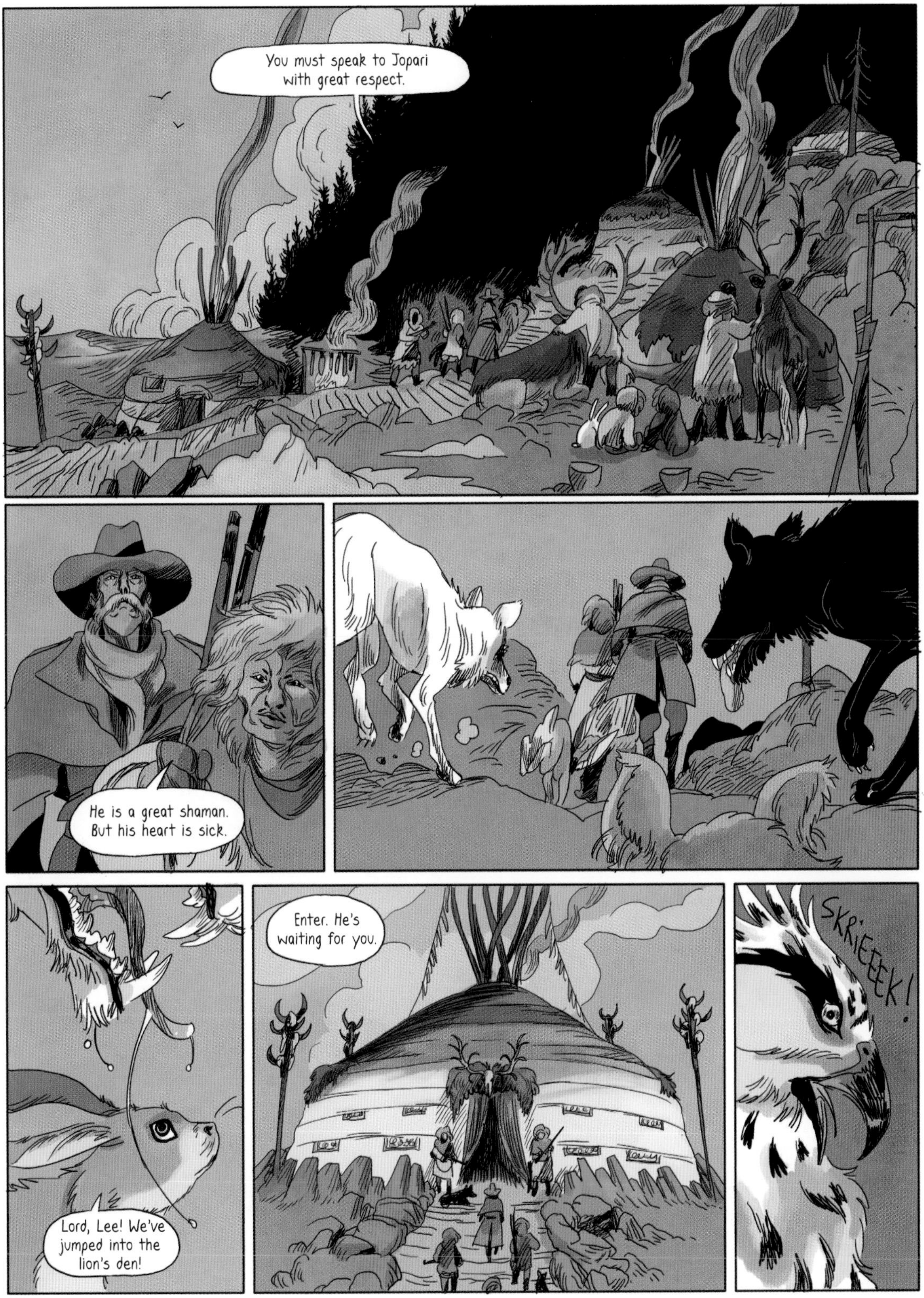

You must speak to Jopari with great respect.
He is a great shaman. But his heart is sick.
Lord, Lee! We've jumped into the lion's den!
Enter. He's waiting for you.
SKRIEEEEK!

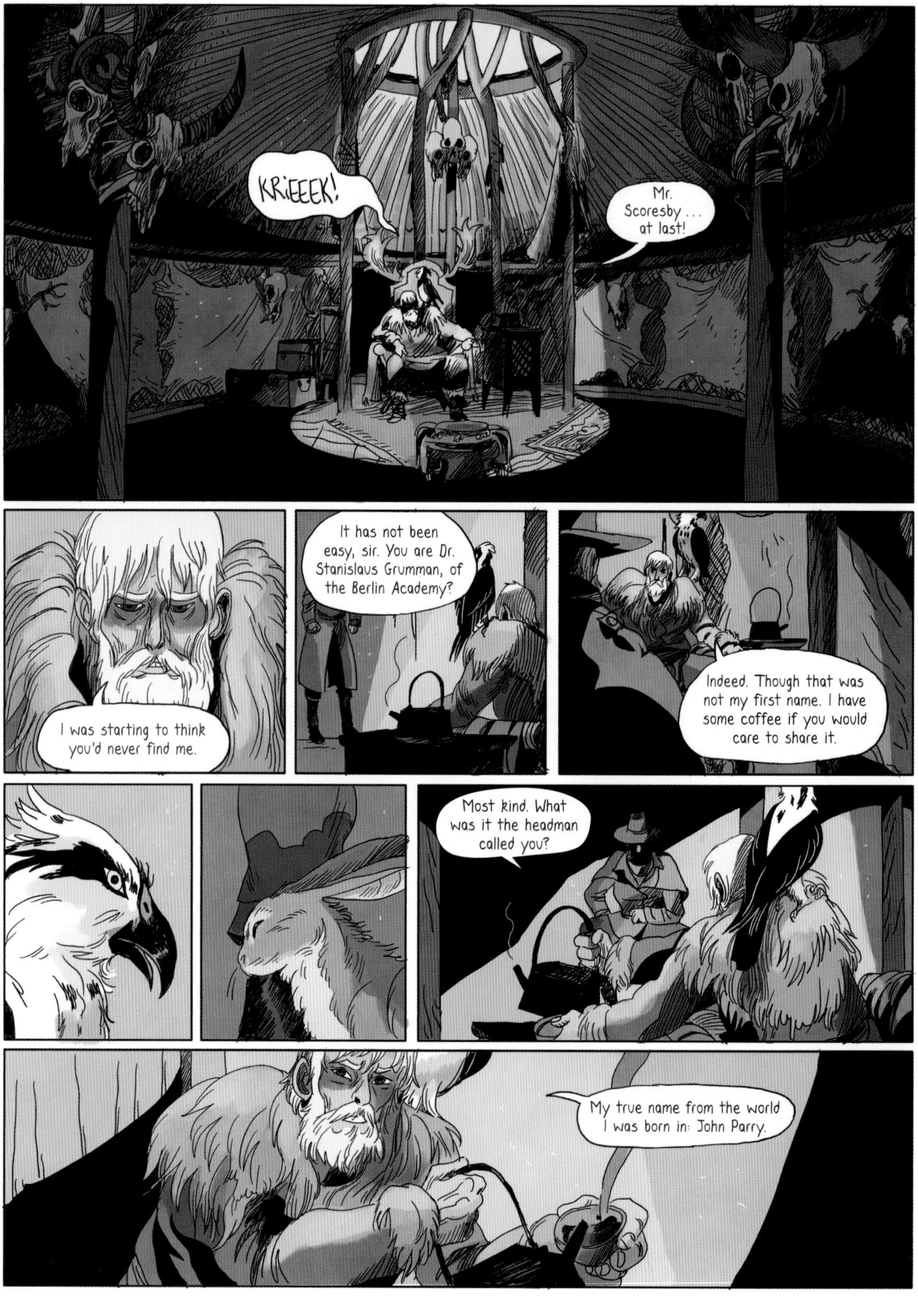
KRiEEEK!
Mr. Scoresby . . . at last!
I was starting to think you'd never find me.
It has not been easy, sir. You are Dr. Stanislaus Grumman, of the Berlin Academy?
Indeed. Though that was not my first name. I have some coffee if you would care to share it.
Most kind. What was it the headman called you?
My true name from the world I was born in: John Parry.

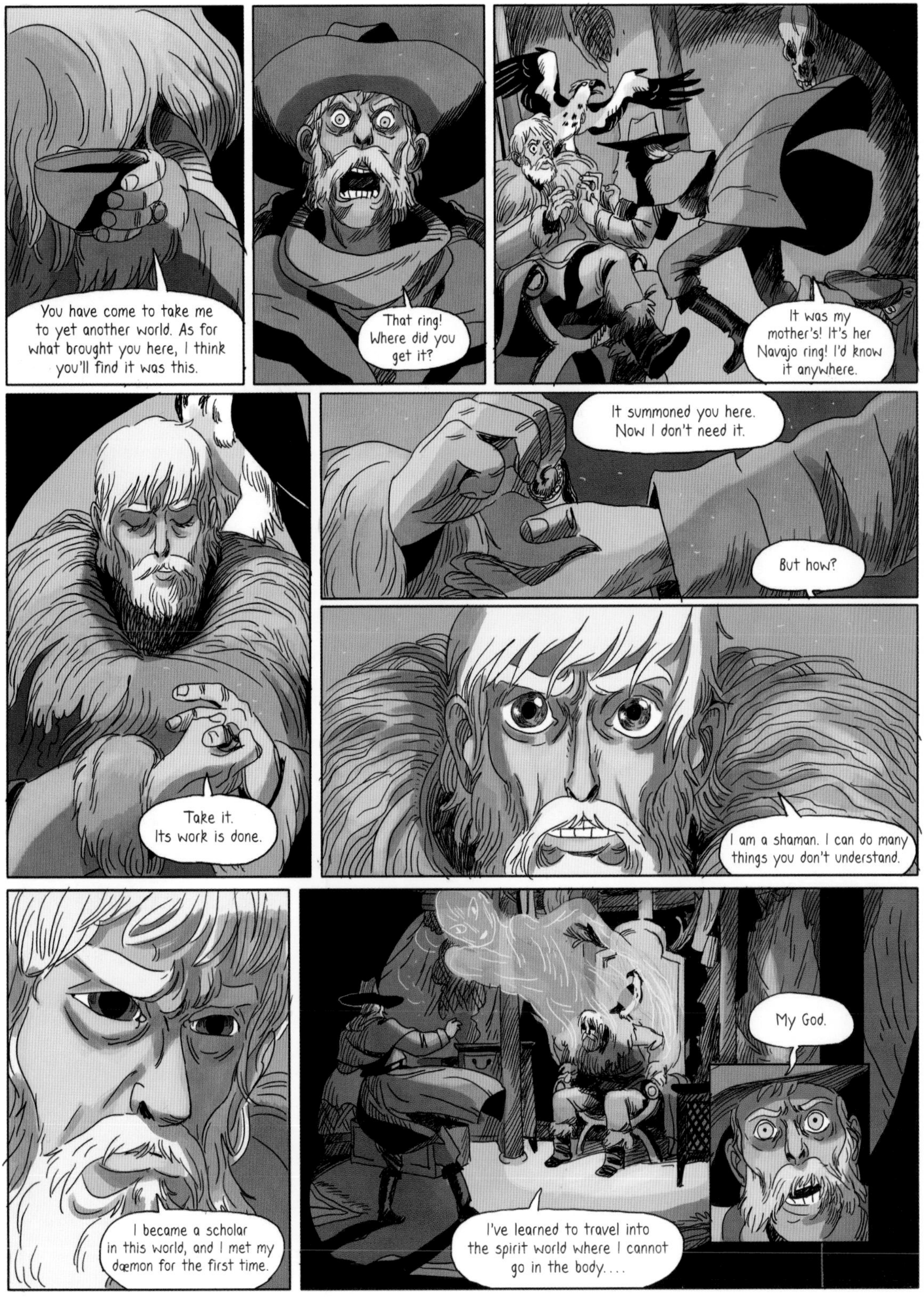
You have come to take me to yet another world. As for what brought you here, I think you'll find it was this.
That ring! Where did you get it?
It was my mother's! It's her Navajo ring! I'd know it anywhere.
Take it. Its work is done.
It summoned you here. Now I don't need it.
But how?
I am a shaman. I can do many things you don't understand.
I became a scholar in this world, and I met my dæmon for the first time.
I've learned to travel into the spirit world where I cannot go in the body. . . .
My God.

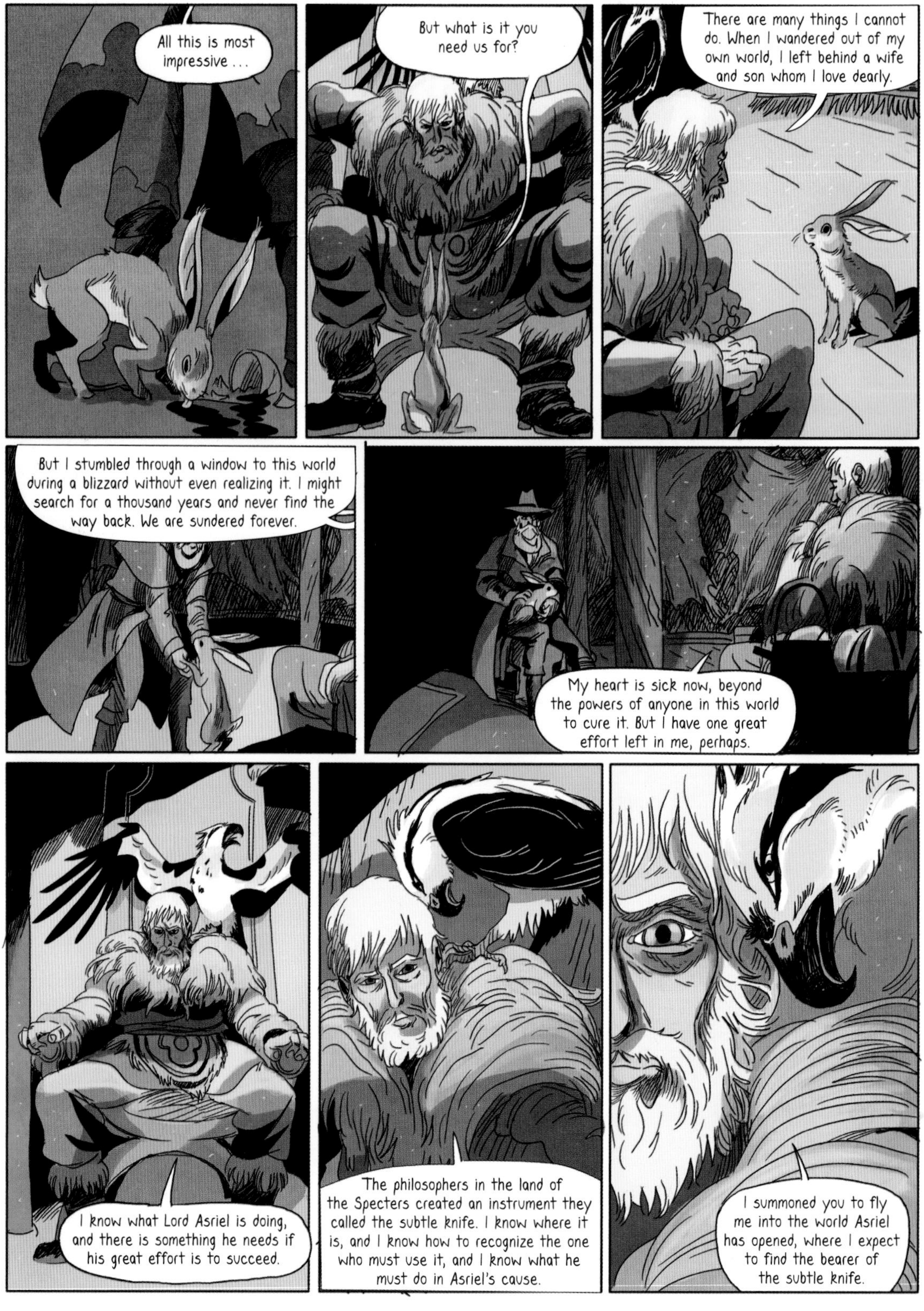
All this is most impressive . . .
But what is it you need us for?
There are many things I cannot do. When I wandered out of my own world, I left behind a wife and son whom I love dearly.
But I stumbled through a window to this world during a blizzard without even realizing it. I might search for a thousand years and never find the way back. We are sundered forever.
My heart is sick now, beyond the powers of anyone in this world to cure it. But I have one great effort left in me, perhaps.
I know what Lord Asriel is doing, and there is something he needs if his great effort is to succeed.
The philosophers in the land of the Specters created an instrument they called the subtle knife. I know where it is, and I know how to recognize the one who must use it, and I know what he must do in Asriel's cause.
I summoned you to fly me into the world Asriel has opened, where I expect to find the bearer of the subtle knife.

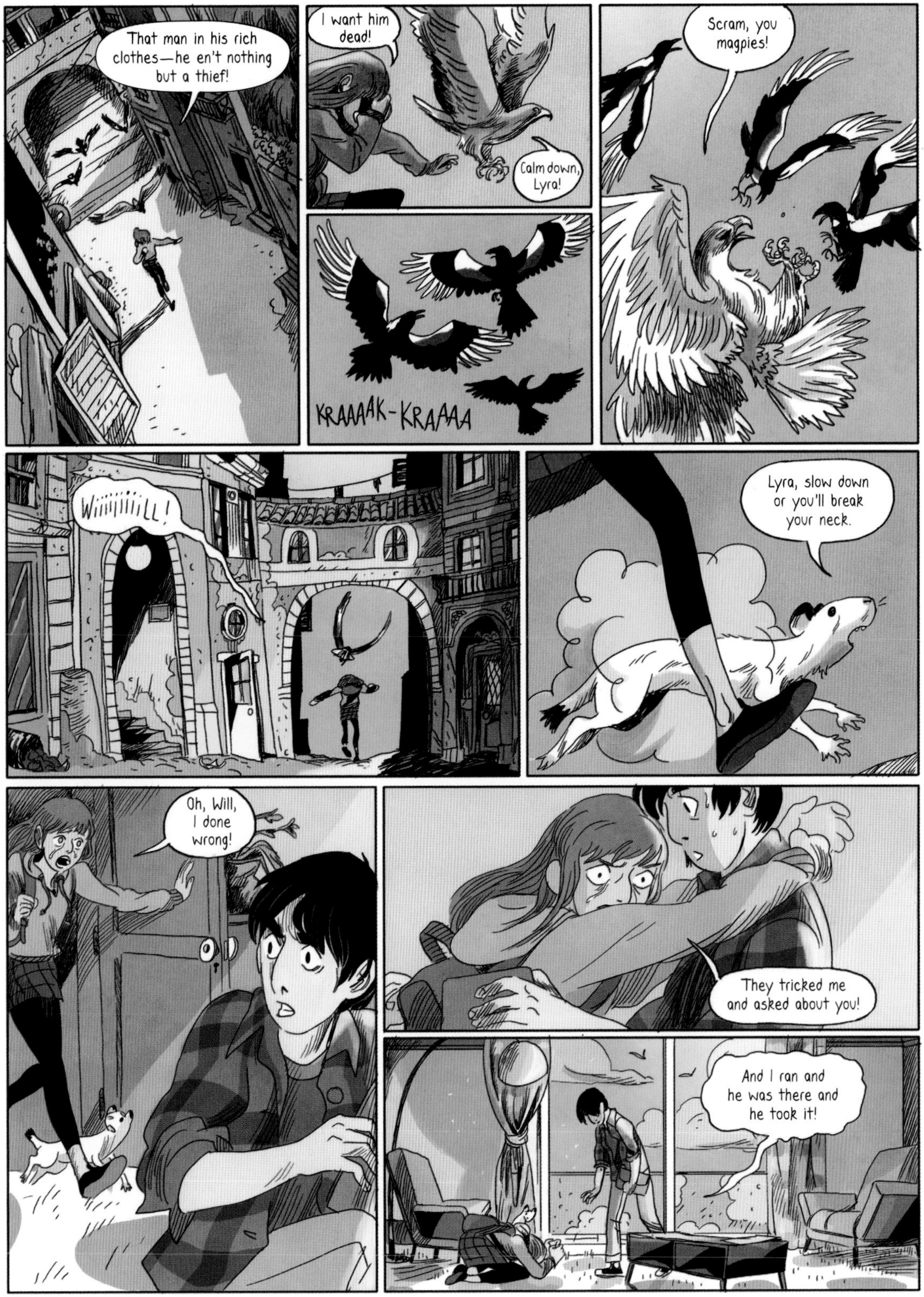
That man in his rich clothes—he en't nothing but a thief!
I want him dead!
Calm down, Lyra!
KRAAAAK-KRAAAA
Scram, you magpies!
WiiiiiiiLL!
Lyra, slow down or you'll break your neck.
Oh, Will, I done wrong!
They tricked me and asked about you!
And I ran and he was there and he took it!

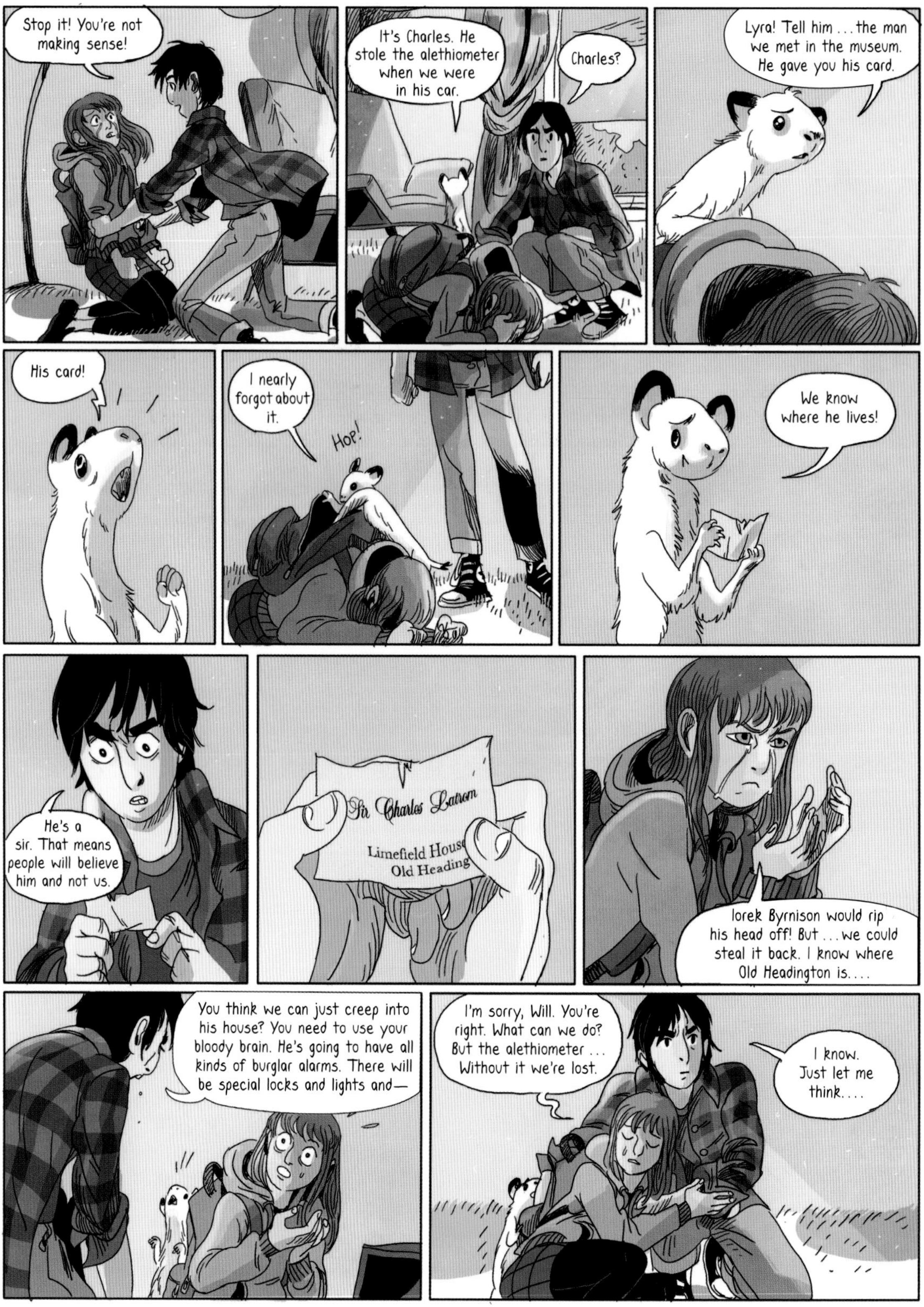
Stop it! You're not making sense!
It's Charles. He stole the alethiometer when we were in his car.
Charles?
Lyra! Tell him . . . the man we met in the museum. He gave you his card.
His card!
I nearly forgot about it.
Hop!
We know where he lives!
He's a sir. That means people will believe him and not us.
Sir Charles Latrom
Limefield House
Old Heading
Iorek Byrnison would rip his head off! But . . . we could steal it back. I know where Old Headington is. . . .
You think we can just creep into his house? You need to use your bloody brain. He's going to have all kinds of burglar alarms. There will be special locks and lights and—
I'm sorry, Will. You're right. What can we do? But the alethiometer . . . Without it we're lost.
I know. Just let me think. . . .

I will speak to these angels, whatever they may be. If they are going to join Lord Asriel, I'll go with them. If not, I'll search on by myself.

May the wind be with you, sister. The angels were flying fast.

I'll go faster still!

And we'll find Lyra!

They're blending in with the constellation of Ophiuchus. We may lose them....

Don't worry, Sergi, I'm keeping a close eye on them.

We're catching up!

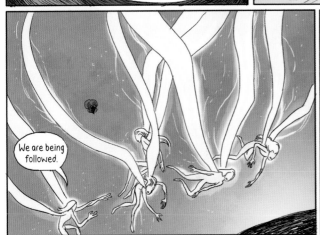

We are being followed.

Angels! Halt and listen! I am the witch Ruta Skadi, and I want to talk to you.

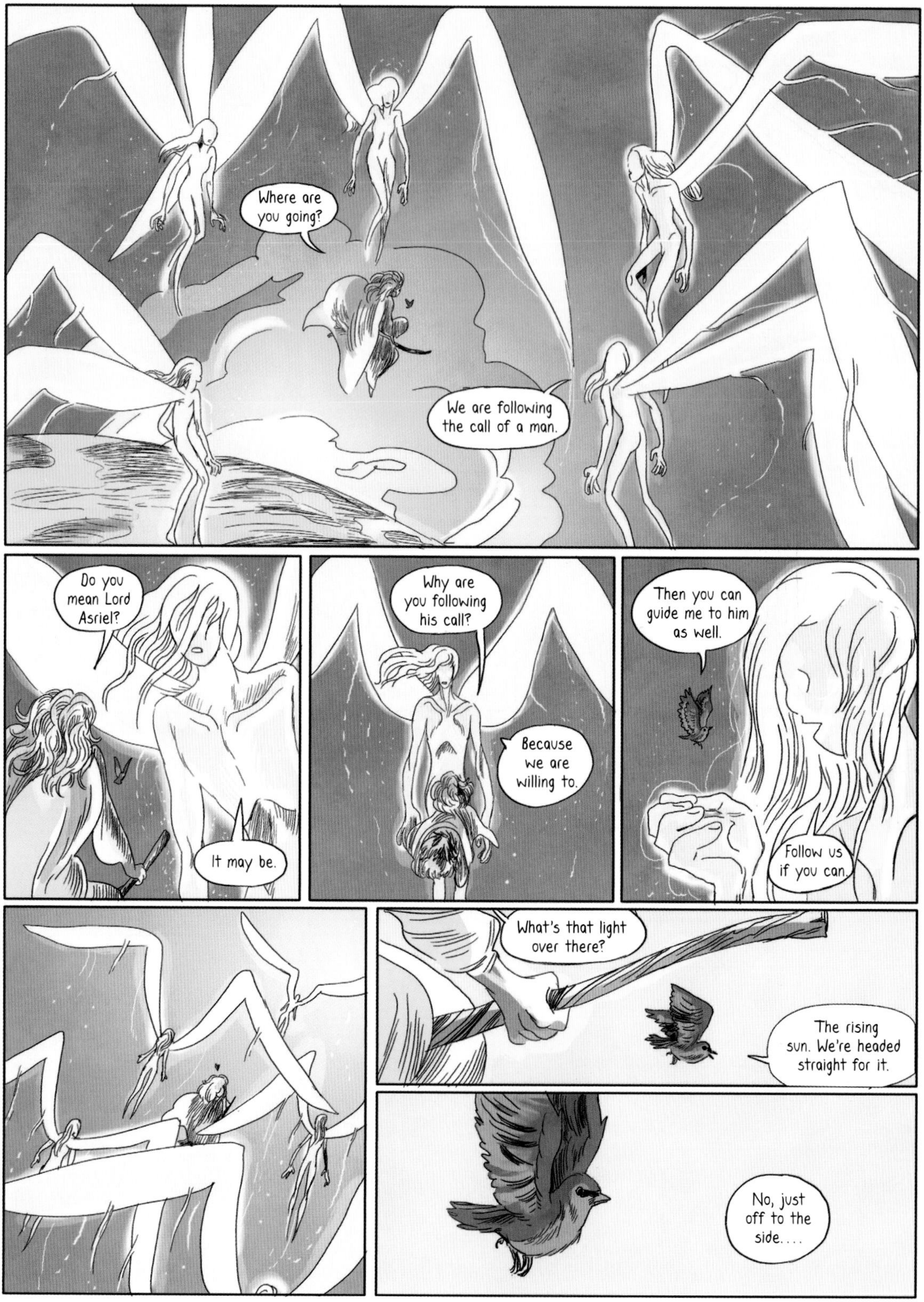
Where are you going?
We are following the call of a man.
Do you mean Lord Asriel?
It may be.
Why are you following his call?
Because we are willing to.
Then you can guide me to him as well.
Follow us if you can.
What's that light over there?
The rising sun. We're headed straight for it.
No, just off to the side. . . .

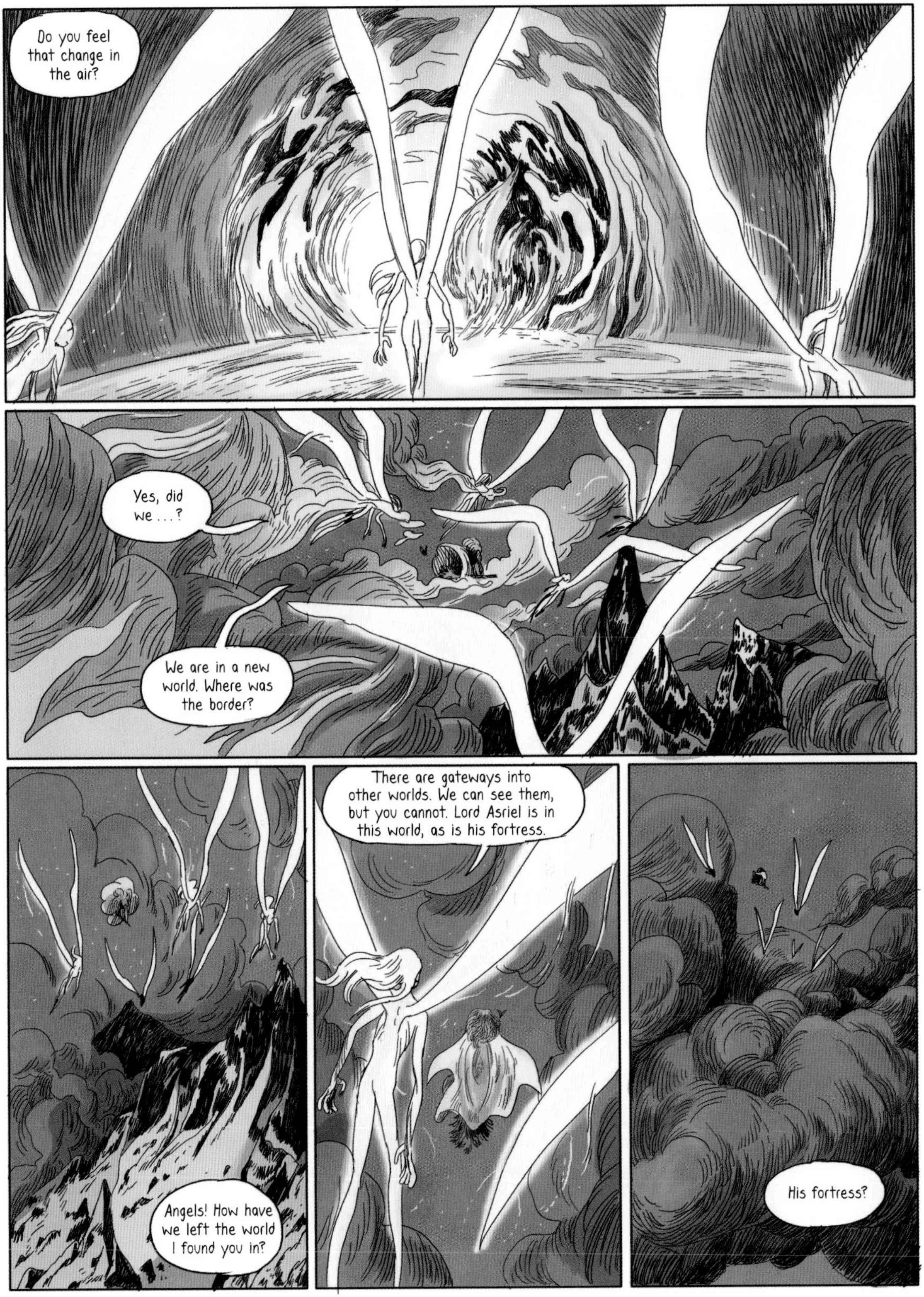
Do you feel that change in the air?
Yes, did we . . . ?
We are in a new world. Where was the border?
Angels! How have we left the world I found you in?
There are gateways into other worlds. We can see them, but you cannot. Lord Asriel is in this world, as is his fortress.
His fortress?

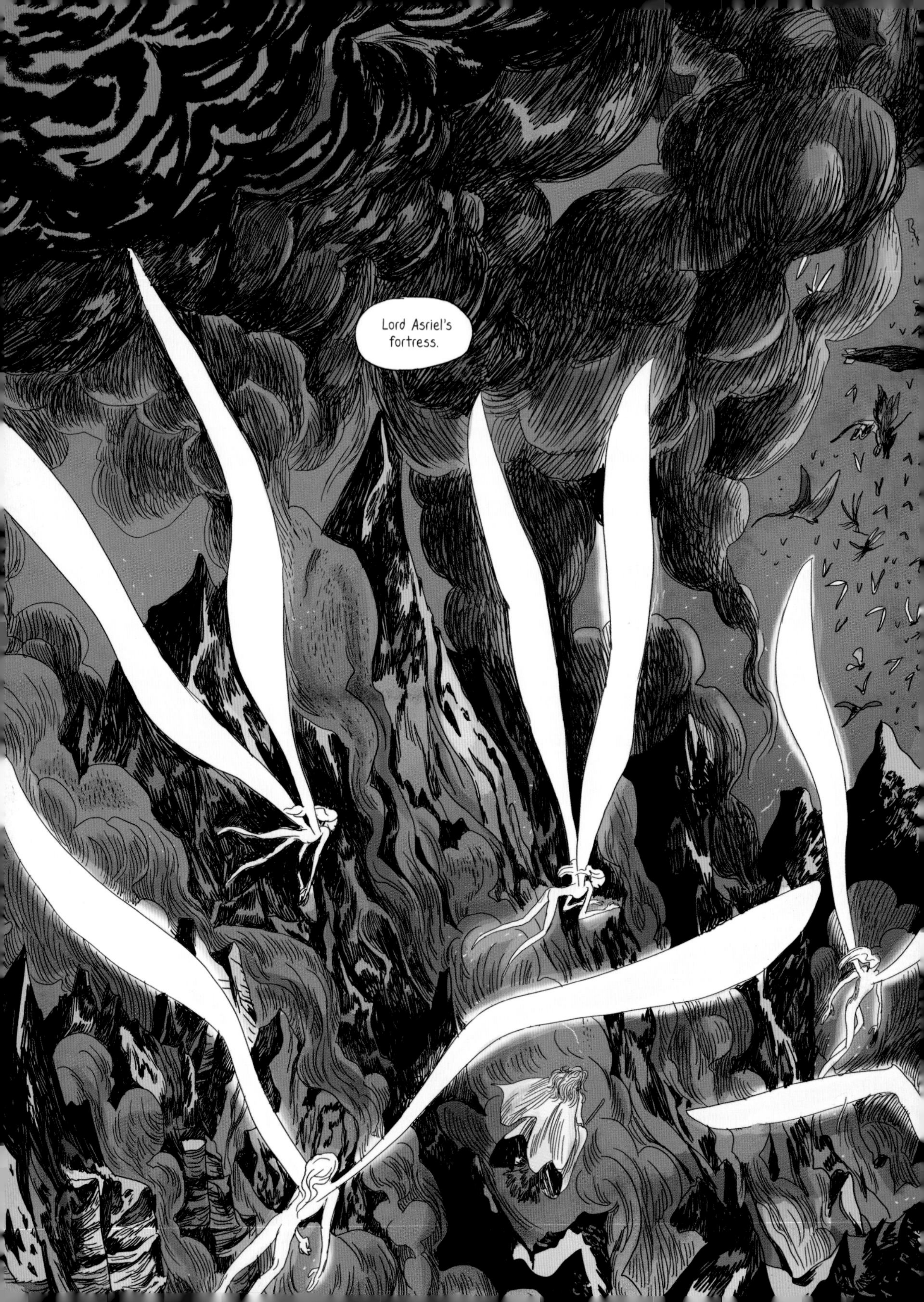
Lord Asriel's fortress.

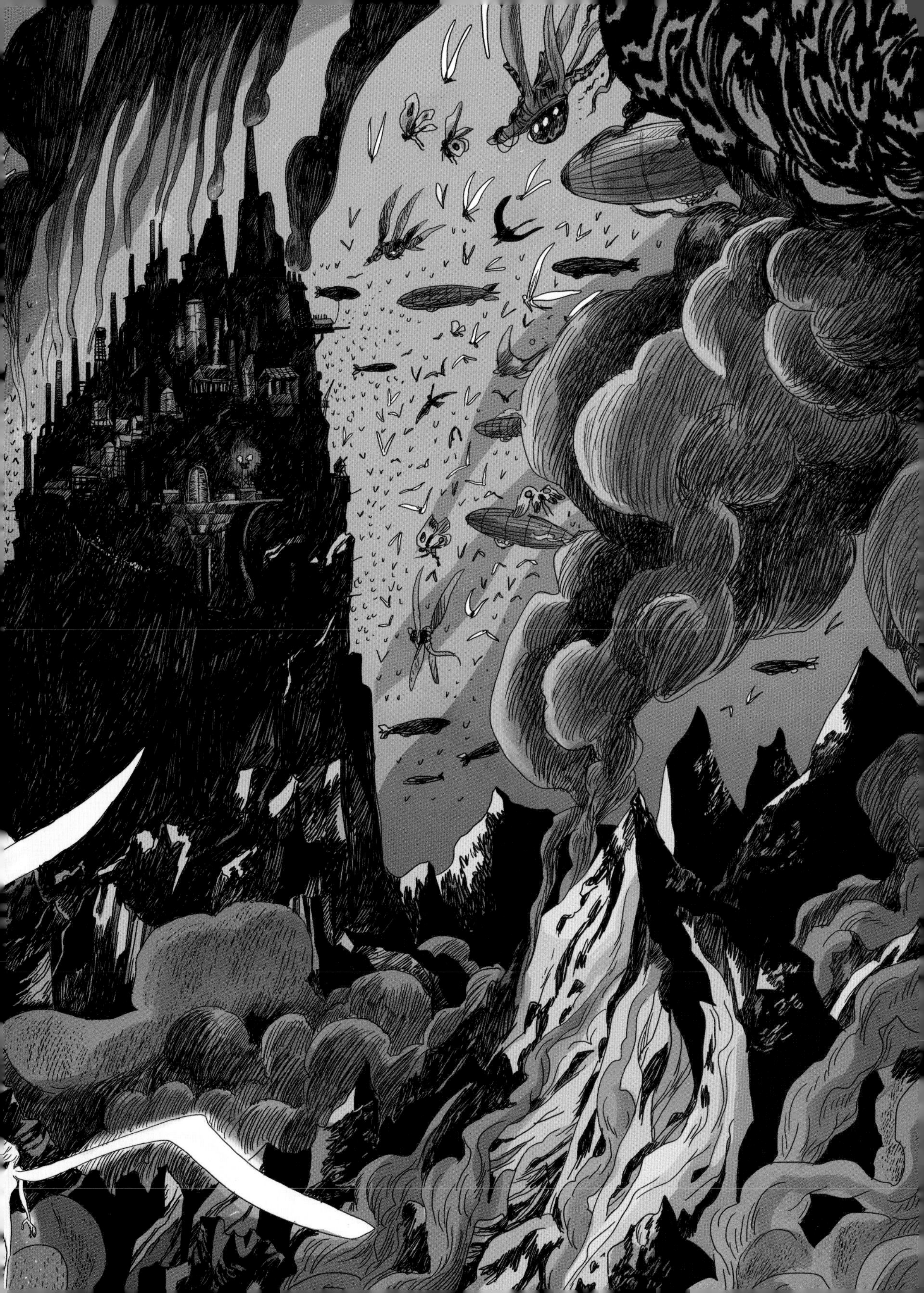

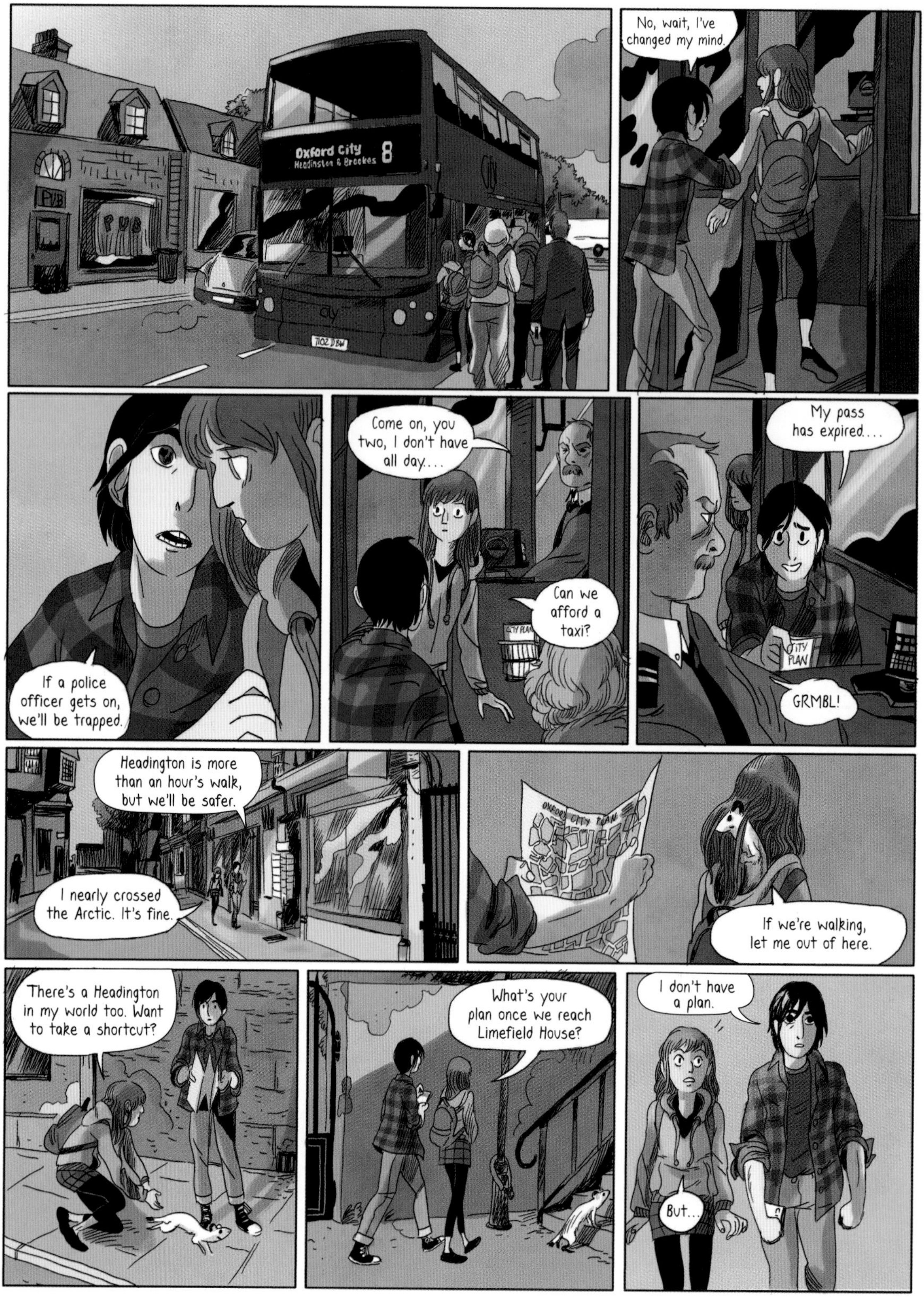
Oxford City 8 Headington & Brookes
PUB
PUB
No, wait, I've changed my mind.
If a police officer gets on, we'll be trapped.
Come on, you two, I don't have all day...
Can we afford a taxi?
My pass has expired...
CITY PLAN
GRMBL!
Headington is more than an hour's walk, but we'll be safer.
I nearly crossed the Arctic. It's fine.
OXFORD CITY PLAN
If we're walking, let me out of here.
There's a Headington in my world too. Want to take a shortcut?
What's your plan once we reach Limefield House?
I don't have a plan.
But...

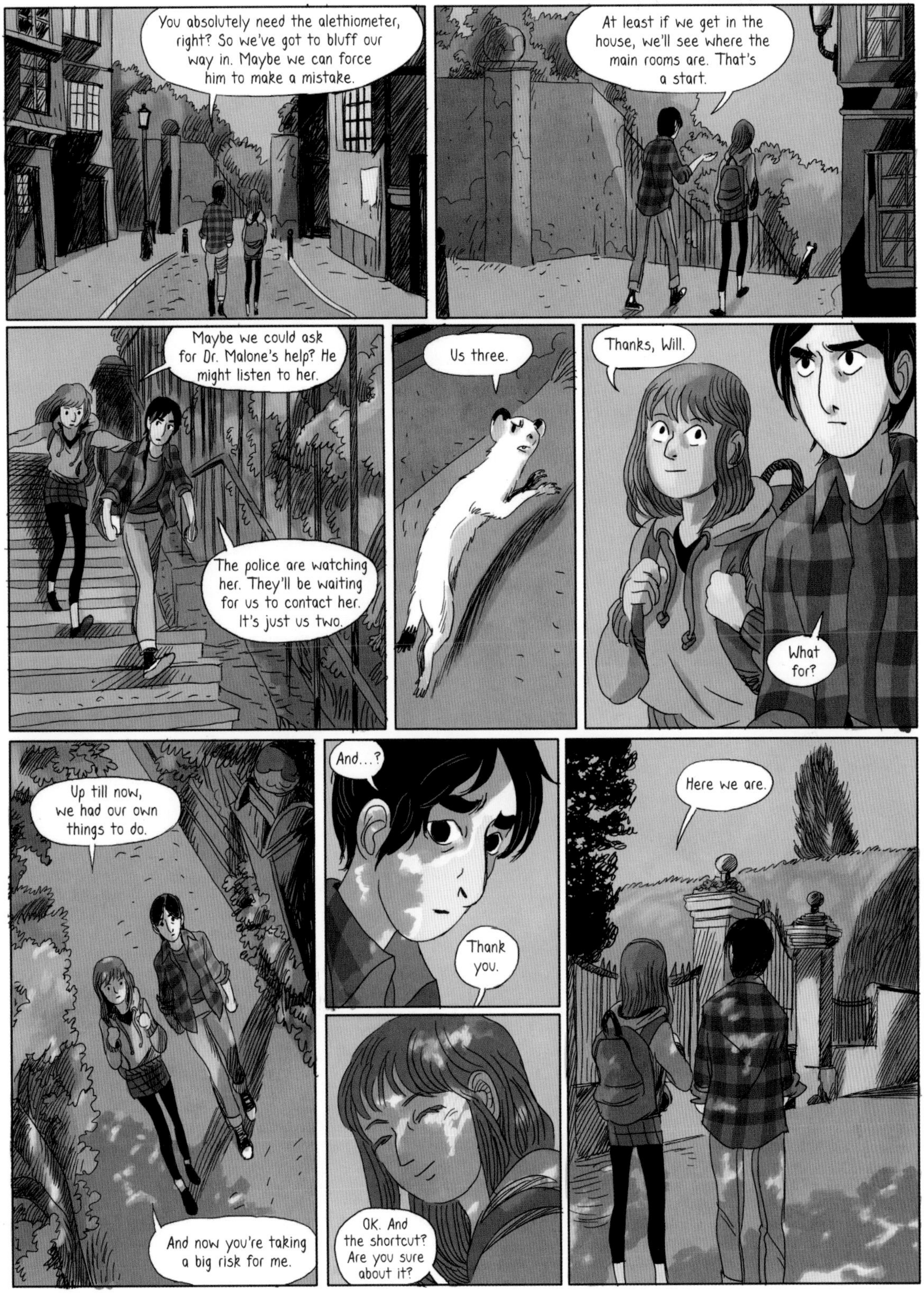
You absolutely need the alethiometer, right? So we've got to bluff our way in. Maybe we can force him to make a mistake.
At least if we get in the house, we'll see where the main rooms are. That's a start.
Maybe we could ask for Dr. Malone's help? He might listen to her.
The police are watching her. They'll be waiting for us to contact her. It's just us two.
Us three.
Thanks, Will.
What for?
Up till now, we had our own things to do.
And now you're taking a big risk for me.
And...?
Thank you.
OK. And the shortcut? Are you sure about it?
Here we are.

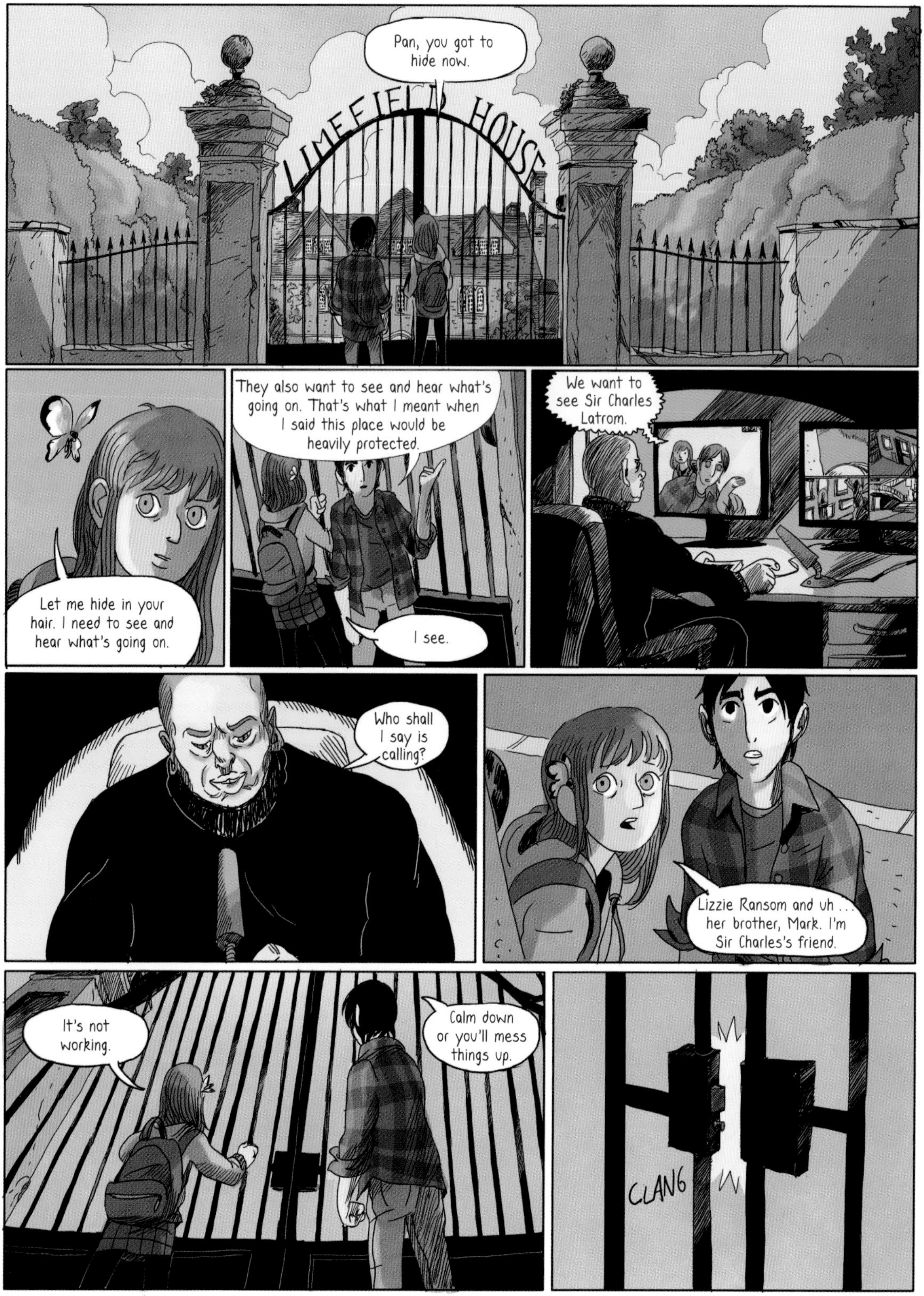
LIMEFIELD HOUSE
Pan, you got to hide now.
Let me hide in your hair. I need to see and hear what's going on.
They also want to see and hear what's going on. That's what I meant when I said this place would be heavily protected.
I see.
We want to see Sir Charles Latrom.
Who shall I say is calling?
Lizzie Ransom and uh . . . her brother, Mark. I'm Sir Charles's friend.
It's not working.
Calm down or you'll mess things up.
CLANG

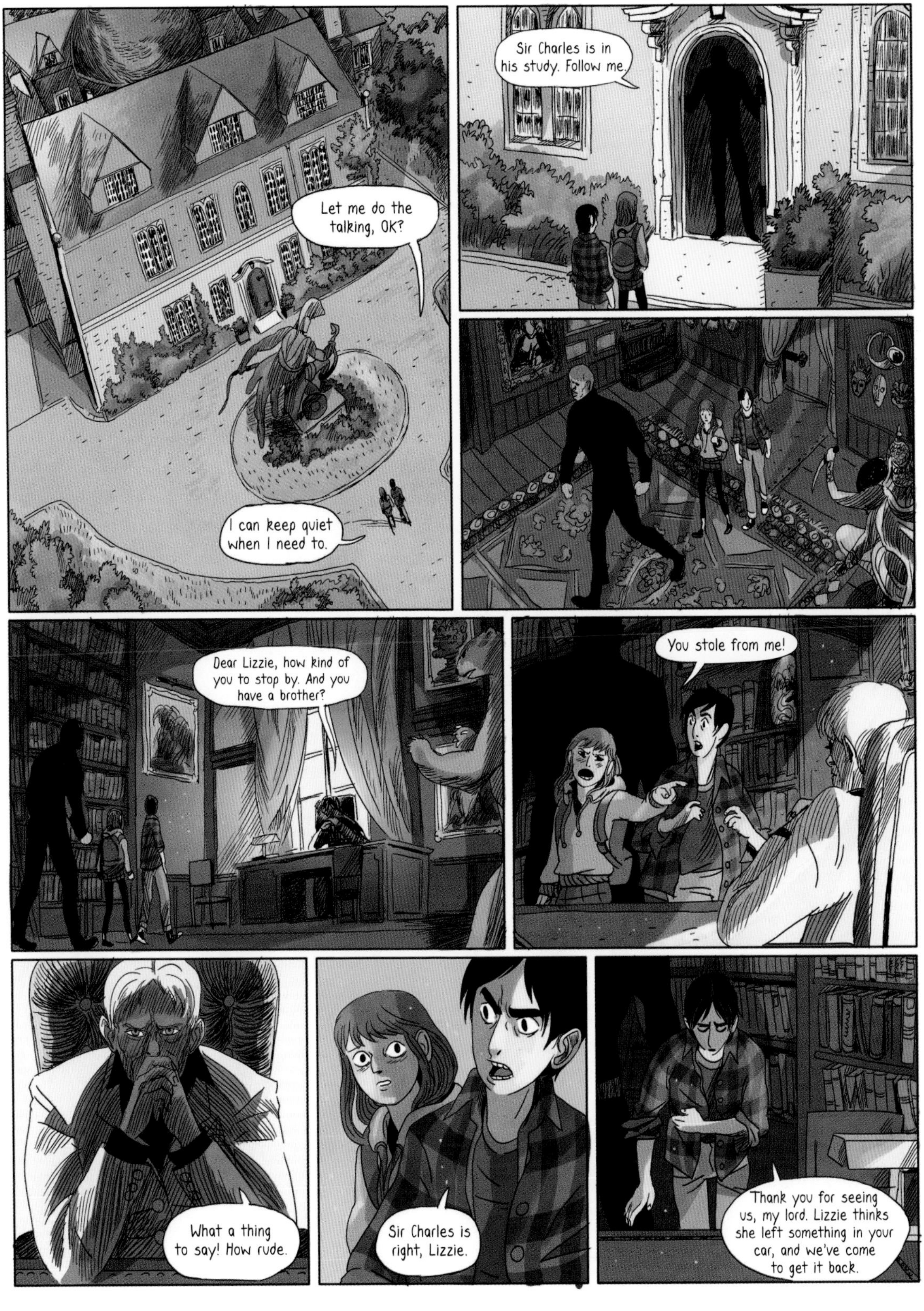

Let me do the talking, OK?
I can keep quiet when I need to.
Sir Charles is in his study. Follow me.
Dear Lizzie, how kind of you to stop by. And you have a brother?
You stole from me!
What a thing to say! How rude.
Sir Charles is right, Lizzie.
Thank you for seeing us, my lord. Lizzie thinks she left something in your car, and we've come to get it back.

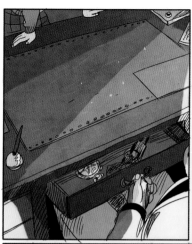

Is this the object you mean?

Yes! That's my alethiometer!

Can you prove it?

The Master of Jordan College gave it to me. Give it back, you dirty thief, or I'll call the police.

Oh yes? And who will they believe? It'll be your word against mine, and this object is certainly too precious to be yours.

You don't even know what you stole! You're worse than my mother! I hope you die!!

PTiUUU

You filthy brat!

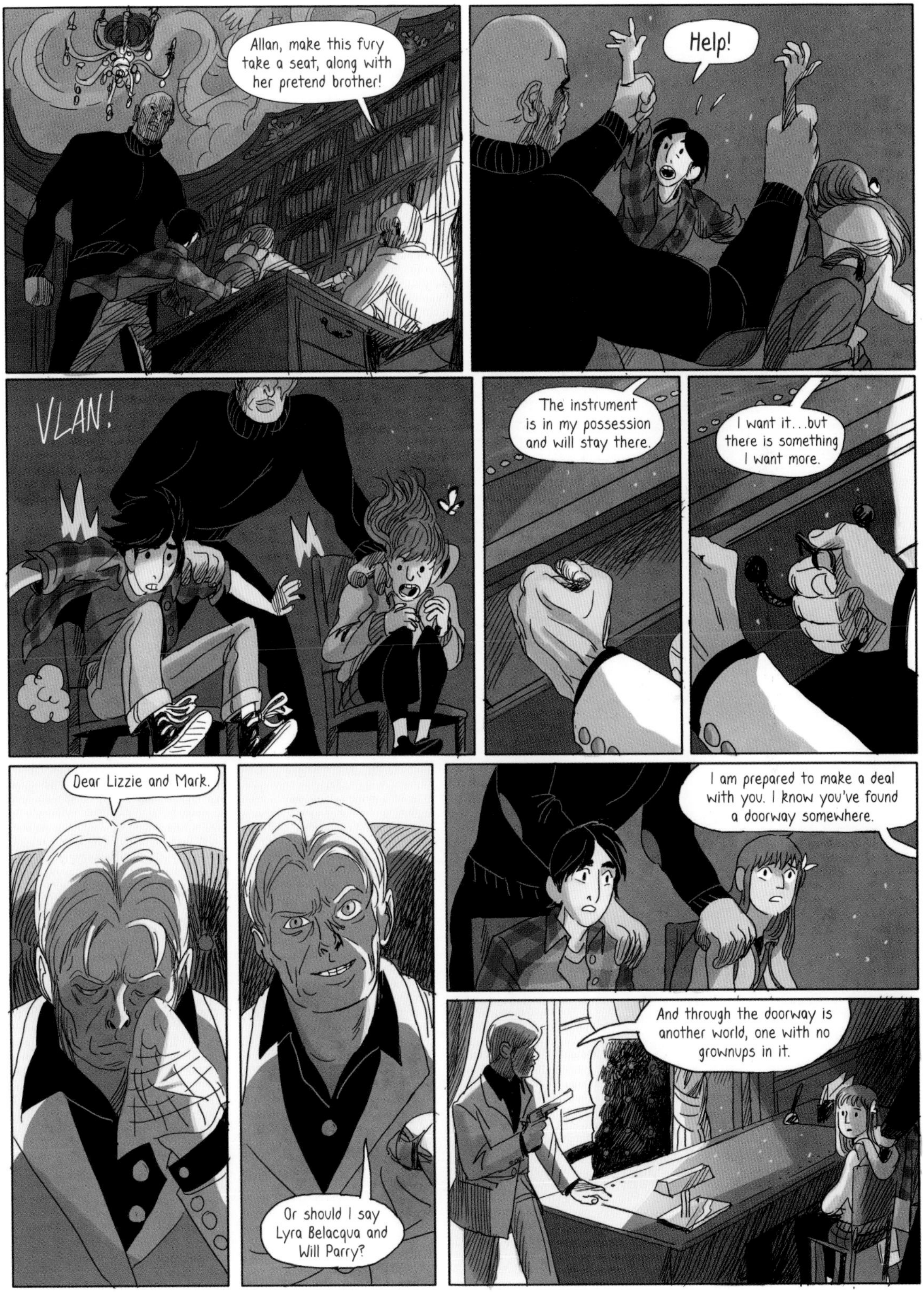
Allan, make this fury take a seat, along with her pretend brother!
Help!
VLAN!
The instrument is in my possession and will stay there.
I want it...but there is something I want more.
Dear Lizzie and Mark.
Or should I say Lyra Belacqua and Will Parry?
I am prepared to make a deal with you. I know you've found a doorway somewhere.
And through the doorway is another world, one with no grownups in it.

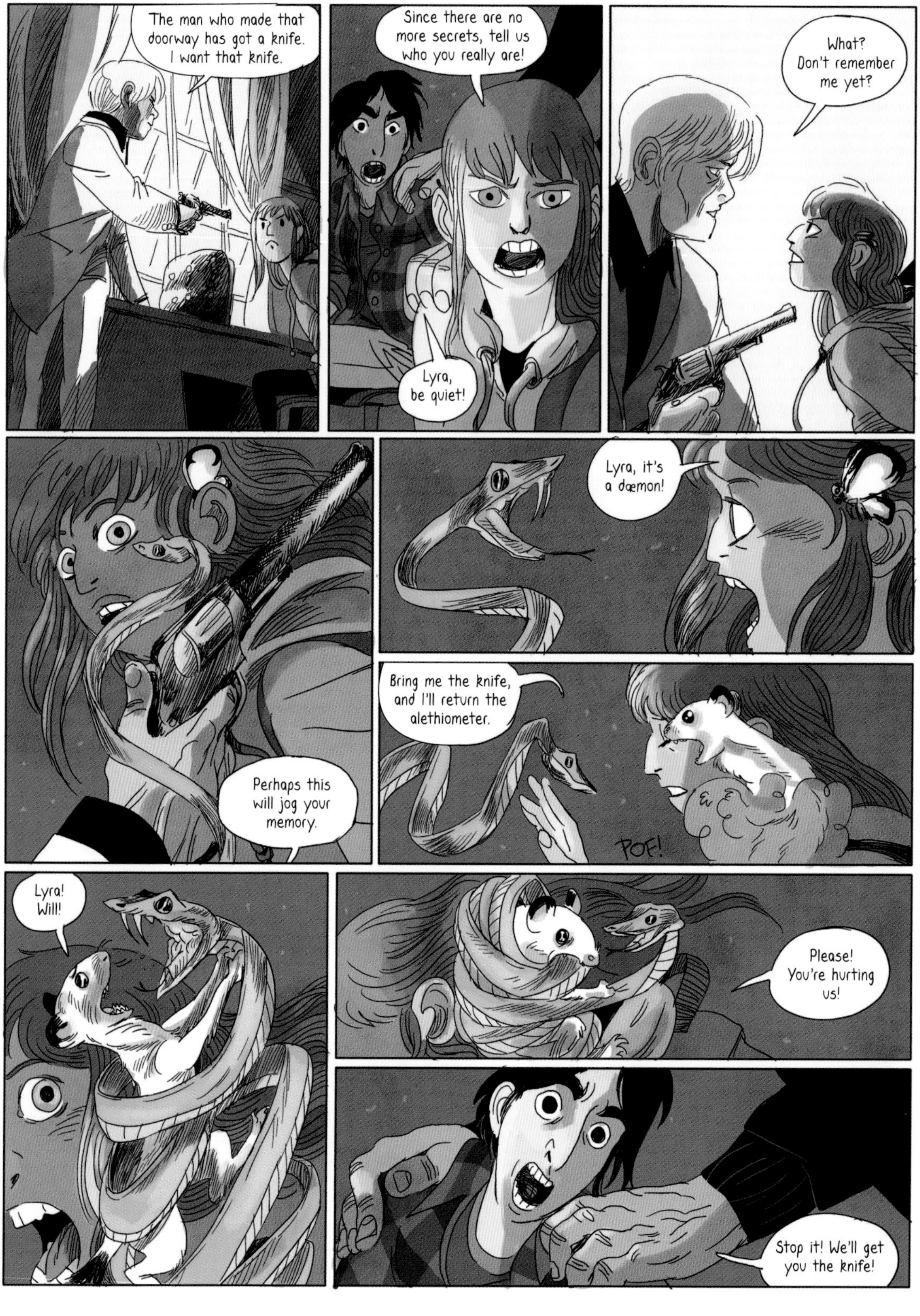
The man who made that doorway has got a knife. I want that knife.
Since there are no more secrets, tell us who you really are!
Lyra, be quiet!
What? Don't remember me yet?
Perhaps this will jog your memory.
Lyra, it's a dæmon!
Bring me the knife, and I'll return the alethiometer.
POF!
Lyra! Will!
Please! You're hurting us!
Stop it! We'll get you the knife!

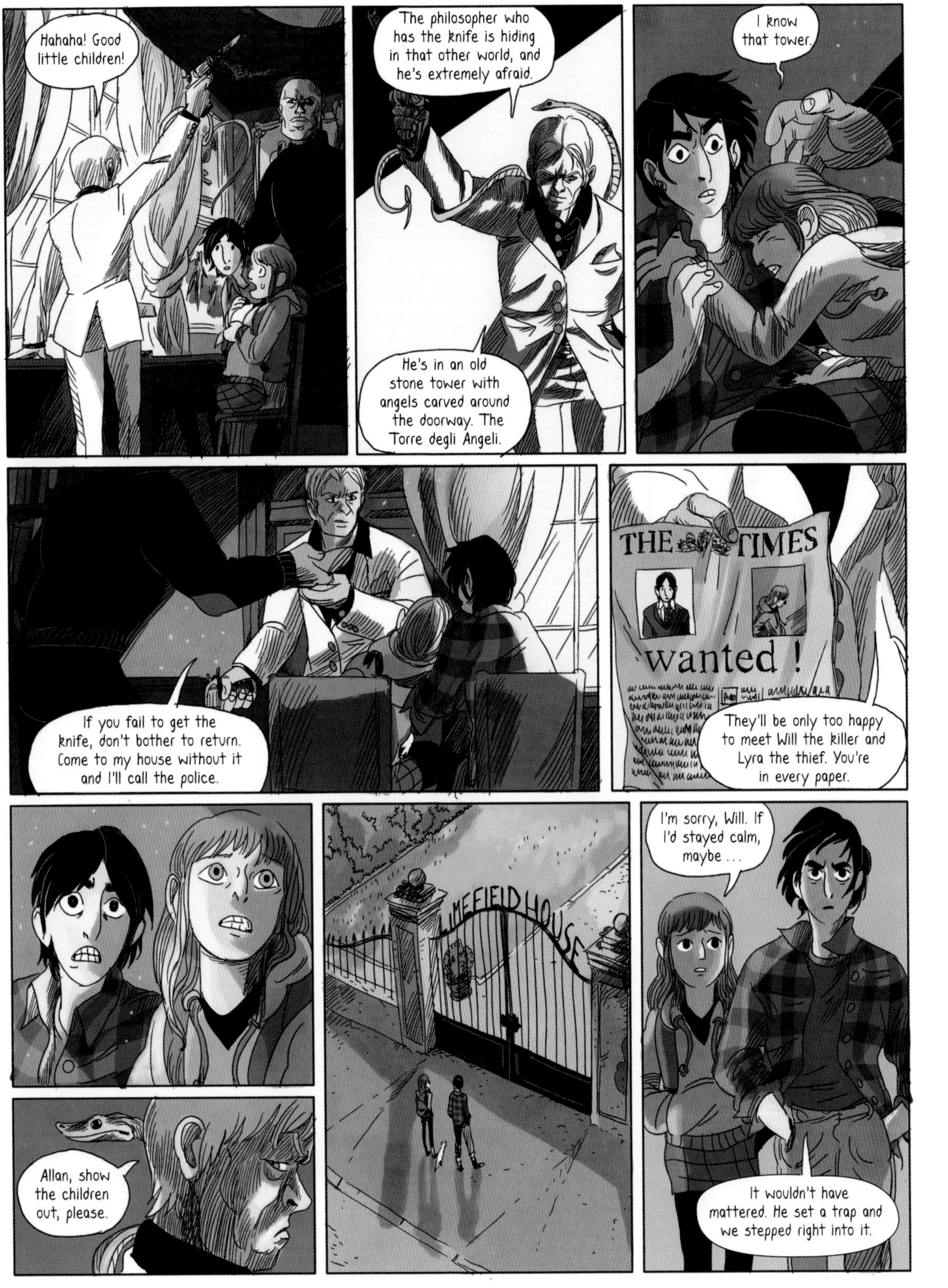
Hahaha! Good little children!
The philosopher who has the knife is hiding in that other world, and he's extremely afraid.
He's in an old stone tower with angels carved around the doorway. The Torre degli Angeli.
I know that tower.
If you fail to get the knife, don't bother to return. Come to my house without it and I'll call the police.
THE TIMES
wanted !
They'll be only too happy to meet Will the killer and Lyra the thief. You're in every paper.
Allan, show the children out, please.
LIMEFIELD HOUSE
I'm sorry, Will. If I'd stayed calm, maybe . . .
It wouldn't have mattered. He set a trap and we stepped right into it.

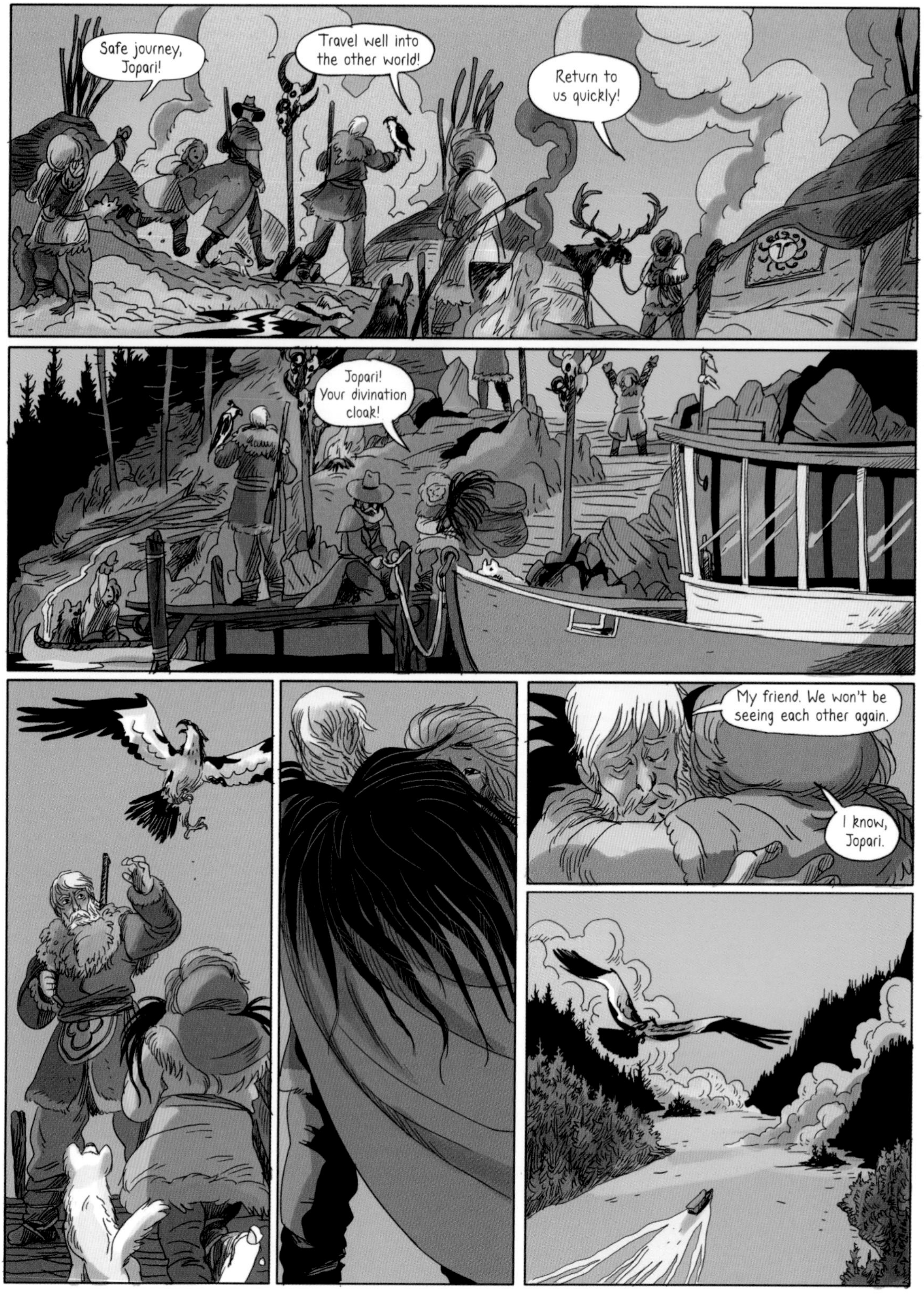
Safe journey, Jopari!
Travel well into the other world!
Return to us quickly!
Jopari! Your divination cloak!
My friend. We won't be seeing each other again.
I know, Jopari.

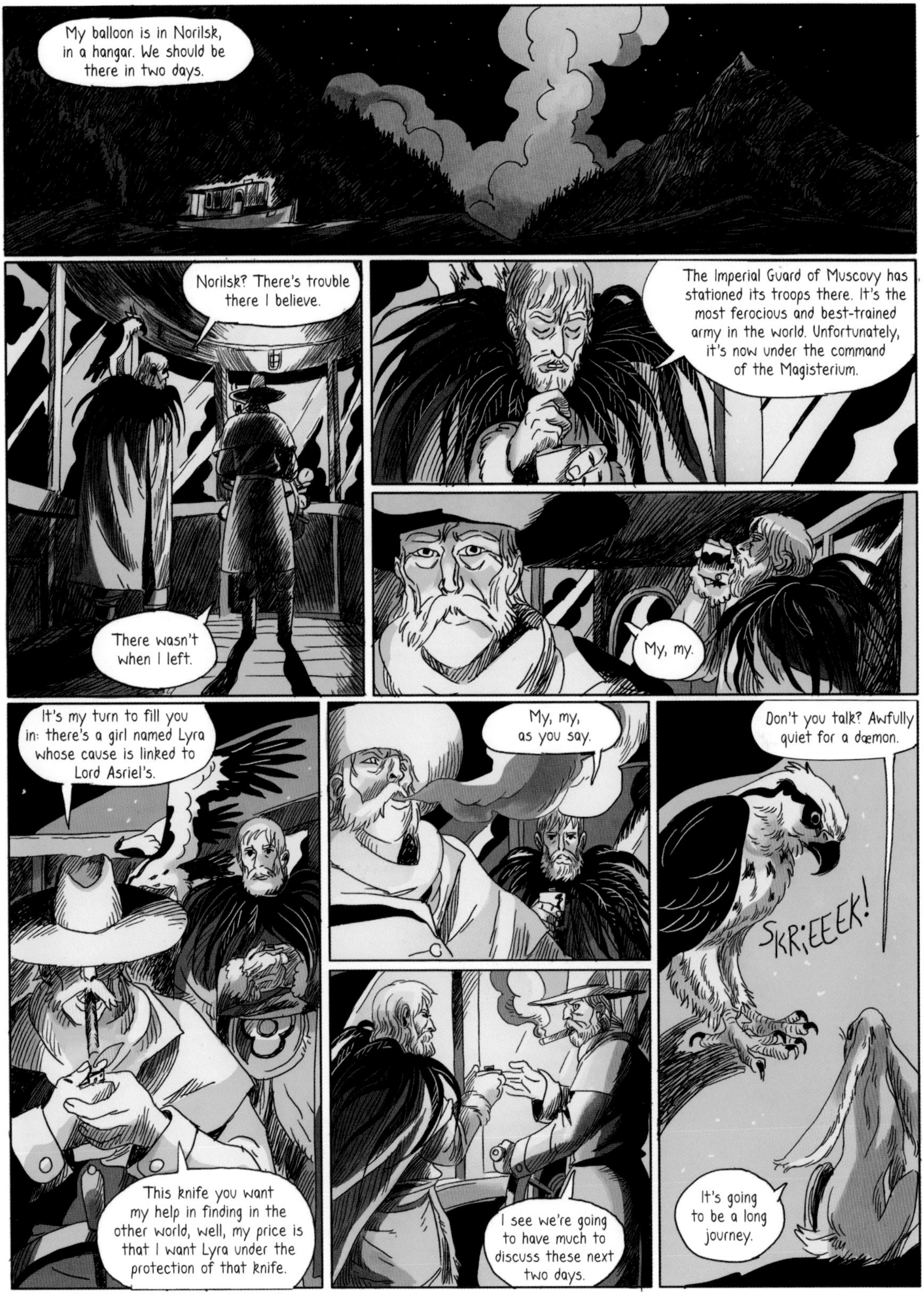
My balloon is in Norilsk, in a hangar. We should be there in two days.
Norilsk? There's trouble there I believe.
There wasn't when I left.
The Imperial Guard of Muscovy has stationed its troops there. It's the most ferocious and best-trained army in the world. Unfortunately, it's now under the command of the Magisterium.
My, my.
It's my turn to fill you in: there's a girl named Lyra whose cause is linked to Lord Asriel's.
This knife you want my help in finding in the other world, well, my price is that I want Lyra under the protection of that knife.
My, my, as you say.
I see we're going to have much to discuss these next two days.
Don't you talk? Awfully quiet for a dæmon.
SKRiEEEK!
It's going to be a long journey.

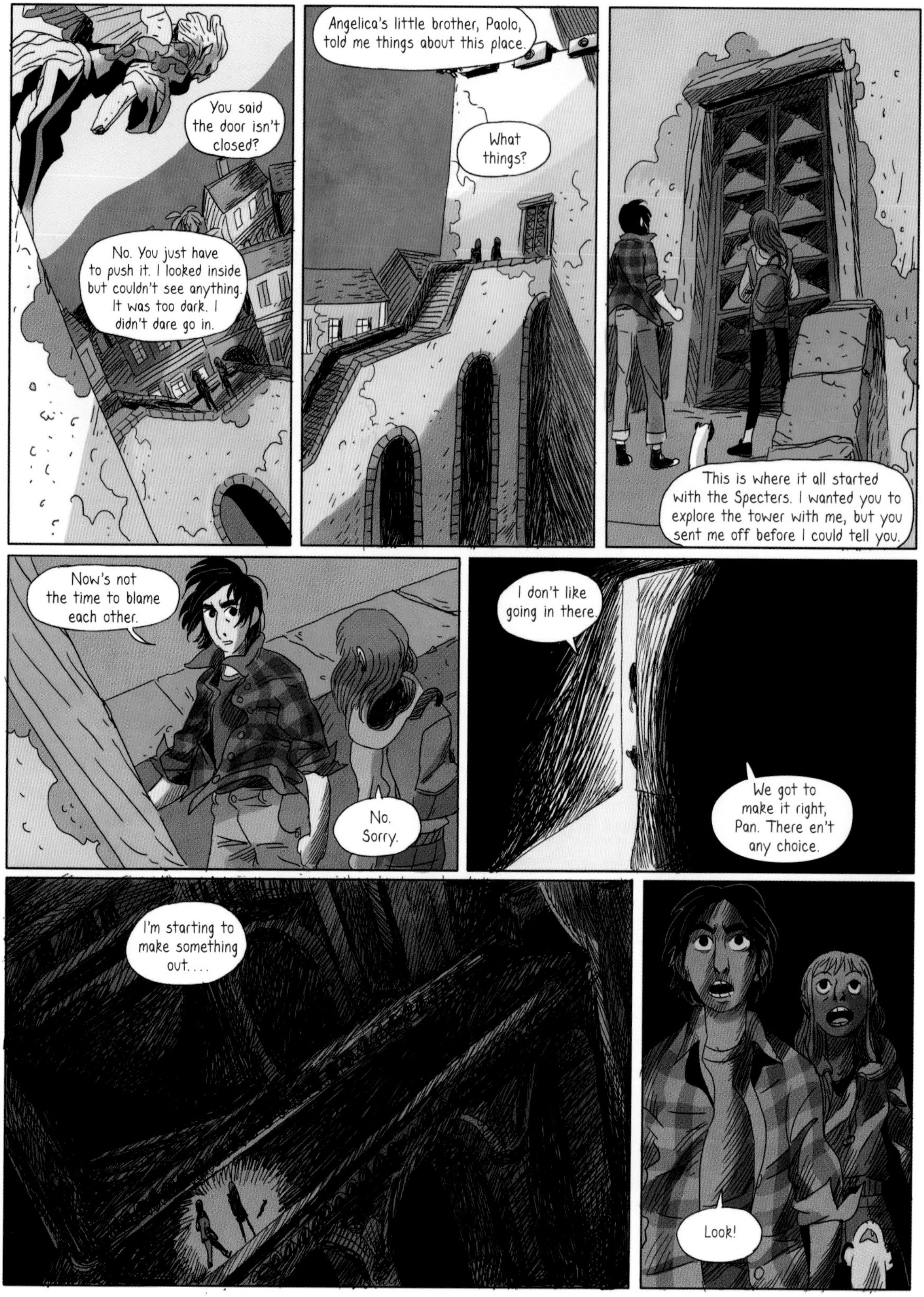
You said the door isn't closed?
No. You just have to push it. I looked inside but couldn't see anything. It was too dark. I didn't dare go in.
Angelica's little brother, Paolo, told me things about this place.
What things?
This is where it all started with the Specters. I wanted you to explore the tower with me, but you sent me off before I could tell you.
Now's not the time to blame each other.
No. Sorry.
I don't like going in there.
We got to make it right, Pan. There en't any choice.
I'm starting to make something out. . . .
Look!

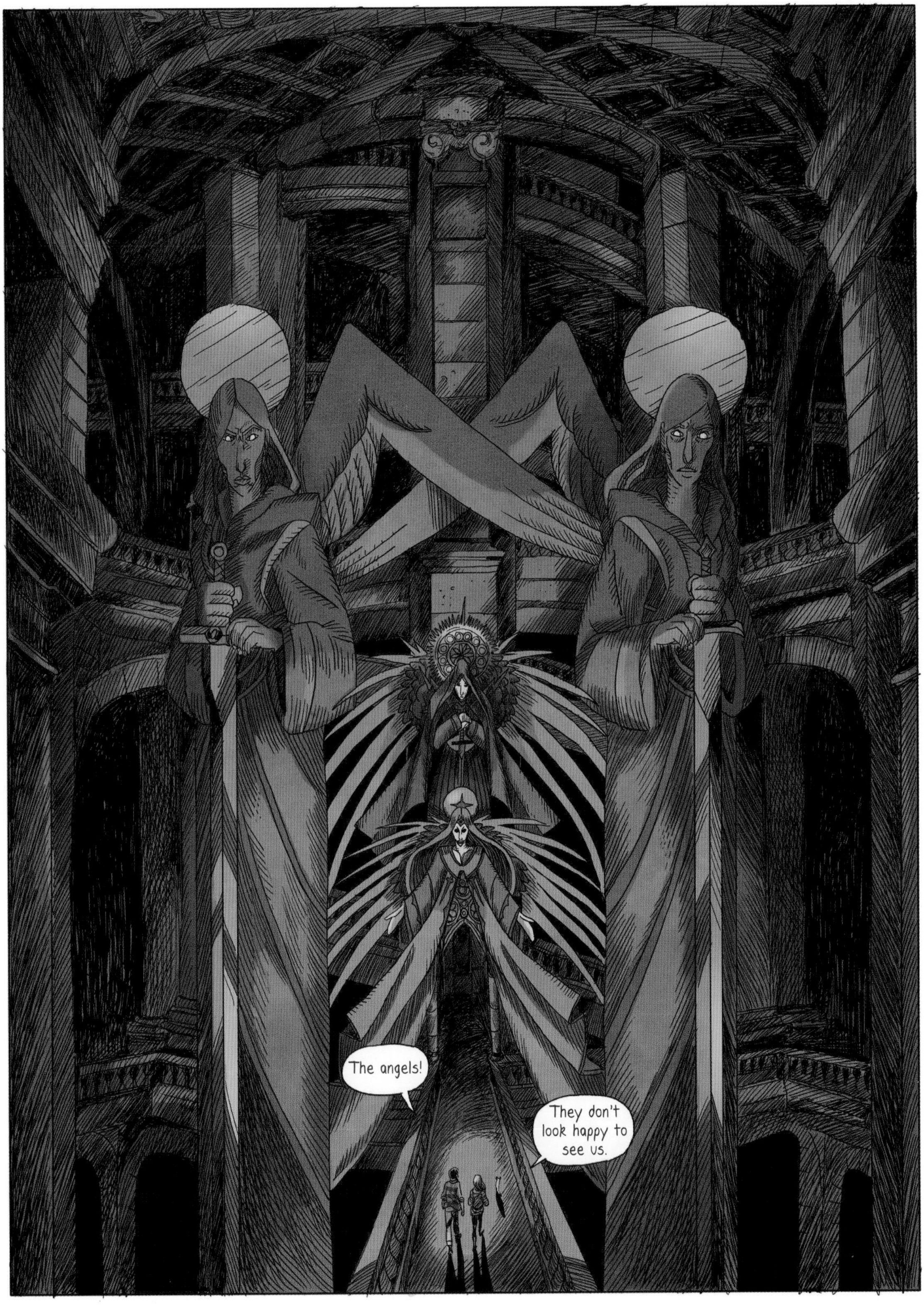
The angels!
They don't look happy to see us.

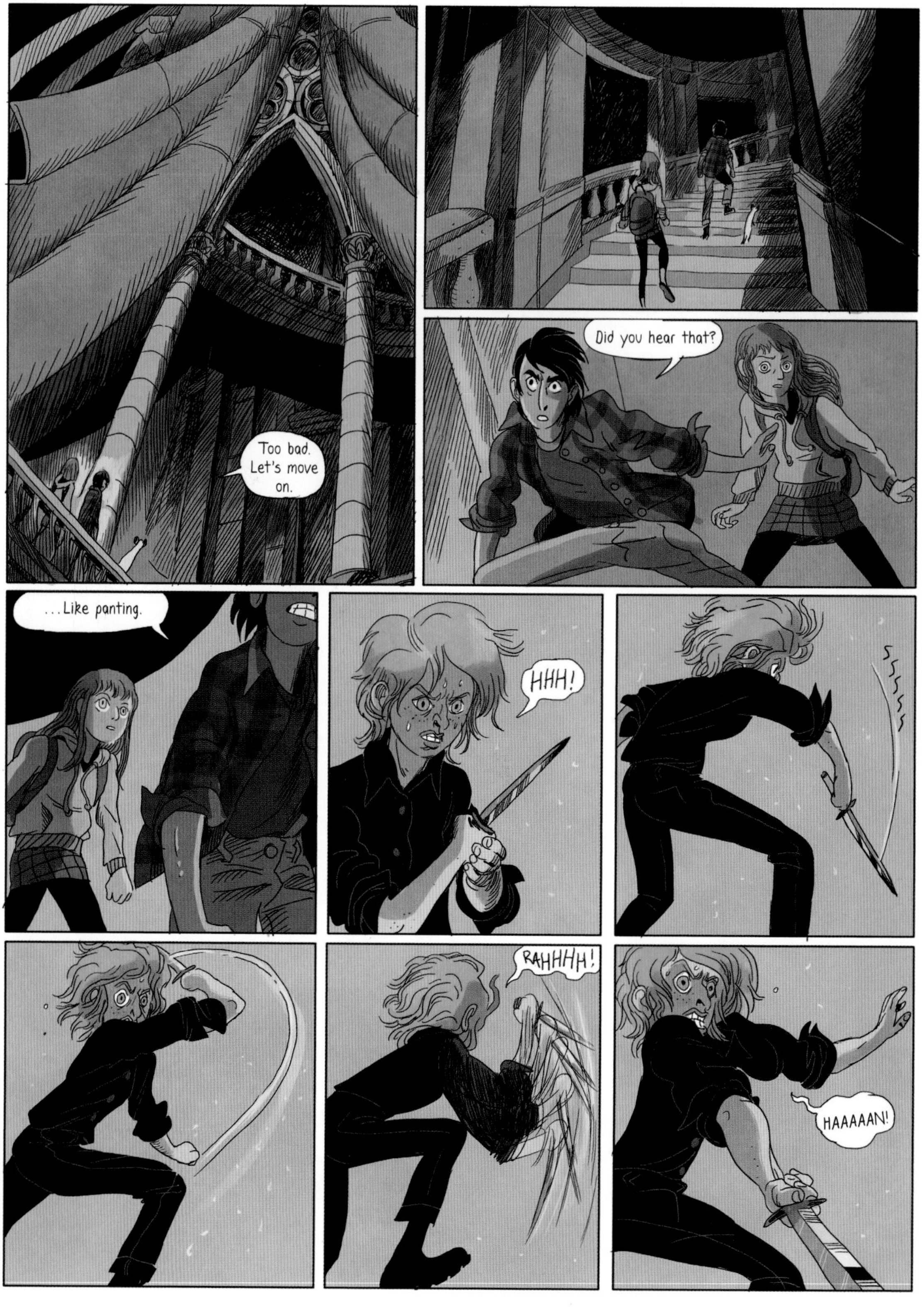
Too bad. Let's move on.
Did you hear that?
...Like panting.
HHH!
RAHHHH!
HAAAAAN!

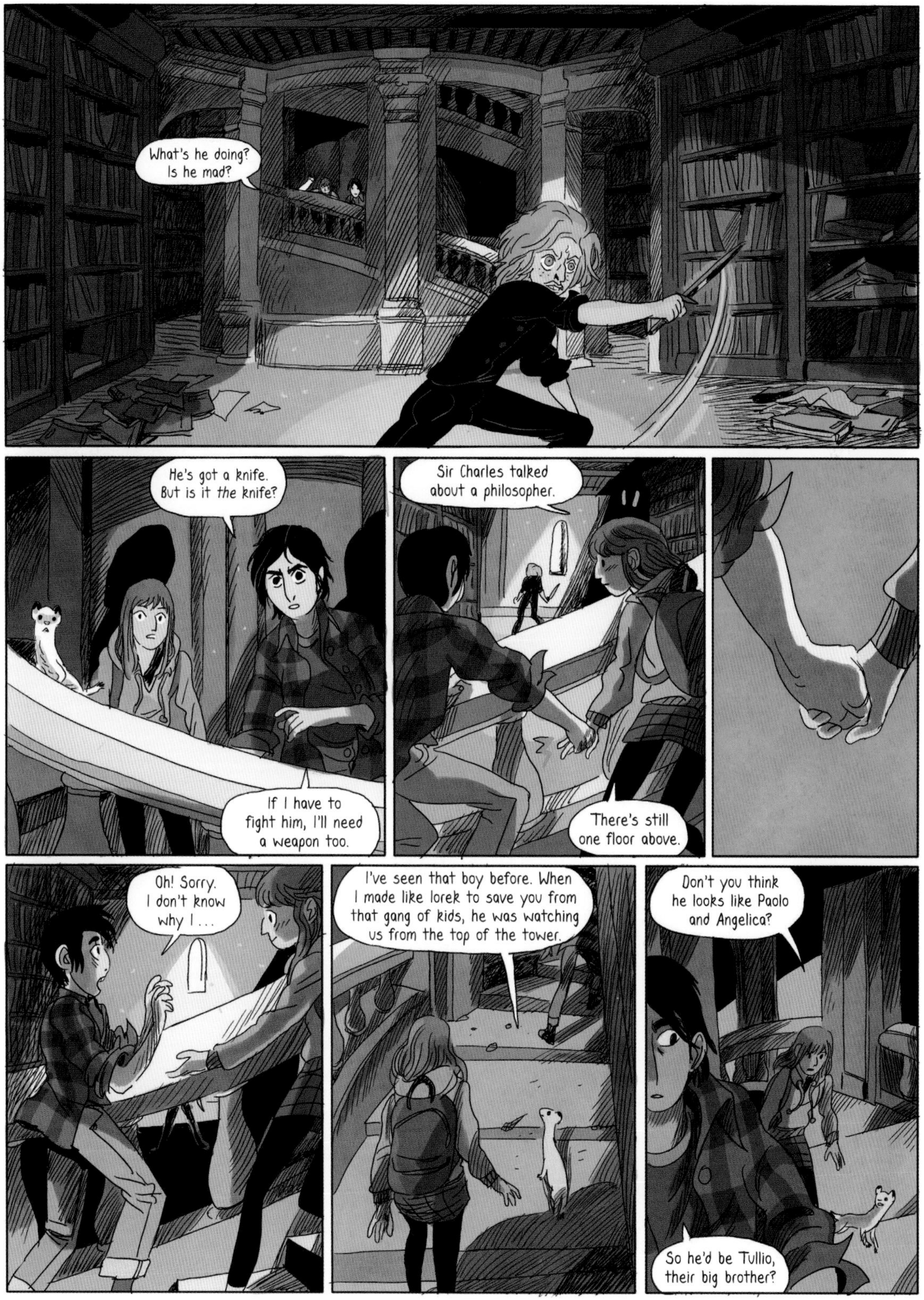
What's he doing?
Is he mad?
He's got a knife.
But is it *the* knife?
If I have to fight him, I'll need a weapon too.
Sir Charles talked about a philosopher.
There's still one floor above.
Oh! Sorry.
I don't know why I . . .
I've seen that boy before. When I made like Iorek to save you from that gang of kids, he was watching us from the top of the tower.
Don't you think he looks like Paolo and Angelica?
So he'd be Tullio, their big brother?

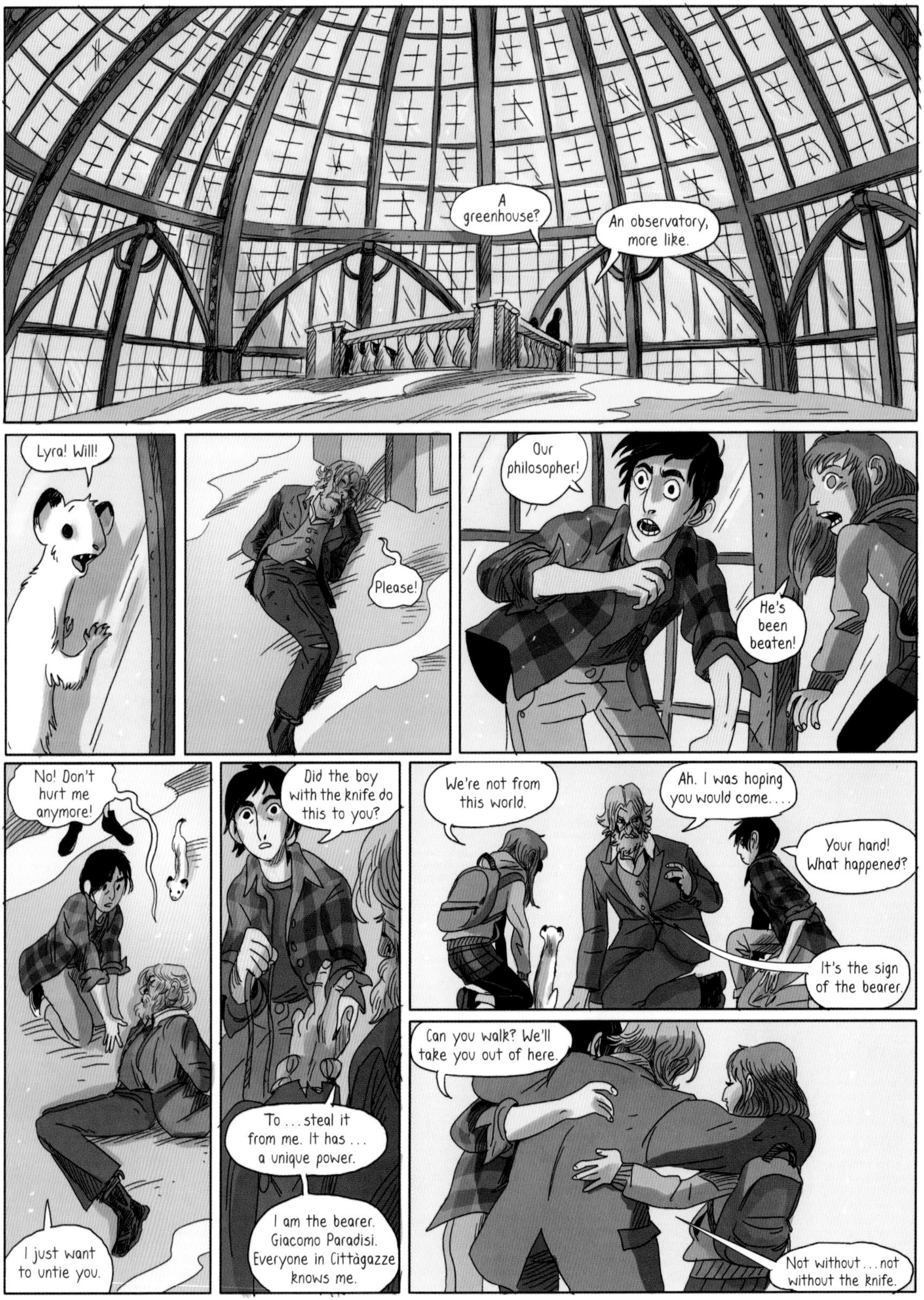
A greenhouse?
An observatory, more like.
Lyra! Will!
Please!
Our philosopher!
He's been beaten!
No! Don't hurt me anymore!
I just want to untie you.
Did the boy with the knife do this to you?
To . . . steal it from me. It has . . . a unique power.
I am the bearer. Giacomo Paradisi. Everyone in Cittàgazze knows me.
We're not from this world.
Ah. I was hoping you would come. . . .
Your hand! What happened?
It's the sign of the bearer.
Can you walk? We'll take you out of here.
Not without . . . not without the knife.

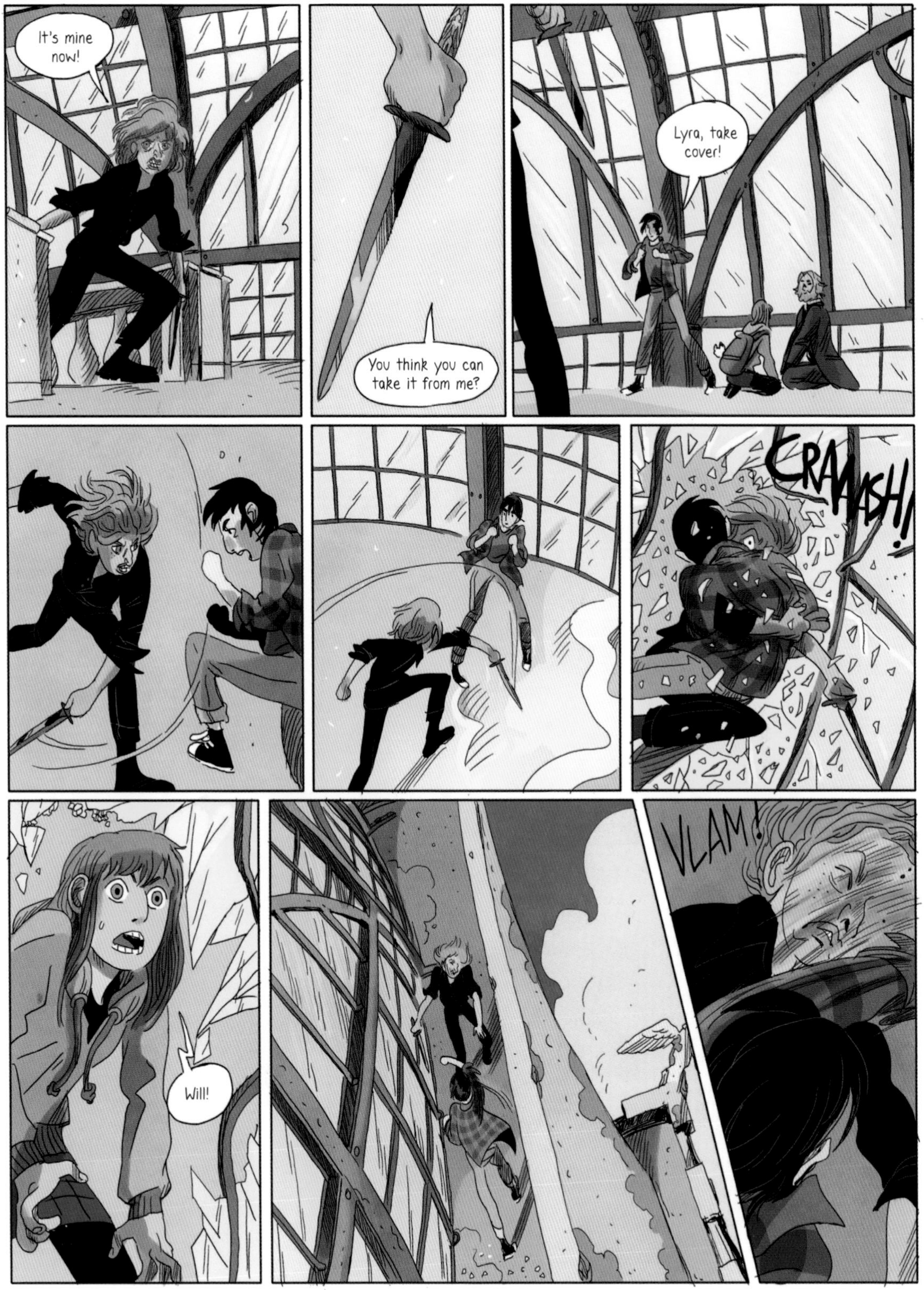

It's mine now!
You think you can take it from me?
Lyra, take cover!
CRAAASH!
Will!
VLAM!

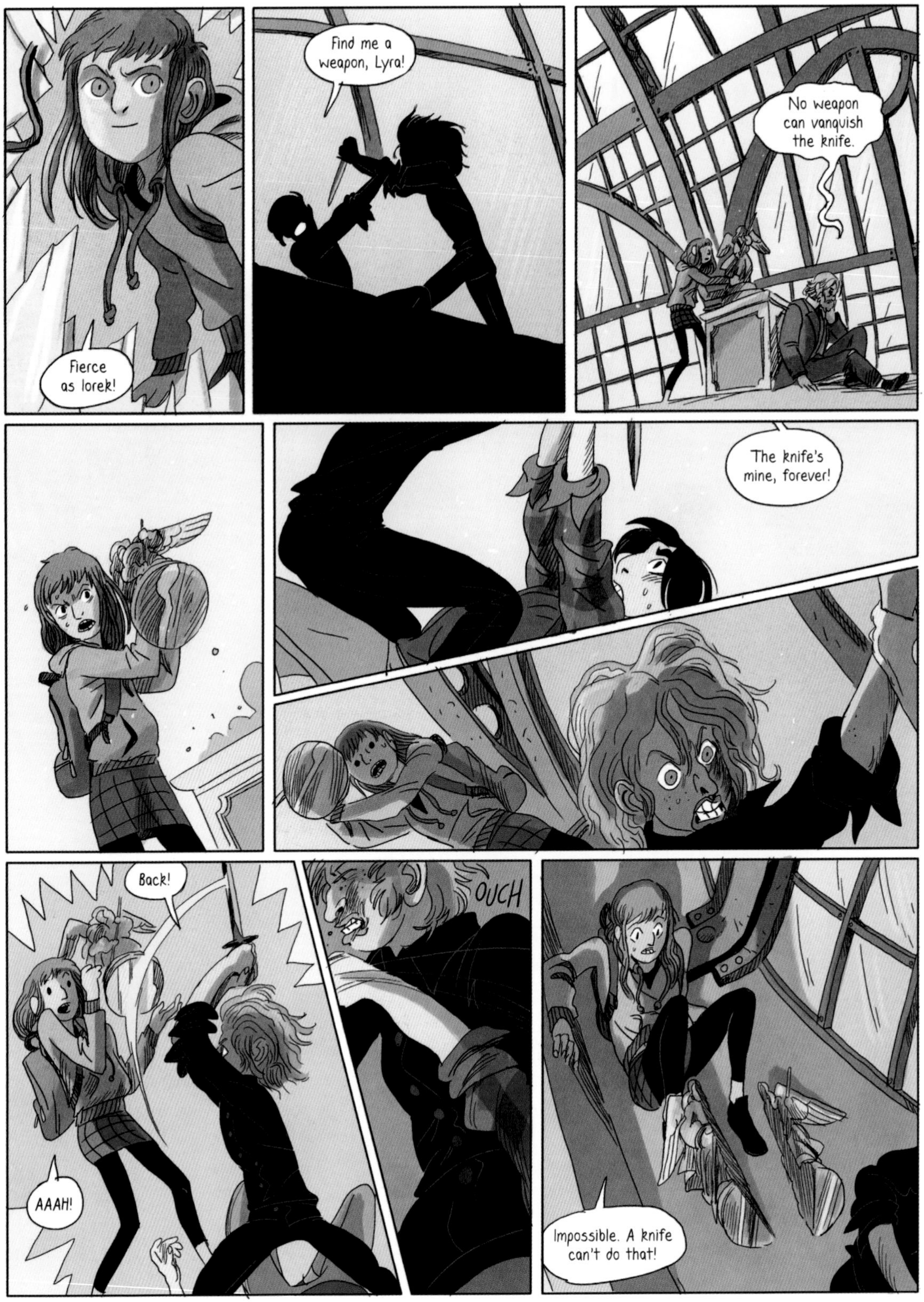
Fierce
as Iorek!
Find me a
weapon, Lyra!
No weapon
can vanquish
the knife.
The knife's
mine, forever!
Back!
AAAH!
OUCH
Impossible. A knife
can't do that!

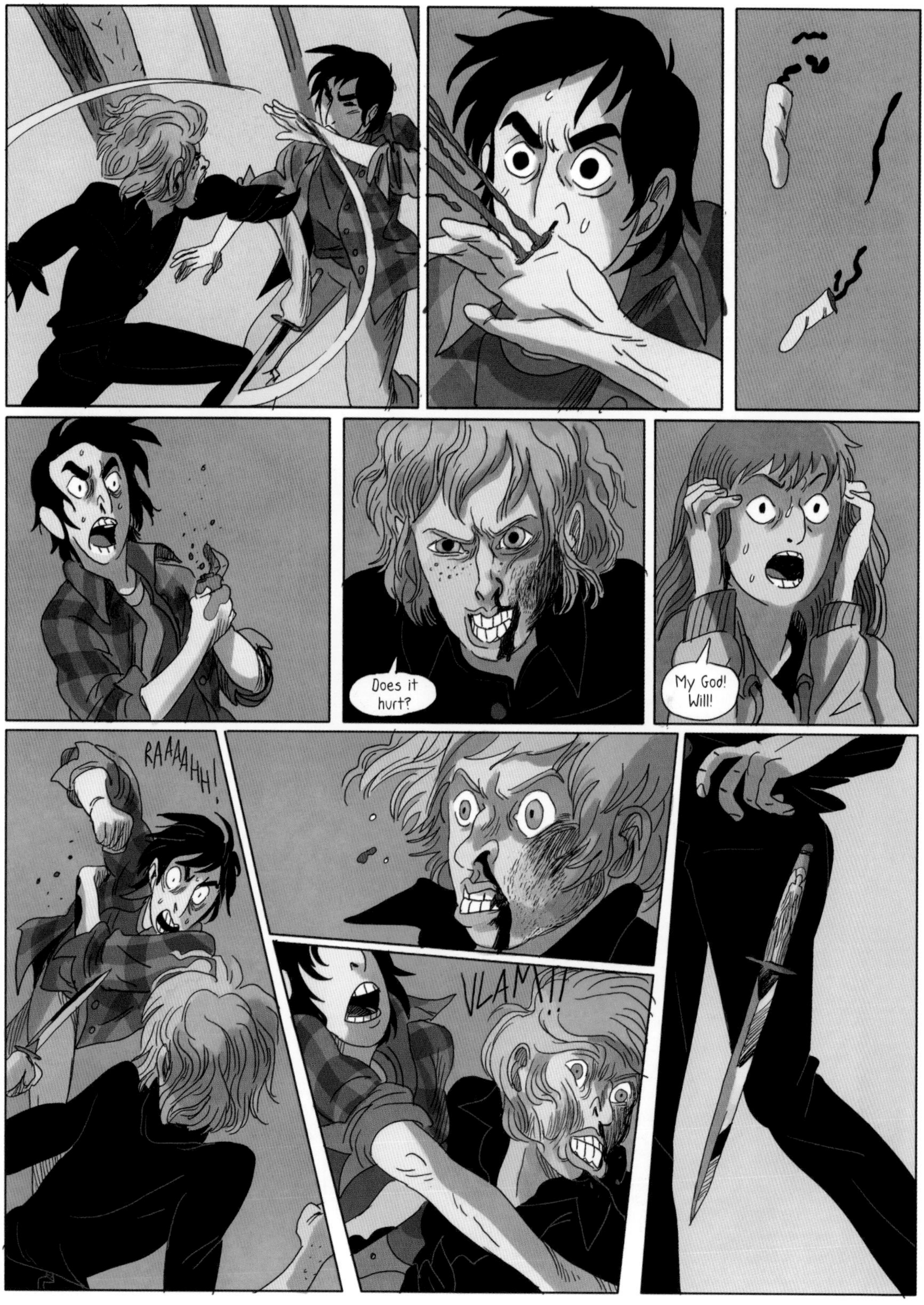
Does it hurt?
My God! Will!
RAAAAHH!
VLAM!!

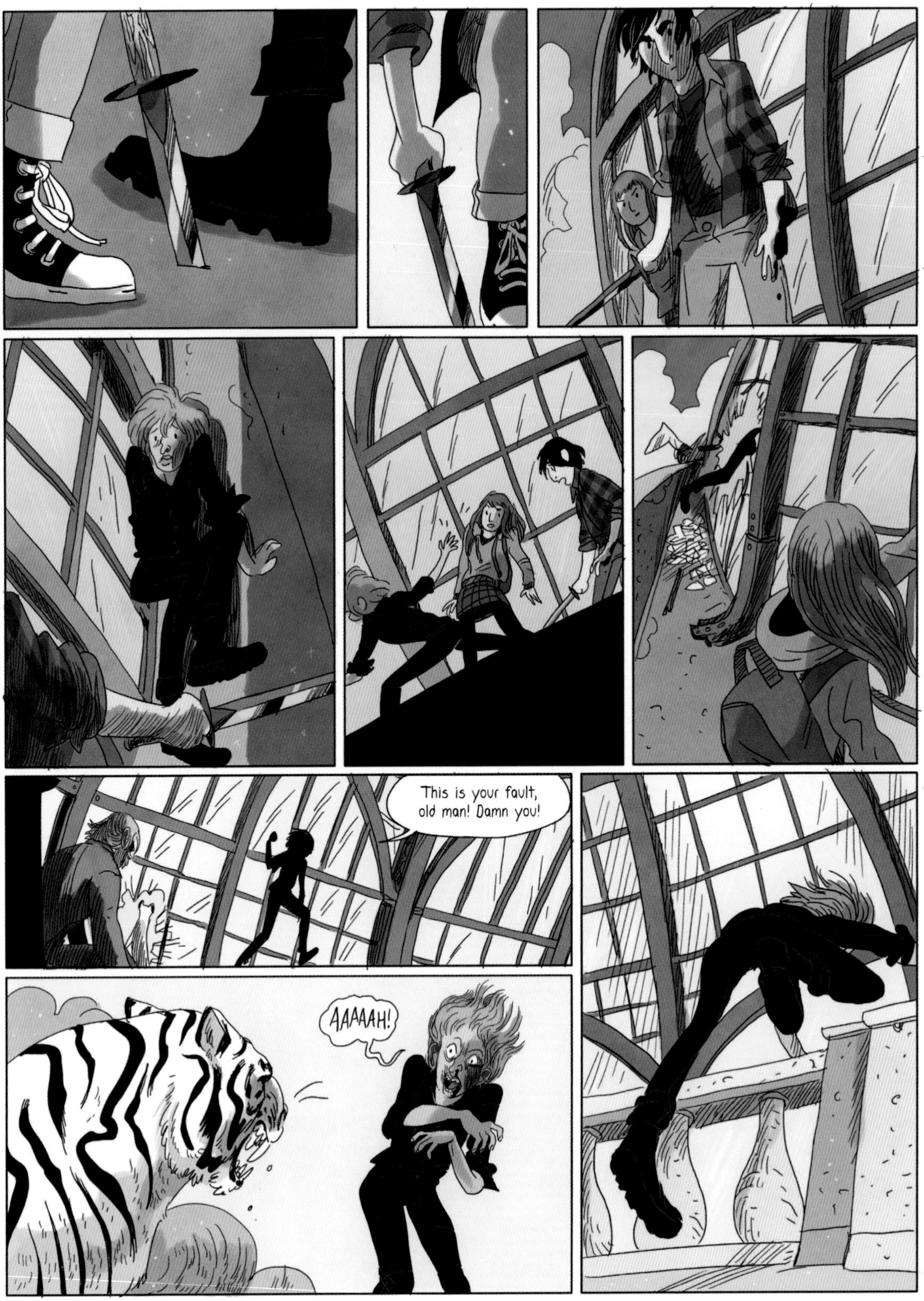
This is your fault, old man! Damn you!
AAAAAH!

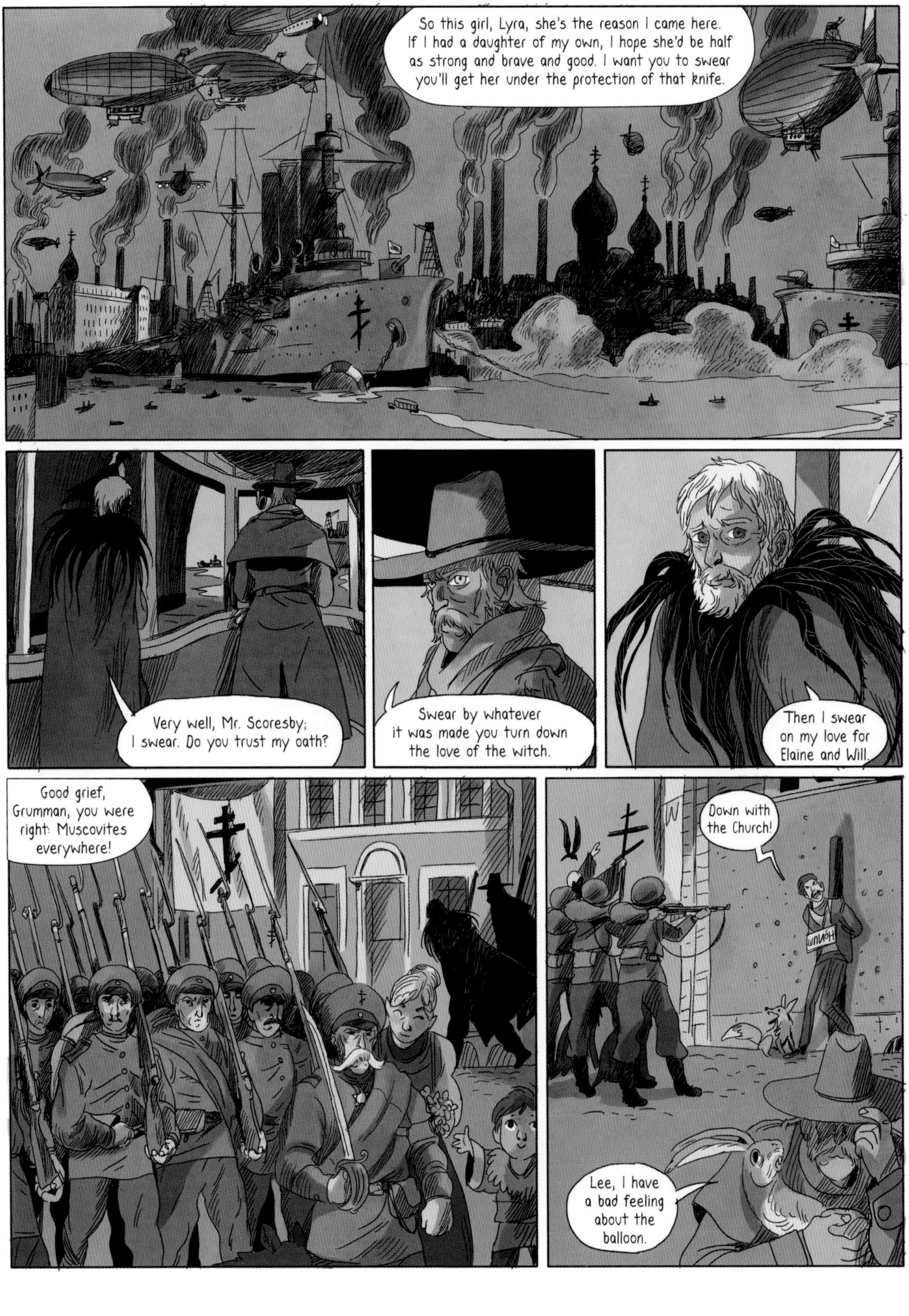
So this girl, Lyra, she's the reason I came here. If I had a daughter of my own, I hope she'd be half as strong and brave and good. I want you to swear you'll get her under the protection of that knife.
Very well, Mr. Scoresby; I swear. Do you trust my oath?
Swear by whatever it was made you turn down the love of the witch.
Then I swear on my love for Elaine and Will.
Good grief, Grumman, you were right: Muscovites everywhere!
Down with the Church!
Lee, I have a bad feeling about the balloon.

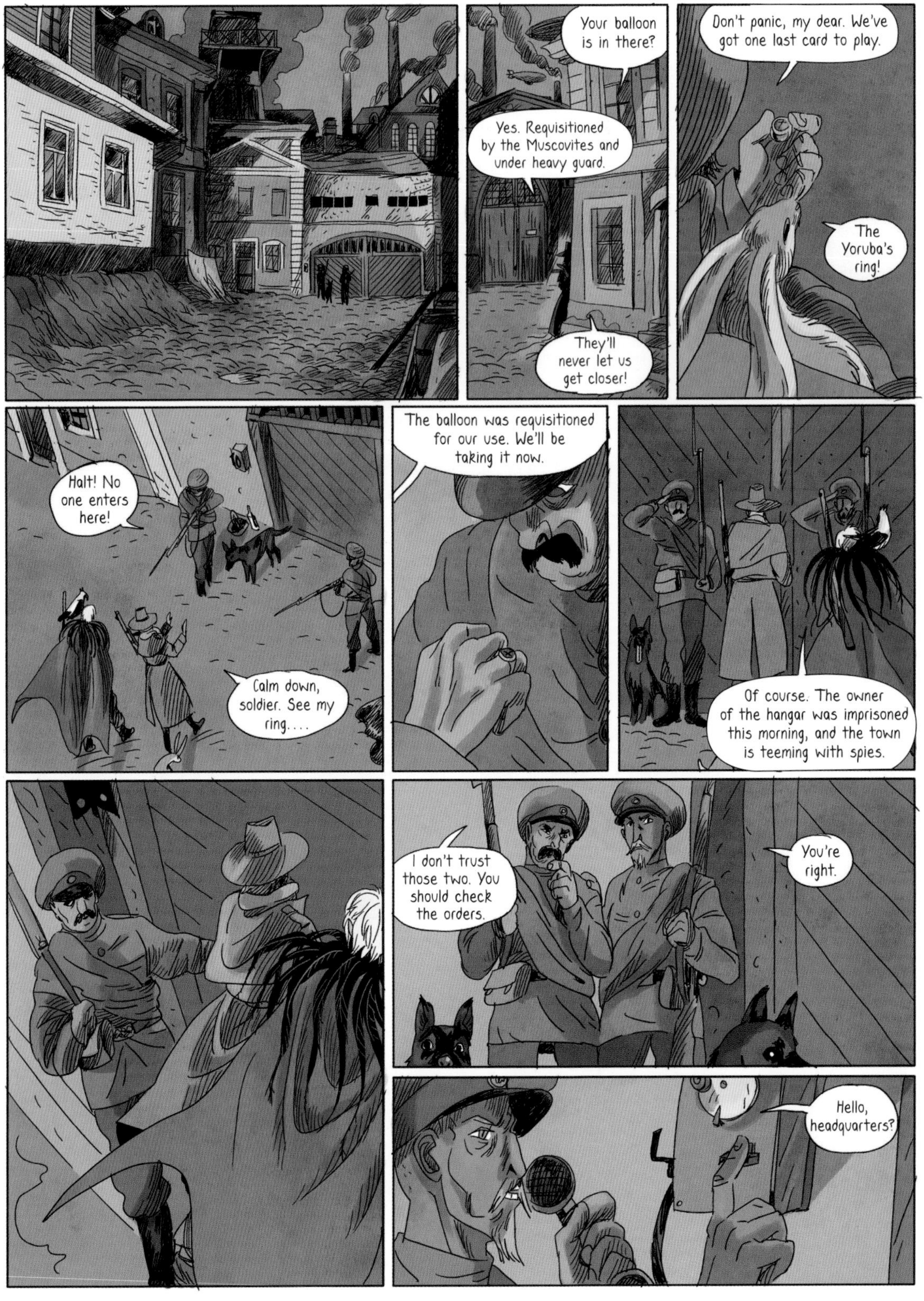
Your balloon is in there?
Yes. Requisitioned by the Muscovites and under heavy guard.
They'll never let us get closer!
Don't panic, my dear. We've got one last card to play.
The Yoruba's ring!
Halt! No one enters here!
Calm down, soldier. See my ring. . . .
The balloon was requisitioned for our use. We'll be taking it now.
Of course. The owner of the hangar was imprisoned this morning, and the town is teeming with spies.
I don't trust those two. You should check the orders.
You're right.
Hello, headquarters?

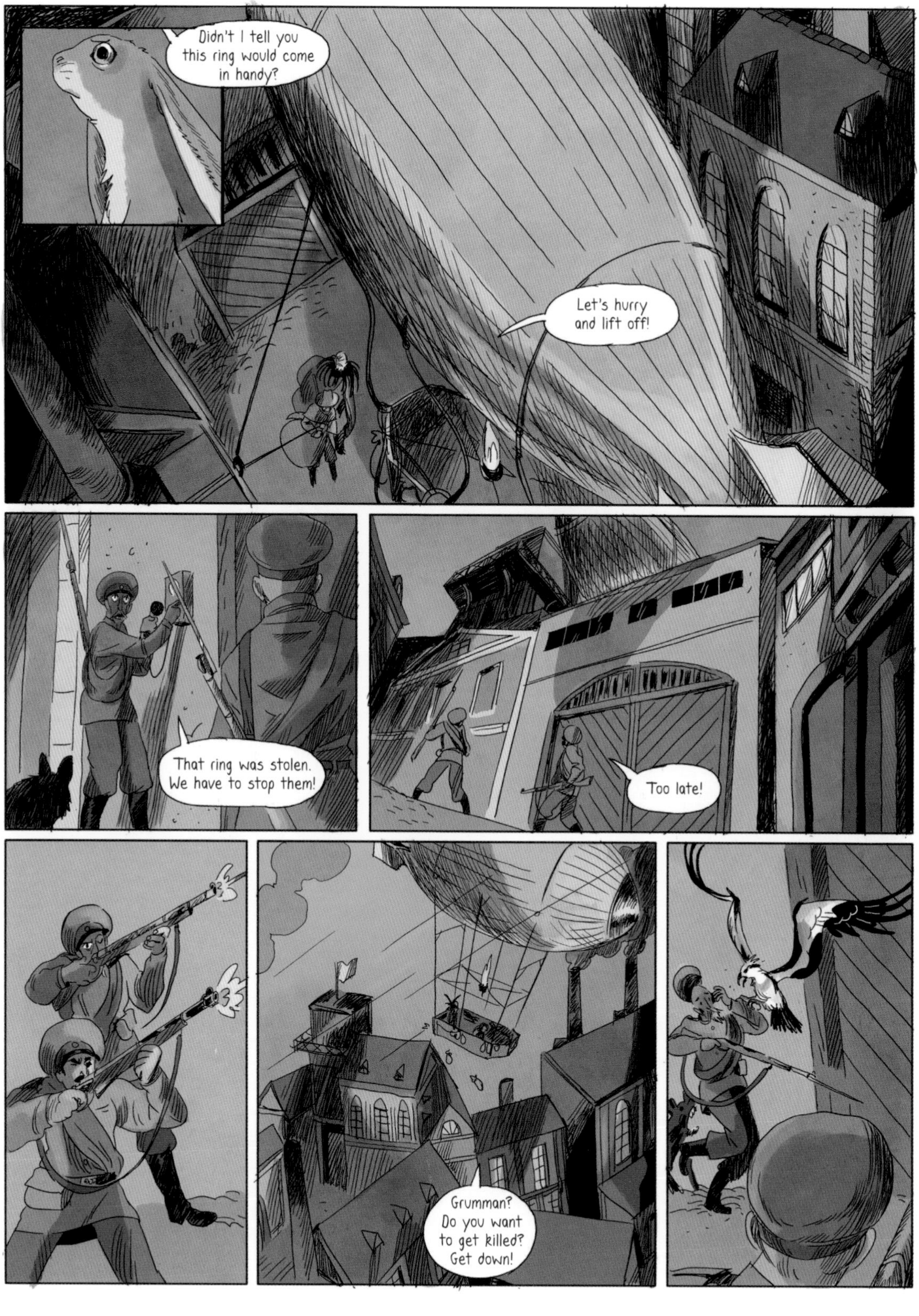
Didn't I tell you this ring would come in handy?
Let's hurry and lift off!
That ring was stolen. We have to stop them!
Too late!
Grumman? Do you want to get killed? Get down!

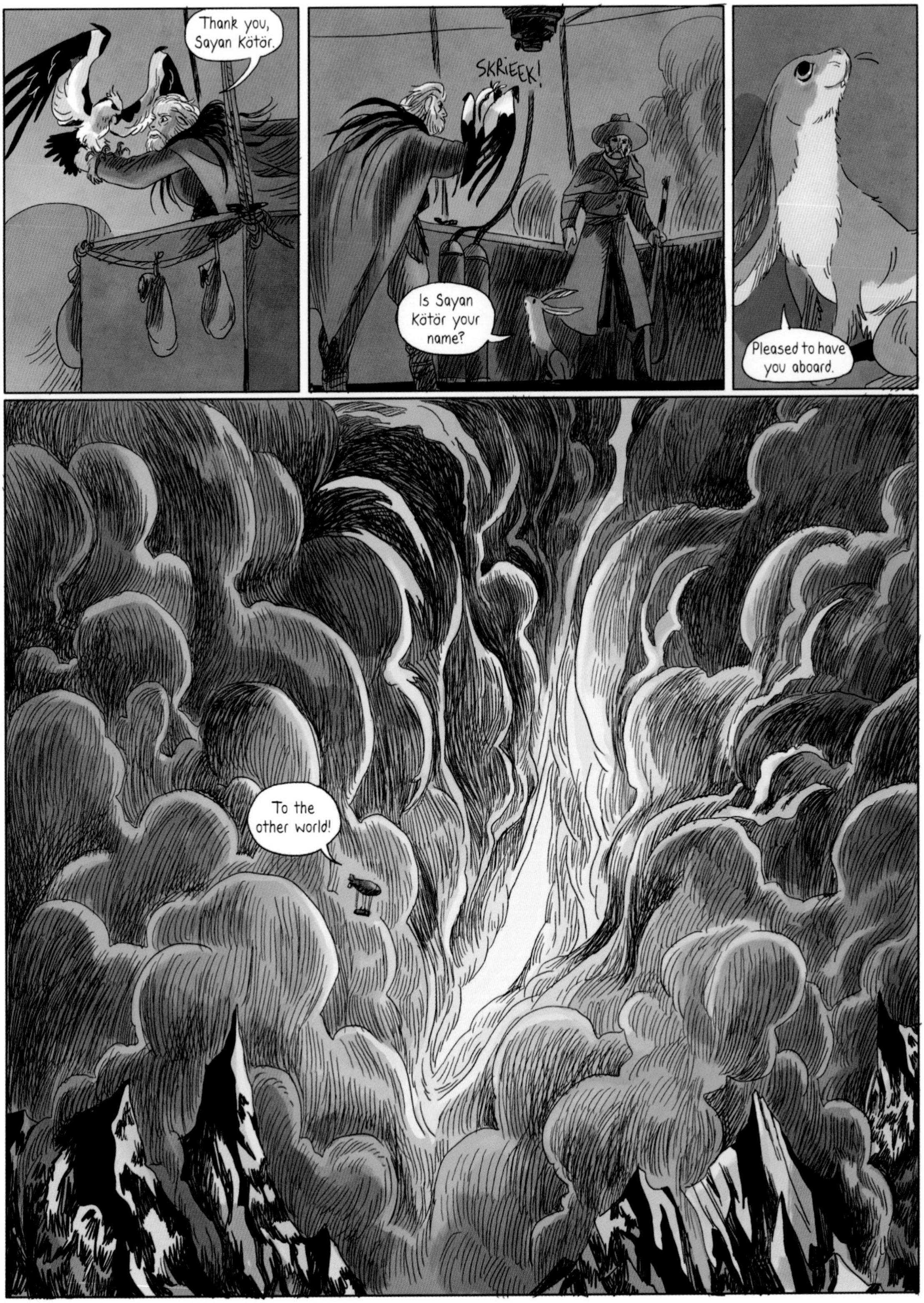
Thank you, Sayan Kötör.
SKRIEEK!
Is Sayan Kötör your name?
Pleased to have you aboard.
To the other world!

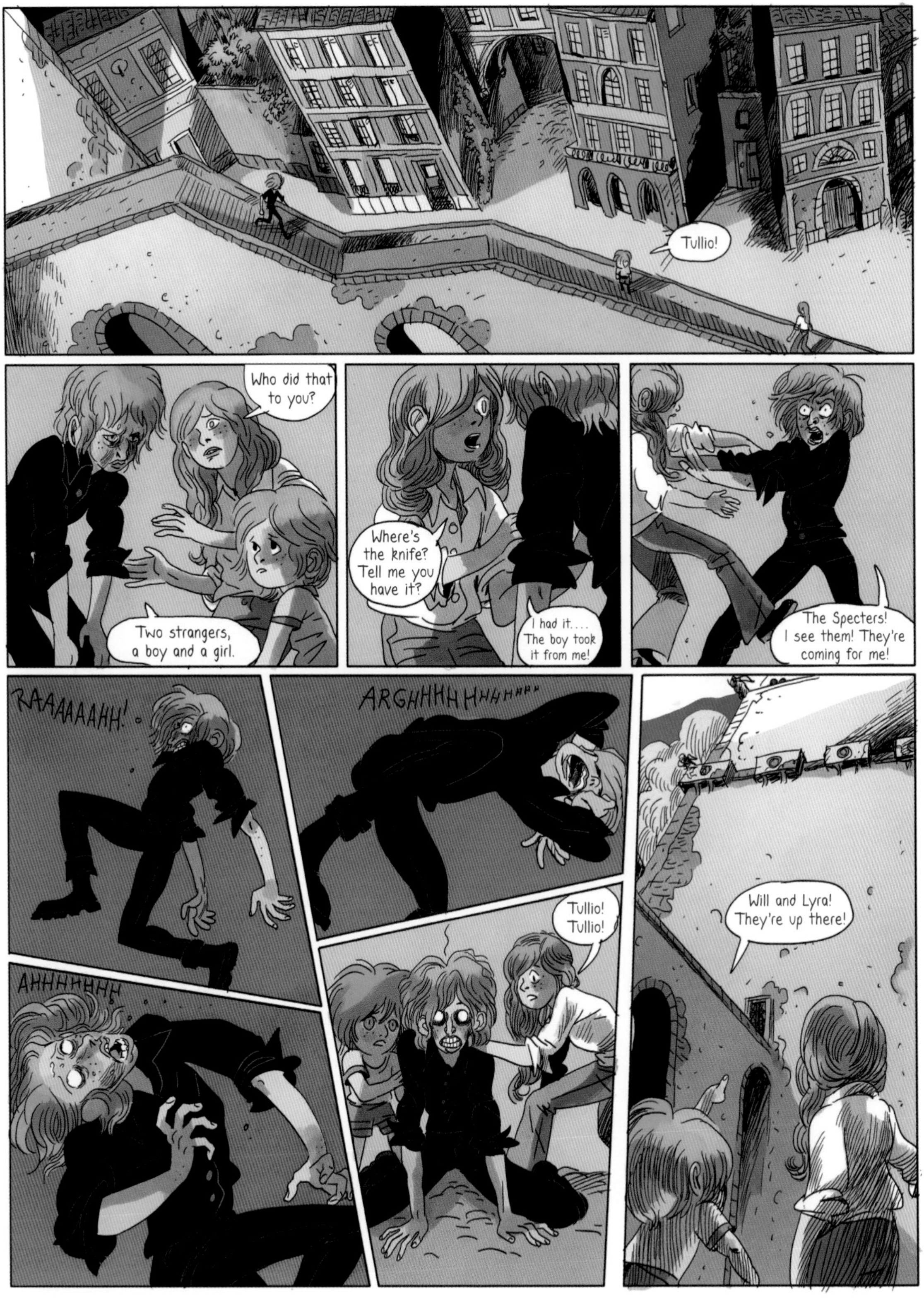

Tullio!
Who did that to you?
Two strangers, a boy and a girl.
Where's the knife? Tell me you have it?
I had it.... The boy took it from me!
The Specters! I see them! They're coming for me!
RAAAAAAHH!
ARGHHHHHhhhhhh
AHHHHHHH
Tullio! Tullio!
Will and Lyra! They're up there!

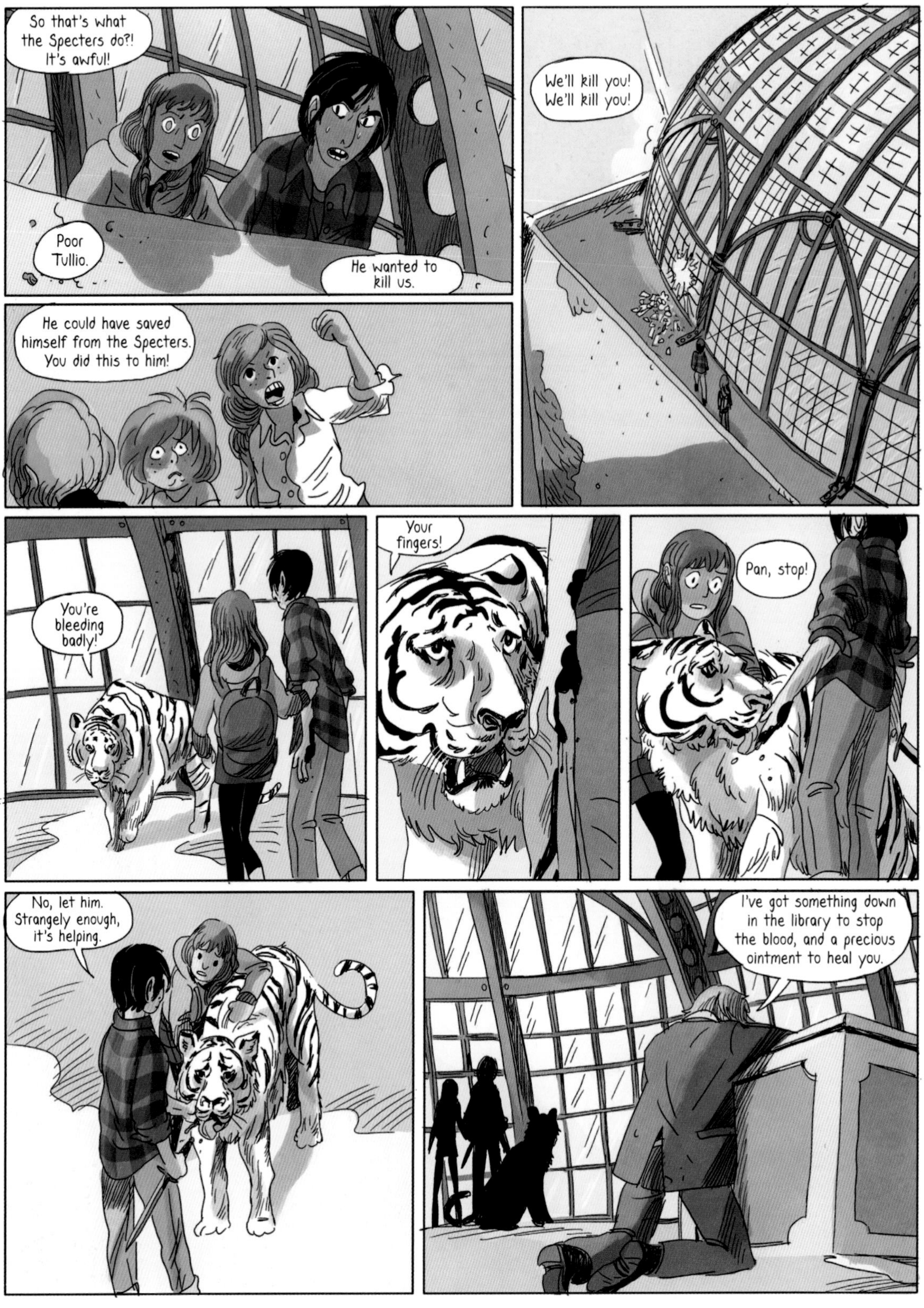
So that's what the Specters do?! It's awful!
Poor Tullio.
He wanted to kill us.
We'll kill you! We'll kill you!
He could have saved himself from the Specters. You did this to him!
You're bleeding badly!
Your fingers!
Pan, stop!
No, let him. Strangely enough, it's helping.
I've got something down in the library to stop the blood, and a precious ointment to heal you.

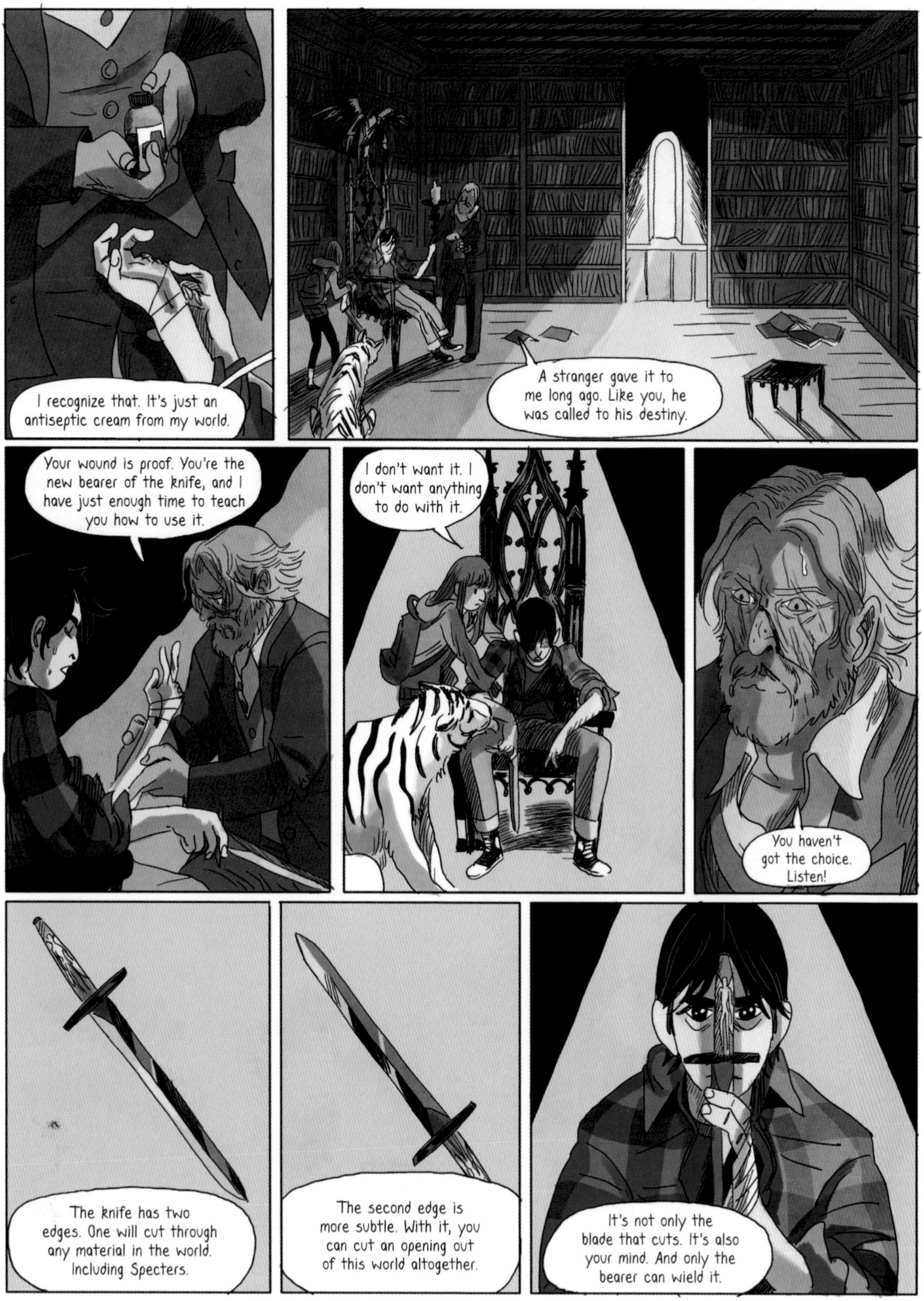
I recognize that. It's just an antiseptic cream from my world.
A stranger gave it to me long ago. Like you, he was called to his destiny.
Your wound is proof. You're the new bearer of the knife, and I have just enough time to teach you how to use it.
I don't want it. I don't want anything to do with it.
You haven't got the choice. Listen!
The knife has two edges. One will cut through any material in the world. Including Specters.
The second edge is more subtle. With it, you can cut an opening out of this world altogether.
It's not only the blade that cuts. It's also your mind. And only the bearer can wield it.

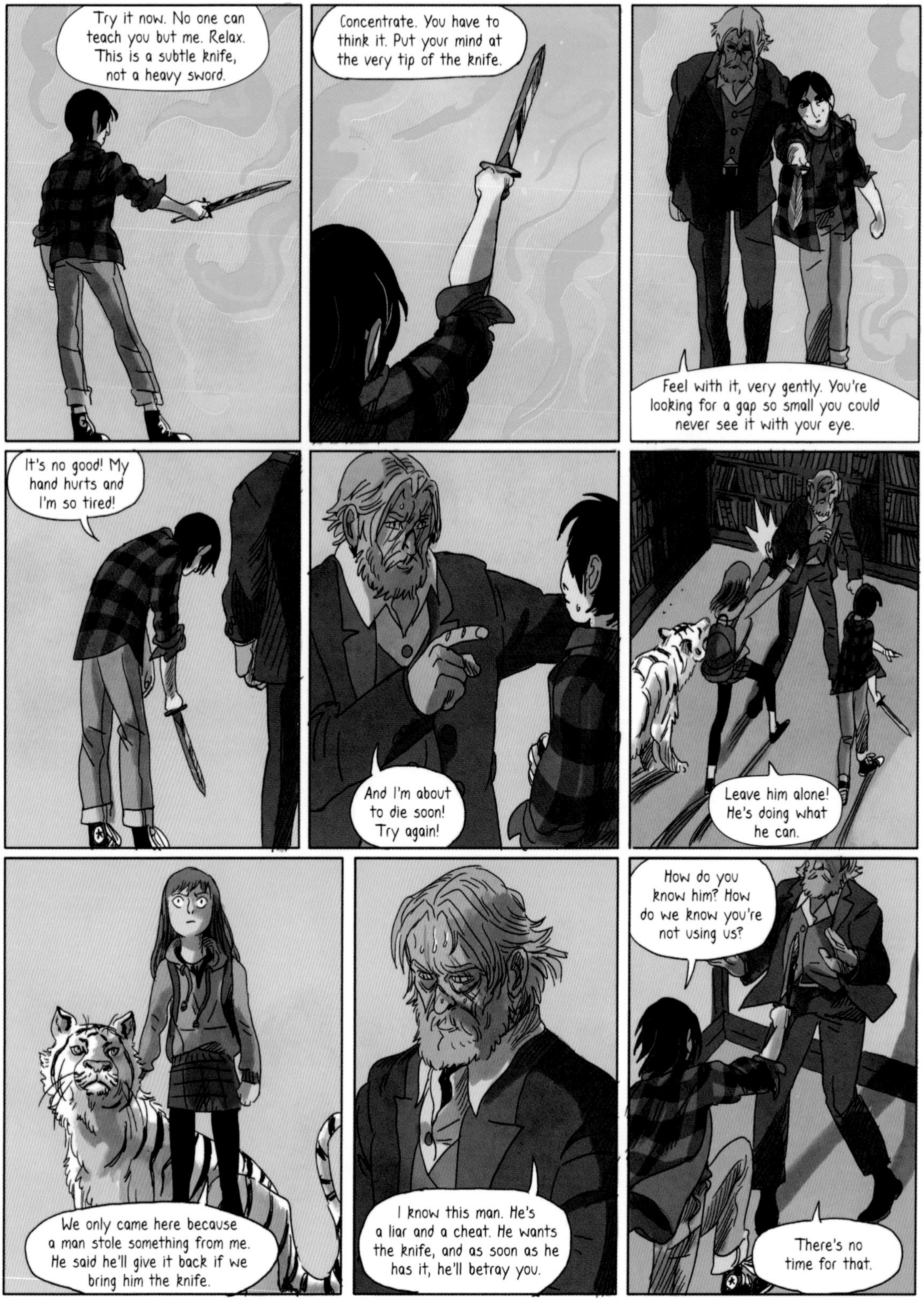
Try it now. No one can teach you but me. Relax. This is a subtle knife, not a heavy sword.
Concentrate. You have to think it. Put your mind at the very tip of the knife.
Feel with it, very gently. You're looking for a gap so small you could never see it with your eye.
It's no good! My hand hurts and I'm so tired!
And I'm about to die soon! Try again!
Leave him alone! He's doing what he can.
We only came here because a man stole something from me. He said he'll give it back if we bring him the knife.
I know this man. He's a liar and a cheat. He wants the knife, and as soon as he has it, he'll betray you.
How do you know him? How do we know you're not using us?
There's no time for that.

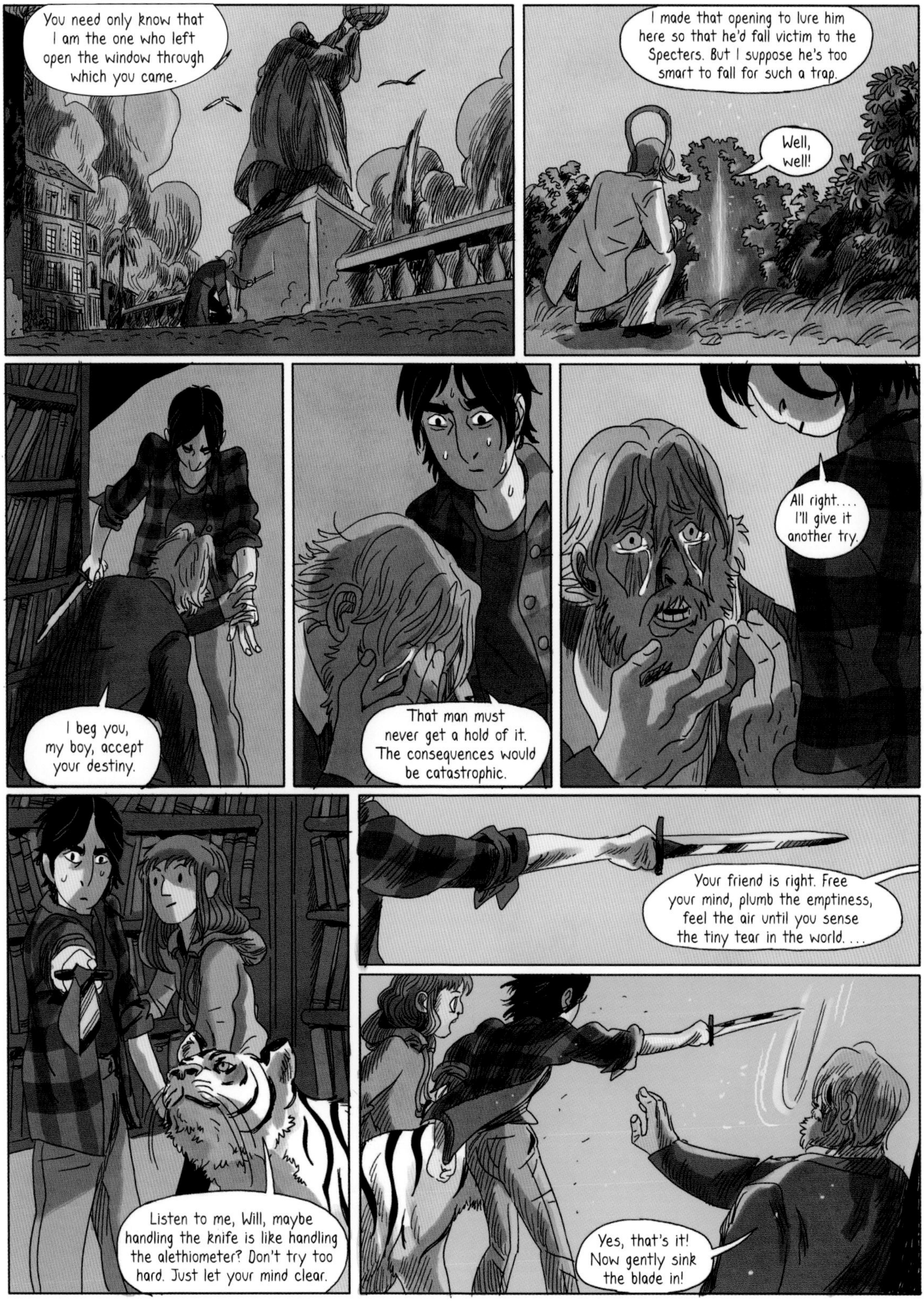

You need only know that I am the one who left open the window through which you came.
I made that opening to lure him here so that he'd fall victim to the Specters. But I suppose he's too smart to fall for such a trap.
Well, well!
I beg you, my boy, accept your destiny.
That man must never get a hold of it. The consequences would be catastrophic.
All right. . . . I'll give it another try.
Listen to me, Will, maybe handling the knife is like handling the alethiometer? Don't try too hard. Just let your mind clear.
Your friend is right. Free your mind, plumb the emptiness, feel the air until you sense the tiny tear in the world. . . .
Yes, that's it! Now gently sink the blade in!

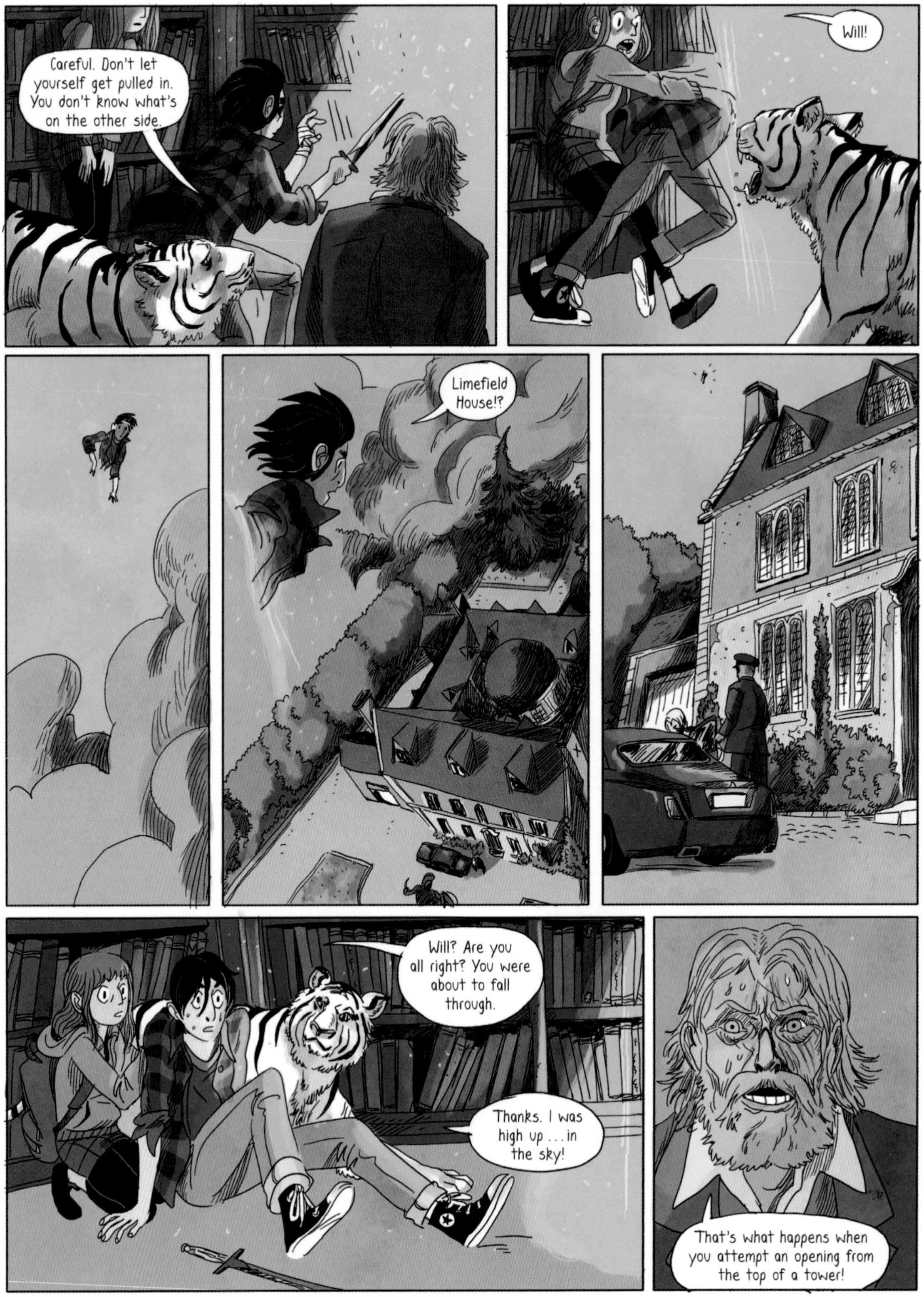
Careful. Don't let yourself get pulled in. You don't know what's on the other side.
Will!
Limefield House!?
Will? Are you all right? You were about to fall through.
Thanks. I was high up . . . in the sky!
That's what happens when you attempt an opening from the top of a tower!

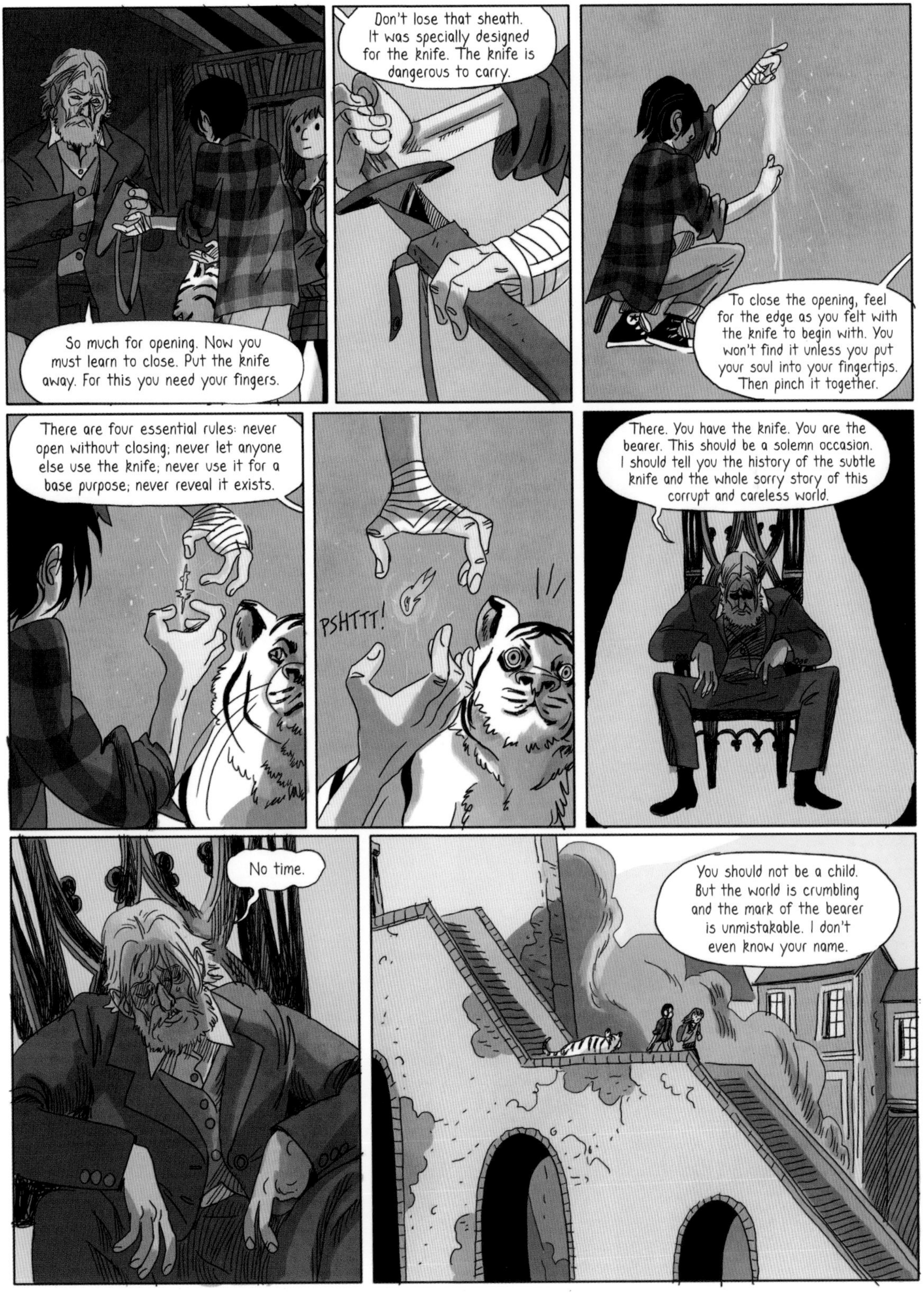
So much for opening. Now you must learn to close. Put the knife away. For this you need your fingers.
Don't lose that sheath. It was specially designed for the knife. The knife is dangerous to carry.
To close the opening, feel for the edge as you felt with the knife to begin with. You won't find it unless you put your soul into your fingertips. Then pinch it together.
There are four essential rules: never open without closing; never let anyone else use the knife; never use it for a base purpose; never reveal it exists.
PSHTTT!
There. You have the knife. You are the bearer. This should be a solemn occasion. I should tell you the history of the subtle knife and the whole sorry story of this corrupt and careless world.
No time.
You should not be a child. But the world is crumbling and the mark of the bearer is unmistakable. I don't even know your name.

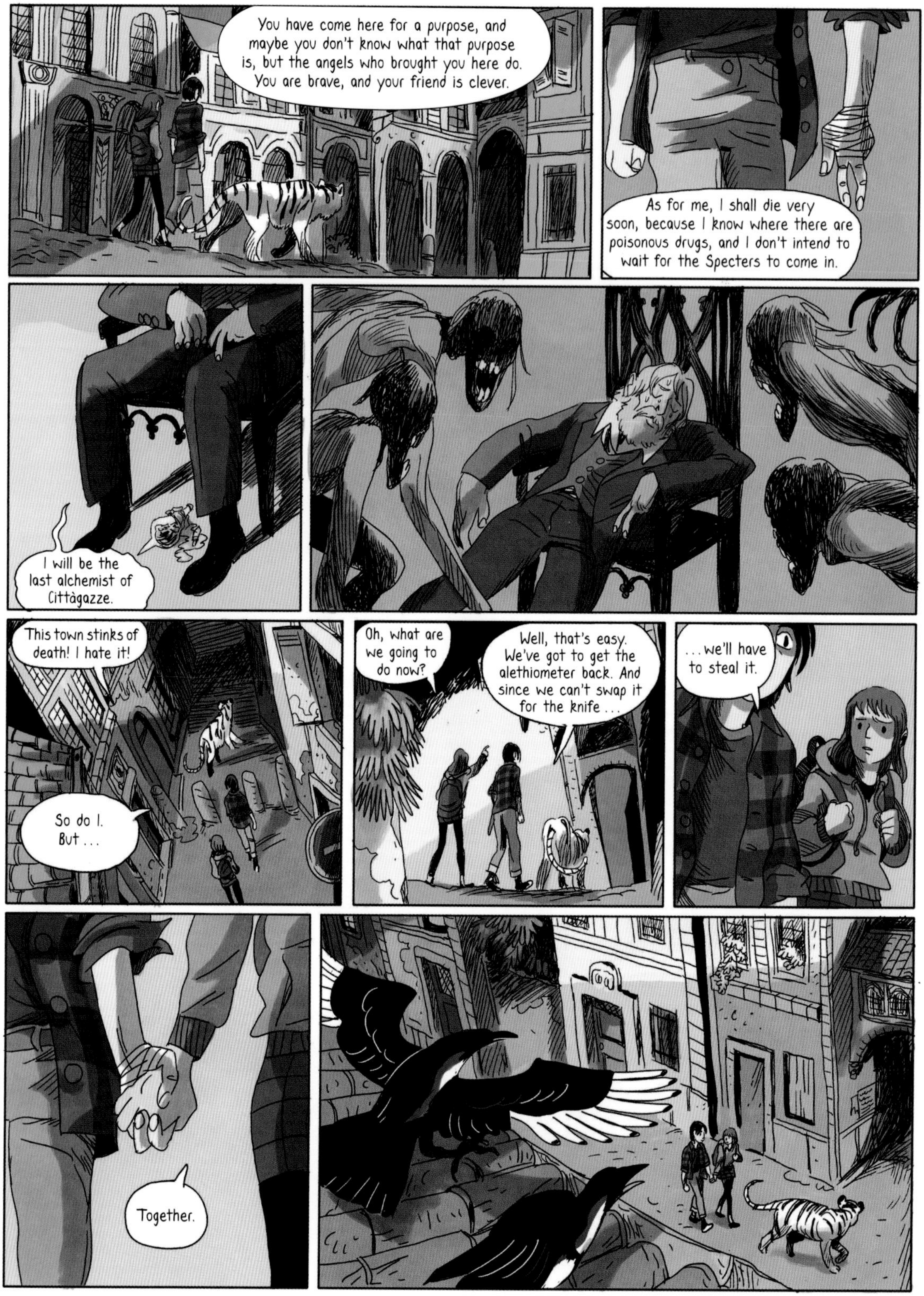
You have come here for a purpose, and maybe you don't know what that purpose is, but the angels who brought you here do. You are brave, and your friend is clever.
As for me, I shall die very soon, because I know where there are poisonous drugs, and I don't intend to wait for the Specters to come in.
I will be the last alchemist of Cittàgazze.
This town stinks of death! I hate it!
So do I. But . . .
Oh, what are we going to do now?
Well, that's easy. We've got to get the alethiometer back. And since we can't swap it for the knife . . .
. . . we'll have to steal it.
Together.

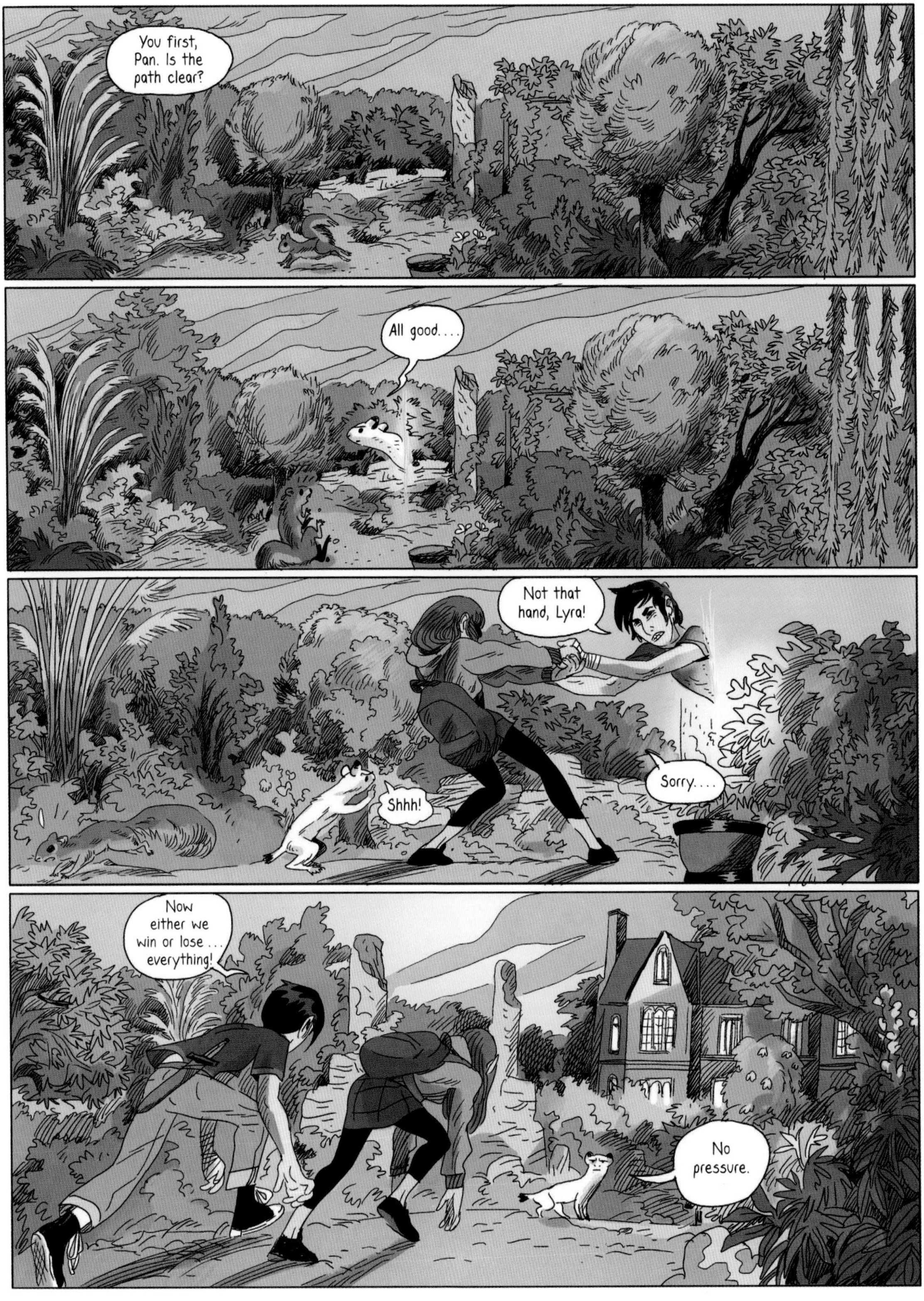
You first, Pan. Is the path clear?
All good. . . .
Not that hand, Lyra!
Shhh!
Sorry. . . .
Now either we win or lose . . . everything!
No pressure.

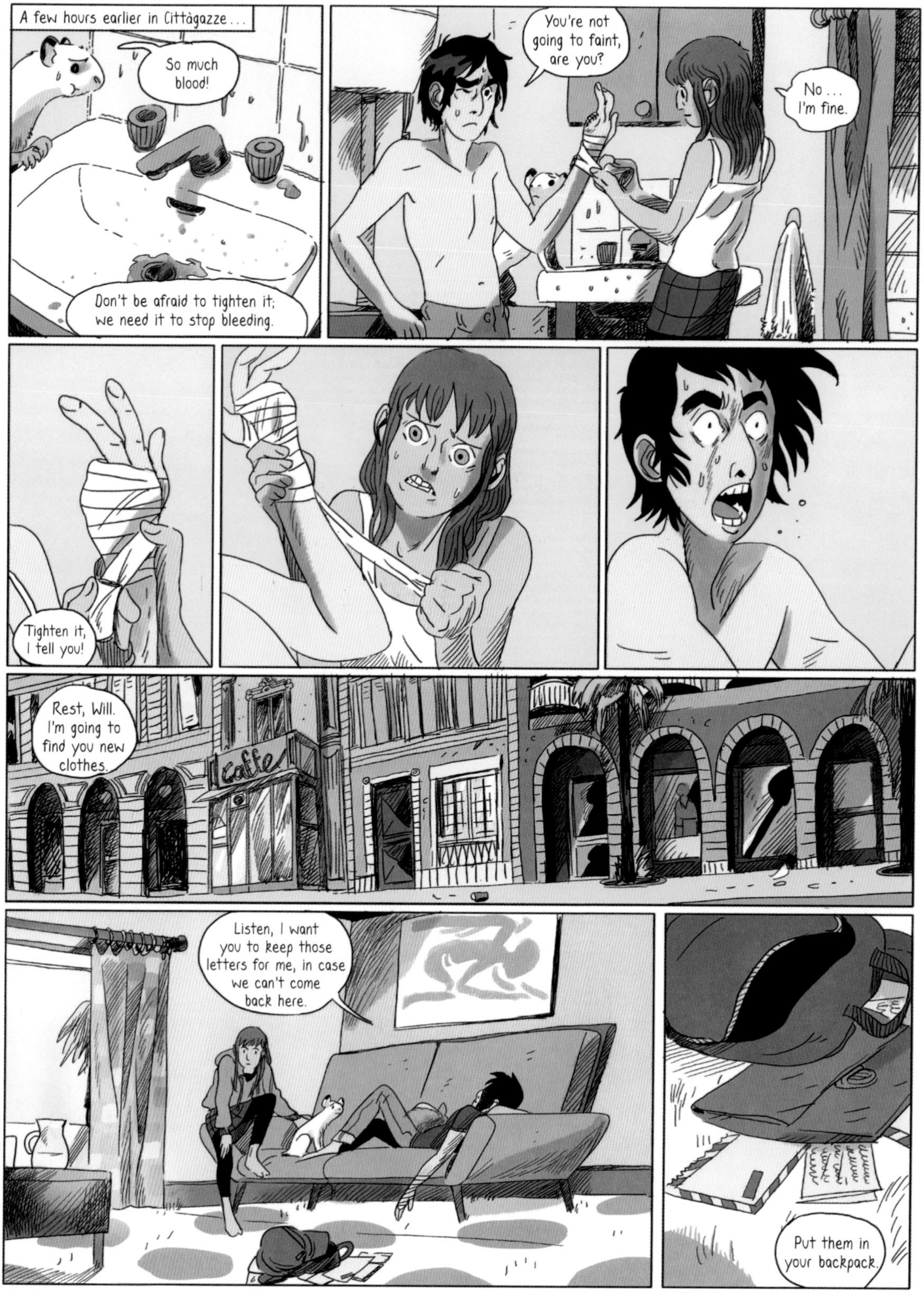
A few hours earlier in Cittàgazze . . .
So much blood!
Don't be afraid to tighten it; we need it to stop bleeding.
You're not going to faint, are you?
No . . . I'm fine.
Tighten it, I tell you!
Rest, Will. I'm going to find you new clothes.
Caffe
Listen, I want you to keep those letters for me, in case we can't come back here.
Put them in your backpack.

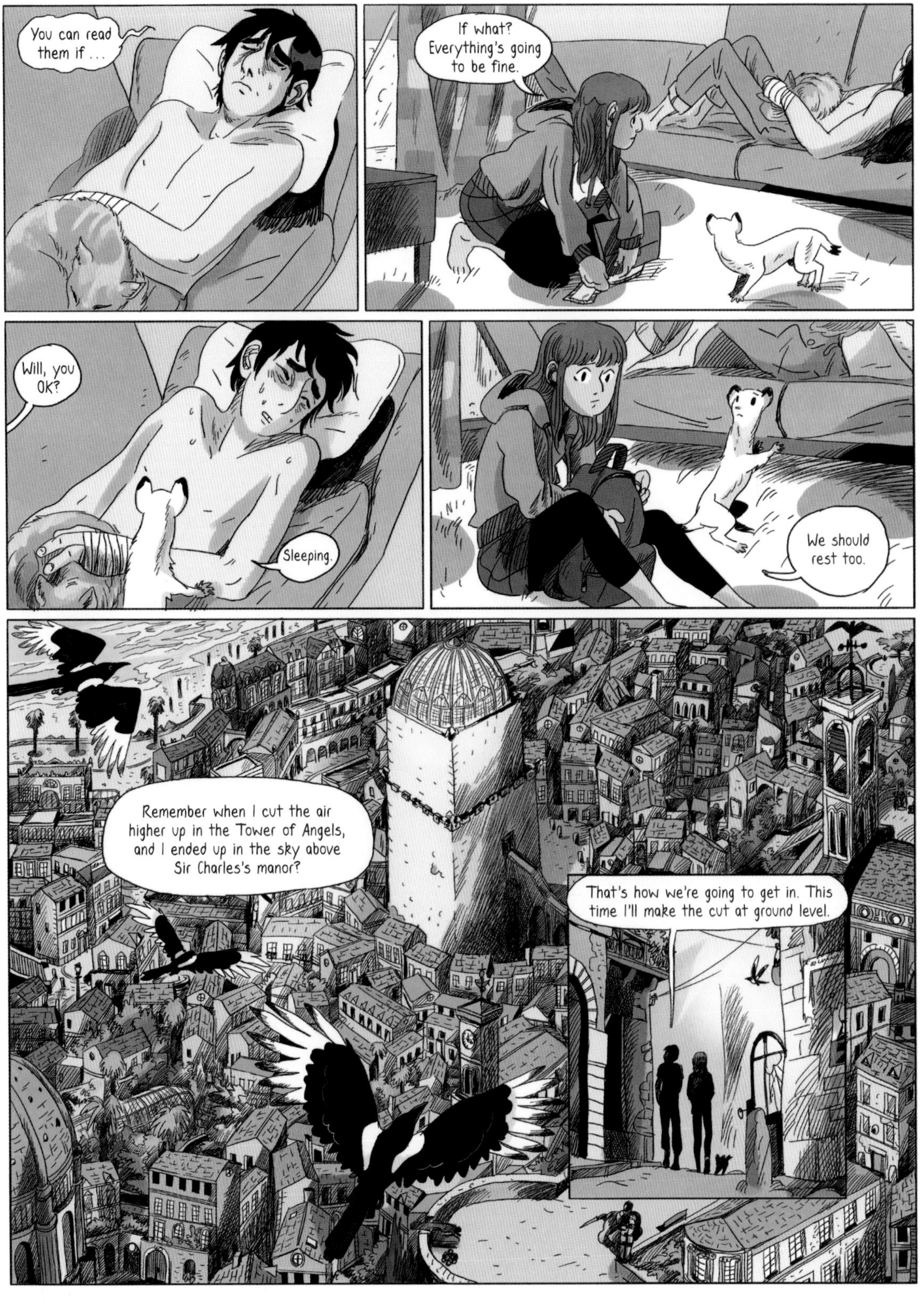
You can read them if . . .
If what? Everything's going to be fine.
Will, you OK?
Sleeping.
We should rest too.
Remember when I cut the air higher up in the Tower of Angels, and I ended up in the sky above Sir Charles's manor?
That's how we're going to get in. This time I'll make the cut at ground level.

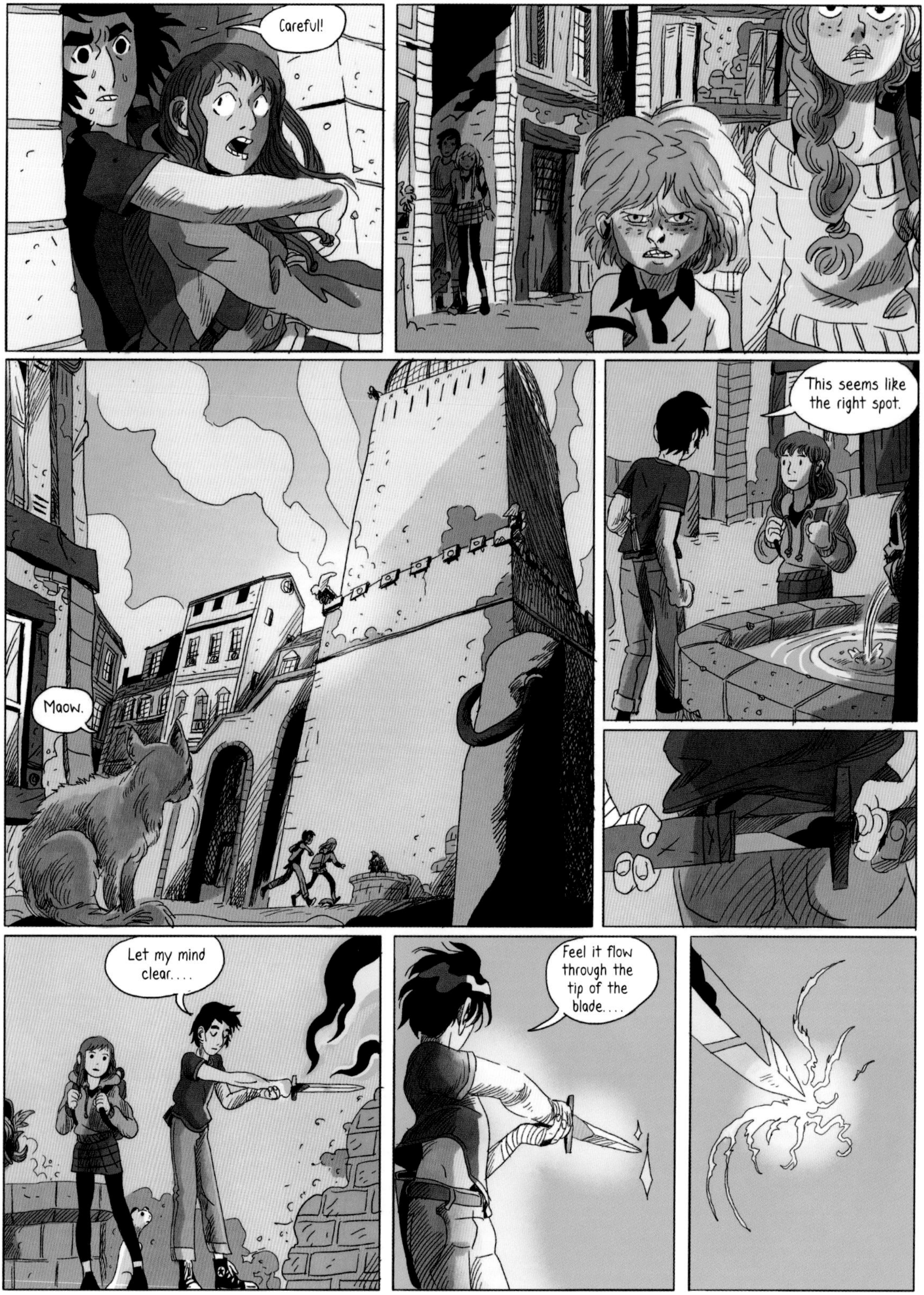
Careful!
This seems like the right spot.
Maow.
Let my mind clear....
Feel it flow through the tip of the blade....

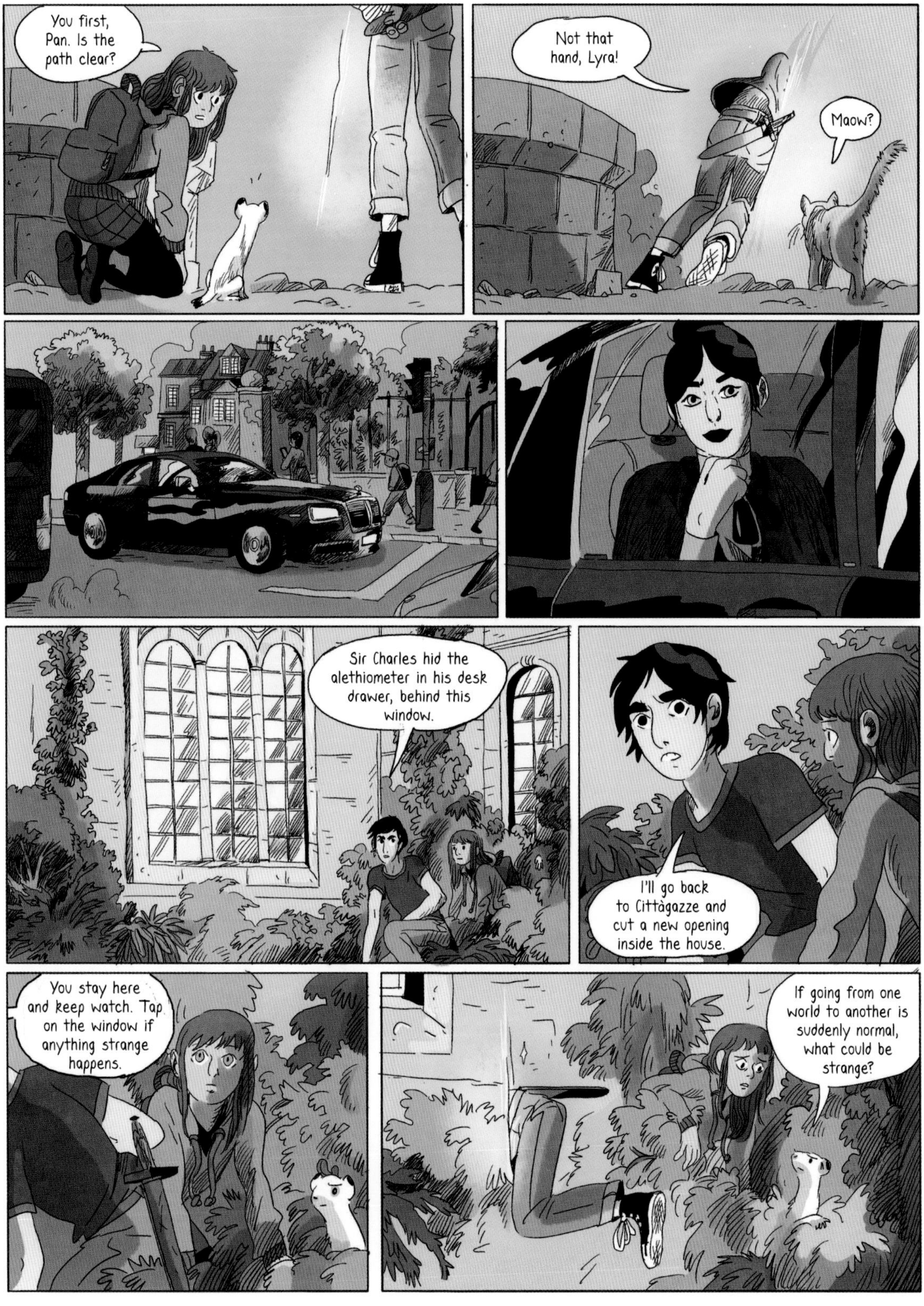
You first, Pan. Is the path clear?
Not that hand, Lyra!
Maow?
Sir Charles hid the alethiometer in his desk drawer, behind this window.
I'll go back to Cittàgazze and cut a new opening inside the house.
You stay here and keep watch. Tap on the window if anything strange happens.
If going from one world to another is suddenly normal, what could be strange?

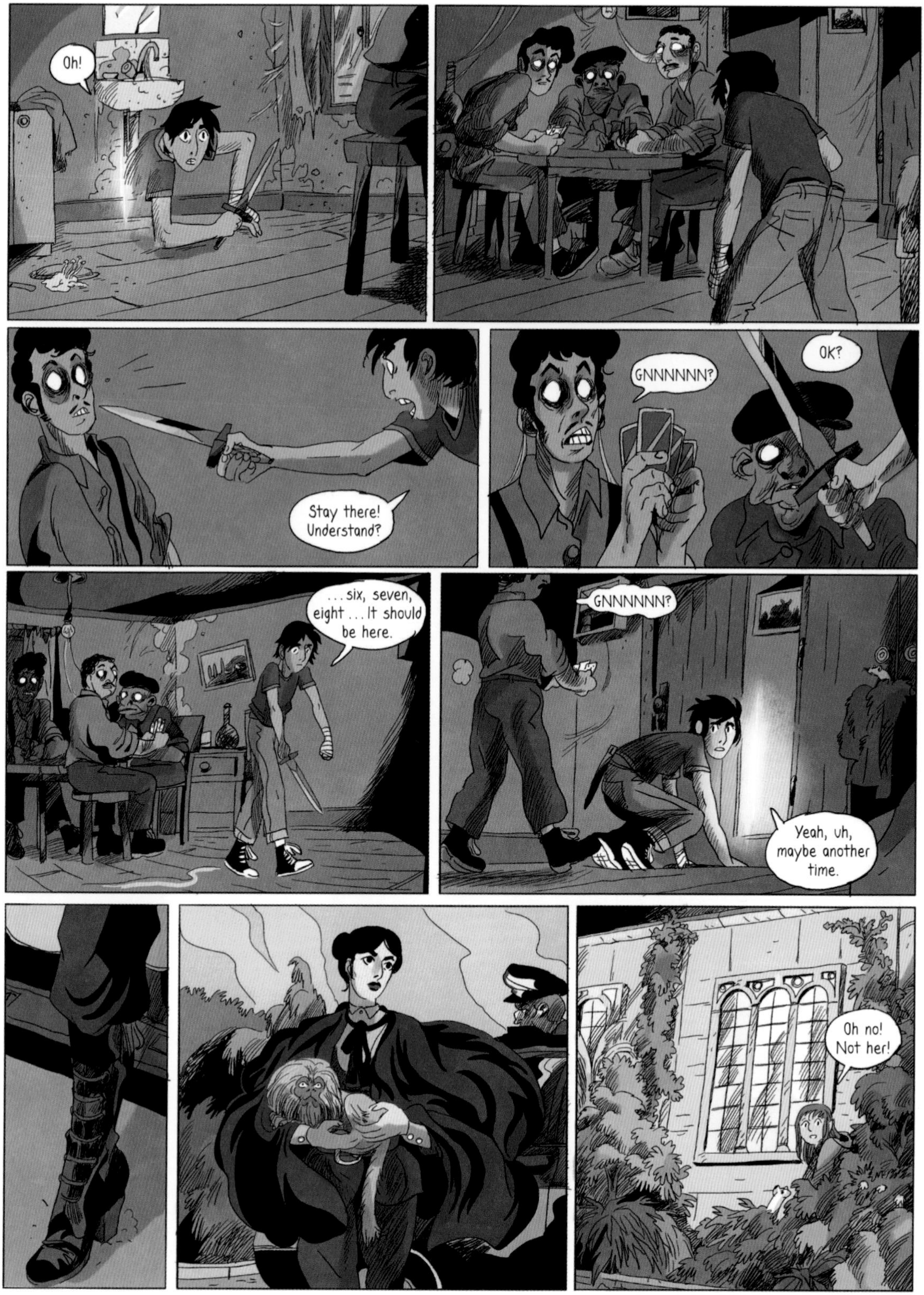

Oh!
Stay there! Understand?
GNNNNNN?
OK?
. . . six, seven, eight . . . It should be here.
GNNNNNN?
Yeah, uh, maybe another time.
Oh no! Not her!

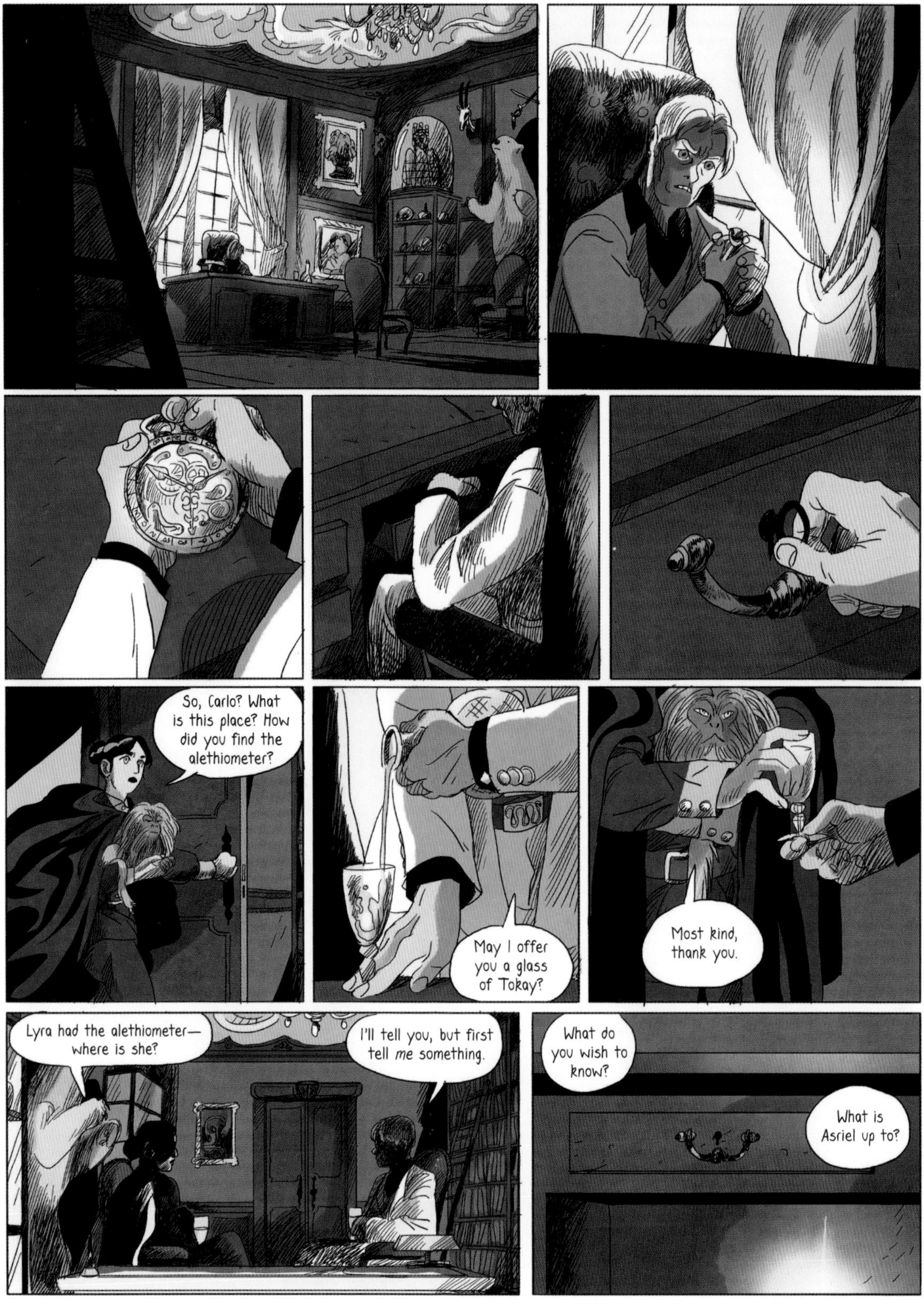
So, Carlo? What is this place? How did you find the alethiometer?
May I offer you a glass of Tokay?
Most kind, thank you.
Lyra had the alethiometer—where is she?
I'll tell you, but first tell *me* something.
What do you wish to know?
What is Asriel up to?

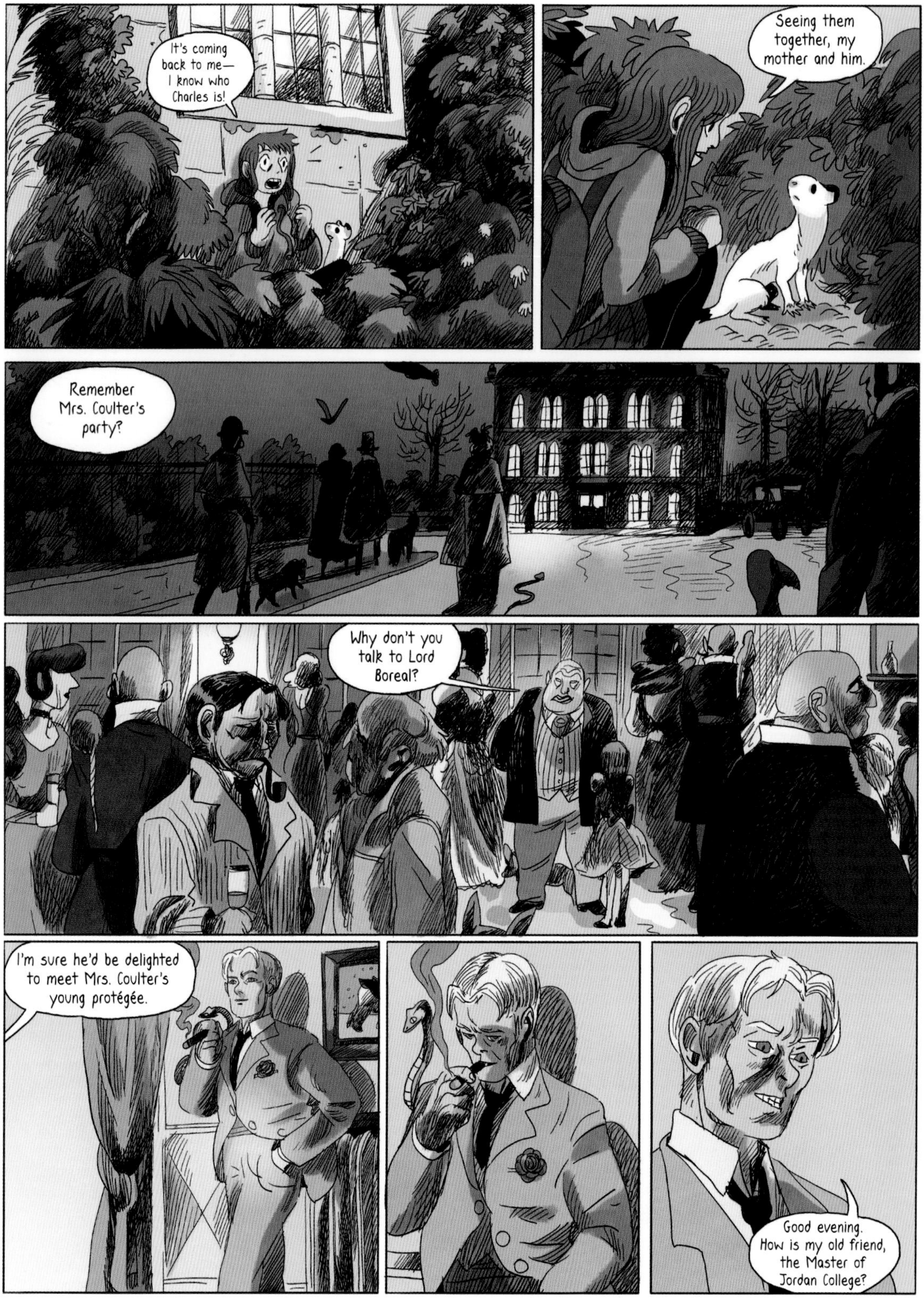
It's coming back to me—I know who Charles is!
Seeing them together, my mother and him.
Remember Mrs. Coulter's party?
Why don't you talk to Lord Boreal?
I'm sure he'd be delighted to meet Mrs. Coulter's young protégée.
Good evening. How is my old friend, the Master of Jordan College?

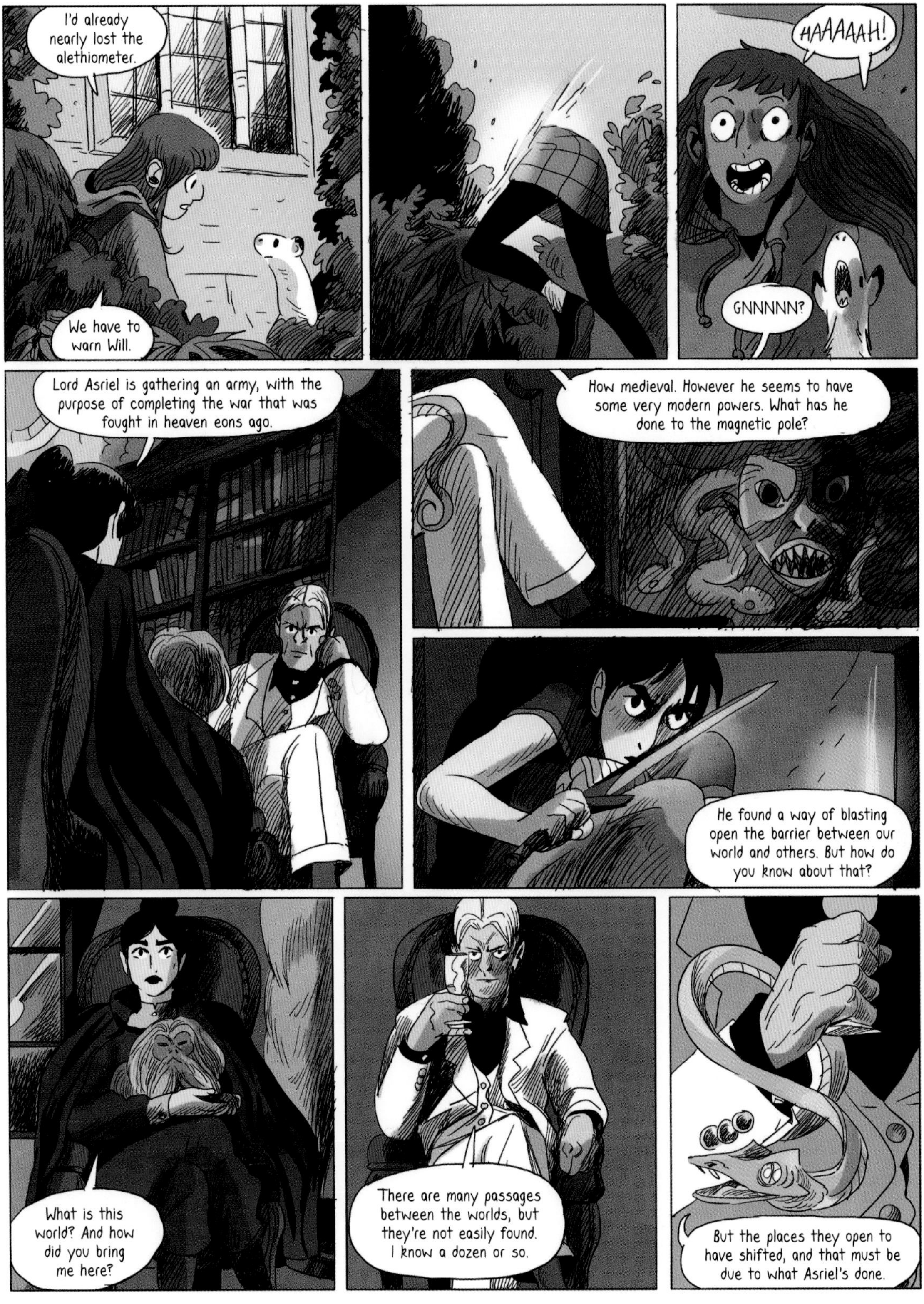

I'd already nearly lost the alethiometer.
We have to warn Will.
HAAAAAH!
GNNNNN?
Lord Asriel is gathering an army, with the purpose of completing the war that was fought in heaven eons ago.
How medieval. However he seems to have some very modern powers. What has he done to the magnetic pole?
He found a way of blasting open the barrier between our world and others. But how do you know about that?
What is this world? And how did you bring me here?
There are many passages between the worlds, but they're not easily found. I know a dozen or so.
But the places they open to have shifted, and that must be due to what Asriel's done.

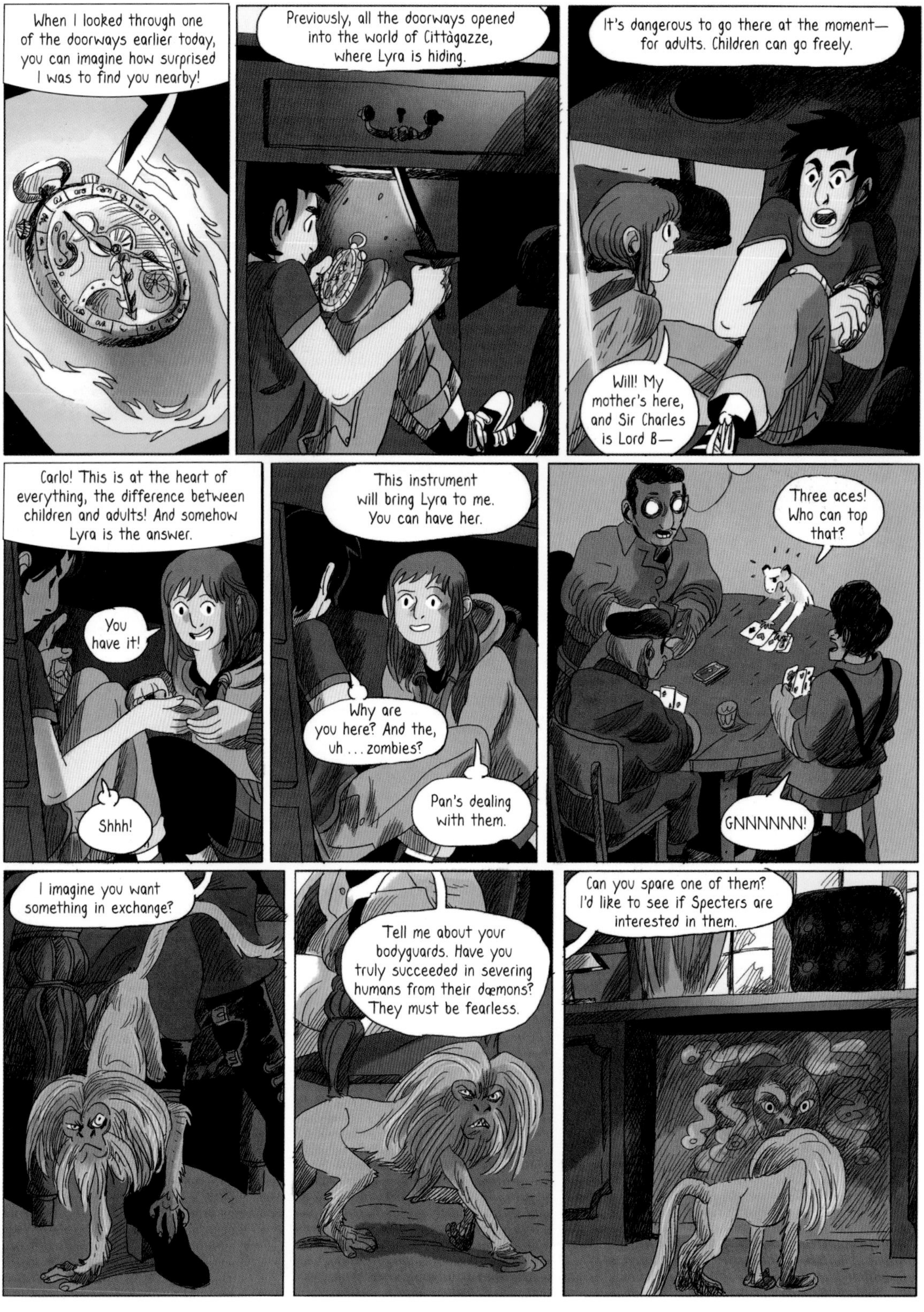
When I looked through one of the doorways earlier today, you can imagine how surprised I was to find you nearby!
Previously, all the doorways opened into the world of Cittàgazze, where Lyra is hiding.
It's dangerous to go there at the moment— for adults. Children can go freely.
Will! My mother's here, and Sir Charles is Lord B—
Carlo! This is at the heart of everything, the difference between children and adults! And somehow Lyra is the answer.
You have it!
Shhh!
This instrument will bring Lyra to me. You can have her.
Why are you here? And the, uh . . . zombies?
Pan's dealing with them.
Three aces! Who can top that?
GNNNNNN!
I imagine you want something in exchange?
Tell me about your bodyguards. Have you truly succeeded in severing humans from their dæmons? They must be fearless.
Can you spare one of them? I'd like to see if Specters are interested in them.

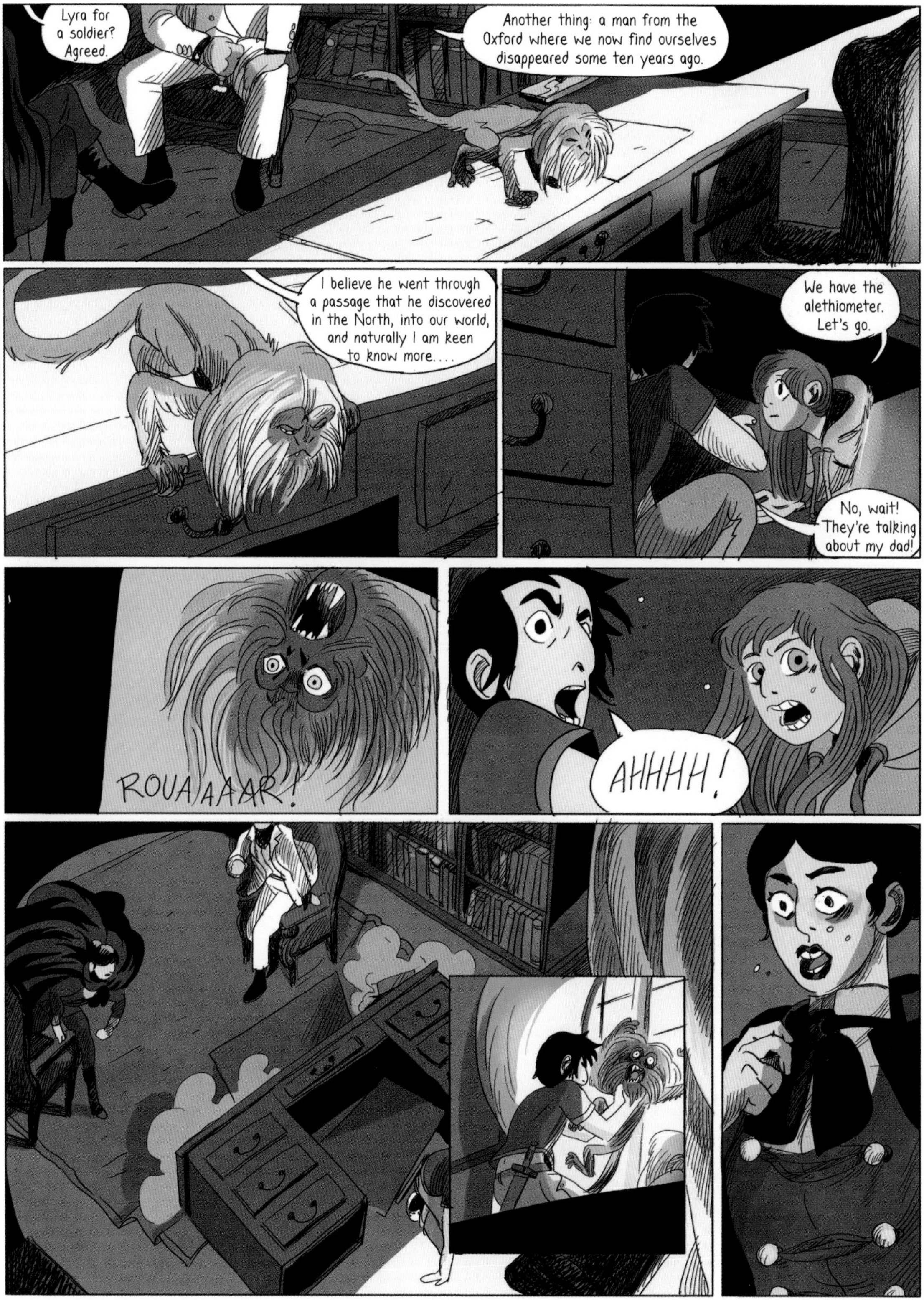
Lyra for a soldier? Agreed.
Another thing: a man from the Oxford where we now find ourselves disappeared some ten years ago.
I believe he went through a passage that he discovered in the North, into our world, and naturally I am keen to know more. . . .
We have the alethiometer. Let's go.
No, wait! They're talking about my dad!
ROUA AAAR!
AHHHH!

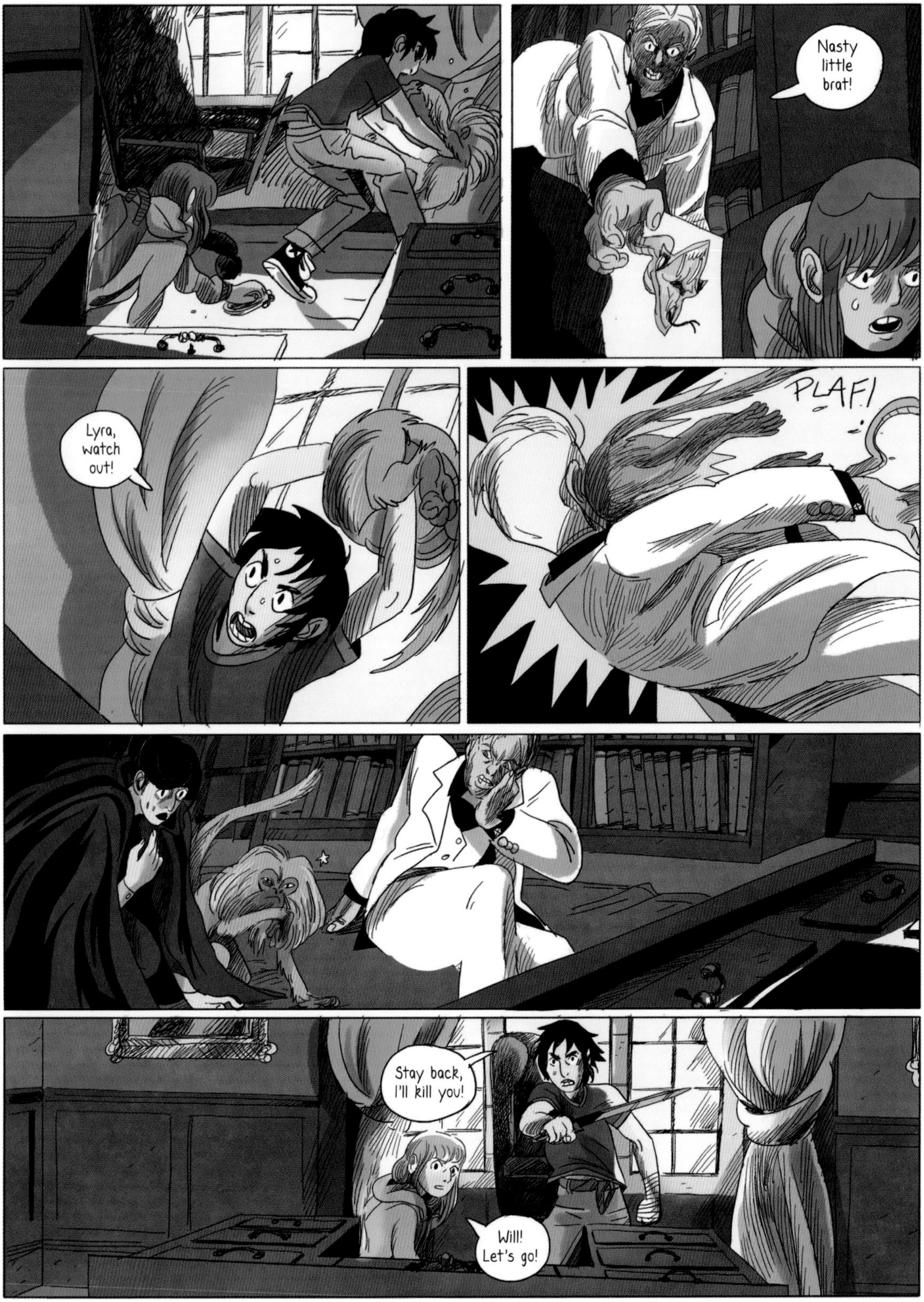
Nasty little brat!
Lyra, watch out!
PLAF!
Stay back, I'll kill you!
Will! Let's go!

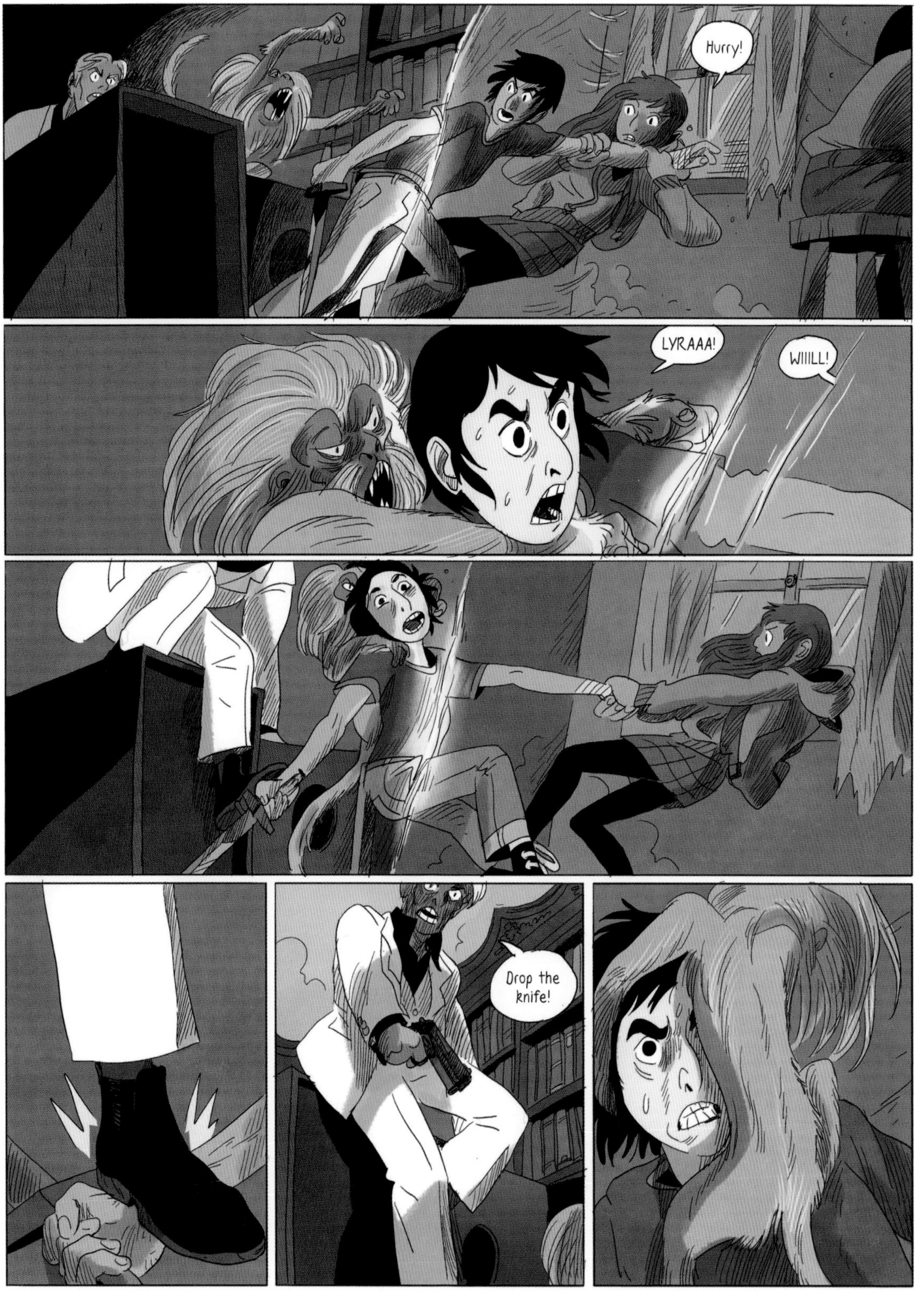
Hurry!
LYRAAA!
WIIILL!
Drop the knife!

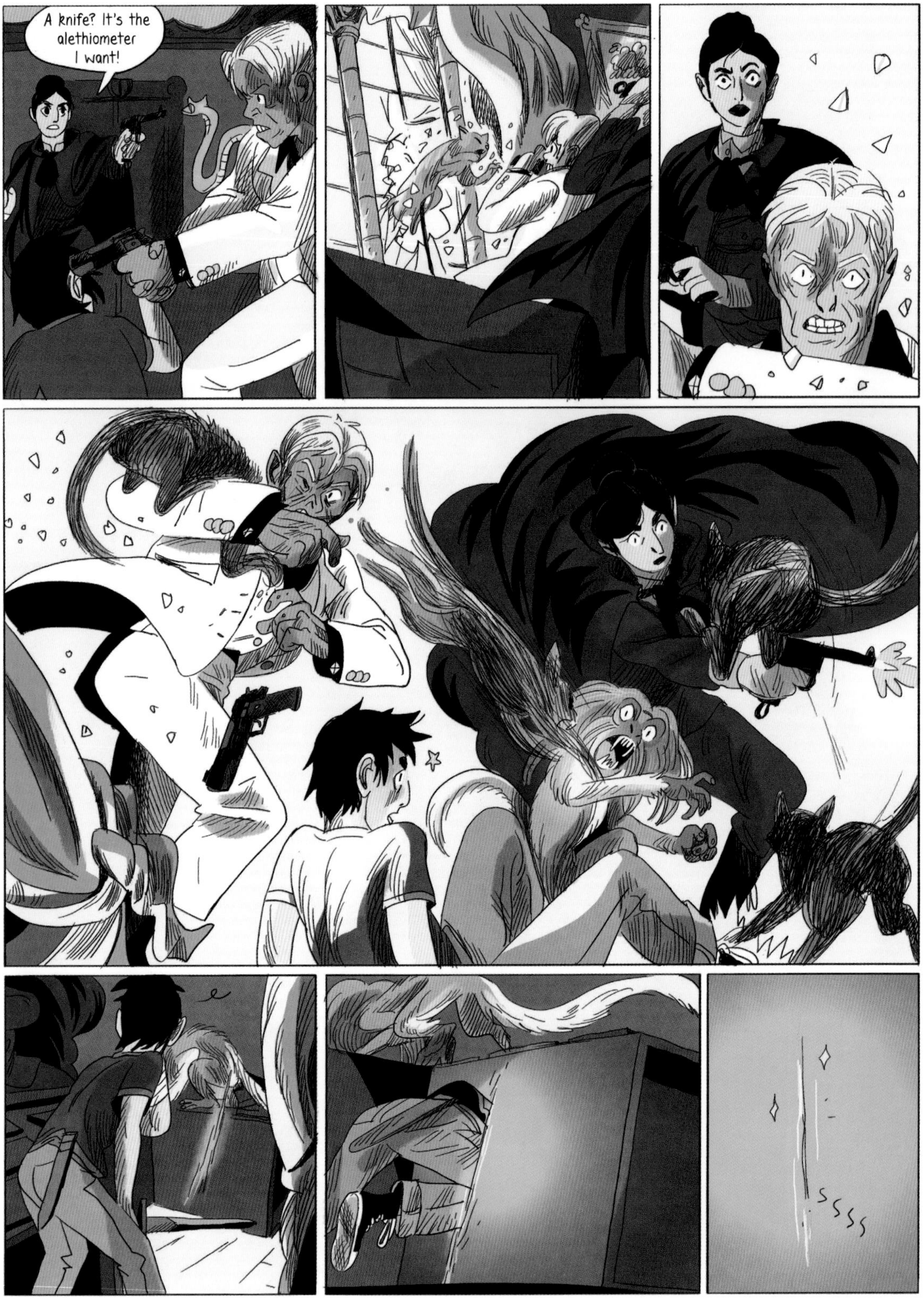
A knife? It's the alethiometer I want!
ssss

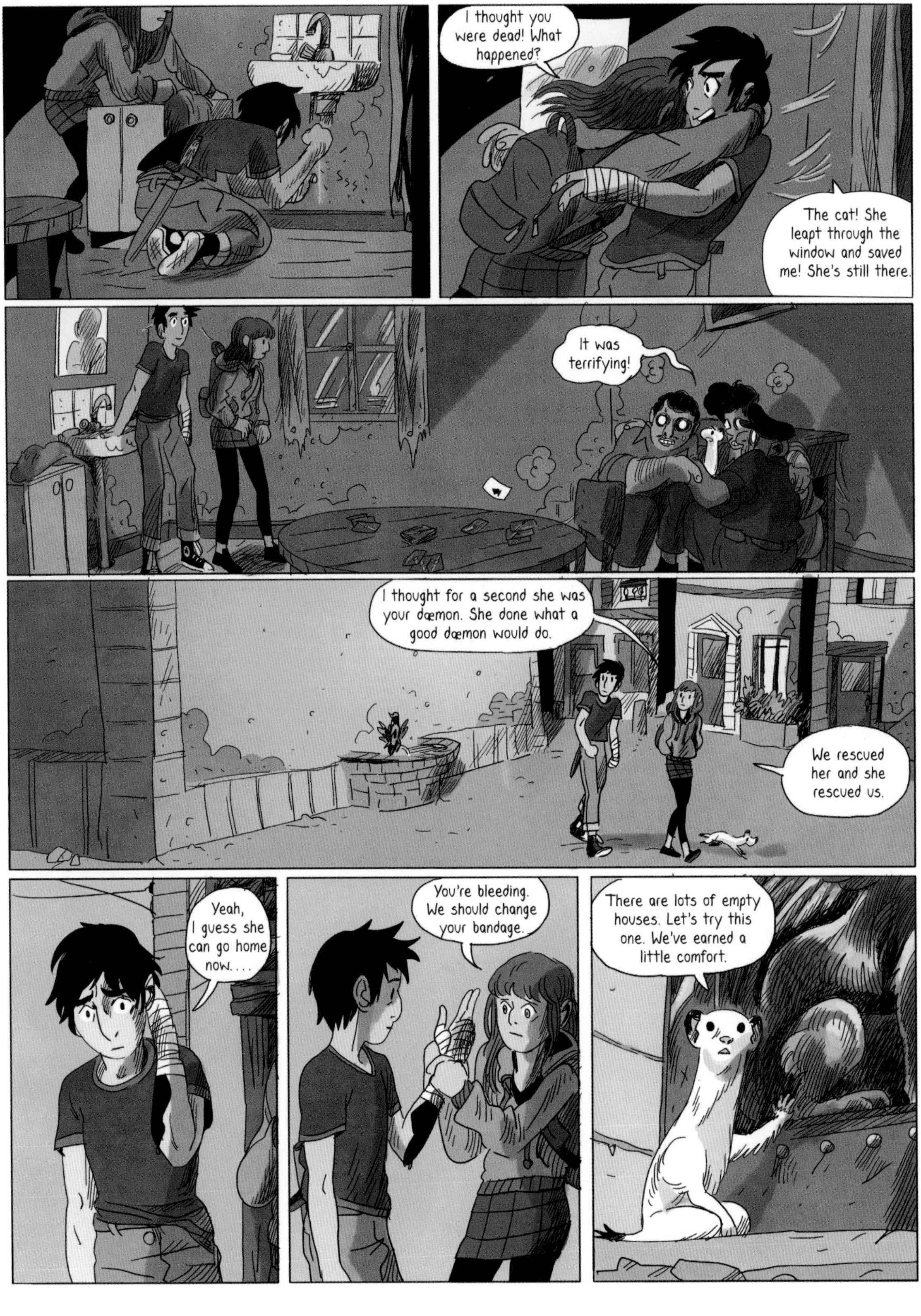
I thought you were dead! What happened?
The cat! She leapt through the window and saved me! She's still there.
It was terrifying!
I thought for a second she was your dæmon. She done what a good dæmon would do.
We rescued her and she rescued us.
Yeah, I guess she can go home now. . . .
You're bleeding. We should change your bandage.
There are lots of empty houses. Let's try this one. We've earned a little comfort.

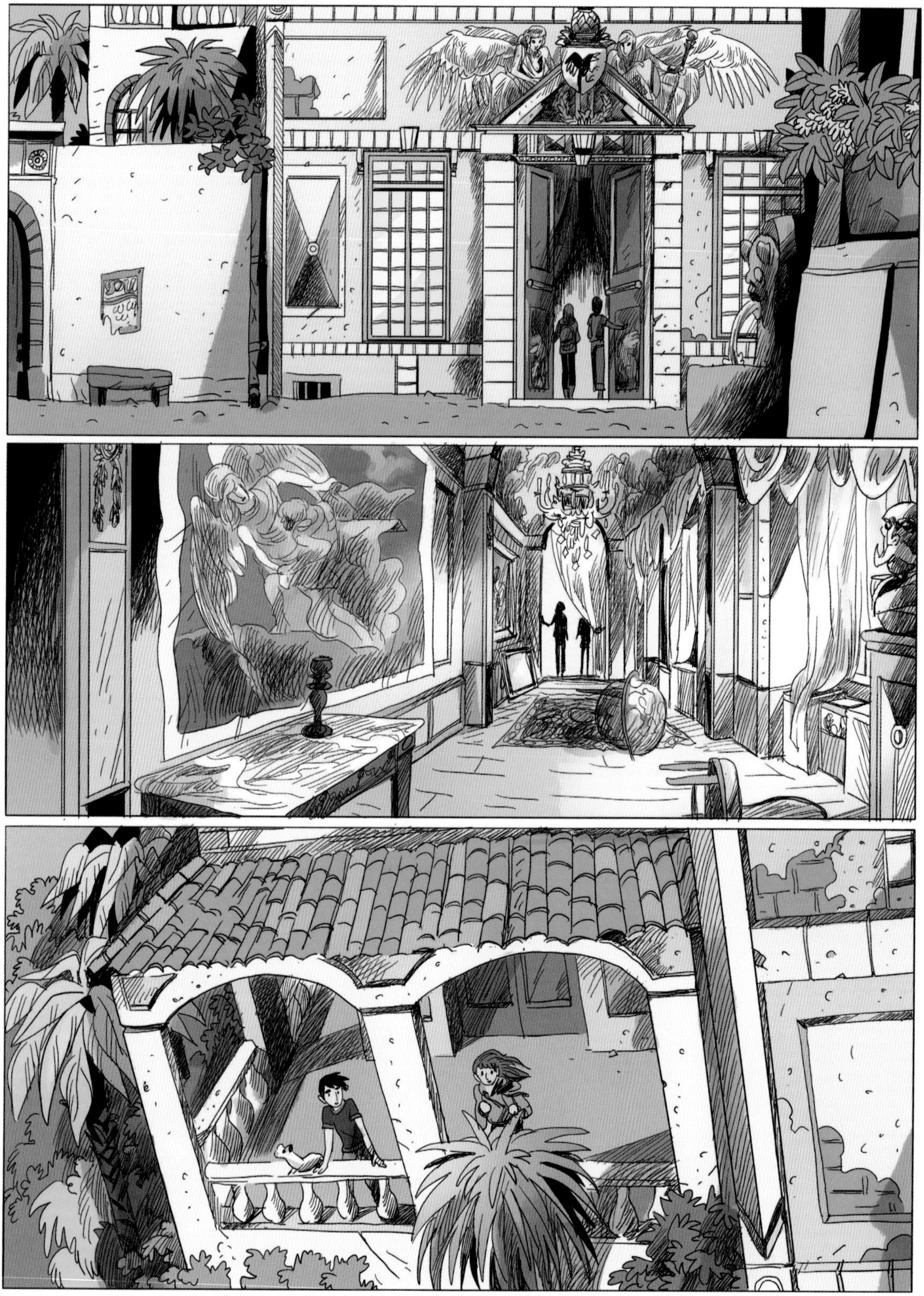

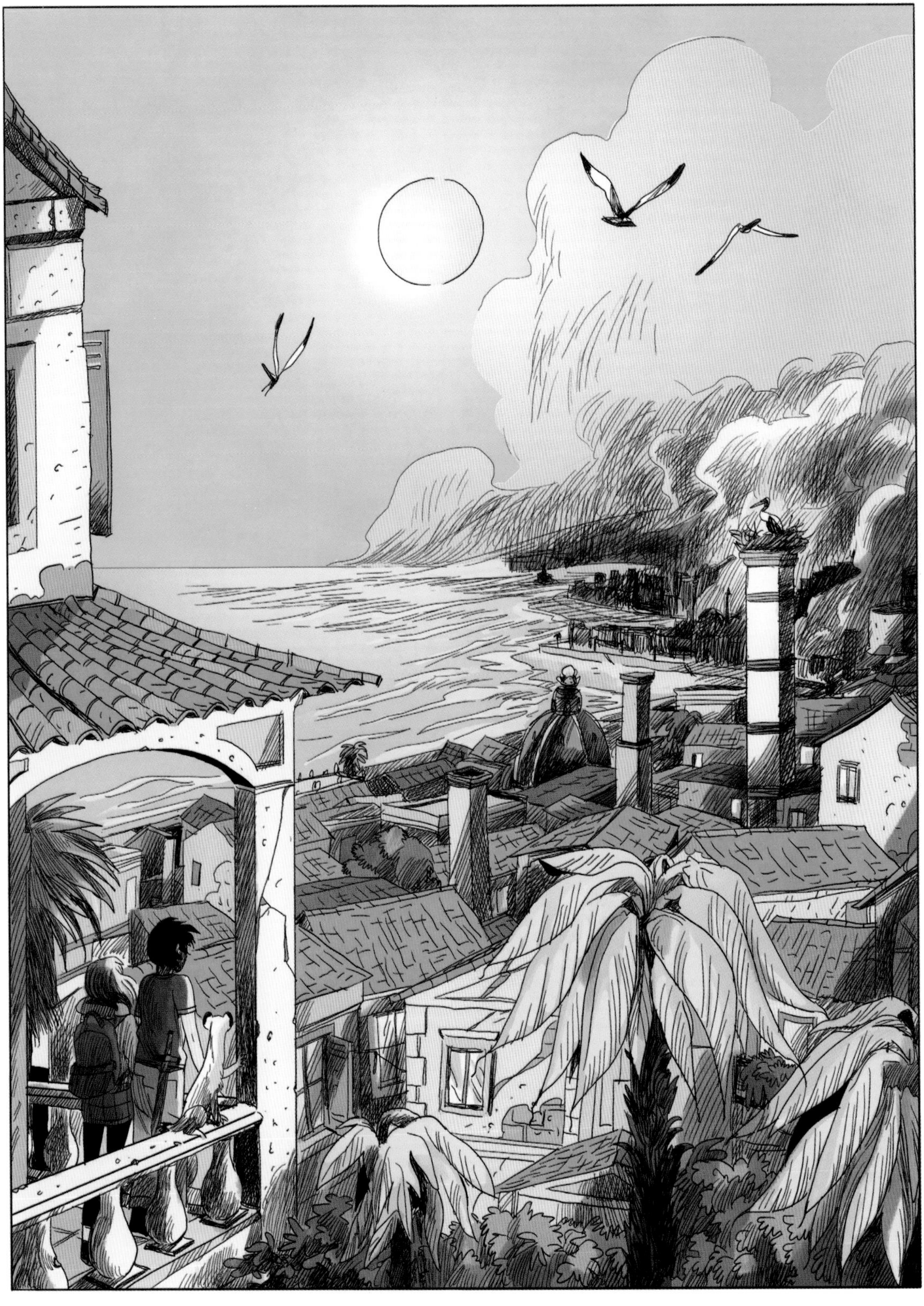

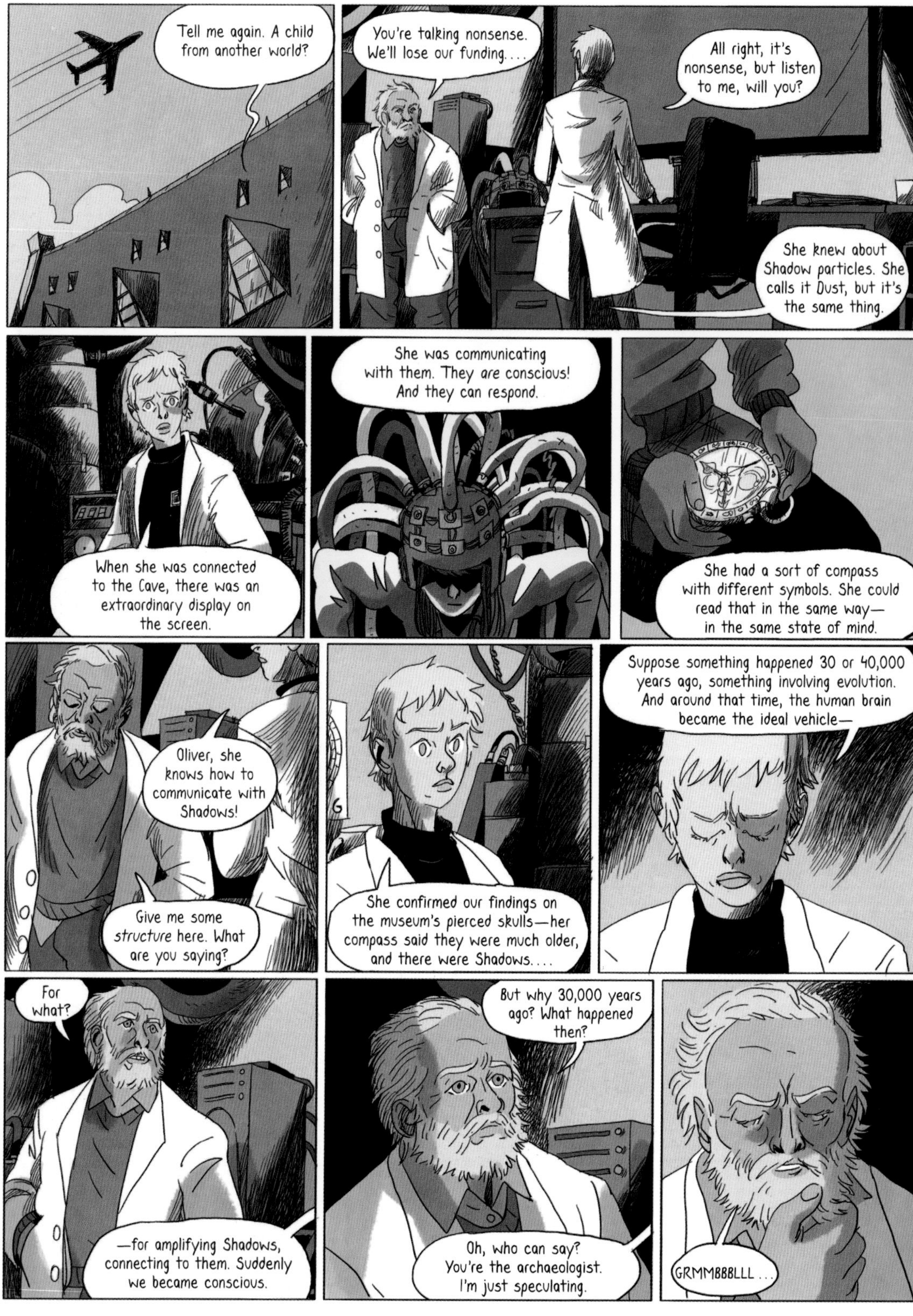
Tell me again. A child from another world?
You're talking nonsense. We'll lose our funding. . . .
All right, it's nonsense, but listen to me, will you?
She knew about Shadow particles. She calls it Dust, but it's the same thing.
When she was connected to the Cave, there was an extraordinary display on the screen.
She was communicating with them. They *are* conscious! And they can respond.
She had a sort of compass with different symbols. She could read that in the same way—in the same state of mind.
Oliver, she knows how to communicate with Shadows!
Give me some *structure* here. What are you saying?
She confirmed our findings on the museum's pierced skulls—her compass said they were much older, and there were Shadows. . . .
Suppose something happened 30 or 40,000 years ago, something involving evolution. And around that time, the human brain became the ideal vehicle—
For what?
—for amplifying Shadows, connecting to them. Suddenly we became conscious.
But why 30,000 years ago? What happened then?
Oh, who can say? You're the archaeologist. I'm just speculating.
GRMMBBBLLL . . .

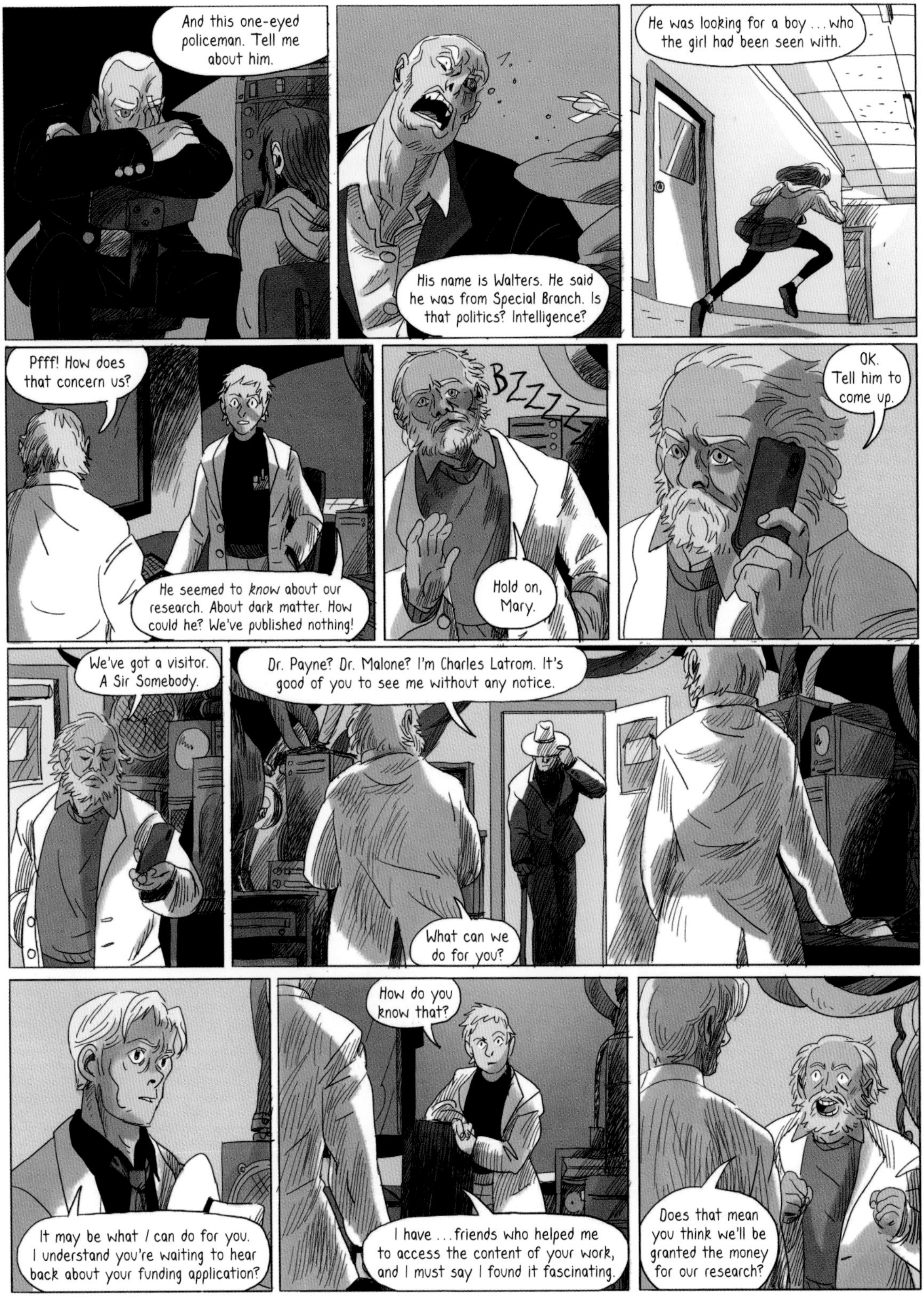
And this one-eyed policeman. Tell me about him.
His name is Walters. He said he was from Special Branch. Is that politics? Intelligence?
He was looking for a boy . . . who the girl had been seen with.
Pfff! How does that concern us?
He seemed to *know* about our research. About dark matter. How could he? We've published nothing!
BZZZZ
Hold on, Mary.
OK. Tell him to come up.
We've got a visitor. A Sir Somebody.
Dr. Payne? Dr. Malone? I'm Charles Latrom. It's good of you to see me without any notice.
What can we do for you?
It may be what *I* can do for you. I understand you're waiting to hear back about your funding application?
How do you know that?
I have . . . friends who helped me to access the content of your work, and I must say I found it fascinating.
Does that mean you think we'll be granted the money for our research?

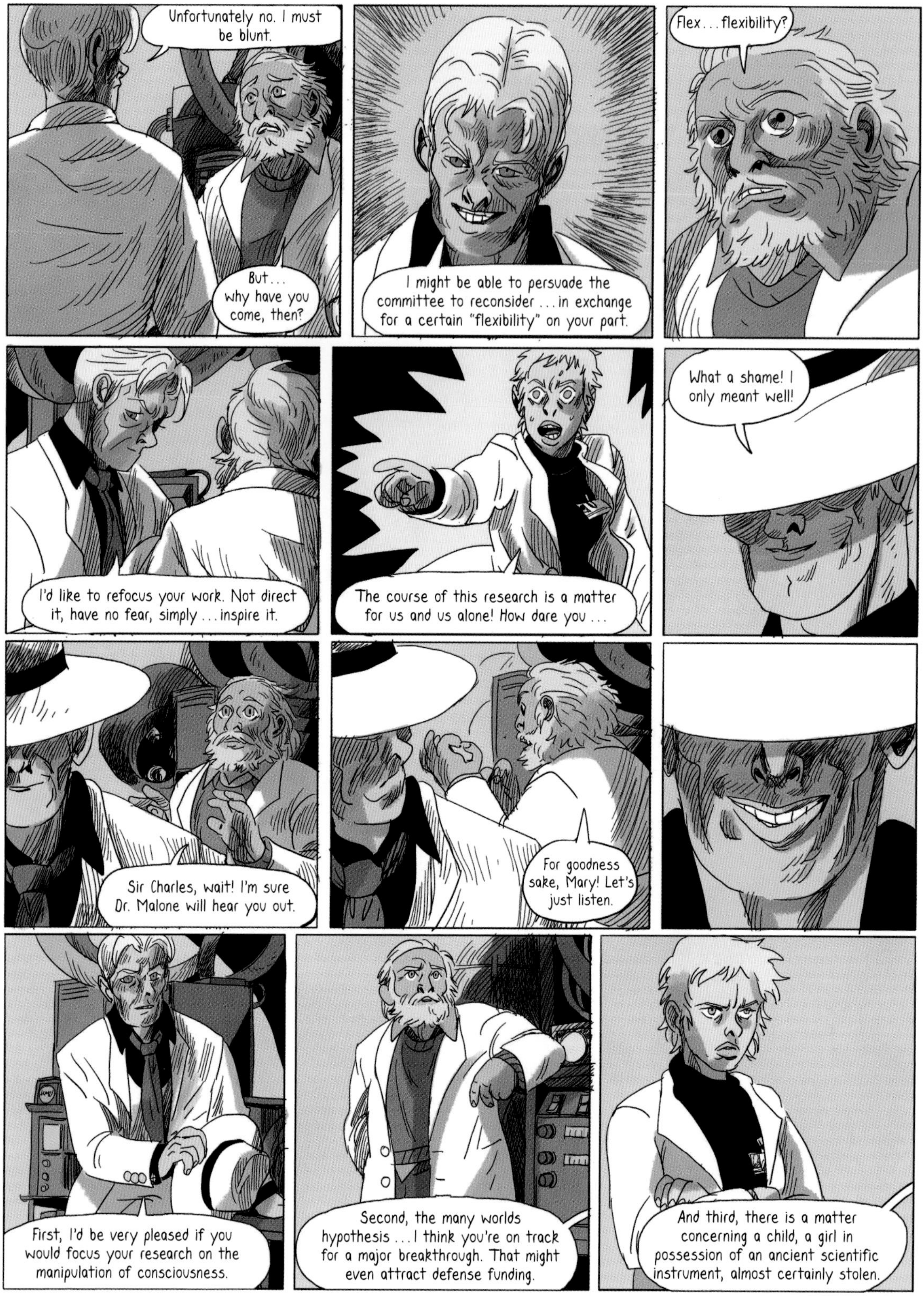
Unfortunately no. I must be blunt.
But... why have you come, then?
I might be able to persuade the committee to reconsider ... in exchange for a certain "flexibility" on your part.
Flex... flexibility?
I'd like to refocus your work. Not direct it, have no fear, simply ... inspire it.
The course of this research is a matter for us and us alone! How dare you ...
What a shame! I only meant well!
Sir Charles, wait! I'm sure Dr. Malone will hear you out.
For goodness sake, Mary! Let's just listen.
First, I'd be very pleased if you would focus your research on the manipulation of consciousness.
Second, the many worlds hypothesis ... I think you're on track for a major breakthrough. That might even attract defense funding.
And third, there is a matter concerning a child, a girl in possession of an ancient scientific instrument, almost certainly stolen.

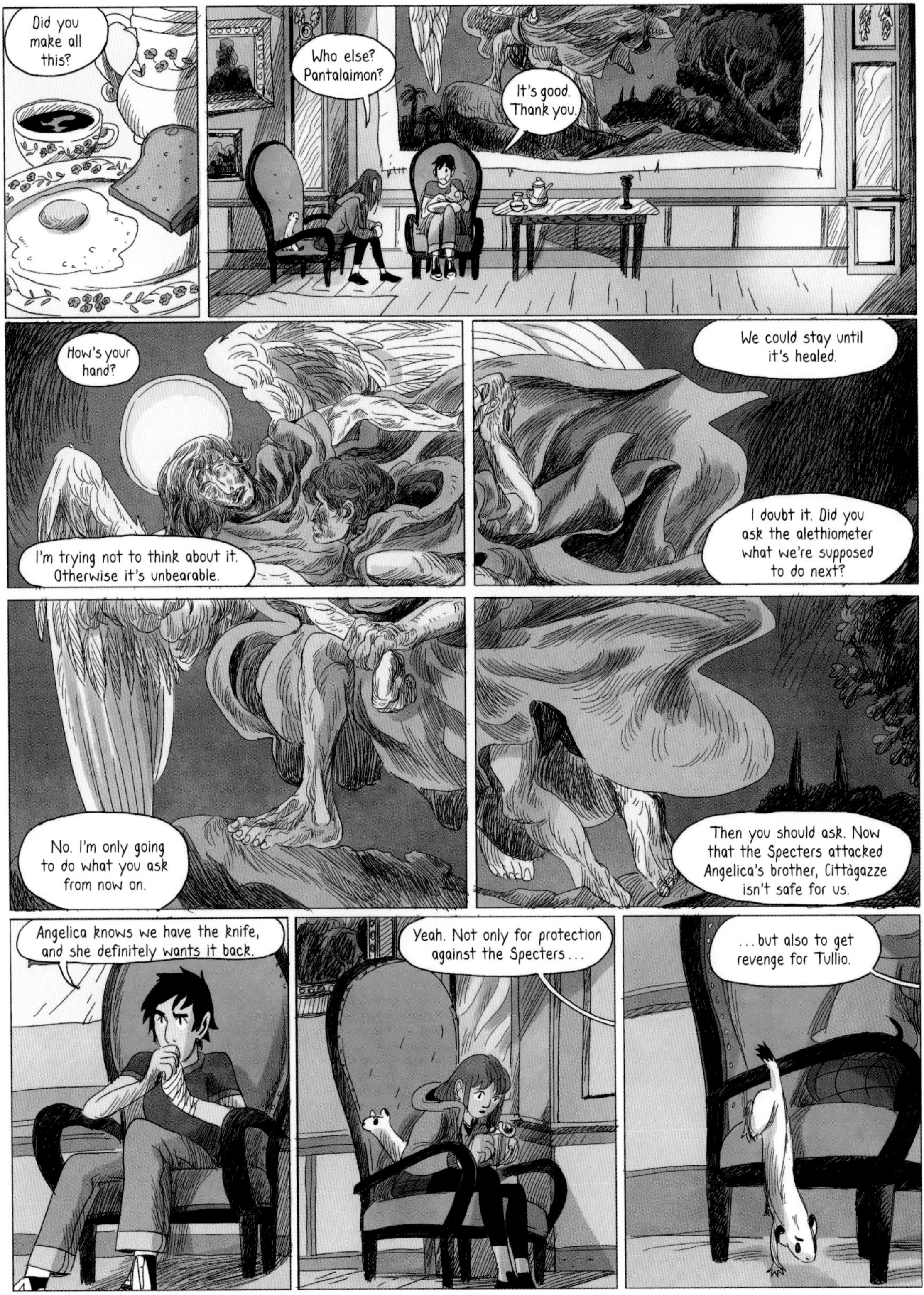
Did you make all this?
Who else? Pantalaimon?
It's good. Thank you.
How's your hand?
I'm trying not to think about it. Otherwise it's unbearable.
We could stay until it's healed.
I doubt it. Did you ask the alethiometer what we're supposed to do next?
No. I'm only going to do what you ask from now on.
Then you should ask. Now that the Specters attacked Angelica's brother, Cittàgazze isn't safe for us.
Angelica knows we have the knife, and she definitely wants it back.
Yeah. Not only for protection against the Specters...
...but also to get revenge for Tullio.

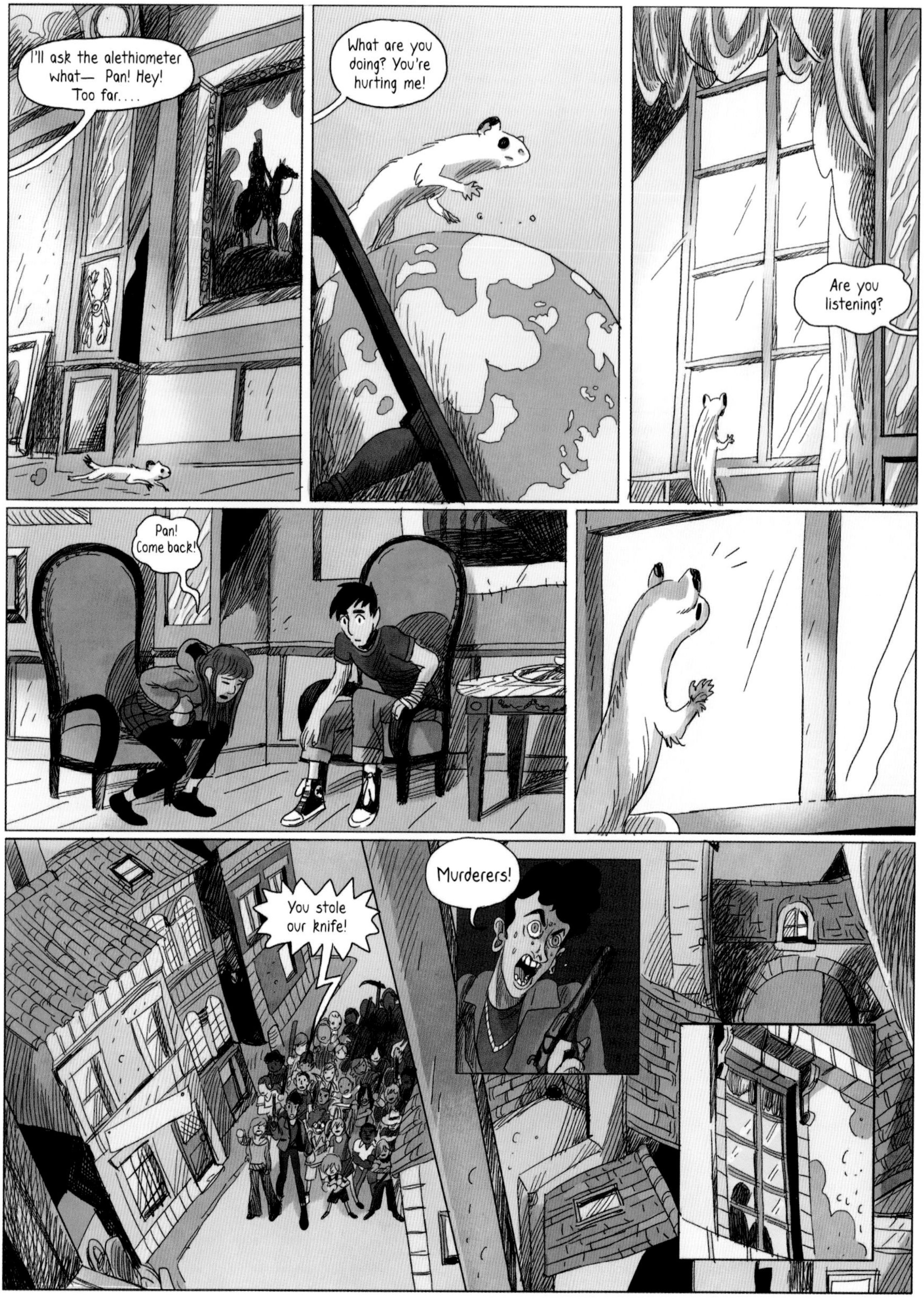
I'll ask the alethiometer what— Pan! Hey! Too far. . . .
What are you doing? You're hurting me!
Are you listening?
Pan! Come back!
You stole our knife!
Murderers!

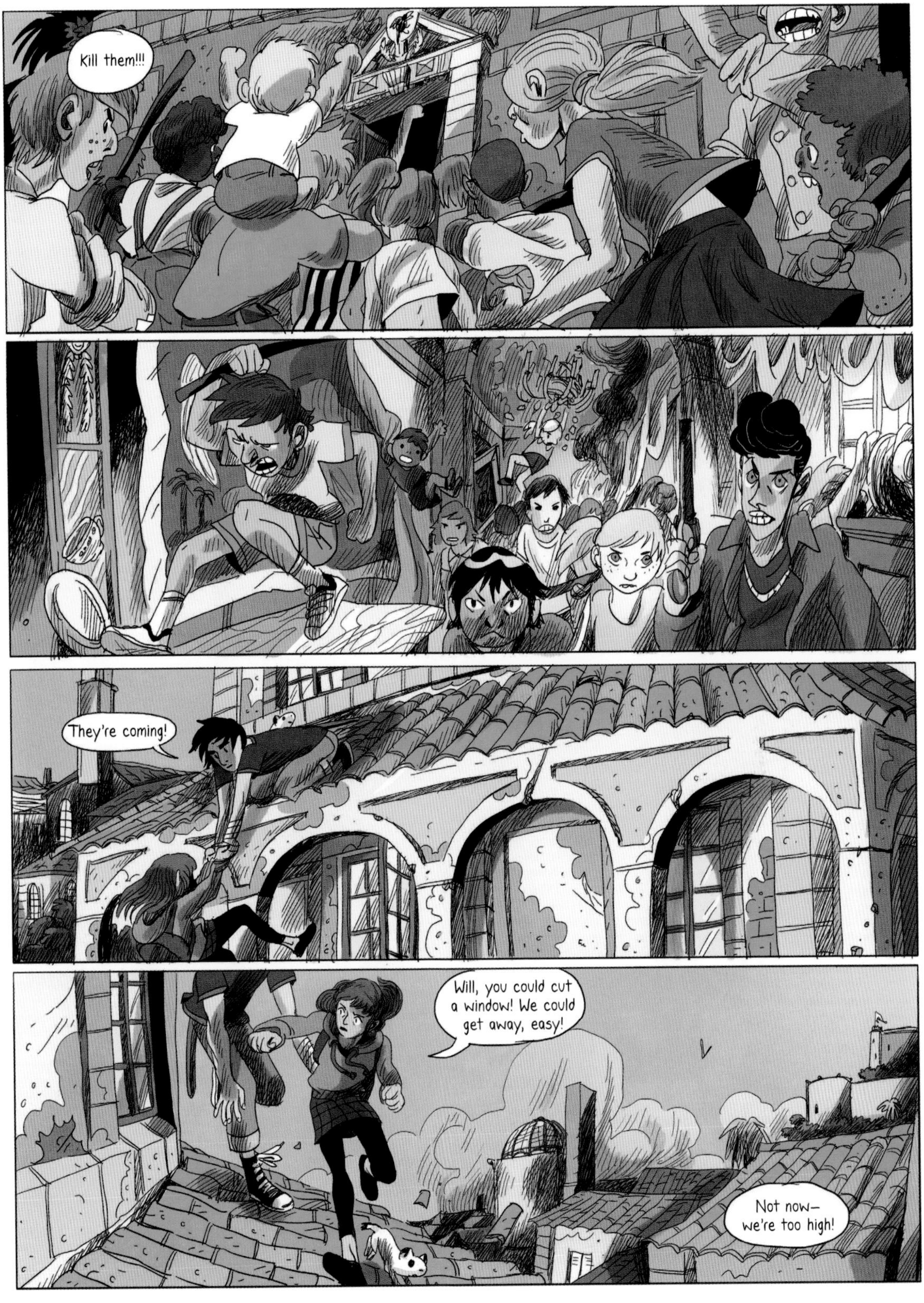
Kill them!!!
They're coming!
Will, you could cut a window! We could get away, easy!
Not now— we're too high!

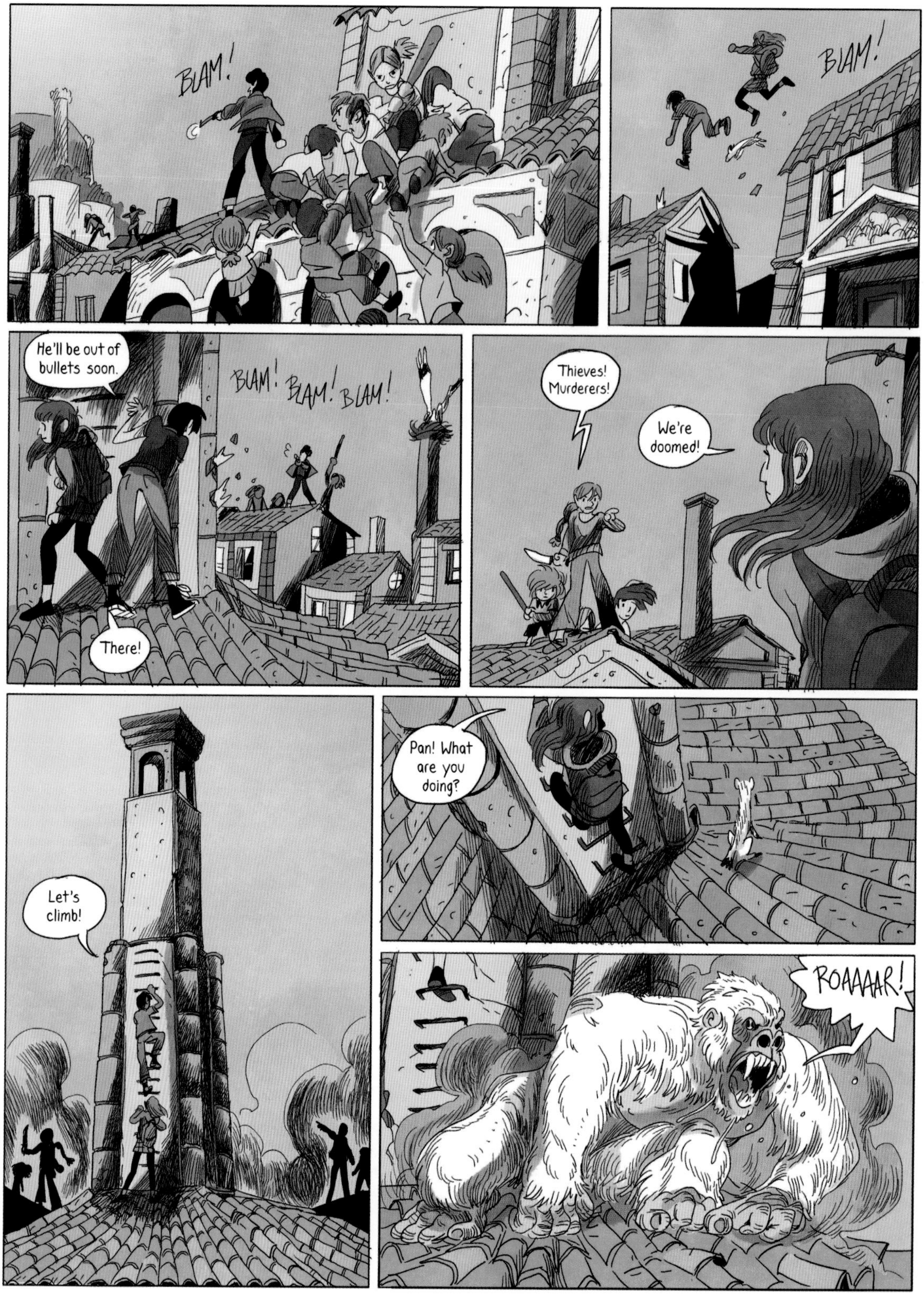
BLAM!
BLAM!
He'll be out of bullets soon.
BLAM! BLAM! BLAM!
There!
Thieves! Murderers!
We're doomed!
Let's climb!
Pan! What are you doing?
ROAAAAR!

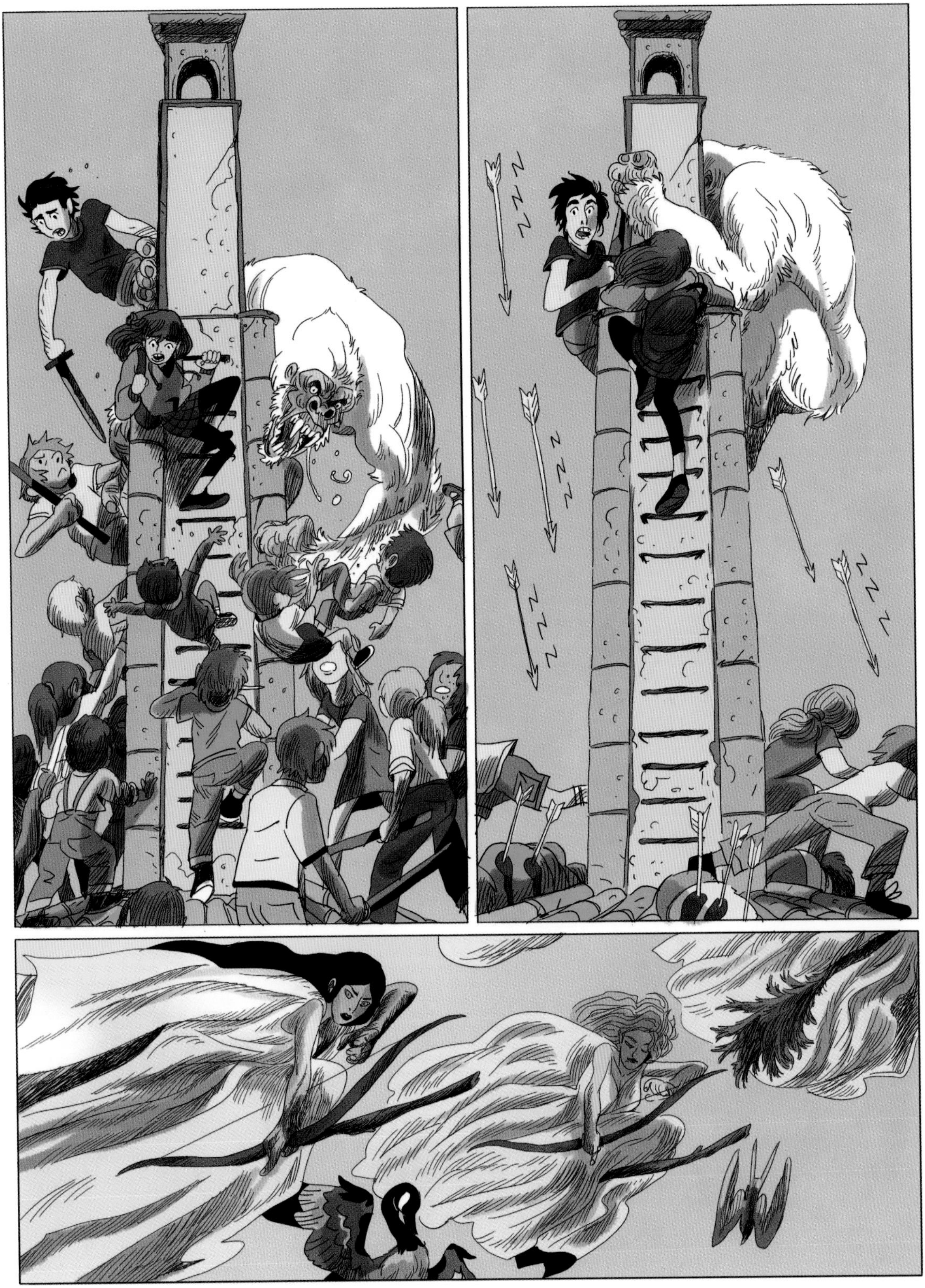

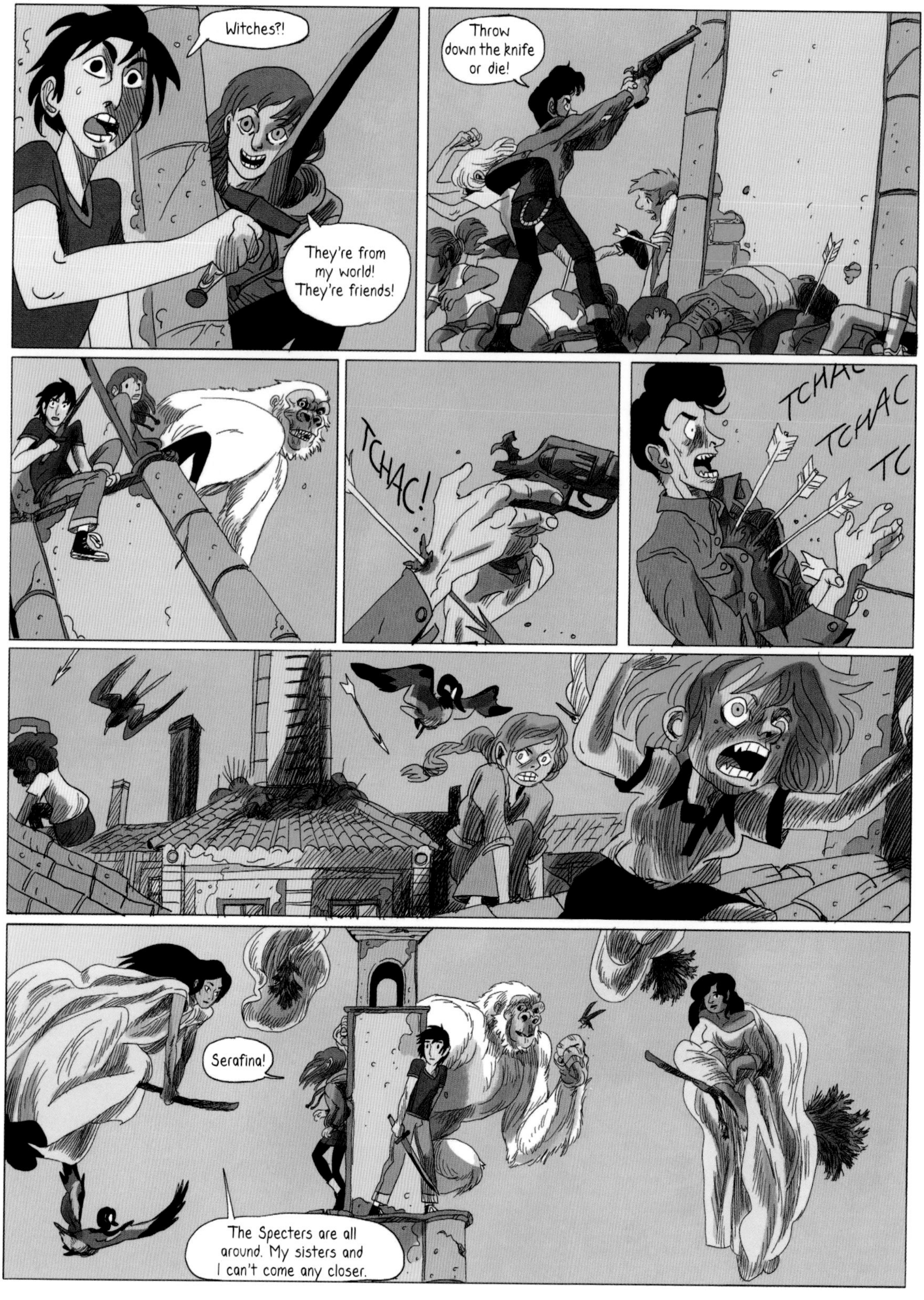
Witches?!
They're from my world! They're friends!
Throw down the knife or die!
TCHAC!
TCHAC
TCHAC
TC
Serafina!
The Specters are all around. My sisters and I can't come any closer.

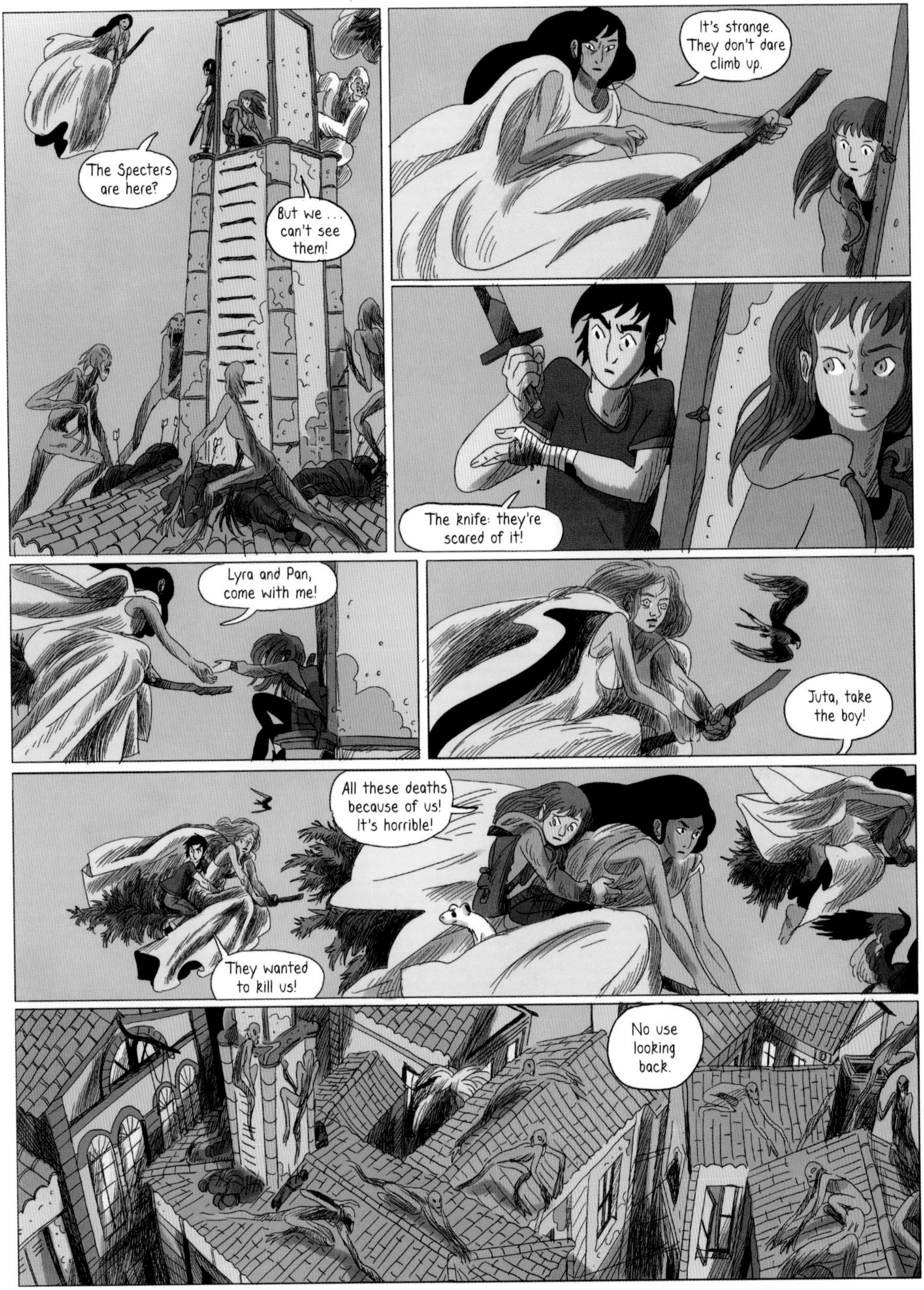
The Specters are here?
But we . . . can't see them!
It's strange. They don't dare climb up.
The knife: they're scared of it!
Lyra and Pan, come with me!
Juta, take the boy!
All these deaths because of us! It's horrible!
They wanted to kill us!
No use looking back.

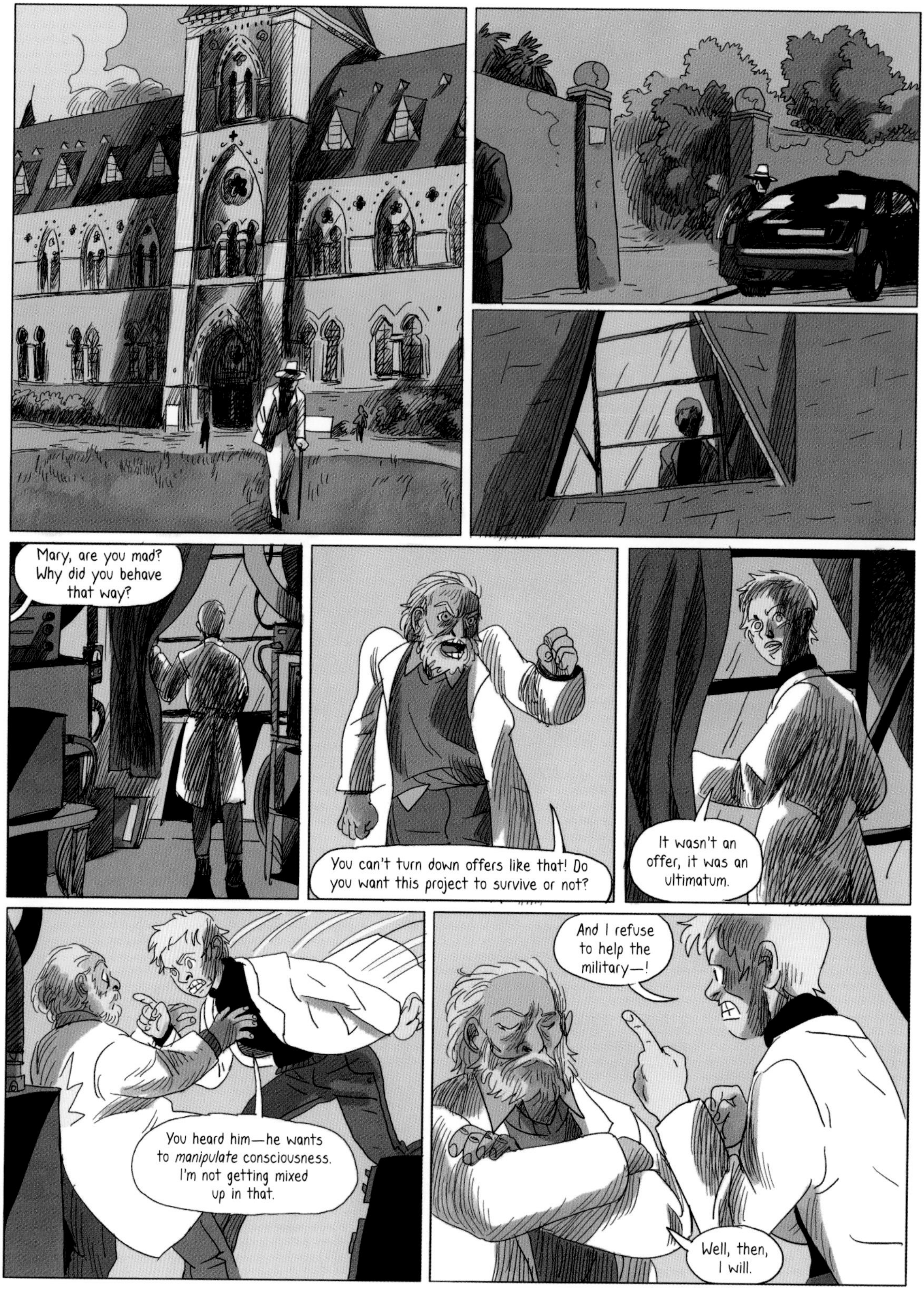
Mary, are you mad? Why did you behave that way?
You can't turn down offers like that! Do you want this project to survive or not?
It wasn't an offer, it was an ultimatum.
You heard him—he wants to *manipulate* consciousness. I'm not getting mixed up in that.
And I refuse to help the military—!
Well, then, I will.

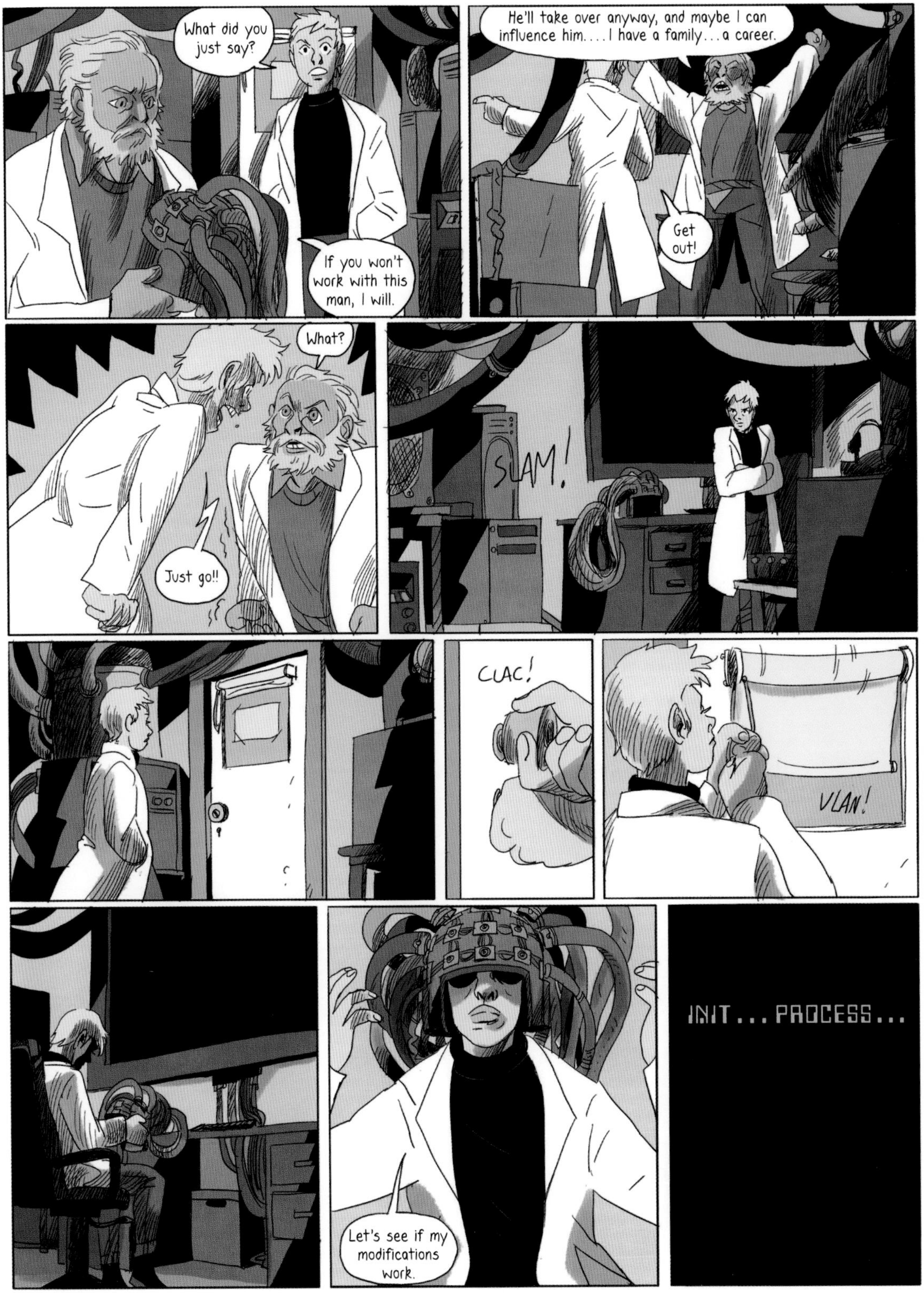
What did you just say?
If you won't work with this man, I will.
He'll take over anyway, and maybe I can influence him. . . . I have a family . . . a career.
Get out!
What?
Just go!!
SLAM!
CLAC!
VLAN!
Let's see if my modifications work.
INIT . . . PROCESS . . .

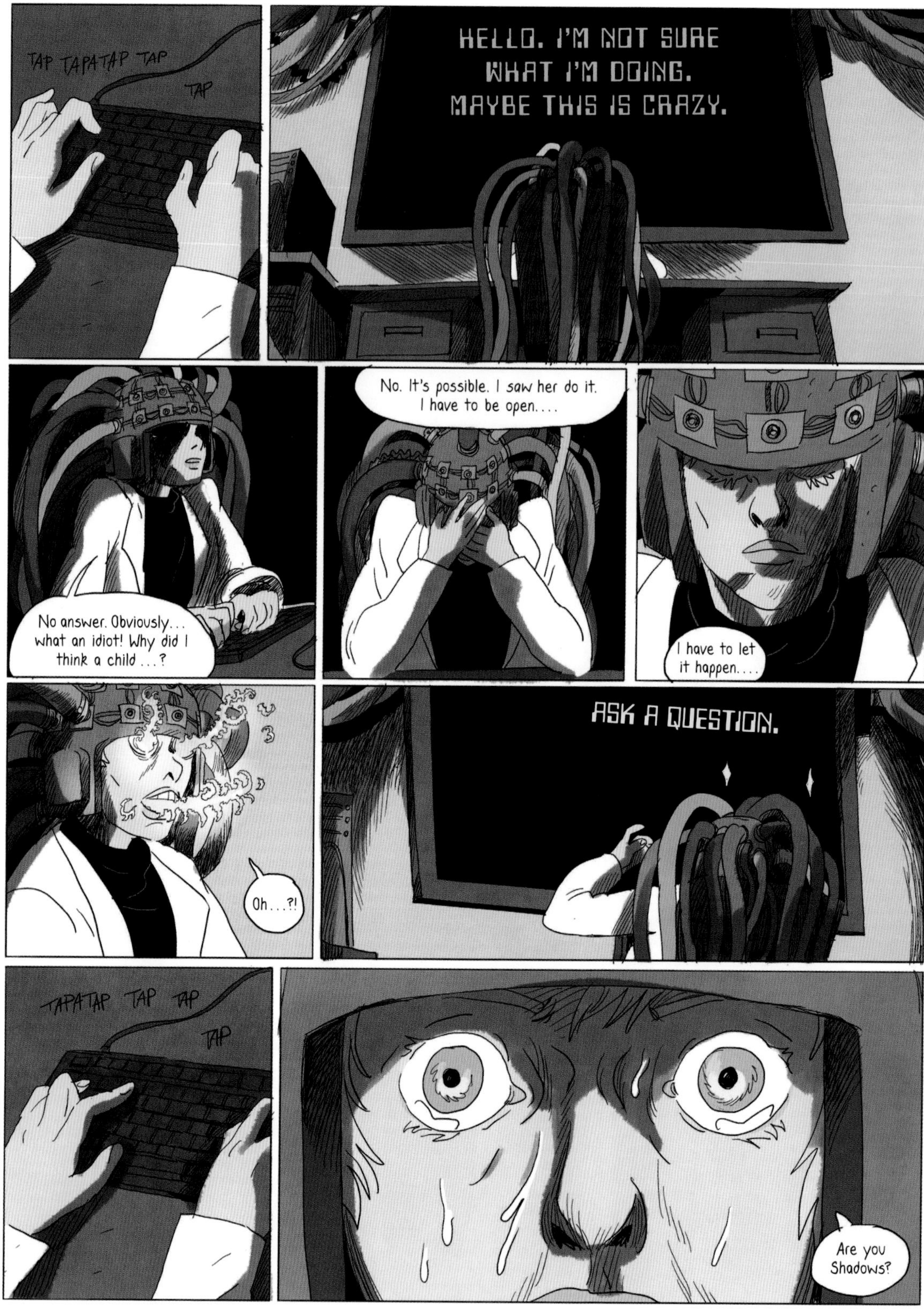
TAP TAPATAP TAP
TAP
HELLO. I'M NOT SURE
WHAT I'M DOING.
MAYBE THIS IS CRAZY.
No answer. Obviously... what an idiot! Why did I think a child ...?
No. It's possible. I saw her do it. I have to be open....
I have to let it happen....
Oh...?!
ASK A QUESTION.
TAPATAP TAP TAP
TAP
Are you Shadows?

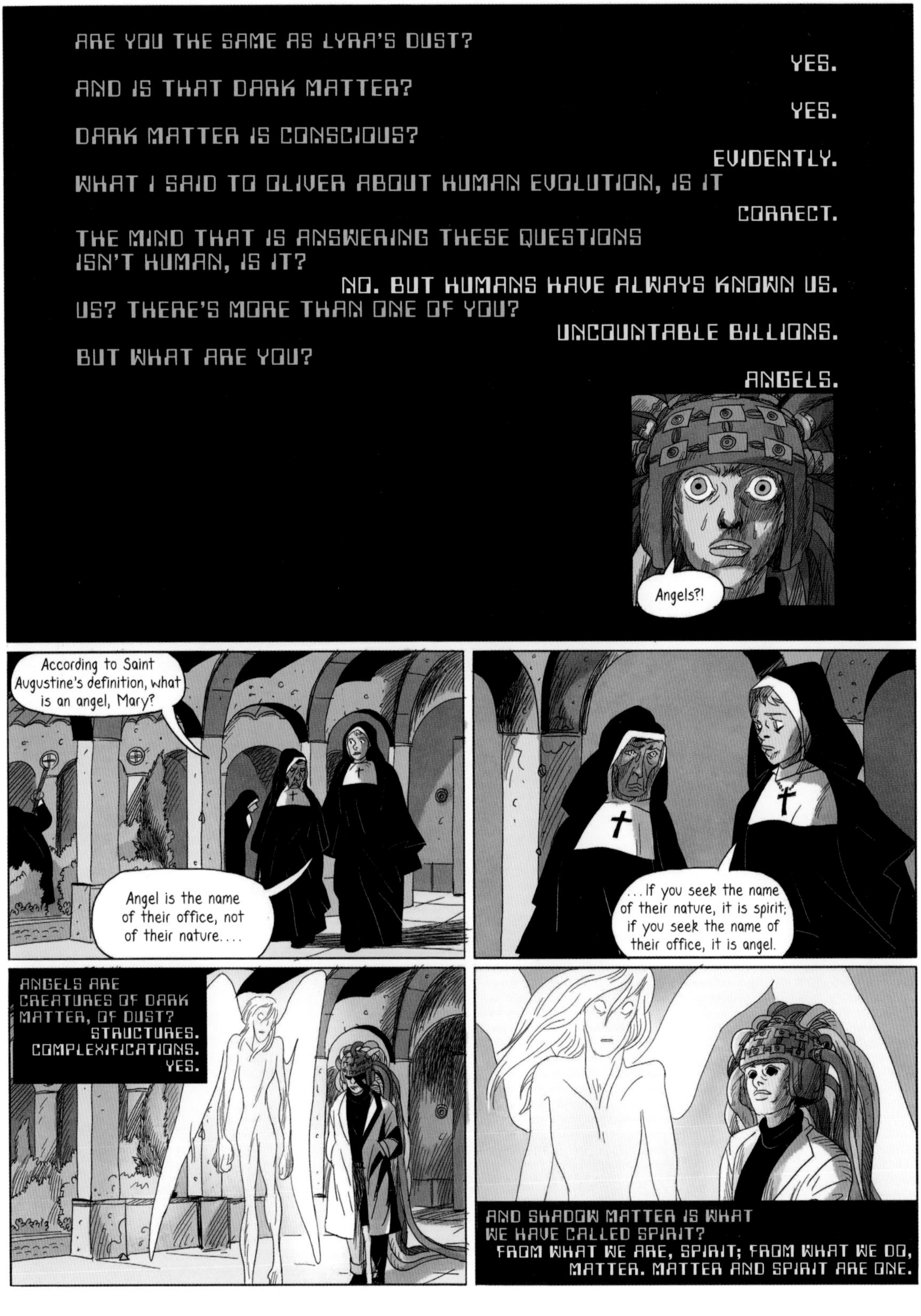
ARE YOU THE SAME AS LYRA'S DUST?
YES.
AND IS THAT DARK MATTER?
YES.
DARK MATTER IS CONSCIOUS?
EVIDENTLY.
WHAT I SAID TO OLIVER ABOUT HUMAN EVOLUTION, IS IT
CORRECT.
THE MIND THAT IS ANSWERING THESE QUESTIONS ISN'T HUMAN, IS IT?
NO. BUT HUMANS HAVE ALWAYS KNOWN US.
US? THERE'S MORE THAN ONE OF YOU?
UNCOUNTABLE BILLIONS.
BUT WHAT ARE YOU?
ANGELS.
Angels?!
According to Saint Augustine's definition, what is an angel, Mary?
Angel is the name of their office, not of their nature....
...If you seek the name of their nature, it is spirit; if you seek the name of their office, it is angel.
ANGELS ARE CREATURES OF DARK MATTER, OF DUST?
STRUCTURES. COMPLEXIFICATIONS. YES.
AND SHADOW MATTER IS WHAT WE HAVE CALLED SPIRIT?
FROM WHAT WE ARE, SPIRIT; FROM WHAT WE DO, MATTER. MATTER AND SPIRIT ARE ONE.

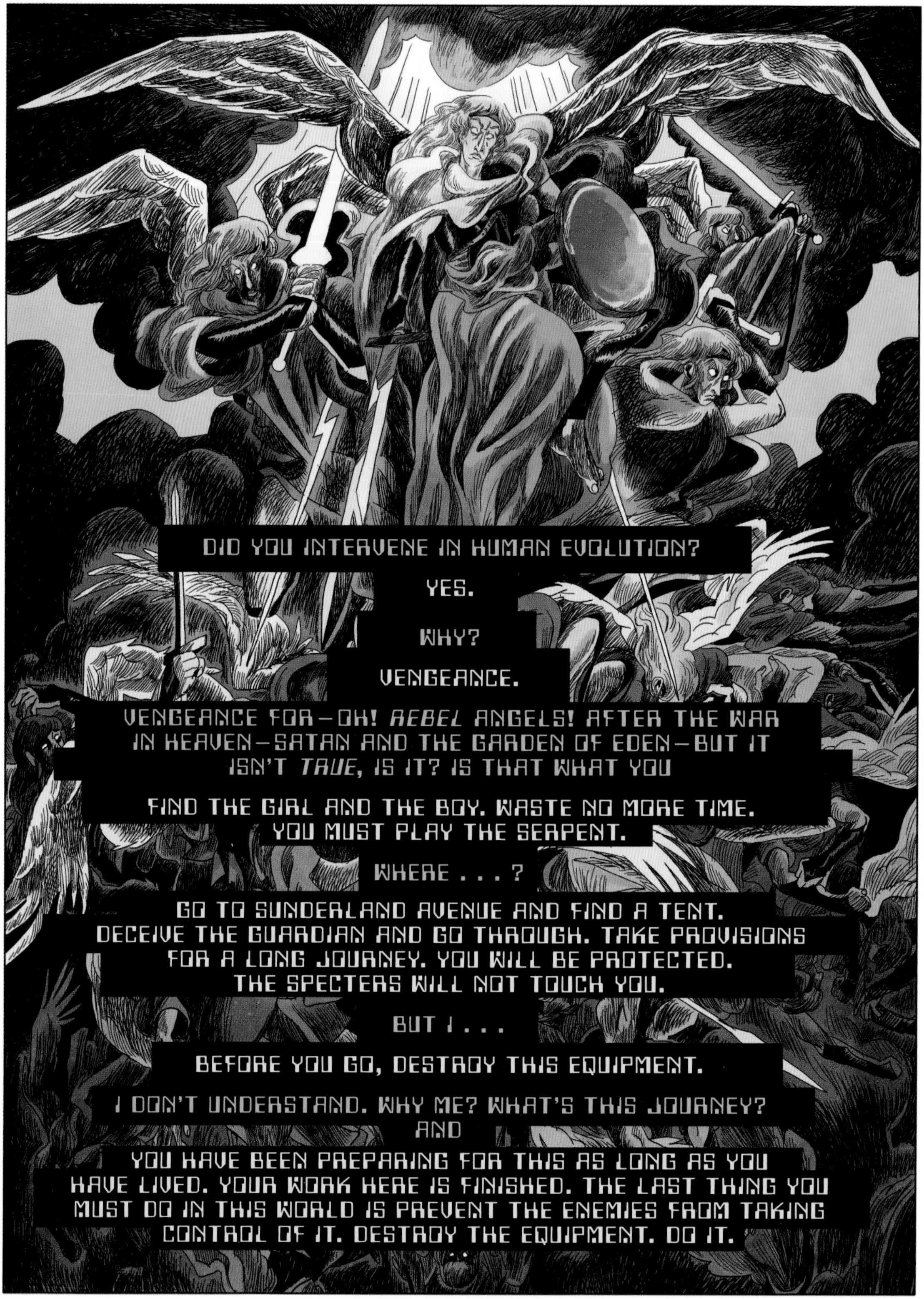
DID YOU INTERVENE IN HUMAN EVOLUTION?
YES.
WHY?
VENGEANCE.
VENGEANCE FOR—OH! *REBEL* ANGELS! AFTER THE WAR IN HEAVEN—SATAN AND THE GARDEN OF EDEN—BUT IT ISN'T *TRUE*, IS IT? IS THAT WHAT YOU
FIND THE GIRL AND THE BOY. WASTE NO MORE TIME. YOU MUST PLAY THE SERPENT.
WHERE . . . ?
GO TO SUNDERLAND AVENUE AND FIND A TENT. DECEIVE THE GUARDIAN AND GO THROUGH. TAKE PROVISIONS FOR A LONG JOURNEY. YOU WILL BE PROTECTED. THE SPECTERS WILL NOT TOUCH YOU.
BUT I . . .
BEFORE YOU GO, DESTROY THIS EQUIPMENT.
I DON'T UNDERSTAND. WHY ME? WHAT'S THIS JOURNEY? AND
YOU HAVE BEEN PREPARING FOR THIS AS LONG AS YOU HAVE LIVED. YOUR WORK HERE IS FINISHED. THE LAST THING YOU MUST DO IN THIS WORLD IS PREVENT THE ENEMIES FROM TAKING CONTROL OF IT. DESTROY THE EQUIPMENT. DO IT.

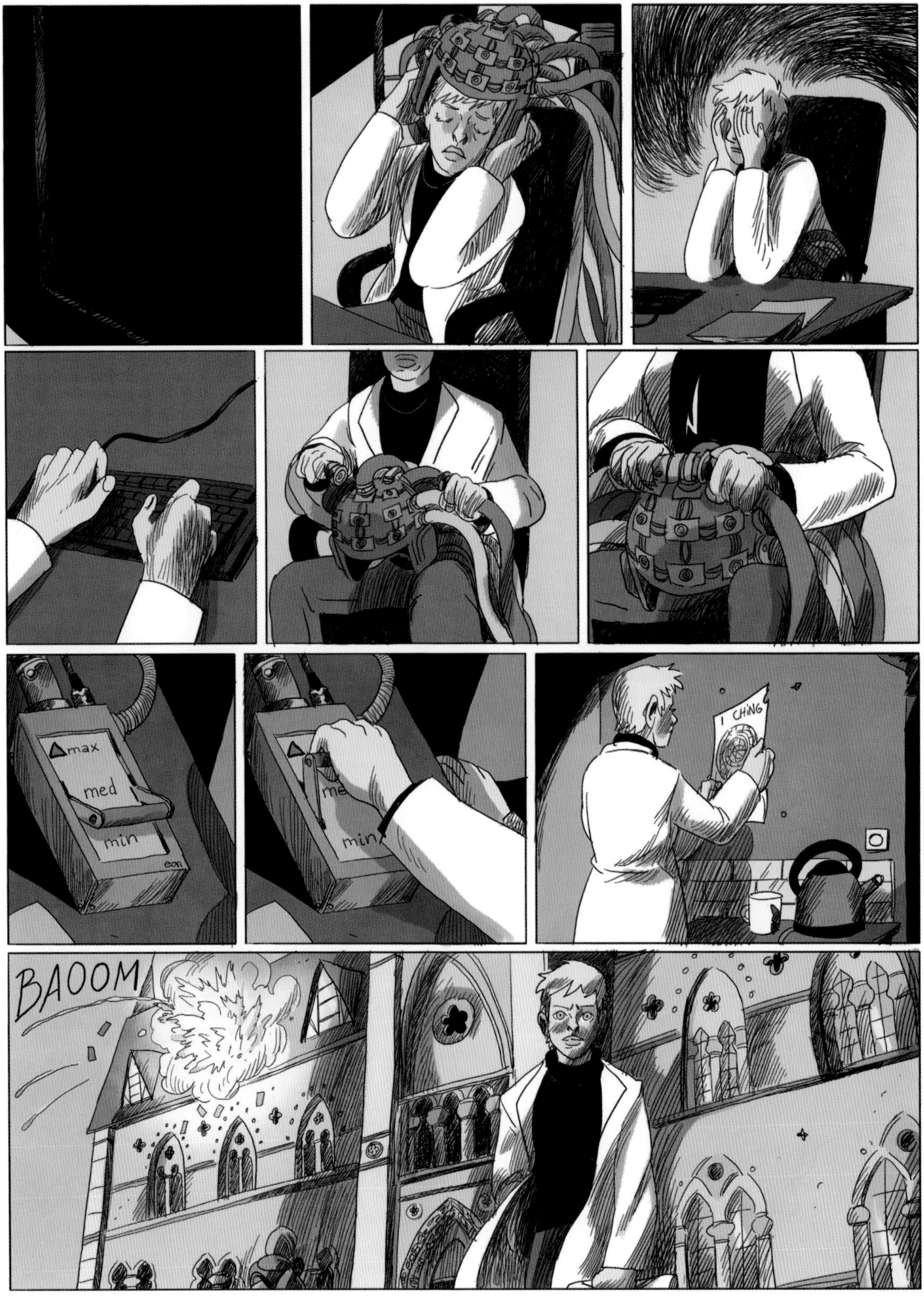
max
med
min
I CHING
BAOOM

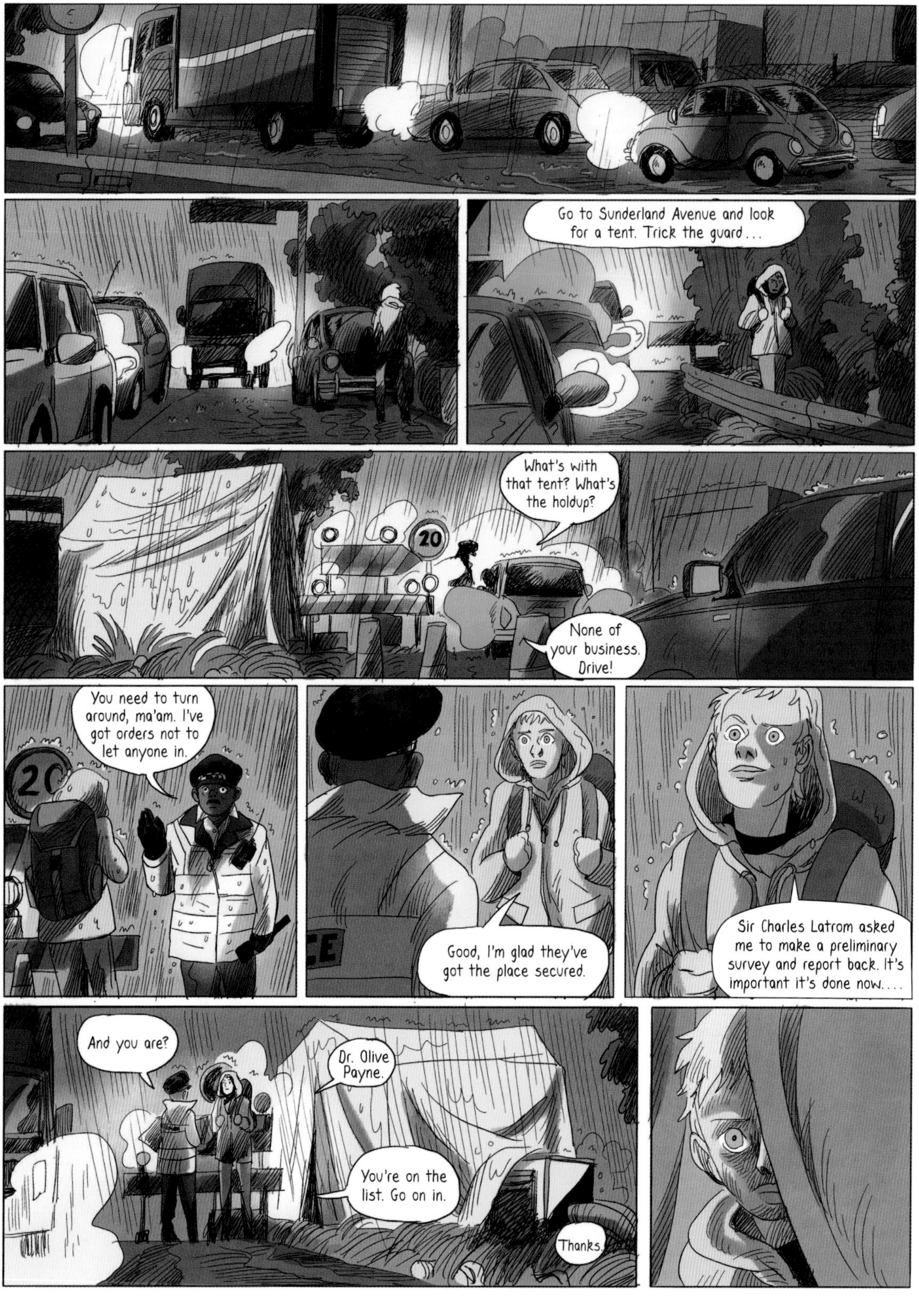
Go to Sunderland Avenue and look for a tent. Trick the guard . . .
What's with that tent? What's the holdup?
None of your business. Drive!
You need to turn around, ma'am. I've got orders not to let anyone in.
Good, I'm glad they've got the place secured.
Sir Charles Latrom asked me to make a preliminary survey and report back. It's important it's done now. . . .
And you are?
Dr. Olive Payne.
You're on the list. Go on in.
Thanks.

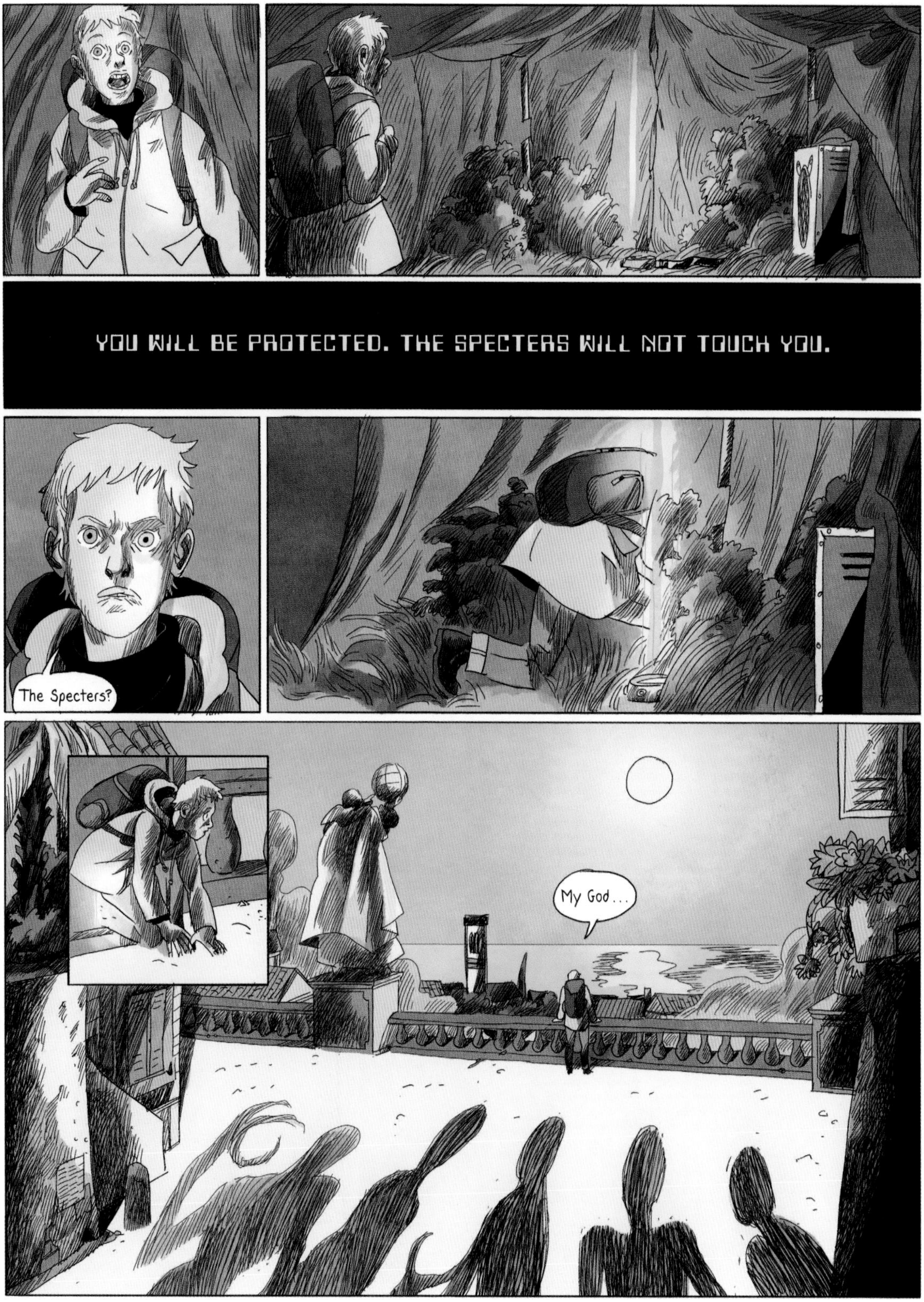
YOU WILL BE PROTECTED. THE SPECTERS WILL NOT TOUCH YOU.
The Specters?
My God...

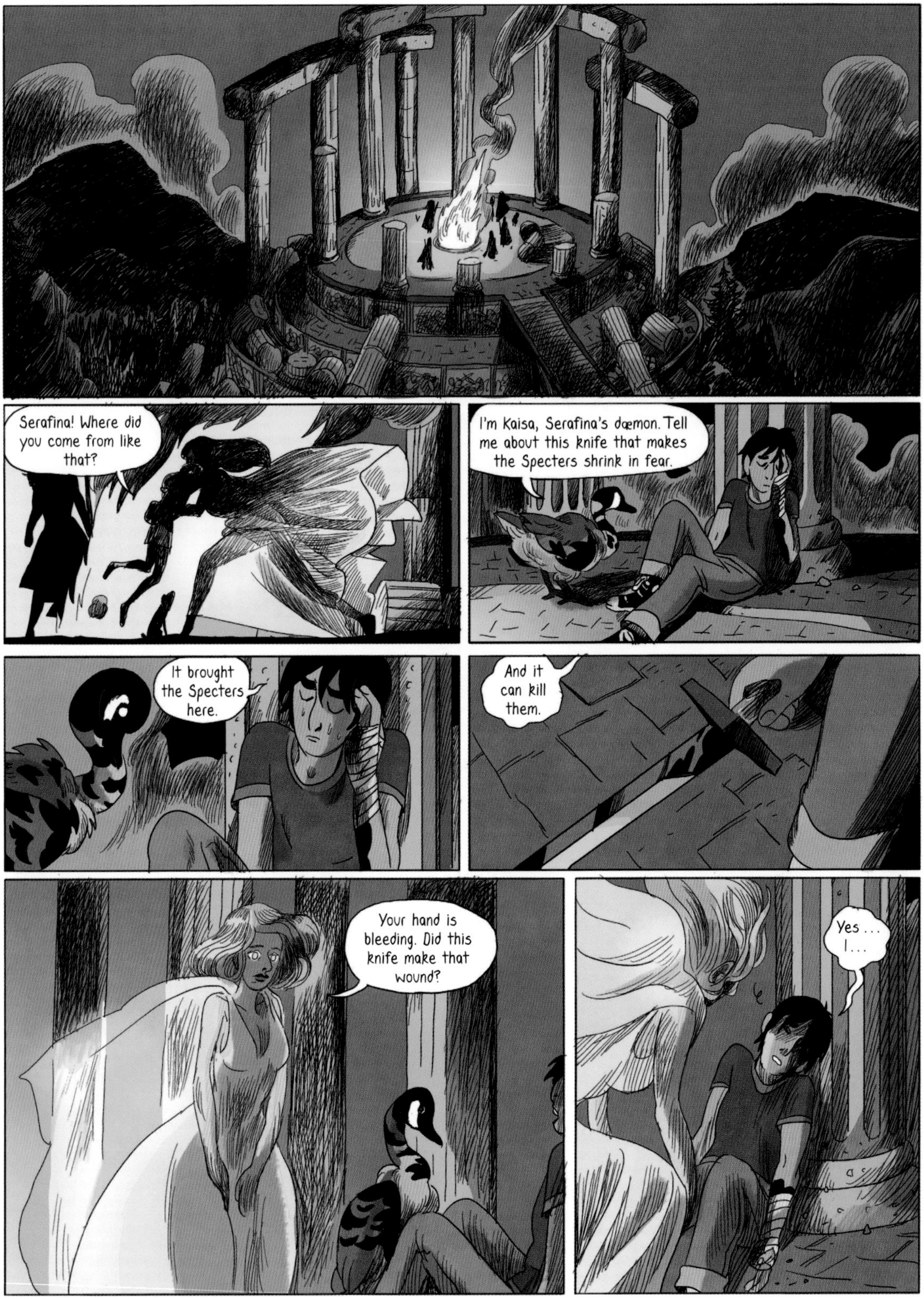
Serafina! Where did you come from like that?
I'm Kaisa, Serafina's dæmon. Tell me about this knife that makes the Specters shrink in fear.
It brought the Specters here.
And it can kill them.
Your hand is bleeding. Did this knife make that wound?
Yes . . . I . . .

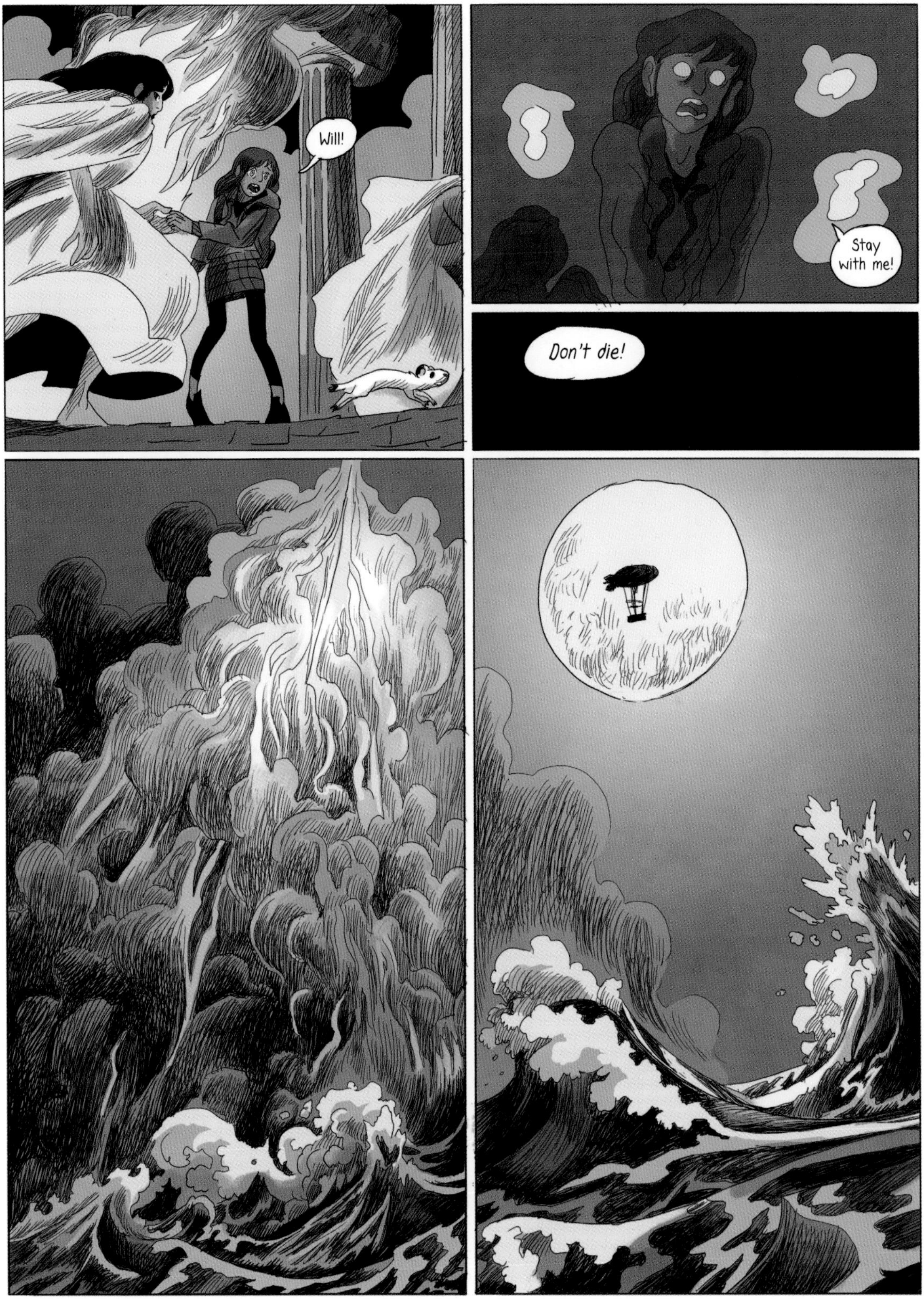
Will!
Stay with me!
Don't die!

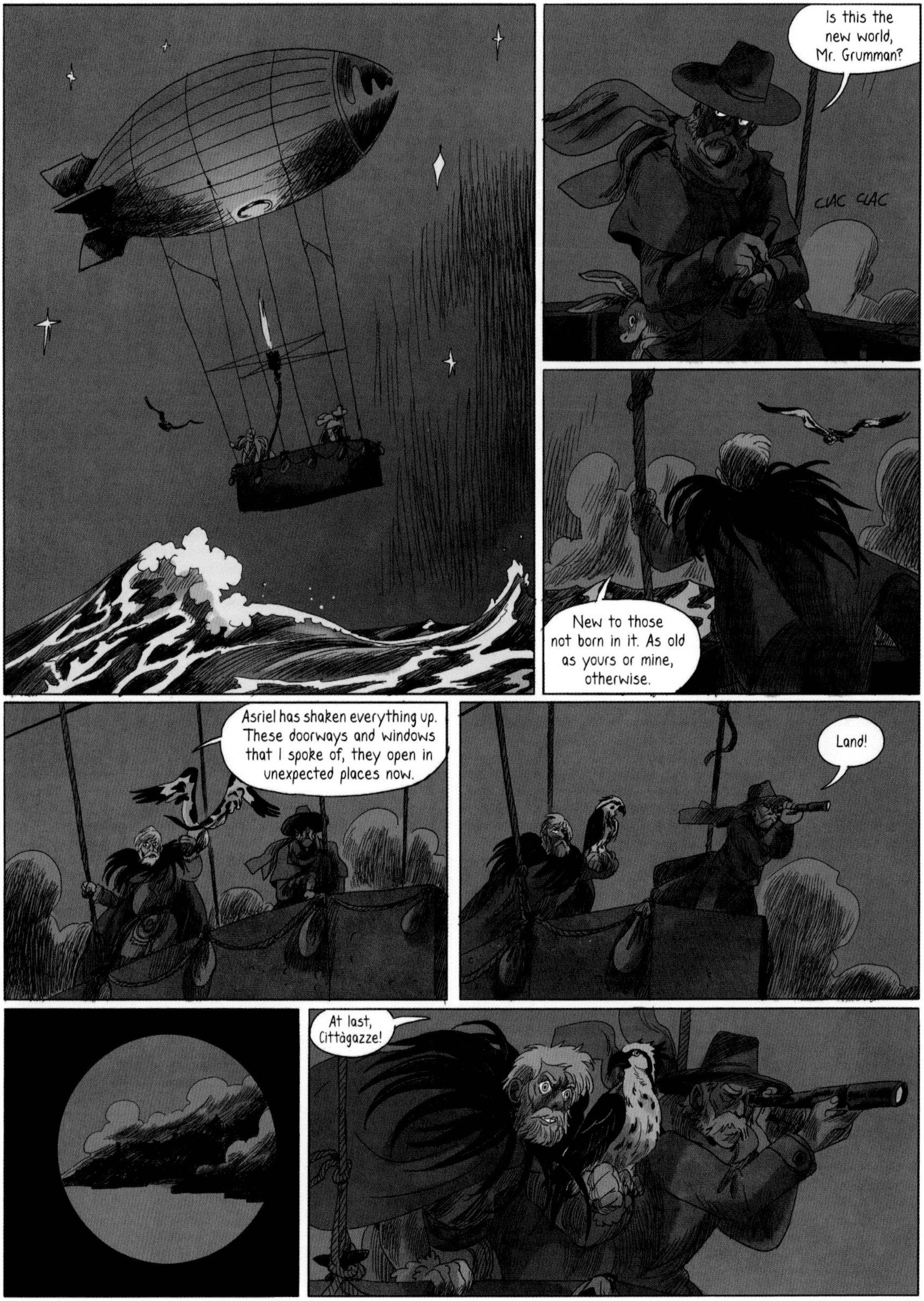
Is this the new world, Mr. Grumman?
CLAC CLAC
New to those not born in it. As old as yours or mine, otherwise.
Asriel has shaken everything up. These doorways and windows that I spoke of, they open in unexpected places now.
Land!
At last, Cittàgazze!

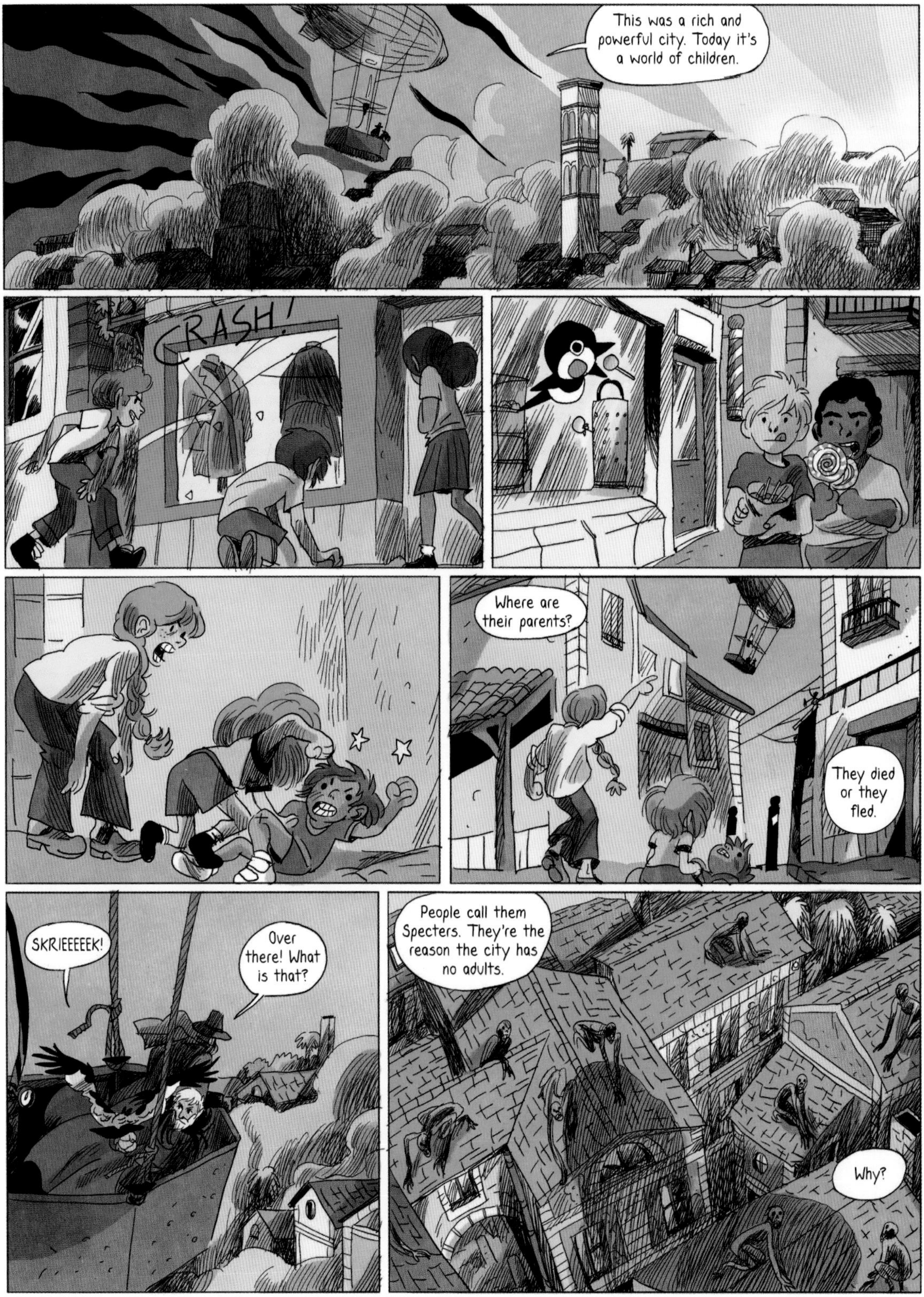
This was a rich and powerful city. Today it's a world of children.
CRASH!
Where are their parents?
They died or they fled.
SKRIEEEEEK!
Over there! What is that?
People call them Specters. They're the reason the city has no adults.
Why?

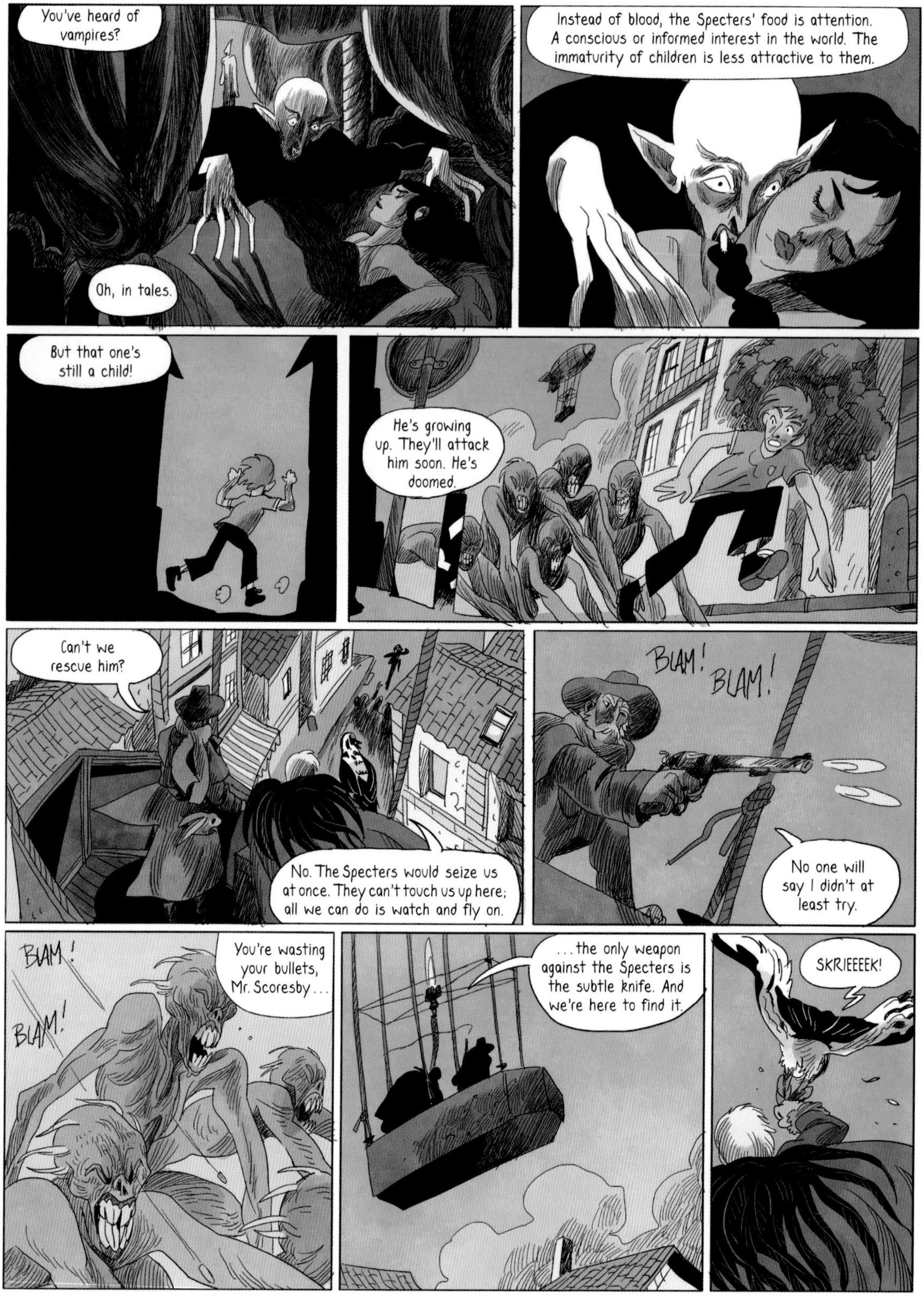
You've heard of vampires?
Oh, in tales.
Instead of blood, the Specters' food is attention. A conscious or informed interest in the world. The immaturity of children is less attractive to them.
But that one's still a child!
He's growing up. They'll attack him soon. He's doomed.
Can't we rescue him?
No. The Specters would seize us at once. They can't touch us up here; all we can do is watch and fly on.
BLAM! BLAM!
No one will say I didn't at least try.
BLAM! BLAM!
You're wasting your bullets, Mr. Scoresby...
...the only weapon against the Specters is the subtle knife. And we're here to find it.
SKRIEEEEK!

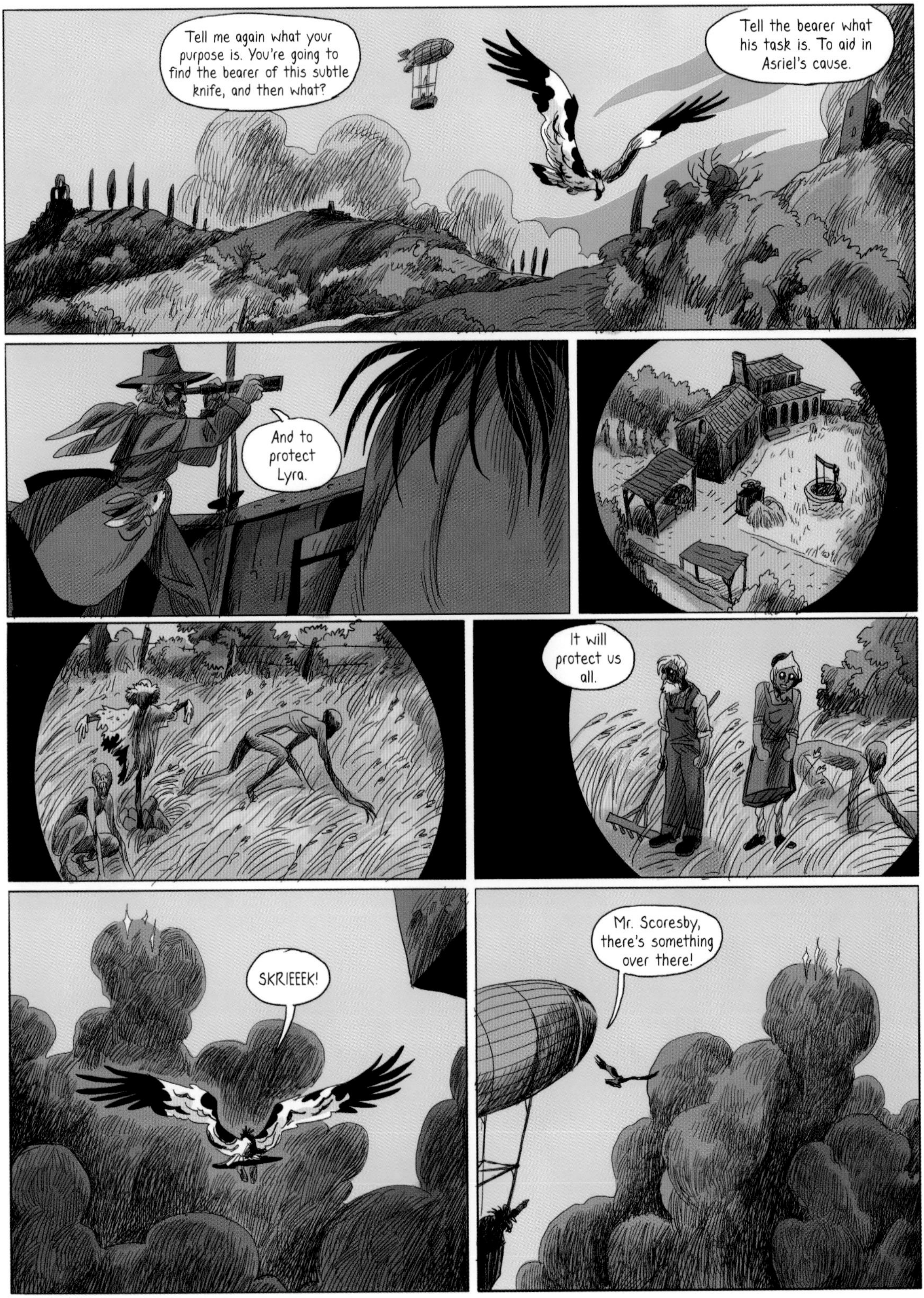
Tell me again what your purpose is. You're going to find the bearer of this subtle knife, and then what?
Tell the bearer what his task is. To aid in Asriel's cause.
And to protect Lyra.
It will protect us all.
SKRIEEEK!
Mr. Scoresby, there's something over there!

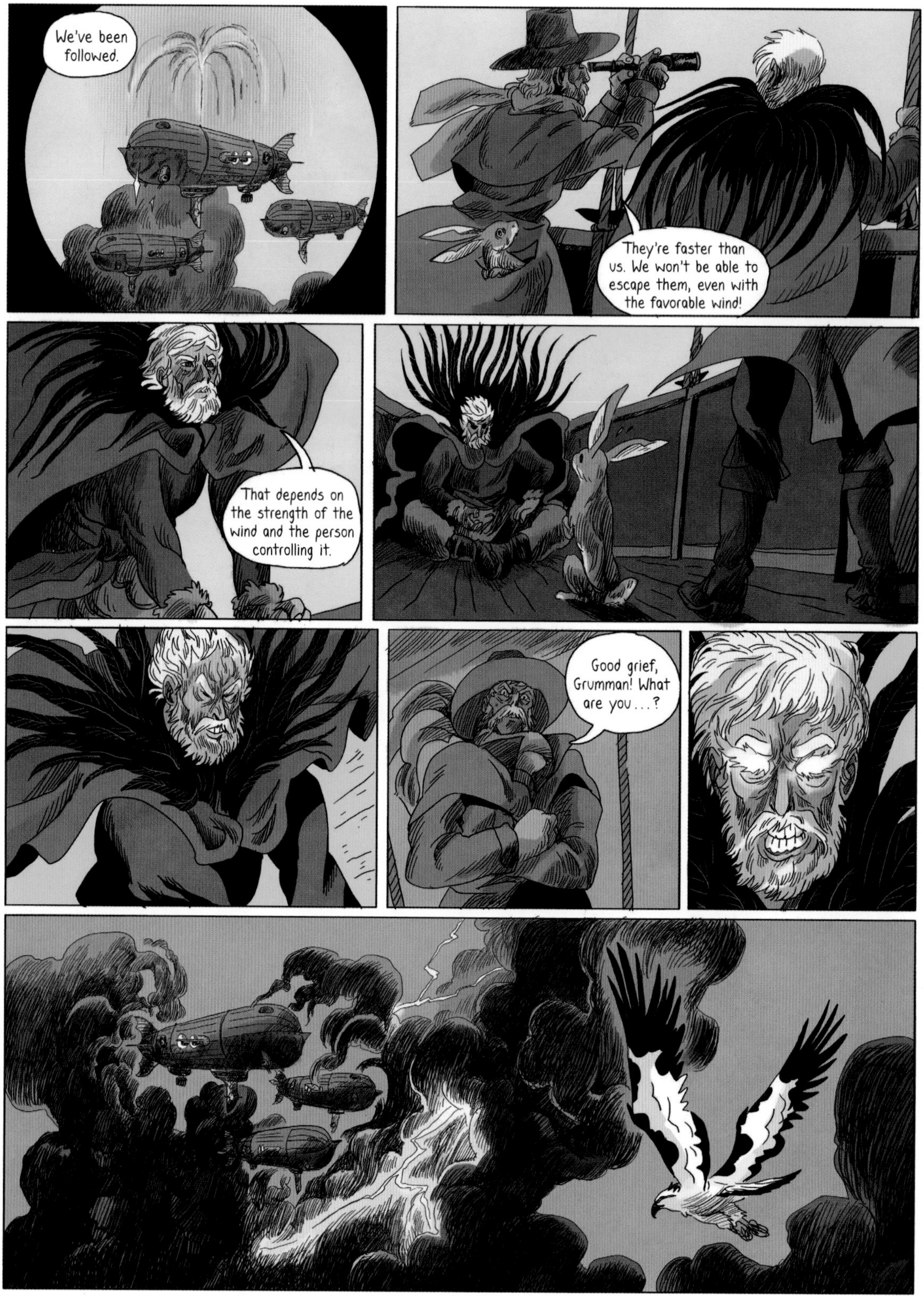
We've been followed.
They're faster than us. We won't be able to escape them, even with the favorable wind!
That depends on the strength of the wind and the person controlling it.
Good grief, Grumman! What are you . . . ?

Amazing!
Keep it up!

SKRIEEEEEEK!

KRAAK!

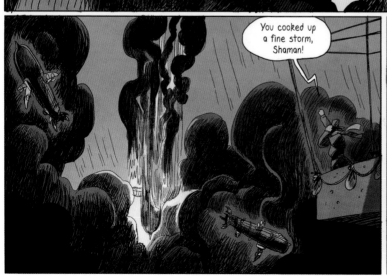

You cooked up
a fine storm,
Shaman!

SCHRAAAAAK!

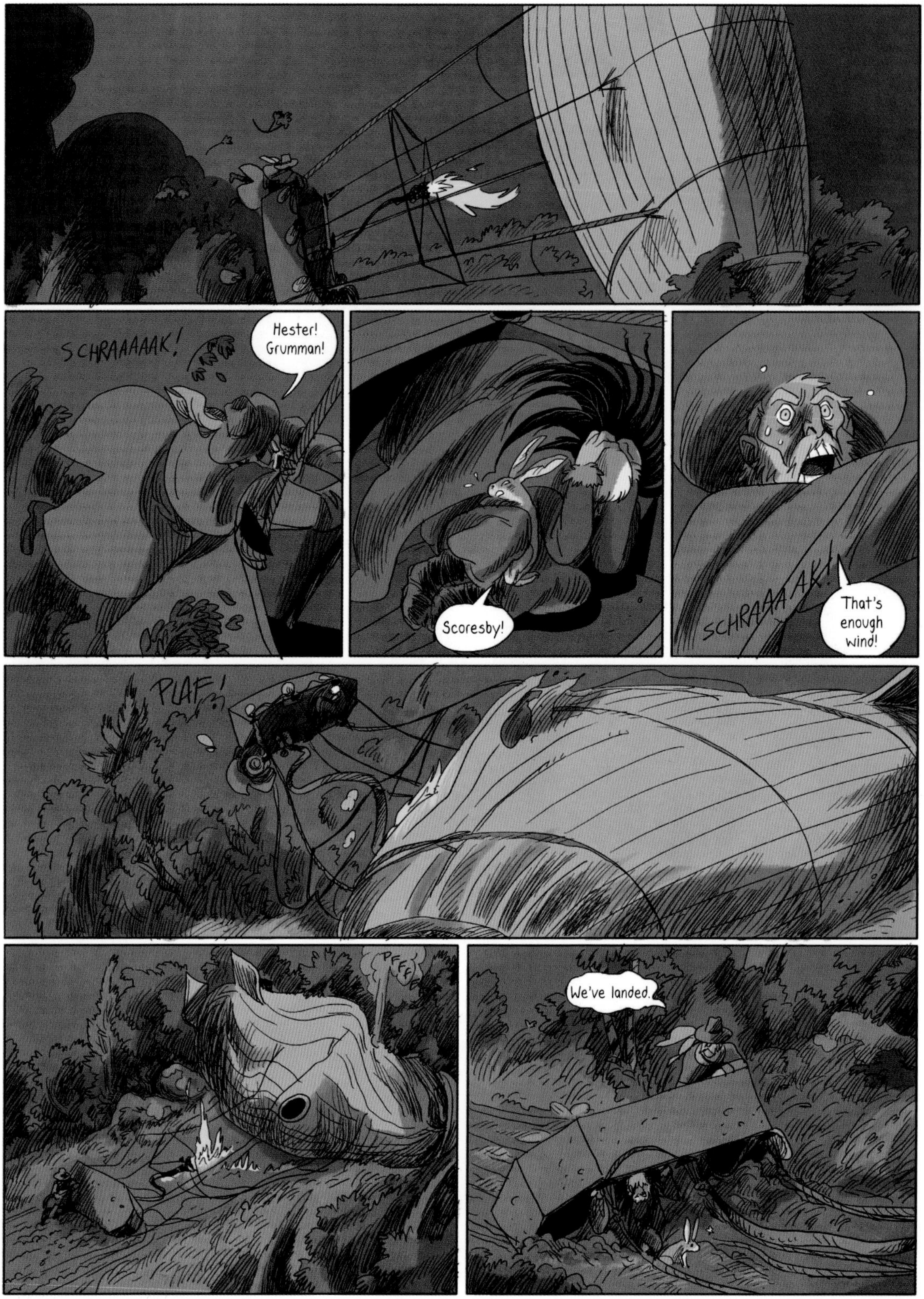
SCHRAAAAAK!
Hester! Grumman!
Scoresby!
SCHRAAAAAK!
That's enough wind!
PLAF!
We've landed.

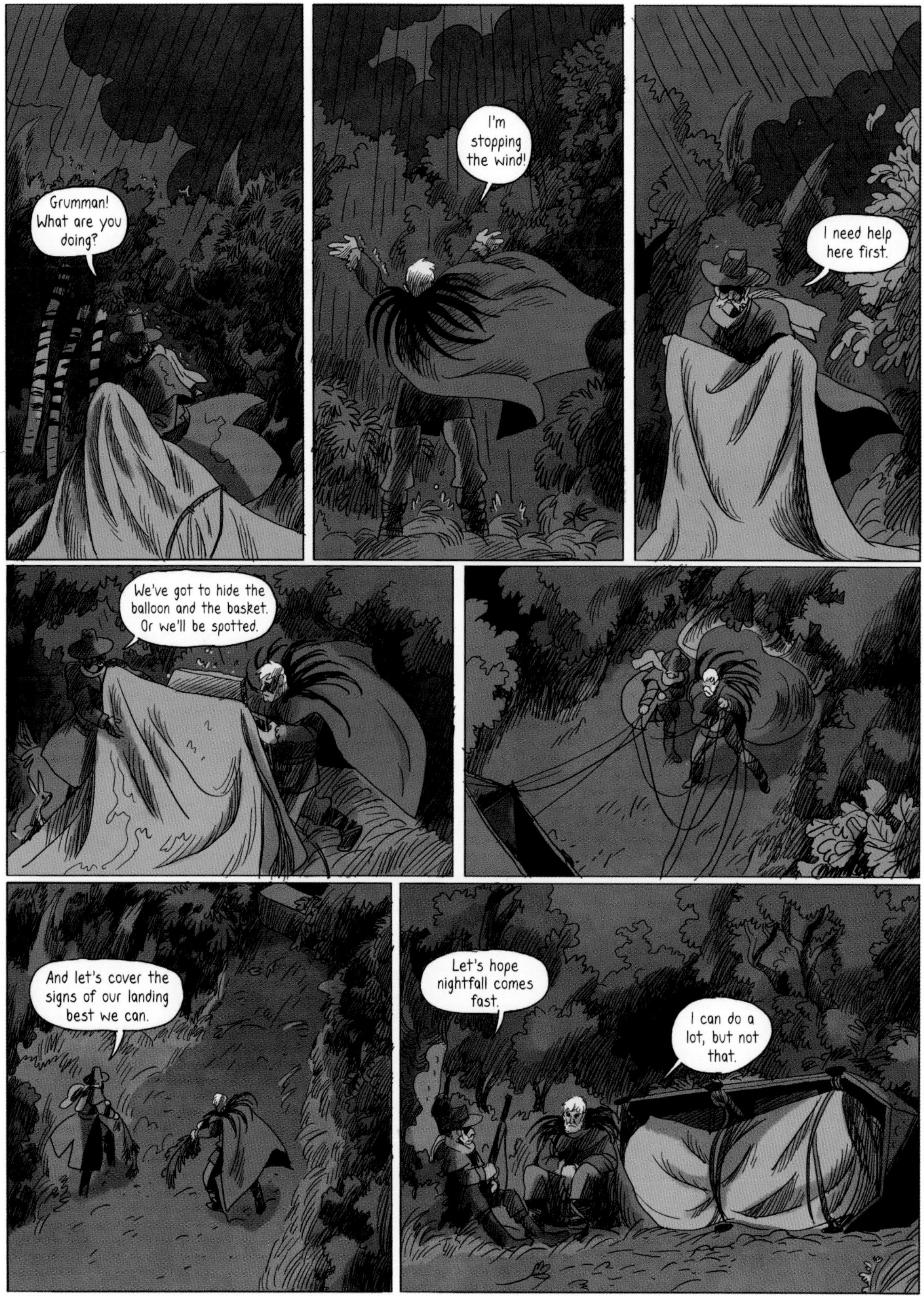
Grumman! What are you doing?
I'm stopping the wind!
I need help here first.
We've got to hide the balloon and the basket. Or we'll be spotted.
And let's cover the signs of our landing best we can.
Let's hope nightfall comes fast.
I can do a lot, but not that.

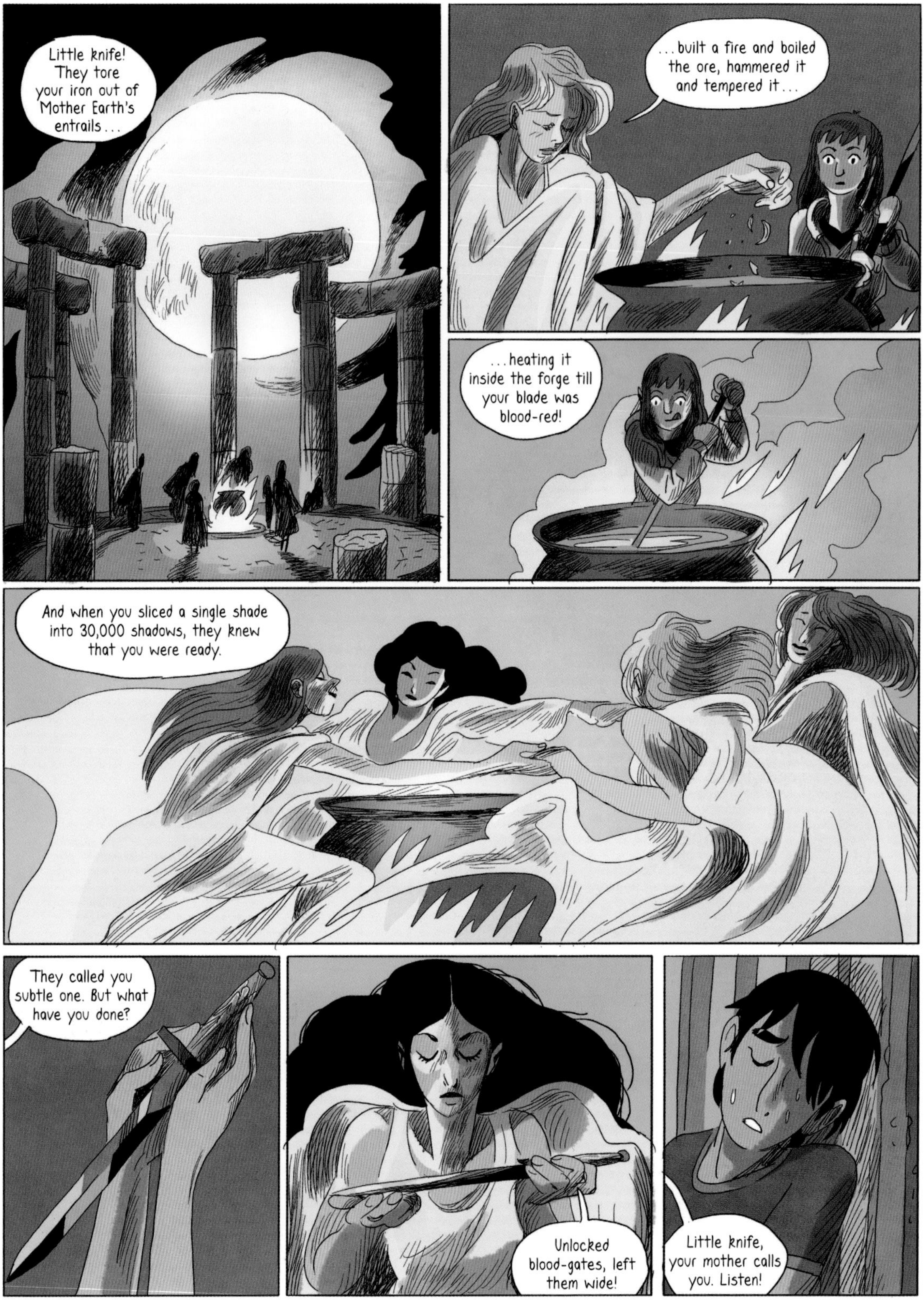
Little knife! They tore your iron out of Mother Earth's entrails . . .
. . . built a fire and boiled the ore, hammered it and tempered it . . .
. . . heating it inside the forge till your blade was blood-red!
And when you sliced a single shade into 30,000 shadows, they knew that you were ready.
They called you subtle one. But what have you done?
Unlocked blood-gates, left them wide!
Little knife, your mother calls you. Listen!

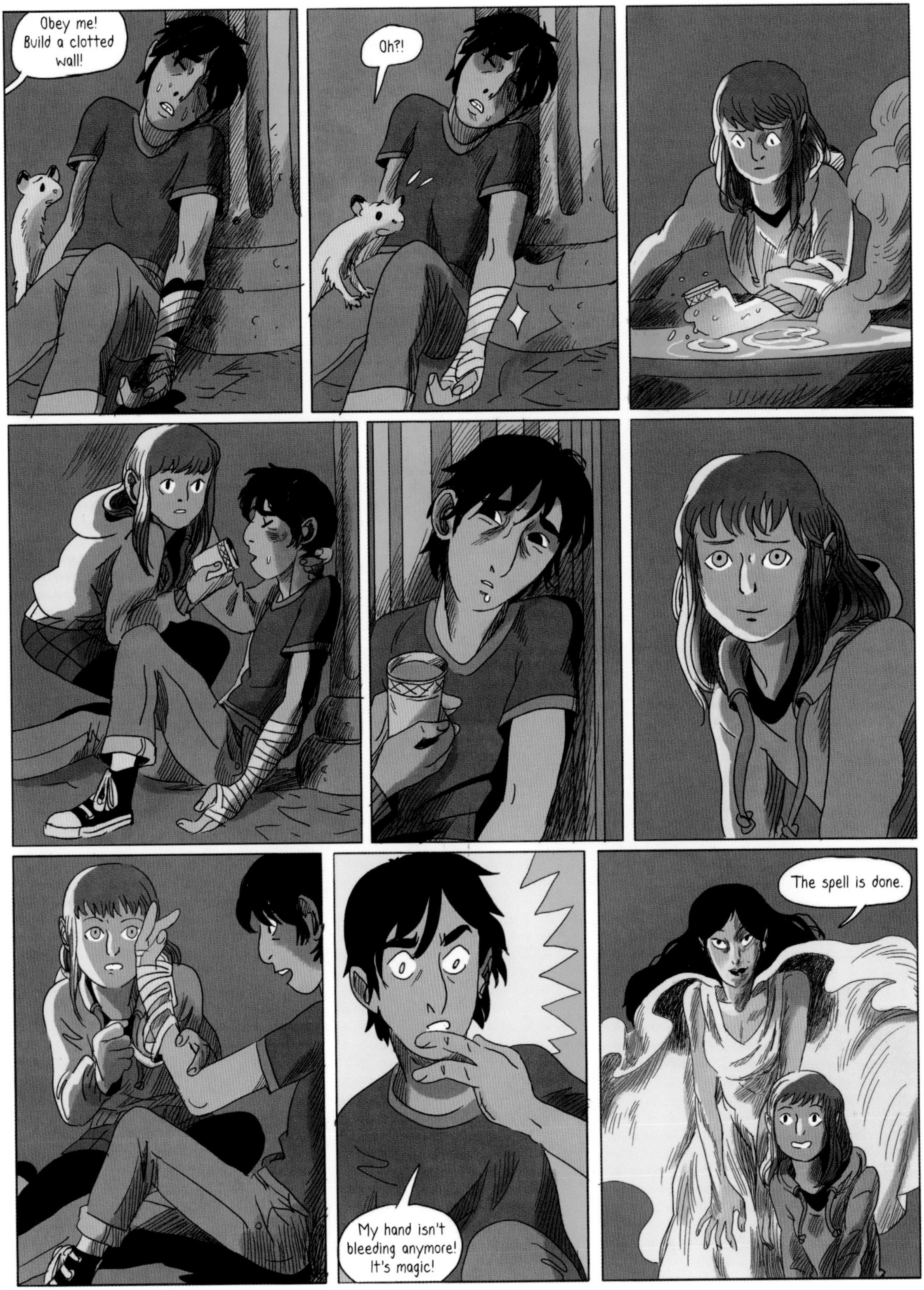
Obey me!
Build a clotted wall!
Oh?!
My hand isn't bleeding anymore! It's magic!
The spell is done.

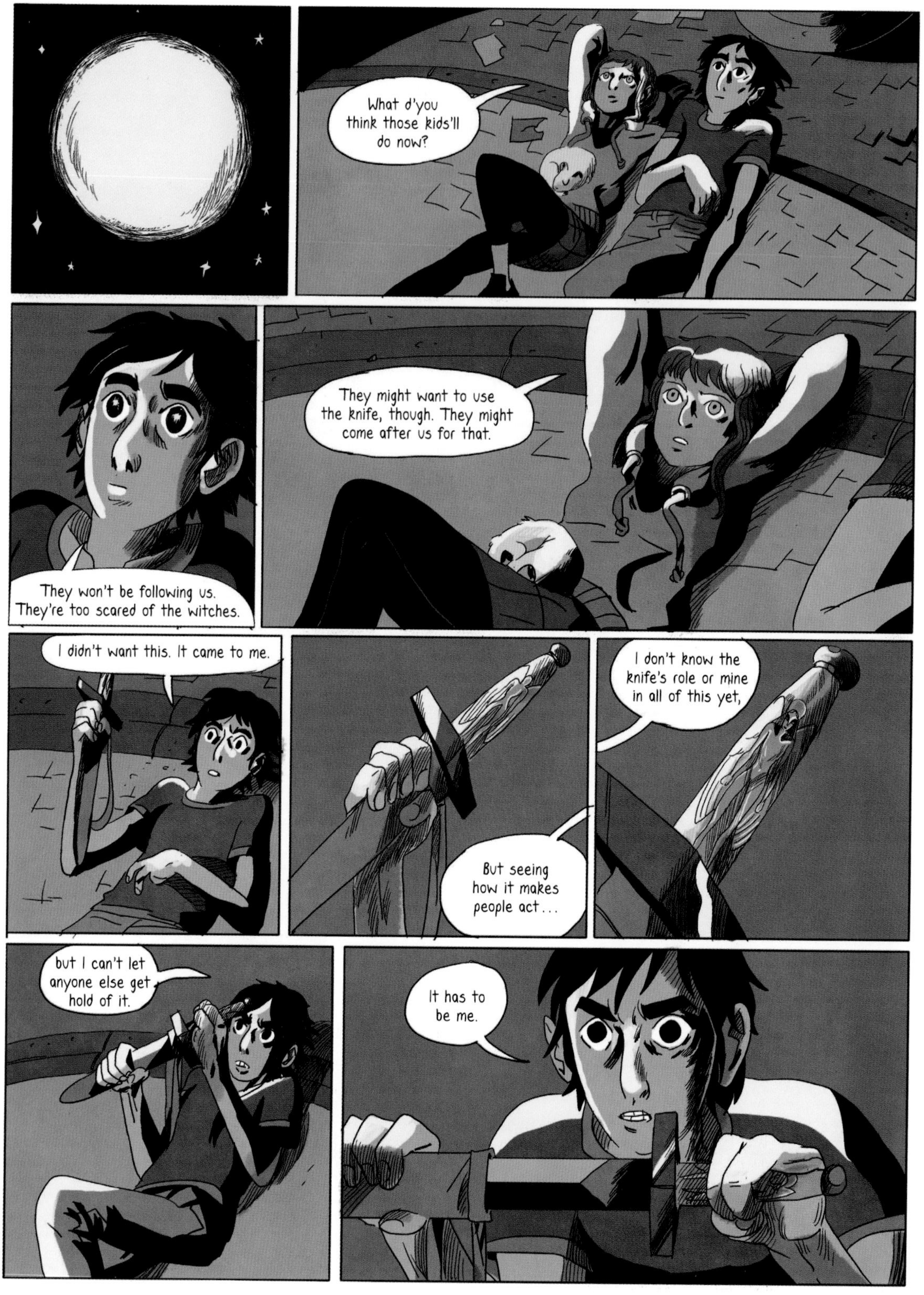
What d'you think those kids'll do now?
They won't be following us. They're too scared of the witches.
They might want to use the knife, though. They might come after us for that.
I didn't want this. It came to me.
I don't know the knife's role or mine in all of this yet,
But seeing how it makes people act...
but I can't let anyone else get hold of it.
It has to be me.

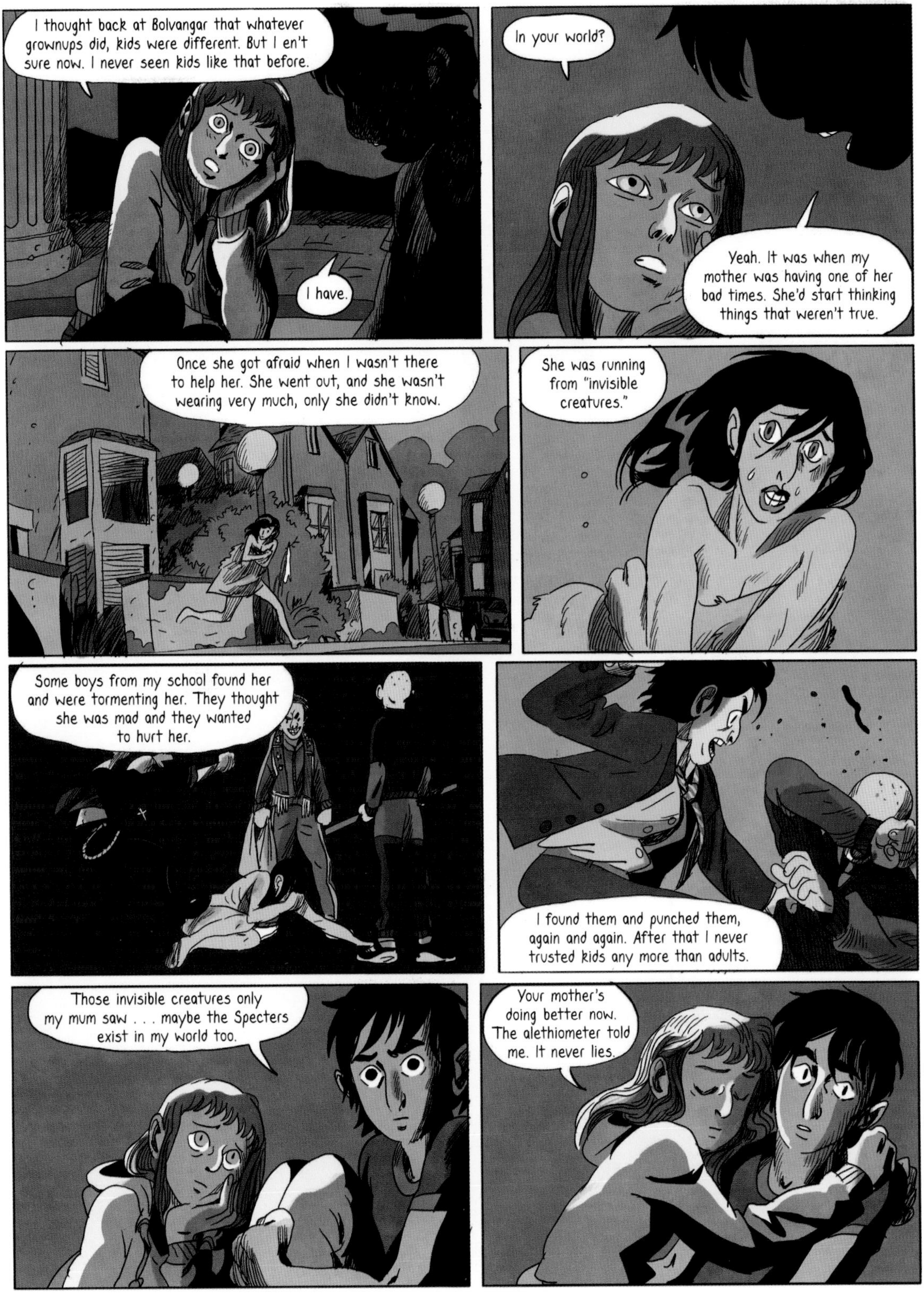
I thought back at Bolvangar that whatever grownups did, kids were different. But I en't sure now. I never seen kids like that before.
I have.
In your world?
Yeah. It was when my mother was having one of her bad times. She'd start thinking things that weren't true.
Once she got afraid when I wasn't there to help her. She went out, and she wasn't wearing very much, only she didn't know.
She was running from "invisible creatures."
Some boys from my school found her and were tormenting her. They thought she was mad and they wanted to hurt her.
I found them and punched them, again and again. After that I never trusted kids any more than adults.
Those invisible creatures only my mum saw . . . maybe the Specters exist in my world too.
Your mother's doing better now. The alethiometer told me. It never lies.

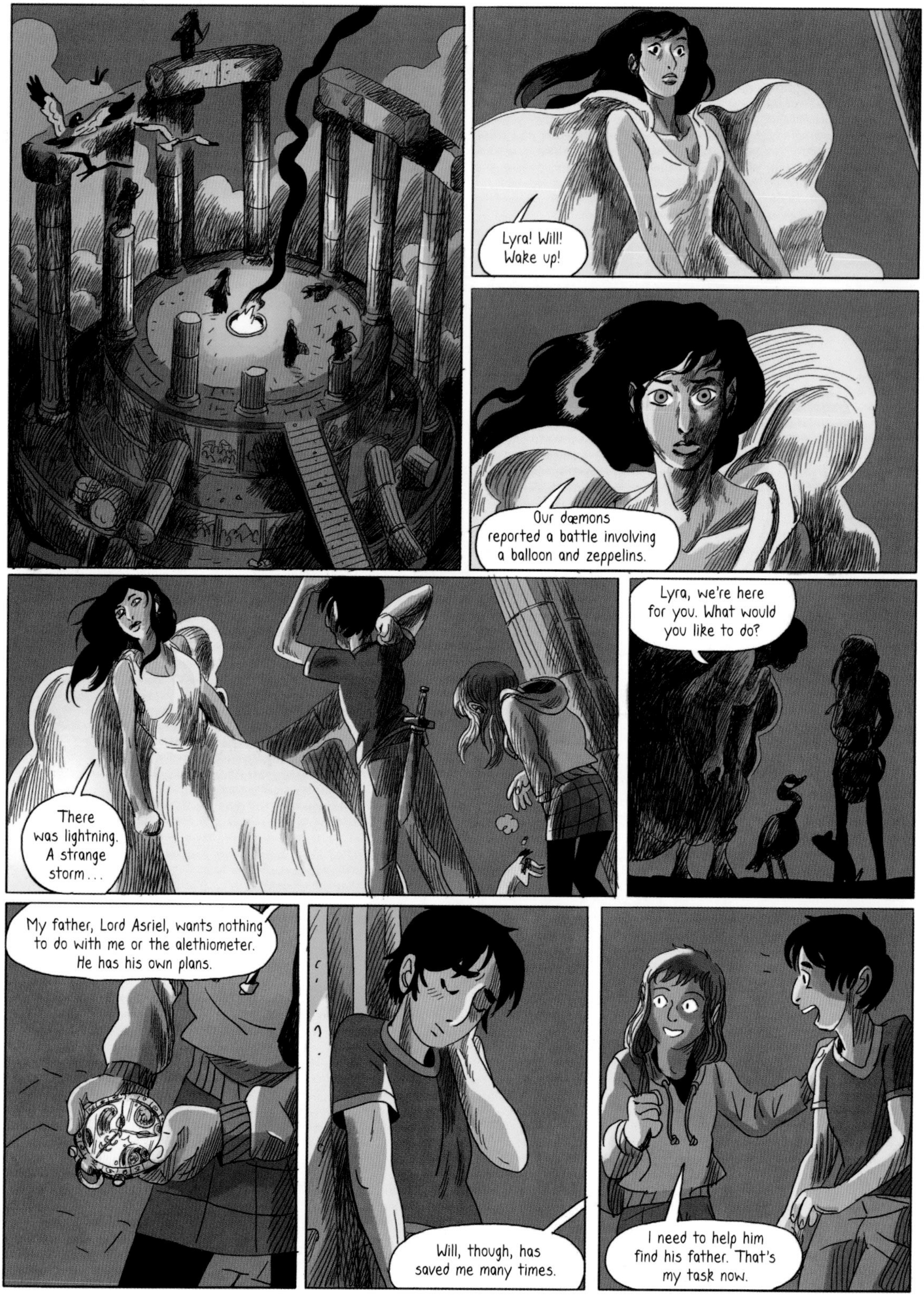
Lyra! Will! Wake up!
Our dæmons reported a battle involving a balloon and zeppelins.
There was lightning. A strange storm . . .
Lyra, we're here for you. What would you like to do?
My father, Lord Asriel, wants nothing to do with me or the alethiometer. He has his own plans.
Will, though, has saved me many times.
I need to help him find his father. That's my task now.

The alethiometer will tell us where to look.

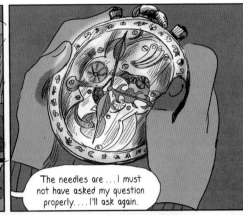
The needles are ... I must not have asked my question properly. ... I'll ask again.

Will! It's saying that your father is here!

What? Where? Can't you be more precise?

I can't ask the alethiometer a direct question. It doesn't work like that.

But it's saying that the path that leads to your father cuts through the mountains.

Either he's there, or we'll find another window ... that will bring us closer to him.

So far and so near.

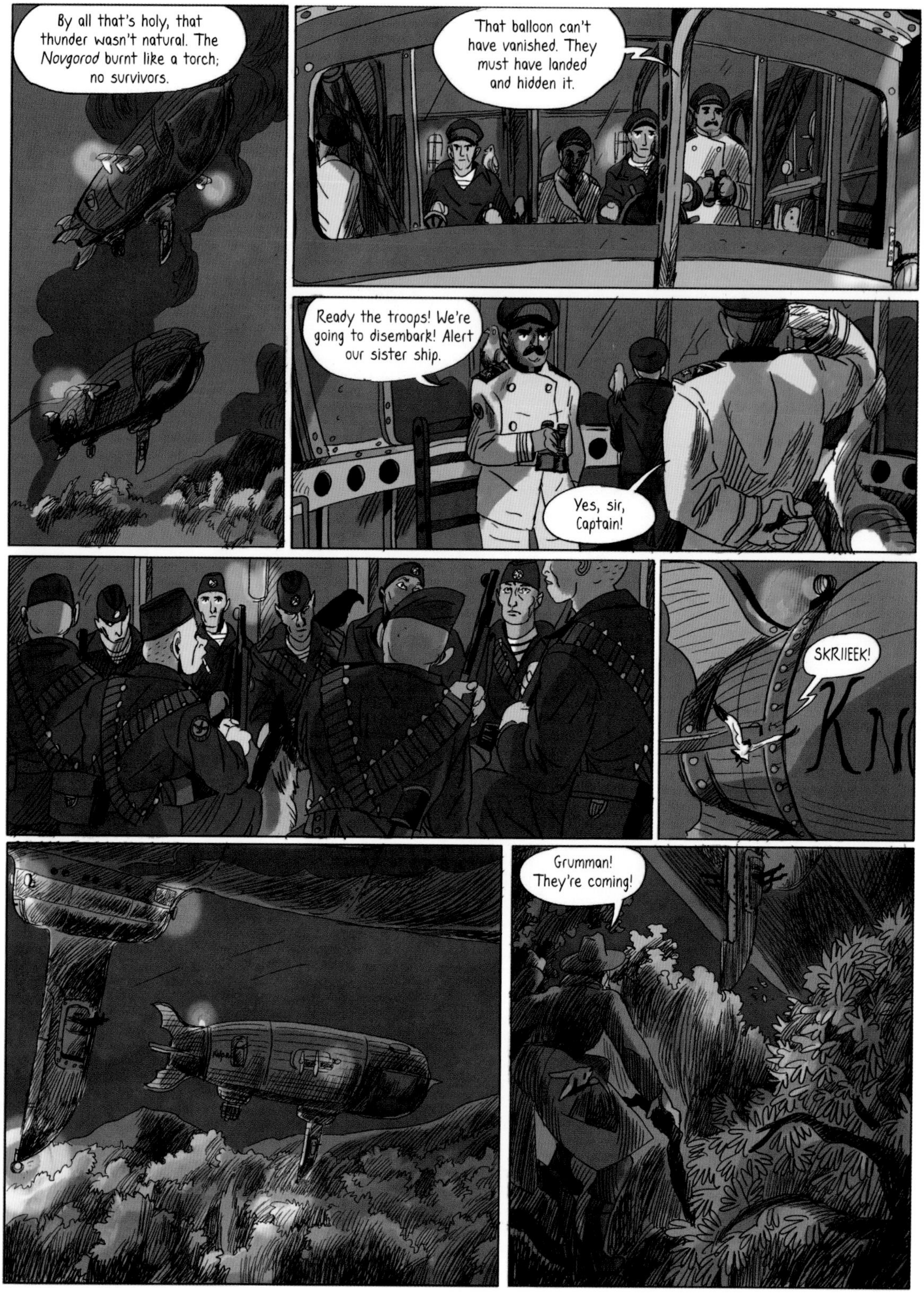
By all that's holy, that thunder wasn't natural. The *Novgorod* burnt like a torch; no survivors.
That balloon can't have vanished. They must have landed and hidden it.
Ready the troops! We're going to disembark! Alert our sister ship.
Yes, sir, Captain!
SKRIIEEK!
Grumman! They're coming!

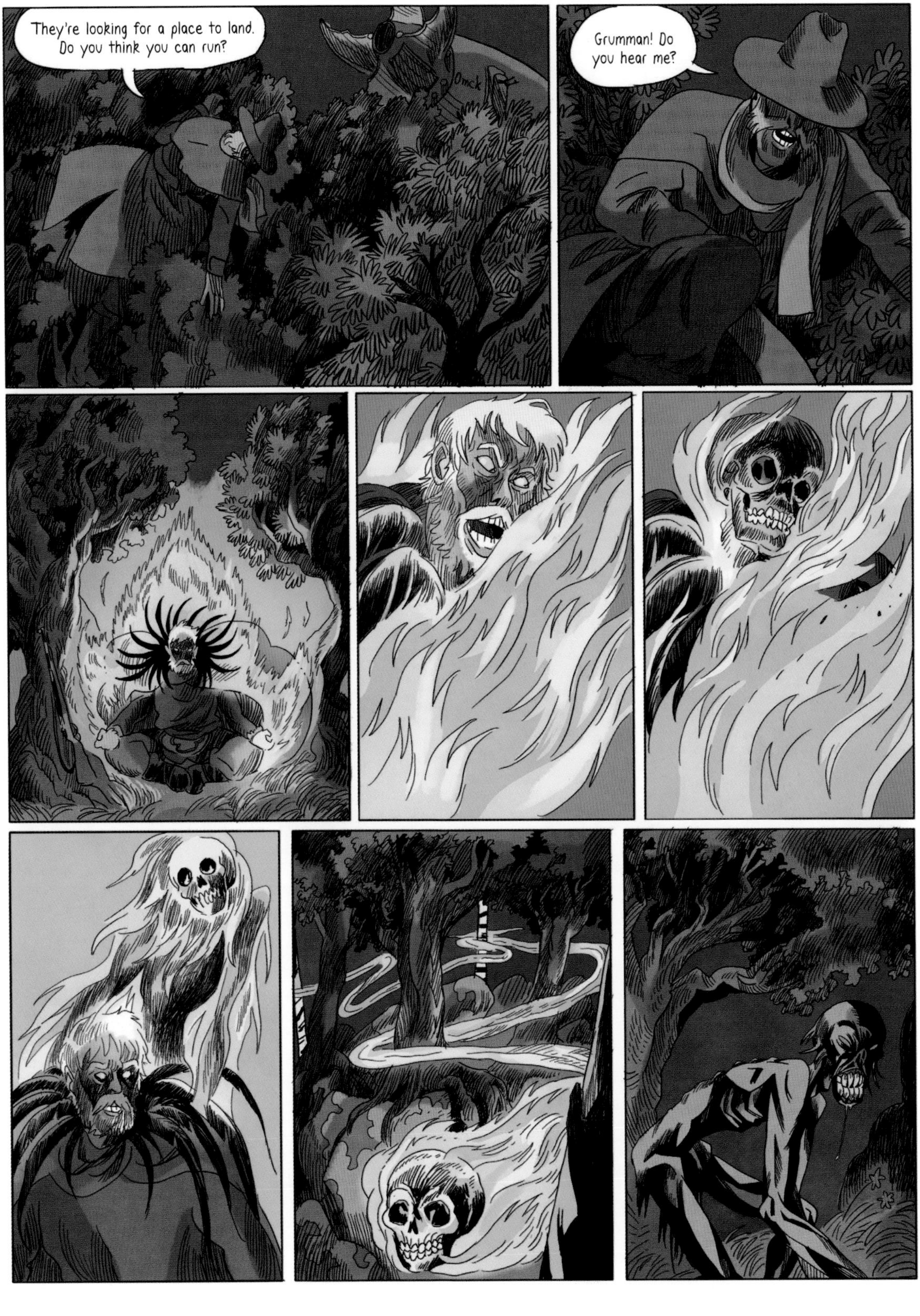
They're looking for a place to land. Do you think you can run?
Grumman! Do you hear me?

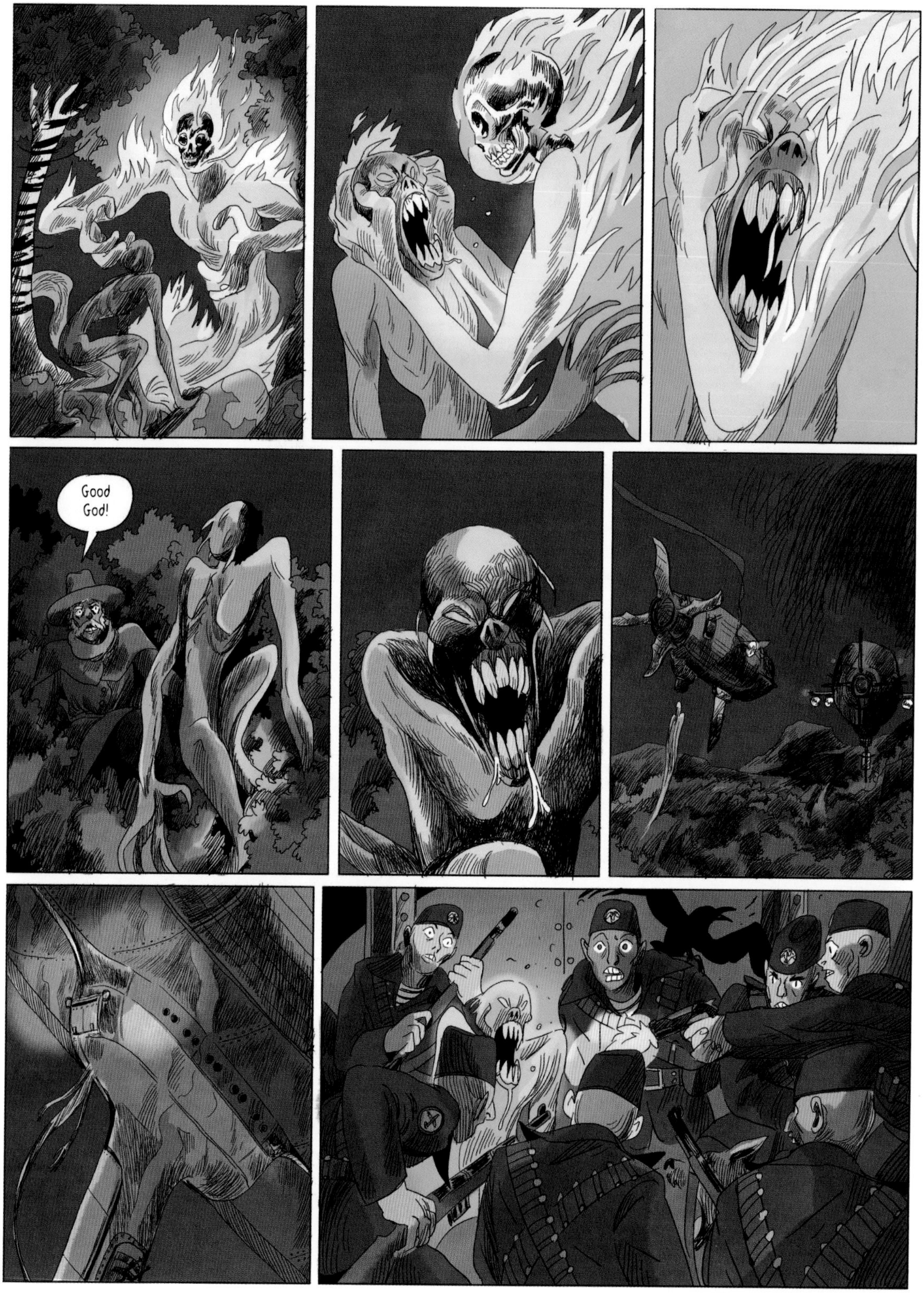
Good God!

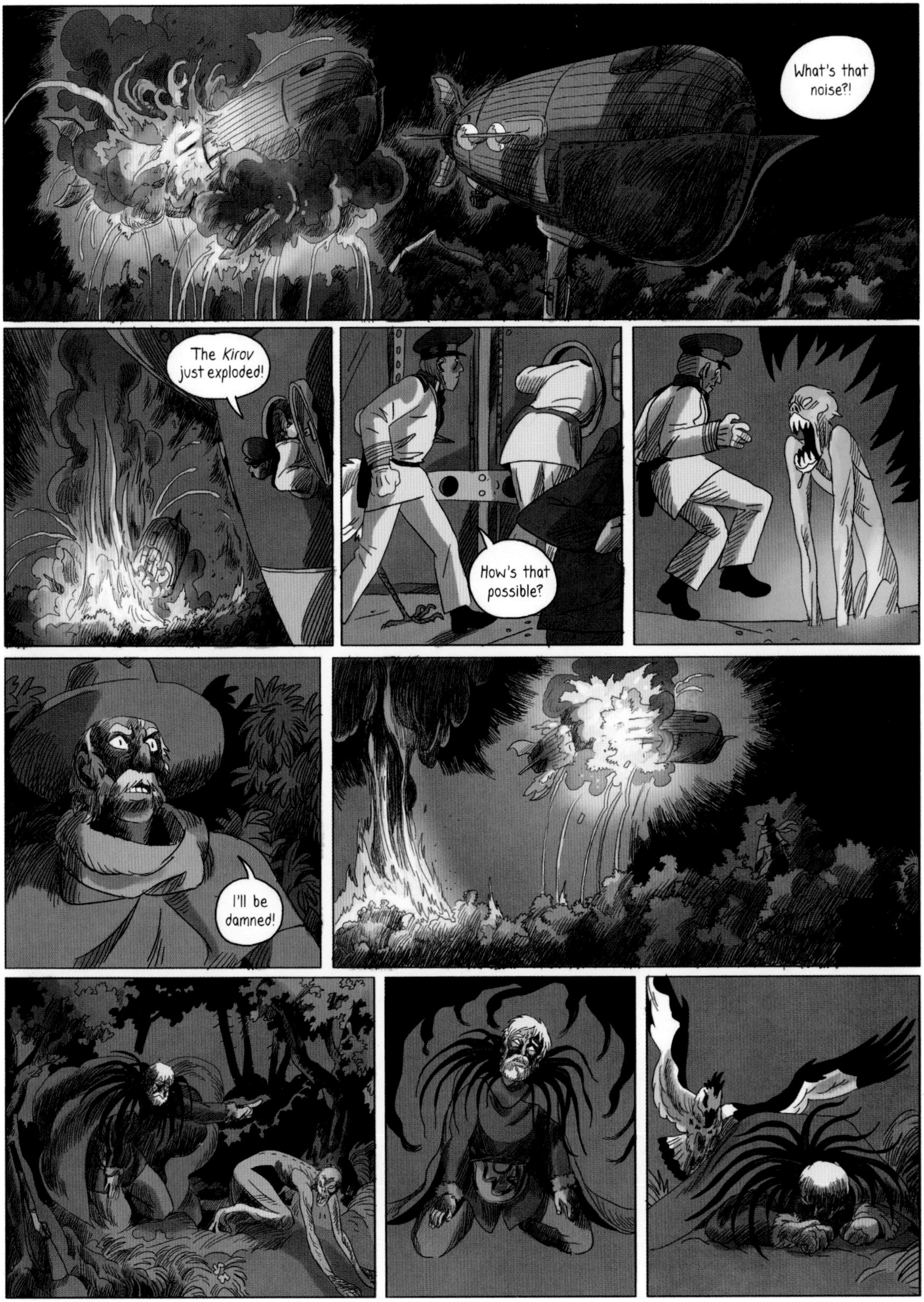

What's that noise?!
The *Kirov* just exploded!
How's that possible?
I'll be damned!

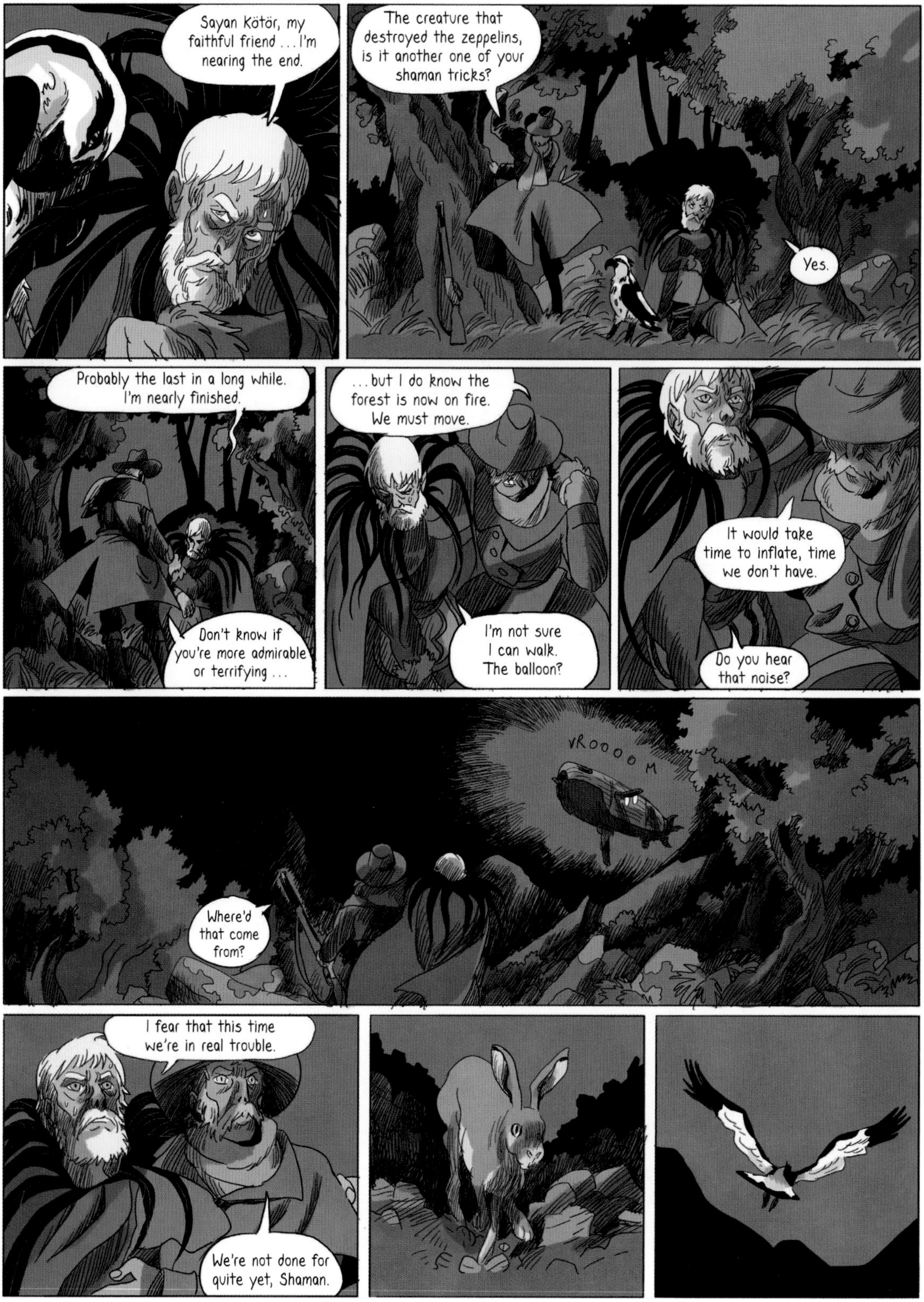
Sayan Kötör, my faithful friend . . . I'm nearing the end.
The creature that destroyed the zeppelins, is it another one of your shaman tricks?
Yes.
Probably the last in a long while. I'm nearly finished.
Don't know if you're more admirable or terrifying . . .
. . . but I do know the forest is now on fire. We must move.
I'm not sure I can walk. The balloon?
It would take time to inflate, time we don't have.
Do you hear that noise?
VROOOOOM
Where'd that come from?
I fear that this time we're in real trouble.
We're not done for quite yet, Shaman.

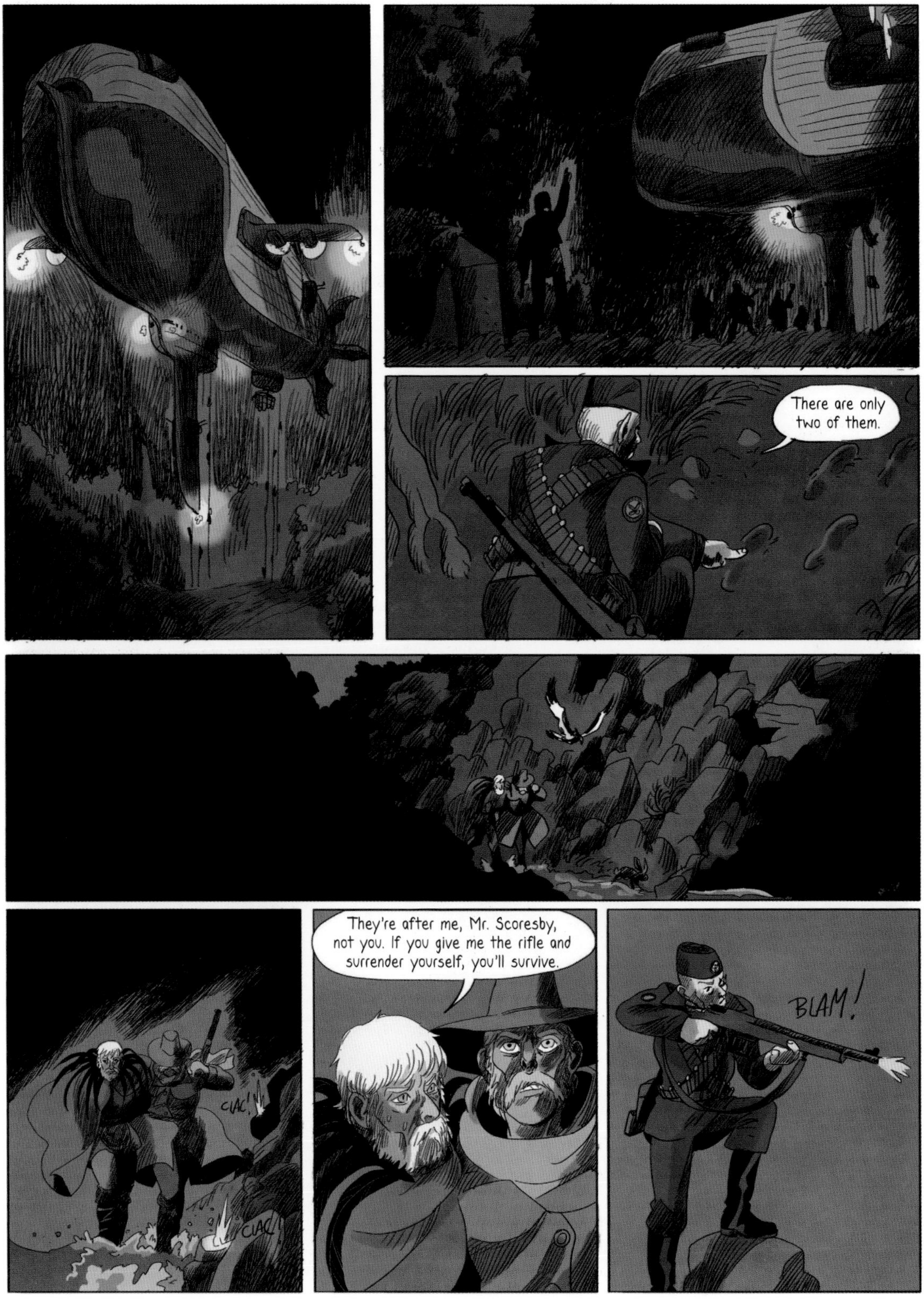
There are only two of them.
CLAC!
CLAC!
They're after me, Mr. Scoresby, not you. If you give me the rifle and surrender yourself, you'll survive.
BLAM!

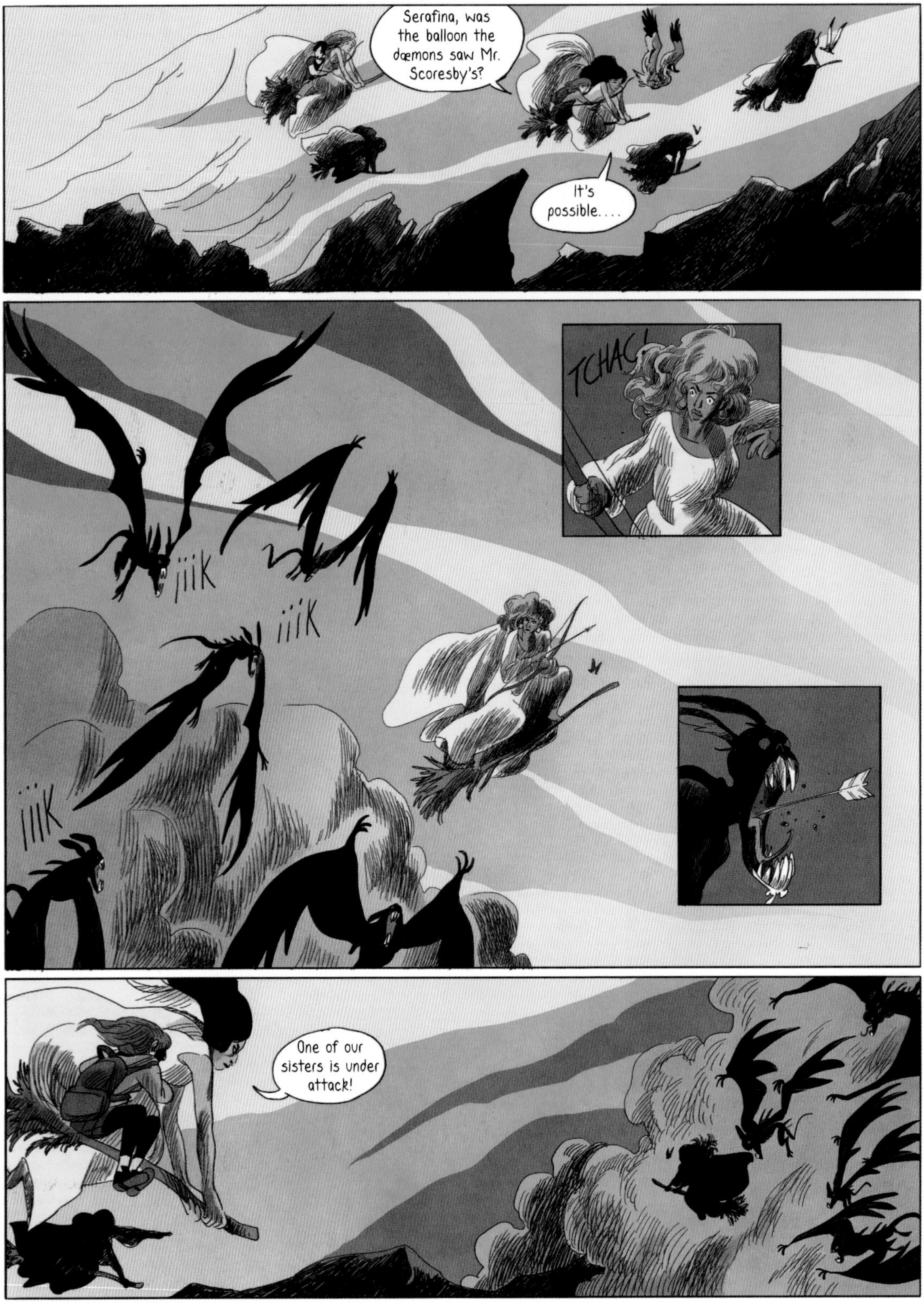
Serafina, was the balloon the dæmons saw Mr. Scoresby's?
It's possible. . . .
TCHAC!
iiik
iiik
. . . iiik
One of our sisters is under attack!

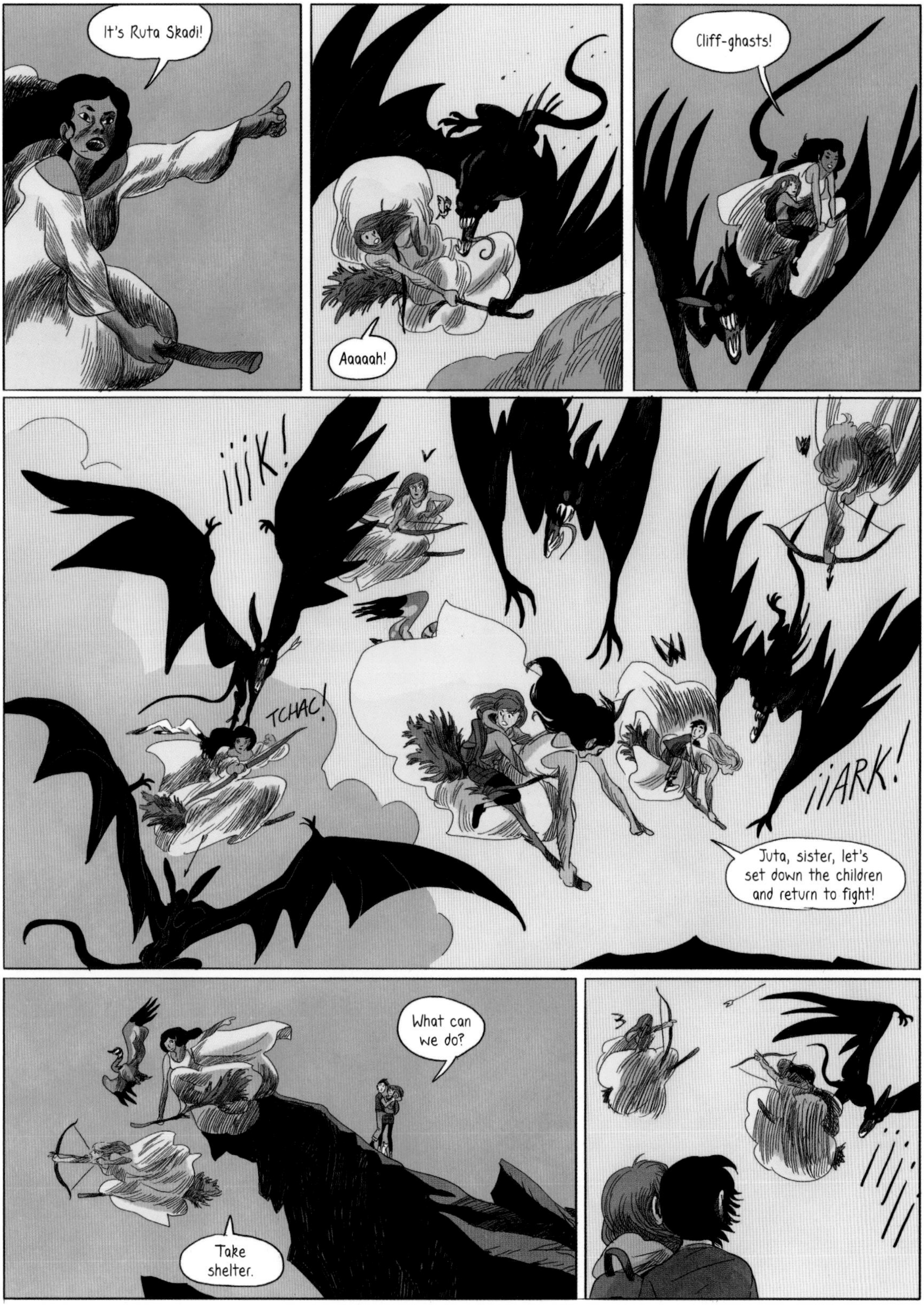
It's Ruta Skadi!
Aaaaah!
Cliff-ghasts!
¡¡¡K!
TCHAC!
¡¡ARK!
Juta, sister, let's set down the children and return to fight!
What can we do?
Take shelter.

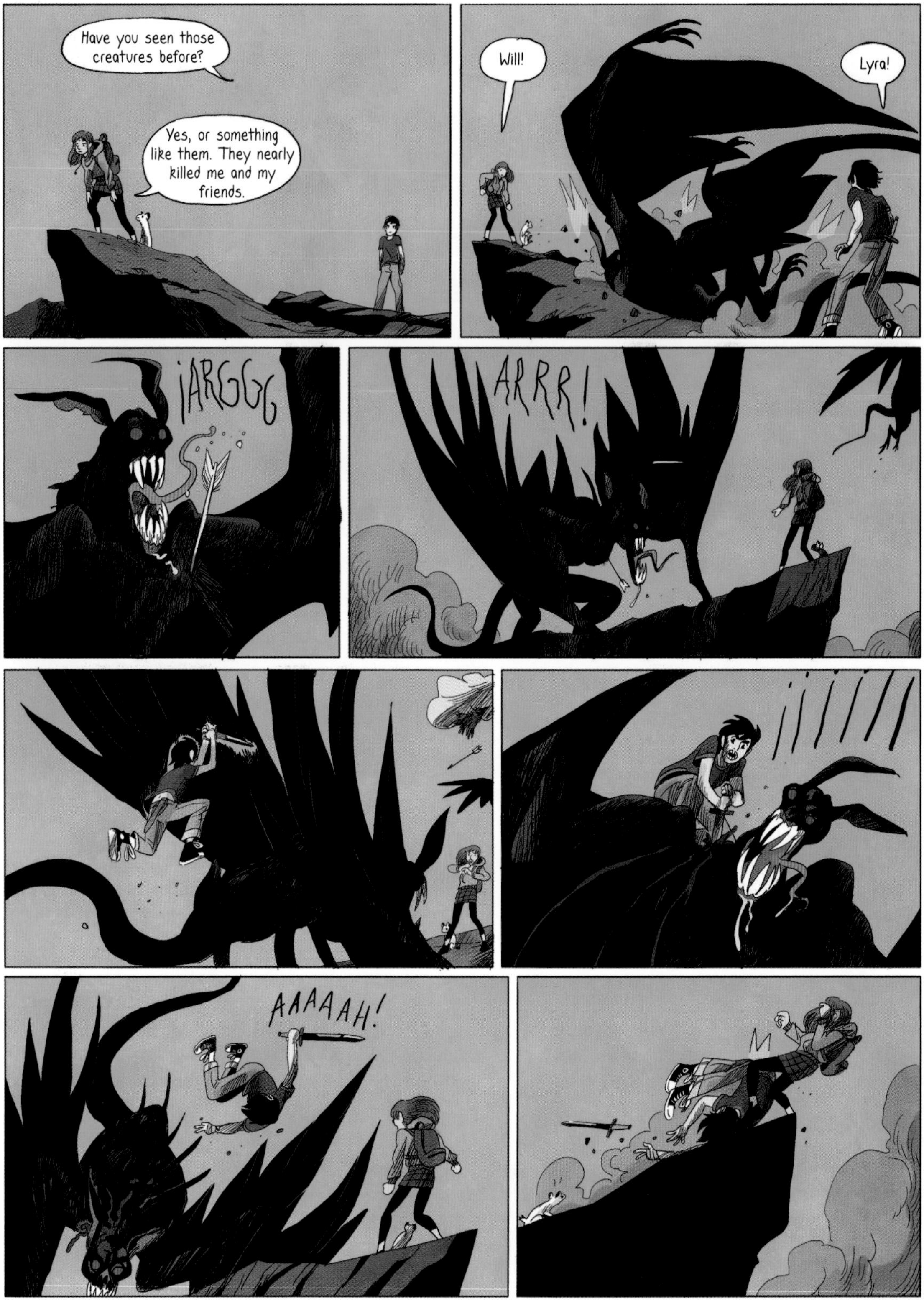
Have you seen those creatures before?
Yes, or something like them. They nearly killed me and my friends.
Will!
Lyra!
¡ARGGG
ARRR!
¡!!!!
AAAAAH!

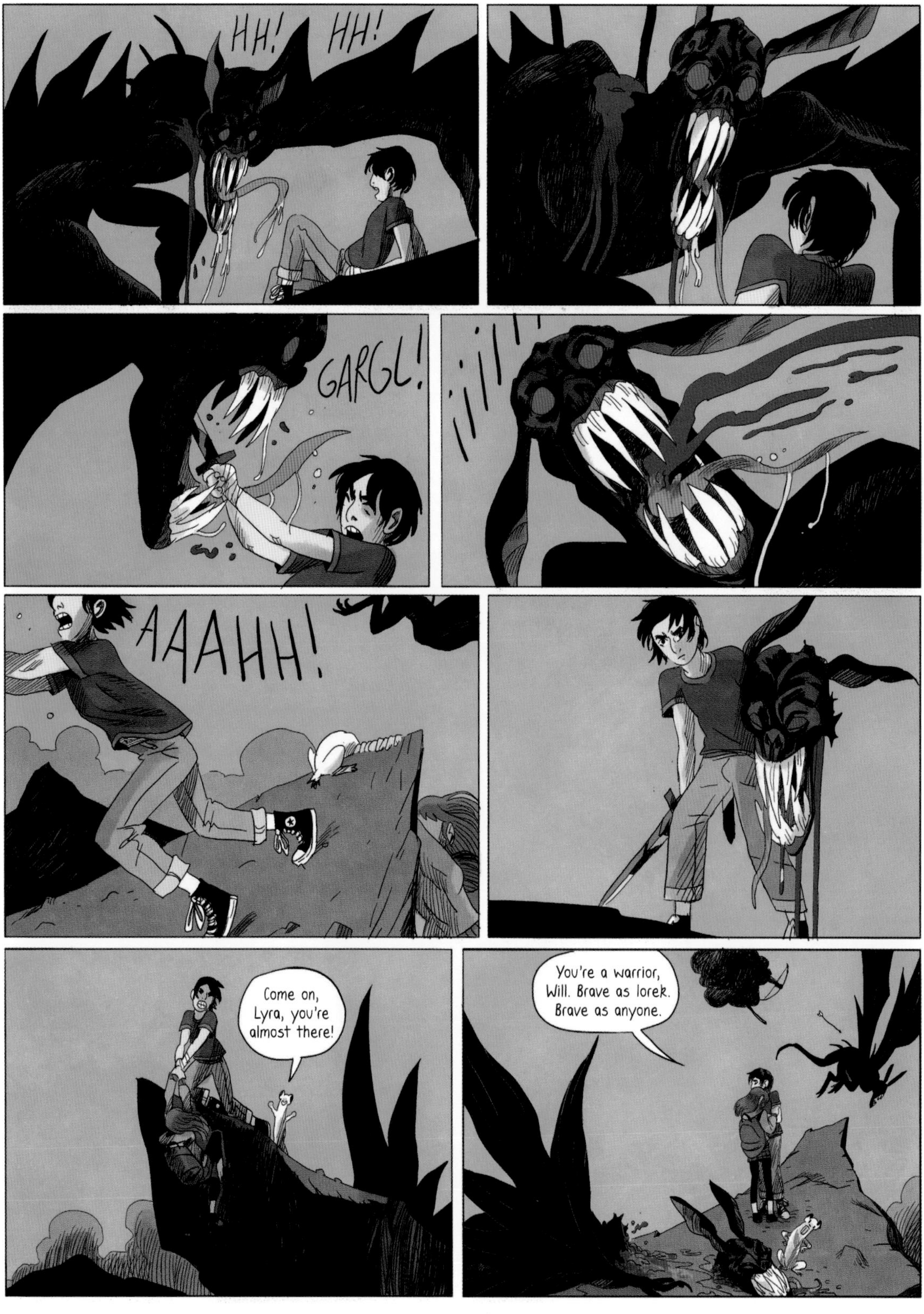
HH! HH!
GARGL!
AAAHH!
Come on, Lyra, you're almost there!
You're a warrior, Will. Brave as Iorek. Brave as anyone.

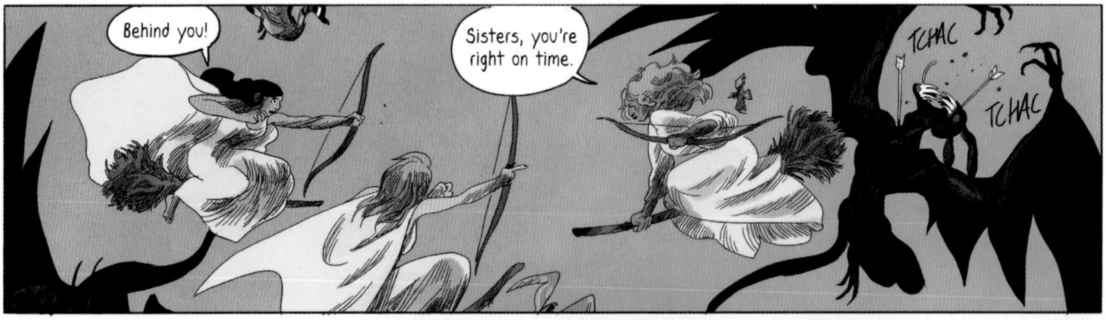
Behind you!
Sisters, you're right on time.
TCHAC
TCHAC

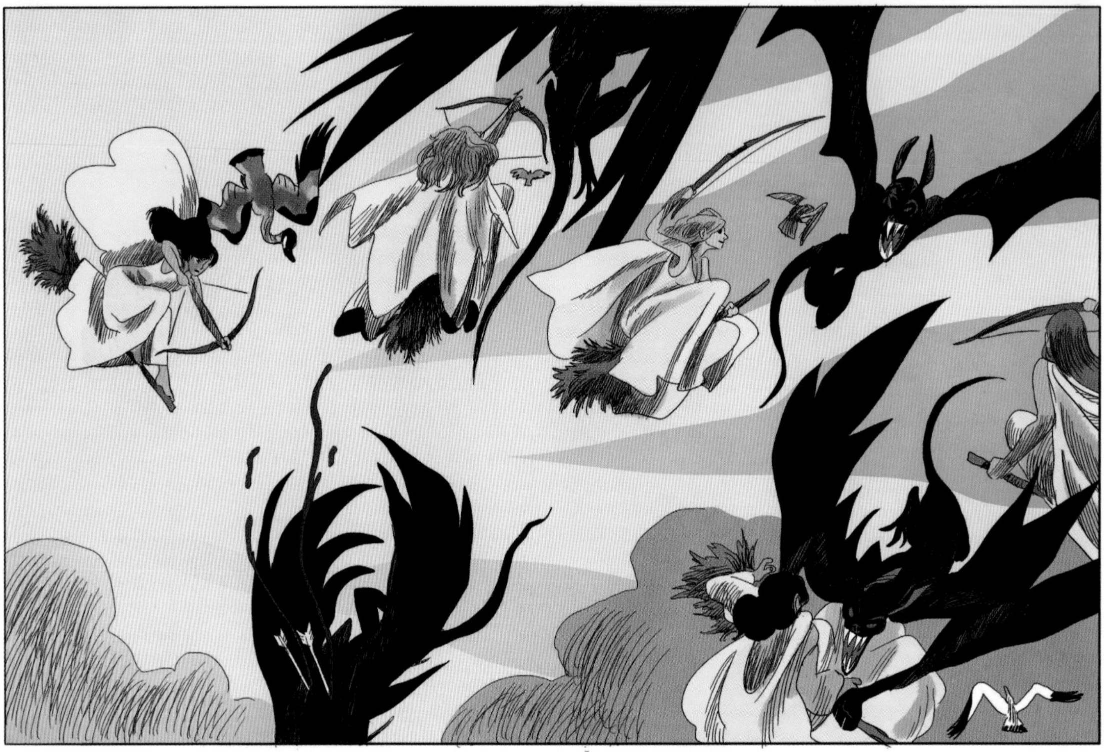

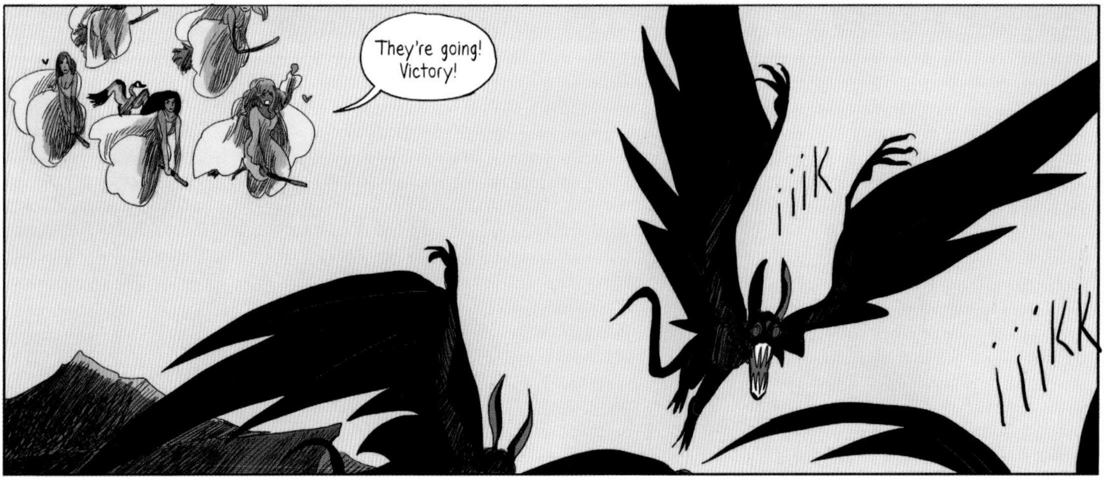
They're going! Victory!
iiiK
iiiKK

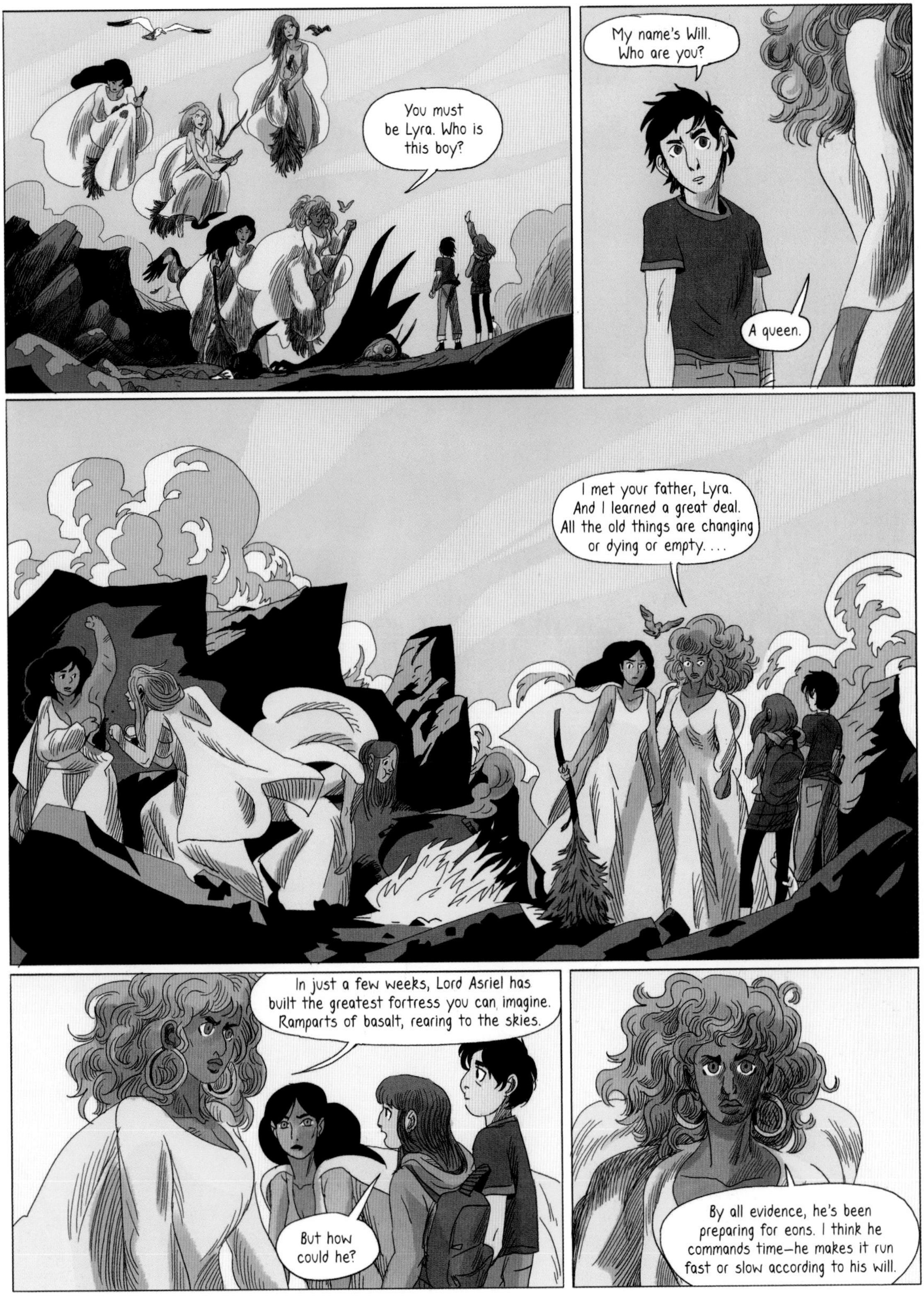
You must be Lyra. Who is this boy?
My name's Will. Who are you?
A queen.
I met your father, Lyra. And I learned a great deal. All the old things are changing or dying or empty. . . .
In just a few weeks, Lord Asriel has built the greatest fortress you can imagine. Ramparts of basalt, rearing to the skies.
But how could he?
By all evidence, he's been preparing for eons. I think he commands time—he makes it run fast or slow according to his will.

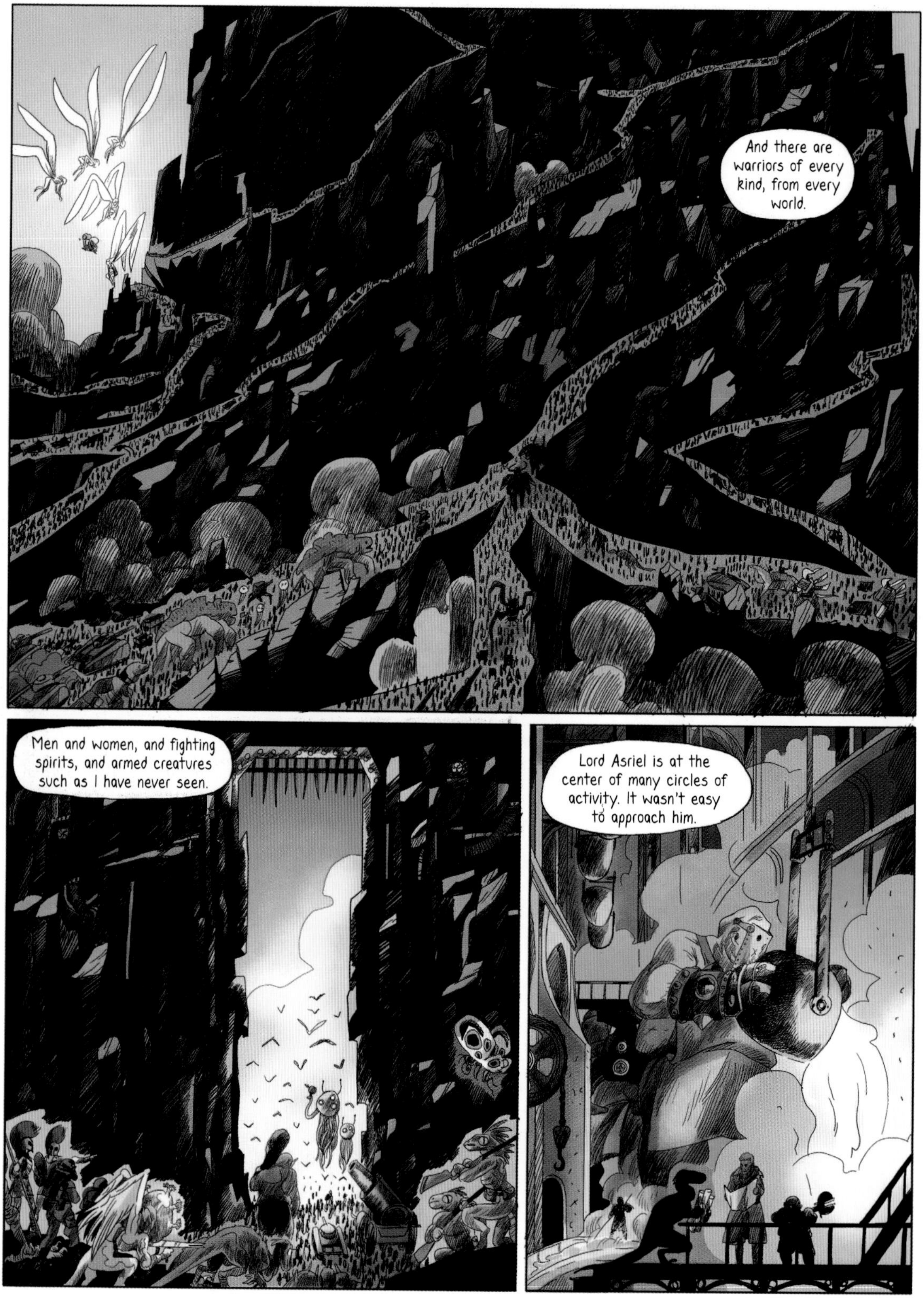
And there are warriors of every kind, from every world.
Men and women, and fighting spirits, and armed creatures such as I have never seen.
Lord Asriel is at the center of many circles of activity. It wasn't easy to approach him.

But I made myself invisible and went to his innermost chamber.

Queen Skadi! What good wind brings you?

A whirlwind of questions, Asriel . . .

He said it was true, that he wants to destroy the Authority. And he invited us to join him, sister.

What's the Authority?

The Authority creates all things. Or it destroys them. Since the beginning of time, it alone decides what is good or bad, for itself and for us.

Its power is without limit. It's both feared and revered.

I see. . . . In my world, that goes by another name.

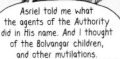

Asriel told me what the agents of the Authority did in His name. And I thought of the Bolvangar children, and other mutilations.

In some worlds they even capture witches and burn them alive.

He opened my eyes. Oh, sisters, I longed to join him!

We're eager too, Queen Skadi. You must convene the council of witches.

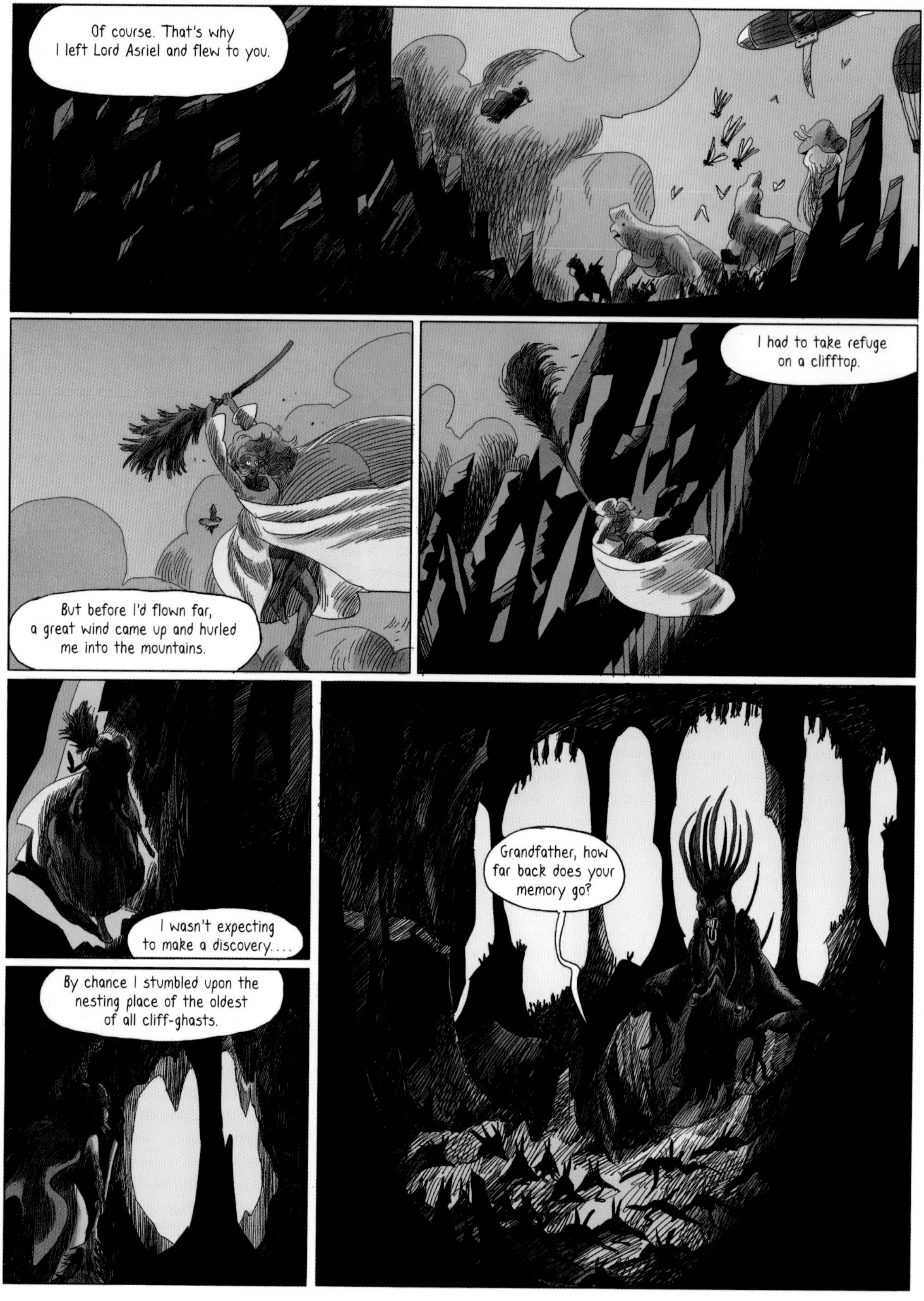
Of course. That's why I left Lord Asriel and flew to you.
But before I'd flown far, a great wind came up and hurled me into the mountains.
I had to take refuge on a clifftop.
I wasn't expecting to make a discovery....
By chance I stumbled upon the nesting place of the oldest of all cliff-ghasts.
Grandfather, how far back does your memory go?

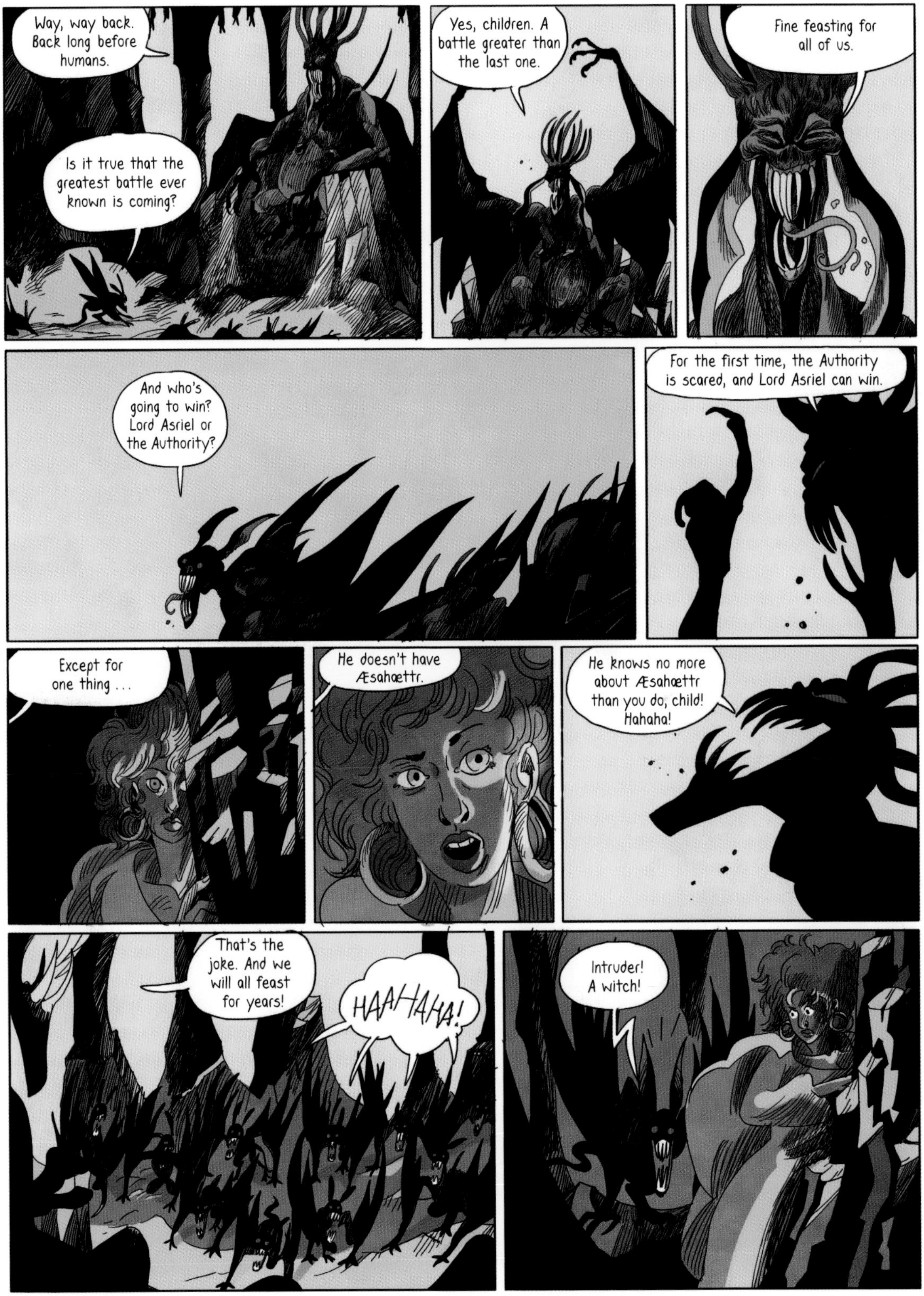
Way, way back. Back long before humans.
Is it true that the greatest battle ever known is coming?
Yes, children. A battle greater than the last one.
Fine feasting for all of us.
And who's going to win? Lord Asriel or the Authority?
For the first time, the Authority is scared, and Lord Asriel can win.
Except for one thing . . .
He doesn't have Æsahættr.
He knows no more about Æsahættr than you do, child! Hahaha!
That's the joke. And we will all feast for years!
HAAHAHA!
Intruder! A witch!

And so I fled back through the gateway in the air, and a flock of them came after me, as you saw.

Whoever this Æsahættr is, Lord Asriel needs us. We have no mission more urgent than to join our forces to his.

Not us. Our task now is to help Lyra, and her task is to guide Will to his father.

You should fly back, to the council of witches, Ruta. I'm staying with Lyra.

Well, if you must.

Thank you, Serafina. I can't explain it, but I'm convinced that finding Will's father is very important, not only for Will, but for all of us.

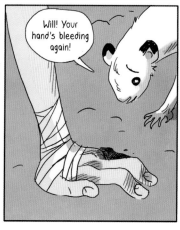

Will! Your hand's bleeding again!

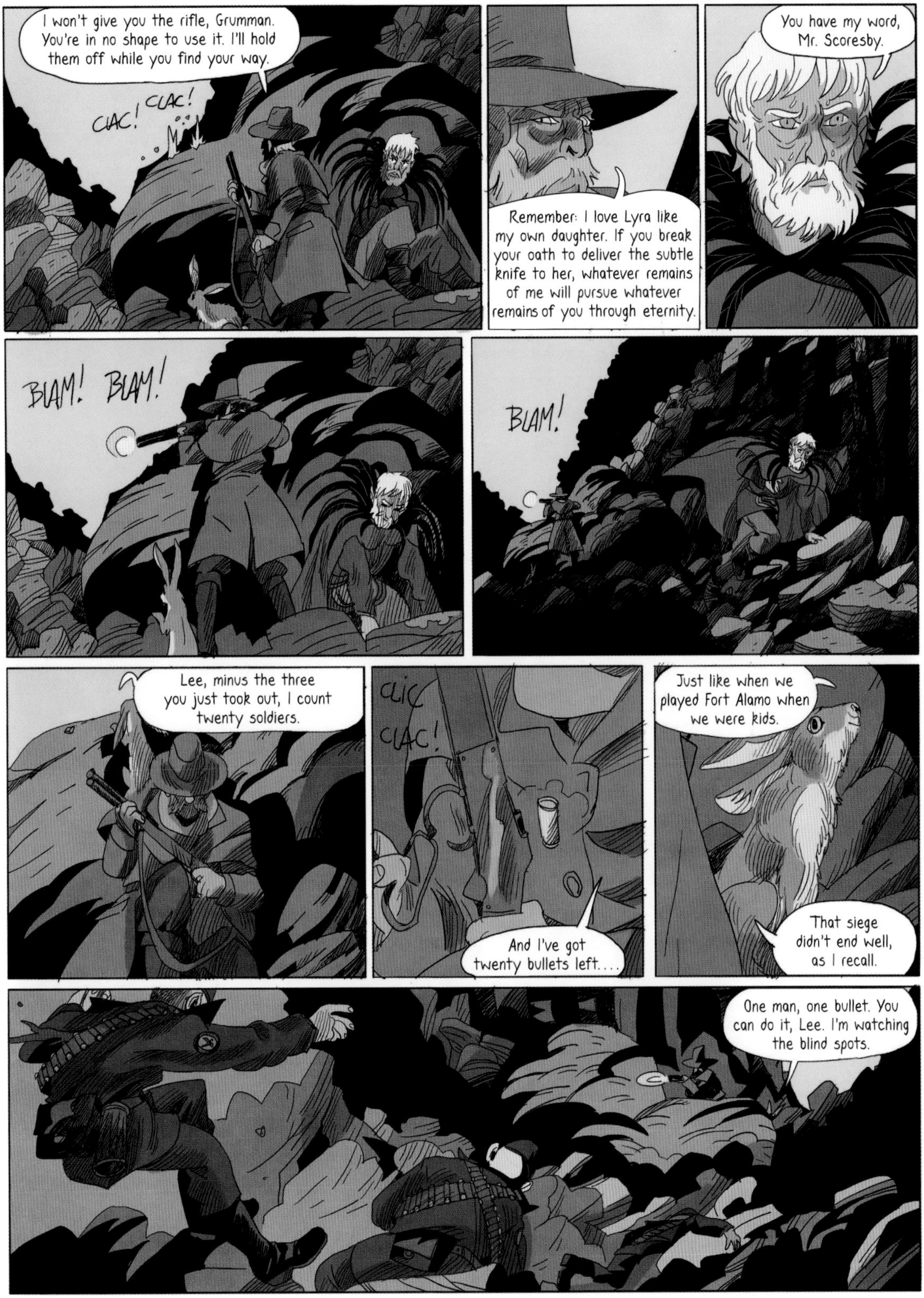
I won't give you the rifle, Grumman. You're in no shape to use it. I'll hold them off while you find your way.
CLAC! CLAC!
Remember: I love Lyra like my own daughter. If you break your oath to deliver the subtle knife to her, whatever remains of me will pursue whatever remains of you through eternity.
You have my word, Mr. Scoresby.
BLAM! BLAM!
BLAM!
Lee, minus the three you just took out, I count twenty soldiers.
CLIC CLAC!
And I've got twenty bullets left. . . .
Just like when we played Fort Alamo when we were kids.
That siege didn't end well, as I recall.
One man, one bullet. You can do it, Lee. I'm watching the blind spots.

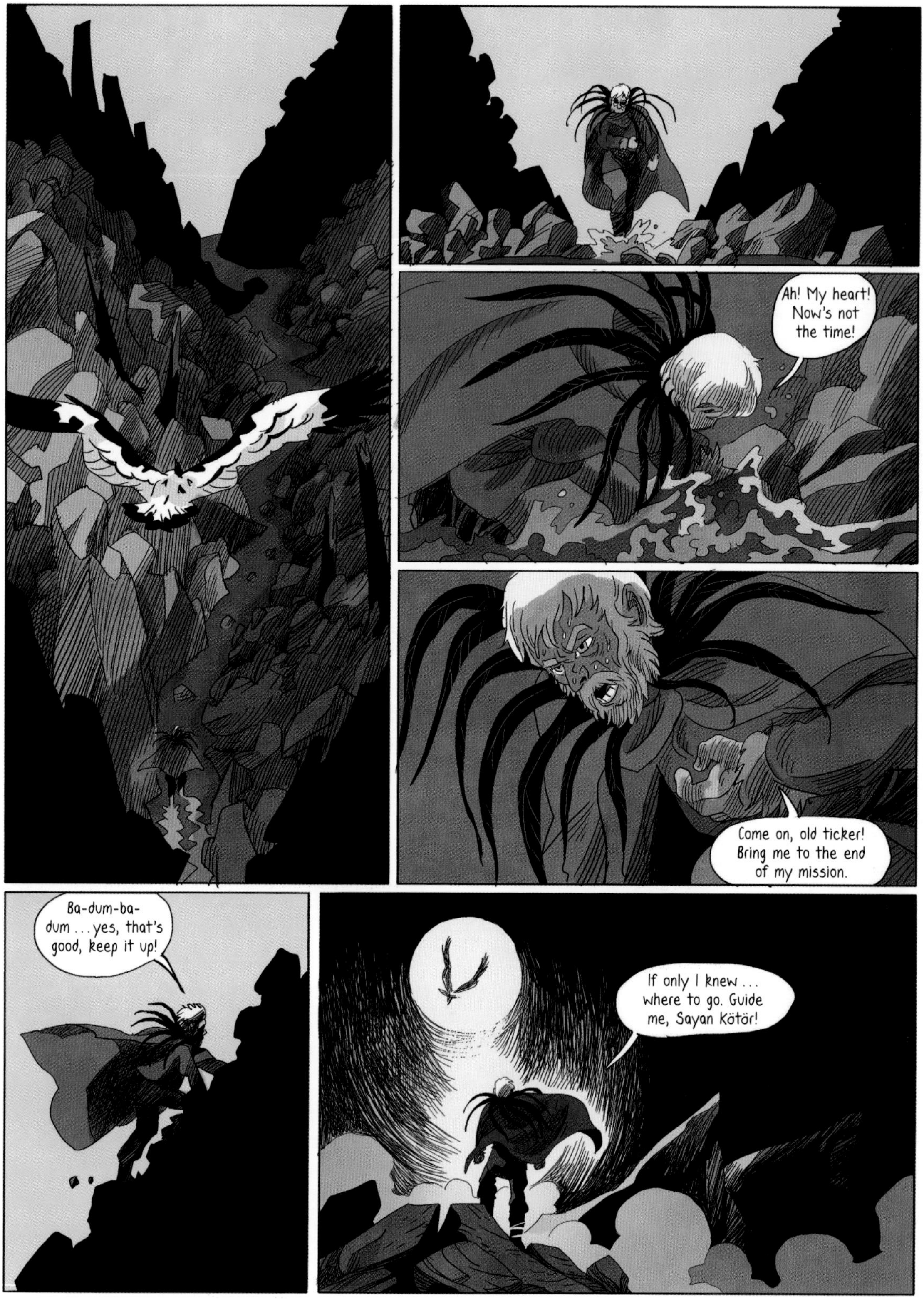
Ah! My heart! Now's not the time!
Come on, old ticker! Bring me to the end of my mission.
Ba-dum-ba-dum . . . yes, that's good, keep it up!
If only I knew . . . where to go. Guide me, Sayan Kötör!

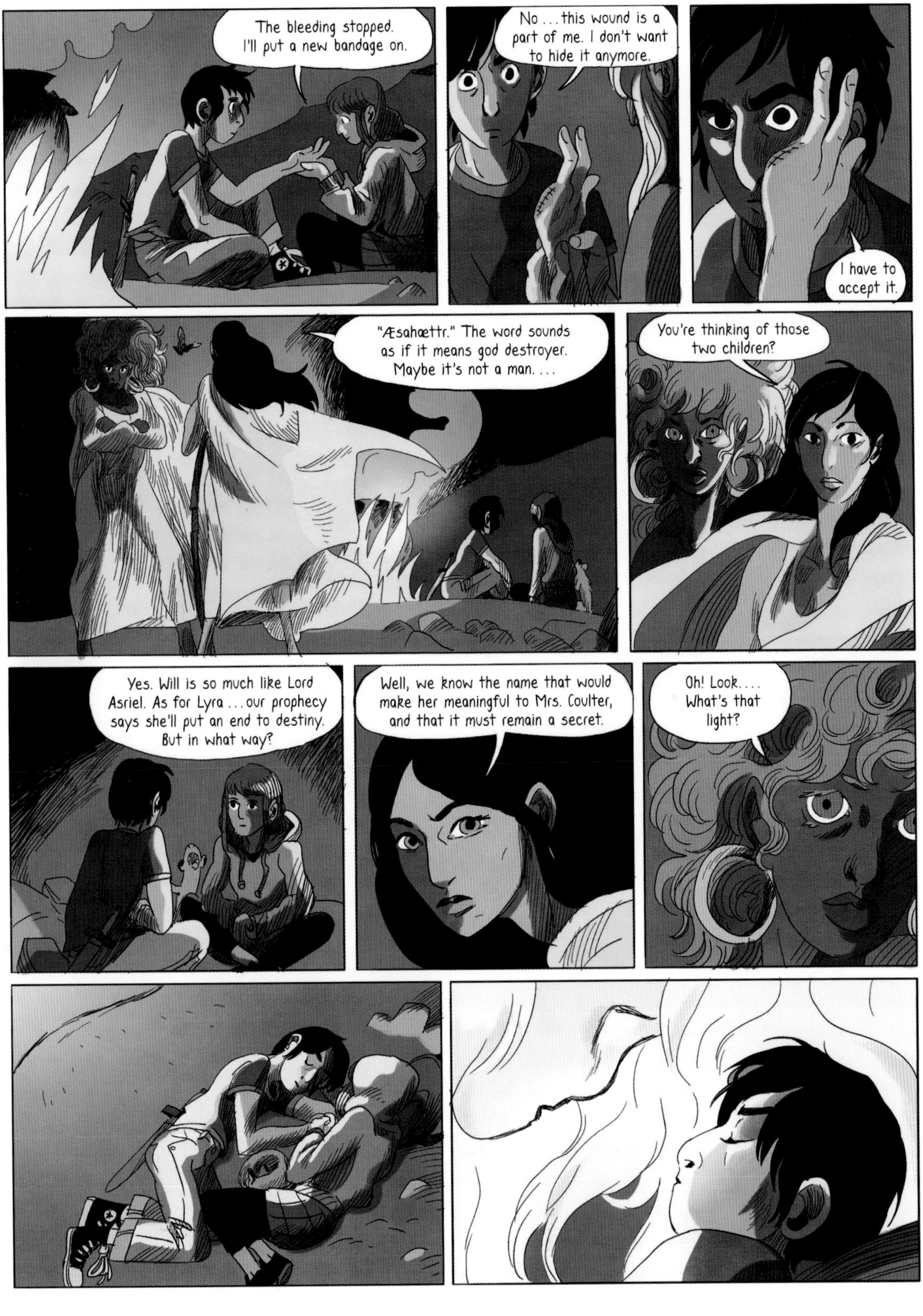
The bleeding stopped. I'll put a new bandage on.
No . . . this wound is a part of me. I don't want to hide it anymore.
I have to accept it.
"Æsahættr." The word sounds as if it means god destroyer. Maybe it's not a man. . . .
You're thinking of those two children?
Yes. Will is so much like Lord Asriel. As for Lyra . . . our prophecy says she'll put an end to destiny. But in what way?
Well, we know the name that would make her meaningful to Mrs. Coulter, and that it must remain a secret.
Oh! Look. . . . What's that light?

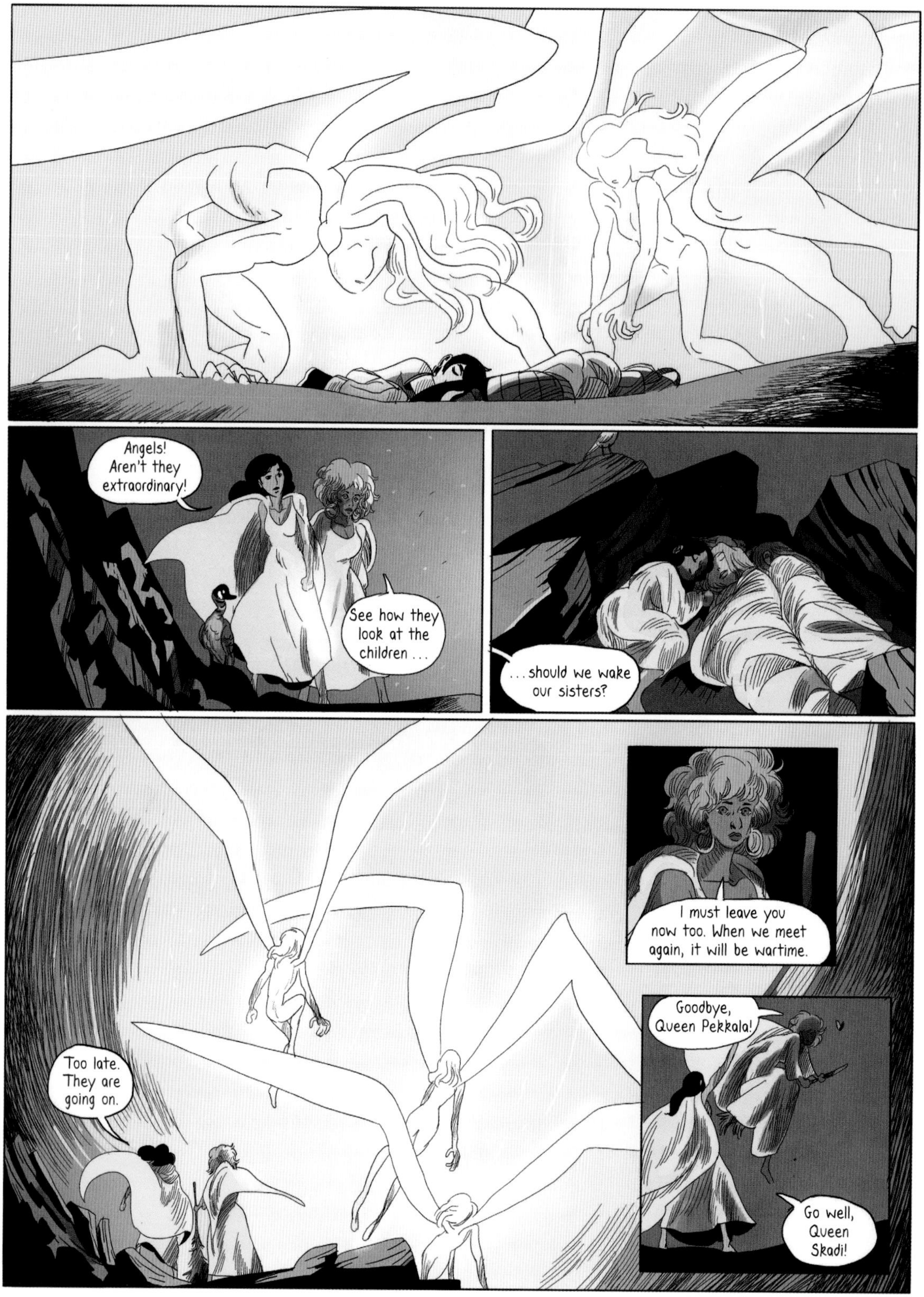
Angels! Aren't they extraordinary!
See how they look at the children . . .
. . . should we wake our sisters?
Too late. They are going on.
I must leave you now too. When we meet again, it will be wartime.
Goodbye, Queen Pekkala!
Go well, Queen Skadi!

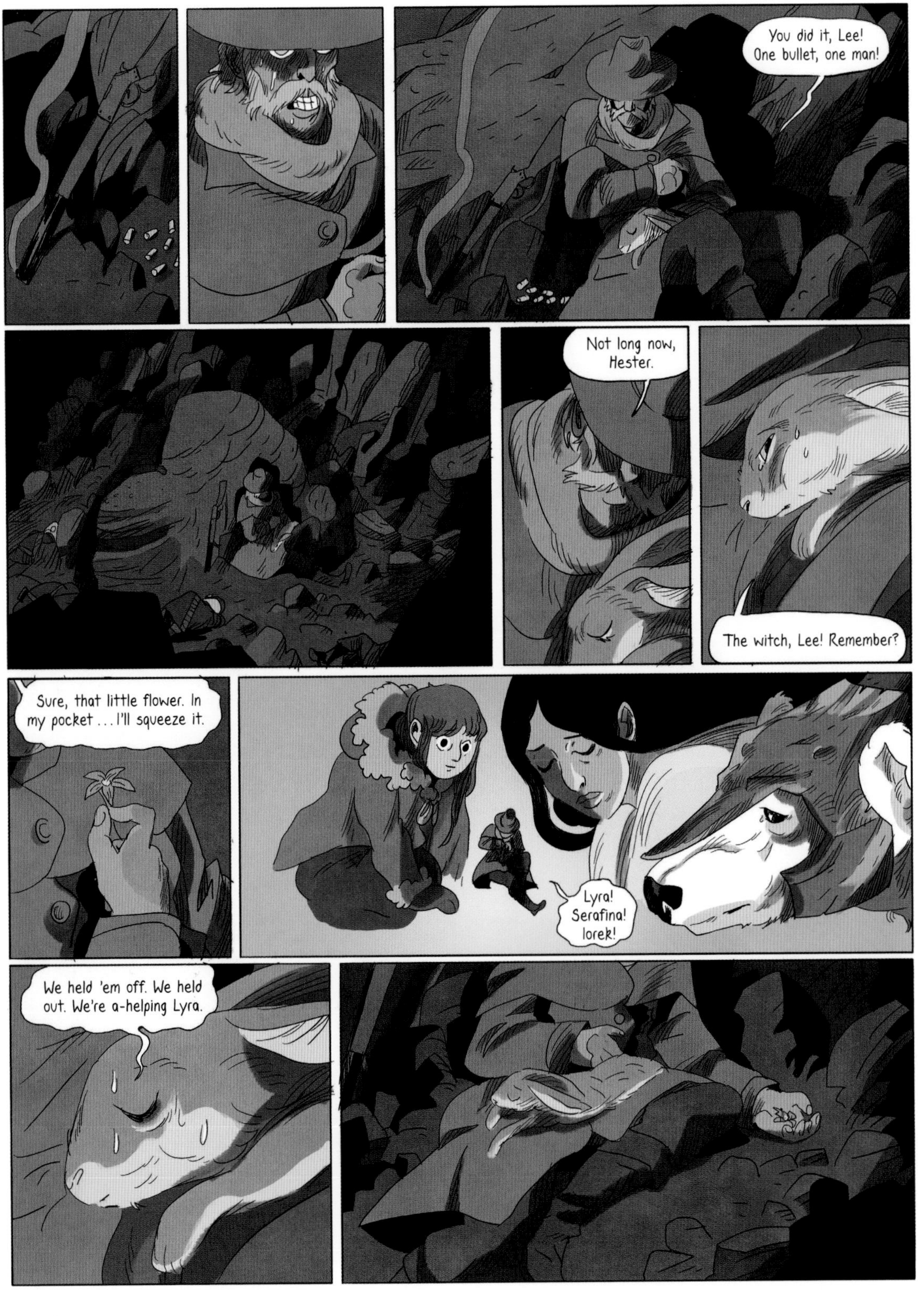
You did it, Lee! One bullet, one man!
Not long now, Hester.
The witch, Lee! Remember?
Sure, that little flower. In my pocket . . . I'll squeeze it.
Lyra! Serafina! Iorek!
We held 'em off. We held out. We're a-helping Lyra.

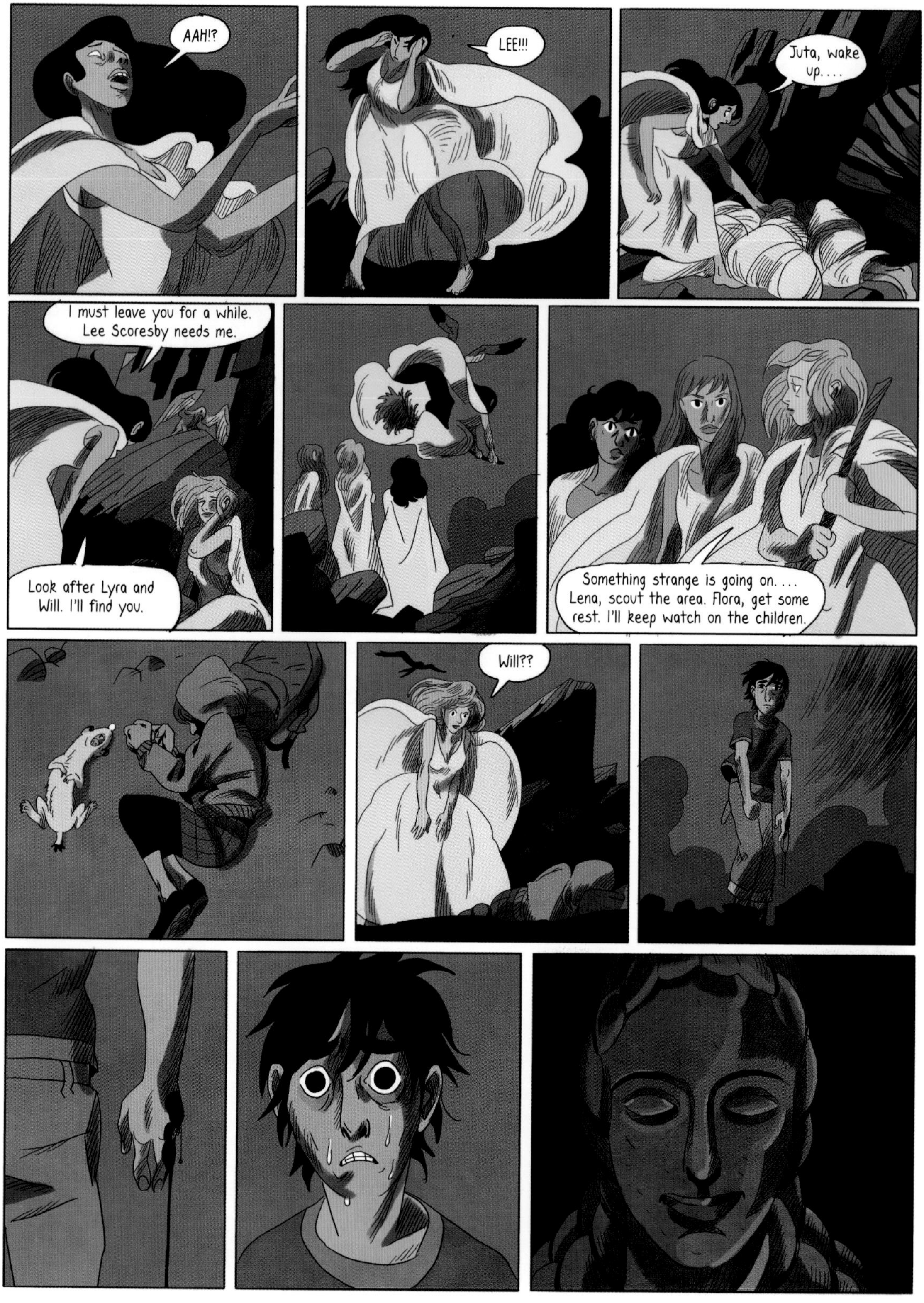
AAH!?
LEE!!!
Juta, wake up. . . .
I must leave you for a while. Lee Scoresby needs me.
Look after Lyra and Will. I'll find you.
Something strange is going on. . . . Lena, scout the area. Flora, get some rest. I'll keep watch on the children.
Will??

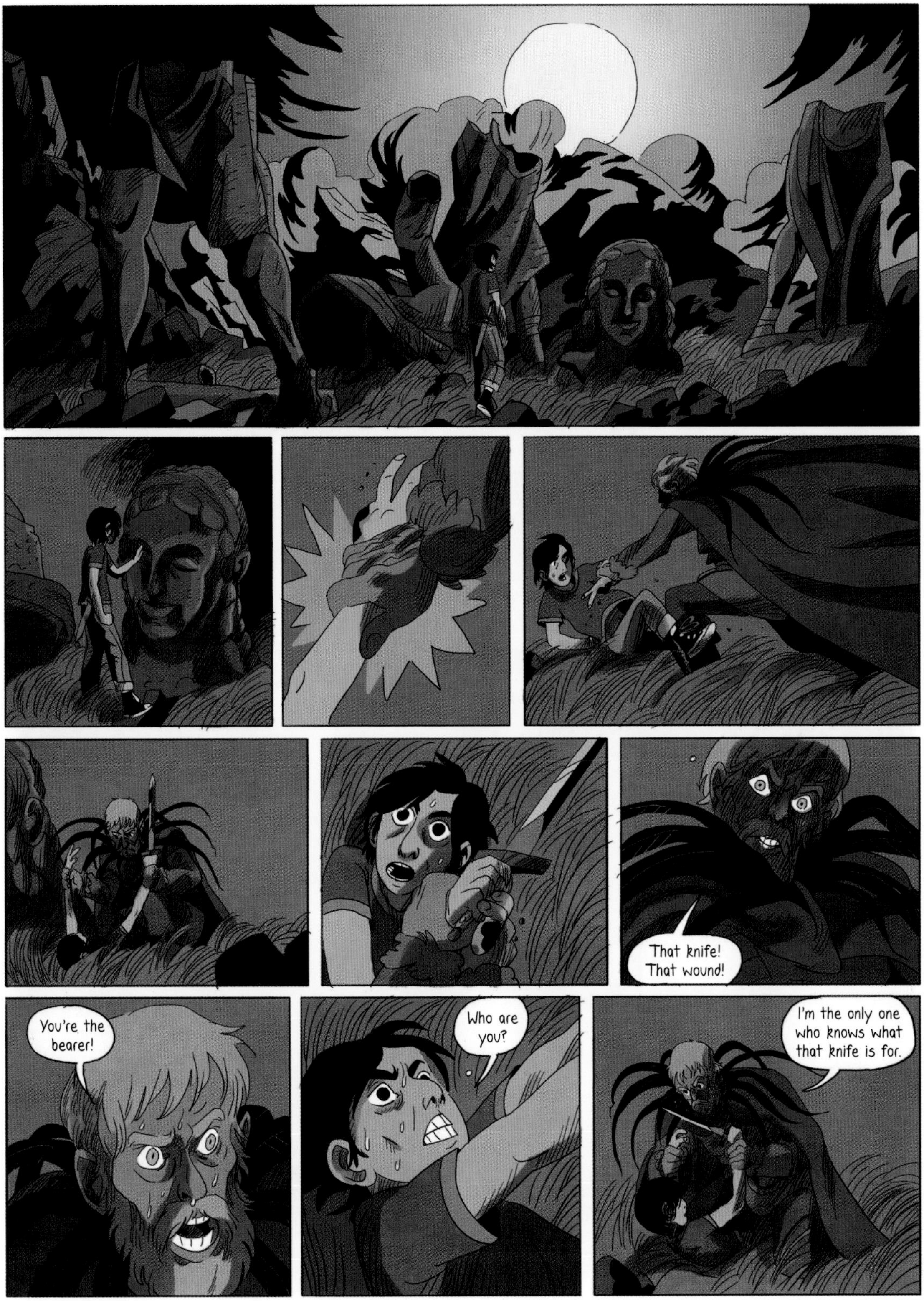
That knife! That wound!
You're the bearer!
Who are you?
I'm the only one who knows what that knife is for.

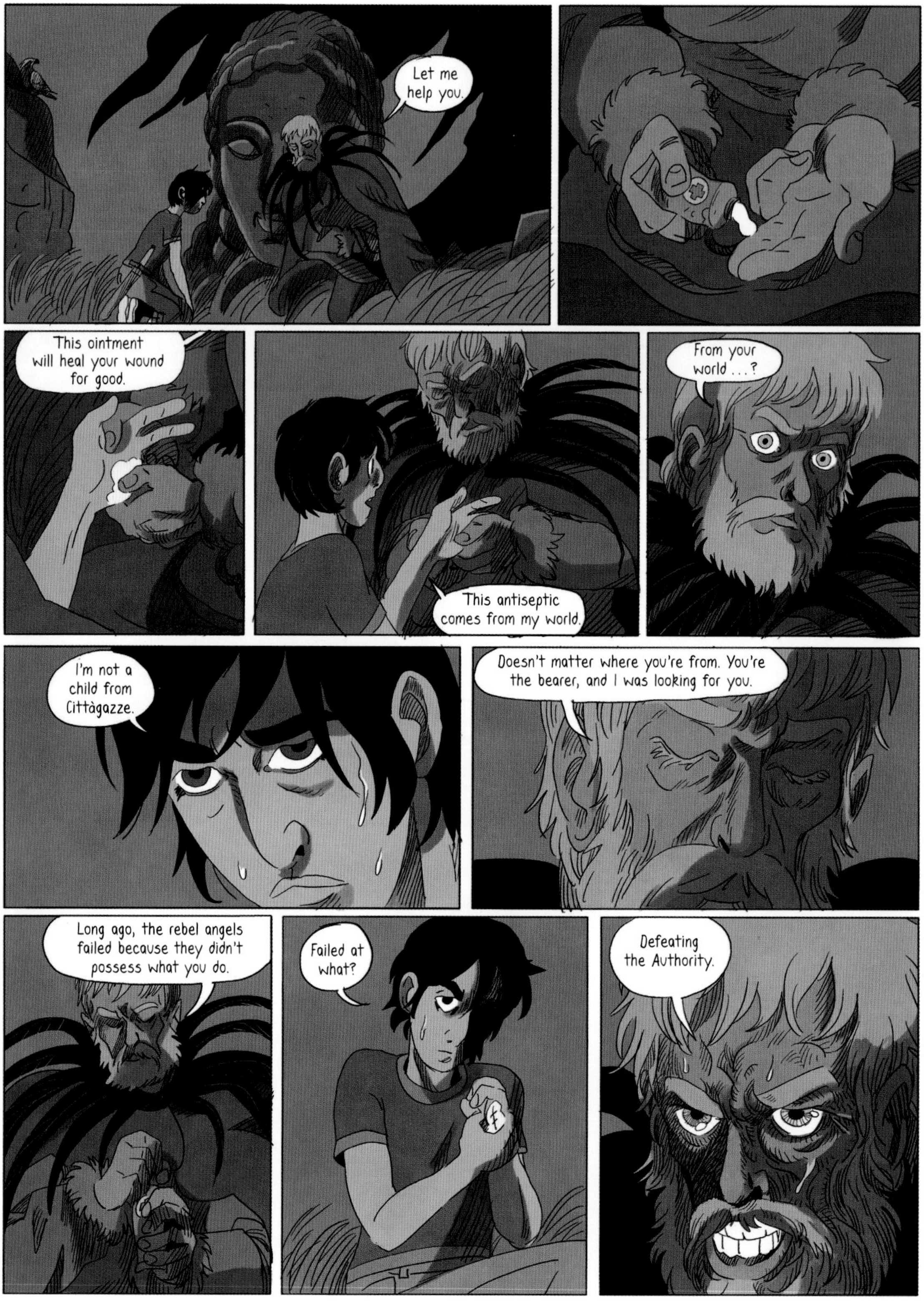
Let me help you.
This ointment will heal your wound for good.
This antiseptic comes from my world.
From your world . . . ?
I'm not a child from Cittàgazze.
Doesn't matter where you're from. You're the bearer, and I was looking for you.
Long ago, the rebel angels failed because they didn't possess what you do.
Failed at what?
Defeating the Authority.

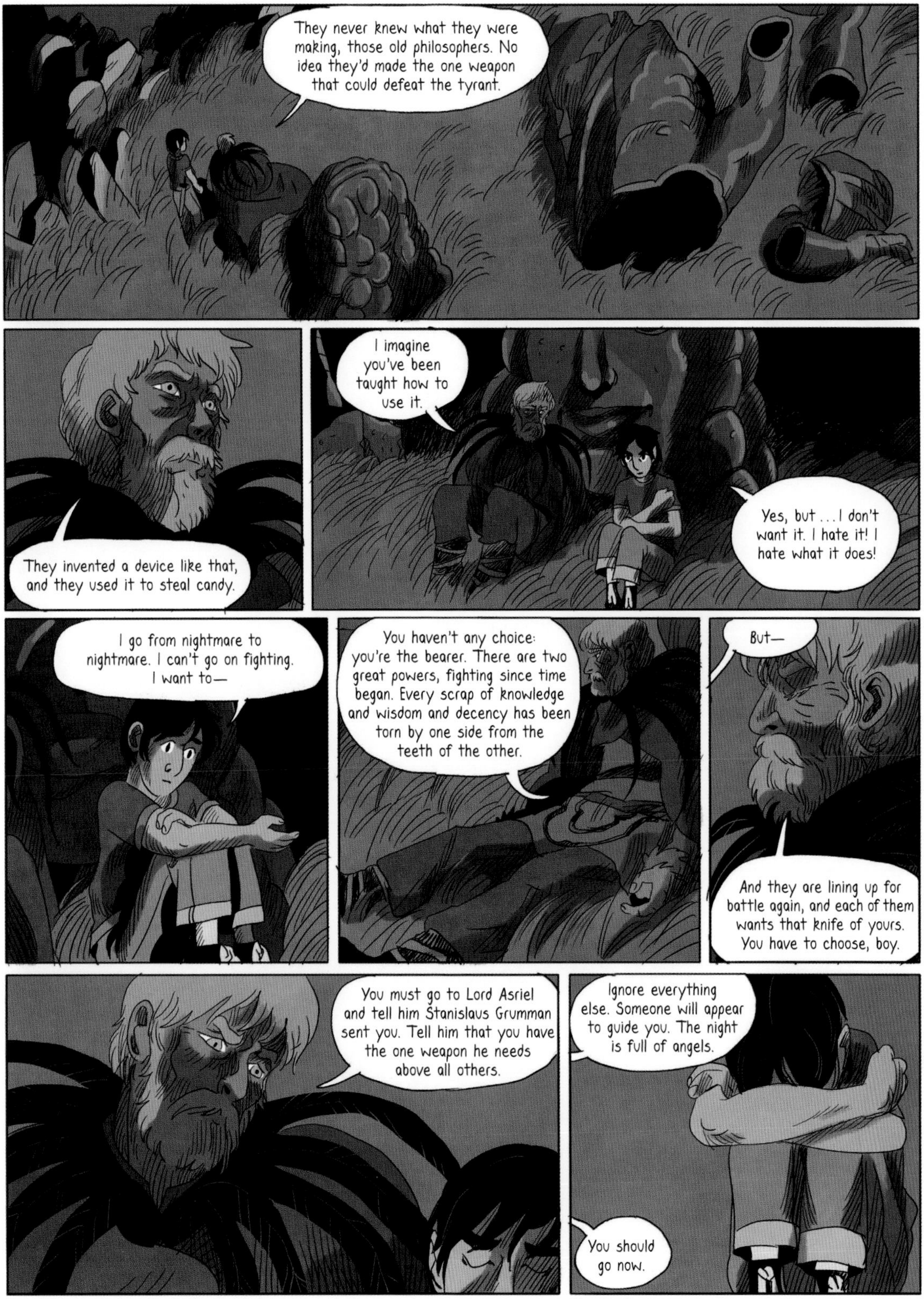
They never knew what they were making, those old philosophers. No idea they'd made the one weapon that could defeat the tyrant.
They invented a device like that, and they used it to steal candy.
I imagine you've been taught how to use it.
Yes, but . . . I don't want it. I hate it! I hate what it does!
I go from nightmare to nightmare. I can't go on fighting. I want to—
You haven't any choice: you're the bearer. There are two great powers, fighting since time began. Every scrap of knowledge and wisdom and decency has been torn by one side from the teeth of the other.
But—
And they are lining up for battle again, and each of them wants that knife of yours. You have to choose, boy.
You must go to Lord Asriel and tell him Stanislaus Grumman sent you. Tell him that you have the one weapon he needs above all others.
Ignore everything else. Someone will appear to guide you. The night is full of angels.
You should go now.

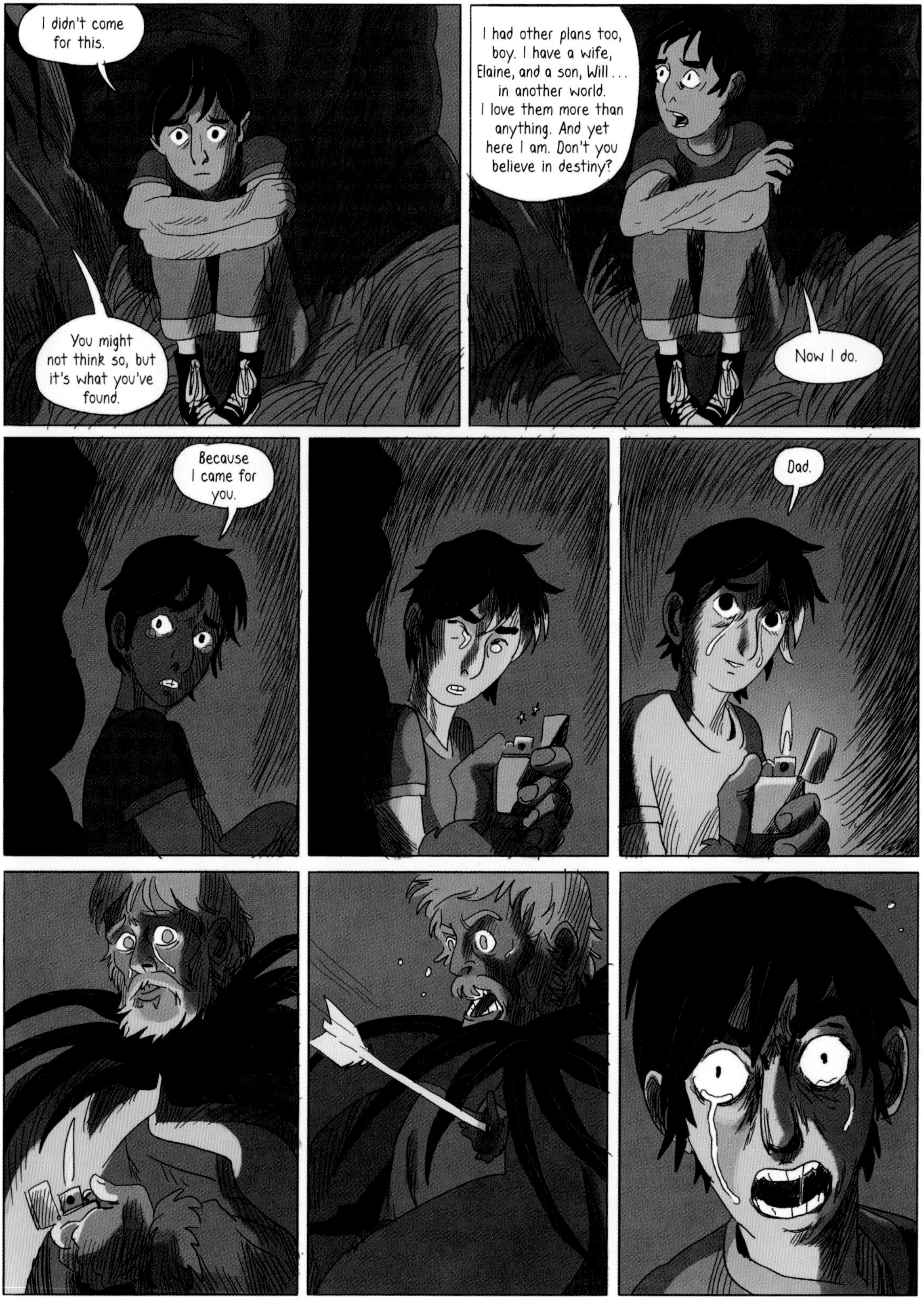
I didn't come for this.
You might not think so, but it's what you've found.
I had other plans too, boy. I have a wife, Elaine, and a son, Will . . . in another world. I love them more than anything. And yet here I am. Don't you believe in destiny?
Now I do.
Because I came for you.
Dad.

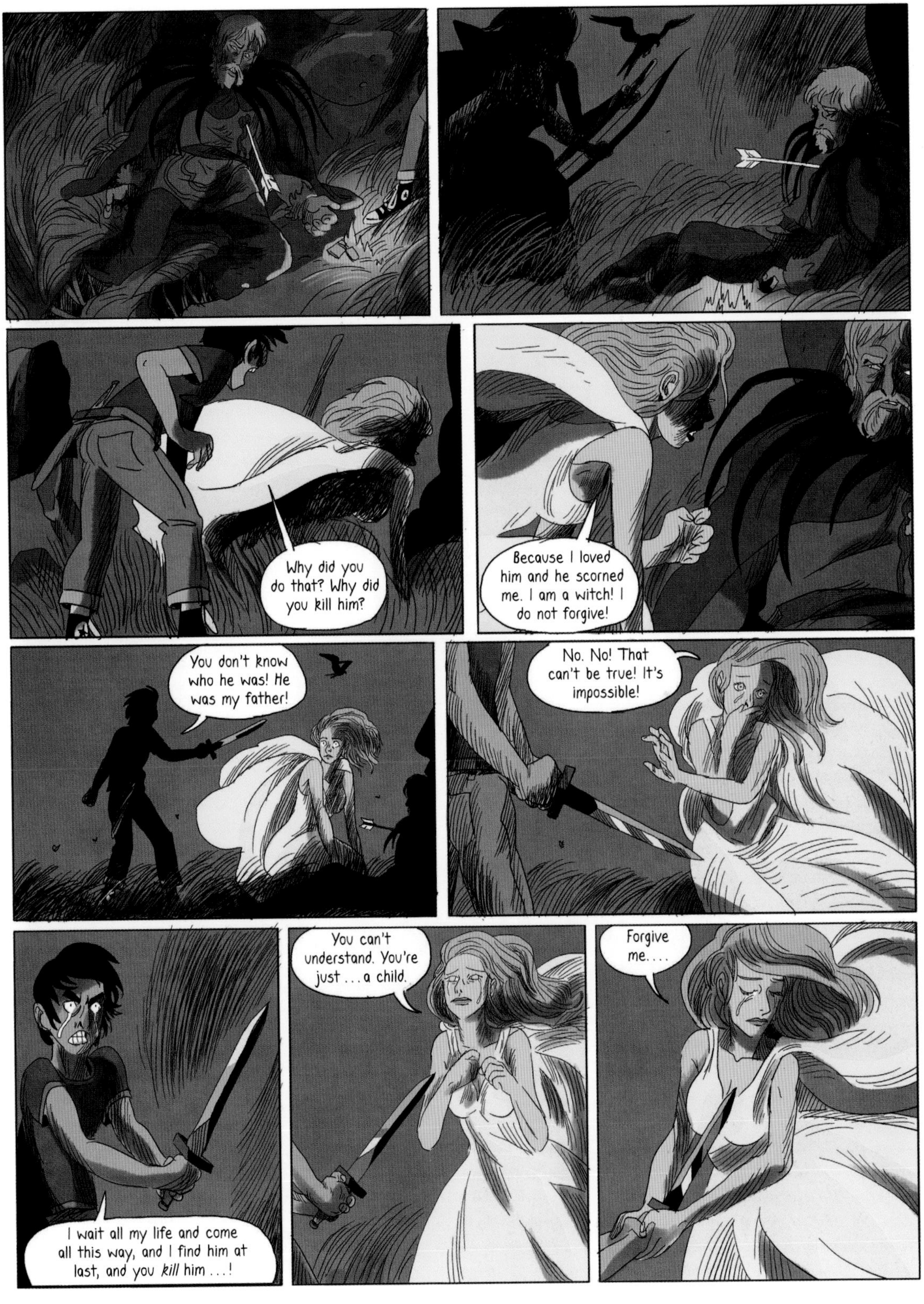
Why did you do that? Why did you kill him?
Because I loved him and he scorned me. I am a witch! I do not forgive!
You don't know who he was! He was my father!
No. No! That can't be true! It's impossible!
I wait all my life and come all this way, and I find him at last, and you *kill* him . . . !
You can't understand. You're just . . . a child.
Forgive me. . . .

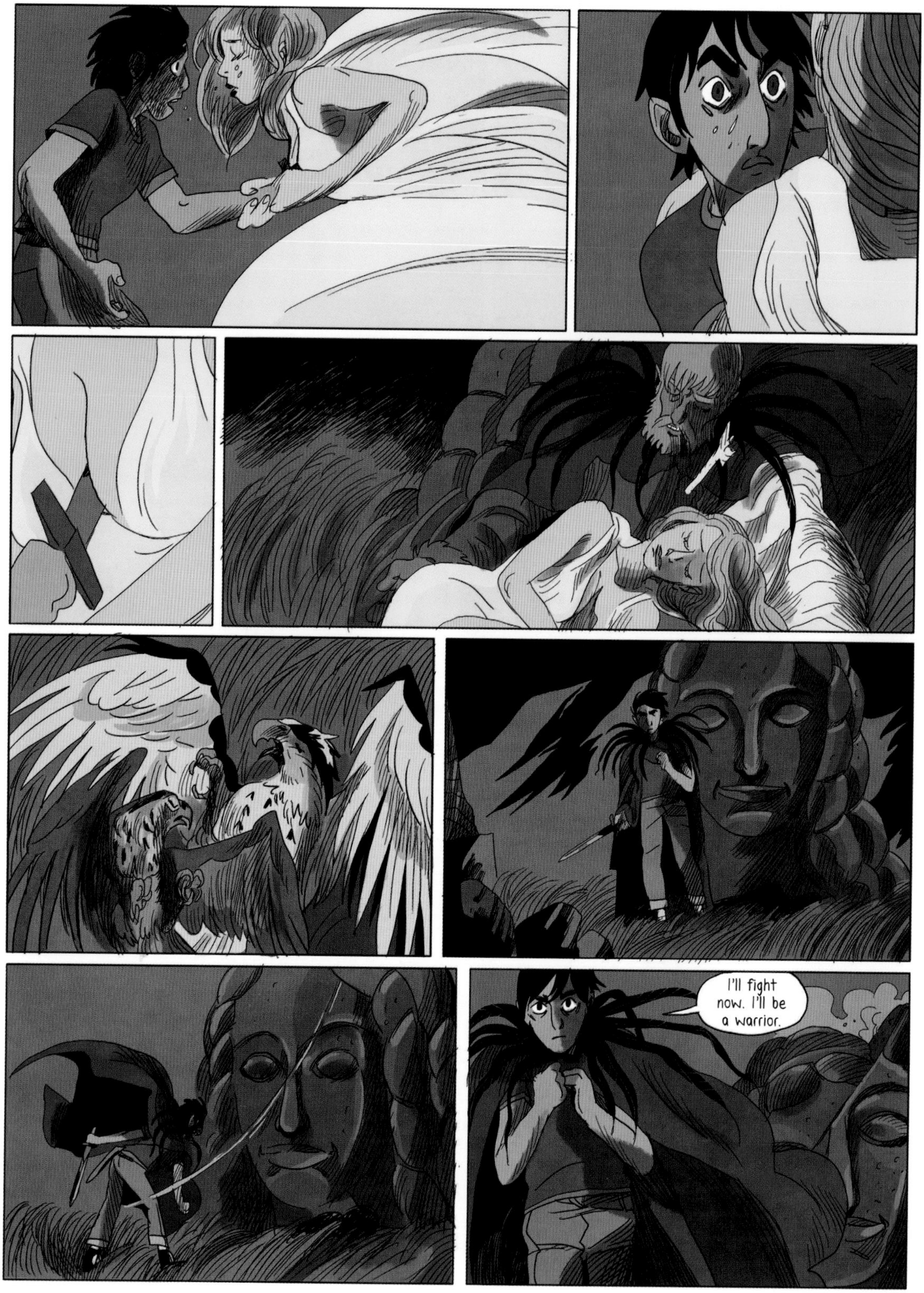
I'll fight now. I'll be a warrior.

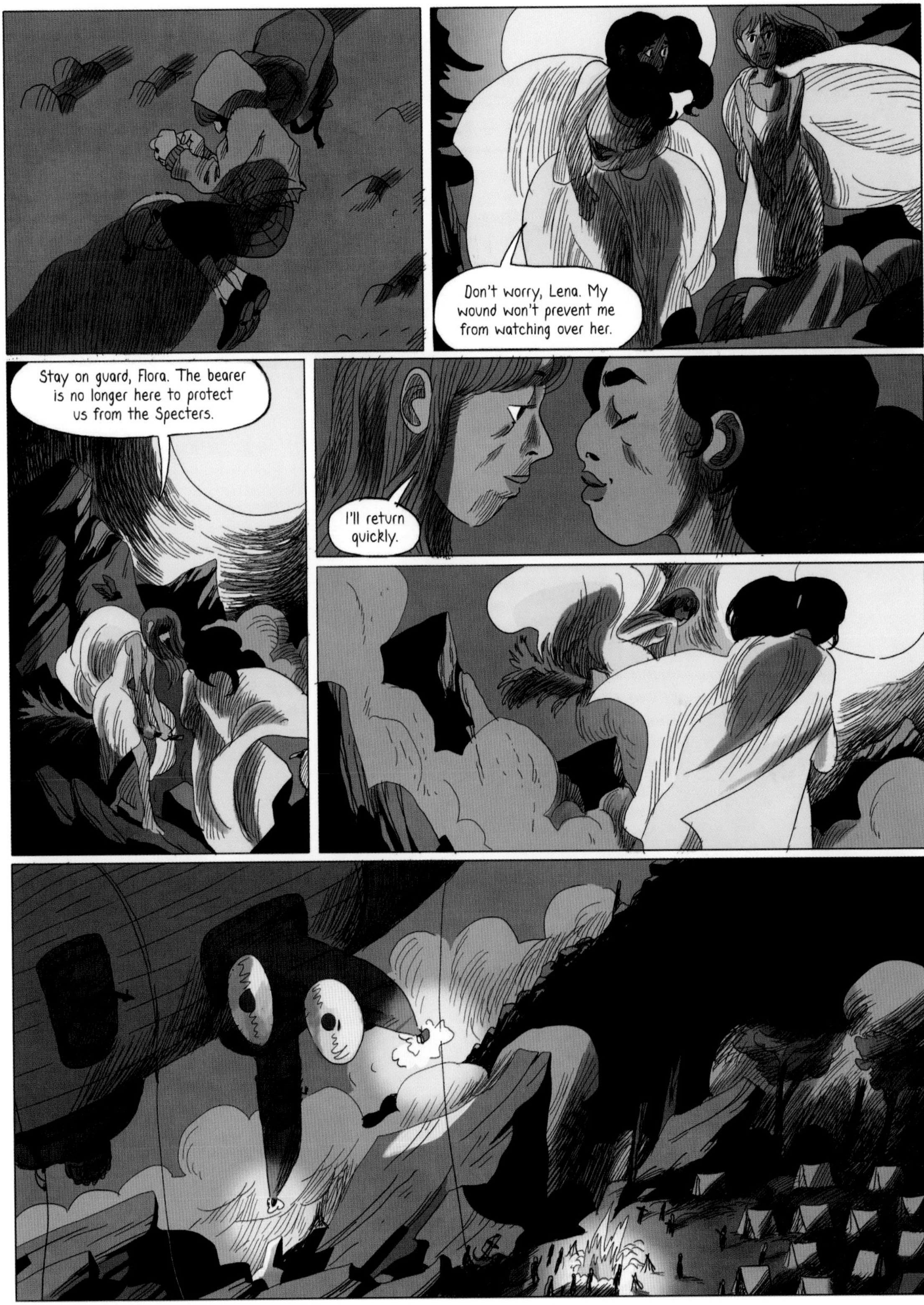
Don't worry, Lena. My wound won't prevent me from watching over her.
Stay on guard, Flora. The bearer is no longer here to protect us from the Specters.
I'll return quickly.

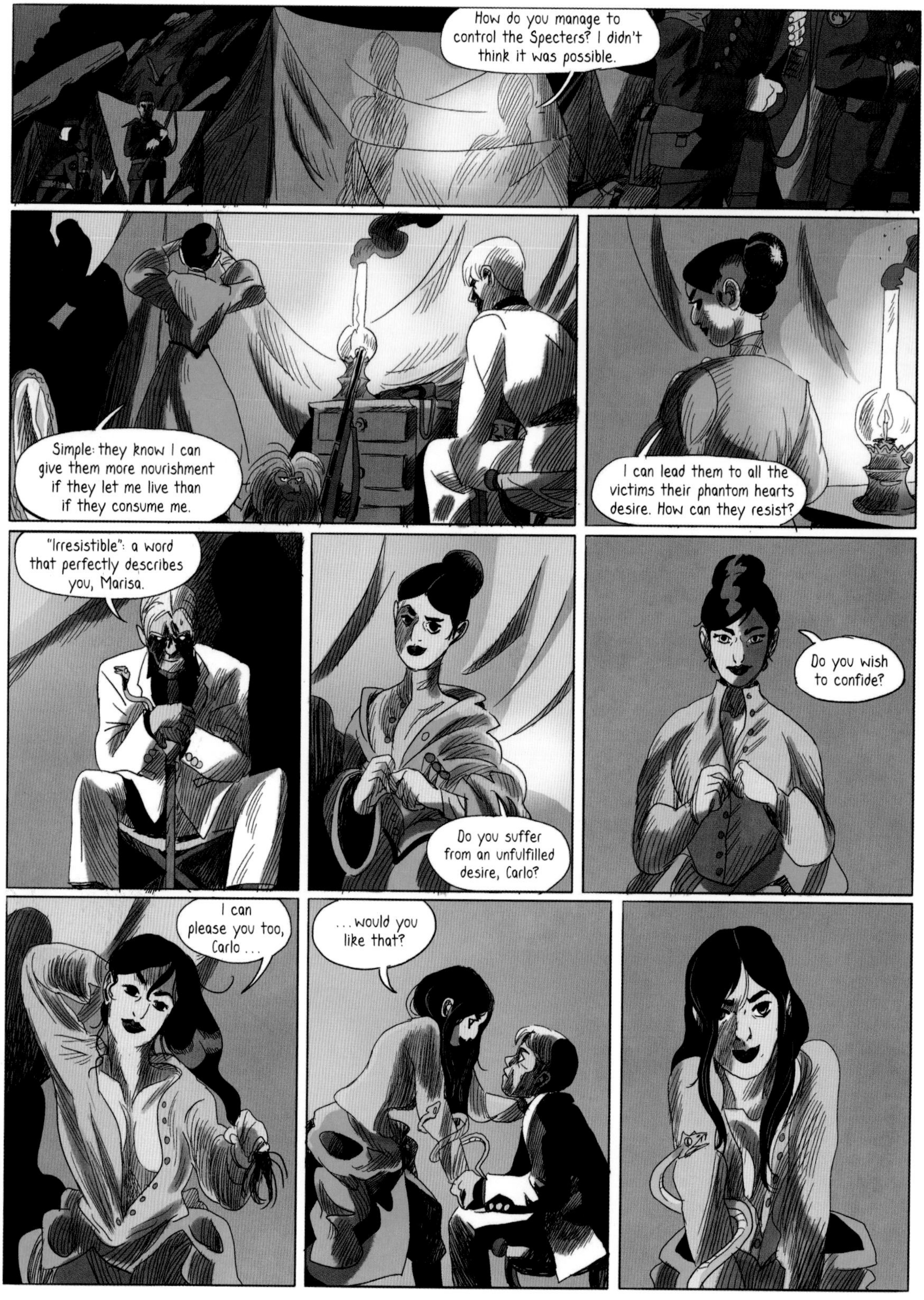
How do you manage to control the Specters? I didn't think it was possible.
Simple: they know I can give them more nourishment if they let me live than if they consume me.
I can lead them to all the victims their phantom hearts desire. How can they resist?
"Irresistible": a word that perfectly describes you, Marisa.
Do you suffer from an unfulfilled desire, Carlo?
Do you wish to confide?
I can please you too, Carlo . . .
. . . would you like that?

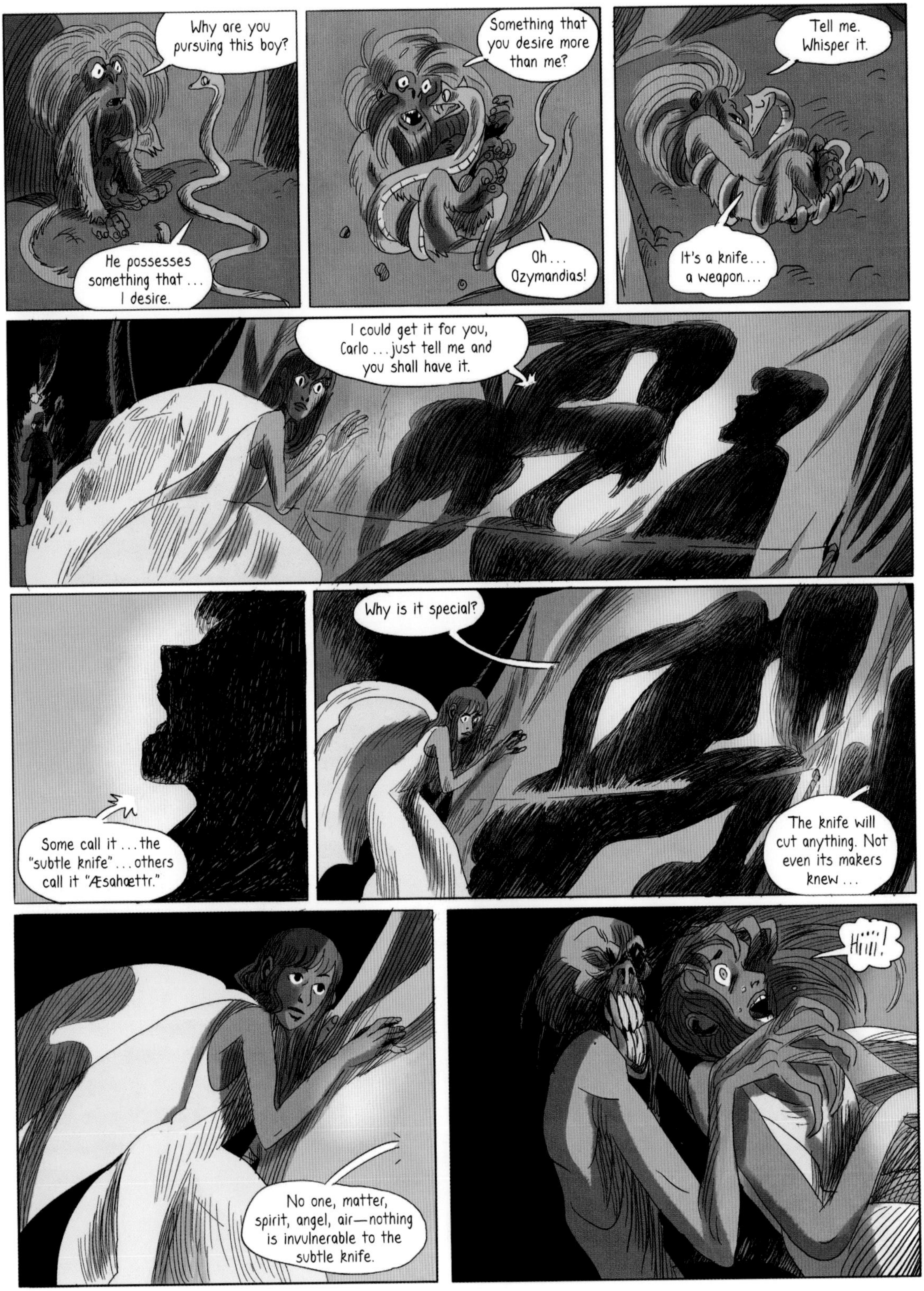
Why are you pursuing this boy?
He possesses something that . . . I desire.
Something that you desire more than me?
Oh . . . Ozymandias!
Tell me. Whisper it.
It's a knife . . . a weapon. . . .
I could get it for you, Carlo . . . just tell me and you shall have it.
Some call it . . . the "subtle knife" . . . others call it "Æsahættr."
Why is it special?
The knife will cut anything. Not even its makers knew . . .
No one, matter, spirit, angel, air—nothing is invulnerable to the subtle knife.
Hiiii!

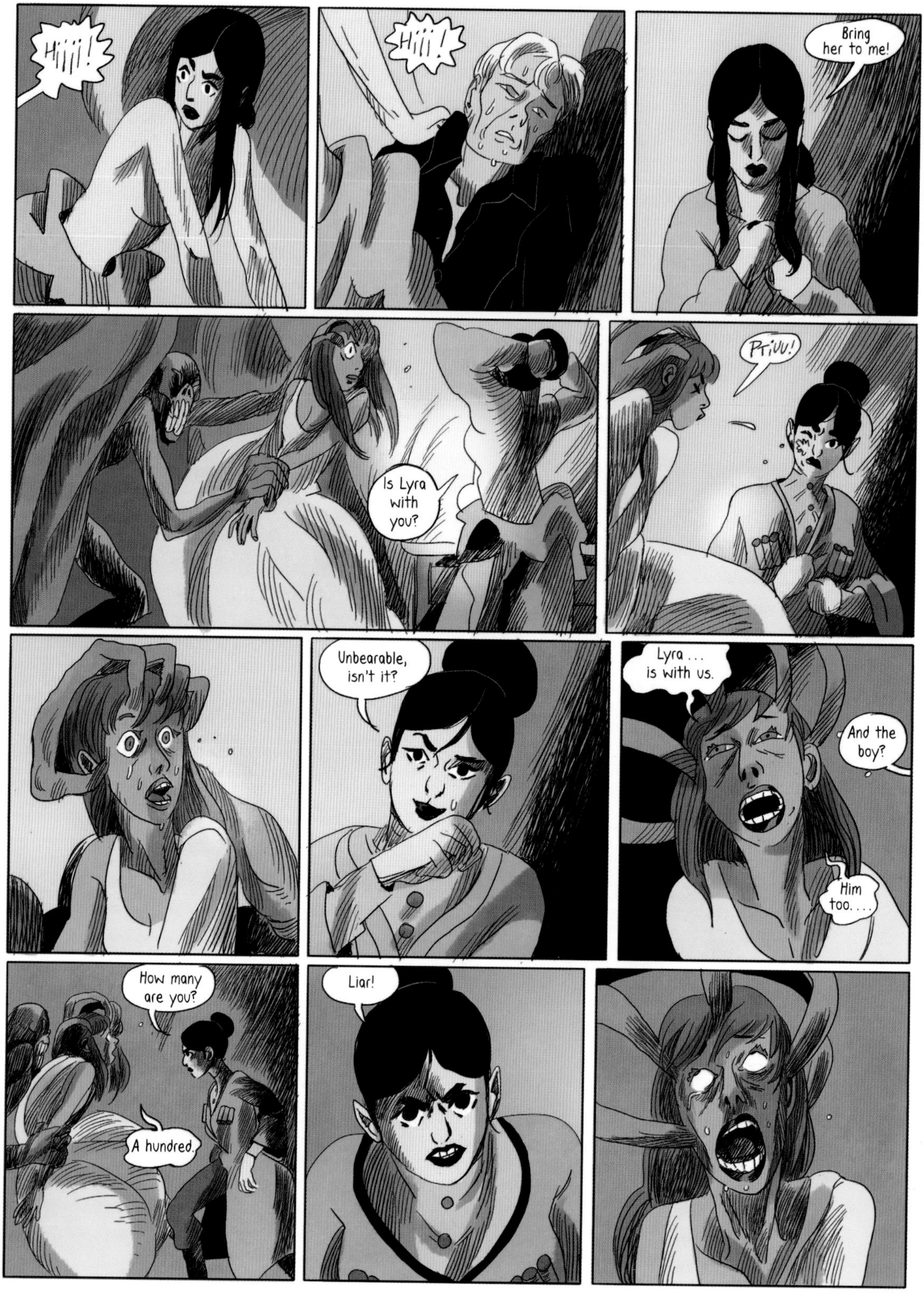
Hiiii!
Hiii!
Bring her to me!
Is Lyra with you?
Ptiuu!
Unbearable, isn't it?
Lyra . . . is with us.
And the boy?
Him too. . . .
How many are you?
A hundred.
Liar!

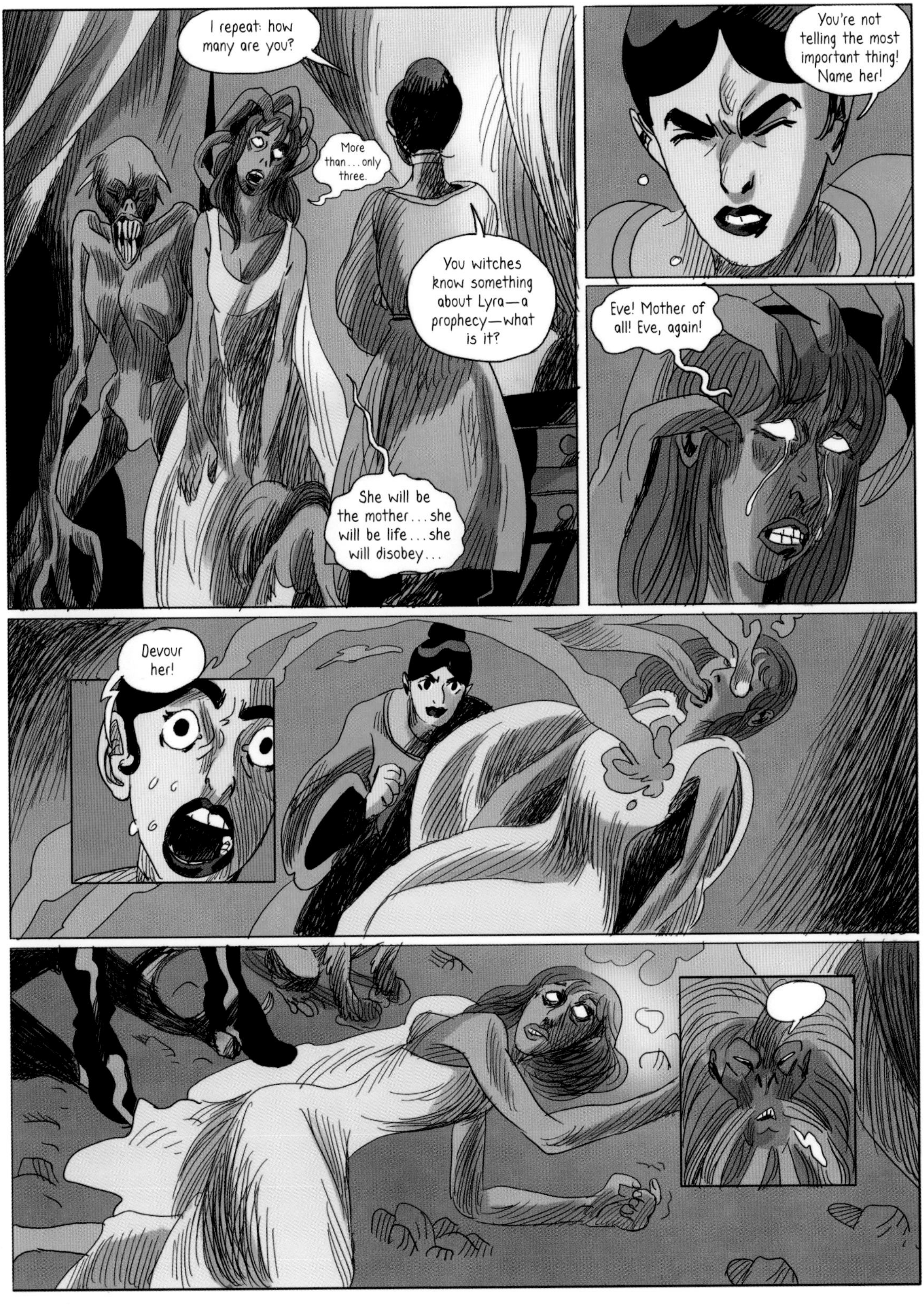
I repeat: how many are you?
More than . . . only three.
You witches know something about Lyra—a prophecy—what is it?
She will be the mother . . . she will be life . . . she will disobey . . .
You're not telling the most important thing! Name her!
Eve! Mother of all! Eve, again!
Devour her!

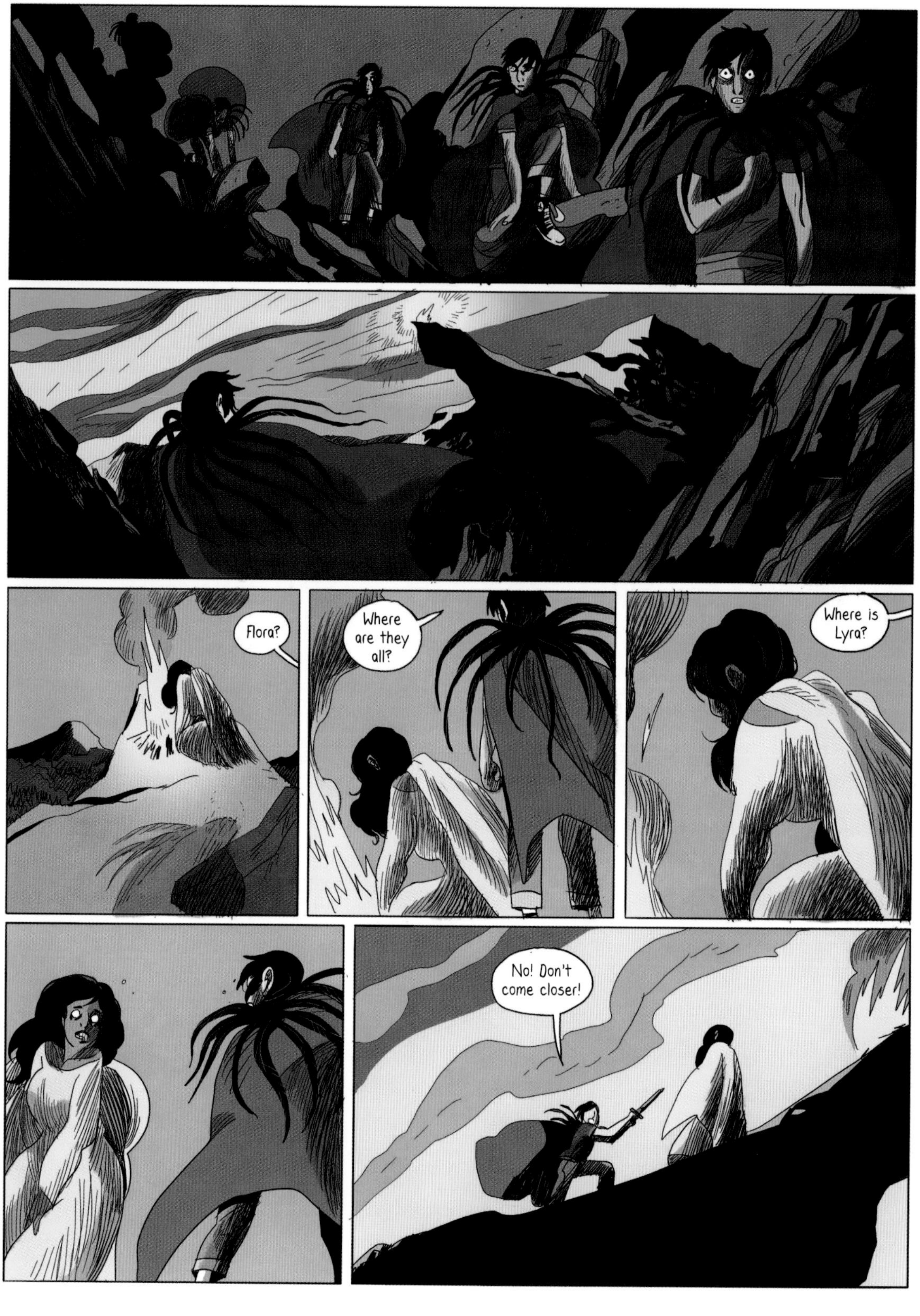
Flora?
Where are they all?
Where is Lyra?
No! Don't come closer!

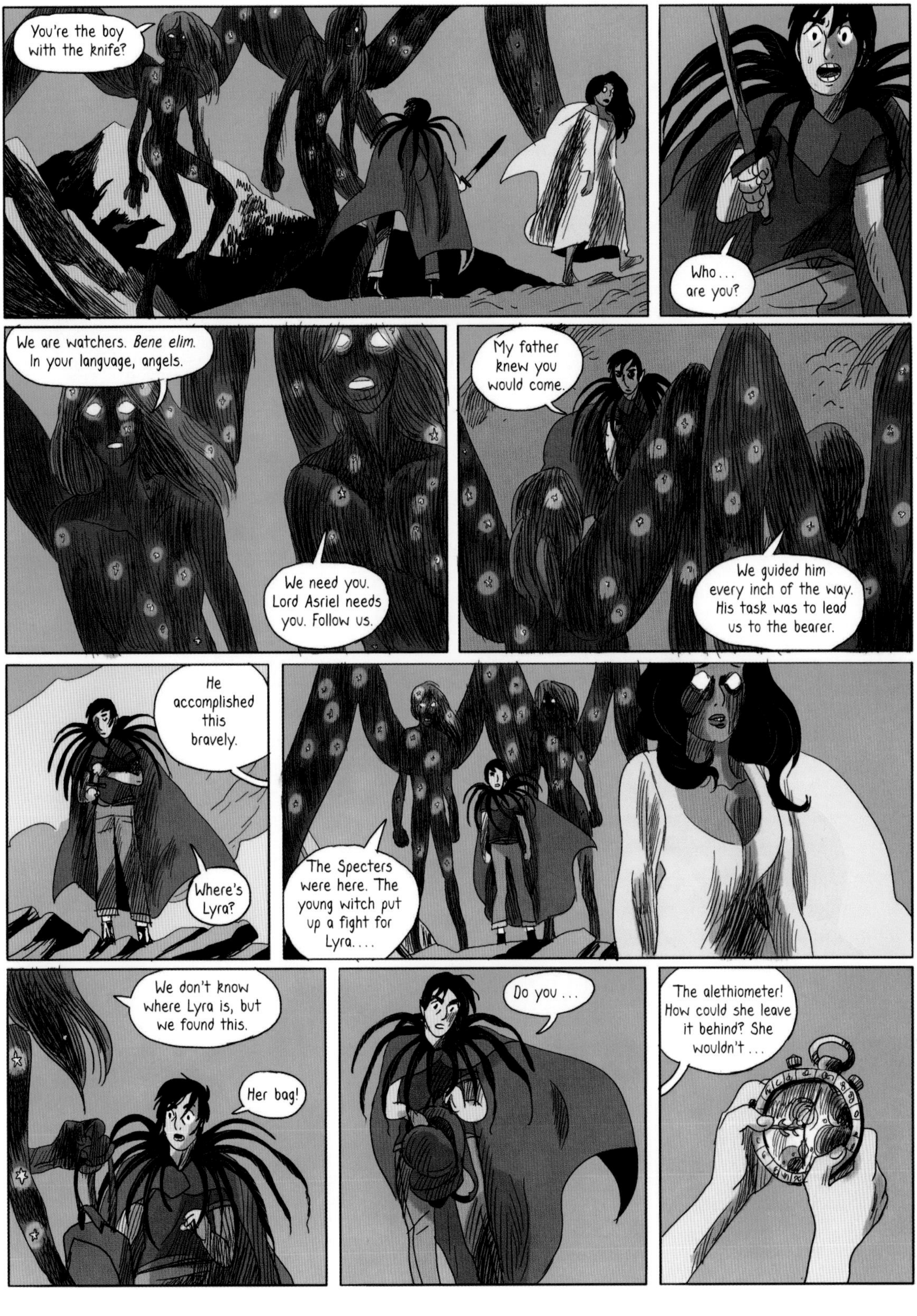
You're the boy with the knife?
Who . . . are you?
We are watchers. *Bene elim.* In your language, angels.
We need you. Lord Asriel needs you. Follow us.
My father knew you would come.
We guided him every inch of the way. His task was to lead us to the bearer.
He accomplished this bravely.
Where's Lyra?
The Specters were here. The young witch put up a fight for Lyra. . . .
We don't know where Lyra is, but we found this.
Her bag!
Do you . . .
The alethiometer! How could she leave it behind? She wouldn't . . .

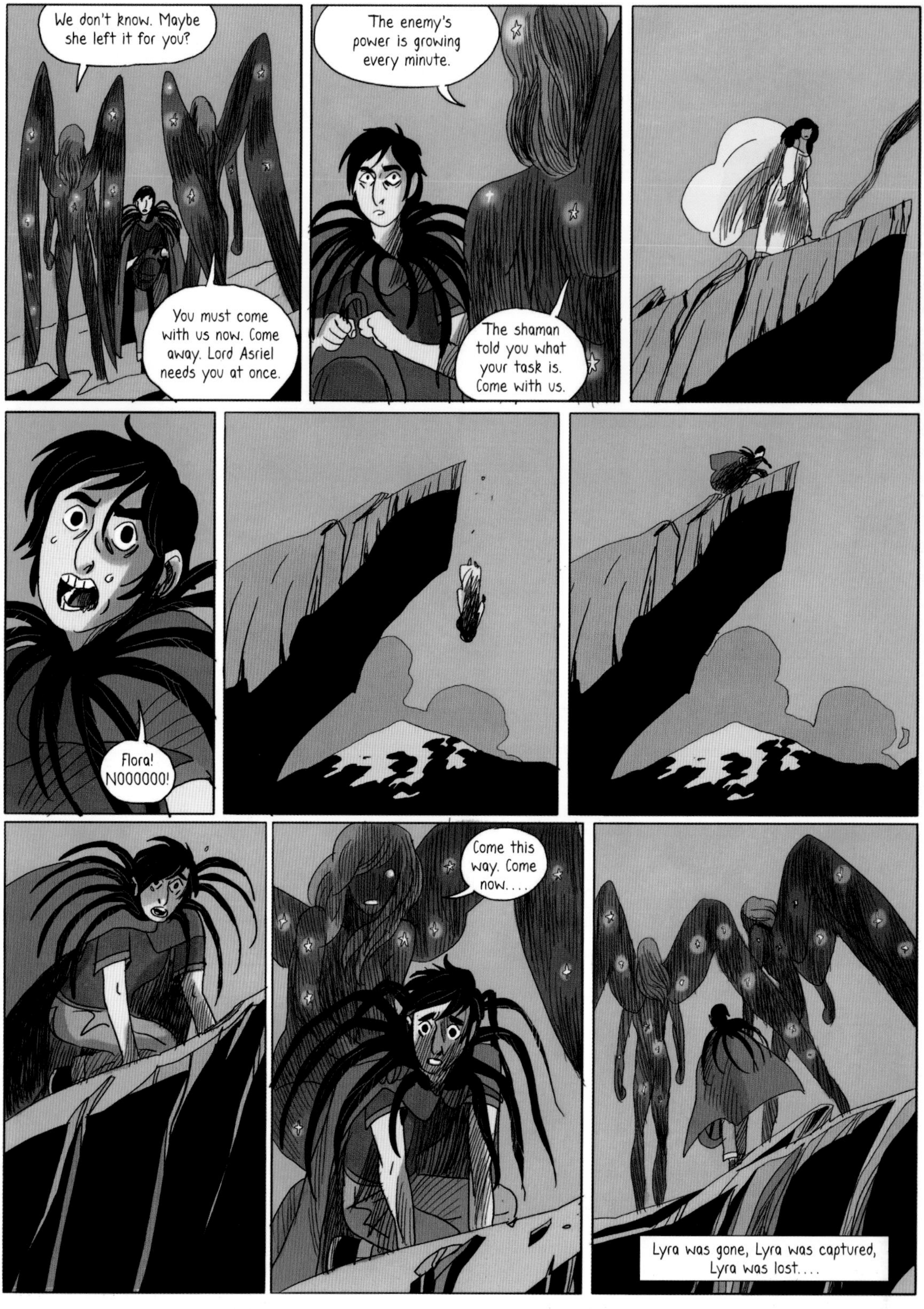
We don't know. Maybe she left it for you?
You must come with us now. Come away. Lord Asriel needs you at once.
The enemy's power is growing every minute.
The shaman told you what your task is. Come with us.
Flora! NOOOOOO!
Come this way. Come now. . . .
Lyra was gone, Lyra was captured, Lyra was lost. . . .

THE WORLD OF
HIS DARK MATERIALS

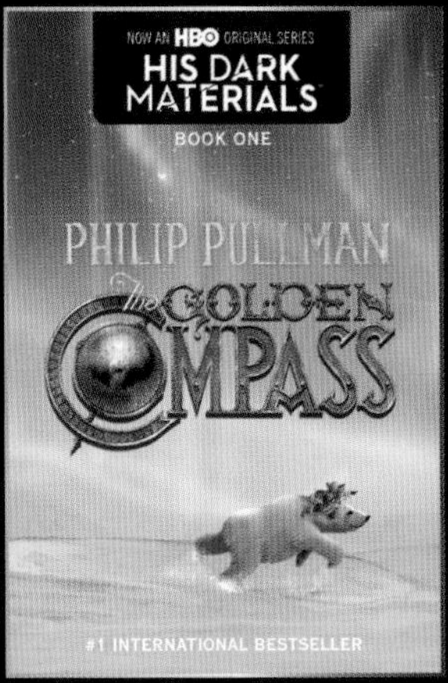
NOW AN HBO ORIGINAL SERIES
HIS DARK MATERIALS
BOOK ONE
PHILIP PULLMAN
The GOLDEN COMPASS
#1 INTERNATIONAL BESTSELLER

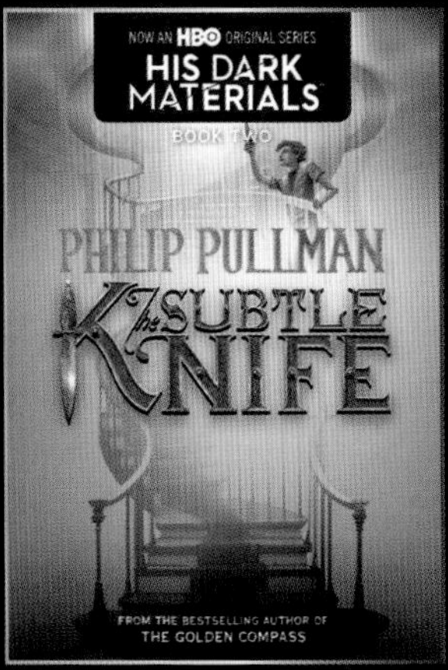
NOW AN HBO ORIGINAL SERIES
HIS DARK MATERIALS
BOOK TWO
PHILIP PULLMAN
The SUBTLE KNIFE
FROM THE BESTSELLING AUTHOR OF
THE GOLDEN COMPASS

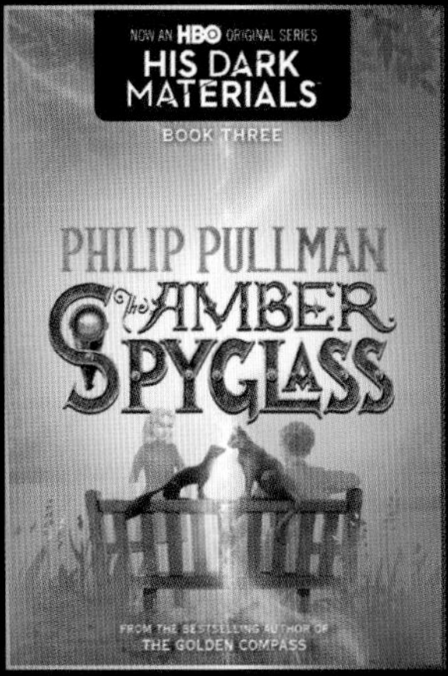
NOW AN HBO ORIGINAL SERIES
HIS DARK MATERIALS
BOOK THREE
PHILIP PULLMAN
The AMBER SPYGLASS
FROM THE BESTSELLING AUTHOR OF
THE GOLDEN COMPASS

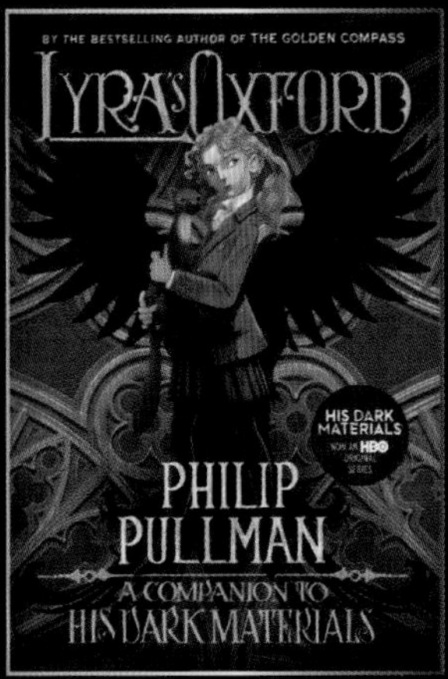
BY THE BESTSELLING AUTHOR OF THE GOLDEN COMPASS
LYRA'S OXFORD
HIS DARK MATERIALS
NOW AN HBO ORIGINAL SERIES
PHILIP PULLMAN
A COMPANION TO
HIS DARK MATERIALS

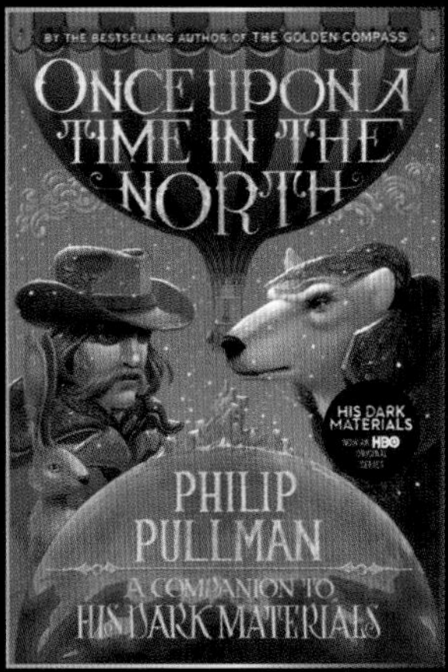
BY THE BESTSELLING AUTHOR OF THE GOLDEN COMPASS
ONCE UPON A TIME IN THE NORTH
HIS DARK MATERIALS
NOW AN HBO ORIGINAL SERIES
PHILIP PULLMAN
A COMPANION TO
HIS DARK MATERIALS

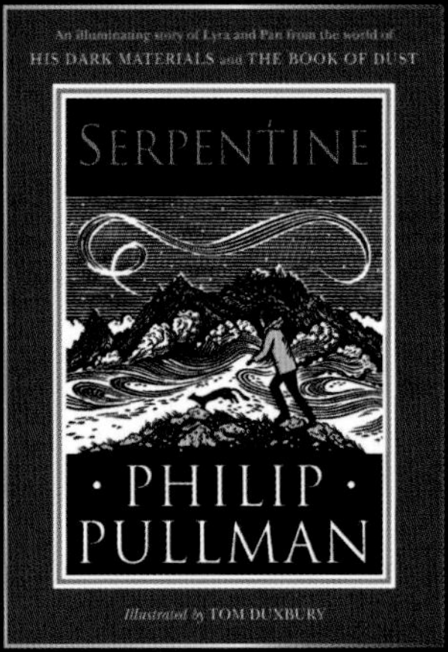
An illuminating story of Lyra and Pan from the world of
HIS DARK MATERIALS and THE BOOK OF DUST
SERPENTINE
PHILIP PULLMAN
Illustrated by TOM DUXBURY

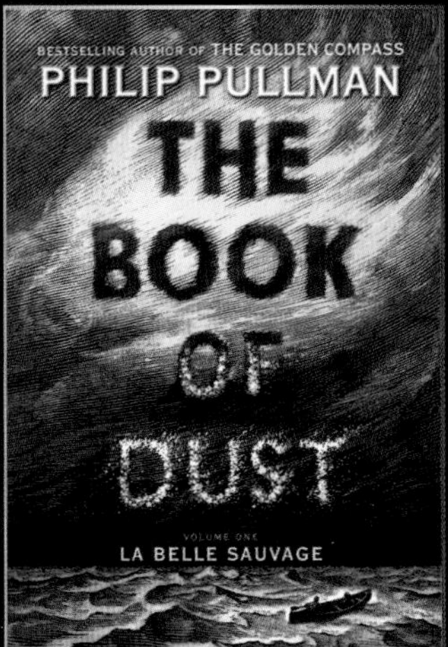
BESTSELLING AUTHOR OF THE GOLDEN COMPASS
PHILIP PULLMAN
THE BOOK OF DUST
VOLUME ONE
LA BELLE SAUVAGE

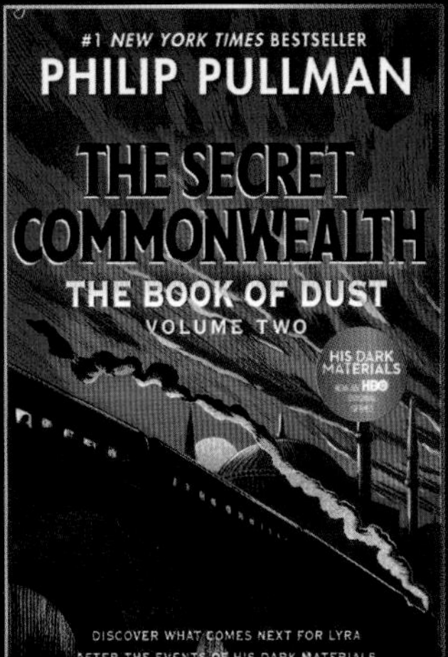
#1 NEW YORK TIMES BESTSELLER
PHILIP PULLMAN
THE SECRET COMMONWEALTH
THE BOOK OF DUST
VOLUME TWO
HIS DARK MATERIALS
DISCOVER WHAT COMES NEXT FOR LYRA
AFTER THE EVENTS OF HIS DARK MATERIALS

RETURN TO THE BEGINNING OF LYRA'S JOURNEY IN:

Adapted from *The Golden Compass* © 1995 by Philip Pullman.

Excerpt text translation © 2015 by Annie Eaton, art © 2014 by Gallimard Jeunesse. Published by Alfred A. Knopf, an imprint of Random House Children's Books, a division of Penguin Random House LLC, New York.

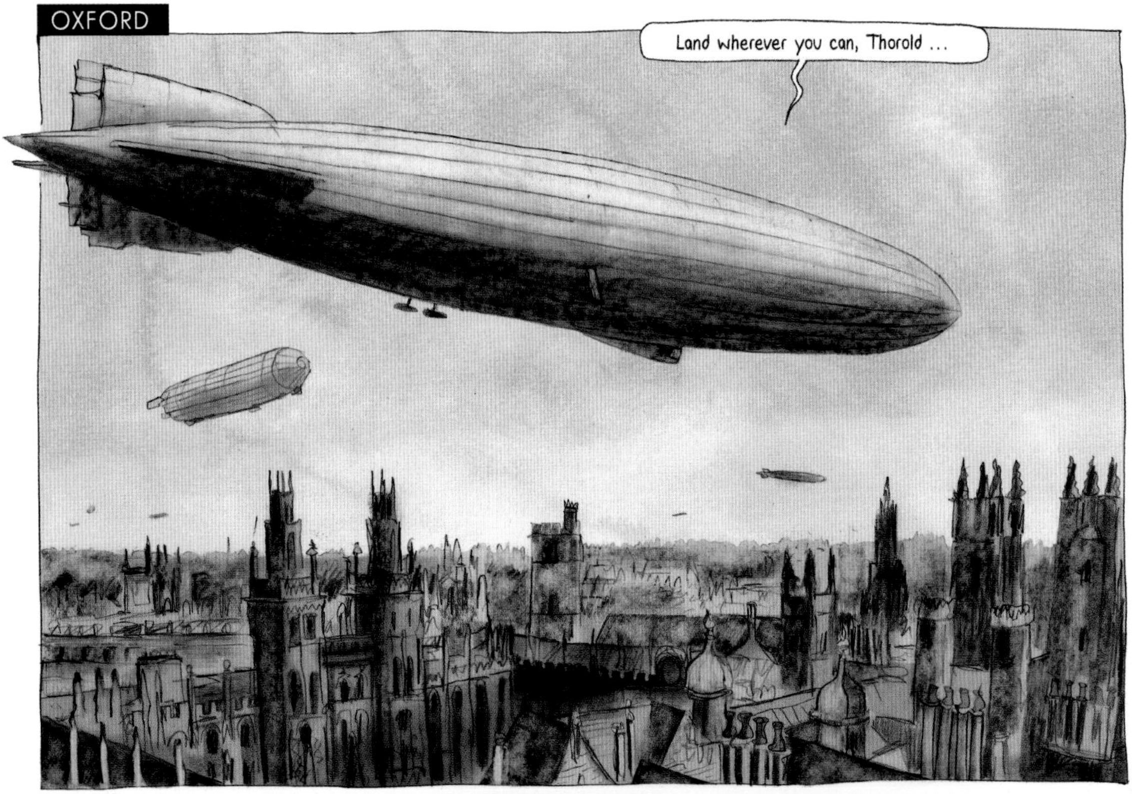
OXFORD
Land wherever you can, Thorold ...

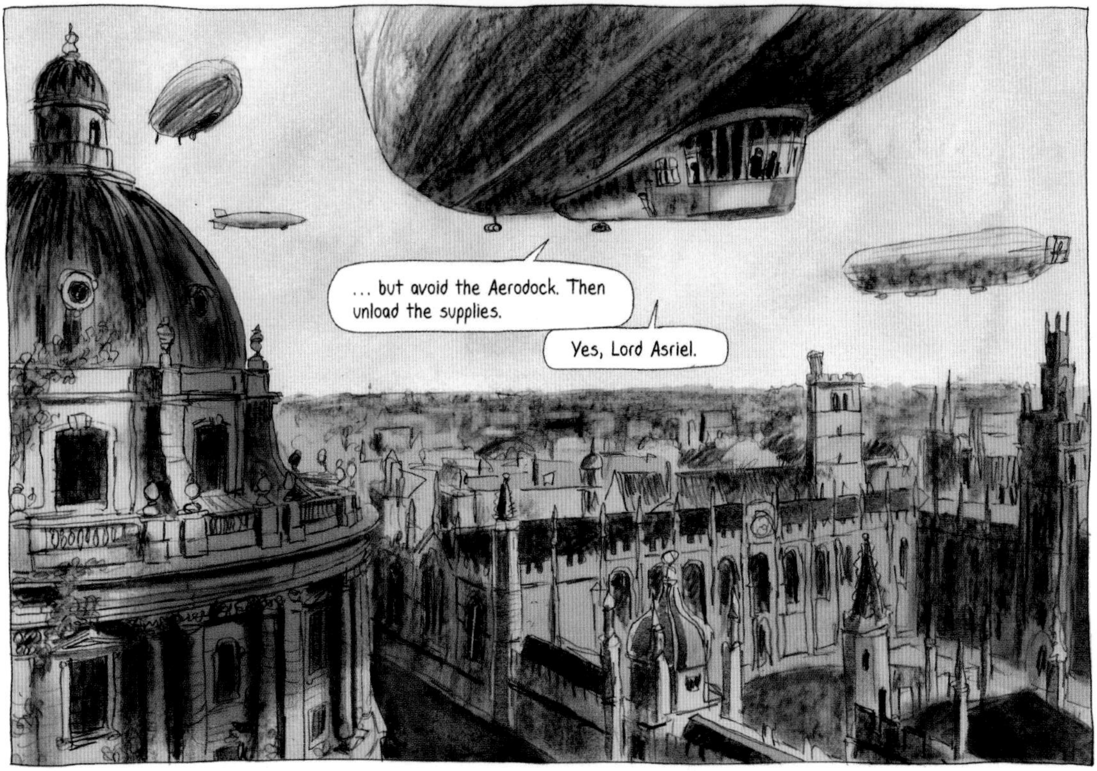
... but avoid the Aerodock. Then unload the supplies.
Yes, Lord Asriel.

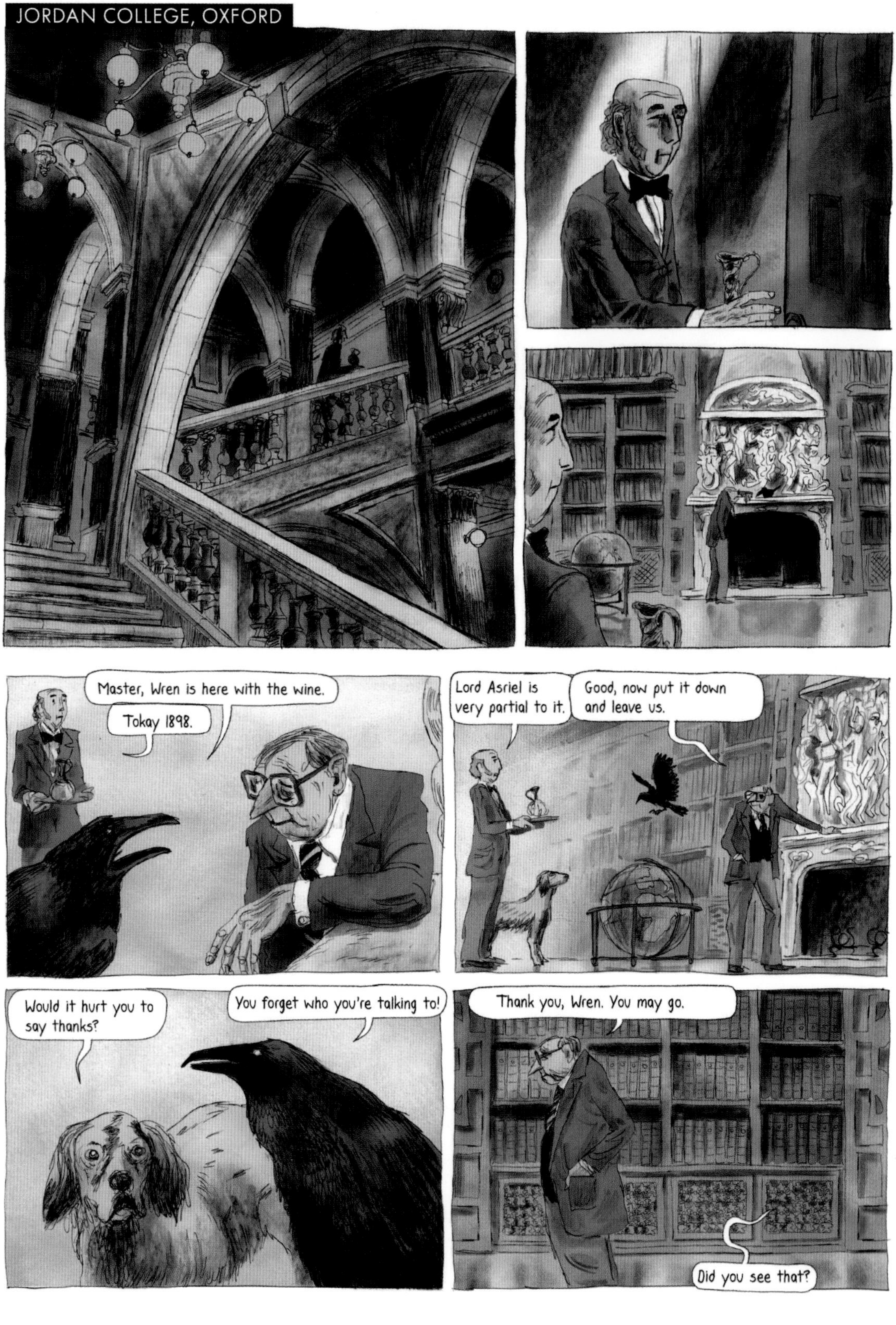
JORDAN COLLEGE, OXFORD
Master, Wren is here with the wine.
Tokay 1898.
Lord Asriel is very partial to it.
Good, now put it down and leave us.
Would it hurt you to say thanks?
You forget who you're talking to!
Thank you, Wren. You may go.
Did you see that?

The Master's not in a good mood, Pan.

He'll be in an even worse mood if he catches you here.

I'm not scared of him.

Liar!

I've had enough of Jordan College. I feel as if I've been here forever.

Lord Asriel is coming. I wish he'd take me away with him.

Your uncle is even scarier than the Master.

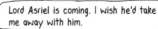

Look!

?

Poison!

Are you mad?

Why are you always imagining things?

Come!

Let's go and greet Lord Asriel when he arrives.

Phew! It's a relief to stretch our legs!

Let's go!

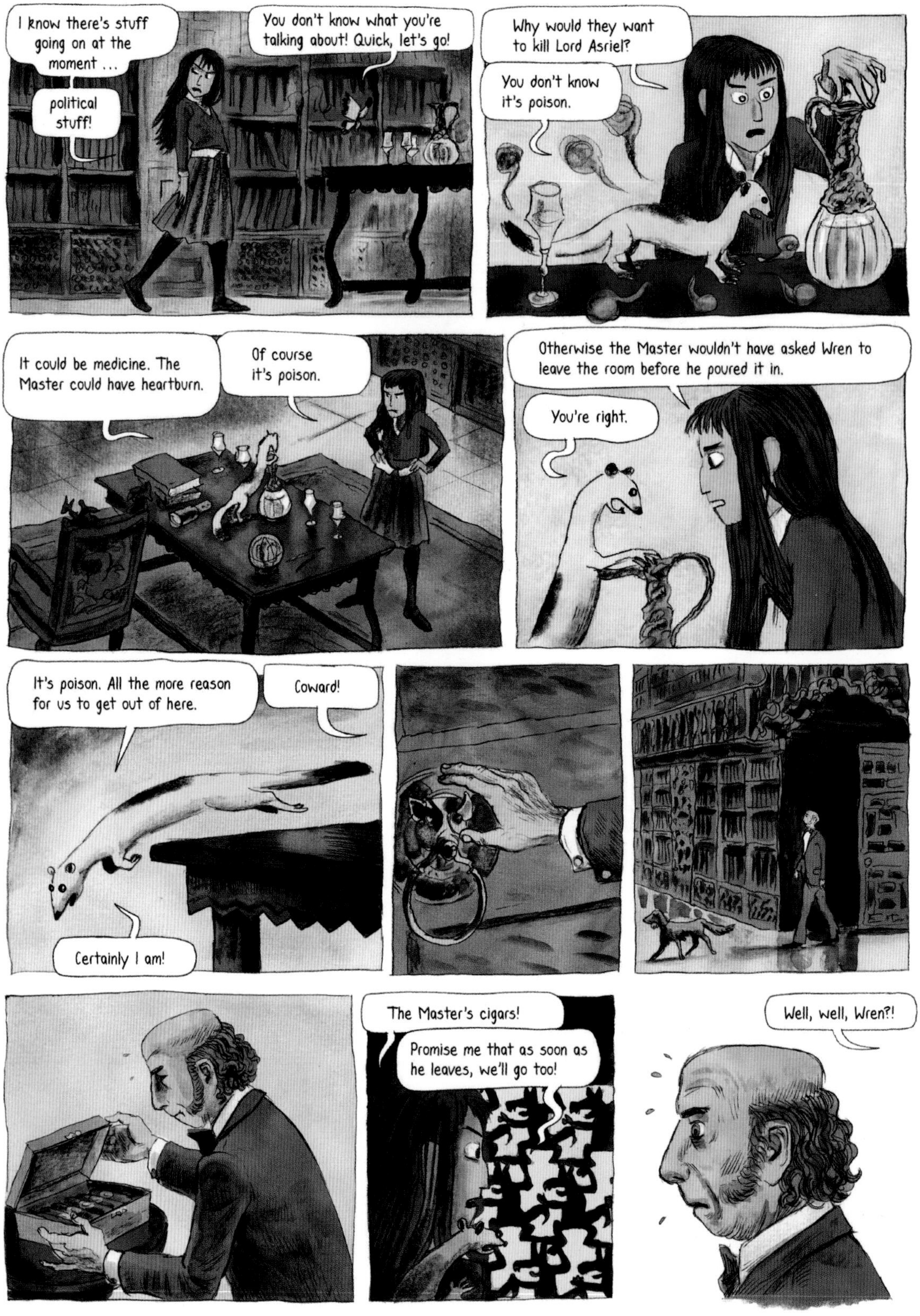
I know there's stuff going on at the moment ...
political stuff!
You don't know what you're talking about! Quick, let's go!
Why would they want to kill Lord Asriel?
You don't know it's poison.
It could be medicine. The Master could have heartburn.
Of course it's poison.
Otherwise the Master wouldn't have asked Wren to leave the room before he poured it in.
You're right.
It's poison. All the more reason for us to get out of here.
Coward!
Certainly I am!
The Master's cigars!
Promise me that as soon as he leaves, we'll go too!
Well, well, Wren?!

Lord Asriel! How long have you been here?

A little while.

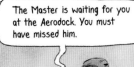

The Master is waiting for you at the Aerodock. You must have missed him.

We like to show up where we're least expected.

You can leave us, Wren, unless you're waiting for the Master to arrive so that he can offer you a cigar?

Your favorite wine is in the carafe. Welcome to Jordan College, my lord.

What a hypocrite. Do you think he's in on it?

You know absolutely nothing about anything.

We must stop him from drinking.

If your uncle finds us spying on him, he'll skin us alive.

No!

?!

Lyra!

So is that what they're teaching you here? Spying?

Ouch, that hurts!

The wine! It's poisoned!

A spy and a liar. They've really done well with your education.

I was hiding! I saw!

The Master poured powder into the wine.

The Master, eh?

?!

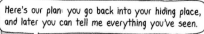

Here's our plan: you go back into your hiding place, and later you can tell me everything you've seen.

WELL DONE! Because of you, we're back in this rat hole.

This time it's different. We're on a mission: he said "our plan"!

I'm sure he'll take me with him.

Why would you want that? He scares me.

Pan, you're a coward.

And you're reckless.

SHUT UP, BOTH OF YOU, OR I'LL MAKE YOU WISH YOU WERE DEAD!

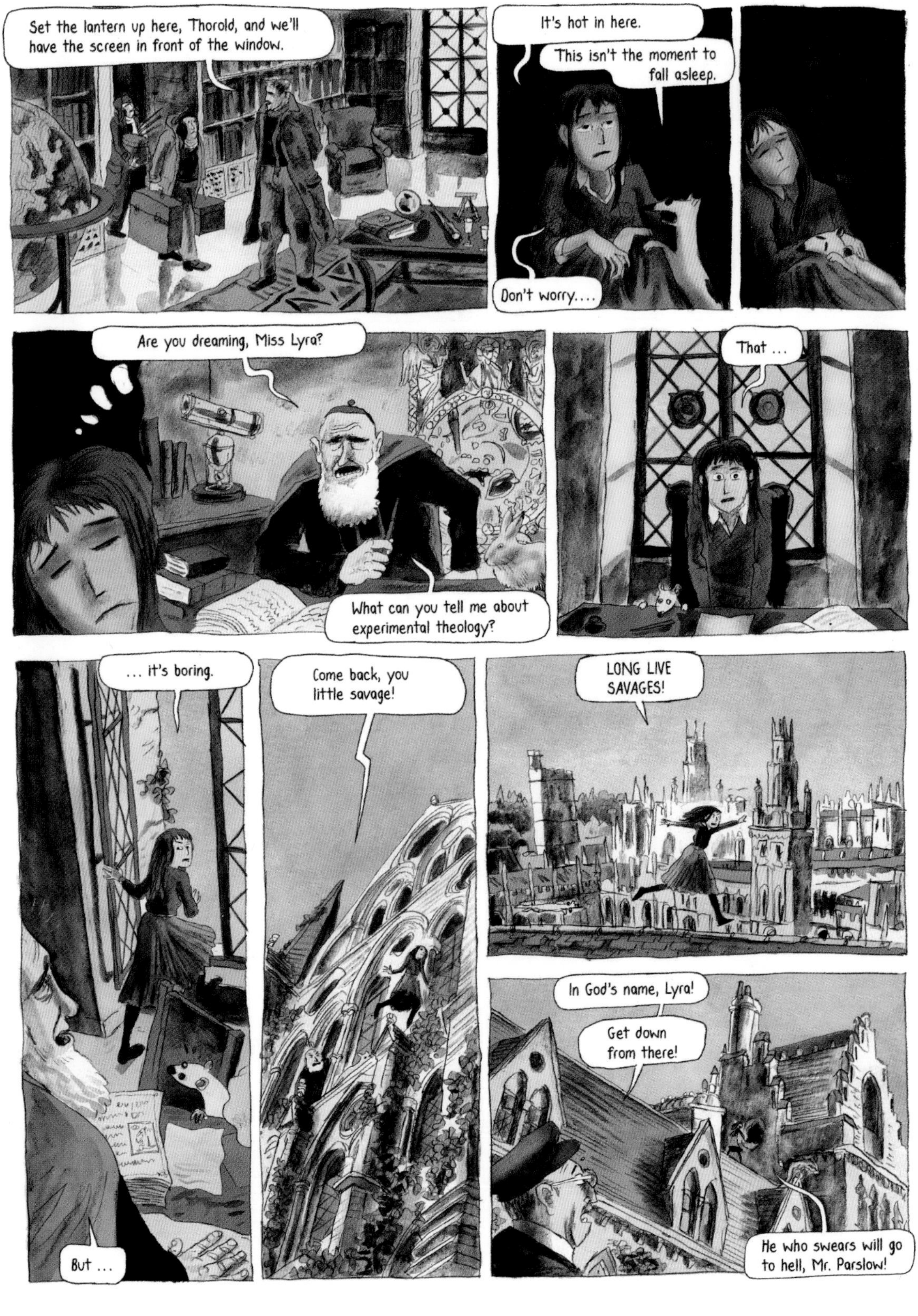
Set the lantern up here, Thorold, and we'll have the screen in front of the window.
It's hot in here.
This isn't the moment to fall asleep.
Don't worry....
Are you dreaming, Miss Lyra?
What can you tell me about experimental theology?
That ...
... it's boring.
But ...
Come back, you little savage!
LONG LIVE SAVAGES!
In God's name, Lyra!
Get down from there!
He who swears will go to hell, Mr. Parslow!

What's the use of learning? There are more books than I could ever read here.

That's what it's like in all libraries, Lyra.

They all claim to believe in God, and yet they keep searching for him with their philosophical instruments.

If the Chaplain could hear you!

LYRA! COME BACK TO YOUR LESSON IMMEDIATELY OR I'LL TELL THE MASTER!

Ha ha ha!

Miss Lyra! Who gave you permission to leave the college?

I gave myself permission, Mr. Wood.

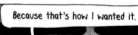

Why wasn't I told that you had arrived?

Because that's how I wanted it.

Lord Asriel, I'm confused!

Wake up, Lyra.

How is it that ...

I wasn't asleep!

The Master's here.